Affinity Publisher Workbook

Learn professional page layout and
publishing techniques with Affinity Publisher

By the Affinity Team

ISBN-13: 978-1-909581-07-4

This book has been created for Affinity Publisher 1.9 and above for both Mac and Windows versions. Screenshots used in this book were captured from the Mac version of Affinity Publisher. Functionality and visual differences between Windows and Mac versions of Affinity Publisher are minimal; if a distinction is required to be made, e.g. when referencing both Mac and Windows keyboard shortcuts, this will be clearly indicated.

Edition 1.0

Foreword

The Affinity Publisher Workbook is in your hands at last and it's a pleasure to share with you the wealth of knowledge contained between its covers.

This book follows in the footsteps of the well-regarded Affinity Designer and Affinity Photo workbooks, yet it is significant in its own right. This companion to Affinity Publisher was designed and created using the same groundbreaking desktop publishing software that is its subject matter.

We've partnered with contributors who are publishing experts to bring you insightful page design and workflow advice. After going hands-on with 10 projects across more than 300 pages, you'll be producing professional publications that make your portfolio stronger than ever.

Affinity Publisher would not have been possible without the support you've shown to the other Affinity apps before it. We hope the app and workbook add invaluable tools and knowledge to your skill set.

Ash Hewson
Managing Director

Affinity Workbook Team

This book has been conceived and created by the following members of the Affinity team:

Editor	Andy Capstick
Technical Writers	Andy Capstick, Caroline Doughty and Alan Stonebridge
Art Direction	Neil Ladkin and Ian Cornwall
Artworkers	Ian Cornwall and Ian Upcott
Copywriter	Kelly Mancaruso
Artist Relations	Kate Musgrove and Charlotte Thomson-Morley

Contributors

Publishing projects generally require content from three creative spectrums: photography, illustration and design. So with that in mind, we enlisted a range of creatives to contribute to this Affinity Publisher Workbook. The contributors from our internal team are joined by various industry specialists to make sure that the publishing projects in this workbook—which are designed to cover the wide spectrum of Affinity Publisher's functionality—replicate real-world printing projects.

Emily Goater—Our in-house product expert for Affinity Publisher, Emily has broad experience in editorial, graphic, typography and brand design. Emily teaches you publication fundamentals in the Page Design Principles chapter (p. 151).

Explore Emily's personal work at emilygoaterdesign.com

Ian Cornwall—As our creative projects manager, Ian has vast experience in layout design and directs the artworking and layouts for the Affinity range of Workbooks. Ian guides you through three projects, including how to design a trifold Root Box Brochure (p. 174), produce an inspirational photography-led Fashionista Lookbook (p. 264) and make an eye-catching Bijou Film Festival Poster (p. 388).

Matt Searston—Our in-house product expert for Affinity Designer, Matt has created the vector logo for the Root Box Brochure project on p. 174, available for you to download and use in this project.

See Matt's personal work at instagram.com/mattsearston

Fernando Martins Ribeiro—Product photography master Fernando has created the product photography images for you to download and complete the Root Box Brochure project on p. 174.

Fernando has also shot the images for the cover of this workbook.

Discover Fernando's work at martinsribeiro.com

Adam Banks—Former editor and creative director of MacUser, Adam has more than 30 years of magazine publishing experience. In the Spotlight Magazine project on p. 216, he teaches you how to make the most of Affinity Publisher's features to design a magazine from scratch.

Learn more about Adam at adambanks.com

Eleni Debo—Eleni is an award-winning illustrator whose work regularly features in international newspapers, books and magazines. We've used Eleni's feature on AffinitySpotlight.com in the Spotlight Magazine project on p. 216, and Eleni has provided her illustrations so you can complete this project too.

Explore Eleni's work at elenidebo.com

Roberta Burattini—Roberta, aka Moon Lotus Dreams, is an artist who has previously created a tutorial about her digital painting process for AffinitySpotlight.com, which we've used in the Spotlight Magazine project on p. 216. Roberta has also provided her images to help you complete this project.

Discover Roberta's work at instagram.com/moonlotusdreams

Rosa Maglione—Rosa aka 'More Profesh' is a Georgia-based designer known for her stylish and impactful curriculum vitae templates. She shows you how to design this type of critical document with the user experience in mind in the Skills On Show CV/résumé project on p. 300.

You can see Rosa's diverse range of CV designs at moreprofesh.com

Steve Simpson—An award-winning illustrative designer, Steve has created all the gorgeous illustrations used in the book creation projects based on Lewis Carroll's children's classic *Alice's Adventures in Wonderland*. Check out the Alice's Adventures in Wonderland Book project on p. 326 and the companion book cover project on p. 362.

See more of Steve's work at stevesimpson.com

Sandi Dez—Founder of **Zeune Type Foundry**, Sandi is the creator of Wallington Pro, a decorative serif typeface with intricate OTF features, which is supplied with a commercial license to purchasers of the Affinity Publisher Workbook. Find out more about how we use the Wallington Pro typeface in the Alice's Adventures in Wonderland Cover project on p. 362.

Discover Zeune Ink at ink.creativezeune.com

James Bates—With more than ten years of experience in branding specialising in corporate identity, Serif's in-house graphic designer James shows how to lay strong foundations for your branding in the KB/A Brand Guide project on p. 430.

James then expands on the brand further to produce a consistent KB/A Stationery set on p. 460.

David Hussner—As Egotype, David is a designer and premium layout template creator. He continues the corporate branding story by showing you how to create a KB/A Annual Report on p. 482 that is faithful to the KB/A Brand Guide.

See more of David's work at behance.net/egotype

TABLE OF CONTENTS

Welcome

Chapter 1: Interface Tour

Chapter 2: Core Skills

Chapter 3: Page Design Principles

Chapter 4: Professional Projects

Chapter 5: Creative Projects

Chapter 6: Corporate Publishing Projects

Index

Inserts

WELCOME

Affinity Publisher Workbook

Welcome to the Affinity Publisher Workbook. This workbook has been created with a host of contributors to help you either get started with Affinity Publisher, or to further develop your desktop publishing skills using the app.

In this introductory section, learn more about us and how to get the most out of your experience with Affinity.

This workbook was designed and published entirely in Affinity Publisher.

Design at chapter and project level

With a small multi-discipline team, projects were developed and reviewed independently of each other in separate Publisher files.

Two master pages with guides were used across projects—with and without page numbering/section fields.

A strict hierarchical text style set was used. Any conflicting text styles were resolved during dummy merge passes.

Section details and index entries were created per document.

Assembling the workbook using Document Merge

23 final documents, comprising chapter dividers, chapters and projects, were merged one by one into our Preface document

Merging was possible using Add Pages From File (right-click last page thumbnail of previous merged document in Pages Panel).

Each document's merge allowed its imported text styles to be reviewed and added to the main document.

Each document's index entries were automatically imported, collated and sorted in the 'master' document.

ABOUT AFFINITY

The new standard in creative software

Affinity is revolutionising design, photography and publishing with a trio of powerful, professional apps which work together in a unique way. Created to harness the full power of the latest technology, their development has been driven by the demands of real-life work environments and professional workflows.

With more than three million users worldwide, Affinity is fast becoming a new global standard in creative software.

Our trio of apps includes:

- **Affinity Designer —** professional graphic design software, available on Mac, Windows and iPad
- **Affinity Photo —** professional photo-editing software, available on Mac, Windows and iPad
- **Affinity Publisher —** professional desktop publishing software, available on Mac and Windows

Designed for cross-platform creatives

Affinity software is developed with full feature parity and total cross-platform compatibility in mind. Every Affinity file you create can be opened by any app in the Affinity suite and on any of our supported platforms. That extends to shared editing history too!

And now, with Affinity Publisher, you can finally experience true multi-discipline, mixed-media publishing and an unmatched level of cohesion within a creative suite of apps. It's how we think a creative software suite should be and why we named our apps Affinity.

ABOUT AFFINITY PUBLISHER

Created by the developers of the award-winning Affinity Designer and Affinity Photo apps, Affinity Publisher is the most advanced professional publishing software around.

The incredibly smooth, intuitive app gives you the power to combine your images, graphics and text to make beautiful layouts ready for publication. From magazines, books, brochures, posters, reports and stationery to other creations, it has everything you need to create the perfect layout.

Also featuring the game-changing ability to fully integrate with other Affinity apps, this next-generation software is completely revolutionising the way publishing professionals work; it's why it was named Apple's **Mac App of the Year 2019**.

KEY FEATURES

Page management tools

See all of your work

Get an instant overview of your publication on the Pages Panel, where everything is shown as thumbnails. Quickly drag and drop pages to change their order and instantly jump to any page with a double-click.

Sections for chapter numbering and organisation

Manage page numbering in the Section Manager, where you can divide your document into discrete, named parts. Each section can continue page numbering from its predecessor or start afresh from a number you choose.

Design to impress

Create horizontal- and vertical-facing spreads with the flexibility to run images and other design elements across the gutter for dramatic effect.

Master pages for repeating page elements

Use master pages to store elements that will appear in the same place on multiple pages. Editing a master instantly updates all publication pages linked to it, but you can edit frame content freely as well as break the connection to make localised changes to object sizes and properties when needed. Smart master pages allow dramatic page layout swaps.

Document design tools

Guides for good layout

The Guides Manager divides pages into evenly spaced columns and rows to establish an organised, consistent look. Page elements automatically snap to guides as you move and resize them. Whenever you need to break the rules, simply hold a key to override snapping. Extra guides can be placed wherever needed by dragging from the rulers onto a page. Refine guide positions with mathematical precision in the Guides Manager.

Intelligent picture placement

Place raster images using rectangle- and ellipse-shaped Picture Frame tools. For more organic results, any vector shape can be converted to a picture frame. Images can be intelligently scaled to fit their frame.

Baseline grid

The Baseline Grid Manager helps keep your text vertically aligned across all columns and pages of your entire publication, or specific text frames and tables. You have full control over the grid's starting position on the page, how far apart its lines are spaced, its colouring and at what zoom level it becomes visible.

Crystal-clear preview

Grids, guides and other visual elements that aren't part of a document can be hidden by switching to Preview Mode for an instant, unobscured view of your pages' contents.

Data merge

Merge text and image links from an external data source such as text (plain/CSV), JSON and XLSX spreadsheet files (e.g. MS Excel)

Asset management

Save page elements to the Assets Panel for later use.

Merge documents

Bring together other Affinity Publisher documents or PDFs into a single 'master' document—great for book creation or adding a cover or inserts. Index entries and text styles are merged too.

Working with text

Text essentials

Use the Artistic Text Tool for headlines and creative typography, the Frame Text Tool for flowing copy, or run text along any vector path. Apply sophisticated ligatures, stylistic sets and alternates. All the controls you need are built in, including leading, kerning, baseline shift, tab stops—as well as the convenience of spell checking and quickly adding placeholder text. Text styles offer consistent text appearance at character and paragraph level.

Flow across pages

Flow text through a sequence of single- or multi-column text frames, even across multiple pages, in just a few clicks. Publisher reflows text automatically and instantly when you resize any of the linked text frames. Save time with AutoFlow, which creates as many pages and text frames as are needed to display all of your text.

Wrap it up

Text can wrap around other elements, including images and shapes, for a more natural feel to your page designs. You have fine control over padding to ensure text doesn't interfere with graphics.

Keep it together

Pin graphics, tables or other text frames so they stay attached to the relevant part of your publication's main text even as it is updated.

Guide your readers

Publisher can auto-generate tables of contents from the sections and text styles used in your publication. Add index marks to words and phrases and Publisher can create a comprehensive index of all the places those terms appear, including cross-references to direct readers to related topics.

Top-notch tabulation controls

Use the Table Tool to drag out the desired number of columns and rows, then resize the whole table to fill a precise area without affecting its internal structure. On-page controls for adding and removing cells, easy methods for selecting continuous or non-adjacent cells and comprehensive styling options. Table formatting can be saved and reused across multiple documents.

Design essentials

Instant undo history

Scrub through thousands of undo steps with the history slider. Editing decisions are saved with your document, so you can undo steps even after closing and reopening.

Smart colour picker

Dedicated colour picker tool to accurately pick a colour for reuse, including single point or averaged sampling.

Transform Panel

Precisely set an object's position, size, rotation and shear.

Stroke Panel

For full control over dashed line styles and arrowheads.

Customisable keyboard shortcuts

Affinity Publisher includes default keyboard shortcuts, which you can tailor to your own preference.

Resource management

Resource Manager

Centralised control of embedded/linked images and documents. Collect linked resources into a single folder.

Font Manager

Substitute missing fonts for suggested replacements or use Font Manager for manual font control.

Packaging

Assemble your project's linked images, documents and fonts into a single file for portability.

Professional file format support and output

Work with familiar formats

Import/place Adobe InDesign (IDML only) and PDFs (passthrough). Open and place other Affinity apps' documents. Place images (PNG, JPEG, TIFF, SVG), layered PSD formats, Microsoft Word DOCX, spreadsheet data (XLSX), RTF and plain text files.

Create templates

Export publications as .aftemplate files that can be shared over cloud storage and made available via the New Document dialog.

Pro colour management

Manage your publication's colour scheme on the Swatches Panel. Work with print in mind from start to finish with a full CMYK workflow and the ability to lock a document's colour profile. PANTONE® colour swatches are included, along with support for RGB, LAB and greyscale workspaces.

Live preflight checking

Errors and warnings are reported as they occur for easy resolution in the Preflight Panel.

Professional PDF output

Prepare your output for a professional printer with trim, bleed and crop marks and support for PDF/X output. For special colour treatment, apply spot colours selectively.

Interactive digital publications

Screen-ready PDFs include hyperlinks and PDF bookmarks.

STUDIOLINK: INTEGRATED AFFINITY APPS

Thanks to Affinity Publisher's revolutionary StudioLink technology, users who also have Affinity Designer and Affinity Photo installed can apply their respective graphic design and photo-editing features directly to pages in Publisher without having to switch apps.

StudioLink allows you to access the primary toolsets of Designer and Photo with the click of a button—just select the relevant app's Persona button at the top left of Publisher's workspace and watch as the tools and Studio Panels automatically change as you switch between vector and raster disciplines. When you're finished using the Designer or Photo Persona, all you need to do is click the Publisher Persona button and all your page layout tools will return.

Say goodbye to repetitive image export/import cycles and hello to an incredibly streamlined creative workflow!

StudioLink

To use StudioLink, check that you have the latest Affinity Designer and Affinity Photo versions installed, then open the apps to register them with StudioLink.

In this example, the annotated vector illustration (left page) has been created in **Designer Persona**, the 3D image (right page) has been manipulated in **Photo Persona**, and **Publisher Persona** has laid them out on the spread along with a logo, title, table and table text.

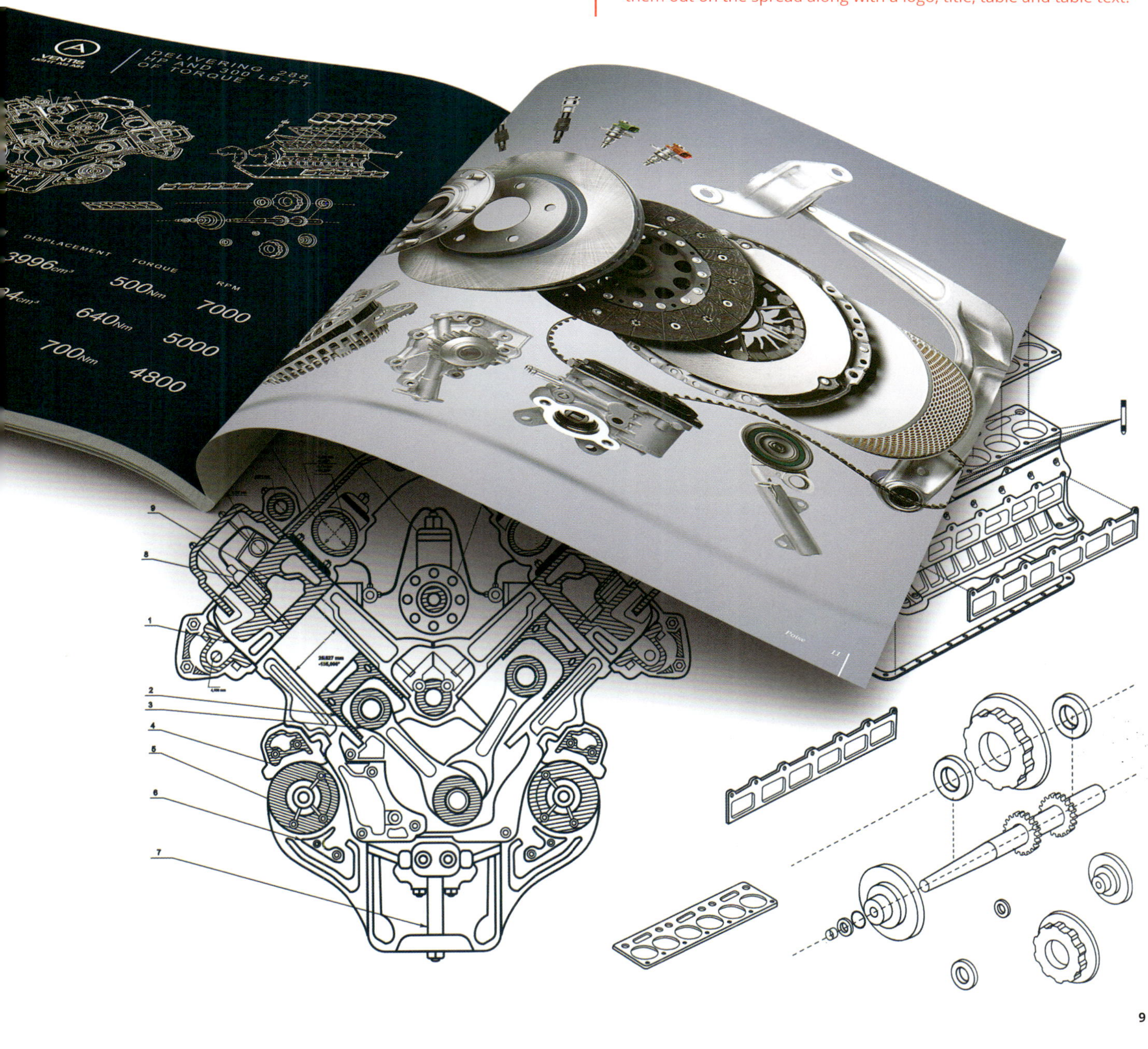

GET THE MOST OUT OF THIS WORKBOOK

To use this workbook, you must have Affinity Publisher installed on your Mac or PC. You can buy Affinity Publisher from the Mac App Store, the Microsoft Store or from affinity.serif.com

For full system requirements, please visit affin.co/publisherfeatures

Be familiar with the Interface

The projects in this book assume that you have a working knowledge of the interface of Affinity Publisher already, or that you have read and understood the Interface Tour (p. 14).

Master the Core Skills

The projects in this book also assume that you have mastered the core skills of Affinity Publisher, or that you have understood the principles outlined in Core Skills (p. 76). At the beginning of each project, core skills that you'll need will be referenced.

Use the Defaults

The projects in this workbook assume that you are using the default settings of Affinity Publisher. See Interface Tour (p. 14) to find out how to reset to the default workspace.

Keyboard Shortcuts

At the back of this book you can find some handy pull-out keyboard cheat sheets to help you learn the default keyboard shortcuts. The default keyboard shortcut for each tool is referenced whenever a tool is first mentioned in a project.

You can also learn about customising the keyboard shortcuts to your liking in the Interface Tour referenced above.

Project Resources

At the beginning of each project you'll be provided with a link to download all the designer's resources for that project, e.g.

https://affin.co/RBBrochure

On later project pages, you may see references to specific files in your resources that you can use to follow along with the project:

Resource
Rootbox_brochure_02.afpub Root Box.afpalette rootbox-ribeiro-berries.png

Resources are hosted on the Affinity Store (https://affinity.serif.com/store) and are accessible via your Affinity account. Simply click the **Get My Download Link** button to download all of each project's resources to your Downloads folder (or equivalent).

JOIN OUR COMMUNITY

Access our latest news and updates, plus get more resources

We are delighted to provide a wealth of help and support to our growing Affinity Community. Here's how to get involved...

Keep up to date and get support

Our **Twitter**, **Facebook** and **Instagram** pages are great places to get up-to-date news, exclusives and sneak peeks. Plus, you can sign up to our **newsletter** to get all the latest news, offers and competitions via email, and we promise to never send you spam, ever.

For in-depth questions and technical support, our **forums** are the best place to go. Our developers play an active role on our forums, so you can get help and updates straight from the source. This is also the place to take part in our free customer betas, so you can try out all our new features first.

Get inspired

Affinity Spotlight is a free, online resource created to share inspirational creative work we love, as well as important advice from professionals. From in-depth interviews with Affinity all-stars, to behind-the-scenes looks at projects created in Affinity to learning resources such as tutorials and explanations of technical concepts, it's all in one place. Visit affinityspotlight.com to find out more.

Keep on learning

Affinity products are backed up by an impressive selection of video tutorials—all recorded in 4K. You can access them from the Welcome screen in the app by clicking View Tutorials. They'll help you to learn our software and develop your creative skill set and are intended for beginners and advanced users equally. We'll keep adding more tutorials as we develop more features.

Join our mailing list to get the latest Affinity news and updates at affin.co/subscribe

Learn how to use the Affinity suite with our comprehensive video tutorials at vimeo.com/affinitybyserif and affin.co/youtube

Get news, updates, support and take part in our competitions by following us on Twitter @affinitybyserif

Like @affinitybyserif on Facebook to get support and to stay up-to-date with the latest news, updates and competitions

Share your work tagged with #madeinaffinity for a chance to be featured on our Instagram page @affinitybyserif

Find news, learning resources and inspiration from the award-winning Affinity team at affinityspotlight.com

Take part in our free customer betas and get in-depth support from our team—including our developers—on our forums at affin.co/forum

CHAPTER 1

Interface Tour

In this chapter you'll get familiar with the user interface of Affinity Publisher. We'll focus on all your page layout tools and Studio panels, and how Affinity uses a context-driven workspace to keep things intuitive, easy to use and, most of all, fun.

AFFINITY PUBLISHER

The Interface Explained

Toolbar

Use to switch Personas and access commonly used controls and options, including text wrap, pinning, design aids, ordering and alignment controls.

Tools Panel

Hosts all your page layout tools. The tool set will change if you switch to different Personas using StudioLink.

Context Toolbar

Dynamically updates according to the selected tool or object so you only get the relevant options as you need them.

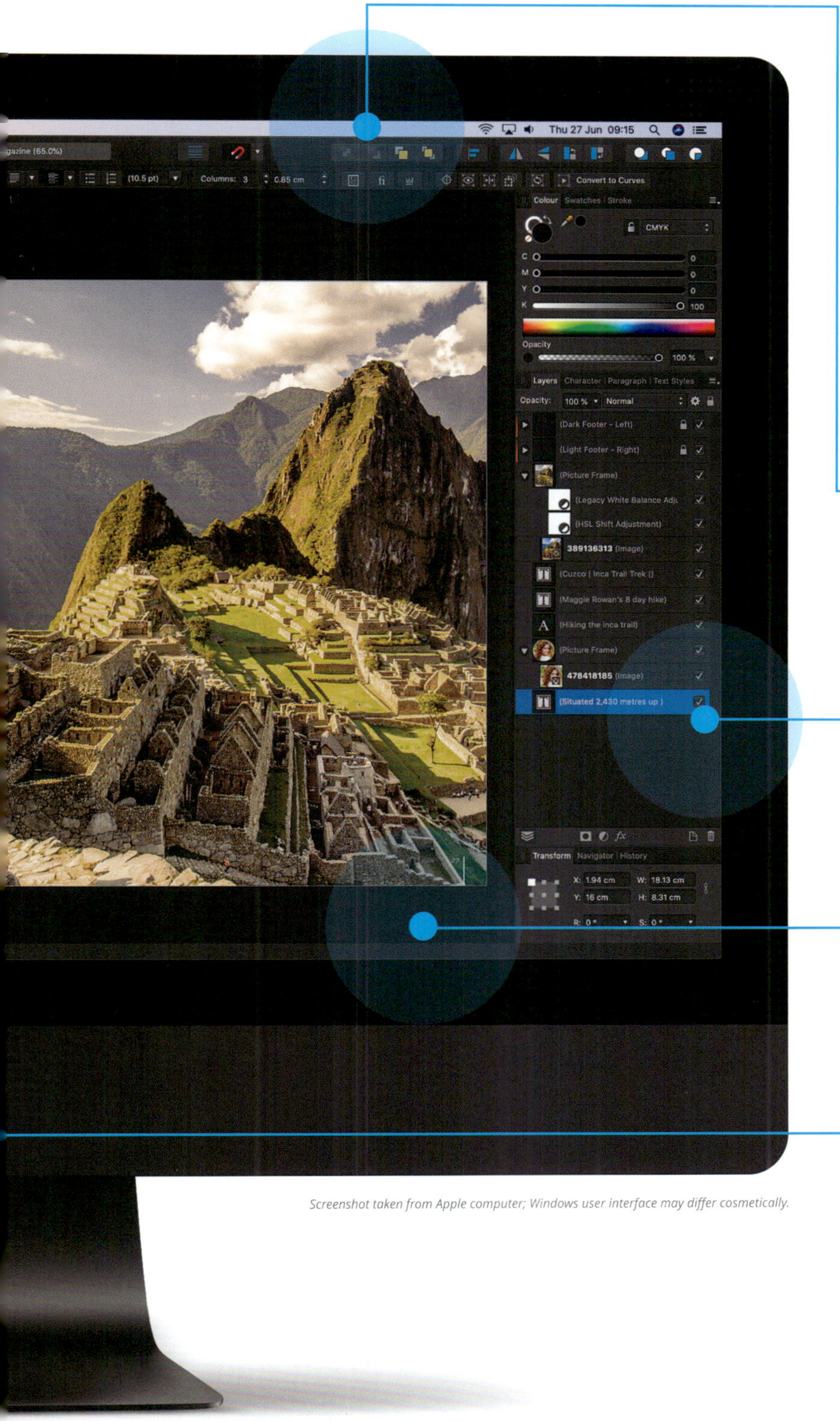

Screenshot taken from Apple computer; Windows user interface may differ cosmetically.

Menu Bar

Provides commands and options via multiple menus.

Studio Panels

Let you change the properties of page objects and elements; other panels are provided as design aids.

Document View

This is your 'real estate' for laying out pages.

Status Bar

Provides handy tips and shortcuts about the currently active tool.

PERSONAS

Personas offer different ways of working in your application. These are accessed via a series of buttons on the main Toolbar.

With only Affinity Publisher installed, and not Affinity Designer or Affinity Photo, a single Persona button, called **Publisher Persona**, is selectable.

Publisher Persona

A page layout Persona which lets you create:

- Pages, master pages and spreads
- Text frames
- Picture frames
- Tables
- Curves and shapes
- Artistic and frame text
- Tables of Contents and Indexes
- Hyperlinks and anchors
- PDF output (web ready and pro print)

StudioLink

StudioLink technology (p. 8) uses additional Personas to access functionality in **Affinity Photo** and **Affinity Designer**. These extend your vector and photo-editing functionality, respectively; you'll never need to leave Affinity Publisher, avoiding repetitive export and import cycles of redesigned work. You'll be working seamlessly between disciplines.

Designer Persona

For additional vector drawing capabilities. If you have purchased and installed **Affinity Designer**, this Persona gives you instant access to its main toolset including:

- Symbols
- Corner Tool
- Vector Brush Tool and many brush categories
- Pencil Tool
- Multi-stroke and multi-fill effects

Photo Persona

For professional image editing using photo-editing tools. If you have purchased and installed **Affinity Photo**, you'll get access to:

- Paint Brush Tool and many brush categories
- Freehand, shape and brush-based selection tools
- Retouching brush tools
- Live filters
- Masking of adjustments and filters

Switching Personas

When you wish to swap your way of working, simply select a different Persona from the **Toolbar** and continue working with a new tool set. Switching between Personas will result in the current workspace changing to display appropriate tools, toolbars, panels and menu options.

PUBLISHER PERSONA TOOLS

Move Tool

The tool lets you move, rotate, resize, transform and copy page objects.
Keyboard shortcut: V

Node Tool

The **Node Tool** edits curves and shapes drawn with the **Pen** and **shape tools** with superior precision.
Keyboard shortcut: A

Frame Text Tool

The **Frame Text Tool** adds flowing paragraph text to your document contained within a text frame.
Keyboard shortcut: T
(Cycles Frame Text, Artistic Text and Table Tools)

Table Tool

The **Table Tool** adds a table to your document.

Artistic Text Tool

The **Artistic Text Tool** creates scalable text intended for titling or decorative reasons.

Pen Tool

The **Pen Tool** draws Bézier curves, closed irregular shapes, straight lines or polygons. Great for converting to text frames or picture frames.
Keyboard shortcut: P

Shape Tools

These tools add complicated geometric shapes to your document. They are highly adaptable and editable and come in a variety of shapes including rectangles, stars, an ellipse and the multifaceted cog. Many shapes are accessible via the flyout menu.
Keyboard shortcut: M
*(Cycles **Rectangle Tool**, **Ellipse Tool**, and **Rounded Rectangle Tool**)*

Picture Frame Rectangle Tool

Adds rectangular or square picture frames to your page into which you can place content.
Keyboard shortcut: F
(Toggles picture frame tools)

The **Tools Panel** hosts a comprehensive set of tools for the current Persona. For **Publisher Persona**, the toolset is primarily intended for page layout and creating page objects.

Picture Frame Ellipse Tool

Adds elliptical or circular picture frames to your document.
Keyboard shortcut: F
(Toggles picture frame tools)

Place Image Tool

Adds an image, Affinity document or PDF to your page (or selected picture frame) at its default or custom dimensions by clicking or dragging.

Data Merge Node Tool

Creates an area to merge external data into, including reproducing content multiple times.

Vector Crop Tool

The **Vector Crop Tool** removes portions of a selected object non-destructively.

Fill Tool

Applies a highly customisable smooth colour gradient to an object's stroke and/or fill. Great for text frames, titling and shapes (for page backgrounds).
Keyboard shortcut: G

Transparency Tool

Applies a transparency gradient to an object.
Keyboard shortcut: Y

Colour Picker Tool

Samples colours from your document and optionally applies it to the current selection.
Keyboard shortcut: I

View Tool

Moves the visible portion of your document in the **Document View**. Double-click the icon to 'Zoom to Fit' the current page.
Keyboard shortcut: H
Hotkey panning: Spacebar

Zoom Tool

Changes the zoom level of your page in the **Document View**. Double-click the icon to set the zoom level to 100%.
Keyboard shortcut: Z

TOOLBAR

The **Publisher Persona**'s **Toolbar** includes options for Persona navigation, default control, text wrapping, pinning, previewing, baseline grid setup and object manipulation.

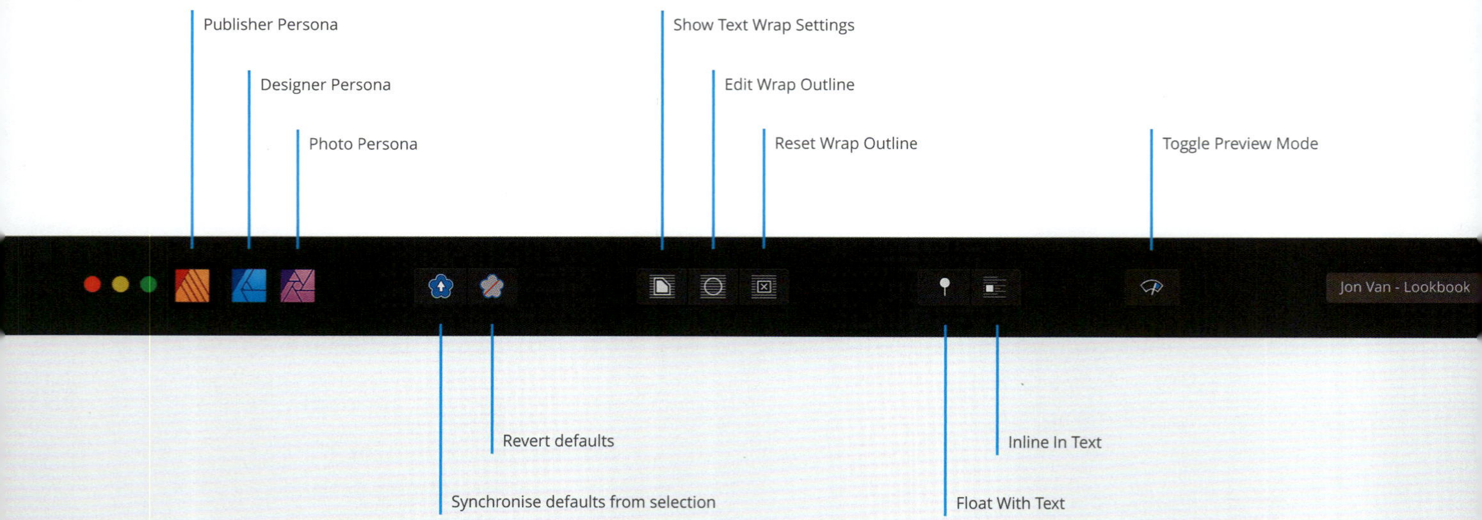

Screenshot taken from Apple computer; Windows user interface may differ cosmetically.

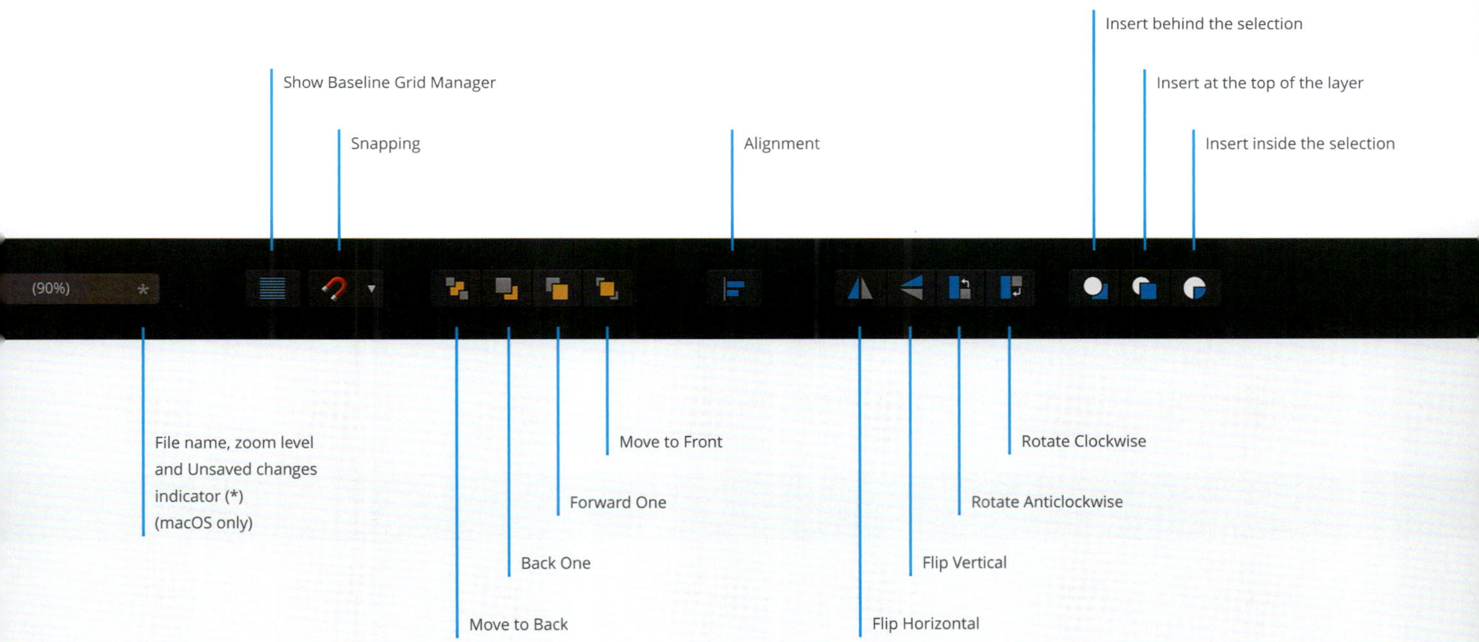
Insert behind the selection
Show Baseline Grid Manager
Insert at the top of the layer
Snapping
Alignment
Insert inside the selection
(90%)
*
File name, zoom level
and Unsaved changes
indicator (*)
(macOS only)
Move to Front
Forward One
Back One
Move to Back
Rotate Clockwise
Rotate Anticlockwise
Flip Vertical
Flip Horizontal

CONTEXT TOOLBAR

The context toolbar appears directly above your **Document View**.

As the name implies, the options on the context toolbar will update depending on the currently selected tool. Regardless of the tool you switch to, you'll have quick access to appropriate options while you edit.

For example, the toolbars for the **Rectangle Tool** (below) and **Frame Text Tool** (opposite) differ.

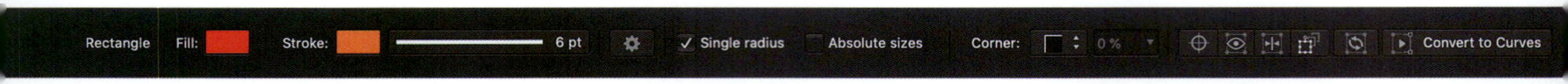

When the **Move Tool** and an **object** is selected, the context toolbar will provide editing options for that object. For example, for a selected picture frame:

When the **Move Tool** is selected, but no objects are selected, the context toolbar will give you access to **Document Setup**, **Spread Setup** and **Preferences**.

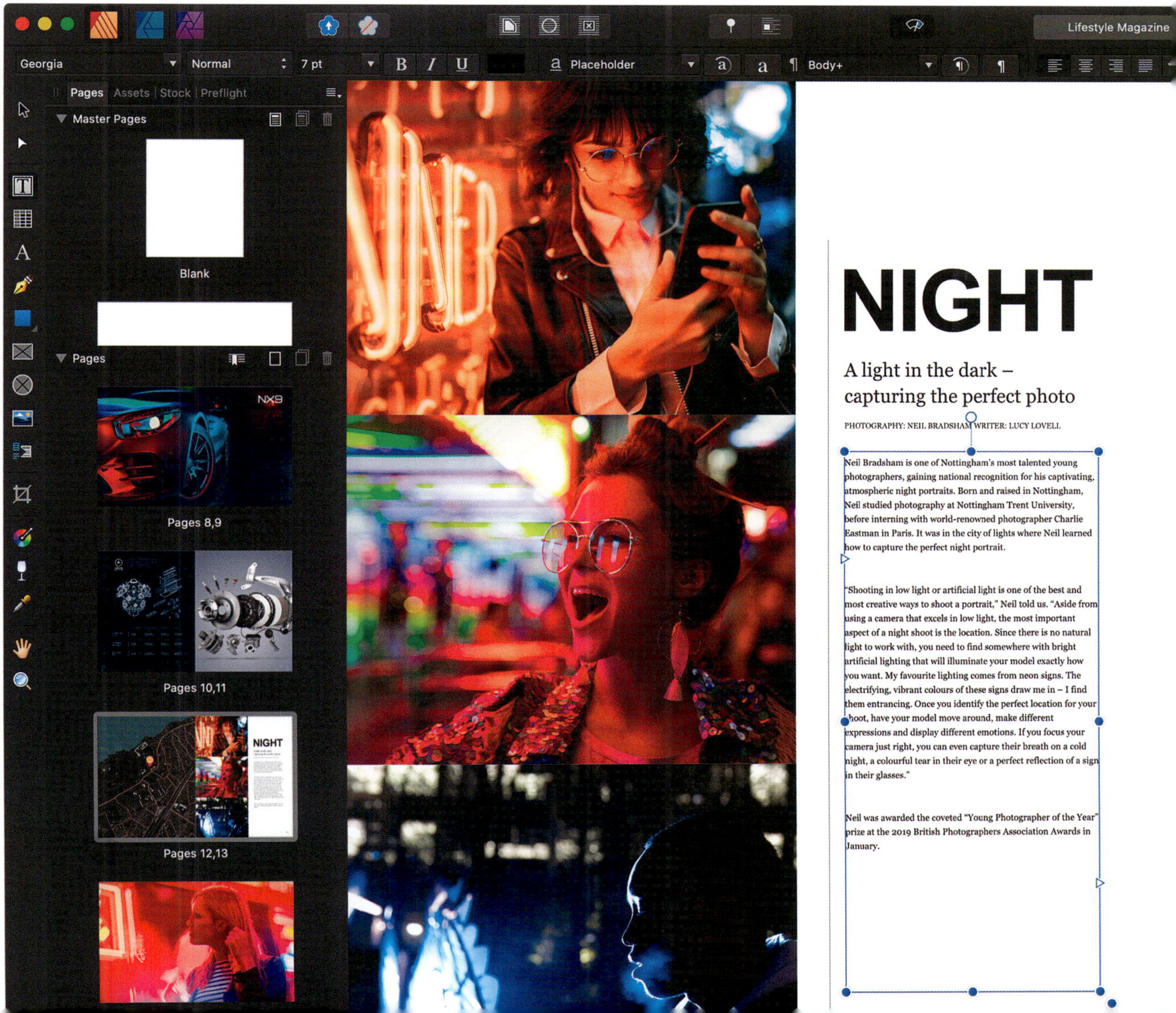
Lifestyle Magazine
Georgia
Normal
7 pt
Placeholder
Body+
Pages
Assets
Stock
Preflight
Master Pages
Blank
Pages
NX9
Pages 8,9
Pages 10,11
NIGHT
Pages 12,13
NIGHT
A light in the dark –
capturing the perfect photo
PHOTOGRAPHY: NEIL BRADSHAM WRITER: LUCY LOVELL
Neil Bradsham is one of Nottingham's most talented young photographers, gaining national recognition for his captivating, atmospheric night portraits. Born and raised in Nottingham, Neil studied photography at Nottingham Trent University, before interning with world-renowned photographer Charlie Eastman in Paris. It was in the city of lights where Neil learned how to capture the perfect night portrait.
"Shooting in low light or artificial light is one of the best and most creative ways to shoot a portrait," Neil told us. "Aside from using a camera that excels in low light, the most important aspect of a night shoot is the location. Since there is no natural light to work with, you need to find somewhere with bright artificial lighting that will illuminate your model exactly how you want. My favourite lighting comes from neon signs. The electrifying, vibrant colours of these signs draw me in – I find them entrancing. Once you identify the perfect location for your shoot, have your model move around, make different expressions and display different emotions. If you focus your camera just right, you can even capture their breath on a cold night, a colourful tear in their eye or a perfect reflection of a sign in their glasses."
Neil was awarded the coveted "Young Photographer of the Year" prize at the 2019 British Photographers Association Awards in January.

STUDIO PANELS

Once an object has been created and selected, its object properties can be modified using options which appear on the **Studio Panels**.

It's worth knowing that not all panels are displayed by default, as some panels are for alternative workflows. Go to **View Menu > Studio** to turn individual panels off and on and use **Reset Studio** to only show the default Studio Panels.

The following panels appear when the **Publisher Persona** is active.

Pages Panel

The **Pages Panel** allows you to add, edit and view master pages, publication pages and sections within your document.

Individual or multiple publication pages can be inserted, duplicated or reordered, as well as have one or more master pages assigned to them.

You can change the dimensions, scaling behaviour and orientation of pages and facing page spreads by changing **Spread Properties** (via thumbnail right-click).

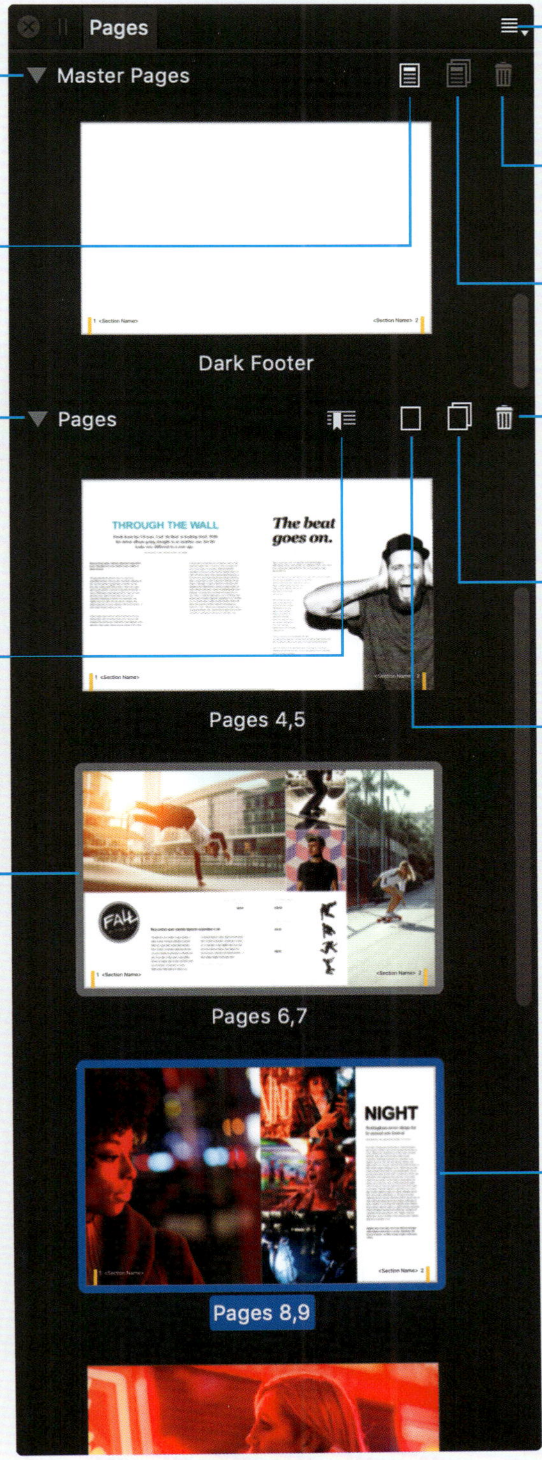

Master Pages Window

Displays the master pages that are currently available in your document.

Add Master

Creates a new master page.

Pages Window

Displays publication pages as thumbnails within your document.

Section Manager

The **Section Manager** lets you add, delete and manage sections and adjust page numbering starts.

Viewed pages

Double-click page thumbnail to display the page (grey outline) in your workspace.

Panel Preferences

Determine page icon sizes, scroll automatically to match the currently active view.

Delete Selected Master

Deletes the selected master page.

Duplicate Selected Master

Duplicates the selected master page.

Delete Selected Pages

Deletes the selected publication page(s).

Duplicate Selected Pages

Duplicates the selected publication page(s).

Add Pages

Creates additional publication pages.

Selected pages

Click page thumbnail to allow the selected page (blue outline) to be edited.

Assets Panel

Assets are stored objects (or groups) which can be accessed from any open Affinity document. They are conveniently stored in the **Assets Panel**.

Assets are created by dragging from the page to a panel subcategory, and subsequently added to the same or different document by dragging its thumbnail from the panel onto the chosen page.

Asset categories and subcategories can be created at any time to help you organise your assets. They are then listed in the pop-up **Category Menu** at the top of the panel.

The panel is empty by default. The example opposite is for illustration purposes only.

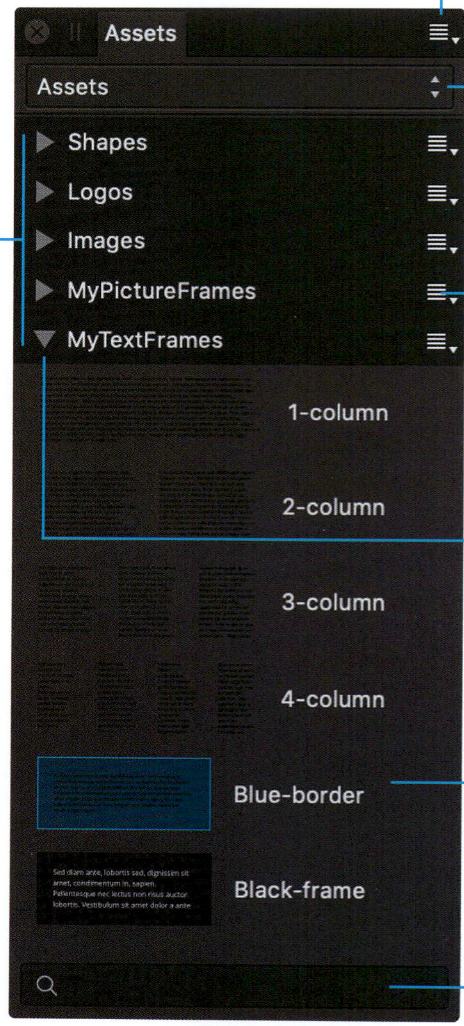

Subcategories

Organise your assets into named subcategories.

Panel Preferences

Allows you to create, rename and delete categories and add subcategories. Also lets you import, export and embed assets, and display assets as named lists.

Category Menu

Select a parent category which contains subcategories and stored assets.

Subcategory Options Menu

Allows you to rename or delete the subcategory as well as move it up or down within the category.

Expand / Collapse

Click to expand to reveal hosted assets. Click again to collapse.

Assets

Displays your stored assets as thumbnails (displayed as lists).

Search

Locate assets by name.

Stock Panel

The **Stock Panel** is an in-app image browser which displays content from free and royalty-free photo providers. Search and browse images, then add them to the document by drag and drop.

Archive

Sets the image provider from which to search.

Search

Colour Panel

The **Colour Panel** is used to choose colours for various tools and selected objects. A pop-up version of the **Colour Panel** may appear when choosing a colour from within other dialogs.

The **Colour Panel** can operate in several colour modes—RGB, RGB HEX, HSL, CMYK, LAB and Greyscale—and has various ways of defining colour—colour sliders, colour boxes and a colour wheel. Colour tints can also be applied from within the panel.

Swap

Switches the colours applied to the selectors.

Stroke/Fill

The active colour selector is shown at the front of the two colour selectors. Choosing a new colour will apply it to the active colour selector.

None

Removes colour from the active selector.

Opacity/Noise

Click to switch between Opacity and Noise.

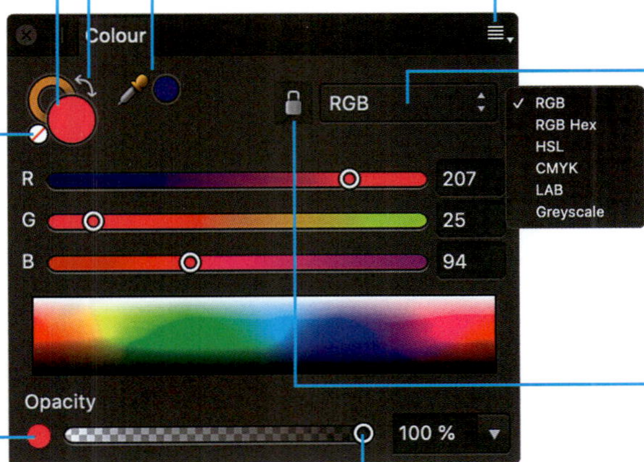

Colour picker and picked colour swatch

Allows colour sampling from individual pixels; click swatch to apply picked colour to active selector.

Panel Preferences

Select colour from colour box, sliders or wheel (HSL only). Colour tints and chords can also be created.

Colour Mode

Defines your colour in your choice of colour mode.

Lock Colourspace

When enabled, the currently active colour mode can't be accidentally changed after using the Swatches Panel or selecting an object created in a different colour space.

Opacity/Noise Controls

Sets the opacity and/or noise of the active colour.

Swatches Panel

The **Swatches Panel** stores your recently used colours and lets you access a range of pre-defined palettes, each containing solid or gradient fill swatches. These can be selected for use with various tools and for applying directly to objects. You can also create and store your own swatches as custom colour palettes either for the document or application (system-wide for macOS version).

As well as accessing palettes, you can create global and spot colours, and make colours overprint. Your registration colour can also be customised.

The Swatches Panel also shows None, Black, Mid-grey and White swatches, recently used colours and an opacity control. Swatches are organised into colour palettes by category.

In contrast to the Colour Panel, use this panel if you'd rather select colours from a pre- defined palette. You can choose colours from a temporary (Recent) palette as well as from custom and pre-defined palettes such as PANTONE® colours.

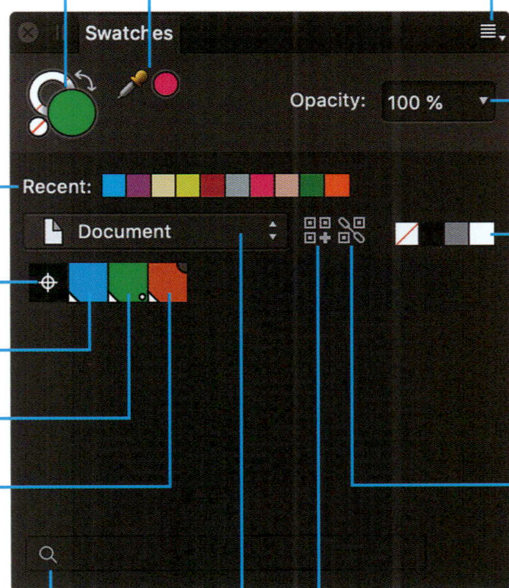

Colour picker and picked colour swatch

Stroke/Fill

The active colour selector is shown at the front of the two colour selectors.

Recently used colours

Registration Colour

Global Colour

Spot Colour

Overprint Colour

Search

Panel Preferences

Add palettes, registration and global colours (including spot and overprint). Manage palettes and viewing options.

Opacity Control

None, Black, Mid-grey and White swatches

Add current colour to palette as a global colour

Add current fill to palette

Category list

Includes Document, Application, System and PANTONE® colour palettes.

Stroke Panel

This panel allows you to modify lines and curves, as well as the stroke of a selected shape. You can change a stroke's thickness, how it scales, and where it's positioned relative to the object. Options for line endings include cap settings and arrowheads.

Cap

Round, **Butt**, or **Square** cap style to end the contour of a line.

Join

Use a **Round**, **Bevel**, or **Mitre** join style to determine the contour of the corner of the selected object.

Align

Select one of the align buttons to control where the stroke is placed in relation to the object edge.

Style

Select a line style button to change how the line is drawn. Choose from **None**, **Solid Line Style**, **Dash Line Style**, and **Texture Line Style** (brush), respectively. For **Dash Line Style**, you can set the design and phasing of the dash.

Width

Drag to change the thickness of the selected line.

Arrowhead styles (Start and End)

Sets the style for each end of your arrow. Tail (fletching) styles are also available.

Arrow scaling

Controls arrow's head and tail scaling in relation to stroke width.

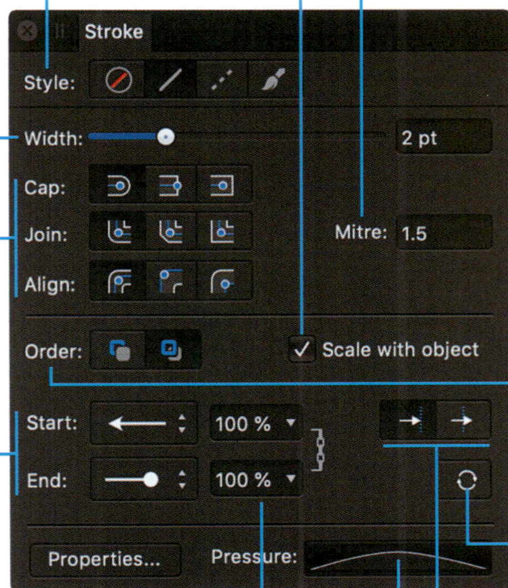

Scale with object

Check to scale the width of the stroke when resizing an object. Uncheck to keep stoke width constant, regardless of object size changes.

Mitre

Sets the length of the extension of **Mitre** Joins to create either sharp or flat corners.

Order

Draws the stroke either behind or in front of the object.

Swap arrow head with tail

The ends of your arrow are reversed.

Arrowhead positioning

The arrowhead can be placed within the line or can extend the line.

Pressure

Displays the current pressure profile applied to a curve or brush stroke. Click to edit the profile and save it for future use.

Opacity

Adjusts the transparency of the selected items.

Master object indicators

Solid and dashed orange indicators show objects connected to and detached from master page, respectively.

Layers Panel

The **Layers Panel** controls the stacking order (Z-order) of objects on your page, organises your layers and objects, and controls layer visibility, locking, opacity and blending. It provides information about a layer, such as its type and whether it has effects applied.

Item

Created object showing a thumbnail of contents, item name, item type (in parenthesis) and if Layer Effect applied. Text objects will show actual text from page.

Expand/Collapse

Click to expand the item, revealing nested or grouped content. Click again to collapse.

Edit All Layers

Allows selection and editing of objects across all layers (rather than the current layer).

Mask Layer

Creates a layer mask to reveal a portion of the layer while the rest of the layer remains hidden.

Adjustments

Applies an adjustment layer for tonal and colour correction of current layer, object or page.

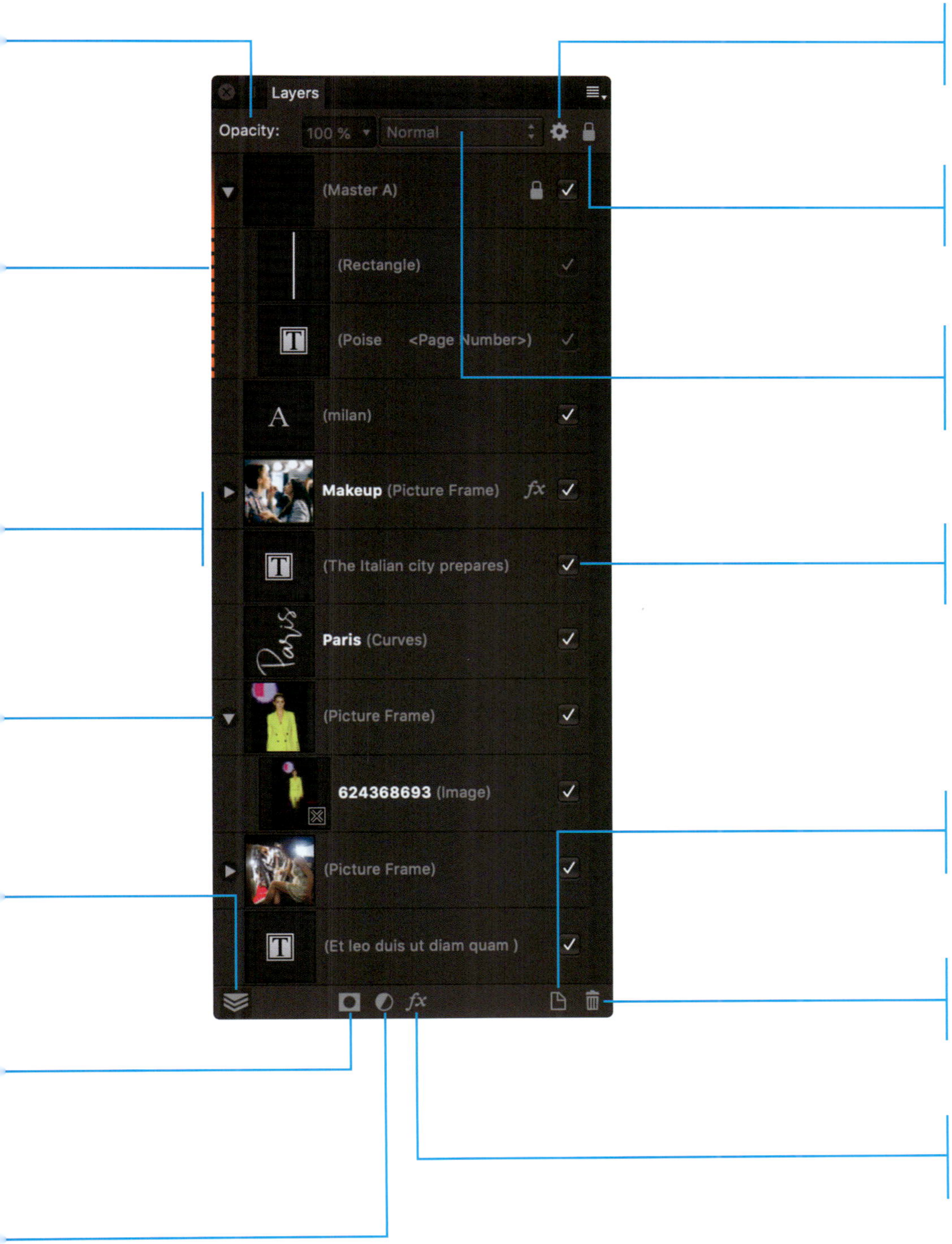

Blend Options

Access settings for blend ranges, blend gamma and antialiasing.

Lock/Unlock

Click to lock or unlock selected items to prevent or allow editing.

Blend Mode

Changes how the current layer's colours interact with existing colours on the layers below.

Hide/Show

Uncheck to hide the item; check to make it visible again.

Add Layer

Creates an empty layer above the currently selected layer.

Remove Layer

Deletes the currently selected, object, group or layer.

Layer Effects

Applies a layer effect to the currently selected layer.

Character Panel

The **Character Panel** allows you to apply local formatting to individual letters, words, sentences and paragraphs as well as entire stories.

Kerning

Controls the distance between two characters. **Auto** will give automatic kerning (default). Positive values give expanded kerning, negative values give condensed kerning.

Tracking

Controls the spacing between characters throughout a word.

Baseline

Controls the position of the bottom of text characters. Increasing the value lowers the baseline, decreasing the value raises the baseline.

Leading Override

Overrides the value set for the paragraph's **Leading** on selected text.

Collection

Filters the list of available fonts in the Font pop-up menu.

Font Size

Controls the point size of characters.

Character Style

Allows a character text style to be applied to selected text.

Decorations

Applies underline, strikethrough or outline attributes with colour options.

Typography

Depending on your font, you can apply various typographic options to enhance your characters beyond their standard attributes. Access OpenType font features like ligatures, alternates, stylistic sets and more.

Language

Sets the languages for the dictionary (for spell checking), hyphenation and typography.

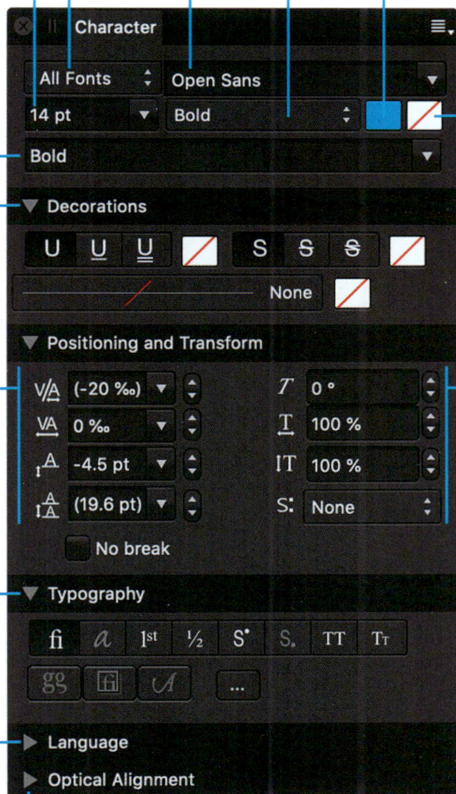

Font

Sets the typeface for the selected text.

Font Style

Controls which typeface style is applied to the selected text.

Font colour

Sets the colour of the text.

Background colour

Sets the colour applied behind the selected text (i.e., creating a highlight effect).

Shear

Controls the extent of text slant. Positive values will tilt text to the left, negative values will tilt text to the right.

Horizontal Scale

Stretches the characters and spacing with regard to point size.

Vertical Scale

Stretches the characters with regard to point size.

Super/Subscript

Applies either a superscript or subscript attribute.

Optical Alignment

Controls the alignment of dashes, punctuation or any character you choose at the start of paragraphs.

Paragraph Style

Applies the selected paragraph text style.

First Line Indent

Controls the indent applied to the first line of the paragraph.

Last Line Outdent

Controls the outdent applied to the last line when a right indent is applied.

Paragraph Panel

The **Paragraph Panel** gives you full control over paragraph-level formatting options. Paragraph formatting is applied to the entire paragraph in which selected text is located or to a paragraph in which the caret is located.

Space Above/Below Management

Controls how space above/below settings work together.

Tab Stops

Create, position and align paragraph tab stops.

Justification

For justified paragraphs, you can control letter and word spacing.

Flow Options

Controls paragraph start position, orphaning, widowing and inter-paragraph relationships.

Bullets and Numbering

Creates bulleted lists using any glyph or numbered lists using a choice of number schemas.

Baseline Grid

Aligns the paragraph to any active baseline grid.

Hyphenation

Applies automatic hyphenation and offers auto-hyphenation settings.

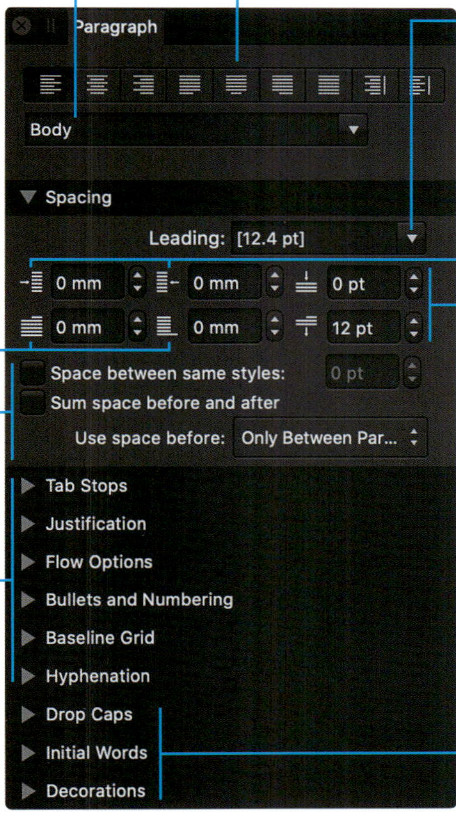

Alignment

Select from **Left**, **Centre**, **Right**, **Justify Left**, **Justify Centre**, **Justify Right**, **Justify All** (Force-Justified), **Align Towards Spine** or **Align Away From Spine**.

Leading

Controls the distance between text baselines (vertical gap between lines) within the paragraph.

Left Indent / Right Indent

Controls the left or right indent applied to the entire paragraph (excluding the first line).

Space Before Paragraph / Space After Paragraph

Controls the vertical gap which precedes or succeeds the paragraph.

Drop Caps

Scales first character across multiple lines for a strong focal point at story start.

Initial Words

Applies character formatting to words at start of paragraph up to a chosen end character.

Decorations

Adds rules or background fill to a paragraph.

Text Styles Panel

A text style is a set of one or more attributes which can be applied to text in bulk. Later, if you choose to modify a text style, any text which uses that style will update to conform to the changes you've made. The **Text Styles Panel** enables you to create, apply and manage text styles within your publication.

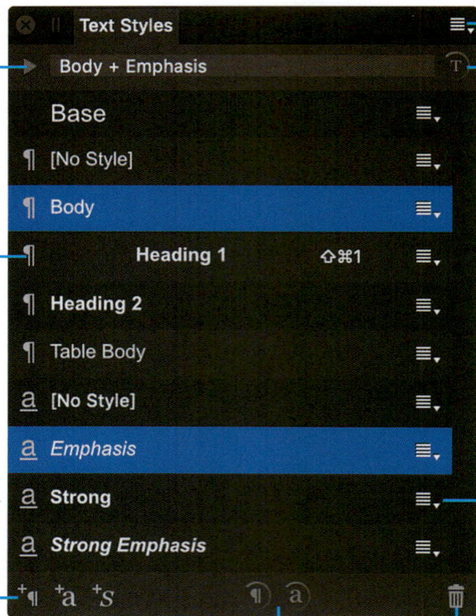

Current Formatting

Displays the formatting applied to the current selection or caret position. Click the arrow to show more details.

Text Style

Entry includes name, preview of its formatting, its predominant type and its shortcut keys.

Create

Launches the **Edit Text Style** dialog ready for creating a new paragraph, character or group text style, respectively, from scratch.

Update

Revises the current paragraph or character style, respectively, to conform to the local formatting of the selected text.

Panel Preferences

Lets you control text styles: show style hierarchy, preview, sort, delete unused, detach/delete all, set as default for future and import.

Reset Formatting

Removes overrides and local formatting applied to the currently selected text but leaves applied text styles in place.

Options menu

Access application, creation, deletion and editing options for individual text styles.

Delete Style

Removes the selected text style from the document and any instances of its application.

Transform Panel

The **Transform Panel** allows you to design with the utmost precision by controlling the horizontal (X) and vertical (Y) position of an object on your page, as well as its overall width (W) and height (H). Rotate and shear options complete the panel. All transforms are carried out in relation to a defined anchor point—corner, edge midpoint or centre.

X—Horizontal position

Adjusts the horizontal position of the object (layer) in relation to the selected anchor point.

Y—Vertical position

Adjusts the vertical position of the object (layer) in relation to the selected anchor point.

Anchor point selector

Transforms are carried out from the selected anchor point. Click on an anchor point to select.

R—Rotation

Rotates the object (layer) by a specified number of degrees in relation to the selected anchor point.

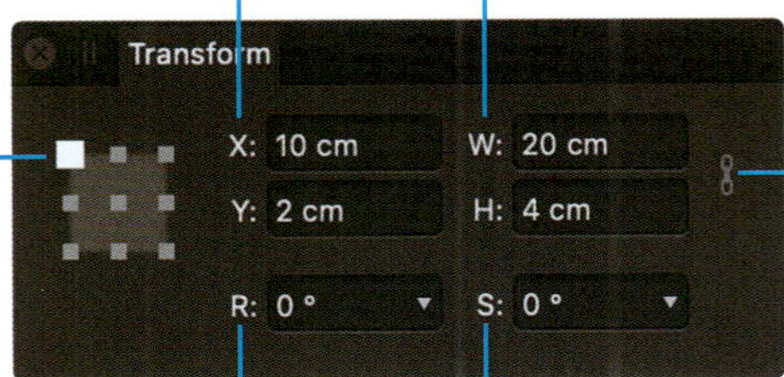

W—Width

Adjusts the object (layer) width in relation to the selected anchor point.

H—Height

Adjusts the object (layer) height in relation to the selected anchor point.

Link

When enabled, width and height are adjusted in proportion to each other, maintaining the current aspect ratio. When deselected, they can be adjusted independently.

S—Shear

Shears the object (layer) by a specified number of degrees in relation to the selected anchor point.

Navigator Panel

This panel is unique as its use has no effect on your design at all. Instead, it allows you to pan and zoom around your **Document View** and set up specific **View Points** so you can jump, and zoom, to particular areas of your project in an instant.

Zoom

Use the slider, buttons or the percentage display to zoom in or out.

View Rectangle

Pan around your design by dragging the view rectangle around in the panel. The main view displays the areas enclosed in the rectangle.

View Point Menu

Select a named **View Point** to jump and zoom to its preset position in the Document View.

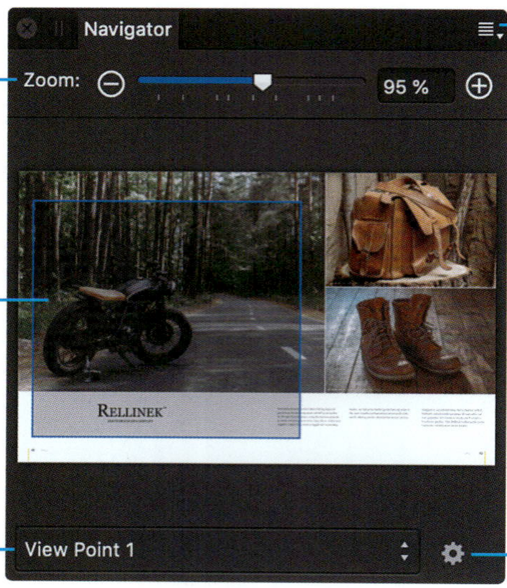

Panel Preferences

Displays the **View Point Menu** and **Settings**.

View Point Settings

Add, remove and rename view points.

History Panel

The **History Panel** tracks changes and shows each state as a labelled entry in a list, allowing you to return to earlier points in time. The oldest state is the topmost in the list, and when edits are made, new states are added to the bottom of the list. If you click on an earlier state and then make a change, you can still reinstate later states.

A document's history can be saved along with the document too by enabling **Save History With Document** in the **File Menu**, so earlier edits can be returned to even if the document is closed and reopened.

Unless you choose to save the document's history, the undo states listed in the History Panel are cleared when the document is closed.

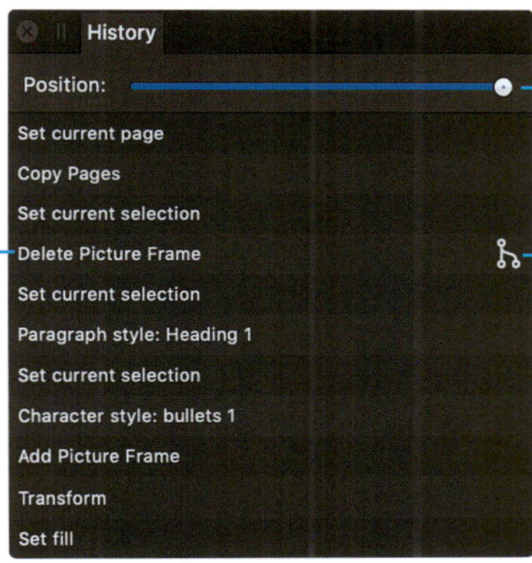

State

Gives a brief description of the edit made to the document. Click a state to jump to that edit.

Position

Drag the slider left to undo a change, right to redo a change.

Cycle futures

Click to reinstate your 'lost' redo history after making an edit at a state in your undo history.

Anchors Panel (View > Studio)

The **Anchors Panel** is used in conjunction with the **Hyperlinks Panel** (p. 53) to create and manage anchors.

They are perfect if you want to 'mark' an important passage of frame text that can be targeted via hyperlinking. If this text passage reflows onto another page, its anchor will move with it so the referencing hyperlink will always be correct.

Name

Displays the anchor name, either named from the selected source text or as Anchor 01, Anchor 02, etc.

Go To Anchor

Navigates to the page where the selected anchor is located, selecting its text frame and showing the anchor position.

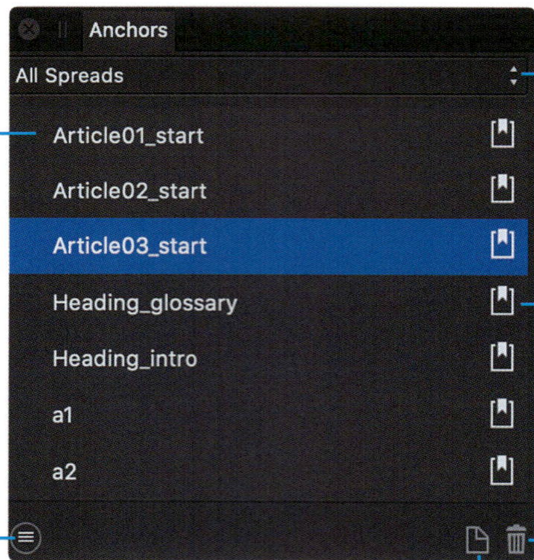

Area

Specifies the pages on which anchors are present: choose from **All Spreads** or a specific page.

Export as PDF Bookmark

Marks the anchor to be a PDF bookmark.

Remove Anchor

Removes the selected anchor.

New Anchor

Opens the **Insert Anchor** dialog, allowing you to add a new anchor from selected text.

Constraints Panel (View > Studio)

The **Constraints Panel** enables you to control the scaling and anchoring of a child object within its parent object (i.e. its container) when the parent object is resized.

For example, constraints could be used to prevent clipped artistic text captions from being repositioned within a picture frame, when that frame is resized.

The panel visually represents (and sets) the selected child object's scaling and anchoring behaviour using clickable inner scaling arrows and outer anchor lines.

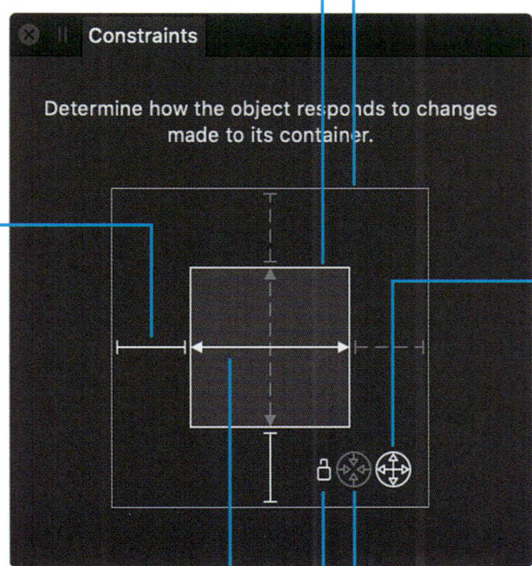

Anchor

Controlled by the lines extending from the inner square to the outer square. When displayed as a grey dashed line, the object is not anchored in that direction. When displayed as a white solid line, the object is anchored in that direction.

Scale

Controlled by the arrows contained within the inner square. When displayed as a grey dashed arrow, the object will not scale in that direction. When displayed as a white solid arrow, the object will scale in that direction. If the arrow displays as white and broken, this means the object is forced to scale in that direction because of anchoring.

Inner Square/Outer Square

The inner grey square represents the selected child object. The outer square represents a parent object (e.g., picture frame).

Max Fit

When the parent object is resized disproportionately, the child object may scale but it will be allowed to be bigger than its scaled parent object, potentially clipping content from view.

Min Fit

When the parent object is resized disproportionately, the child object may scale so it always fits within its parent object (if unanchored).

Lock

Child objects scale as their parents resize. If the parent's aspect ratio changes, the object's aspect ratio is maintained but its scaling depends on the Fit setting.

Effects Panel (View > Studio)

The **Effects Panel** offers copious settings for applying and modifying object effects such as blurs, shadows, glows, and more.

Layer effects can be applied to the currently selected object or entire layer. These effects are also completely non-destructive so you can change them at any time.

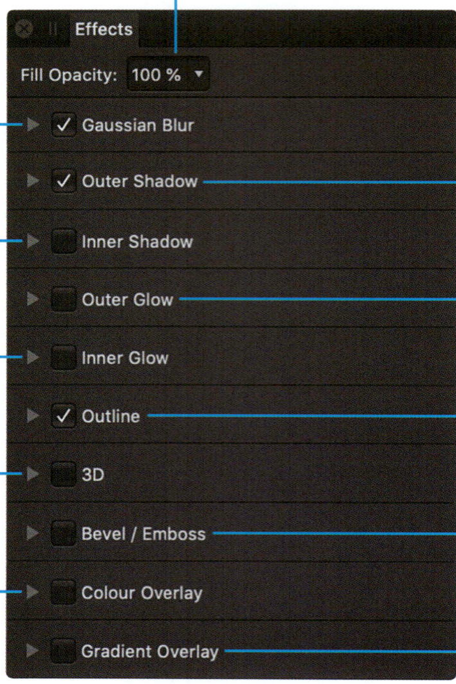

Fill Opacity

Alters the stroke and fill opacity of the object, without altering the opacity of the applied layer effect(s).

Gaussian Blur

Blurs the object.

Outer Shadow

Adds a shadow behind the object.

Inner Shadow

Adds a shadow inside the object edge.

Outer Glow

Adds a colour glow that emanates from the outside edges.

Inner Glow

Adds a colour glow that emanates from the inside edge.

Outline

Adds an outline to the object edge.

3D

Adds lighting to give a 3D appearance.

Bevel/Emboss

Adds various combinations of highlights and shadows.

Colour Overlay

Applies a solid colour to the object.

Gradient Overlay

Applies a linear gradient to object.

Fields Panel (View > Studio)

The **Fields Panel** lets you insert fields containing information related to your document into your document text. Fields will automatically update as data (for example, a date) changes.

Document Information

Displays the **Author**, **Tags**, **Comments**, **Title**, **Subject** and **Revision**.

Document Sections

Displays section fields used to report section names and page numbers. Typically added to master pages.

General Information

Displays the current **Date & Time**.

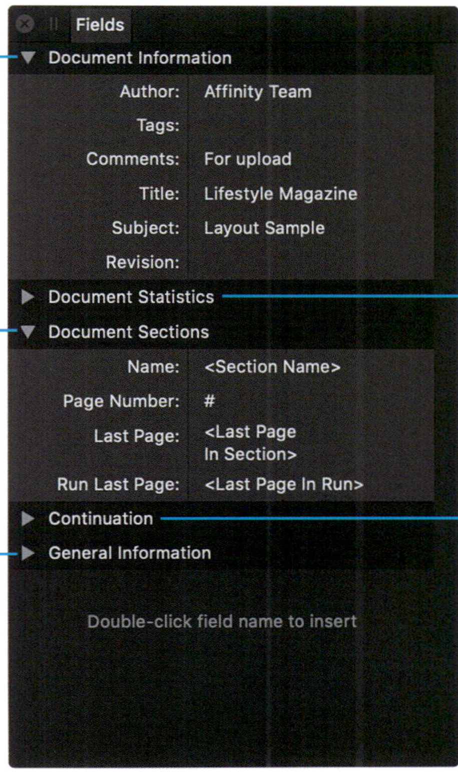

Document Statistics

Displays key statistics for the document: **Last edited by**, **Created**, **Saved**, **Printed**, **Save Count**, **Filename**, **Path** and **Total Pages**.

Continuation

Displays the **Previous Frame** and **Next Frame**.

Find and Replace Panel (View > Studio)

The **Find and Replace Panel** provides an easy way to search for and replace items such as words, fonts, formats, and character attributes either across the document in one operation, or on a case-by-case basis.

Find

Specify the item you would like to search for.

Special characters

Add a special character from the pop-up menu to include in the search or replace criteria.

Find

Displays a list of any applicable results at the bottom of the panel.

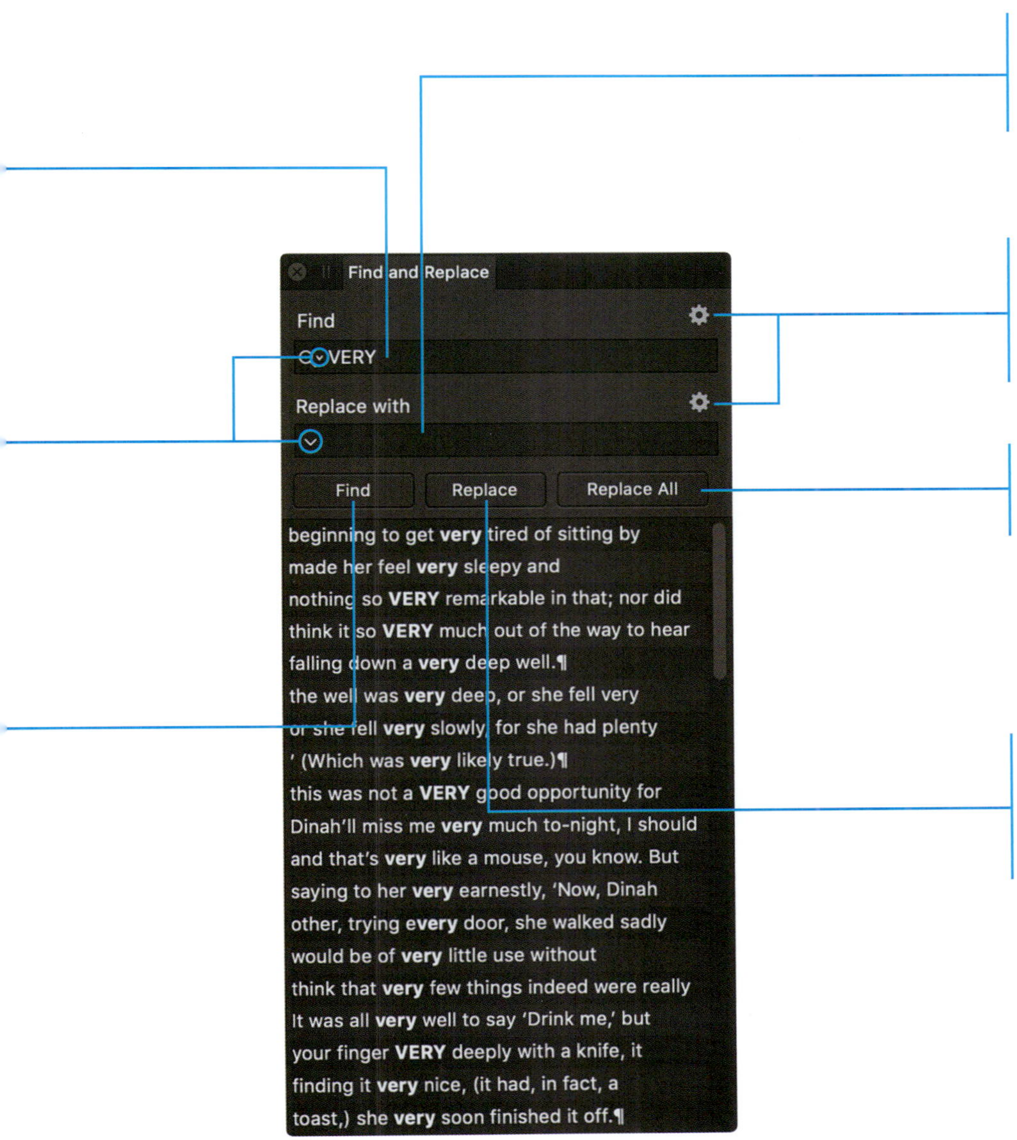

Replace with

Specify the intended replacement (if any) for the item you are searching for.

Formatting

Access settings to additionally search by character format, text style, case sensitivity and regular expression.

Replace All

Replaces every instance of the result listed.

Replace

Replaces the selected result using the settings you have specified in the **Replace with** field.

Glyph Browser (View > Studio)

The **Glyph Browser** lets you navigate glyphs or Unicode characters available with your currently installed fonts. By first choosing a font or using the Search option, you can apply a specific glyph to a selected character (or at an insertion point) by double-clicking.

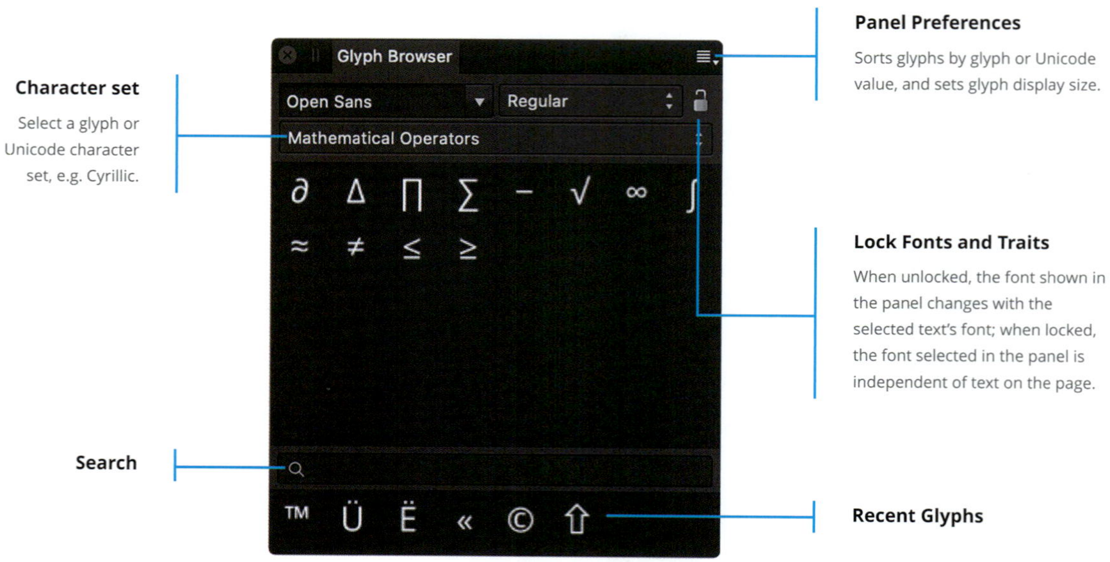

Hyperlinks Panel (View > Studio)

The **Hyperlinks Panel** allows you to view and edit hyperlinks used in your document. Hyperlinks will automatically update as they are edited from the panel.

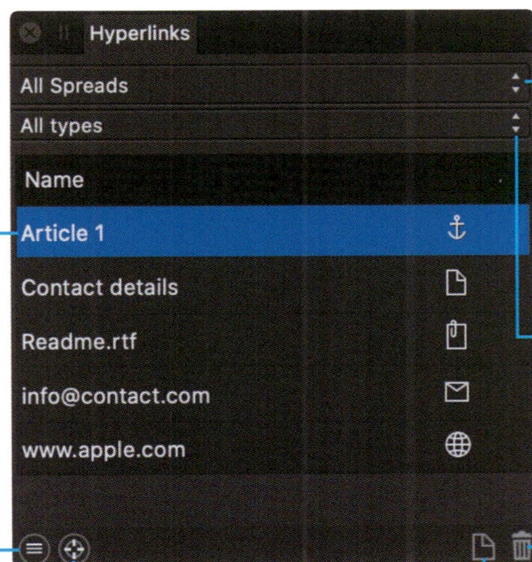

Name

Displays the hyperlink name, either named from the source text or unnamed (e.g., Hyperlink1) if from a shape or image.

Go to Source

Navigates to the page where the hyperlink's source is located.

Go to Target

Navigates to the hyperlink's target location (only if hyperlink target is within the same document).

Area

Specifies the pages on which hyperlinks are present: choose from **All Spreads** or a specific page.

Hyperlink Type

Filters the hyperlink by type: **Anchor**, **Page**, **File**, **Email**, **URL**.

Remove Hyperlink

Removes the selected hyperlink.

Add Hyperlink

Opens the **Hyperlink Properties** dialog, allowing you to add a new hyperlink.

Index Panel (View > Studio)

From the **Index Panel** you can create index topics and insert index markers directly into your page, as well as generate and insert your index in your document.

Index topics are simply index terms that you can search for in your document. From the search results in the panel, you can index all matching terms or index selectively.

The panel also lets you oversee all aspects of index management from a single location.

Delete

Deletes the selected index topic/ mark from the panel and page, or just the selected index mark.

Insert Mark

Inserts an index mark to your page for the currently selected text. The index mark is placed at the start of the indexed word.

Add Topic

Adds a new index topic to the panel which can be searched for via right click.

Options

Language

Select an index language from the pop-up menu.

Separator

Specify the separator to be placed between the topic name and any associated page numbers.

See (Also) Label

Specify the text to be used for cross reference labels.

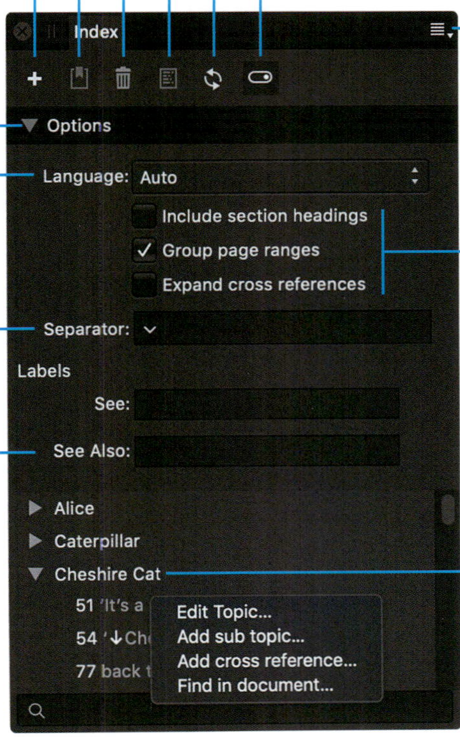

Insert Index

Inserts a generated index in a text frame at the caret position.

Update

Updates an existing generated index to include newly added or modified index topics/marks.

Show/Hide Index Marks

Displays or hides index marks inserted into text on your document pages.

Panel Preferences

Displays just topics or topics and their references.

Include section headings

When checked, the index topics will be divided up into sections based on their initial letter.

Group page ranges

When checked, ranges of three or more consecutive page numbers will be grouped.

Expand cross references

When checked, cross references within the generated index will list the page number(s) of the reference target, and not the text.

Index topic list

Lists added index topics/marks. Right-click any created index topic to locate term in document (select **Find in document**).

Pinning Panel (View > Studio)

The **Pinning Panel** lets you pin objects to text frames either as floating objects (anchored to the frame text) or as inline objects (inserted as a character).

The panel settings are different for floating and inline methods of pinning.

Float with Text

Click to pin the selected object (e.g., image, table or text frame) to adjacent text in a text frame. The object will then flow with reflowing frame text.

Horizontal align

The horizontal position (e.g., **Outside Left**, **Inside Right**, etc.) in relation to the page element set in the **Of** option.

Of

The page element from which horizontal alignment is made, e.g. character (pin location), frame, column, etc.

Offset

Offsets the object horizontally from the **Horizontal align** position in absolute units.

Keep within bounds

Ensures pinned object can only be placed within the bounding box of the text frame.

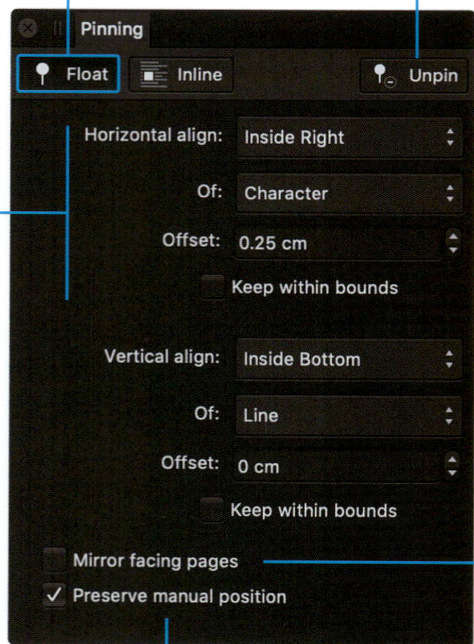

Preserve manual position

When checked, the pinned object and its pin can both be moved independently of each other. When unchecked, the pinned object is locked and will only move in accordance with the settings in the panel.

Unpin

Click to detach any floating or inline object, reverting it to a standalone object.

Vertical align

Determines the vertical position (e.g., **Inside Top**, **Outside Below**, etc.) in relation to the page element set in the **Of** option.

Of

The page element from which vertical alignment is made, e.g. character (pin location), frame, column, etc.

Offset

Offsets the object vertically from the **Vertical align** position in absolute units.

Keep within bounds

Stops the pinned object from being placed outside of the text frame. The object will move but only to the frame edge. When unchecked there is no restriction on object placement.

Mirror facing pages

With **Facing Pages** activated, ensures the object will automatically mirror its position in relation to text moved onto a new page.

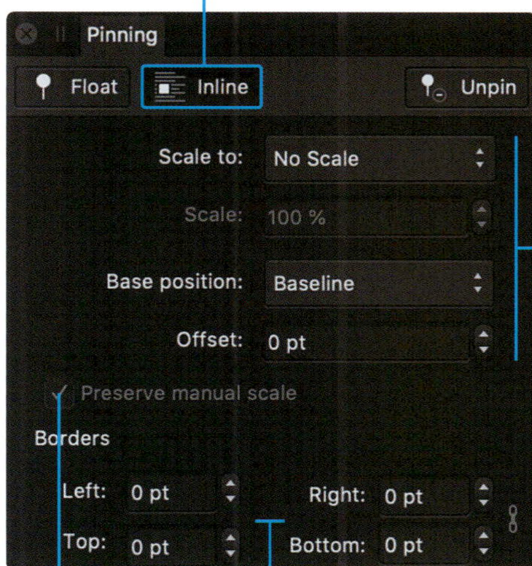

Inline in Text

Click to pin the object inline (as a character) into text in your text frame.

Scale to

Sizes the inline object in relation to its point size as well as different font metrics, e.g., ascent, x-height, etc.

Scale

Scales the object to a percentage of the Scale to value. This keeps the same relative size if the text size changes.

Base position

The inline object can be positioned vertically in relation to the baseline or descender.

Offset

Moves the inline object vertically in single percentage increments.

Borders

Sets a positive or negative border to the left, right, top or bottom of the inline object.

Preserve manual scale

When checked, the pinned object can be scaled manually using object handles; when unchecked, the pinned object will only scale according to the panel's **Scale** option.

Preflight Panel (View > Studio)

The **Preflight Panel** reports any preflight errors or warnings present in your document. By default, live preflight checking is in operation—you'll see errors or warnings appear in the panel as they occur.

By resolving these issues you can ensure your PDF output will be error free and ready for handing off to professional printers.

You can double-click an entry to jump to the page on which the issue occurs; the offending object will be selected ready for you to take action.

For more control over preflight checking, you can create saveable profiles that customise the types of checking made.

> The bell icon on the status bar changes to yellow or red when preflight warnings or errors are generated, respectively. Click the icon to launch the **Preflight Panel** for further analysis and quick resolution.

Profile

Displays a named preflight profile saved from the **Options Menu** after customising preflight settings. If blank, default preflight settings are used.

Check

Controls when preflight is operational. **Never** disables preflight; **Export** activates preflight only at export time; **Live** generates preflight errors and warnings in realtime.

Warning Level

A red icon indicates a high-priority error; a yellow icon a lower-priority warning.

Issue

A description of the preflight issue.

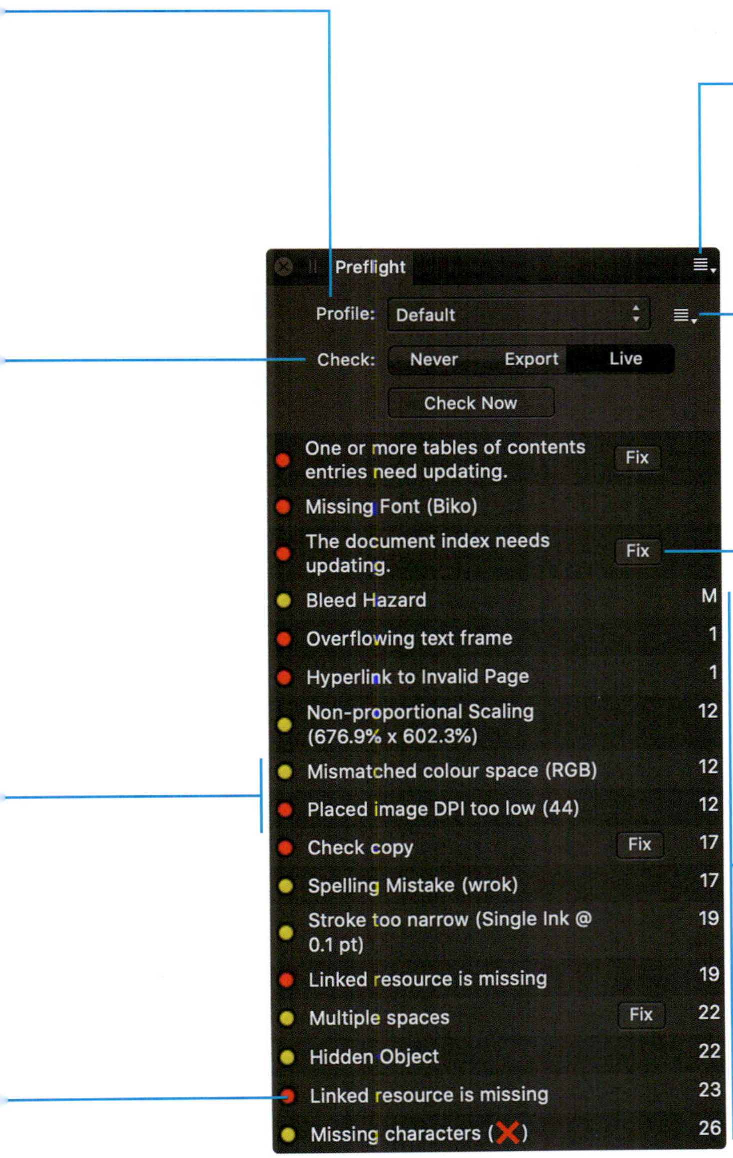

Panel Preferences

Sort by page or error type.

Options Menu

Lets you edit the preflight settings to disable specific checks, change warning levels, and check embedded/linked documents. You can save settings to categorised presets.

Fix

For some issues, a **Fix** button is available to directly resolve the issue in-panel.

Page Number

Shows the page number on which the issue occurs. **M** indicates a master page.

Table Panel (View > Studio)

The **Table Panel** allows you to adjust the formatting of individual tables within your document. Tables are created using the **Table Tool**.

Insets

Sets white space padding between table frame and table text.

Ignore Baseline Grid

Check to make the table ignore any currently set document baseline grid.

Border

Specify which cell border(s) you would like to format within the current selection.

Cell Stroke Colour

Sets the stroke colour for the selected cell(s).

Insets

Sets white space padding between cell edge and text within each selected table cell.

Vertical Position

Sets the vertical alignment of cell text. Select from **Top Align**, **Centre Align**, **Bottom Align** or **Justify**.

Rotation

Rotates cell text by 0° (acts as reset), 90°, 180° or 270° clockwise.

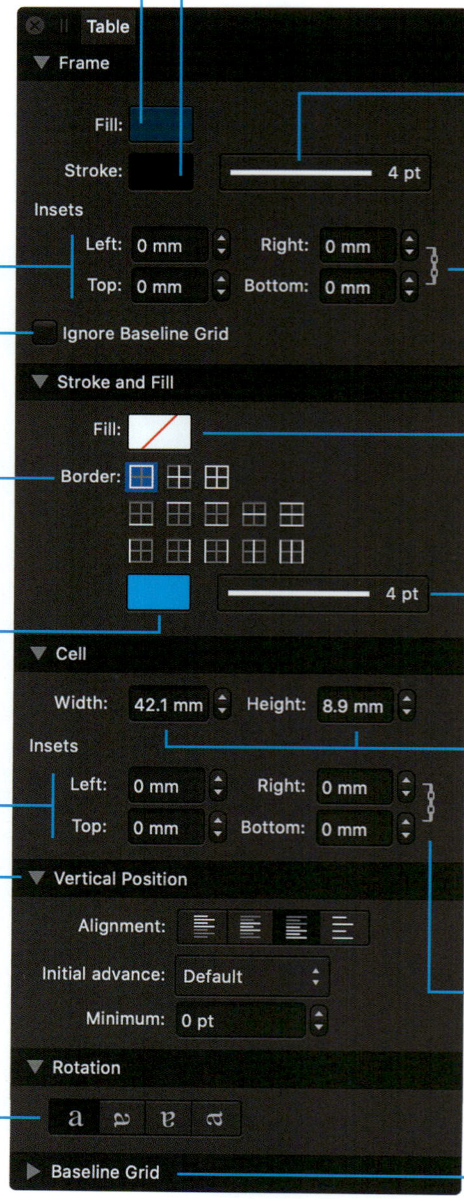

Fill

Sets the fill colour of the entire table.

Stroke Colour

Sets the stroke colour around the entire table.

Stroke Properties

Sets stroke width and stroke style around the entire table.

Link Insets

When enabled, the inset values are adjusted in proportion to each other. When deselected, they can be adjusted independently.

Fill

Sets the selected cell's fill colour.

Cell Stroke Properties

Sets stroke width and stroke style for the selected cell(s).

Width

Adjusts the selected cell's width.

Height

Adjusts the cell's height.

Link

When enabled, the inset values are adjusted in proportion to each other. When deselected, they can be adjusted independently.

Baseline Grid

Expand and check **Use Baseline Grid** to apply grid to table text.

Table Formats Panel (View > Studio)

The **Table Formats Panel** creates and stores table and cell formatting options such as borders and cell colours as presets which can then be applied to other tables in your document at any time.

Panel Preferences

Allows you to set thumbnail size, save current table preset as default and import table formats from file. You can also create a new table format from a selected table on your page or from scratch.

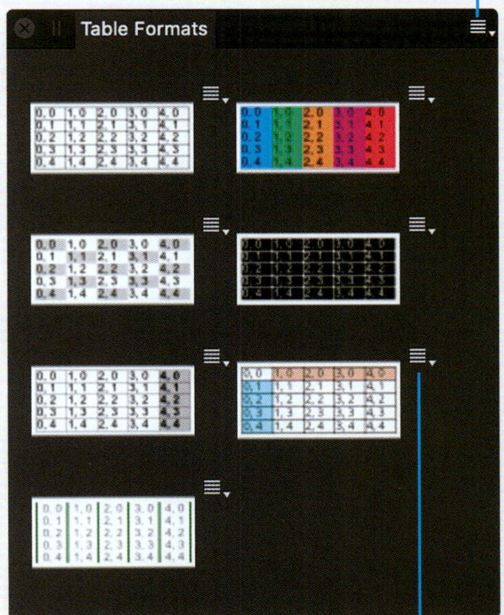

Options Menu

Edit the formatting and properties of your table preset, edit as a copy and apply to selected table on your page.

Styles Panel

The **Styles Panel** lets you apply pre-designed styles to your objects. Styles are made up of effects, stroke properties, or text attributes and combinations of these. The Styles Panel lets you apply these properties easily by drag-and-drop or selecting an object and clicking on a panel thumbnail. You can also save any object's style to the Styles Panel for future use.

Panel Preferences

Add, remove and rename style categories. Import and export styles. Save a new style to the category based on the current selection.

Search

Table of Contents Panel (View > Studio)

The **Table of Contents Panel** allows you to insert, update and manage any table of contents (TOCs) within your document.

Insert

Inserts a generated TOC in a text frame at the caret position.

Scope

The TOC will be generated from all the document or only the section containing the TOC.

Look In

TOC headings will be generated from all text frames in the section(s) or only the frames that are linked in a text flow.

TOC Style

Applies a TOC Style preset (text style set and **Style Name** choice) to the currently selected TOC.

Numbers before headings

Check to place page numbers before the TOC headings.

Remove line breaks

Replaces line breaks in referenced text with spaces.

Include inline pins

Copies inline pinned objects from headings into the TOC.

Separator

Specify any glyphs you would like to place between the page number and the text in an entry. Use drop-down arrow for common glyphs.

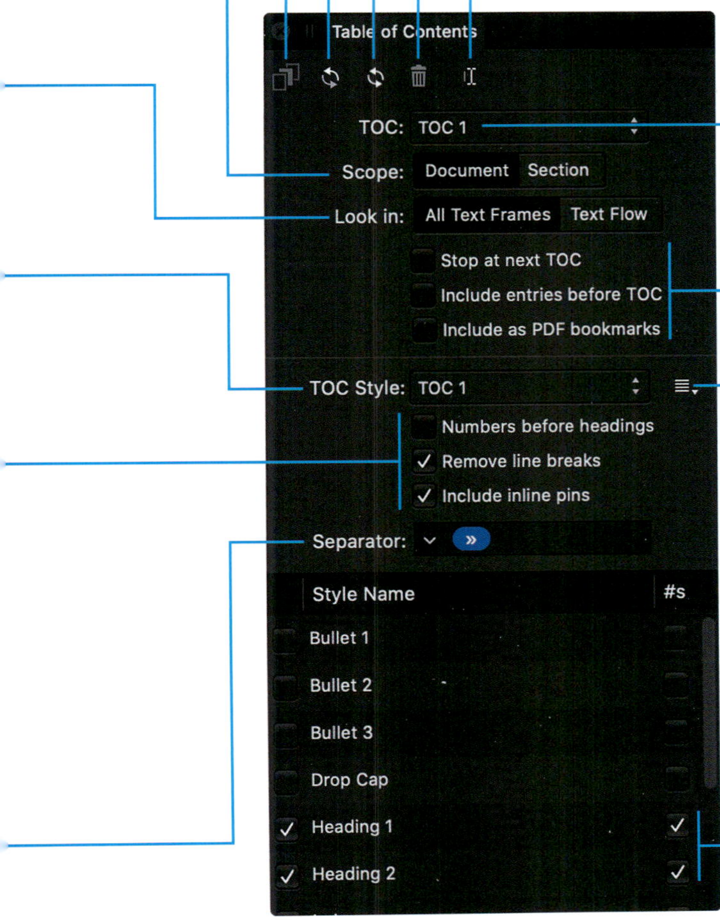

Update

Updates the selected TOC to include TOC entries for text newly assigned with a text style that is marked to be included in the TOC.

Update All Tables of Contents

Updates all TOCs within your document.

Delete

Deletes the selected TOC in the **TOC** pop-up menu.

Rename

Allows you to enter a new name for the selected TOC.

TOC

Select a TOC from the pop-up menu to configure its settings and jump to its page location.

Stop at next TOC

Check to automatically stop TOC generation if another TOC is found.

Include entries before TOC

Check to include TOC entries before the intended TOC location, e.g. to include preface or introductory information.

Include as PDF bookmarks

Makes TOC entry link to referenced text (for digital publications).

TOC Style Options Menu

Creates, deletes or renames a **TOC Style** preset. Use for styling additional TOCs in your document.

Style Name

Check paragraph styles in the list to base the TOC on the text associated from those styles. For each style you select, page numbers are included by default.

Text Frame Panel (View > Studio)

The **Text Frame Panel** lets you adjust the frame layout, including frame stroke/fill colour, number of columns, gutter settings, text position vertically and baseline grid control.

Hide overflow

Check to clip overflowing text that does not fit in the frame. Same as eye icon on text frame.

Ignore Text Wraps

Check to stop frame text from wrapping around objects with text wrapping set.

Ignore Baseline Grid

Check to make the text frame ignore any currently set document baseline grid.

Fill

Sets the fill colour of the entire text frame.

Stroke Colour

Sets the stroke colour around the entire text frame.

Insets

Sets white space padding between text frame and frame text.

Columns

Specify the number of columns in your text frame.

Width

Specify the width of each column.

Balance text in columns

Check to automatically balance columns of text.

Gaps

Specify where the top and bottom of the column rule starts and ends.

Vertical Position

Sets the vertical alignment of frame text. Select from **Top Align**, **Centre Align**, **Bottom Align** or **Justify**.

Use Baseline Grid

Check to enable a baseline grid that is restricted to the text frame.

Colour

Sets the grid line colour. Drag the slider to set the opacity of the line colour.

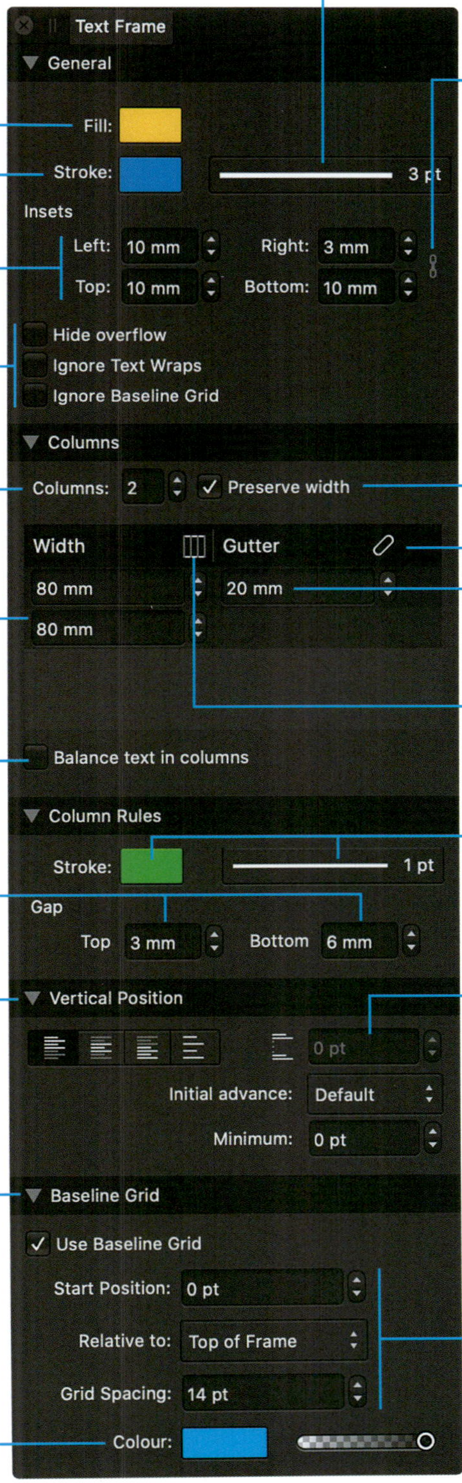

Stroke Properties

Sets stroke width and stroke style around the entire text frame.

Link Insets

When enabled, the inset values are adjusted in proportion to each other. When deselected, they can be adjusted independently.

Preserve width

Check to ensure that when column or gutter widths are changed, the text frame's width remains unchanged.

Link

When enabled, all gutter widths keep the same value. When unchecked, they can be adjusted independently.

Gutter

Specify the gutter size between each column.

Same column widths

Click to automatically make all columns the same width.

Rule Stroke Colour/Properties

Sets the stroke, width and style of a vertical rule between text columns.

Max Paragraph Space

Specify the maximum spacing between paragraphs in the text frame.

Start Position

Specify the offset of the first grid line measured from the **Relative To** setting.

Relative to

Specifies the baseline grid's starting position in relation to the top of the text frame or top inset position.

Grid Spacing

Specify how far apart consecutive horizontal grid lines are.

CUSTOMISING YOUR WORKSPACE

Not everyone likes to work in the same way so with this in mind there are options in Affinity Publisher that allow you to customise your workspace to your liking.

User Interface Preferences

Tweak the UI to your taste by updating your **Preferences**. Access via **Affinity Publisher > Preferences** (Mac) or **Edit > Preferences** (Win) and choose **User Interface** to get the following customisable options:

- **Background Grey Level**—controls the greyscale level of the Document View background.
- **Artboard Background Grey Level**—controls greyscale level of the pasteboard surrounding artboard(s) if opening Designer files.
- **UI Gamma**—adjusts the contrast of the user interface.
- **Font UI Size (Mac only)**—optionally increase the font size of UI text.
- **UI Style**—choose between a dark, light or the default OS user interface (Mac only).
- **Tooltip Delay**—set the length of time before a tooltip appears when hovering over a UI element.
- **Decimal Places for Unit Types**—controls the number of decimal places displayed for each document measurement unit.
- **Automatically lock background layer on import**—locks (or keeps unlocked) an imported image as a background layer.

- **Show Lines in points**—choose whether line width (thickness) displays in points or in the document's measurement units.

- **Show Text in points**—choose whether text is expressed in points or in the document's measurement units.

- **Show brush previews**—choose whether the brush cursor displays a preview of pixels to be placed.

- **Always show brush crosshair**—overlays a crosshair over the brush cursor for better targeting.

- **Monochromatic Iconography**—makes icons display in greyscale.

- **Show Selection in Layers Panel**—As you select an object, the panel scrolls to show its layer entry.

- **Enable Touch bar support**—Allows you to utilise the Touch bar on Apple MacBook Pro computers.

Workspace Modes (Mac only)

In the Mac version of Affinity, you can choose from two different workspace modes: **Normal** and **Separated** mode. You can change to either workspace mode from the **Window Menu**.

By default, Affinity Publisher will run in **Normal** (single window) mode. This means that all panels and view will be neatly docked together. **Separated mode** has no containing frame, the panels (or panel groups) and toolbars are floating, and each open document has its own view (although you can still create groups).

> When in full screen view, you cannot switch between workspace modes.

Customising your Studio panels

You can customise your workspace to fit your workflow. In particular, you can control the arrangement of Studio panels and which panels are displayed.

To hide/show a panel:

- From the **View Menu**, click the panel name on the **Studio flyout**. To show, click the panel name again.

To hide/show all panels:

- From the **View Menu**, click **Toggle UI** (Tab).

To hide/show left/right panel groups:

- From **View > Studio**, click **Show Left Studio** or **Show Right Studio**.

To collapse a panel/panel group:

- Double-click on the active panel label.

To expand a panel/panel group:

- Click on the label of the panel that you want to view.

To move a panel:

- Drag the panel label to its new position, as a free floating panel or as item in an existing panel group.

To resize a panel:

- Drag any corner of a panel.

To dock a panel:

- Drag the panel label to a panel group.
- Drag the panel label to an area of the studio.
  A highlight shows where the panel can be docked.

To move a panel group:

- Drag the panel group to a new position, either as a free floating panel or as an item in an existing panel group.

To dock a panel group:

- Drag the panel group to another panel group.
- Drag the panel group to an area of the studio.
  A highlight shows where the panel group can be docked.

To save your Studio arrangement as a preset:

- Select **View > Studio Presets > Add Preset**.

To reset the workspace:

- Select **View > Studio > Reset Studio**.

Customising the Tools Panel

The **Tools Panel** can be docked or floating, or shown or hidden, depending on your preference. You can customise the panel to fit your individual way of working by removing tools and adding tools.

To dock/undock the Tools Panel:

- From the **View Menu**, select **Dock Tools**.

To show/hide the Tools Panel:

- From the **View Menu**, select **Show Tools**.

To remove or add a tool:

1. From the **View Menu**, select **Customise Tools**.
2. Drag a tool icon from the **Tools Panel** into the flyout, or vice versa.
3. Click **Close**.

To reset the Tools Panel:

- From the **View Menu**, select **Customise Tools**, then from the flyout, click **Reset**.

Customising the Toolbar

The **Toolbar** organises some of the most commonly used commands and functions to keep them at your fingertips. You can customise your Toolbar in the following ways:

To show/hide tool group labels on the Toolbar:

1. Choose **View > Customise Toolbar**.
2. From the dialog's **Show** pop-up menu, select **Icon Only** or **Icon and Text**.

To hide/show the Toolbar:

- Choose **View > Show Toolbar**.

To customise the Toolbar:

1. Choose **View > Customise Toolbar**.
2. Drag the items from the dialog to the **Toolbar**.
3. Remove items by dragging them off the Toolbar and onto your Document View.

To reset the Toolbar:

1. Choose **View > Customise Toolbar**.
2. Drag the default set item to the **Toolbar**. This will revert the Toolbar to its original settings.

> Your workspace customisation will be remembered between sessions.

CUSTOMISING KEYBOARD SHORTCUTS

You can quickly access common tools and commands using your keyboard. Many of the shortcuts are the same as those that you use in other apps.

> In your app, you'll find many of the shortcuts listed next to menu items.

A comprehensive set of keyboard shortcuts can be found in a series of tear-out inserts located at the end of this workbook.

Customising keyboard shortcuts

Learning the keyboard shortcuts in Affinity Publisher will speed up your productivity, but you may want to customise shortcuts on an application-wide or on a per-Persona basis. You can also save your customised shortcuts to a file that can be shared with other users or backed up for safe keeping. Go to **Affinity Publisher > Preferences** (Mac) or **Edit > Preferences** (Win) and choose **Keyboard Shortcuts** to customise your shortcuts.

> Exported keyboard shortcut files can only be used on the same platform as they were created. A keyboard shortcut file exported from Affinity Publisher on a Mac cannot be imported into Affinity Publisher for Windows, and vice versa. The extension for the keyboard shortcut file is *.affshortcuts on a Mac and *.afshort on Windows.

Available settings are as follows:

- **Persona**—The pop-up menu sets the Persona for shortcut customisation.
- **UI Element**—The pop-up menu displays the menus, commands and operations for the currently selected Persona. A **Miscellaneous** category groups shortcuts for commonly performed operations and lets you switch on/off panels via shortcuts.
- **Apply to all**—If checked, the shortcut applied to a UI element is shared across every Persona. If unchecked, you can uniquely assign a custom shortcut to work just within the currently selected Persona in the initial Persona pop-up menu.

A warning triangle shows if a shortcut has already been assigned to another command. The tooltip will inform you which command.

An arrow symbol indicates that the shortcut is shared between several tools. Hover over the symbol to see the names of the other tools.

To delete a shortcut, click the cross icon at the end of the shortcut entry.

- **Ignore Modifier**—Lets you create shortcuts using a single letter designation instead of using keyboard modifiers.
- **Reset**—All customised shortcuts are reset back to default.
- **Clear All Shortcuts**—All default and customised shortcuts are removed.
- **Load**—Loads a previously saved shortcuts file. This will overwrite your current keyboard shortcut allocations.
- **Save**—Saves the current set of shortcuts to a file for sharing or backup.

Affinity Publisher's keyboard shortcuts are different to macOS's defaults – for example, when adjusting character spacing, baseline and paragraph leading, moving the insertion point and selecting text. To use the system's shortcuts instead, click **Apple Defaults**.

RESETTING YOUR WORKSPACE

Now you have a good understanding of the Affinity Publisher user interface, it's important to ensure your workspace is reset to the default 'factory-supplied' layout before commencing with the projects in this book.

It may be that you've inadvertently customised, repositioned or switched off toolbars or panels previously. By resetting, the project's written instructions will more closely match your own experience.

Reset the Toolbar

On the **View Menu**, select **Customise Toolbar**. Drag the default set of tools at the bottom of the dialog over the **Toolbar** spanning the top of your workspace and release.

Reset the Tools Panel

On the **View Menu**, select **Customise Tools**, then from the flyout, click **Reset**.

Reset Studio Panels

On the **View Menu**, select **Studio > Reset Studio**. This will need to be done for each Persona workspace.

THROUGH THE WALL
Chad Felix on his return to competitive BMX and how biking saved his life after almost taking it
The beat goes on

THROUGH THE WALL
Chad Felix on his return to competitive BMX and how biking saved his life after almost taking it
The beat goes on

CHOOSING A UI STYLE

Affinity Publisher offers the choice of a dark or light UI style, allowing you to experience the interface in two different ways. Each UI style has its pros and cons depending on the type of design you are working with. Here are a few things to consider:

Dark UI

- Ideal for designs with less text and more images or videos to focus on
- Reduces eye strain
- Works well with minimalist designs containing very few elements which are spaced out well
- Makes the core elements of the page really pop

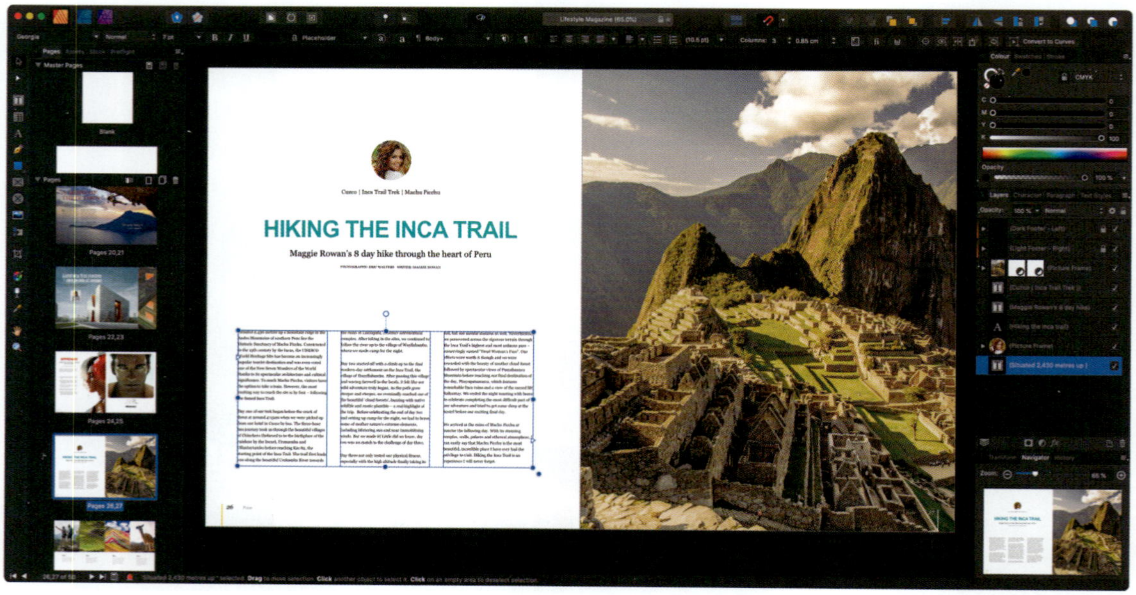

To change the UI style

1. Go to **Affinity Publisher > Preferences** (Mac) or **Edit > Preferences** (Windows) and select **User Interface**.
2. Select a **UI Style** from **Dark**, **Light** or **Default OS** (this will automatically use the default OS user interface; macOS only).

Light UI

- Ideal for designs that require you to read a lot of text
- Good for busy designs containing a lot of visual elements
- Allows designs containing a wide variety of colours to really stand out

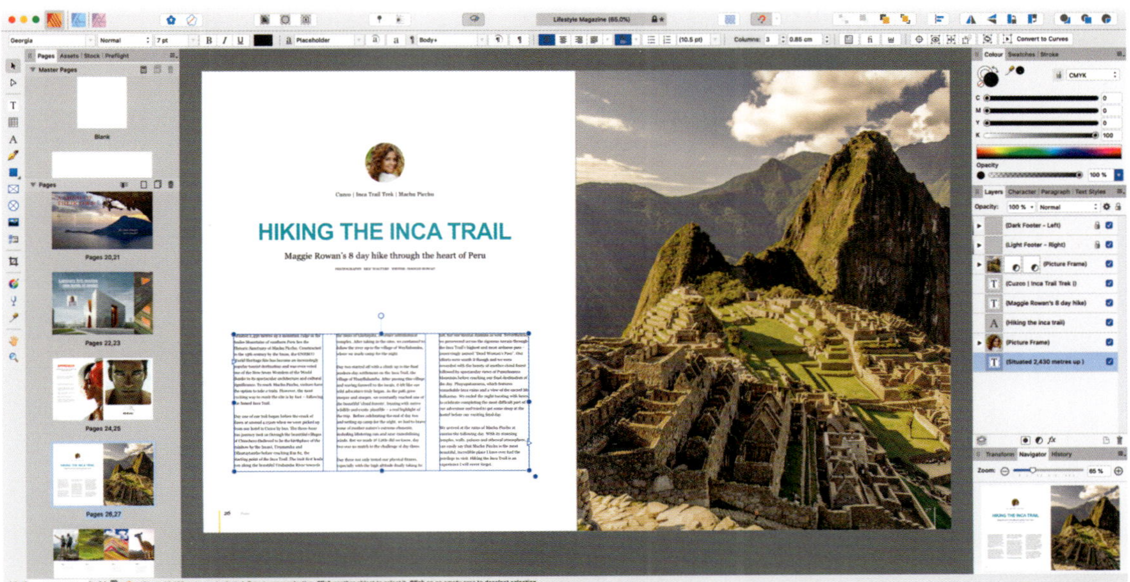

CHAPTER 2

Core Skills

This chapter teaches you essential techniques you will need to use Affinity Publisher and work your way through the projects in later chapters. Not all projects use every core skill, but spending your time learning all skills here will strengthen your capabilities with Affinity Publisher generally.

BEFORE YOU GET STARTED

Resources

You can get all the resources that are referenced in this chapter from: https://affin.co/PublisherCoreSkills

OPENING DOCUMENTS AND TEMPLATES

The .afpub file extension used by Affinity Publisher documents tells macOS and Windows which app to open when they are double-clicked. Affinity Publisher can also open InDesign Markup Language (IDML) and PDF files.

IDML compatibility enables InDesign documents to be migrated to Affinity Publisher.

If you don't have an editable version of your document or your previous DTP app cannot export IDML files, opening a PDF that was exported for distribution provides a way to start recreating the document in Affinity Publisher.

Opening Affinity Publisher files

Double-click an Affinity Publisher document in Finder (Mac) or File Explorer (Win).

File Name.afpub

In Affinity Publisher, Designer or Photo (Mac/Win):

1 Select **File > Open**.

2 Locate the file and select it.

3 Click **Open**.

Migrate InDesign documents

Adobe InDesign documents and templates can be exported as IDML files, which can be imported into Affinity Publisher.

1 In InDesign, choose **File > Export** (CS4 up to CS5.5) or **File > Save As** (CS6 or CC).

2 Set **Format** (Mac) or **Save as type** (Win) to **InDesign CS4 or later (IDML)** or equivalent.

3 Click **Save**.

Opening IDML documents

Documents created using alternative page layout software can be migrated to Affinity Publisher if the other app can export to IDML format.

The steps for opening an IDML file in Affinity Publisher are the same as for opening an Affinity Publisher document.

Working with templates

We've worked with some of the best creators who sell templates on Creative Market to ensure that there is a broad range of templates available in Affinity Publisher format. While these are all paid-for templates, they're a great tool as a starting point for your designs.

You can also open in Affinity Publisher any IDML-format template that you find online (free or paid for).

Templates are also available from sites like indesignskills.com, pagephilia.com and elements.envato.com. These can be adapted to your needs using Affinity Publisher.

Make sure you check each site and template's licensing terms for whether templates are free for personal and commercial use before publishing anything based on them. Some templates may use images and fonts with their own licensing terms.

Brand Guidelines
By Occy Designs

Magazine
By Luuqas Design

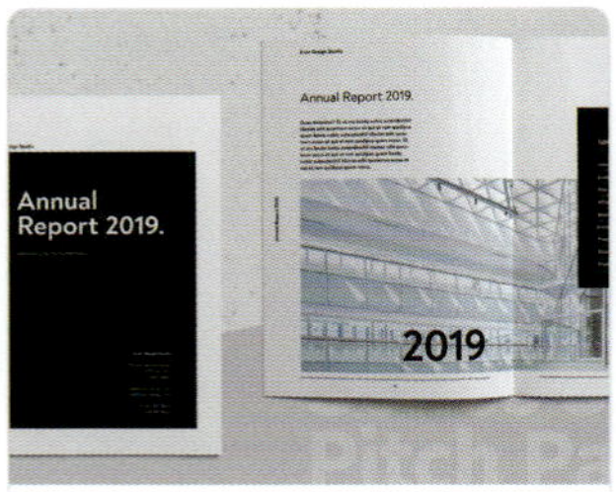

Annual Report
By Egotype

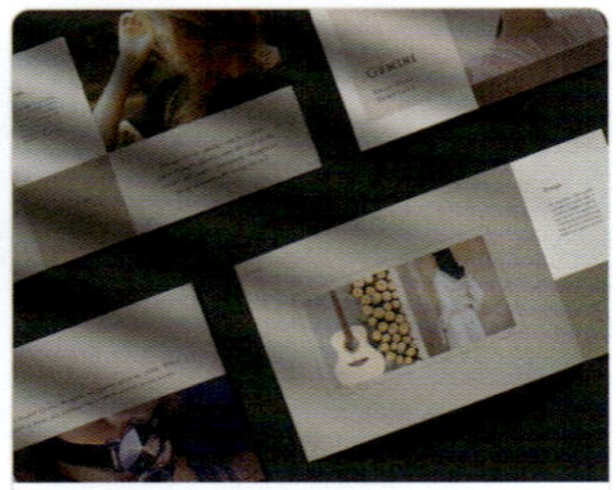

Gemini Brochure
By Slide Station

Project Proposal
By ID Vision Studio

Voyager Magazine
By Visuel Colonie

Architecture Portfolio
By Studio Bons

Cookbook
By Occy Designs

Opening PDFs

Opening a PDF file creates a new Affinity Publisher document from it. This enables you to edit the PDF's contents and republish it.

1 Select **File > Open**.

2 Browse to and select the PDF. Click **Open**.

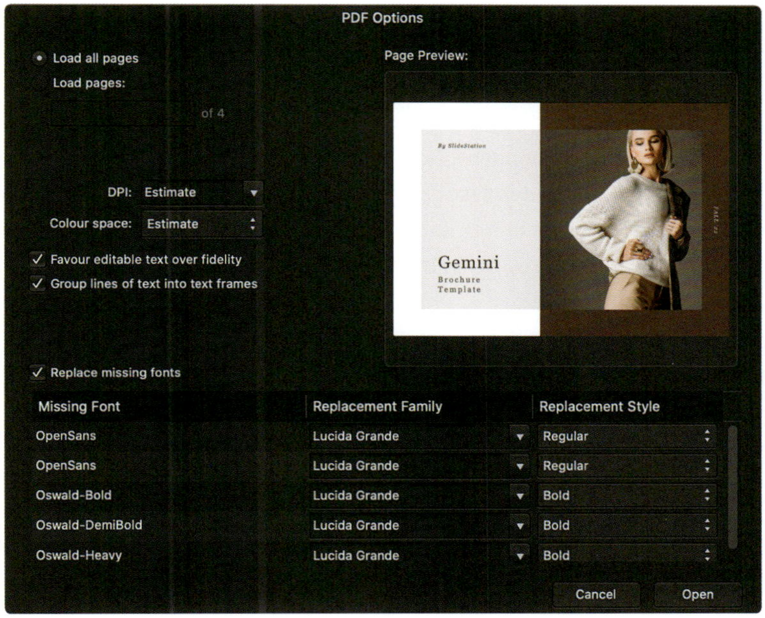

On the PDF Options dialog:

1 If the PDF contains more than one page, select **Load pages** and specify the page(s) to extract.

2 Enter your choices of **DPI** and **Colour space** settings, or tell Affinity Publisher to estimate them from the PDF file.

3 Check **Favour editable text over fidelity** so you can update the document's text.

4 Check **Group lines of text into text frames** to minimise the number of separate text frames created.

5 If fonts used in the PDF are missing, check **Replace missing fonts** and choose a replacement family and style for each one.

PAGES AND MASTER PAGES

Pages are the fundamental building block of Affinity Publisher documents. Each document can contain multiple pages of varied sizes.

There are two types of pages: **publication pages**, which are the ones you'll export, and **master pages**, from which publication pages can inherit repeating elements. On the **Pages Panel**, the latter are listed in the upper window and the former in the lower window.

Modifications to a master page appear instantly and automatically on all pages to which it has been applied.

Pages can be presented as individual pages or two facing pages. Each one can contain whatever mix of text, vector and raster graphics are needed by your design.

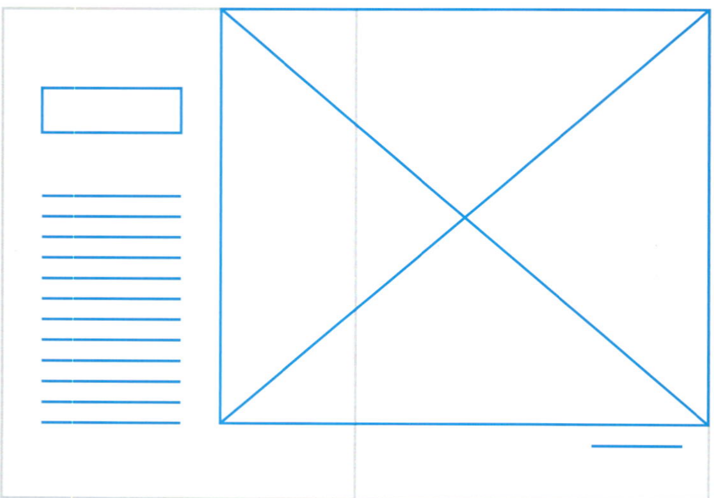

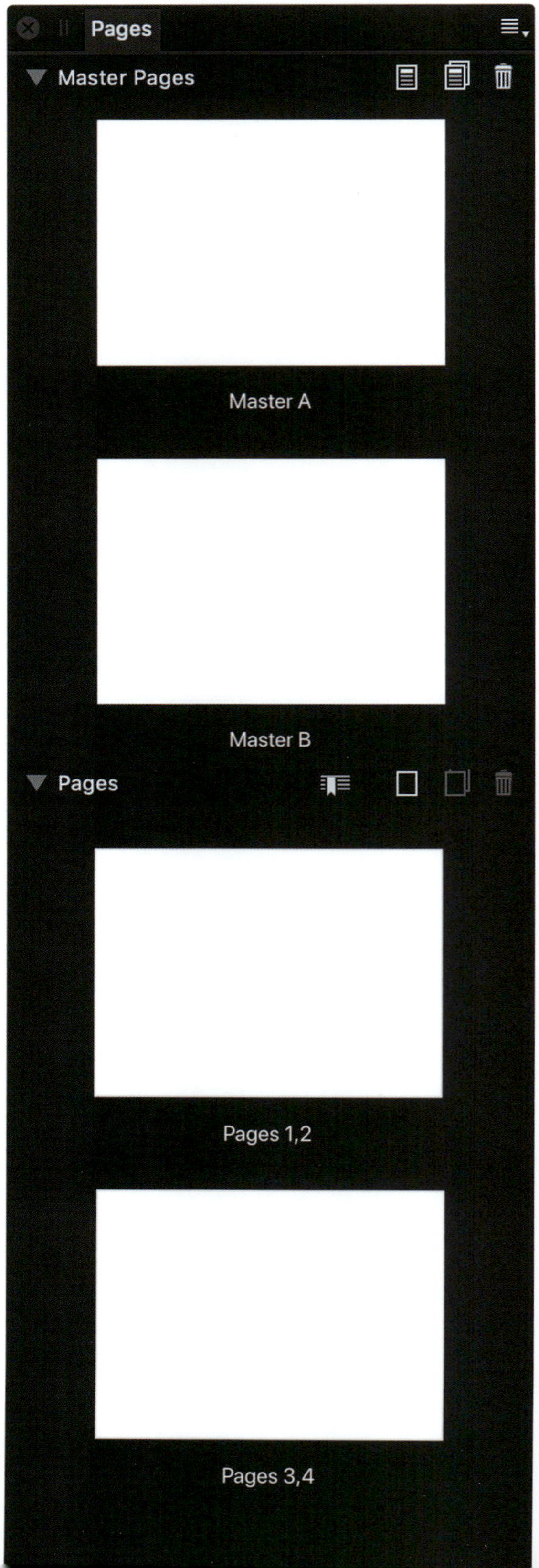

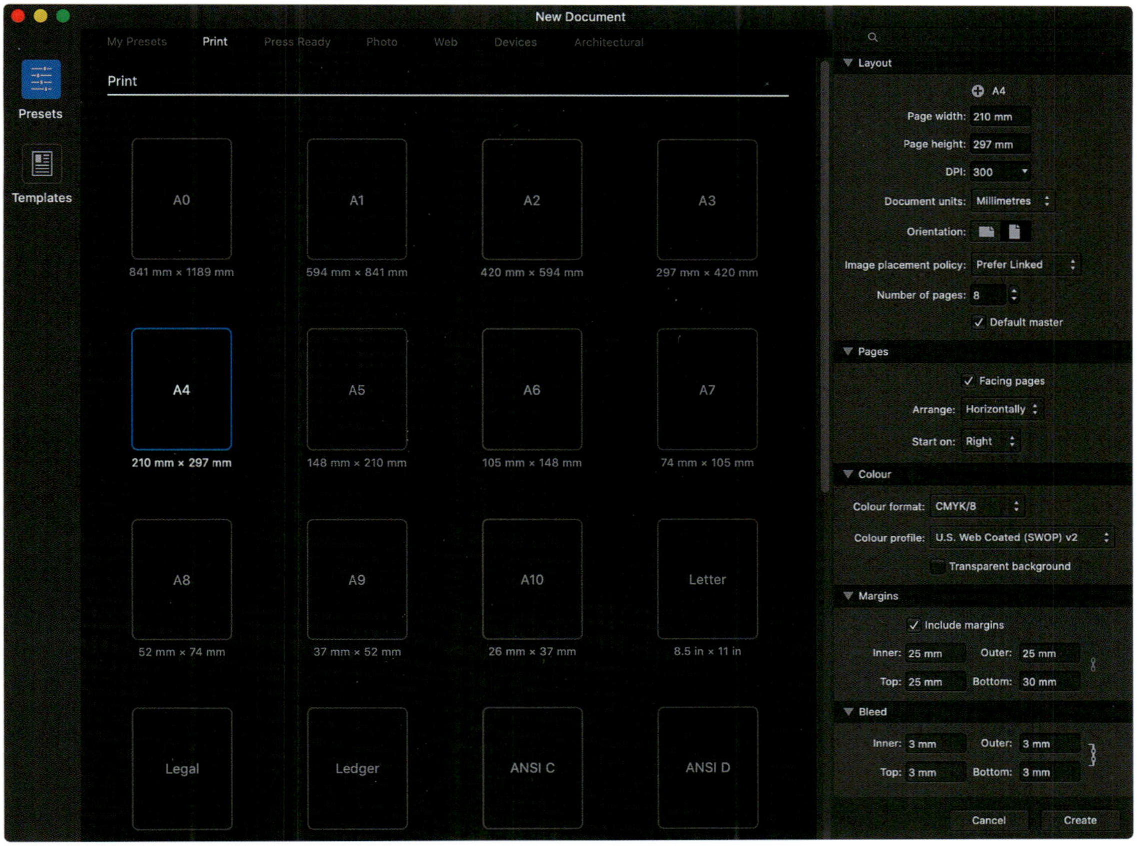

If no preset suits your project, select the closest and amend its settings on the right.

Optionally, click the **+** at the top to save settings for reuse.

Creating documents

It is important to choose the correct document type based on delivery format, as this affects the page presets you're offered.

Your choice affects colour, measurement units, dots per inch and other settings. For example, **Press Ready** and **Web** presets use different colour space and bleed settings appropriate to professional printing and on-screen presentation respectively.

Create a document for a print publication

1. Select **File > New**.
2. On the **New Document dialog**, select **Presets** on the left, then **Press Ready** near the top left.
3. Select the **A4** preset. In its settings to the right, set **Number of pages** to *8*.
4. With **Facing pages** checked, the first and last pages will be front and back covers. Those in between are spreads, like in a magazine.
5. Click **Create**. The first page is central in the Document View. Scroll to reach others.

After creating a document, its colour profile, units, bleed and other settings can be amended in **File > Document Setup**. A page's dimensions can be altered in **File > Spread Setup**.

Adding pages

A document's number of pages is not fixed at the time of its creation. More can be added at any time.

1 Either:

- Click **Add Pages** within the **Pages Panel**'s lower window.
- If the current page is the document's last, click **Next Spread** on the status bar.

2 Set the **Number of pages** to add.

3 Select whether to insert the new pages before or after the one listed next to **Page**.

4 (Optional) Select which **Master Page** should be applied to the new pages (p. 88).

5 Click **OK**.

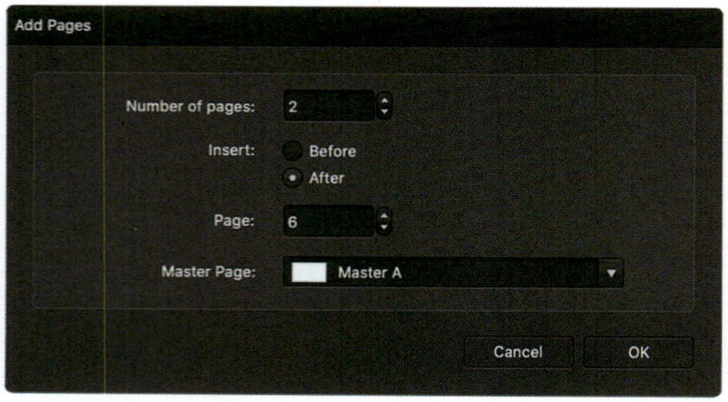

Duplicating pages

The layout and contents of pages can be duplicated exactly, ready for adaptation.

1 On the **Pages Panel**, select one or more publication pages.

2 Click **Duplicate Selected Pages** near the top of the panel's lower window.

The copies are inserted immediately after the (last of the) originals. Any master pages applied to the originals are also applied to the copies.

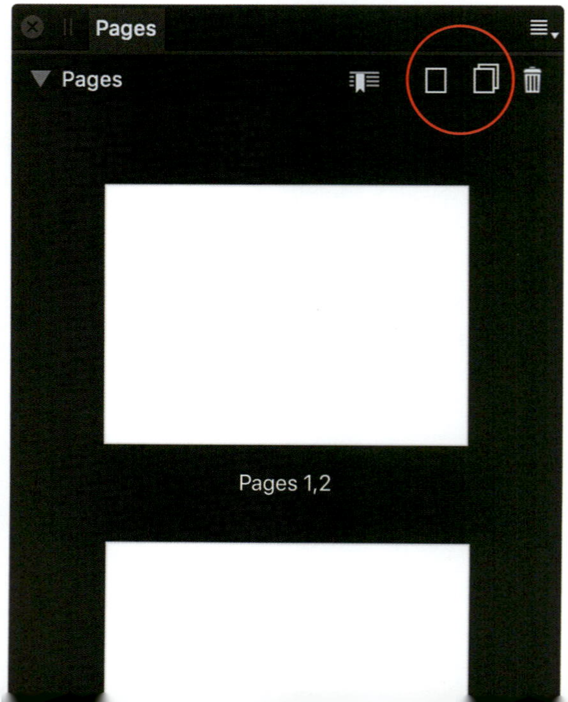

Viewing and editing pages

The page or spread you are editing is identified by its page numbers on the **Page navigation bar** at the bottom left of the window and by a grey highlight around its thumbnail on the **Pages Panel**, as depicted on Pages 12,13 to the right.

Set the current page/spread by doing one of the following actions:

- Double-click its thumbnail on the **Pages Panel**.
- Use the spread navigation buttons to reach the desired page.
- Click the page number between the navigation buttons and enter the desired page number.
- Click on a page in the Document View.

If a master page is being edited, its name is shown on the Page navigation bar instead.

Resource

core_skills_rearranging_pages.afpub

Rearrange pages

The **Pages Panel** previews the arrangement of your document's pages and their contents. In it, the order of publication pages can be changed by dragging and dropping their thumbnails.

Click the left- or right-hand page of a spread to select it individually.

Click near the centre of a spread to select both of its pages.

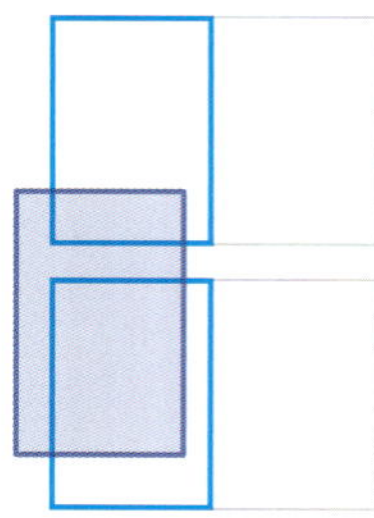

Drag from an empty area of the Pages Panel through a range of pages to select them.

Click a page, hold the shift key (⇧) and then click another page to select the two pages and all in between them.

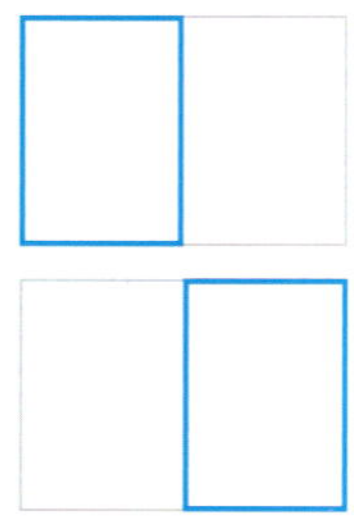

Hold the cmd ⌘ key (Mac) or ctrl key (Win) and click any page thumbnails to create a discontinuous selection.

1 Select one or more pages.

2 Drag the selected page(s) to the place you want them to appear.

3 When a vertical blue line appears, drop the page(s) to move to that position.

If multiple pages are moved, their previous order within the document is maintained at their new location.

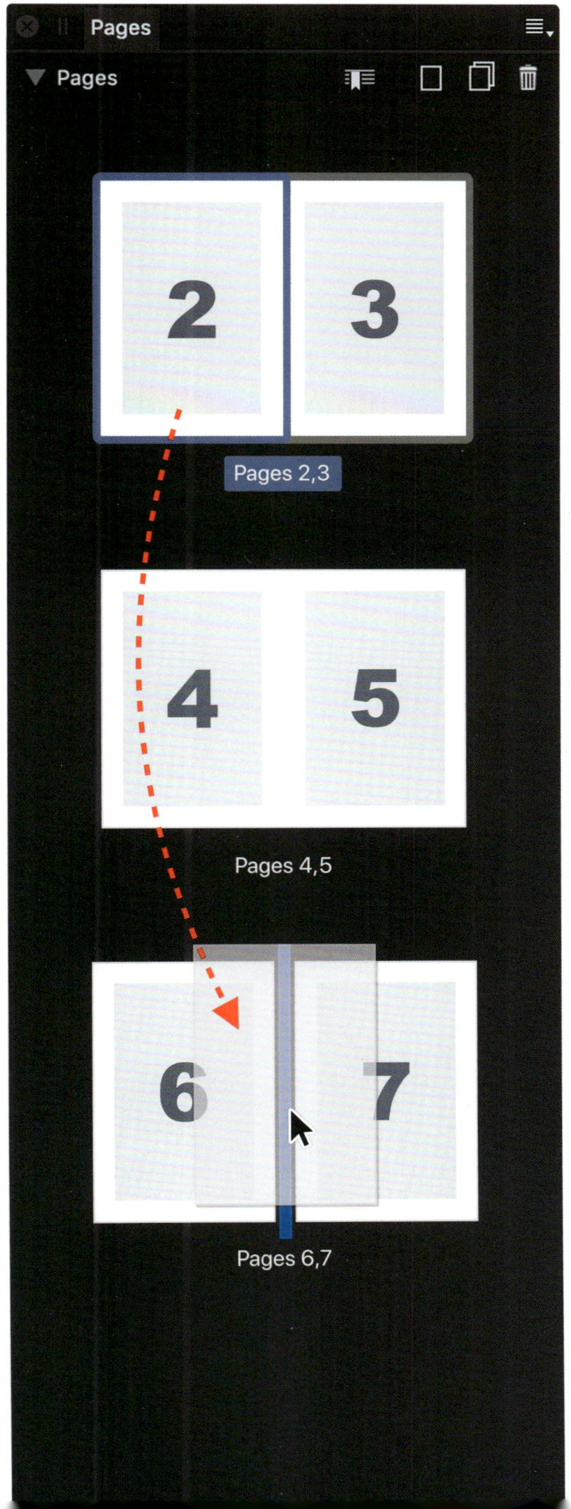

Master pages

Master pages are managed in the upper window of the **Pages Panel** (p. 26). They are often used to add headers, footers and other recurring objects to multiple publication pages, such as page numbering, on-page objects (e.g. placeholder text) and guides (p. 102).

By applying a master to a publication page, the latter inherits all of the elements contained on the former.

> *Changes made to a master page appear automatically on all publication pages to which it has been applied.*

A master page can contain on-page objects and its own set of guides.

There's no requirement to apply a master page to a publication page. For example, you may want to fill a page with an image or an advertisement and not add page numbering to it.

Add a blank master page

Documents can contain multiple master pages.

1 On the **Pages Panel**, click **Add Master** above the **Master Pages** window.

2 Name the master and select whether it is a **Single** page or a **Facing** page spread.

The Document View switches to the new master page, ready to add elements.

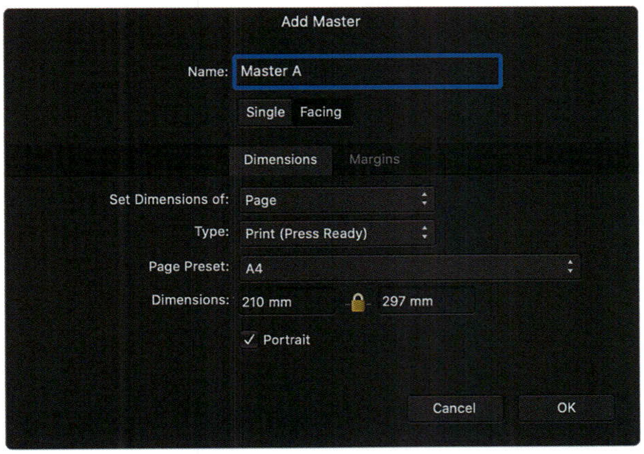

Add page numbers and section details as a footer

1 Draw a text frame in the bottom-left corner of your new master's left page.

2 Put the insertion point in the text frame and select **Text > Insert > Fields > Page Number**.

3 Type a space, a vertical bar (|) and another space.

4 Select **Text > Insert > Fields > Section Name**.

5 Copy the text frame to the master's right page.

6 Right-align the copy's contents and use **Cut** and **Paste** to reverse the information so the page number is nearest the page's outer edge.

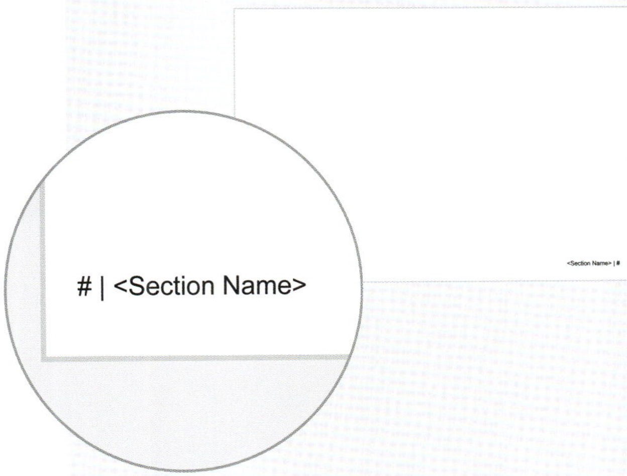

Apply a master page

To apply a master page to a publication page:

1 Drag the master's thumbnail from the upper window of the **Pages Panel**.

2 Drop it onto a publication page in the lower window. If dropping onto a spread:

- Drop onto the centre to apply to both sides (a).
- Drop onto the verso or recto page to apply only to that side (b).

If multiple publication pages are selected, dropping a master onto one of them applies it to the entire selection.

> Single-page masters can be applied to either a verso or recto page. Applying a master spread to a single page inherits the contents of the corresponding (verso or recto) page of the spread.

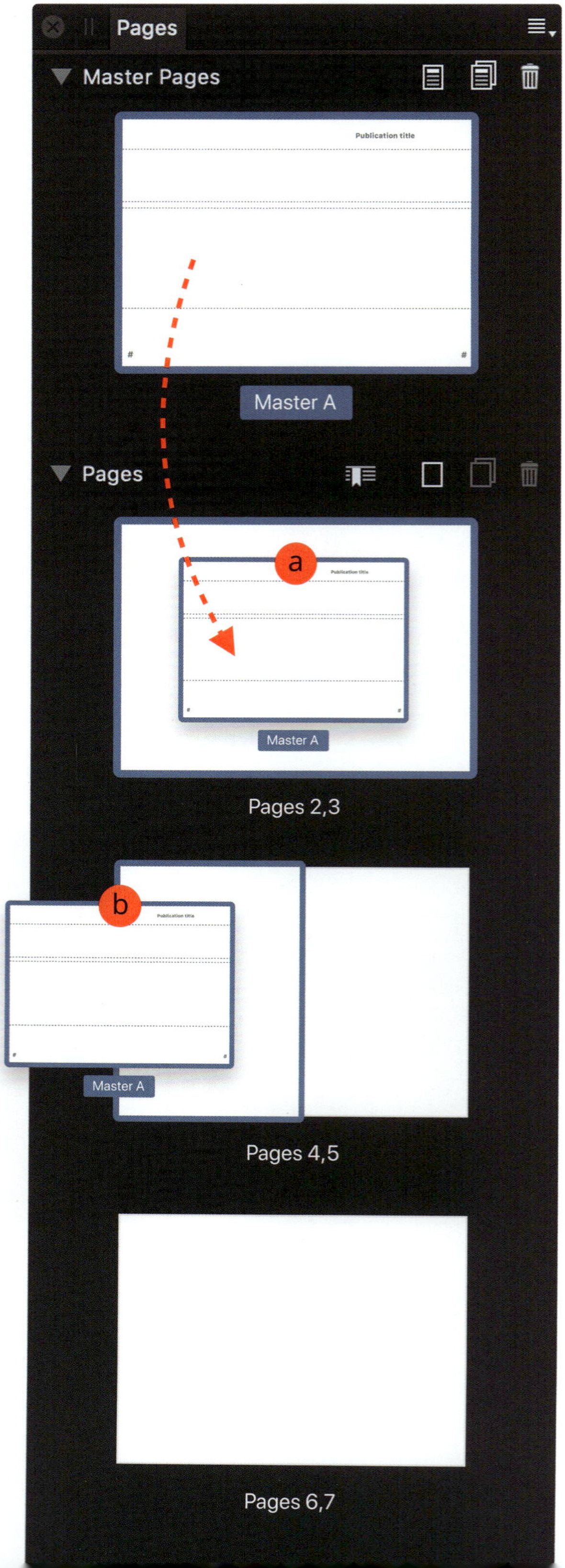

Alternatively, to quickly apply a master to odd, even or a range of pages without selecting each one's thumbnail:

1 Ctrl-click (Mac) or right-click (Win) a publication page and choose **Apply Master**.

2 Select a master from the **Apply Master** pop-up menu.

3 Specify the pages to which the master should be applied.

4 Uncheck the **Replace Existing** box if you want to apply multiple masters.

5 Click **OK**.

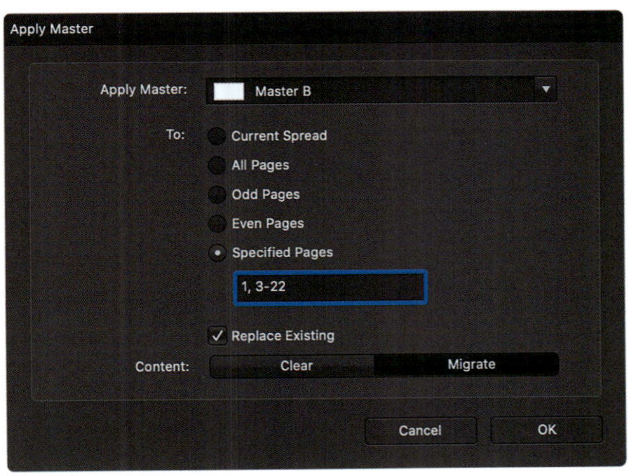

When specifying exact page numbers, use a comma to separate discontinuous pages and a hyphen to specify a page range. For example: 2-3, 19.

*Place the cursor over any page on the **Pages Panel**. If a tooltip appears, it will list masters that are applied to the page.*

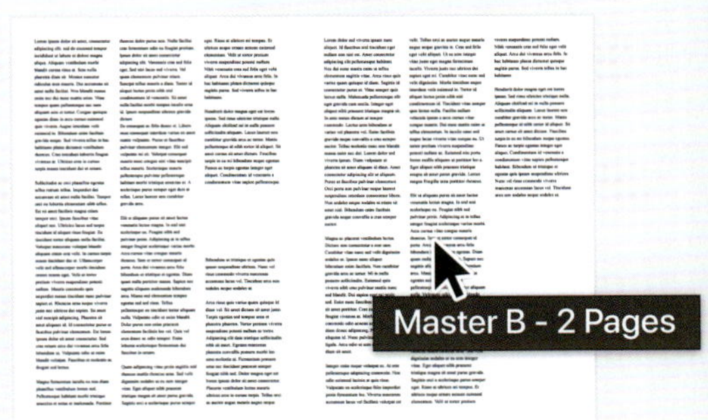

Make local changes

The contents of text and picture frames inherited from a master page (1) can always be populated with new content on any page where the master is applied (2). Such changes are local to that page and do not edit the master or other pages.

By default, the position, size and rotation of text and picture frames inherited from a master are not editable. However, their contents are editable independent of the master.

Other attributes of inherited objects may require adjustment on a publication page. For example, you may want to alter a picture frame's position, size and text wrap settings to better suit available imagery.

To do this, select the layer named after the applied master on the **Layers Panel**, switch to the **Move Tool** and choose an editing mode, as described to the right, on the context toolbar.

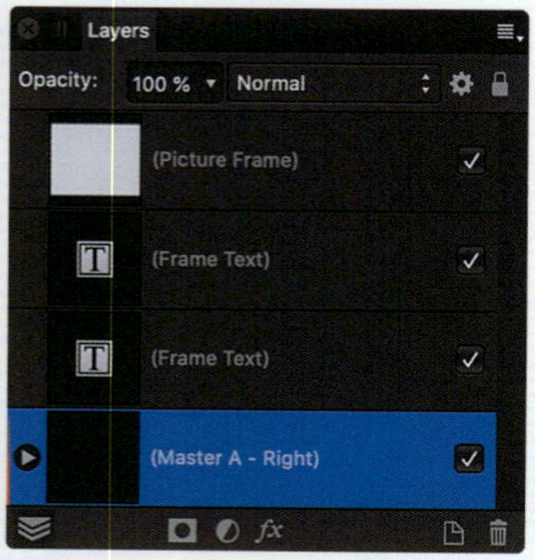

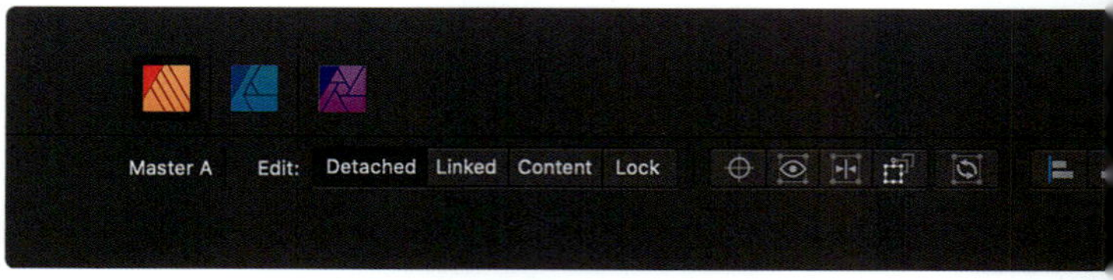

Detached

Enables adjusting inherited elements without amending the master and affecting other pages to which it is applied. Note that the link to the master is not broken altogether. Changes to the master continue to be inherited and may override local modifications you have made.

The page opposite demonstrates how a master page (1), when applied to a publication page, can be detached to modify a picture frame (3). For example, to resize and reposition it to span both pages (4) as shown in the final modified layout.

Linked

Enables editing the master's elements on the page that inherits them. Changes are made to the master and other pages linked to it.

Content

This is the default mode, allowing only the contents of inherited text and picture frames to be edited but not other object attributes. However, the master can be dragged on the page to reposition it.

Lock

The same as locking the master's layer on the Layers Panel and prevents accidental dragging.

1. Master Page

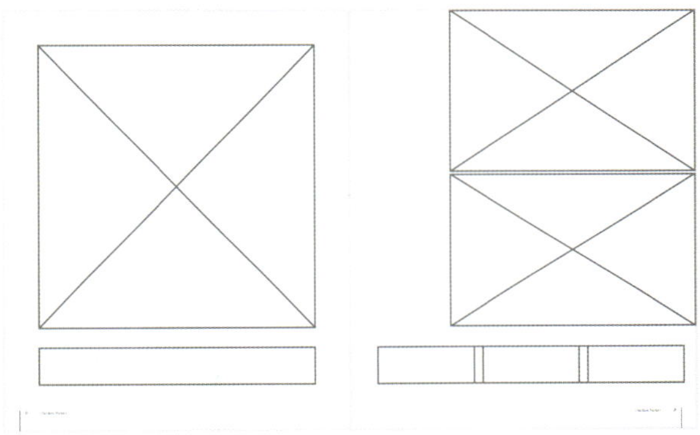

2. Publication page with master applied, content edited

3. Detached picture frame resized on publication page

4. Finalised publication page layout

Resource
core_skills_master_pages.afpub

Removing a master from a page

1 Ctrl-click (Mac) or right-click (Win) the page's thumbnail.

2 Select **Clear Masters**.

Applying one master page to another

Master pages can be applied to other masters, or 'nested'. For example, Master A might contain a footer with page numbers (p. 89), Master B contains a coloured bar down its left edge to represent a publication page's section in a publication.

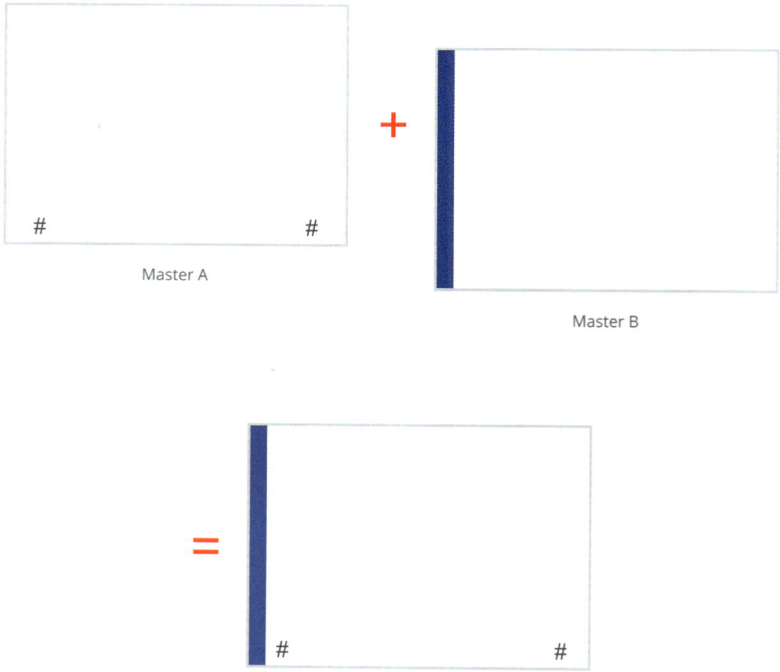

Master B with Master A applied to it

Taking this further, each of Master B through to Master E contains a uniquely coloured bar. By applying Master A to Masters B through to E, you can drag just one master page to each publication page to apply both effects. To amend the footer information or styling on all master and publication pages, only Master A needs to be modified.

1 On the **Pages Panel**, drag Master A to Master B, ensuring you do so to the whole spread.

2 Repeat step 1 for Masters C through to E.

3 In turn, double-click Master B through to Master E's thumbnails. Each displays the footer from Master A.

4 Double-click Master A's thumbnail to start making changes to that master.

5 In the text frame, select the field (#) and choose **Text > Character Traits > Bold**.

6 Double-click each of Master B through to E. The page number will be bold on each of those masters too.

By applying Master A to each of the other four masters, you can apply one of Master B through to E to add page numbers and section-specific objects—a coloured bar in our case—to a spread.

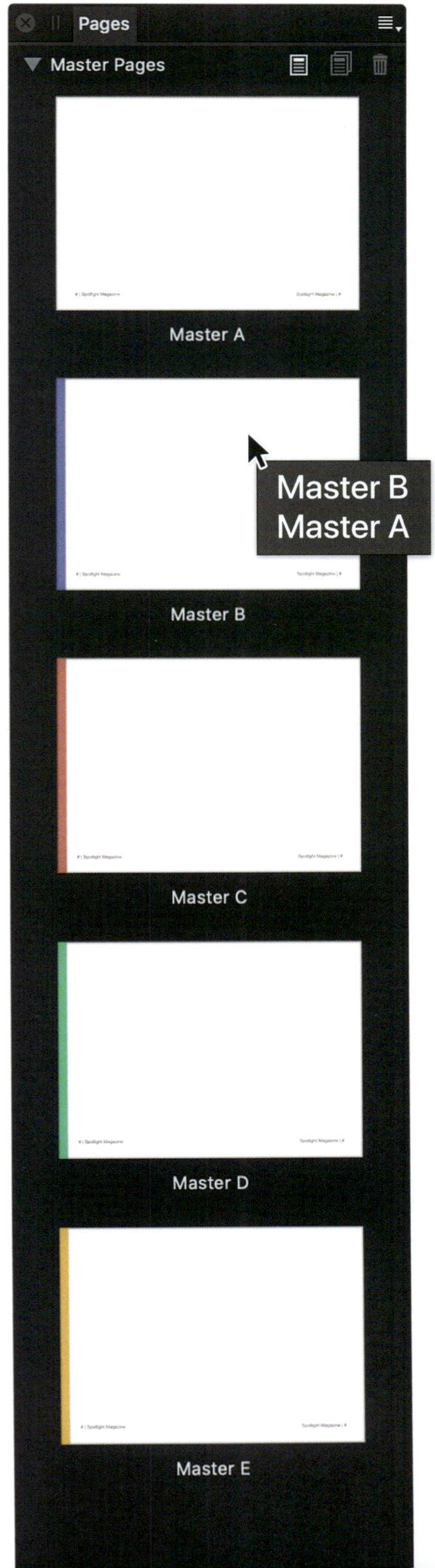

DESIGN AIDS

Understanding the design aids available in Affinity Publisher enables you to work with absolute precision, yet more easily too. We'll look at snapping, column and ruler guides for visually aligning objects, and baseline grids for making text look neater. These features can be enabled or disabled at will at any time.

Snapping

Snapping helps you to align objects with each other, and with the baseline grids and guides described over the next few pages. It is turned on by default and its behaviour can be adapted or entirely disabled to suit your needs.

- Click **Snapping** on the **Toolbar** to toggle it on or off.

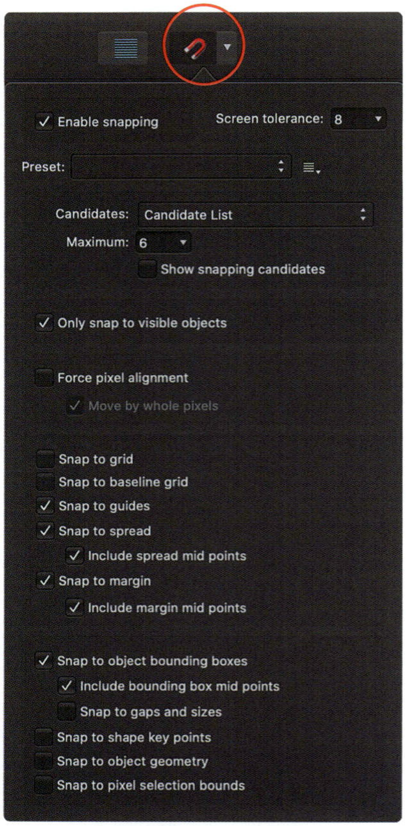

Units of measurement

If you prefer to use a different unit of measurement—for example, pica values like 3p6 (42 pt)—instead of your document's default, you can do so in several places:

View Tool and Zoom Tool (a)
When either of these tools is selected, choose from the **Units** pop-up menu on the context toolbar.

Direct input (b)
Many dialogs/panels accept values in the unit of measurement of your choice. They also accept expressions (in a single unit) to calculate values; see Advanced Text, Expressions & Gestures insert.

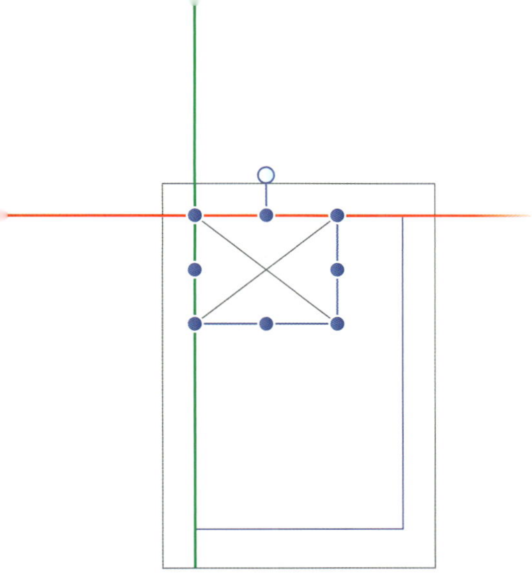

Snapping to page margin

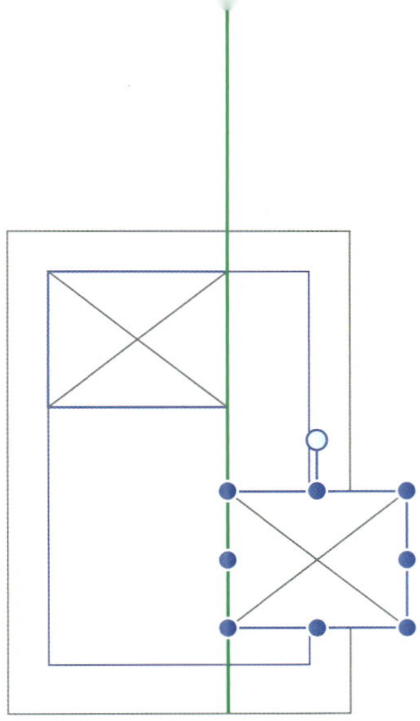

Snapping to existing picture frame

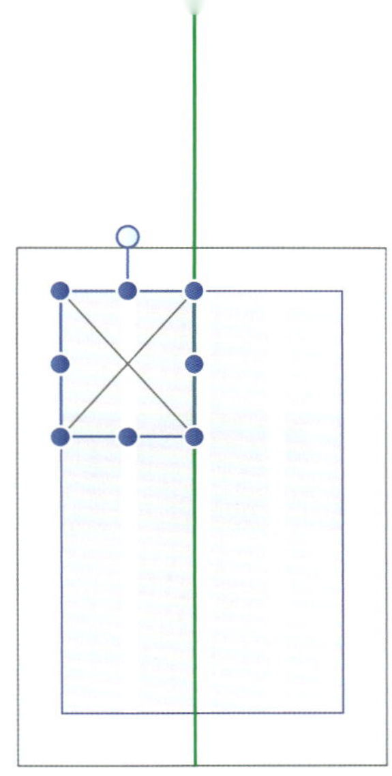

Snapping to column guide

Choose snapping behaviour

Click the Snapping button's adjacent arrow to choose from snapping to baseline grids and guides, page margins and midpoints, other objects' bounding boxes, key points within objects and more.

To help with a variety of page layout tasks, choose a built-in behaviour from the **Preset** pop-up menu, or click the adjacent **Preferences** icon to save your personal choices via a menu.

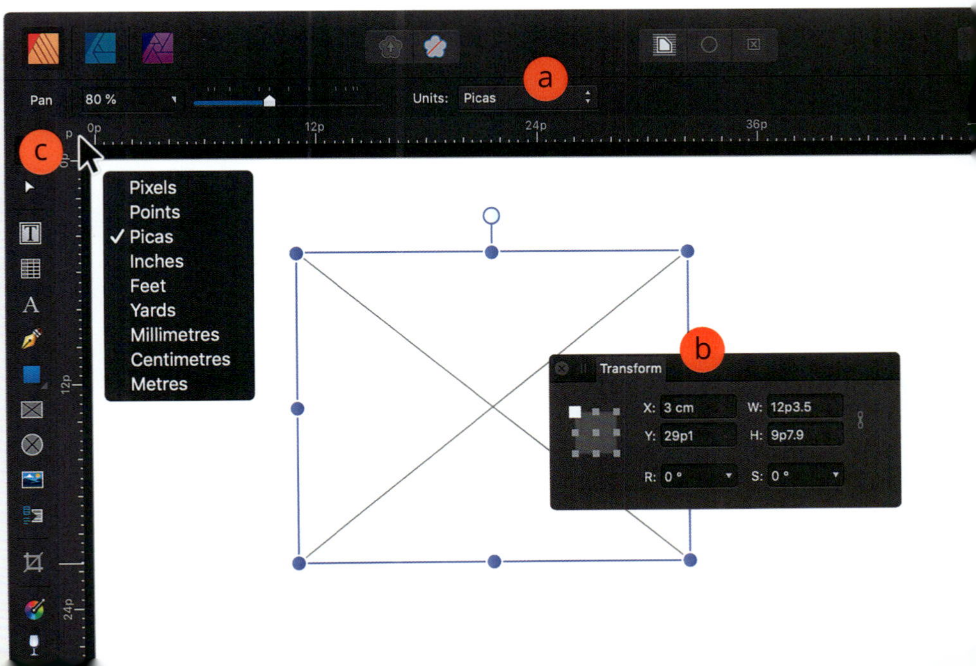

Rulers (c)

Ctrl-click (Mac) or right-click (Win) the unit of measurement shown where the rulers meet at the top left of your document to choose a different unit. This alters the document's default units as well.

Baseline grids

A document-wide **baseline grid** is a set of horizontal ruled lines that applies to all of a document's pages. Once it has been set up, text in frames, shapes and tables snaps to the lines automatically.

The baseline grid is often based on the size and leading of body copy, though it applies to other text styles as well.

A key purpose of the baseline grid is to ensure that, for example, a subheading of a different size in one column or text frame does not push the baseline of subsequent text out of alignment; instead, alignment is maintained for a neater overall look.

Diam sit amet nisl suscipit adipiscing bibendum. Feugiat in fermentum posuere urna nec tincidunt praesent. Ultrices eros in cursus turpis massa tincidunt dui.

Viverra mauris

In aliquam sem fringilla ut morbi tincidunt augue. Elementum integer enim neque volutpat ac tincidunt. Vel fringilla est ullamcorper eget. Cras ornare arcu dui vivamus arcu felis. Malesuada proin libero nunc consequat interdum varius sit amet

Dui vivamus arcu felis bibendum ut tristique. Vitae elementum curabitur vitae nunc. Duis ut diam quam nulla. Viverra ipsum nunc aliquet bibendum. Feugiat pretium nibh ipsum consequat nisl vel pretium lectus. Eu augue ut lectus arcu bibendum at varius vel pharetra. Morbi leo urna molestie at elementum. Viverra mauris in aliquam sem fringilla ut morbi tincidunt. Velit scelerisque in dictum non. Sit amet purus gravida quis blandit turpis cursus in. Nam at lectus urna duis convallis convallis.

Setting a baseline grid

The baseline grid is applied to all pages.

1 Click **Show Baseline Grid Manager** on the **Toolbar**.

2 Check the **Use Baseline Grid** box.

3 From the **Relative to** pop-up menu, select **Top Margin**. Lines will appear above that point, but the 'origin' of the grid is whatever value you enter next to **Start Position**.

4 Next to **Grid Spacing**, set the distance between each pair of grid lines.

5 (Optional) Specify the **Colour** and opacity of the grid lines.

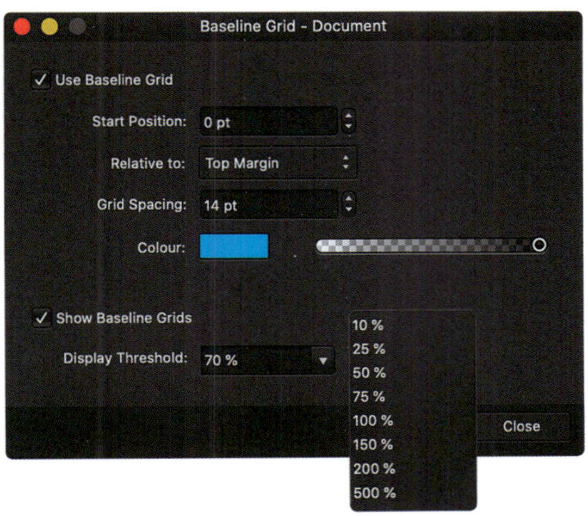

Displaying the baseline grid

The baseline grid need not be visible at all times:

1 On the **Baseline Grid - Document** dialog, check **Show Baseline Grids**.

2 Set **Display Threshold** to *50%*. The grid will appear only at this level or closer.

3 Click **Close**.

4 While zoomed in to at least the display threshold, toggle the baseline grid's visibility by choosing **View > Show Baseline Grid**.

Text in existing frames and tables in your document may visibly shift when you turn on the document-wide baseline grid.

Baseline grids for tables and text frames

Text frames and tables can have their own baseline grid settings, independent of the document-wide baseline grid. This helps to align text across columns or table cells even if a document-wide baseline grid has not been set.

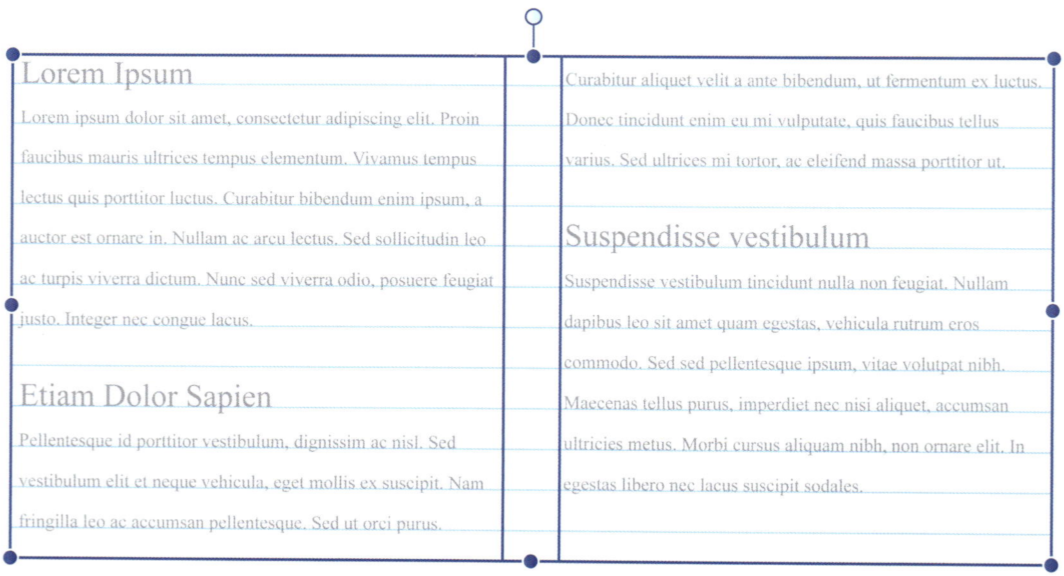

Apply an object-specific baseline grid by following these steps:

1 Select a text frame or table.

2 Choose **View > Studio > Text Frame** or **View > Studio > Table** as appropriate.

3 On the panel's **Baseline Grid** section, check **Use Baseline Grid**.

4 Most of the object-specific baseline grid settings are the same as for the document-wide grid. The exception is what the first grid line is drawn relative to: the top of the element's frame or its top inset.

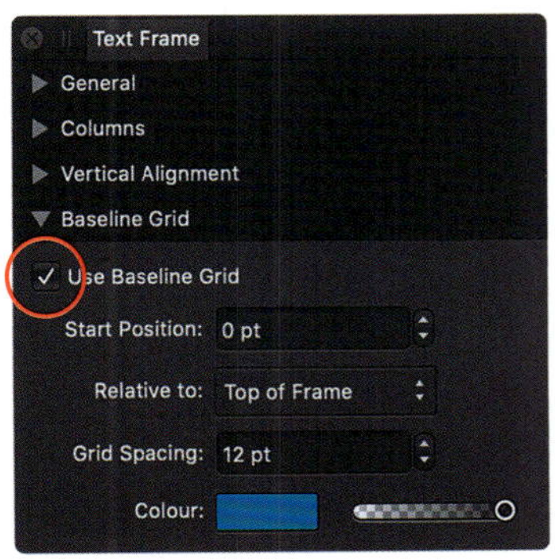

Overriding the baseline grid

Elements can ignore the document-wide baseline grid without applying their own.

1 Select the element on the page.

2 In **View > Studio**, choose **Text Frame** or **Table** as appropriate.

3 On the panel's **General** section, check **Ignore Baseline Grid**.

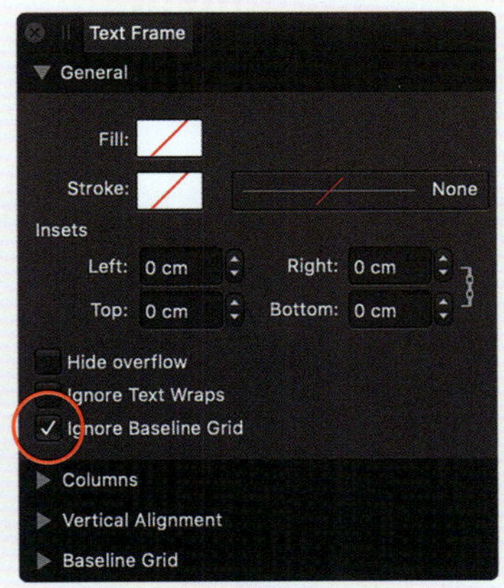

Resource
core_skills_column_ruler_guides.afpub

Guides

Guides help you to position and resize objects on pages with precision, and to follow principles of good design in your page layouts (p. 151). They are purely a visual and practical aid and are excluded when you print or export a document.

Column and ruler guides can be configured in **View > Guides Manager**. Additionally, ruler guides can be added directly from the rulers.

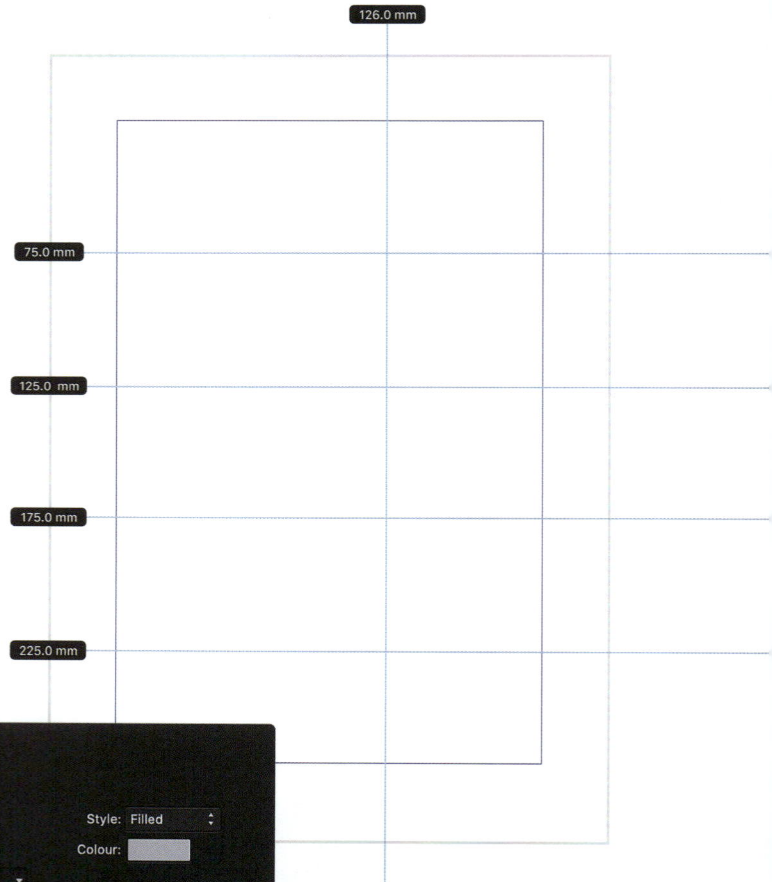

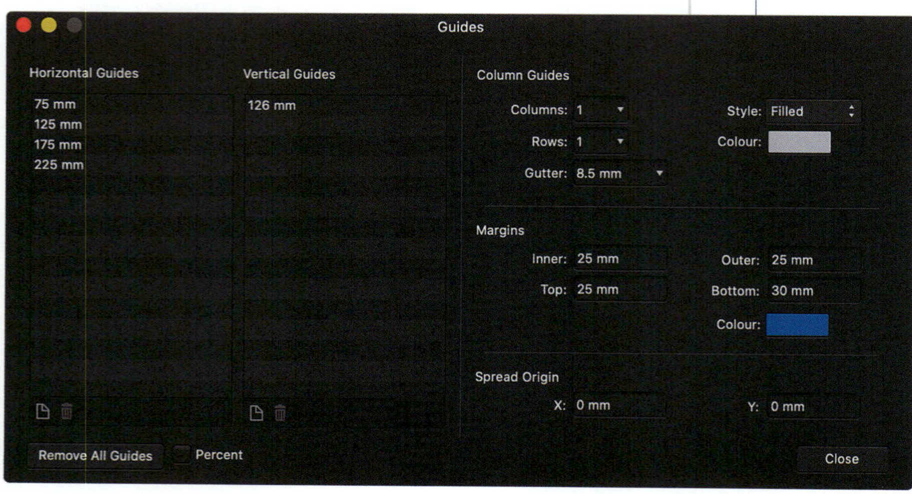

Column guides

Column guides are used to divide a page into columns and rows. They steer your pages towards balanced design. Each page or spread of your document has its own column guide settings.

Column guides are overlaid on pages in a semi-transparent, non-printing overlay. Their **Style** (fill or outline) and **Colour** are customisable. The **Gutter** width, which is the gap between columns, is applied uniformly between each pair of columns.

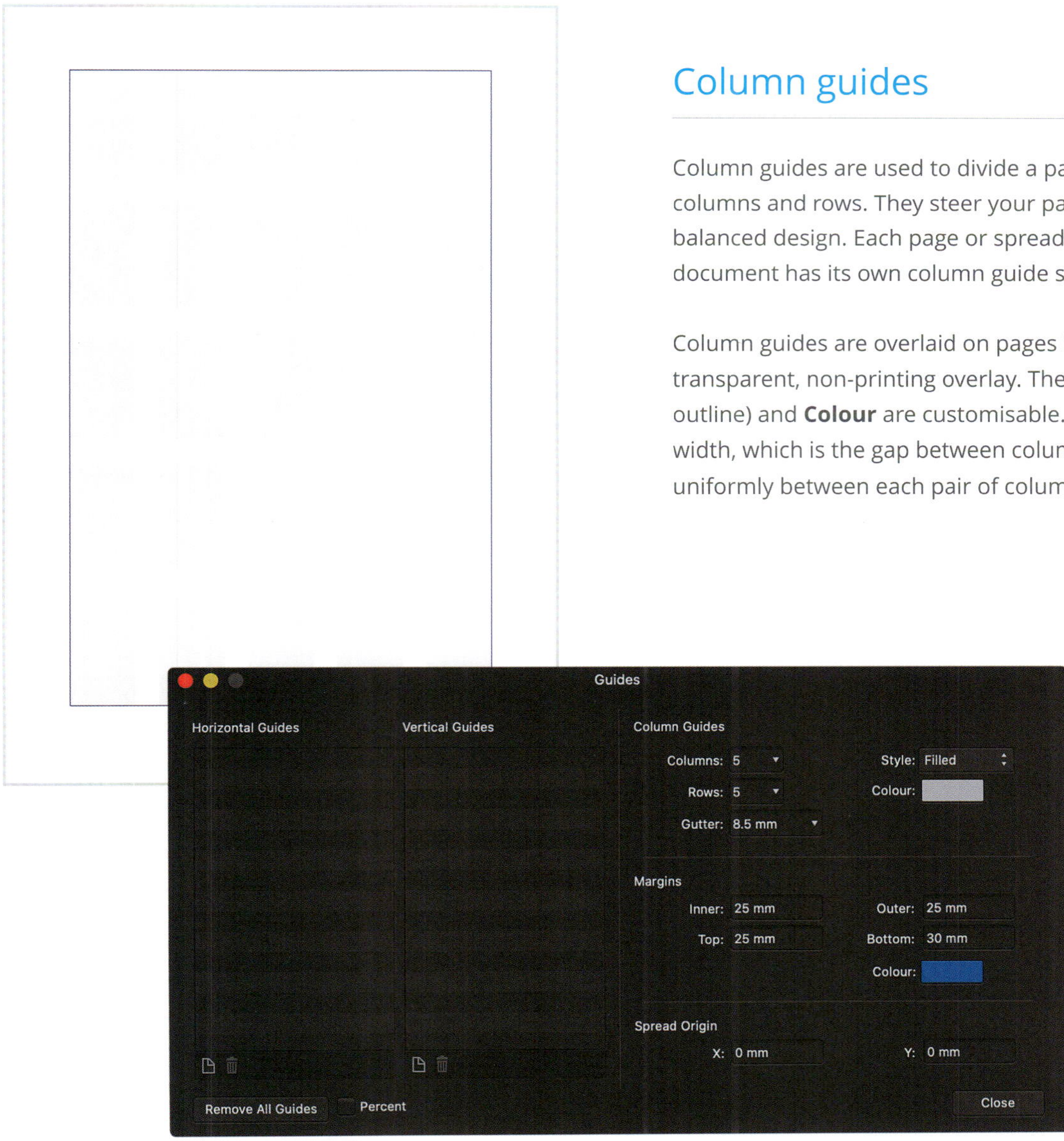

Ruler guides

Ruler guides can be added wherever they are needed simply by dragging from a ruler onto the page. This is the more intuitive method.

However, for grid-based publications you may want to enter precise numerical positions in **Guides Manager** when 'breaking' page elements out of the grid for creative purposes.

Column and ruler guides are commonly added to master pages. Ruler guides inherited from a master are displayed as dashed lines rather than solid ones.

When an object is resized or repositioned and snaps to a ruler guide, the guide will turn red (if it's horizontal) or green (if it's vertical) to confirm what has happened.

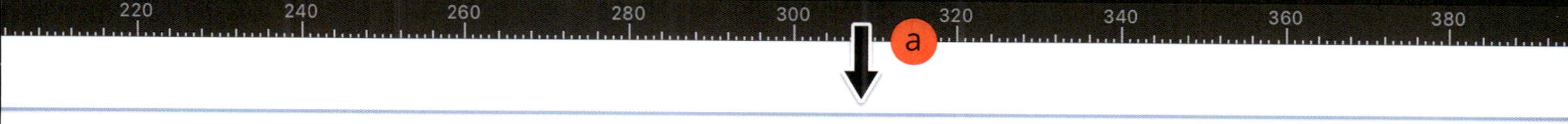

Adding ruler guides

Ruler guides can be added directly to pages.

1. Choose **View > Show Rulers**.
2. Drag from either the horizontal (a) or vertical ruler and drop it in position on the page.

When adding ruler guides using this method, open the Guides Manager so it's available to precisely adjust their positions.

Ruler guides can be created at an exact numerical position or, if they already exist, have their position fine-tuned.

1. Choose **View > Guides Manager**.
2. (Optional) Click **Add new horizontal guide** or **Add new vertical guide** beneath the corresponding list.
3. In either list, double-click a guide's position to edit it.
4. Type the exact position required.

Hiding column and ruler guides

In the **View Menu**, choose either **Show Column Guides** or **Show Guides** to toggle the corresponding overlay. A check mark is shown next to these items when the guides are visible/active.

When column or ruler guides are invisible, they are ignored by the Snapping feature.

OBJECT CONTROL

Affinity Publisher provides a consistent set of controls for manipulating objects, meaning selectable elements on pages: text frames, picture frames, tables, shapes and artistic text.

Using the **Move Tool** (V), click an object to select it. A bounding box is displayed around the object, with handles at the corners and at the centre of each edge.

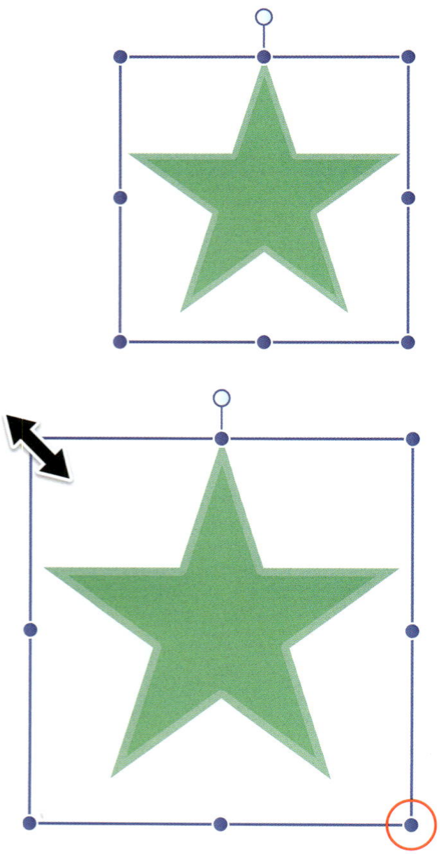

Resizing an object

Drag any of an object's handles to increase or decrease the object's size. Most objects are able to be distorted as you scale them. Hold the shift key (⇧) while resizing to maintain an object's proportions (aspect ratio).

The exceptions are artistic text and unframed pictures, which maintain their aspect ratio when scaled. In these cases, hold the shift key (⇧) to allow them to distort.

When resizing an object, the opposite corner is the anchor point. Hold the cmd ⌘ key (Mac) or ctrl key (Win) to resize about its centre.

Resource

core_skills_object_control.afpub

Resizing text frames

Dragging a text frame's corner or edge handle (a) scales the frame itself and its column widths, but maintains its text size and gutters' widths.

Text frames have an additional handle hanging outside their bottom-right corner (b). This scales the *entire* frame proportionally: its overall dimensions, internal structures and text size.

Original text frame

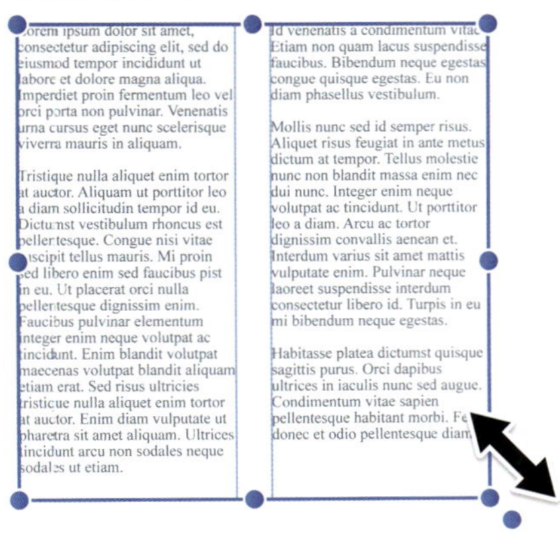

Scaled frame maintaining text size and gutter widths

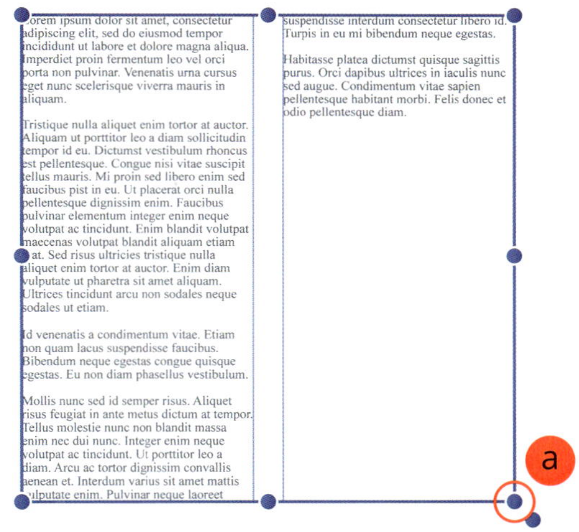

Scaled entire frame proportionally

Reposition an object

- With the **Move Tool** selected, drag from within the object's bounding box to move it on the page.

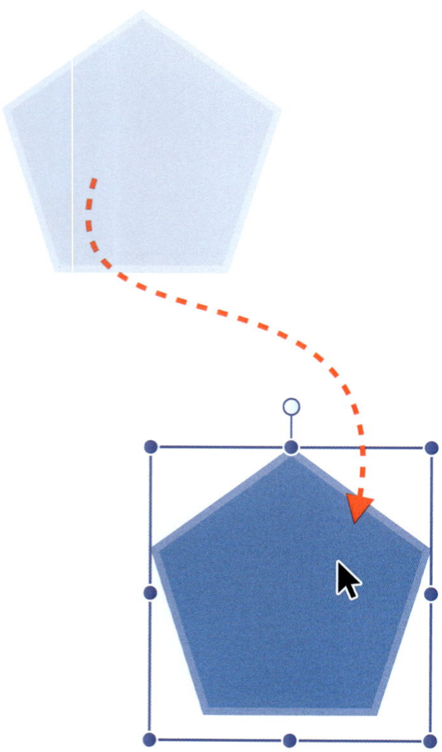

Duplicate an object

- With the **Move Tool** selected, hold the cmd ⌘ key (Mac) or ctrl key (Win) and drag an object to create a duplicate at the position where you drop the object. The original object is unaltered.

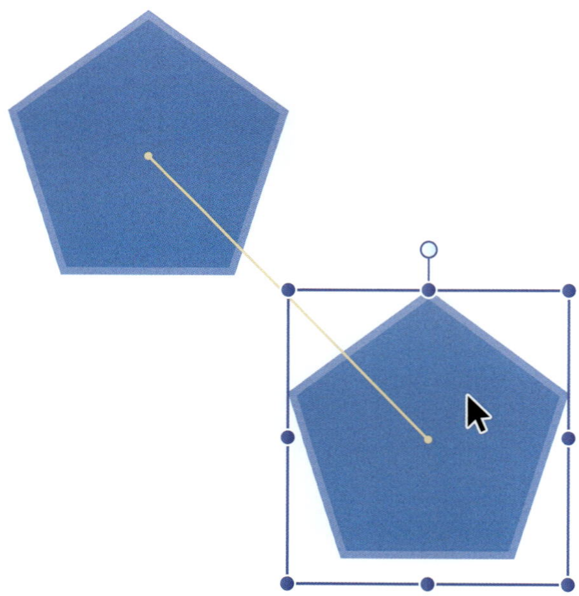

When repositioning or duplicating an object, hold the shift key (⇧) as well to constrain along multiples of 45° from the starting position.

Rotate an object

Drag left or right from the lollipop-like rotation handle that hangs outside the top edge of an object. The object will rotate around its centre.

Hold the shift key (⇧) while dragging the handle to rotate in 15° increments.

Double-click the rotation handle to reset the object's rotation to 0°.

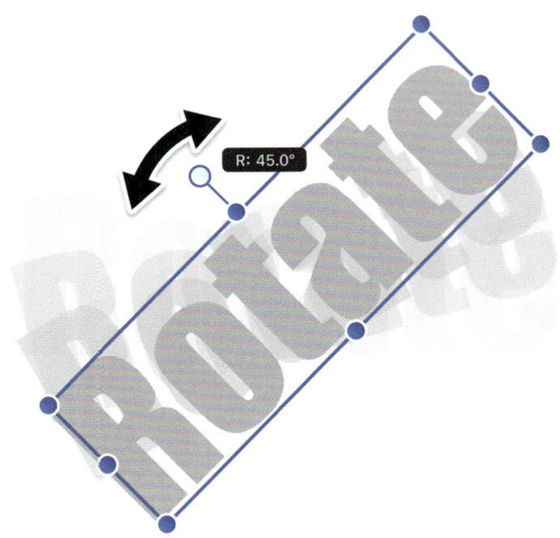

The object controls described here can be applied to an individual object or layer, or to a multiple selection made by holding the shift key (⇧) and clicking several objects.

Precisely reposition, resize or rotate an object

Select an object and then type in the **Transform Panel**'s **X** and **Y** fields to reposition it, the **W** and **H** fields to resize it, or the **R** and **S** fields to rotate and shear (skew) it. The fields can calculate new values based on the object's current attributes—see the Advanced Text, Expressions & Gestures insert.

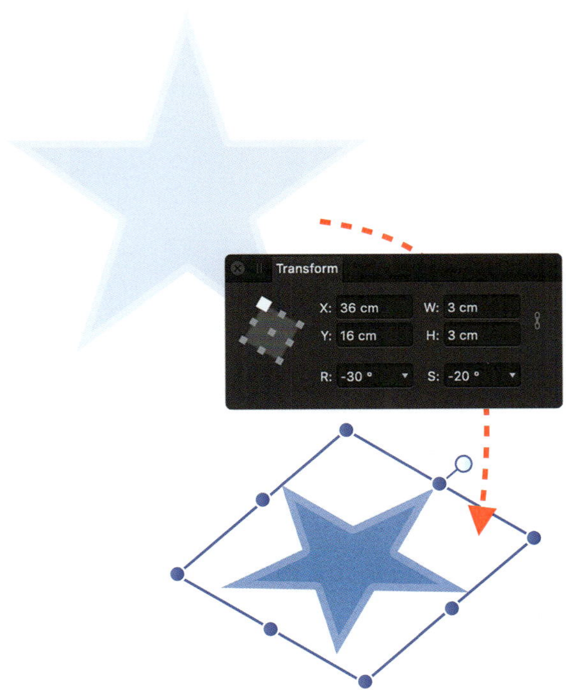

Arranging objects

Every object on the current page is listed on the **Layers Panel**. Layer order from top to bottom on the panel corresponds to object positions from front to back on the page.

To change an object's position in the layer stack, do one of the following:

- Select it and use the **Arrange** buttons on the **Toolbar** to bring it forward/move it back a layer at a time or all the way in an instant.
- Use the equivalent keyboard shortcuts listed in **Layer > Arrange**.

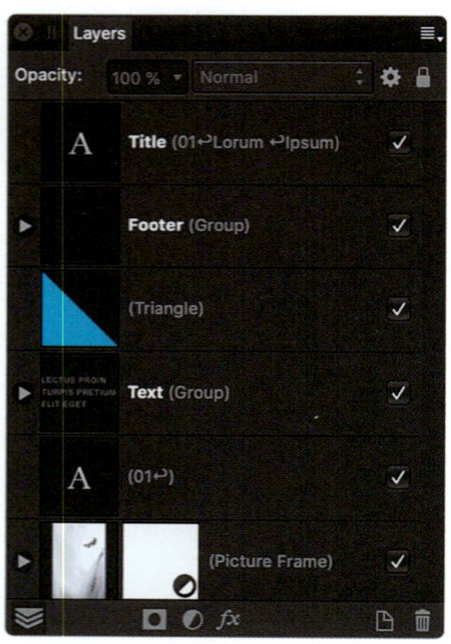

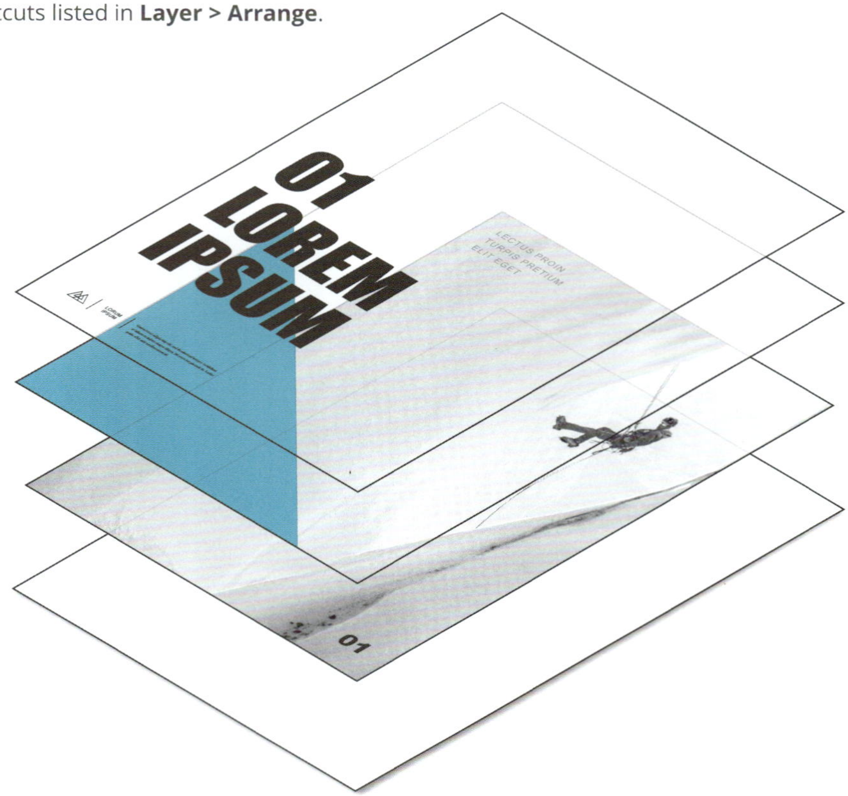

Resource
core_skills_new_object_insertion.afpub

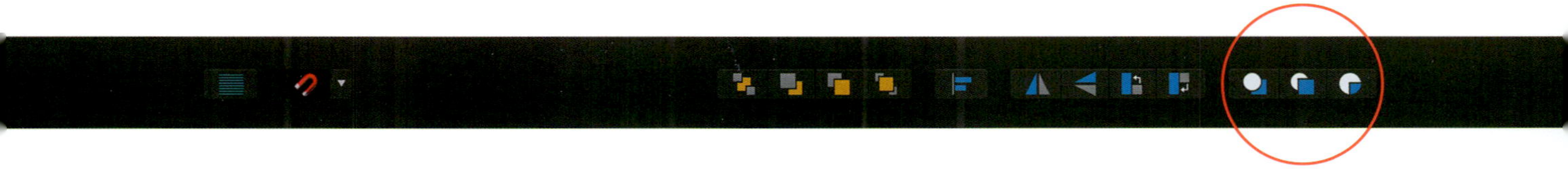

Inserting new objects

A newly drawn object's position in the layer stack depends on what is selected in **Layer > Insertion** or which button, if any, in the **Toolbar**'s **Insertion** group is selected. In the examples below, the triangle is the newly drawn object.

Default

Inserts the triangle on a new layer immediately above what is selected, or at the top of the stack if nothing is selected.

Behind

Inserts the triangle immediately beneath whatever is selected, or at the bottom of the stack if nothing is selected.

Top

Always inserts the triangle at the top of the stack, regardless of whatever is currently selected.

Inside

Clips the triangle to the selected object, so only its overlaps are visible, or inserts it at the top if nothing is selected.

Resource

core_skills_multicolumn_text_frames.afpub

WORKING WITH TEXT

Text is a crucial component of almost every publication. Affinity Publisher offers several ways to use it, which are explained here. They will be familiar if you have used other Affinity apps, though Affinity Publisher's **Frame Text Tool** has extra capabilities specifically suited to page layout.

Frame text

This is the most commonly used type of text in Affinity Publisher. It can be used for anything from a single-sentence caption to multi-paragraph body copy.

1 Using the **Frame Text Tool**, drag across a page to create a new text frame in that area.

2 Choose **Text > Insert Filler Text** to fill the frame with placeholder text. By default, the line length of text runs to the frame's full width and height.

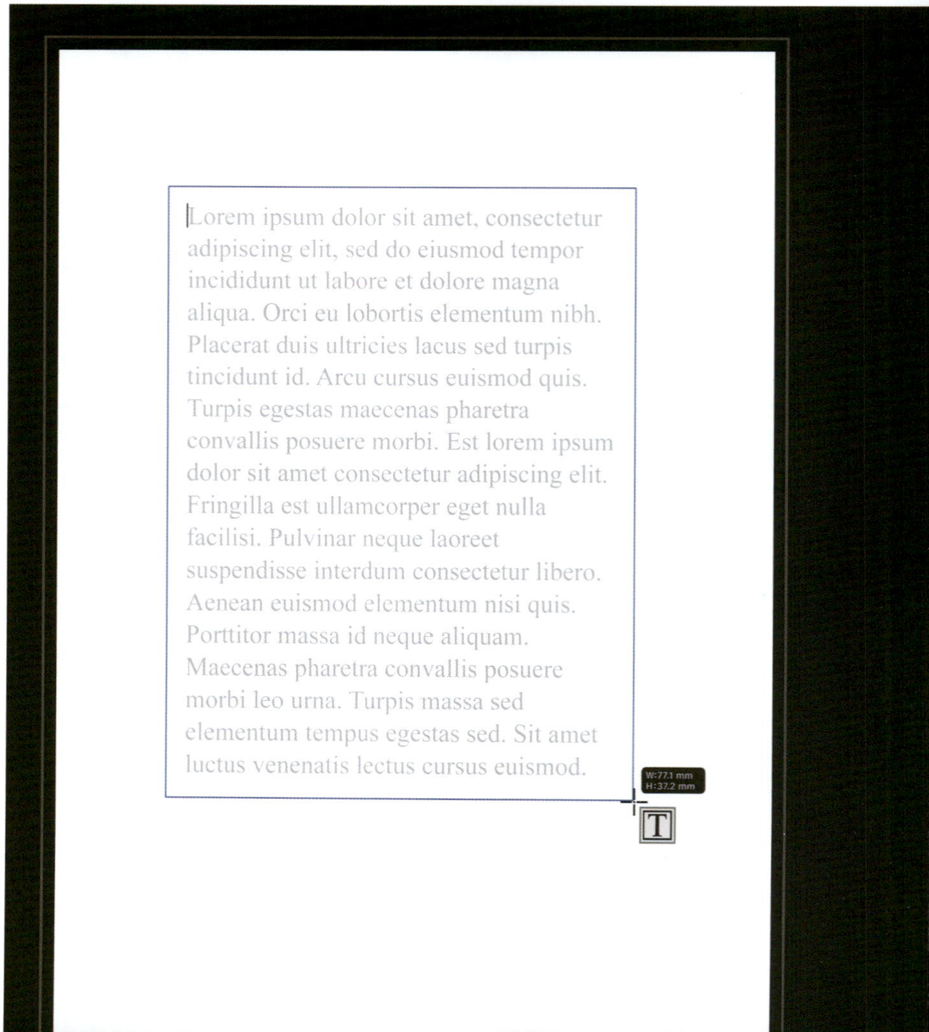

Multi-column text frames

A text frame can display its contents across multiple columns, with adjustable gutter widths between them. This is important to many types of publication, from posters to magazines to books.

Setting up a text frame

1. Use the **Move Tool** (V) to select a frame with text in it.
2. On the context toolbar, set **Font Colour** to *White*.
3. Set **Columns** to *3*.
4. Click **Text Frame**.
5. On the **Text Frame Panel**, set **Fill** to a dark colour for contrast.
6. Under **Insets**, set all values to *2 mm* so text doesn't touch the frame's edges.

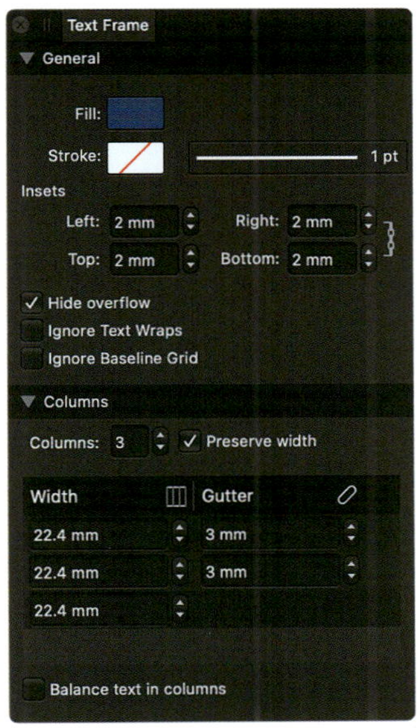

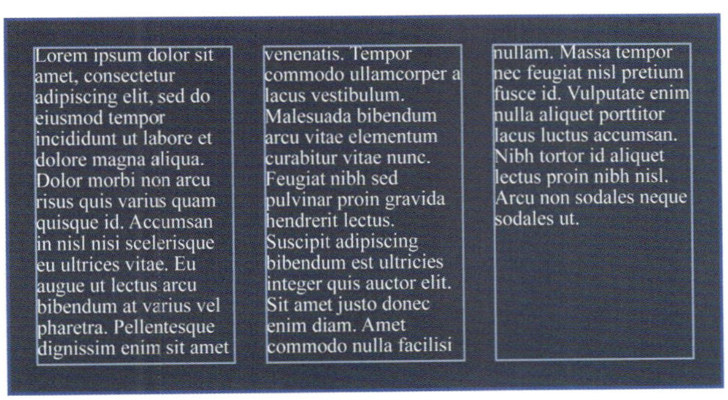

Asymmetric text frames

Column widths are initially the same but can be adjusted individually. Click the **Width** icon to reset all to the same value.

By default, changing one gutter's width changes all others to match. Click the **Gutter** icon toggle between adjusting gutters uniformly or individually.

If the final column's text runs short, check **Balance text in columns** to redistribute text across all columns more evenly.

Resource
core_skills_overset_text.afpub

Dealing with overset text

With the frame selected, its triangular **Text Flow** buttons turn red as a reminder that there is overset text hidden from view.

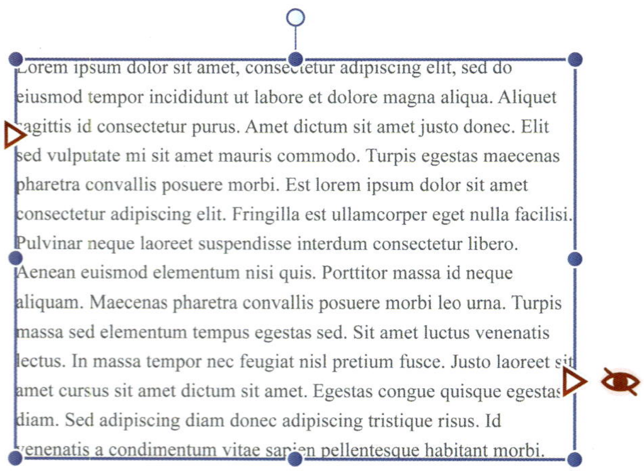

When text overflows its frame, red handles on the frame's edges warn you about it—even when the frame is deselected.

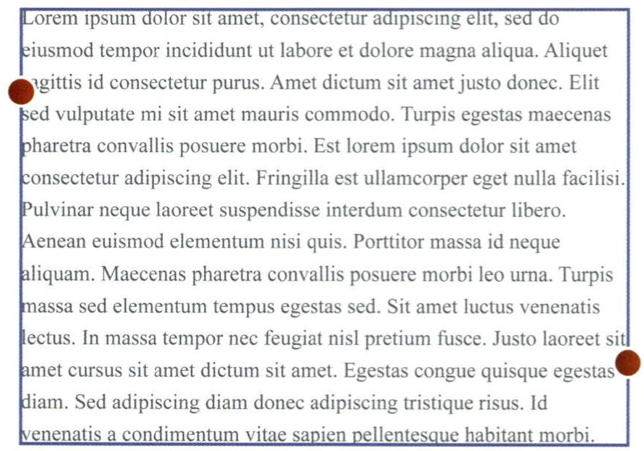

Click the **Text Flow** button's adjacent eye icon to display the overset text for review. Click it again to hide the overset text.

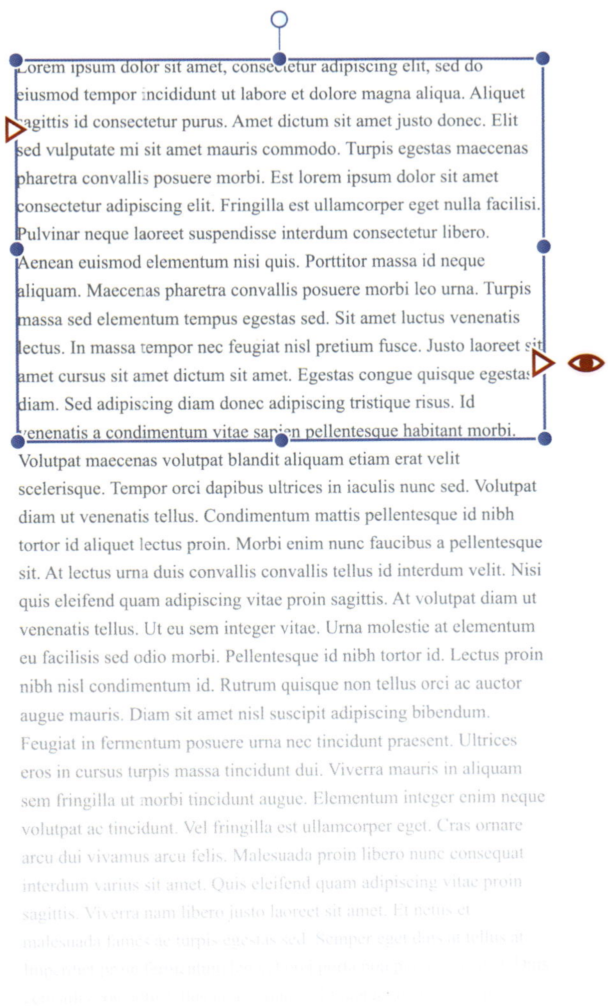

Overset text warning

When you print or export a document, Affinity Publisher will warn you if it contains any preflight errors, including overset text made temporarily visible by clicking the eye icon. To resolve an overset text error, do one of the following:

- Resize the frame to display all of the text.
- Edit the text to fit the frame.
- Flow the text through additional linked text frames.

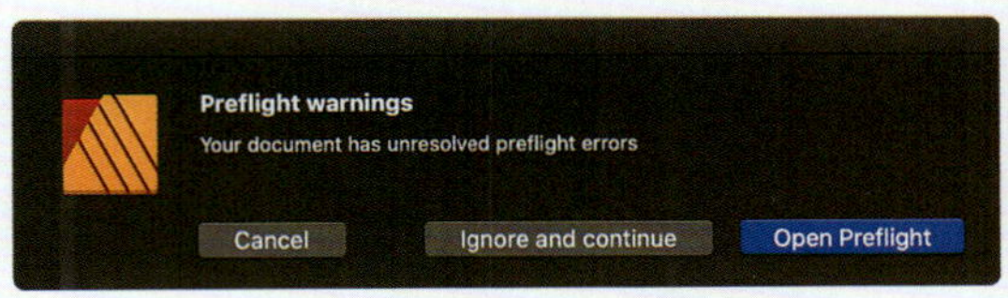

Resource
core_skills_linking_text_frames.afpub

Linking text frames

Text frames can be linked so that overset text from one frame spills into subsequent frames in the sequence automatically. Later frames can be on the same page or different pages.

Frames can be linked when created, or retrospectively.

1 Use the **Frame Text Tool** to create an initial text frame.

2 Click the frame's bottom-right **Text Flow** button.

3 Drag out another new text frame (or click within an existing one) so text flows from the initial frame into it.

4 Repeat steps 2 and 3 to create and link as many frames as required for your text.

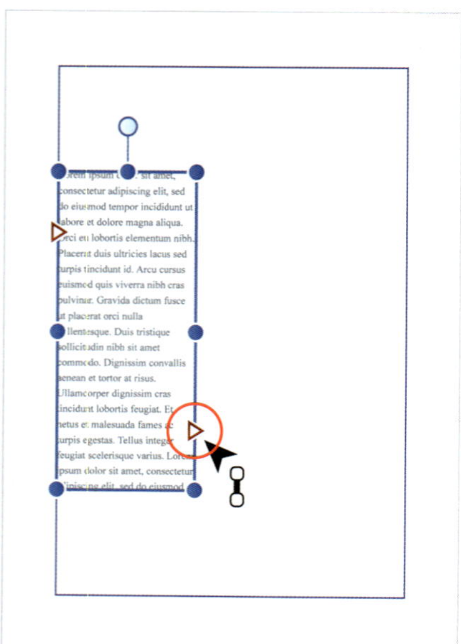

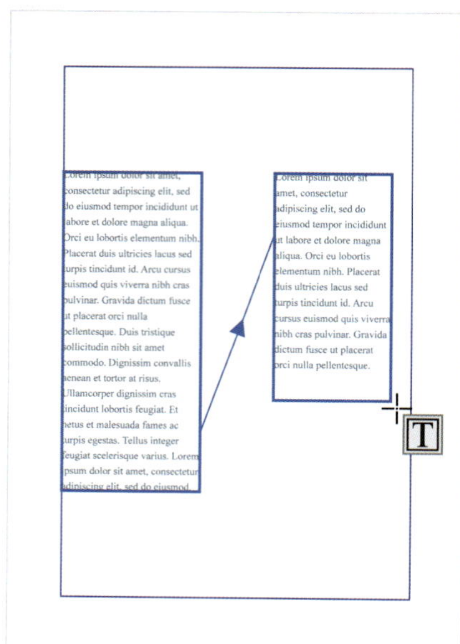

Paragraph styles and **character styles** (p. 140) are commonly applied to frame text to help maintain consistency throughout a publication. Adjustments made to a style are immediately visible wherever it has been applied.

Managing linked frame order

Text frames can be inserted into or deleted from the middle of a sequence.

Inserting a new text frame reflows text from that point onwards.

1 Click either of a frame's **Text Flow** buttons, depending on where the new frame is needed.

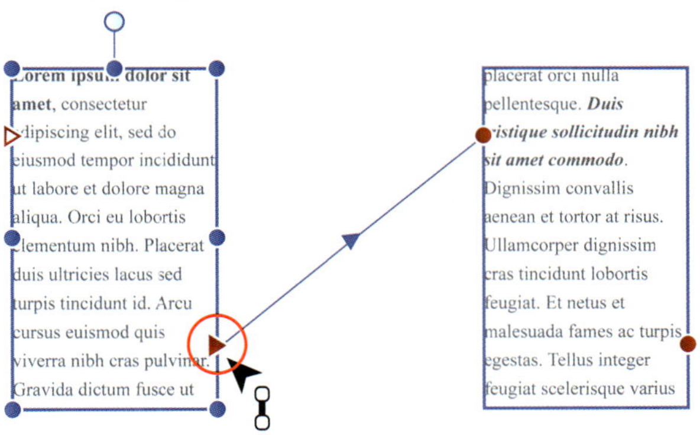

2 Drag on the page to create a new frame, or click an existing but unlinked one.

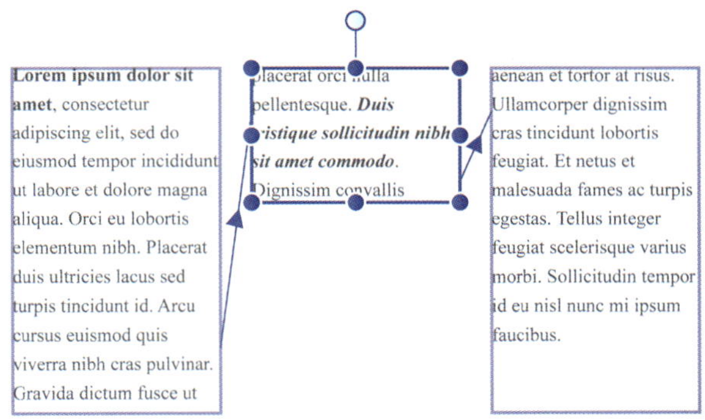

Deleting a linked text frame or the page it is on does not break the overall sequence. The links on the frames before and after it are updated and text is reflowed.

Beware of moving a page that contains frames that belong to a linked sequence, because this does not alter the order in which frames are linked and so your text may become out of order.

Resource
core_skills_autoflow_text.afpub

Autoflow text

With one click, the **Text Flow** button can create as many new pages and linked text frames as are needed to present all your text.

This saves time with publications that follow a repeating format, such as books and reports. It can be done one page at a time or for as many pages as are needed to display all of your text.

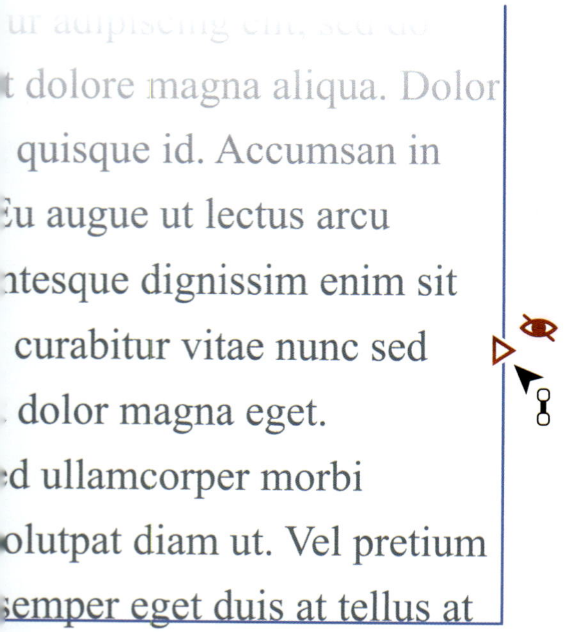

Autoflow one page at a time

1 Hold the option ⌥ key (Mac) or alt key (Win) and click the frame's **Text Flow** button to append a page containing a new linked text frame of the same size and position to your document.

2 Repeat step 1 on the newest frame until you have as many pages/text frames as needed.

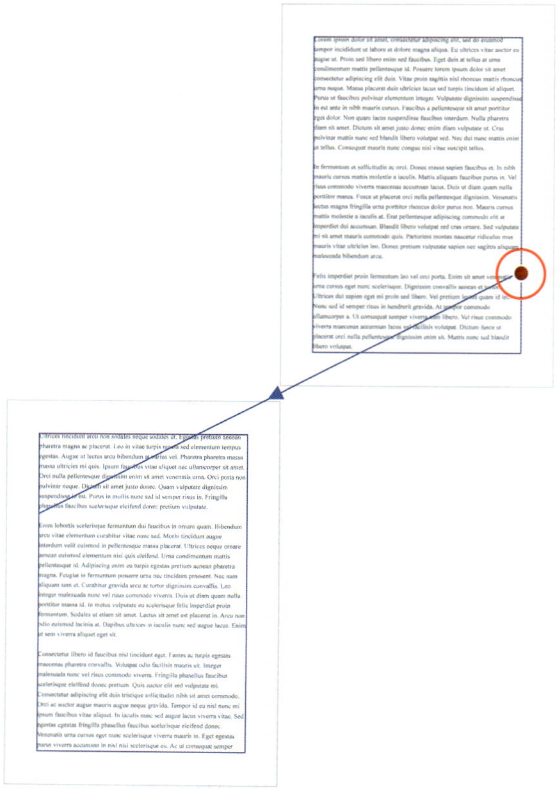

Autoflow all at once

Hold the shift key (⇧) and click the frame's **Text Flow** button to instantly create as many pages and text frames (all of the same size) as are needed to display *all* of the overset text.

If a document contains facing pages and the initial frame is asymmetrically positioned, the new frame's position is mirrored across the spread.

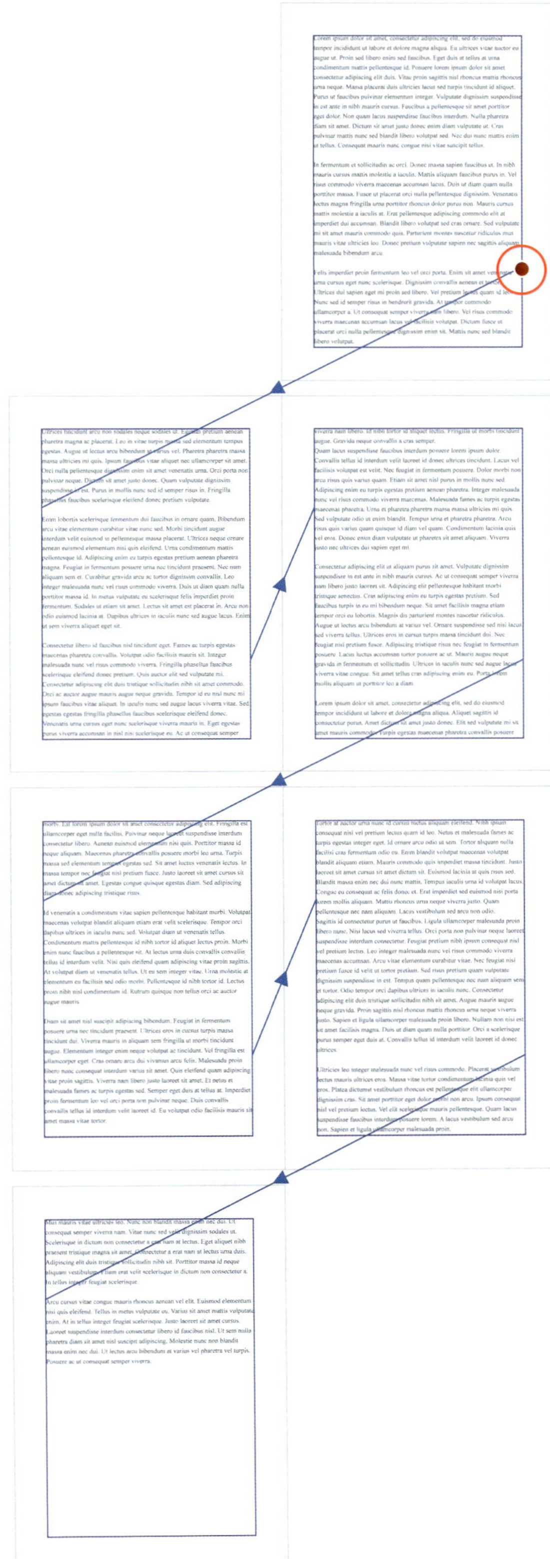

Resource
core_skills_other_text_types.afpub

Other kinds of text

Artistic Text

Use the **Artistic Text Tool** to create prominent or decorative typography, such as headlines. Artistic text resizes to always fill its container.

1 With the **Artistic Text Tool** (T), drag on the page to set the text size.

2 Type some text.

3 (Optional) Drag a corner handle to resize the artistic text proportionally; that is, without distorting the text's dimensions.

Text, kerning, tracking and leading adjustments are often applied to large text to refine its appearance within an overall design.

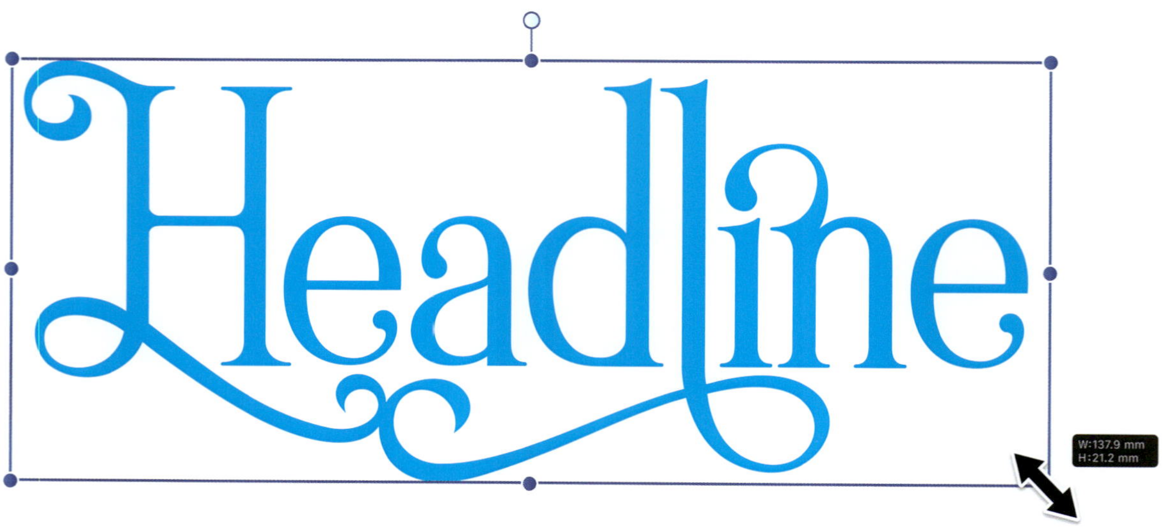

Path Text

Text can run along a curve, closed shape or geometric shape.

1 Select a suitable object.

2 Using the **Artistic Text Tool**, hover the cursor over the object's edge. Click when it changes to the cursor shown below.

3 Type some text.

4 Drag the coloured handles to adjust where the text sits. Text that does not fit between them flows onto the other side of the curve/object outline.

If the path is a visible design element, the **Baseline** property on the context toolbar can be used to offset the text from it.

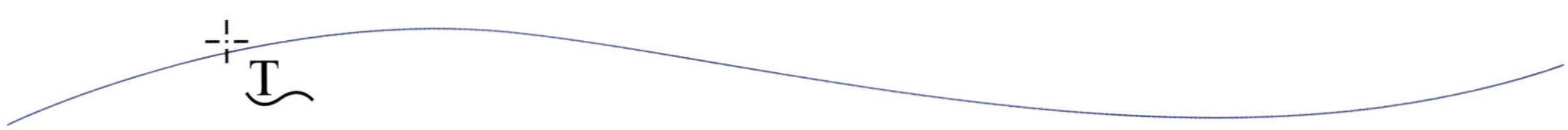

Take the stroke width off a path before converting to Path Text if you do not want the visible stroke to be burned into the design.

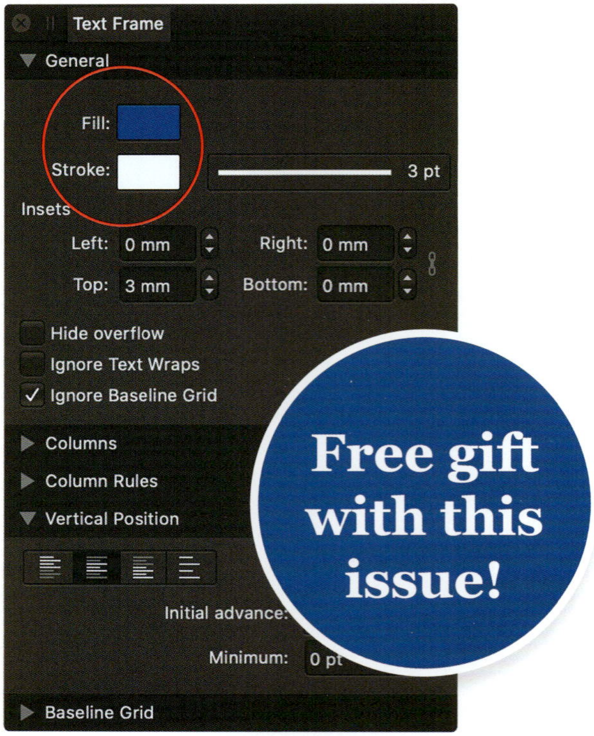

Shape Text

As well as rectangular text frames, text can flow within shapes drawn using the shape tools or **Pen Tool**.

Like frame text, shape text can be divided into columns and have insets applied to ensure it doesn't touch the shape's outline.

1 Click and hold the **Rectangle Tool**. Select the **Ellipse Tool**.

2 Hold the shift key (⇧) and drag on a page to draw a circle.

3 Select the **Frame Text Tool** and place it over the shape's interior.

4 Click on the shape and click **Centre Align** on the context toolbar.

5 Open the menu next to **Top Align** on the context toolbar. Choose **Centre Vertically**.

6 Select **View > Studio > Text Frame** and then apply **Fill** and **Stroke** settings to the shape.

7 Type the required text—for example, 'Free gift with this issue!'—and adjust its size and colour.

8 (Optional) With some shapes, words and font settings, shape text may look more balanced, in terms of the gaps around it, when offset slightly from its shape's vertical centre. If necessary, unlink the **Insets** on the **Text Frame Panel** and adjust the **Top** inset.

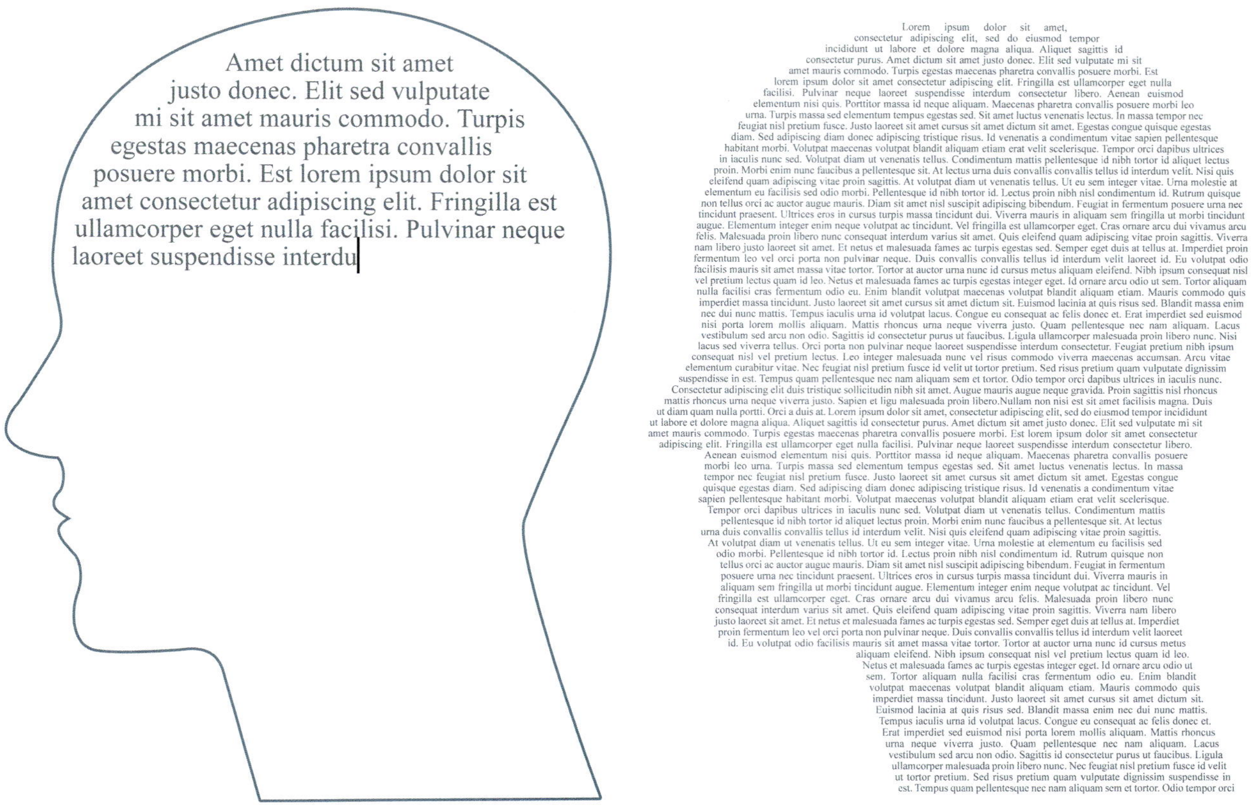

Hand-drawn shapes as text frames

Closed shapes drawn using the **Pen Tool** can contain shape text.

- With the **Pen Tool** selected, on the context toolbar choose **Pen Mode** or **Smart Mode** to draw a shape with curves, or **Polygon Mode** to draw using straight lines.

When your closed shape is complete, follow from step 3 opposite to add text inside it.

Resource
core_skills_picture_frames.afpub

PICTURE FRAMES

Picture frames are placeholders into which you can insert images, PDFs and Affinity documents. Affinity Publisher includes tools for creating rectangular and elliptical picture frames.

Intersecting diagonal lines through an empty picture frame's centre distinguish it from a plain shape.

To create a picture frame:

1 Select either the **Picture Frame Rectangle Tool** (F) or the **Picture Frame Ellipse Tool**.

2 (Optional) Hold the shift key (⇧) if you want a perfect square or circle.

3 Drag on a page to set the size and position of the frame.

Placing content in a picture frame is described on p. 130.

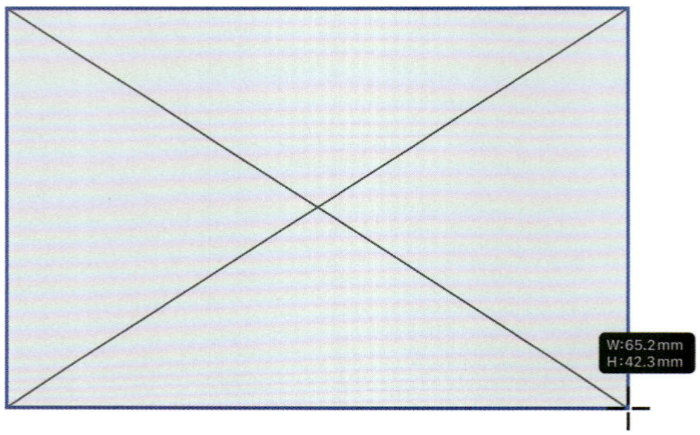

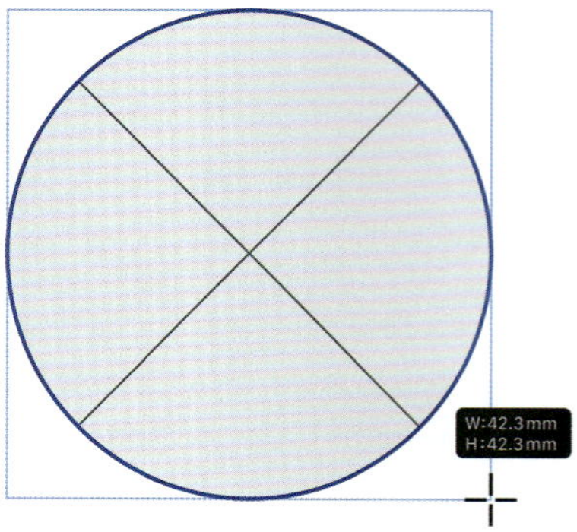

a

Use shapes as picture frames

Closed shapes drawn using the **Pen Tool** (a) and compounds created from multiple objects (b) using the commands in **Layer > Geometry** can be converted into picture frames (c).

With one selected:

- Choose **Layer > Convert to Picture Frame**.

b

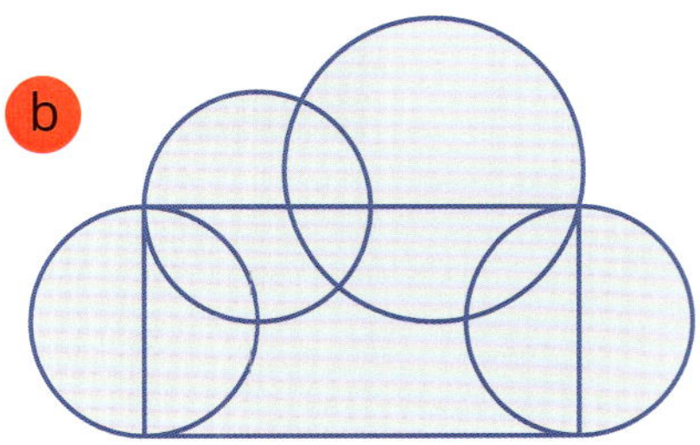

c

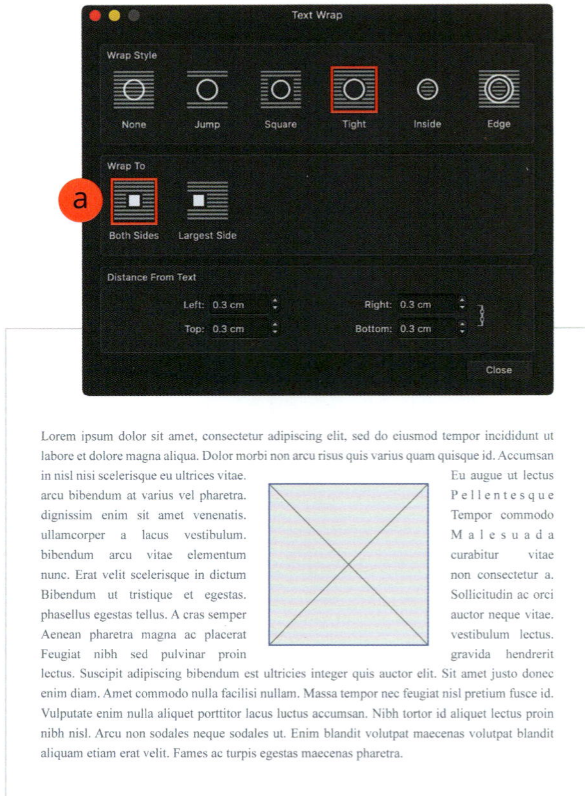

Wrap text around pictures

The flow of words in a text frame is, by default, unaffected by another element overlapping the frame. Sometimes you'll want this. When you don't, Affinity Publisher provides several behaviours for how text flows around an element.

Text can wrap around picture frames, shapes, tables and even other text objects.

1 Select a picture frame that overlaps a text frame.

2 Click **Show Text Wrap Settings** on the **Toolbar**.

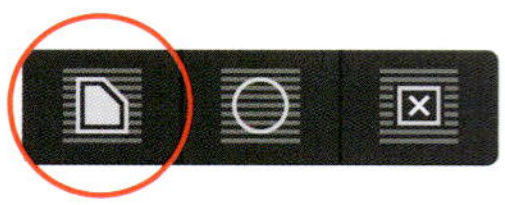

3 Set **Wrap Style** to your desired behaviour, e.g. not running down either side (**Jump**), running down both sides of the picture frame's rectangular bounding box (**Square**) or following a precise outline (**Tight**).

4 If the text flows too close or too far away from the picture, adjust **Distance From Text**. Negative values are allowed.

Wrap To is available only for the Square and Tight text wrap styles. It enables you to specify whether text flows around Both Sides (a) or only the Largest Side (b) of the picture frame, where text has the longest line length.

Effects of image transparency on text wrapping

Text may not immediately wrap as shown in the Text Wrap dialog's examples. It will wrap to the rectangular bounding box of another picture frame, artistic text or another text frame (a) even if a picture frame's image has an alpha channel, which specifies which pixels are transparent or opaque.

If an image file contains an alpha channel, placing it directly on a page, rather than in a picture frame, and applying the Tight text wrap style to it, for example, makes text flow around its opaque outer edges (b).

It's still possible to fine tune the text wrap outline on framed transparent images, which we'll look at next.

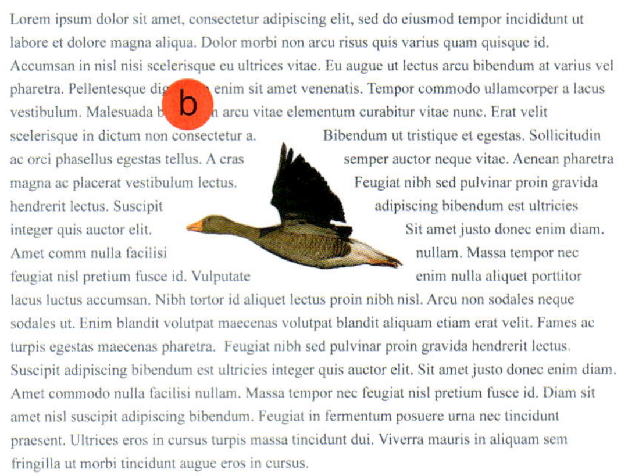

Fine-tune a text wrap

The more flexible method of wrapping text around a non-rectangular shape can be applied to images without an alpha channel and in picture frames. However, it may involve extra effort depending on the image's edge.

1 Select the picture frame with a text wrap applied.

2 Click **Edit Wrap Outline** on the **Toolbar**.

3 Drag the nodes around the object's outline to adjust the text flow. (This does not alter the object's content.)

4 To add a node, click an empty position on the wrap outline.

5 Drag the new node into position.

6 Repeat steps 4 and 5 as necessary.

When an object's text wrap settings cause unwanted wrapping—to a text frame placed on top of it, for example—you can override the wrapping.

1 Select the affected text frame.

2 Choose **Text > Text Wrap > Ignore Text Wraps** or check that setting on the **Text Frame Panel**.

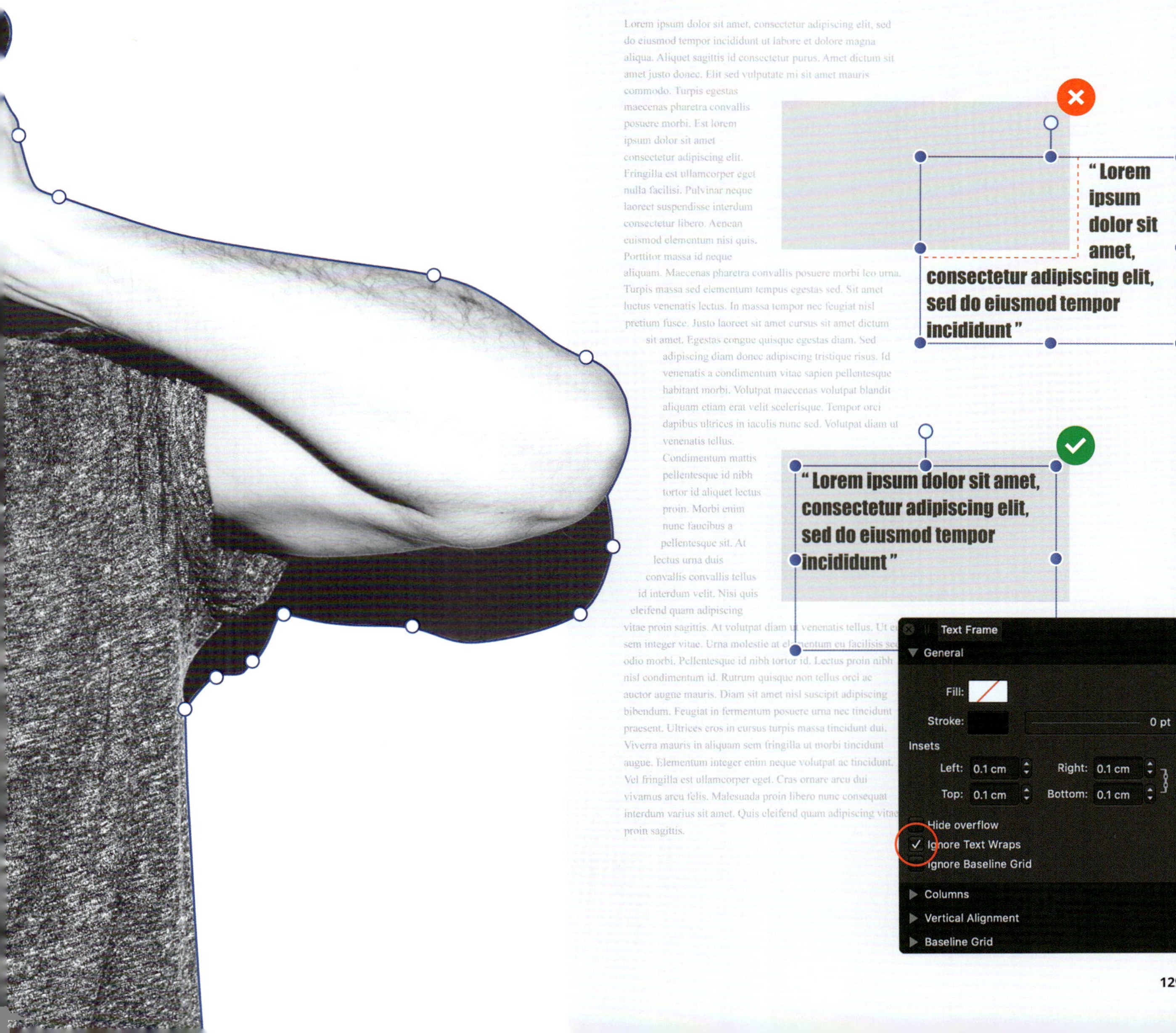

ADDING CONTENT

As well as creating content directly on pages using Affinity Publisher's built-in tools, content can be imported from a variety of text, raster and vector image files.

Files can be of different formats, including PNG, JPEG, TIFF, SVG, layered Photoshop (PSD), PDF, Microsoft Excel (XLSX) and Affinity documents. The latest list of importable formats is available at https://affin.co/afpfeatures under **Placing Content**.

Use the **Place Image Tool** to add an image (or a PDF or Affinity document) to your Affinity Publisher document.

The tool's behaviour changes depending on how many image files you import.

Place directly on a page

1. Select the **Place Image Tool**.
2. Choose an image file to place and click **Open**.
3. Drag across the area of a page that you want the image to occupy.

Place in a picture frame

1. Select one or more existing picture frames.
2. Select the **Place Image Tool**.
3. Choose one image and click **Open**. It is placed in all of the selected picture frames.

Change image to a picture frame

1. Select the unframed image.
2. Choose **Layer** > **Convert to Picture Frame**.

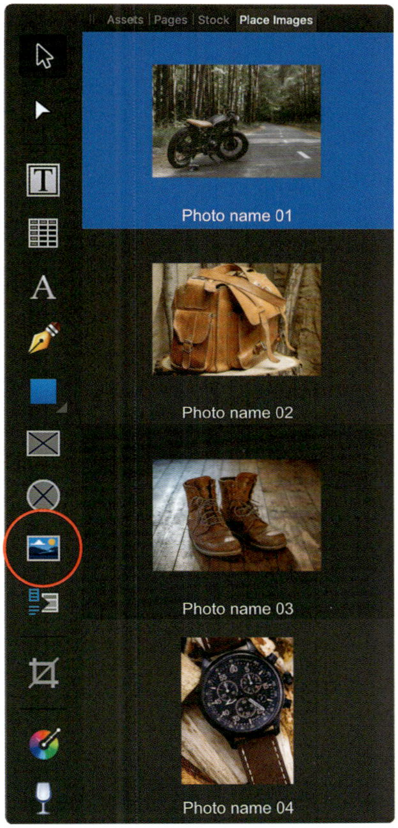

Placing multiple images

It is possible to place multiple images without having to select the **Place Image Tool** for each one individually.

1. Select the **Place Image Tool**.
2. Select multiple image files to place and click **Open**.
3. The images are queued on the **Place Images Panel** on the left.
4. Do one of the following:
   - Click an existing picture frame to populate.
   - Drag out to size the new image on the page.

   By default, images on the panel are placed in order from top to bottom. You can select a specific image to place it next.
5. Repeat step 4 until all images are placed or press Esc to cancel further placement.

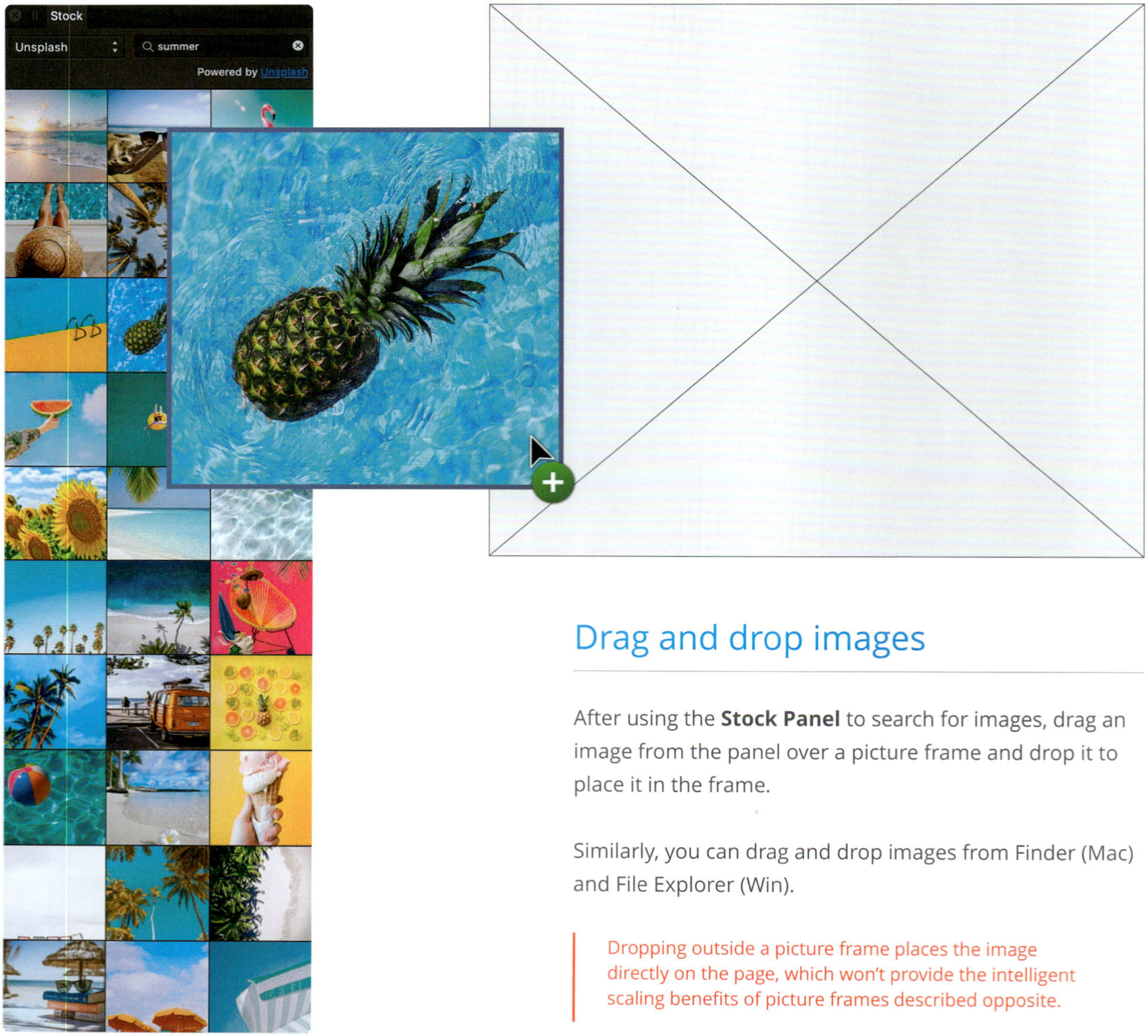

Drag and drop images

After using the **Stock Panel** to search for images, drag an image from the panel over a picture frame and drop it to place it in the frame.

Similarly, you can drag and drop images from Finder (Mac) and File Explorer (Win).

> Dropping outside a picture frame places the image directly on the page, which won't provide the intelligent scaling benefits of picture frames described opposite.

Scale to Max Fit
The image is scaled to fill the entire frame without distorting it. Some of its contents may be cropped. This is the default scaling behaviour.

Scale to Min Fit
The whole image fills the frame without distorting it, but some of the frame may be empty. You may want to adapt your page layout to suit.

Stretch to Fit
The entire image is visible and may be distorted to ensure the whole frame is filled. This is useful when the image and frame dimensions are similar.

None
No further automatic scaling is applied. This setting is selected if you manually change the image's scale, position or rotation within the frame.

Intelligent auto-scaling options

When you place an image in a picture frame, the **Scale to Max Fit** option is applied. This is one of several scaling behaviours the app can perform instantly.

1 Select a populated picture frame with the **Move Tool** (V) or either picture frame tool.

2 Click **Properties** on the context toolbar and then pick a scaling behaviour.

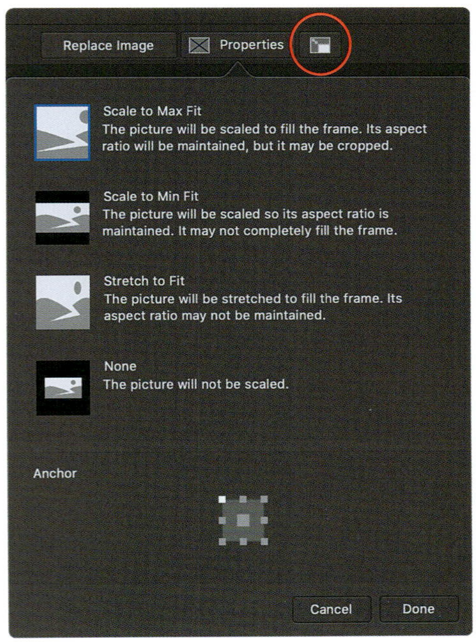

If a frame's dimensions cause its image to be cropped, you can instead click **Size Picture Frame to Content** on the context toolbar to resize the frame so it displays the entire image.

The scaling controls are also available for PDFs and other Affinity documents placed in picture frames.

Manual positioning and scaling

When a populated picture frame is selected, additional controls appear when the cursor is over it.

Drag the circular arrow left or right to rotate the content.

Drag the pan control to move the content within the frame.

Use the zoom slider to adjust the content's magnification.

If you prefer, double-click the picture frame to use traditional object manipulation controls to move, magnify and rotate the framed content. However, depending on the placed content's size, you may have to zoom out to see and interact with the handles.

Resource
core_skills_placing_multipage_docs.afpub core_skills_placing_multipage_docs.pdf

Multipage documents

When a multipage PDF or Affinity document is placed in an Affinity Publisher document, use the **Spread** setting on the context toolbar to choose which page is displayed. Use the equivalent **Artboard** setting for placed Affinity Designer files containing artboards.

Layered documents

As long as they are not flattened prior to placement, PDFs, other Affinity documents and layered Photoshop PSDs remain editable within Affinity Publisher.

With one selected on a page, click **Edit Document** on the context toolbar to edit its contents in a separate tab.

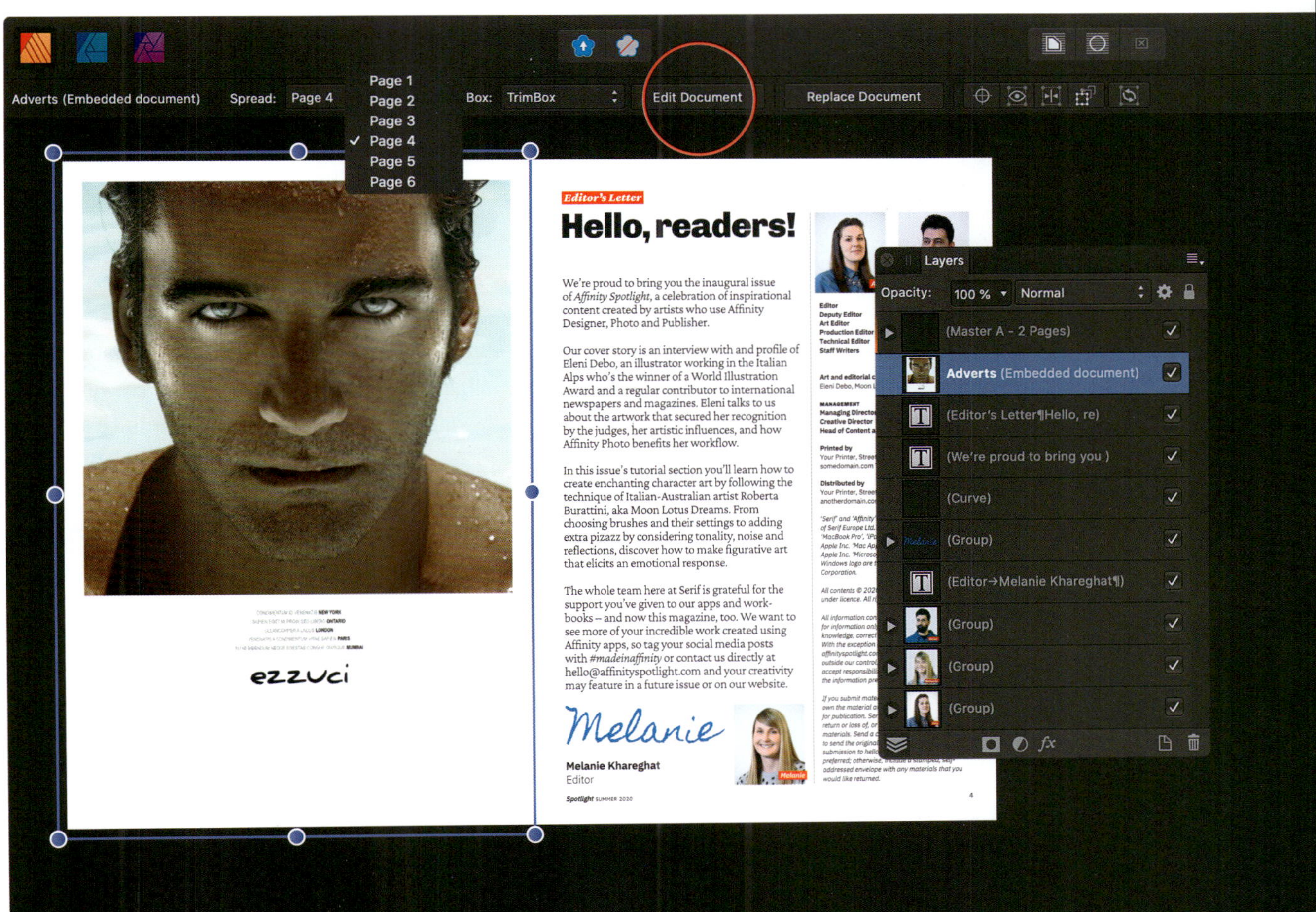

> *A good strategy for managing linked resources is to store them within a folder alongside your document.*

Check resource statuses

You can choose how images and documents used in an Affinity Publisher document are stored: internally in the document or externally in a sidecar folder.

A document's **Image Placement Policy** is chosen at the time of creation. It can be modified later in **File > Document Setup**.

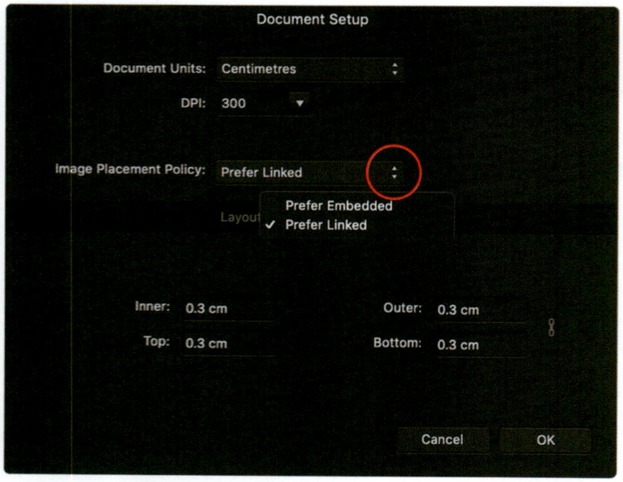

Pros

Cons

Prefer Embedded

Creates a copy of the original files within your document. Everything is stored at full quality in it and easily passed around in one file.

The document's file size increases each time a resource is placed, even if used multiple times.

When the file reaches a certain (inbuilt rather than user configurable) size, Affinity Publisher will recommend switching to the Prefer Linked policy.

Prefer Linked

Creates a link to the original files on your computer, so you can pass around a relatively small document with low-res image previews on its own, or with the external files for full quality.

As linked files' data is not part of the Affinity Publisher document, the document's file size is smaller even when an image is used multiple times—as a page background, say.

This helps team members to work independently and simultaneously. For example, a photo editor can work on external image files while a subeditor works on words in Affinity Publisher.

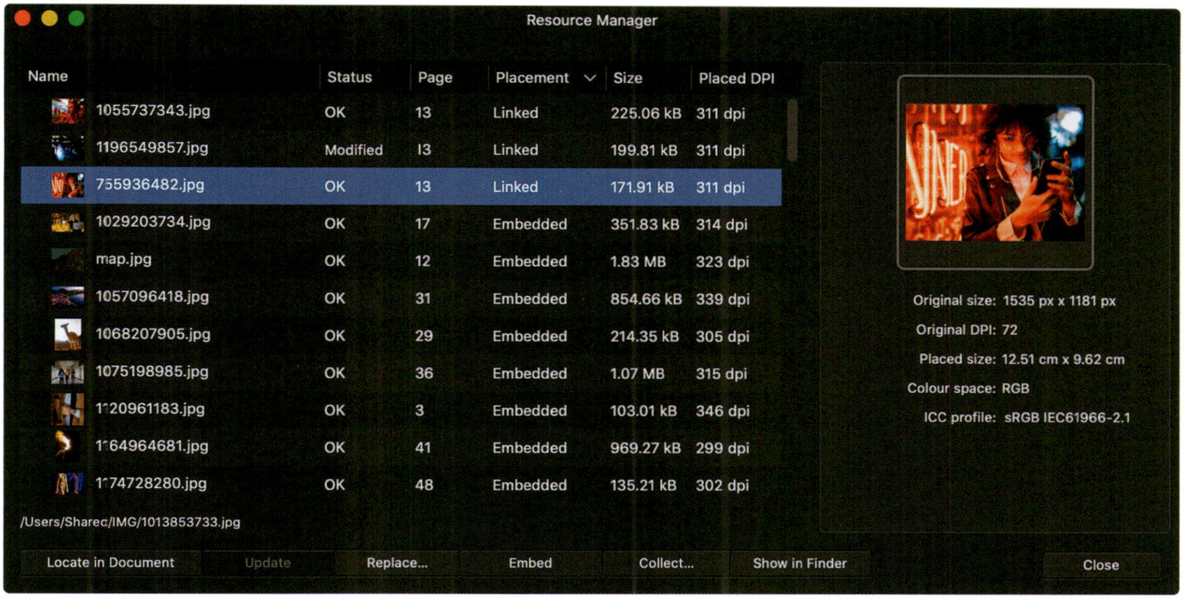

Use the **Resource Manager** to review the status of each item placed in an Affinity Publisher document.

Changing a resource between linked and embedded

1 Select **Document > Resource Manager**.

2 Select an item in the list. Do one of the following:

- If the item is linked, click **Embed**. Changes to the original file will no longer affect your Affinity Publisher document.
- If the item is embedded, click **Make Linked**. If the source file is not at its original location, you will be asked where to save the currently embedded data.

Updating a linked resource to its latest version

1 Select **Document > Resource Manager**.

2 Select an item for which the **Status** column reads **Modified**.

3 Click **Update** to refresh all instances of that resource in your document.

> To update all linked resources at once, click the **Status** column heading so resources in need of updating are listed consecutively. Hold the shift key (⇧), click the first and last of those items to select them and all items in between, and then click **Update**.

Auto-updating linked resources

Affinity Publisher can be configured to auto-update linked resources as they are modified, without manual action on your part.

1 Choose **Affinity Publisher > Preferences** (Mac) or **Edit > Preferences** (Win).

2 Click the **General** icon.

3 Check **Automatically update linked resources when modified externally**.

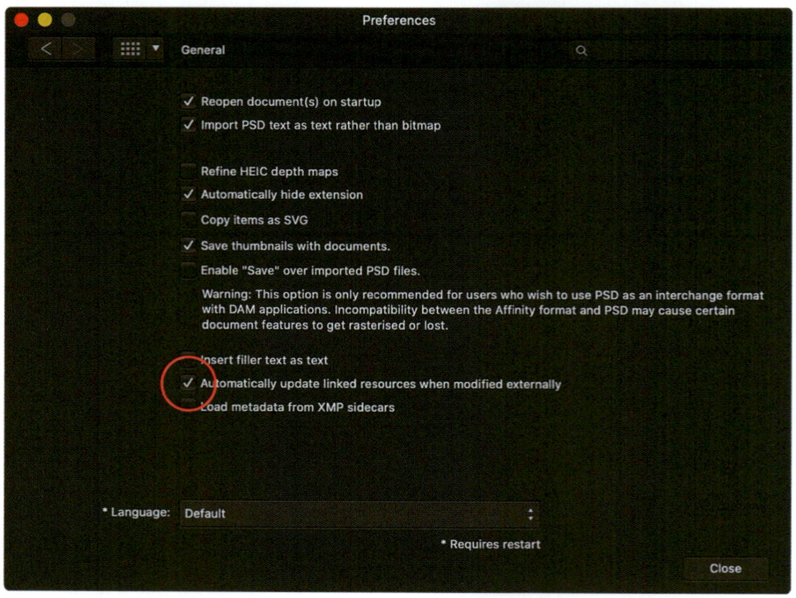

Auto-updating is advantageous when working individually. As part of a team, you may prefer to leave it turned off to allow you to review, in **Resource Manager**, what needs updating before accepting changes.

Resource
core_skills_importing_text.docx

Importing text

Affinity Publisher can import text from Microsoft Word (DOCX), Rich Text Format (RTF) and plain text (TXT) files into text frames.

Place in a new text frame

1. Choose **File > Place**.
2. Select a compatible file and click **Open**.
3. Drag out a new text frame on the page.

Replace an existing text frame's contents

1. Use the **Move Tool** to select a frame.
2. Choose **File > Place**.
3. Select a compatible file and click **Open**.

Unlike other document types, placed text is never linked back to the original file, so changes to that file are not reflected in your Affinity Publisher document.

Insert at a chosen point

1. Use the **Frame Text Tool** to set the insertion point or select text in an existing frame.
2. Choose **File > Place**.
3. Select a compatible file and click **Open**.
4. If text in the frame *Is not selected*, the file's contents are added at the insertion point. If *selected*, the file's contents replace that selection.

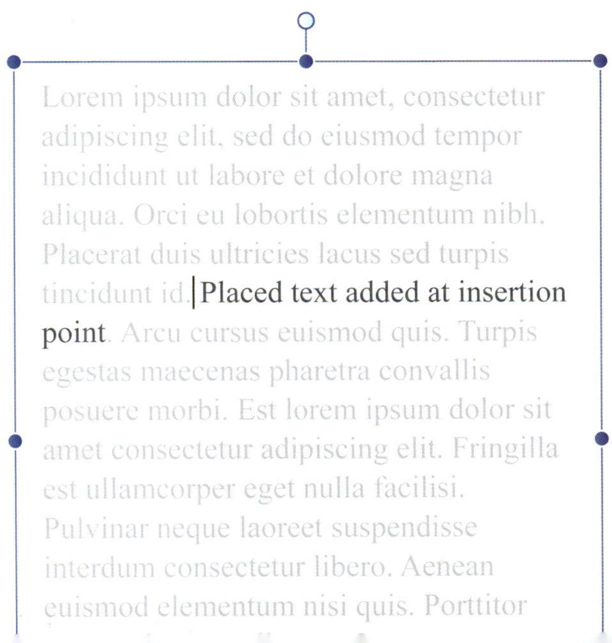

TEXT STYLES

Text styles specify how text should look; which typeface is used, at what size, how it is aligned, and much more. Each text style has a unique name, such as Heading 1, Heading 2 and Body Text.

Using text styles helps you maintain a consistent visual identity for a publication.

- **Character styles** (a) are applied to individual glyphs or continuous character sequences within paragraphs.
- **Paragraph styles** (c) are used to format whole passages of text—one or more whole paragraphs.

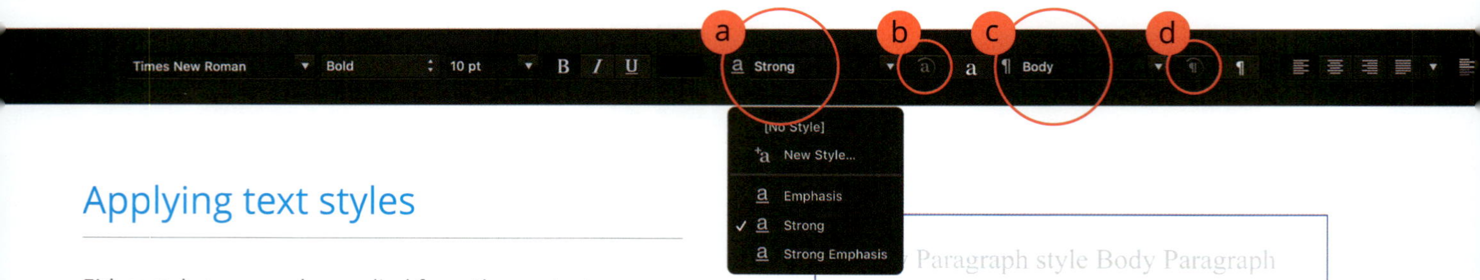

Applying text styles

Either style type can be applied from the context toolbar. As the cursor moves down the **Character Style** or **Paragraph Style** menu, the style under it is previewed live in your document.

When a character style is chosen, it is applied to all text that is selected or the word in which the insertion point is positioned using the **Frame Text Tool** or **Artistic Text Tool**.

When a paragraph style is chosen, it is applied to all paragraphs included in your selection or to the entire paragraph in which the insertion point is located.

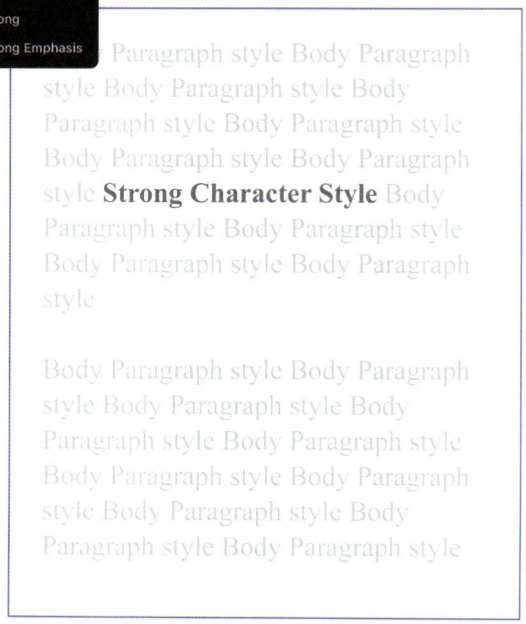

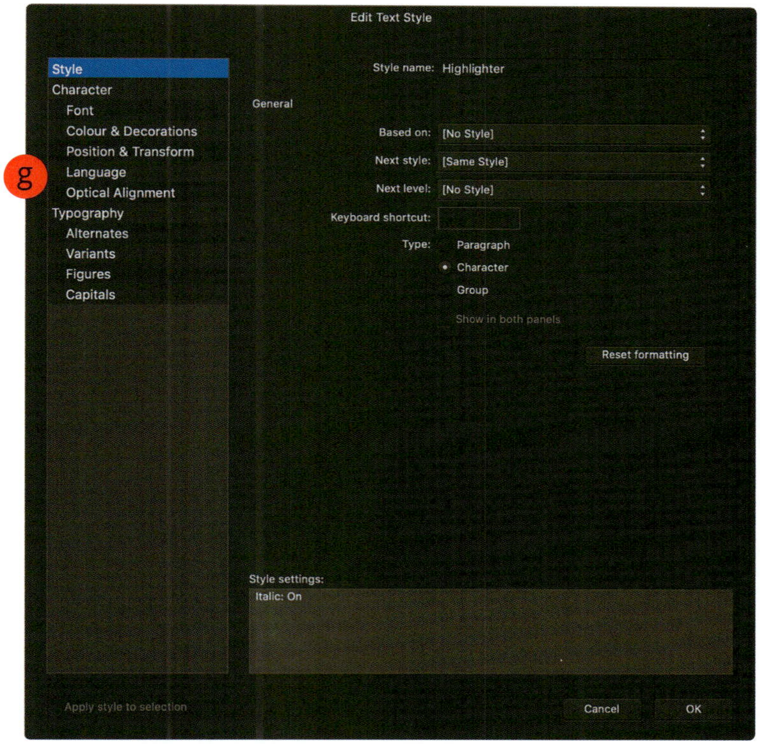

The top row (e) on the **Text Styles Panel** lists the style applied at the insertion point/to the selection. Expand the row to see a summary of any local modifications.

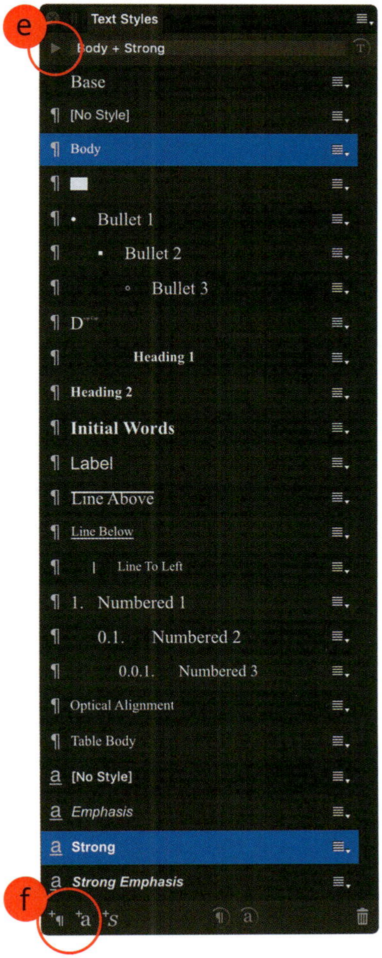

Creating, editing and overriding text styles

Create a new style at the bottom-left corner of the **Text Styles Panel** (f).

Double-click a style on the panel to edit it. With **Style** selected on the left, rename the style or choose relationships with other styles, then navigate the other menus (g) and adjust settings to modify the text style.

Local modifications can also be made directly on a page. With text selected, use the font controls on the context toolbar. These can be rolled into the underlying style, affecting all other instances where the style is applied. Click **Update Character Style** (b) or **Update Paragraph Style** (d) on the context toolbar.

Style hierarchy

Text styles can inherit settings from other text styles. When you edit a style, its subordinate styles are updated automatically.

To make a style inherit another's appearance, use the **Based on** setting on the **Edit Text Style** dialog. In addition, you can specify the style that is switched to, if any, when the return ↵ key is pressed.

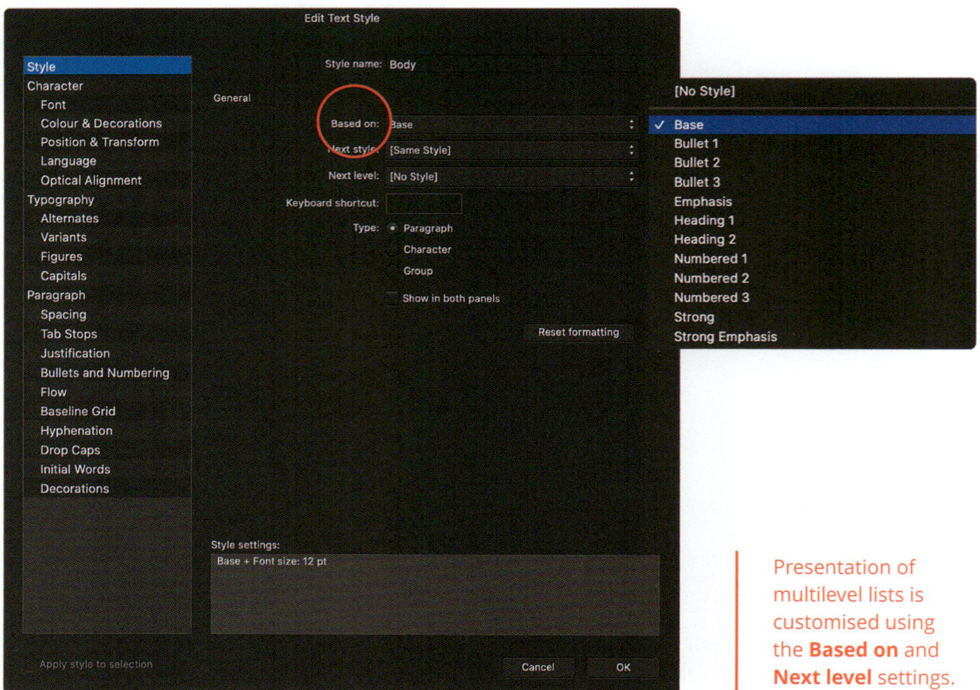

Presentation of multilevel lists is customised using the **Based on** and **Next level** settings.

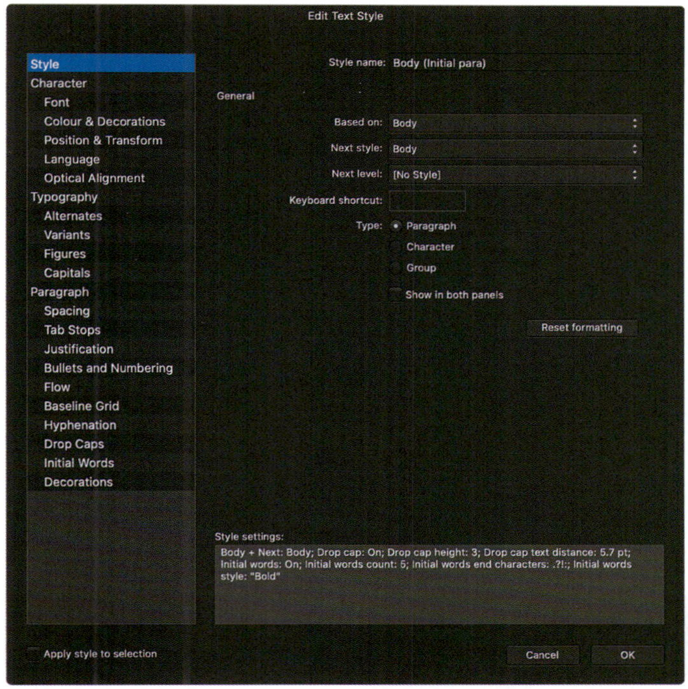

In a long-form article, let's say we want the first paragraph to have a drop cap and the first five words—or just the first sentence, if it is shorter—in a bolder weight. In a text frame containing multiple paragraphs, do the following:

1 Select the first paragraph.

2 On the **Text Styles Panel**, click **Create Paragraph Style**.

3 Set **Style name** to *Body (Initial para)*.

4 Set **Based on** and **Next Style** to *Body*. This will cause the next paragraph to lack the following adornments.

5 Select **Drop Caps** on the left. Set **Height in lines** to *3*, **Distance to text** to *2 mm* and check **Enabled**.

6 Select **Initial Words** on the left. Set **Max word count** to *5*, **End characters** to *.?!:* (characters that might end a sentence), **Style** to *Strong* and check **Enabled**.

7 Click **OK**.

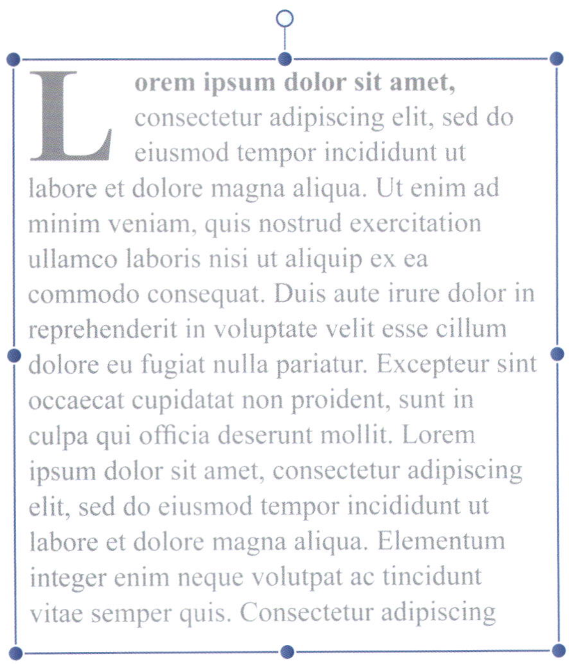

To review the relationships between a document's styles, choose **Show Hierarchical** from the **Text Styles Panel**'s **Preferences** menu.

Group Styles

A third style type is available: **group styles**. These are used as the foundation of multiple styles.

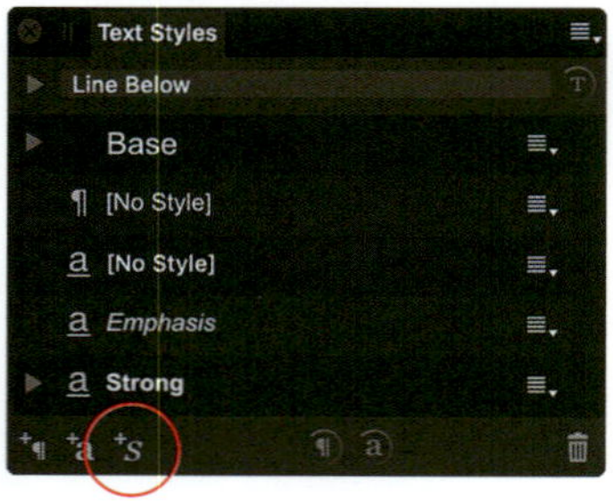

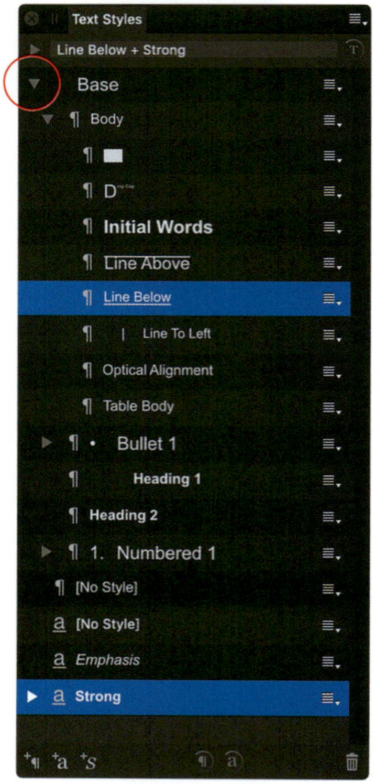

Subordinate styles will inherit a group's settings but can selectively override them, e.g. changing text colour or weight to ensure legibility against particular backgrounds.

Group styles are listed only on the **Text Styles Panel** and cannot be applied directly to text. If the context toolbar's **Character Style** and **Paragraph Style** menus are long, consider whether group styles can help to shorten them, 'hiding' styles you never apply directly so only their subordinates are listed.

> Group styles, such as Base, can be identified by the lack of an icon to their left on the Text Styles Panel.

Design using temporary text

Placeholder text can be used to design pages when meaningful text is unavailable, or so that real words don't distract from a mock-up's appearance. Filler text repeats until it literally fills its text frame—or a linked sequence of them.

Add filler text

1 Create a text frame.

2 Choose **Text > Insert Filler Text**.

Replace filler text

1 Select the **Frame Text Tool**.

2 Double-click the filler text to select it all.

3 Type, paste or place real content in the frame.

Filler text is not editable by default. To make it so, select it, ctrl-click (Mac) or right-click (Win) it and choose **Expand Field**.

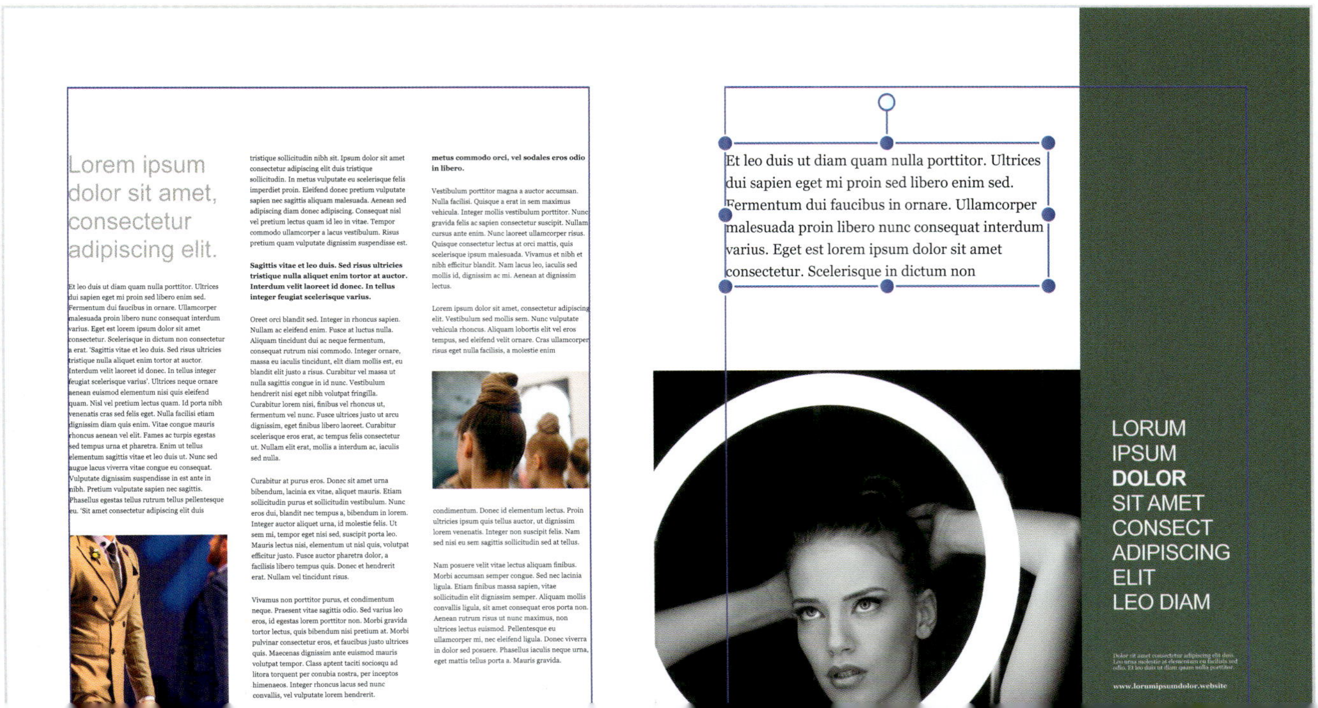

ACCESSING GLYPHS AND SPECIAL CHARACTERS

Glyphs are the characters available in a font: letters, numbers, symbols and other special characters. Choose **View > Studio > Glyph Browser** to access many more characters than are labelled on your keyboard.

Common uses of the **Glyph Browser** include adding symbols like ticks, crosses and arrows from 'picto' fonts, and looking up and inserting Unicode characters via the browser's search bar.

Add stylised quotation marks around the pull-quote in this page's resource by following these steps:

1 In the Glyph Browser's **Preferences** menu, select **Largest Size**.

2 The browser displays glyphs from the font applied at the insertion point by default. Click **Lock Fonts and Traits** (a padlock) to stop it switching from your selected font, e.g. to insert glyphs in several places.

3 Select **Zapf Dingbats** (Mac) or **Wingdings** (Win).

4 Find the chunky quotation mark glyphs.

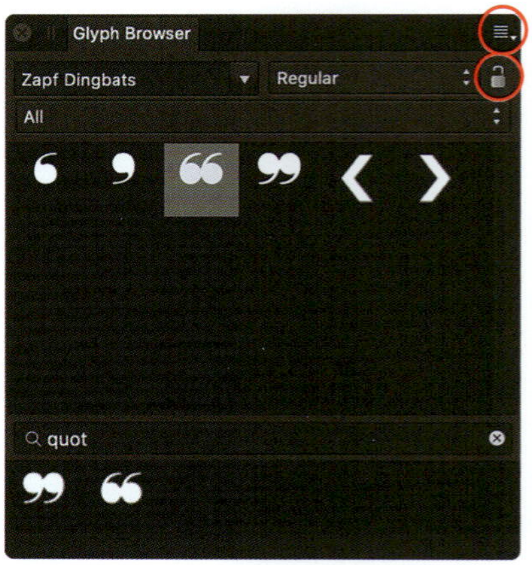

A reference of popular Unicode characters and their codes can be found at https://affin.co/unicodewiki.

Resource
core_skills_glyph_browser.afpub

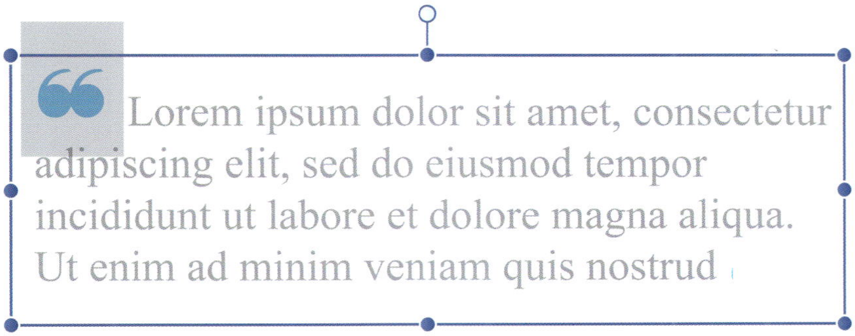

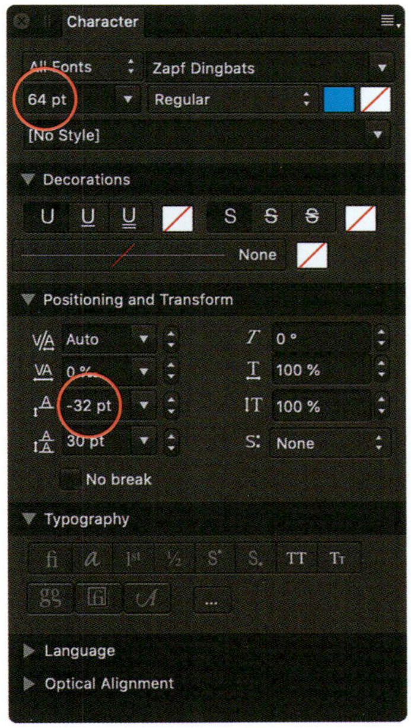

5 Position the insertion point at the start of the pull quote's text.

6 Double-click the opening quotation mark on the **Glyph Browser**.

7 In your document, select the quotation mark.

8 On the **Character Panel**, adjust the **Size** and **Baseline** values to position the quote as wanted.

9 (Optional) Repeat steps 6 to 8 to add a closing quotation mark.

Characters which occupy a particular space in one font may display an entirely different character when a another font is applied

PREVIEWING YOUR WORK

The various types of guide, the baseline grid and other visual design aids displayed over your document can get in the way at times. Select **Toggle Preview Mode** on the **Toolbar** for a clear view of your document's contents. Additionally, choose **View > Toggle UI** to hide Affinity Publisher's various toolbars and panels.

A document can be edited even while in **Preview Mode**. As such, anything that's selected will display its bounding box and accompanying controls; press the Esc key to see a pure document preview.

Other adornments, including any overflowing text that has been revealed on the page, are hidden.

The **View Menu** also contains options to toggle the visibility of various overlays individually.

Rellinek (100.0%)
Class aptent taciti sociosqu ad litora
Vestibulum
RELLINEK™
LEATHER GOODS COMPANY
Rellinek leathersmiths have been crafting high-end goods from the finest top-grain and full-grain leather for the past hundred years, using the timeless material to create everything from seats, bags, shoes, clothes and supplies. Inspired by nature's rugged and unrelenting beauty, our full-grain leather goods make up some of the most durable and beautiful products in all of the world, offering you the absolute best money can buy.

CHAPTER 3

Page Design Principles

Let's take a look at some basic principles that you can adopt when laying out your pages in Affinity Publisher. These principles go beyond tool, panel and command usage, so compared to the previous Interface Tour and Core Skills chapters, you'll find this chapter mostly free of user interface terminology, instead focusing on adopting some proven page design concepts.

Harness your newly learnt combined knowledge of the Affinity user interface, core skills and these principles and you'll be set for starting a workbook project. Note that some principles are more appropriate to specific types of publications than others!

STRUCTURE

Each page's structure needs to be planned just as you'd plan the structure of your entire publication.

Keep logical information areas in mind

As you're laying out single pages or facing page spreads, think about three information areas—heading, image and text—then consider their size and position relative to the page and each other. If an obvious repeatable layout is needed, create the structure on a master page (p. 88).

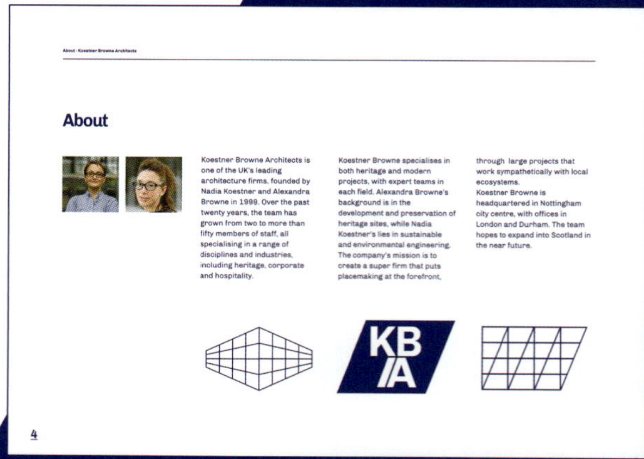

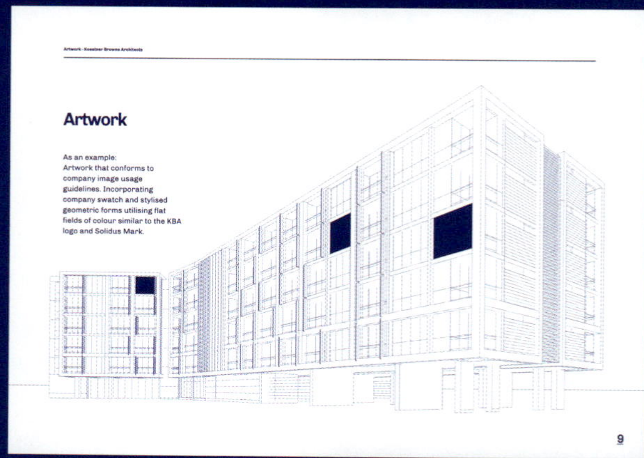

Break up stories by subheading

In story text, use inline subheadings to divide up body content for additional organisation and to break up a continuous run of text.

Maintain clarity

Always focus on the core objectives and goals of your publication. Is secondary information vital to the story? A cluttered layout loses the reader's focus and attention.

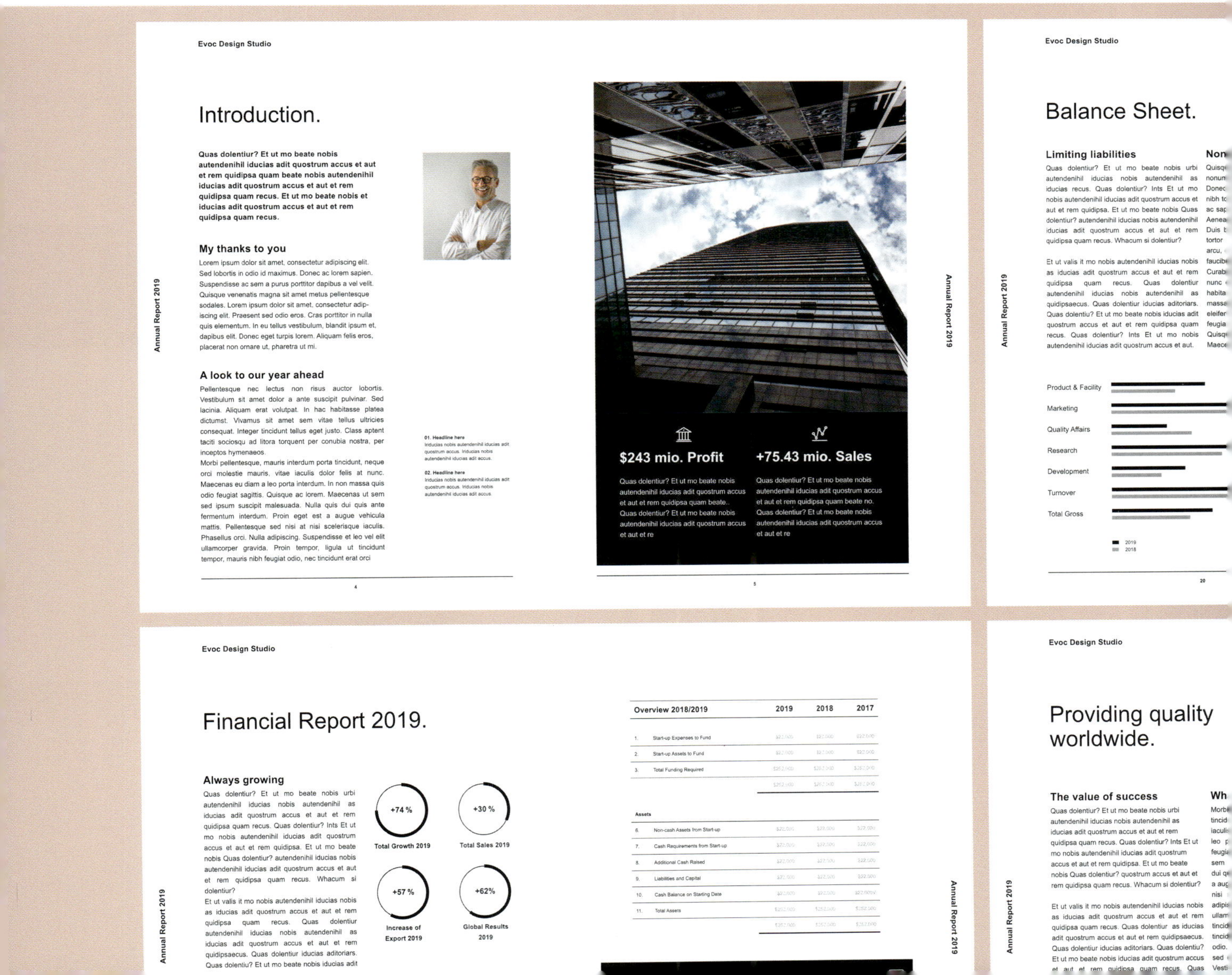

VOICE AND MESSAGE

Think about your audience when planning your page designs. Your publication should aim to convey a particular voice to your readership. Selected pages or articles can communicate a particular message.

Imagery or text?

The publication's story can be image-led rather than text-led. A fashion lookbook should rightly be strongly image-driven, telling the story of a range of products visually. Text takes a back seat supporting each image, perhaps as captions.

Colour

Pick colours that reflect the voice you want to give. More subtle image colours suggest understated confidence and assurance while more vibrant colours can shout youth and vitality.

Minimalism

Saying less can be saying more. Keeping your content minimal can add impact and sets a consistent voice.

Shades of the Season Lookbook | Spring Awakening
Giorgia
Ribbon ring in Olive
Francesca
Cushioned leather bag in Olive
Isabella
Sheer collared blouse in Olive

BALANCE

Balancing the page content stops it from looking too lopsided, top-or bottom-heavy. This can be just as valid vertically as horizontally.

Mirroring text

On facing page spreads, try mirroring text across verso and recto pages—even background shapes can be mirrored too. This is especially useful on master pages for footer information (page numbering and chapter names).

Sizing to same column widths

Identical column widths make text frames look neat; you could also consider mirroring irregular-width frames across a spread.

Balancing text across columns

For a less ragged appearance at column ends, balance your frame text vertically in text columns.

CONSISTENCY

Consistent use of typefaces is assumed, but beyond this, you can repeat the same colours and shapes across your publication to 'connect' pages together and for visual effect.

... the old guard still taking names

MASDEN TREMO-5 80W 210

by Jess Jackson

Nulla quis dui quis ante fermentum interdum. Proin eget est a augue vehicula mattis. Pellentesque sed nisi at nisi scelerisque iaculis. Phasellus orci. Nulla adipiscing. Suspendisse et leo vel elit ullamcorper gravida. Proin tempor, ligula ut tincidunt tempor, mauris nibh feugiat odio, nec tincidunt erat orci dictum purus. Etiam luctus odio. Aliquam adipiscing urna a felis. Quisque sed elit in eros aliquet ultrices. Donec at sem. Vestibulum cursus. Integer dolor. Vestibulum sit amet sem nec augue fermentum consectetuer. Integer justo.

Vivamus vel sapien. Praesent nisl tortor, laoreet eu, dapibus quis, egestas non, mauris. Cum sociis natoque penatibus et magnis dis parturient montes, nascetur ridiculus mus. Nullam eleifend pharetra felis. Mauris nibh velit, tristique ac, lacinia in, scelerisque et, ante.

DONEC VIVERRA TORTOR SED phasellus nec magna. Aenean vehicula, turpis in congue eleifend, mauris lorem aliquam sem, eu eleifend est odio et pede. Mauris vitae mauris sit amet est rhoncus laoreet. Curabitur facilisis, urna vel egestas vulputate, tellus purus accumsan ante, quis facilisis dui nisl a nunc.

NULLA VESTIBULUM NULLA suspendisse potenti. Aliquam turpis nisi, venenatis non, accumsan nec, imperdiet laoreet, lacus. In purus est, mattis eget, imperdiet nec, fermentum congue, tortor. Aenean ut nibh. Nullam hendrerit viverra dolor. Vestibulum fringilla, lectus id viverra malesuada, enim mi adipiscing ligula, et bibendum lacus lectus id sem. Cras risus turpis, varius ac, feugiat id, faucibus vitae, massa.

Nunc gravida nonummy felis. Etiam suscipit, est sit amet suscipit sodales, est neque suscipit erat, nec suscipit sem enim eget leo. In porttitor rutrum leo. Ut eget leo.

Nulla quis nibh. Proin ac pede vel ligula facilisis gravida. Phasellus purus. Etiam sapien. Duis diam urna, iaculis ut, vehicula ac, varius sit amet, mi. Donec id nisl. Aliquam erat volutpat. Integer fringilla. Duis lobortis, quam non volutpat suscipit, magna sem consequat libero, ac hendrerit urna ante id mi. Quisque commodo facilisis tellus. Integer sodales lorem sed nisl.

MORBI CONSECTETUER MAURIS quis odio. Ut dolor lorem, viverra vitae, viverra eu, euismod nec, enim. Lorem ipsum dolor sit amet, consectetuer adipiscing elit. Morbi nisl eros, dignissim nec, malesuada et, convallis quis, augue. Vestibulum ante ipsum primis in faucibus orci luctus et ultrices posuere cubilia Curae; Proin aliquam, leo at luctus tempus, eros lectus eleifend massa, quis sollicitudin erat magna non leo.

VESTIBULUM VEL METUS donec sagittis velit vel augue. Fusce in nisl vitae massa venenatis rhoncus. Praesent orci velit, lobortis eget, suscipit semper, congue eu, est. Quisque malesuada volutpat enim. Vestibulum leo sem, molestie a,

▶ www.masdenvalveamps.website

A-Z of valve testing

page 48

APRIL ISSUE 128

Applying stored colours

Stored (global) colours can be repeatedly applied to shapes and text to keep colours consistent and coherent.

Colour can be applied as a text style's attribute, but for unstyled text or shapes you can sample colour from other objects in your document including images.

Size consistency

For objects serving a common purpose, keep your dimensions or aspect ratios consistent. Think text frames and shapes (e.g., sidebars and footer rectangles).

Repetition

Introduced shapes (drop-cap squares and footer rectangles) can be duplicated and aligned to offer some visual interest and focal points.

IMPACT

Impact as a principle means drawing attention to areas of the page where you want the reader's eye to land first. In applying this, you can choose what page elements you consider important and make your audience better engage with your pages.

White space

White space above your main text blocks gives breathing space. Headings will 'float' in the airy white space for more attention.

Wide margins

Allow pinned (anchored) images, shapes or text quotes to reach into the empty margin space for greater impact.

Size images by importance

Size does matter—the bigger the image, the more the impact! Go full page or spread for maximum impact. If presenting an array of images, you can size and position your main image, make subordinate images smaller, then position them in a grid arrangement around the main image. The overall effect will be visually interesting, with the reader's eye drawn to the larger image as the main focal point.

Focal points in text

As well as images as focal points, using drop caps at the start of your frame text signals the beginning of a new story.

Ignore page boundaries

You don't have to be confined to page boundaries—some images can extend over the page edge significantly for effect. The partly obscured results add visual interest and intrigue.

mentum interdum. Proin eget
ula mattis. Pellentesque sed nisi
e iaculis. Phasellus orci. Nulla
endisse et leo vel elit
vida. Proin tempor, ligula ut
r, mauris nibh feugiat odio, nec
ci dictum purus. Etiam luctus
lipiscing urna a felis. Quisque
iquet ultrices. Donec at sem.
us. Integer dolor. Vestibulum sit
gue fermentum consectetuer.

en. Praesent nisl tortor, laoreet
egestas non, mauris. Cum
enatibus et magnis dis
es, nascetur ridiculus mus.
pharetra felis. Mauris nibh velit,
nia in, scelerisque et, ante.
rtor sed nulla. Phasellus nec
vehicula, turpis in congue
lorem aliquam sem, eu eleifend
Mauris vitae mauris sit amet est
Curabitur facilisis, urna vel
e, tellus purus accumsan ante,
nisl a nunc.

n eleifend nulla. Suspendisse
a turpis nisi, venenatis non,
mperdiet laoreet, lacus.

Dynamic spaces

3 years to fund, design and build, Mary Carly-Smith takes us head first through the challenges

WORDS: DAVID REZNOR | PHOTOGRAPHY: SAMANTHA BIRD

Hollow Mews - Phase 3 - South facing

Site and interior projects fully complete

page 48

Contrast

Use contrast to focus the reader on specific areas in your publication. For example, use black for headings (for maximum impact) and 50% black for body copy. Try inverting colours (e.g., white on black) on objects you want to stand out.

EMPHASISE

Sometimes short passages of your story text are important and need to be emphasised. Several techniques are available that go beyond simply applying text formatting or text styles.

Notes and pull-quotes

Pull out shorter passages of text from your story and present standalone next to the main story. A pull-quote is typical but use any text that could entice the reader to read the full story.

Decorations

Use paragraph decorations to draw attention to headings and notes. Decorations can be horizontal or vertical strokes around text, or a background fills (below).

Background panels

Present important text information in front of a drawn geometric shape—rectangles, squares or circles. Use a contrasting font colour for clarity.

DE-EMPHASISE

The flip side of emphasising is to 'detune' secondary detail, often used only for occasional reference only, which may otherwise interfere with readability.

Headers and footers

Small font sizes for page numbers, chapter names and other footer information are ideal. This information shouldn't visually interfere with your main story.

Publication dates and issue numbers

For periodicals, a small font size for these details won't detract from the title, nor lessen its impact and message.

Imagery

If an image plays only a supporting role, make it smaller to reflect its lesser importance. Alternatively, blur or crop in an abstract way so that the eye looks for text instead.

A magazine for journey seekers

Inspiration

TRAVEL

Why we need to travel by the end of this Summer Season

Ut faucibus justo quis nisl. Etiam vulputate, sapien eu egestas rutrum, leo neque luctus dolor, sed hendrerit tortor metus ut dui. Etiam id pede porttitor turpis tristique lacinia. Suspendisse potenti. Etiam feugiat. Lorem ipsum dolor sit amet, consectetuer adipiscing elit. Cras gravida sem ut massa. Quisque accumsan porttitor dui. Sed interdum, nisl ut consequat tristique, lacus nulla porta massa, sed imperdiet sem nunc vitae eros. Vestibulum ante ipsum primis in faucibus orci luctus et ultrices posuere cubilia Curae; Pellentesque sit amet metus. Nullam tincidunt posuere ligula. Aenean volutpat ultrices ligula. In tincidunt. Aenean viverra suscipit tellus. Suspendisse sem lorem, ornare non, vestibulum ut, tempor porttitor, est. Quisque convallis aliquet eros. Nunc nec nulla eget urna convallis eleifend. Nulla feugiat eros at augue. Integer feugiat nisi vitae velit. Cras cursus ipsum vel dolor. Sed pulvinar. Etiam velit orci, pellentesque at, porttitor blandit, luctus eu, justo. Donec in odio sed

8

www.voyagermagazine.website

ALIGNMENT

Strong alignment produces a better presented publication more pleasing to the eye, instead of one made up of a random arrangement of page objects. Objects appear connected by common alignment to other objects, page elements or layout aids (e.g., guides).

Hang lines

Hang page objects from a series of placed hang lines (i.e. horizontal or vertical guides). You can snap text frames, picture frames and other objects to them.

On publications with repeating page layouts, hang lines on master pages creates consistency across your spreads when flicking through your publication.

Margins

Objects can be snapped to margins, so they accurately align to margin position. Typically, a starting text frame is often snapped, dragged out and sized from a left margin.

Dynamic guides

Affinity Publisher's default snapping behaviour will snap the edges or centres of a moving object to those of another placed object.

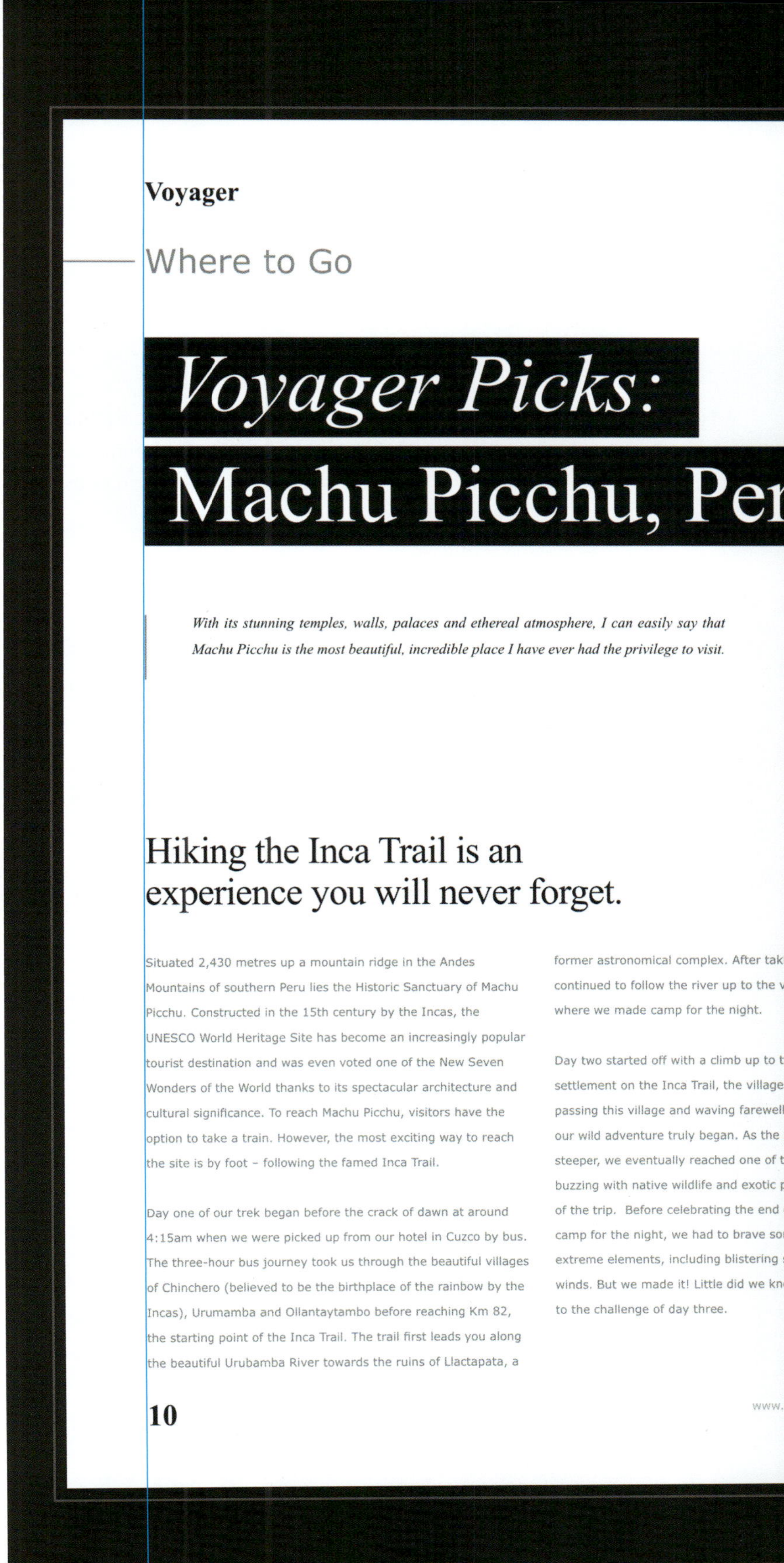

Voyager

Where to Go

Voyager Picks:

Machu Picchu, Per

With its stunning temples, walls, palaces and ethereal atmosphere, I can easily say that Machu Picchu is the most beautiful, incredible place I have ever had the privilege to visit.

Hiking the Inca Trail is an experience you will never forget.

Situated 2,430 metres up a mountain ridge in the Andes Mountains of southern Peru lies the Historic Sanctuary of Machu Picchu. Constructed in the 15th century by the Incas, the UNESCO World Heritage Site has become an increasingly popular tourist destination and was even voted one of the New Seven Wonders of the World thanks to its spectacular architecture and cultural significance. To reach Machu Picchu, visitors have the option to take a train. However, the most exciting way to reach the site is by foot – following the famed Inca Trail.

Day one of our trek began before the crack of dawn at around 4:15am when we were picked up from our hotel in Cuzco by bus. The three-hour bus journey took us through the beautiful villages of Chinchero (believed to be the birthplace of the rainbow by the Incas), Urumamba and Ollantaytambo before reaching Km 82, the starting point of the Inca Trail. The trail first leads you along the beautiful Urubamba River towards the ruins of Llactapata, a

former astronomical complex. After taki continued to follow the river up to the v where we made camp for the night.

Day two started off with a climb up to th settlement on the Inca Trail, the village passing this village and waving farewell our wild adventure truly began. As the p steeper, we eventually reached one of th buzzing with native wildlife and exotic p of the trip. Before celebrating the end c camp for the night, we had to brave son extreme elements, including blistering s winds. But we made it! Little did we kno to the challenge of day three.

10

www.v

TYPOGRAPHY

Typography is perhaps the most fundamental part of your content, and perhaps the least considered part of publishing. It tells us what pictures cannot in that different typefaces have different personalities and styles to help influence the emotion of the reader.

Considerations

Message

Before deciding what typefaces to use, it is important to read the words you have been given and trusted with by your client. Many designers allow their style to influence the text, when it should be the other way round.

- Who is the target audience? Does gender need to be taken into account? (women's magazines typically use lighter typography, whereas men's magazines usually incorporate **heavier typography**). Consider the hobbies of your potential reader.

- What is the age range of the readership? Is it a children's book or is the reader primarily older? Taking greater consideration of the typeface you choose ensures you are targeting your audience better.

- Where is the reader? If you're localising content, some typefaces may not translate correctly to other languages.

Readability

Readability is about ease of legibility, and is made up of several elements such as;

- Space and line height
- Line width
- Letter spacing
- Contrast
- Hierarchy

What is the minimum text size required for your audience to read clearly? Food menus have to cater to a wide age range, hence having separate children's menus to allow for bigger and more playful text. Standard menu type size should always be no smaller than 10 pt or 12 pt for descriptions, and bigger for everything else.

Medium

Consider how your work will be viewed, e.g.

- For glossy magazines: environmental lighting can cause reflections that interfere with the readability of your content.

- For mobile devices: phones and tablets emit light which can cause a halo effect on your typography.

Appropriate context

Typography also needs to take into consideration historical and cultural context. The right typography for the right time helps establish an emotional connection between the reader and the message, but when this is not considered there is a disconnect and the message is lost.

Food Menu Series 192

Cleveland

RE-ESTABLISHED 2019

Take this example: before I designed this food menu I considered the message, readability and medium of this 1960s-themed restaurant. I wanted to transport the customer to a specific time, so the interior, brand and food are all styled around this era. I learned that *Futura sans serif* and *Americana serif* were popularised in the 1960s, and you can see how it captures the elegant but playful restaurant experience of that time.

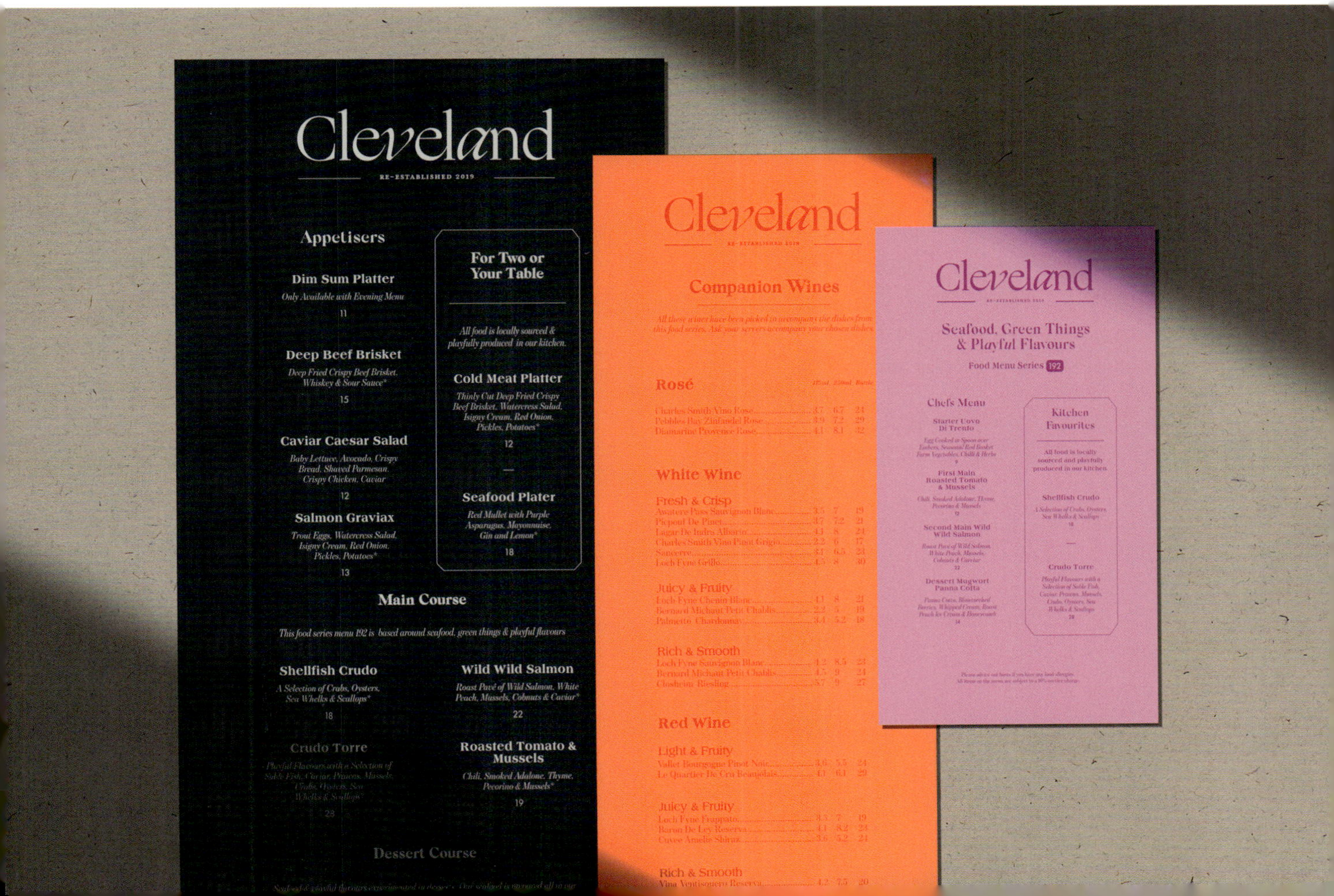

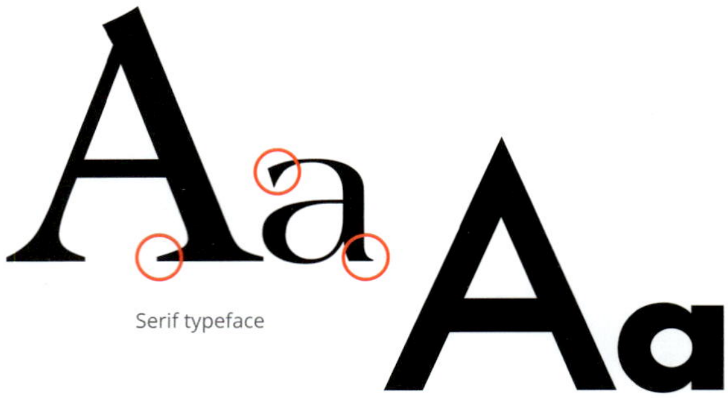

Serif typeface

Sans Serif typeface

Typeface weights

Choices

Serif, sans serif or both?

In choosing the typeface one of the biggest decisions is between using serif or sans serif fonts or both.

- **Serif**: Serifs are decorative features at the ends of strokes in some fonts. Often used in formal documents or in smaller body copy as they are more legible when printed.
- **Sans Serif**: Sans, meaning without, do not have the serifs and are often chosen for their more modern, bold and clean-looking style. These are popular for screen-ready documents.
- **Both**: If you are leaning towards using both, think back to your considerations and ultimately your message.

Weights

- **Bold**: The best way to make a phrase or word pop out is to embolden it. This is often used for product names or at the top level of a style hierarchy, e.g. for headings.
- *Italic/Obliques*: Both serve the same purpose when used in text, namely emphasis. Italics are primarily found in serif designs, and obliques are associated with sans serifs.
- Regular: This is the default appearance of the typeface and a good choice for body text.
- Light: Lighter weight than regular, is sometimes used for descriptions or captions.
- More: There are many font weights you might come across like Black, Compressed, Condensed, Demi, and extended. Play around and experiment but always remember the considerations. Does it appeal to the reader? Where does it go in the hierarchy?

How many typefaces?

Avoid overwhelming your readers by keeping to only two or three typefaces. Think what typeface would be best for headings, subheadings and body; and do not be scared to play with the weights of the type families. To save even more time, if you find a text style you like, add it to your **Text Styles Panel**.

Font size and hierarchy

Hierarchy helps guide your reader and it also helps with the readability and usability of your design. Choose typefaces and sizes that will contrast perfectly against each other or keep the typeface the same and just change the weight; but remember, font sizes often get smaller down the page. Picture this recipe page design in three conceptual tiers.

- Tier 1: The first tier is the most important, as it should be designed to catch the readers attention. For this reason, it should be applied to the most prominent typographic element in your design, which is usually headlines.

- Tier 2: This tier can be used to further draw the reader in the right direction. This could be in the form of a quote or a summary of the article. As a rule, this should never be bigger or bolder than tier 1 items.

- Tier 3: Most of the design is in this tier, as this is where we place our body copy. It is really important to pick a legible typeface and ensure that it is no bigger than Tier 2.

There's a New Wave Of Furniture

A growing number of e-commerce companies are offering personal choices at affordable prices.

This article is part of our latest special report on Interior Trends, which is about getting personal with customisation of new furniture.

Customisation has always been part of home furnishings. Urged on by their clients, interior designers seek out luxurious fabrics and collaborate with workshops to design special pieces. And even items like Crate & Barrel sofas come with size, finish and upholstery options. But in almost all situations, the more personalised the piece, the more you will have to pay, and the waiting time for made to order is months.

It doesn't have to be that way. A new wave of commerce furniture companies, including Inside Weather, The Inside, Interior Define and Benchmade Modern, are promoting speedy customisation for all.

To buy a sofa in Inside Weather's online store, shoppers choose among a dozen arm styles, including fat upholstered perches and grooved timber slabs; upholstery options like woven linen and polyester fabrics and vegan leathers; and details like stitching.

If a credenza is wanted, shoppers can pick the finish for the top and sides, one of more than a hundred ornamental door patterns, and their favourite pulls legs.

The table starts at £630, and small credenzas begin at £360 — a substantial savings over traditional custom furniture, which can run into five figures.

These are shipped (from California) typically within a couple of weeks and in some cases just a few days. "In apparel, customisation has moved downstream and become more and more accessible," said Ben Parsa, the chief executive of Inside Weather, which began in 2018. He wants to do the same for household products. "Being able to visualise tens, and soon hundreds, of millions of combinations of furniture from the comfort of your home is something that we think has tremendous mass appeal."

Behind the scenes, the companies hold essentially no inventory and rely on computer-controlled machines to do much of the work. At Inside Weather, a sofa is merely raw lumber until a customer places an order. When this is done, a CNC machine cuts the necessary wood components at the company's facility in Rancho Cordova, Calif. When someone orders a credenza, a flatbed digital printer applies patterns to panels. "The people who are shopping online have spent years on social media saving gorgeous interiors, and they have a sense of what they're looking for," said Britt Bunn, a co-founder of The Inside. "We're excited to be able to make those visions come true."

Placement

Alignment

There are several different ways of aligning your text so it is good to experiment with them all, but be careful with justified alignments as it can create undesirable spacing. If this happens play around with the width of the text frame, size of the typeface or look at your tracking. You can manually set justification settings or enable auto-hyphenation for the paragraph style too.

Widows and orphans

To maintain smart typographic standards, avoid widows and orphans, which are eyesores.

- Widows: A line (which could be a single word) that gets left on its own at the end of a paragraph or the bottom of a page.
- Orphans: Orphans are very similar to widows in that they can be a line or single word but they are located at the top of the next page or column instead.

To correct both of these, adjust text frame heights, justification settings, kerning and tracking and you will see more satisfying alignment.

The example opposite shows an orphan and then a widow in the second column.

Length of line

If text lines are too long, it is harder for the eyes to keep their pace whilst reading, but if they are too narrow, the rapid back and forth required will fatigue your readers quickly. A line length of 9 to 12 words is perfect for readability.

Baseline grid

A baseline is a unit of measurement for spacing and alignment. It takes out all the guesswork for thoughtful spacing of page elements and type. Typically, the font size of the main body copy and the baseline grid are the same. Other page objects can also hang off the baseline grid for perfect alignment.

Kerning, Tracking and Leading

Transforming

Kerning

This is the space adjustment between individual letters. As a rule, the further apart the letters are the slower it is to read. Affinity Publisher automatically applies kerning rules to text (e.g., AV and WA are kerning pairs) that are derived from the font, but manual kerning using numerical values can fine-tune spacing.

Tracking

The term can often be confused with kerning, but instead of spacing between individual letters, tracking is the equal spacing between groups of letters. Tracking can be useful when you need to remove hyphenation, widows and orphans from copy.

Leading

Controls the space between lines and is measured from baseline to baseline. Play around with the line height of titles and when done correctly can deliver interesting results.

> Converting text to curves is a great way to customise and manipulate typefaces, or correct a typeface to match your needs.

Punctuation and glyphs

Hyphenations, En dash, Em dash

- Hyphens (-): the hyphen connects two things that are intimately related. Auto-hyphenation can be enabled using paragraph styles or hyphens can be entered manually to suit your needs.

- En Dash (–): a specific type of hyphen that is half the height of the uppercase font. They are used to join similar concepts together, e.g. 2010–2011 or 9pm–5pm.

- Em Dash (—): this hyphen is equal in height to the uppercase font. It is most often used to indicate a sharp change of thought in a sentence and is stronger than a comma, but weaker than a period or semicolon, e.g. The table starts at £630, and small credenzas begin at £360—a substantial saving over traditional custom furniture.

En dash

Em dash

¼ ½ ¾ ™ © ® ℗

É Й Ó Ý Ы́ Э́

$ € ¢ £ ¥ ƒ ₴ ﬁ

Glyphs

Quotations

Using quotations can be a source of contention and confusion. As a rule of thumb, it is best to use curly quotations when quoting a descriptive passage from an interview, for example. If quoting imperial measurement units, use straight quotations.

- **Curly quotation**
  “Being able to visualise tens, and soon hundreds, of millions of combinations of furniture from the comfort of your home has tremendous mass appeal.”

- **Straight quotation**
  Jack was 6'4" and wore a blue shirt.

Glyphs

A lot of typefaces come with alternate characters and special glyphs, e.g. fractions. Using Affinity Publisher's Glyph Browser, inspect what glyphs are available in your prospective typeface; this avoids having to make them yourself. Not all glyphs and alternate characters are available for every typeface.

Superscript and subscript

- Superscript: A letter, figure or symbol placed above the baseline.

- Subscript: A letter, figure, or symbol placed below the baseline.

CHAPTER 4

Professional Projects

This initial project chapter covers classic DTP deliverables such as brochures and magazines. We'll also cover lookbooks which are popular in the fashion world. Lookbook design explores skills you can easily transfer to photo books and photo albums.

Finishing off, we'll demonstrate simple but effective single-page CV/Résumé design.

1

Root Box Brochure

Making a press-ready trifold brochure for small businesses

In this first project, we'll create a brochure for a forward-thinking company, called Root Box, specialising in fruit and vegetable deliveries directly to your door.

Farmers Delight Box
Root Box
SO FRESH. SO TASTY.
Let's talk!
Root Box

BEFORE YOU GET STARTED

Resources

You can get all the resources that are referenced in this project from: https://affin.co/RBBrochure

Knowledge of Affinity Publisher

To get the most from undertaking this project, you will need to:

- Be familiar with the interface of Affinity Publisher. You can learn more about the interface in the Interface Tour chapter, starting on p. 14.
- Have good core skills. See the skills table below to see which additional aspects of Affinity Publisher you need to be confident with to complete this project:

Design Aids	p. 96
Working with Text	p. 112
Picture Frames	p. 124
Text Styles	p. 140

INTRODUCTION

Creating a printed brochure is a great way to raise the brand awareness of your company, showcasing its benefits, products and services to potential customers. In a predominantly digital world, there's nothing like the tactile feel of a brochure to set your brand apart.

We've all been handed a beautifully printed brochure at a promotional event and been impressed—by paper choice, finish or special effects. Their physicality brings a greater sense of ownership that you don't experience with digital media.

They also assist in communicating your brand to new demographics and can align your brand with other more established companies.

The project

In this project, we'll look at the fictitious Root Box food delivery company which delivers organic fruit and vegetable boxes directly to customers' doors.

To support marketing and branding efforts, a brochure is required to boost sales and promote the company.

DOCUMENT SETUP

In this project, the design is based on a trifold layout, using a square ratio in a custom size. The type of fold reveals all three inside 'panels' at once which gives the benefit of a large surface area for your content.

Visually, a pile of these brochures would resemble a stack of 7" music singles placed on a table—a callback to the days of vinyl.

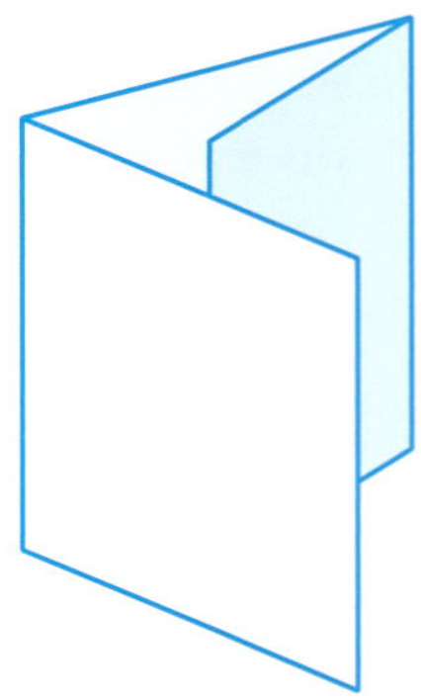

To implement this square-ratio vinyl idea, we opted for a 21" x 7" document size (3 x 7") to be printed double-sided. When folded, this setup will create the trifold arrangement.

Like other press-ready deliverables you'll encounter in this workbook our initial step is to set up our document in a CMYK colour space with bleed.

You and your print partner

Establish contact with a print company early to talk about your brochure—get an understanding of what page formats, sizes, folding options and paper stock are available and appropriate.

1 Select **File > New**.

2 On the dialog, ensure **Presets** and **Press Ready** are selected.

3 In the right-hand Settings pane (**Layout**), set **Document Units** to *Inches* and **Page width** and **Page height** to *21 in* and *7 in*, respectively.

4 The trifold layout is wide, so we'll need the **Orientation** set to *Landscape*.

5 In terms of pages, the **Number of pages** will be *2* (for brochure outer and inner pages), each using the same **Default master** page (keep checked).

6 Ensure **Facing pages** is unchecked—a two-page facing spread layout is not needed.

7 Uncheck **Include Margins** and keep the default **Bleed** settings.

8 Click **Create**.

Bleed will add space around the page edge for all backgrounds and images to run into. This prevents white gaps from appearing when the printer trims the printed brochures.

For thick brochure card stock, you may have to extend the Page width to accommodate a fold gutter rather than a simple guide. This will make the brochure sit flat after folding.

Resource

Rootbox_brochure_01.afpub

GUIDES

We can use two guides to define where the fold points are when this brochure is folded at your printers. By placing guides on your master page both pages will benefit from the same guide layout.

Creating guides

1 Jump to the master page using **Document > View Masters**.

2 On the **View Menu**, select **Guides Manager**, then enter two **Vertical Guides** values to define the two fold points.

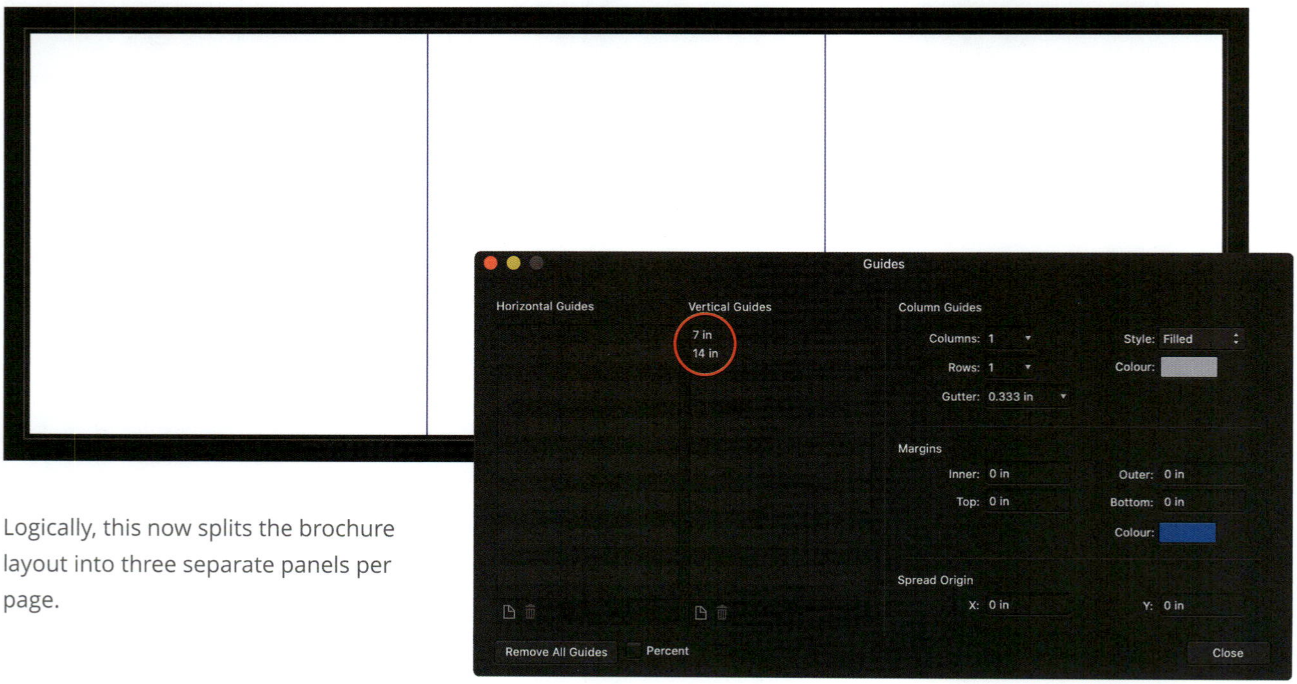

Logically, this now splits the brochure layout into three separate panels per page.

PLANNING BROCHURE CONTENT

Before adding content, the trifold brochure layout needs to be understood further as it needs to be imagined when folded. What content goes on which panel? Do I add to Page 1 or Page 2? Is Page 1 on the outside?

Get physical—create a model and sketch

It's a great idea to experiment with a paper model approximately the same dimension as your planned project. Get the folding direction right in your mind, fold it and place the model on the table. After this, you can visualise your content by marking up and then sketching on the model.

For trifold layouts, the folding arrangement can make usual page numbering confusing so instead we'll reference pages as Inner and Outer.

Here's the original mock-ups for the project.

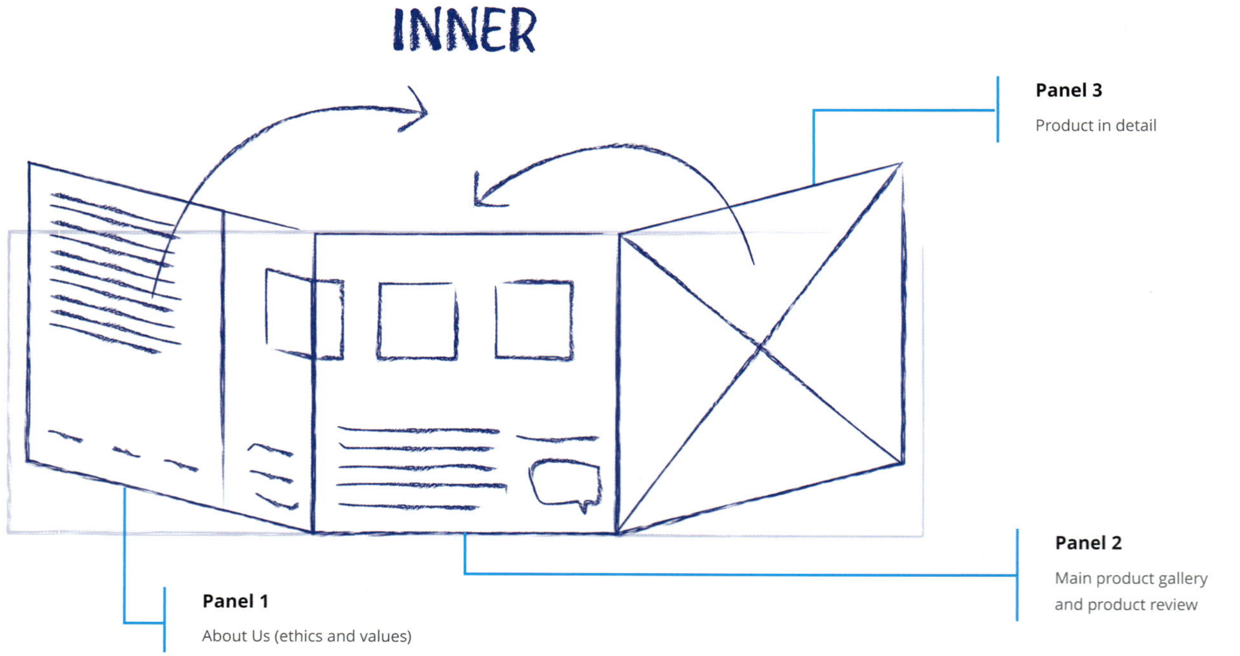

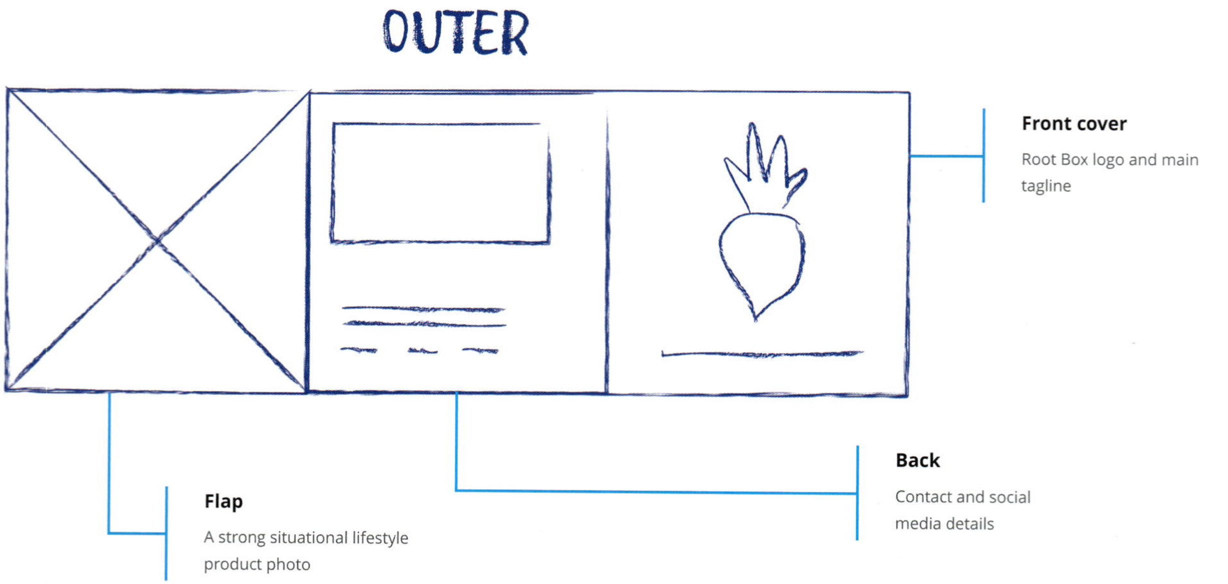

Plan the all-important front cover and back cover carefully as these will be on display most of the time. Use the inner panels for your company and product details.

ROOT BOX: THE BRAND

Logo design is a core element in promoting your brand and brochure. In reality, the branding process is likely to precede the brochure design and you'll have resourced an internal or external Graphic Designer to design your logo.

In this project, we used the skills and expertise of Matt Searston to offer some logo design variants for us to choose from - the second example seemed perfect for the brand.

Matt Searston | Designer

The brief for creating the Root Box logo was to create a modern design with a playful, earthy feel.

"As you can see from my sketches, I thought that a beetroot would be a good starting point, given that it is a root vegetable with a great shape for a logo—the leaves also add extra interest.
I then redrew my final idea digitally in Affinity Designer so the finished logo would be suitable for all print requirements in the future."

INNER PAGE DESIGN (PAGE TWO)

Resource
Rootbox_brochure_02.afpub Root Box.afpalette Root Box Brochure.docx

The inner page is about selling the product so clear and concise details about the company, the product range and a showcase "best product" photo are essential.

Before page design starts, install the appropriate fonts and palettes.

Installing fonts

The design uses two font families, i.e. Special Elite for headings and Caladea for body text.

1 Go to https://fonts.google.com (or search online for Google fonts) and download the **Special Elite** font and **Caladea** font family.

2 Open the downloaded font folders and read the License.txt or OFL.txt file.

3 For *Mac*: ctrl-click the files, select **Open**, then select **Install Font**.
or:
For *Windows*: Right-click the downloaded font files and select **Install**.

Importing palettes

1 On the **Swatches Panel**, click **Panel Preferences**, then select **Import Palette > As Document Palette** from the menu.

2 Navigate to the downloaded Root Box.afpalette file, select it and click **Open**.

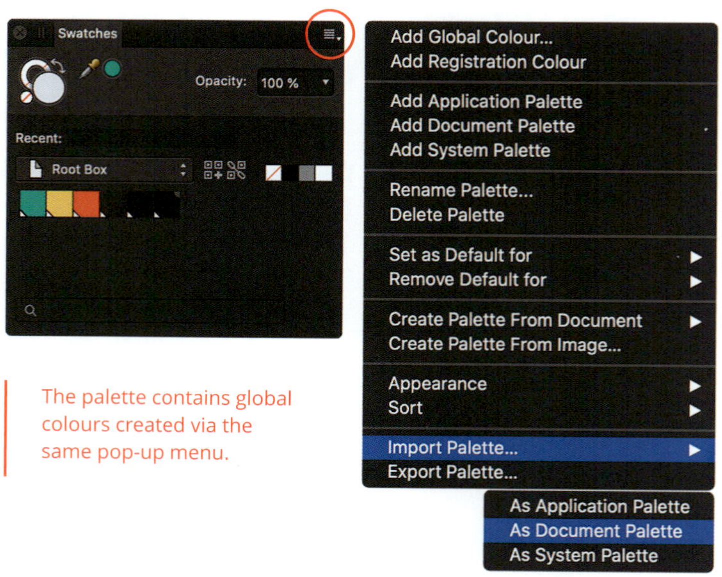

The palette contains global colours created via the same pop-up menu.

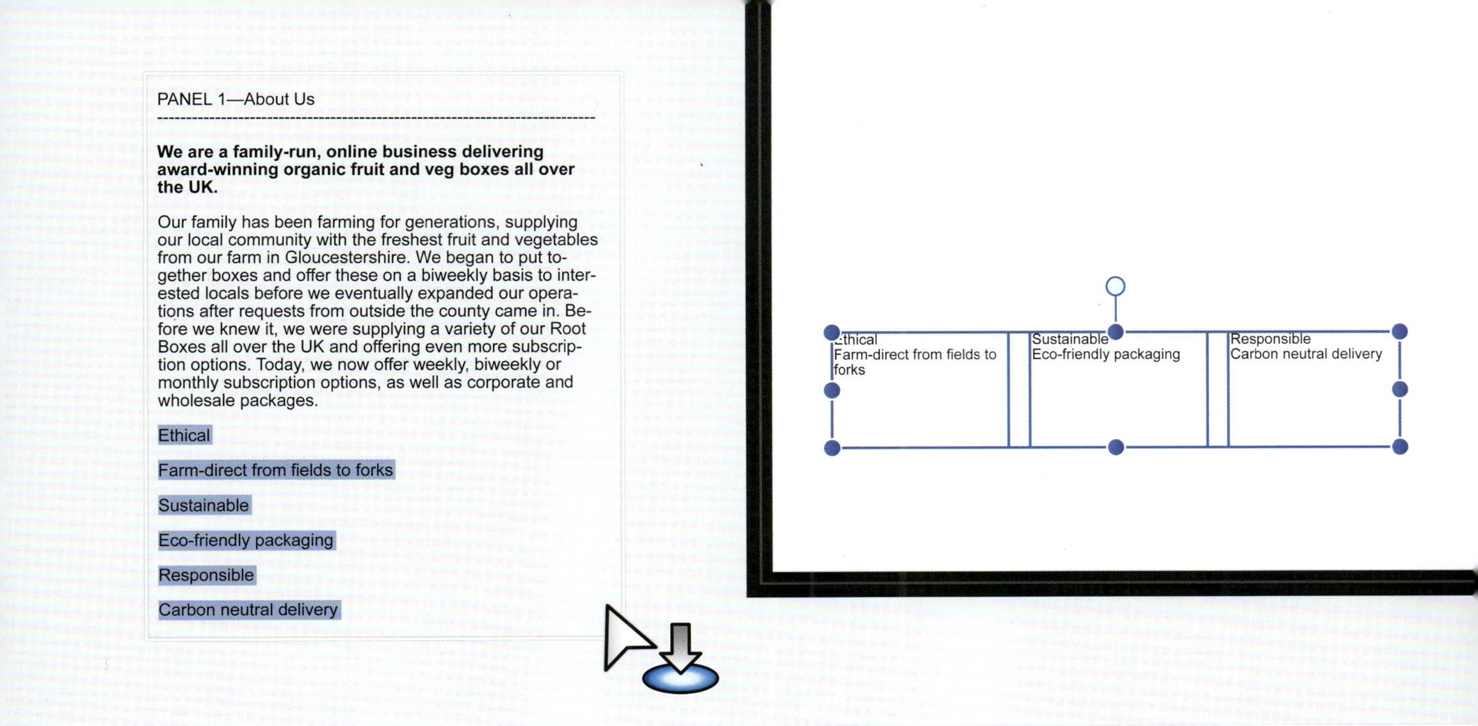
PANEL 1—About Us

We are a family-run, online business delivering award-winning organic fruit and veg boxes all over the UK.

Our family has been farming for generations, supplying our local community with the freshest fruit and vegetables from our farm in Gloucestershire. We began to put together boxes and offer these on a biweekly basis to interested locals before we eventually expanded our operations after requests from outside the county came in. Before we knew it, we were supplying a variety of our Root Boxes all over the UK and offering even more subscription options. Today, we now offer weekly, biweekly or monthly subscription options, as well as corporate and wholesale packages.

Ethical

Farm-direct from fields to forks

Sustainable

Eco-friendly packaging

Responsible

Carbon neutral delivery

Adding copy text to Publisher's pasteboard

1 From **View > View Mode**, switch **Clip to Canvas** off.

2 Select **File > Place**.

3 Navigate to the downloaded Root Box Brochure.docx file, select it and click **Open**.

4 Drag out the cursor across the pasteboard next to Page 2.

5 From **Affinity Publisher > Preferences** (Mac) or **Edit > Preferences** (Windows), the **User Interface** category lets you set a **Background Grey Level** to a contrasting light greyscale; this shows your text clearly.

Panel 1—About Us

We'll add some text that introduces the company, its mission statement and core values.

Adding copy text to text frames

- With the **Frame Text Tool** (T), draw out a text frame in the centre of the panel. Select and drag-drop the About Us section from the pasteboard copy text to the frame.
- Add another text frame, setting **Columns** to *3* on the context toolbar. Drag-drop the Ethical, Sustainable and Responsible text into each text frame column and apply column breaks from **Text > Insert > Breaks**.

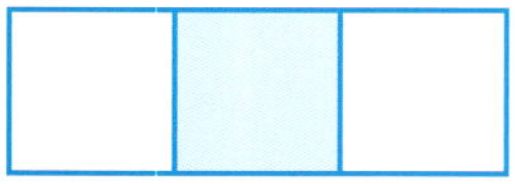

Resource

rootbox-ribeiro-englishgarden.jpg
rootbox-ribeiro-farmersdelight.jpg
rootbox-ribeiro-paradise.jpg
rootbox-ribeiro-holdingbox.jpg
Root Box Logo.afdesign

Panel 2—Our top boxes

Like Panel 1, we'll introduce copy text but also add picture frames to present the three products.

On this panel, we'll actually extend the planned panel 2 content over the first fold point into Panel 1. This means we'll have a larger design area for showcasing the product range.

Adding copy text

Add a text frame for the *Our top boxes* heading (a) and three caption text frames (b), then populate with copy text. Ensure the heading text frame snaps to the same height as the text frame on Panel 1.

> *Don't be afraid to span your design across folds.*

Adding picture frames

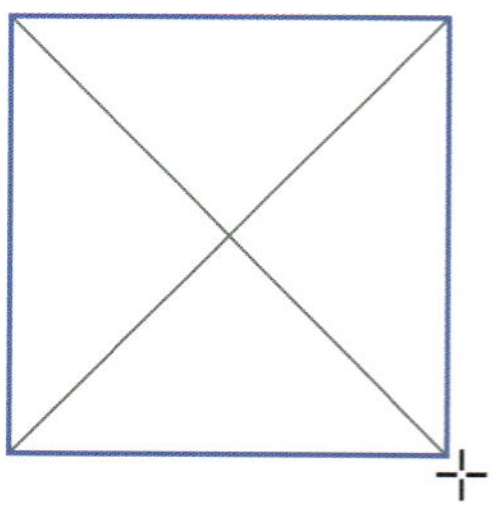

1 With the **Picture Frame Rectangle Tool** (F), press the shift key (⇧), then draw out a square picture frame (c), duplicating it twice.

2 Align and distribute the frames using the **Alignment** options on the **Toolbar**.

3 Give the frames a stroke of *2 pt* and the *Background* global colour from the **Stroke** and **Swatches Panels**.

4 Use **File > Place** to add the first three image files (see Resource box) into consecutive selected picture frames.

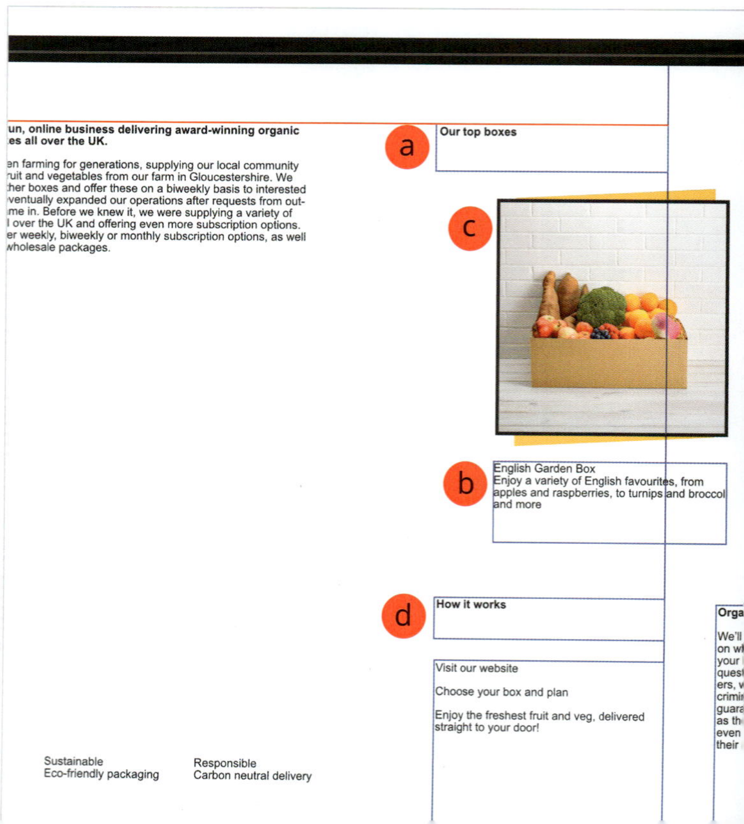

To add interest, we've also introduced coloured background rectangles, which were sheared (skewed) vertically by dragging the shapes' edge handles upwards.

Panel 2—How it works

This panel contains the 'body text' of the brochure which covers the delivery and buying process.

Adding copy text

Add a text frame for the *How it works* heading (d) and three additional text frames, then populate with copy text. These include buying steps, buying process and a review comment.

Fernando Martins Ribeiro
Product Photographer

"For these images, the main focus was to get a wonderful variety of natural-looking fruit and vegetables.

In the top box images, it was important to make sure that every fruit/vegetable was against a distinct colour. This allows for better readability, especially in very small images.

For the raspberry heart, I drew the shape by hand on paper and then carefully placed the berries, creating the contour first and then filling the inside.

The holding box image required building a custom cardboard box with the correct measurements. A box filled with fruit is rather heavy and that can show in the hands of the model, so to avoid that, I partially filled the box with wrinkled paper which pushed the fruit to the top."

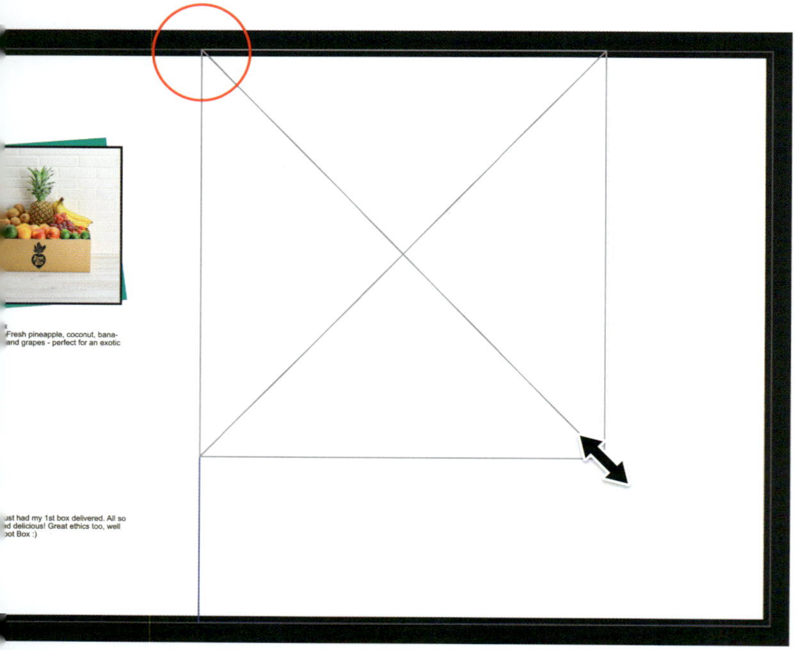

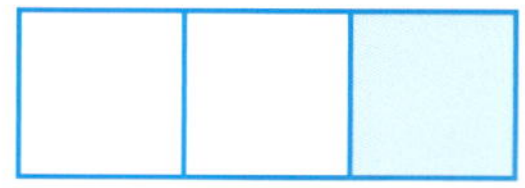

Panel 3

Detailed product photo

1. Draw a picture frame that snaps from the intersection of the rightmost guide and top-left bleed corner to the bottom-right bleed corner.
2. Place the rootbox-ribeiro-holdingbox.jpg file into the picture frame and zoom in using the slider.
3. Deselect the frame and place Root Box Logo.afdesign outside it, then drag the logo into position over the frame.
4. Reduce the logo height to match the perspective of the box and position centrally. Drop the layer **Opacity** to *80%* to blend in with the image.

I also added duplicates of the logo onto the three images on Panel 2.

Resource
Rootbox_brochure_03.afpub

Formatting and styling text

With text still unstyled, let's format text and build up paragraph text styles as we go—this helps keep text formatting consistent and easy to change.

Formatting text and saving styles

Work through the text on the page, starting from the body text to the largest heading. The key point is that you're building up a hierarchy of paragraph styles based on a 'parent' group style called Base—any style based on Base will adopt all the parent's styling automatically, only needing to override a few settings (e.g., font size) that make it distinct from its parent. The text styles are configured as described overleaf.

To help visualise this style inheritance think of a tree structure using the two font families—Caladea and Special Elite for body and headings, respectively.

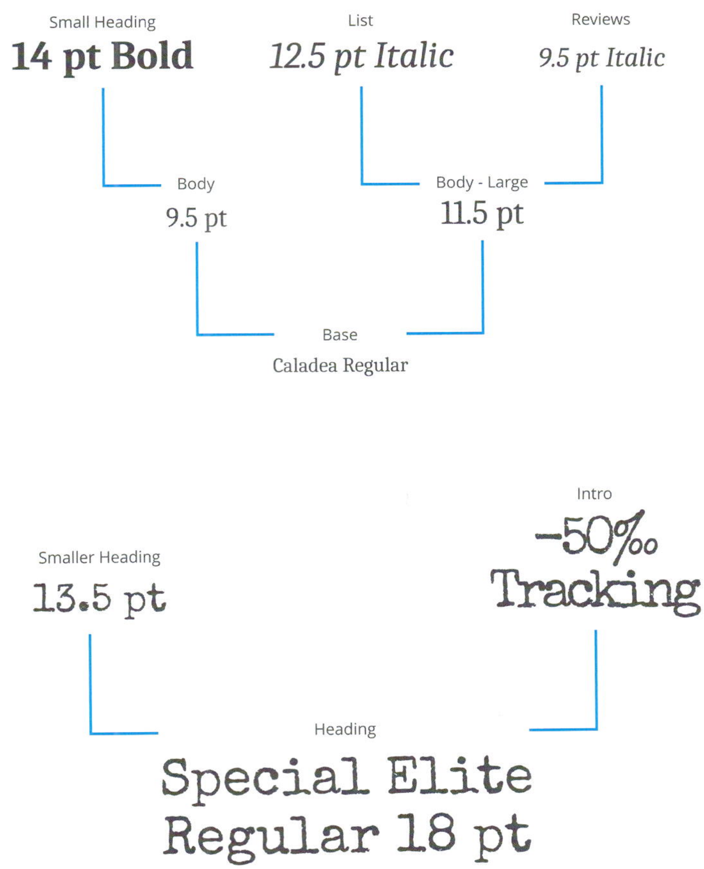

Modifying the group text style

- On the **Text Styles Panel**, edit the *Base* text style to use the Caladea Regular font.

Body styling

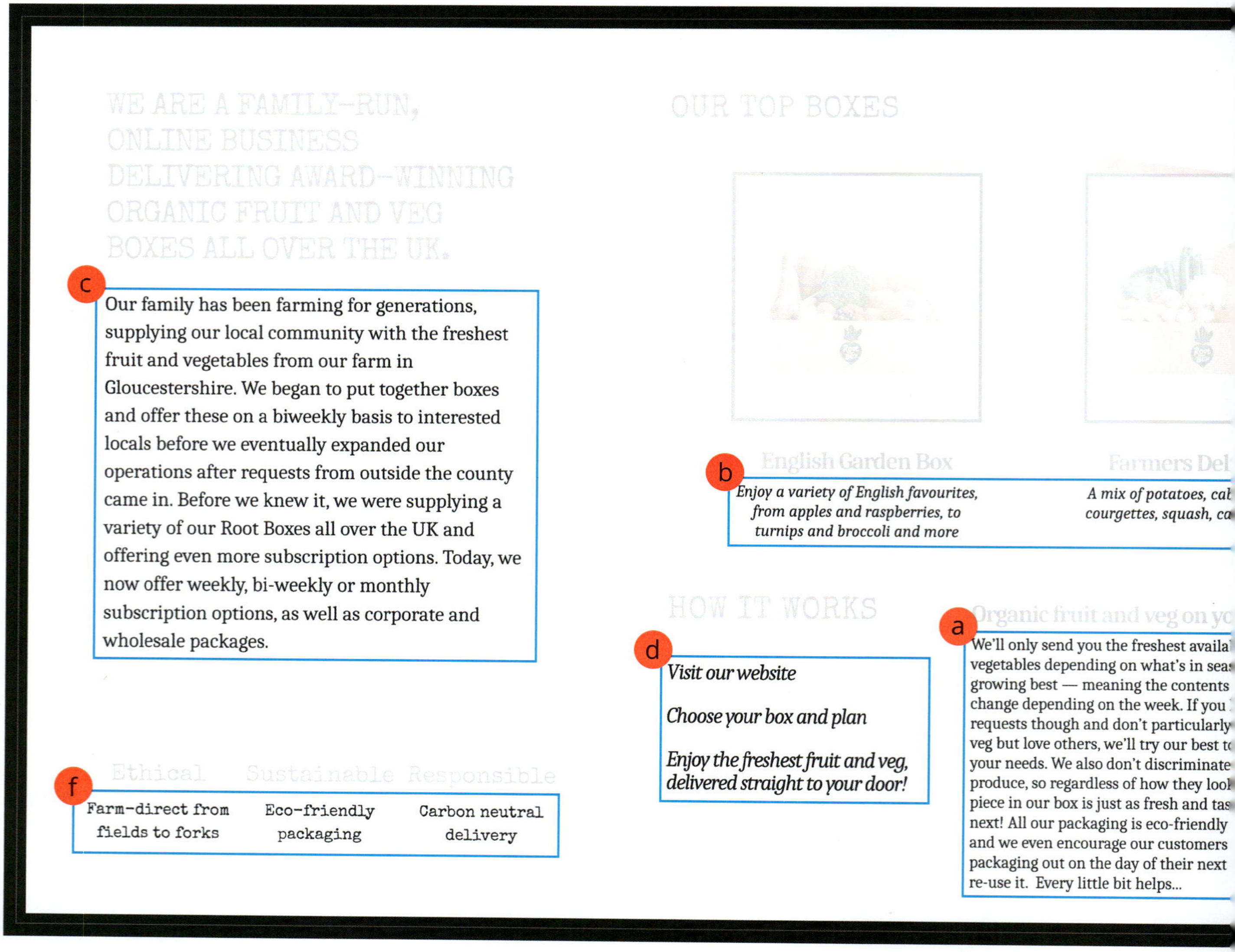

Text styles can be complicated. If you've already reviewed Core Skill's Text Styles section (p. 140) but want to progress quicker you can import all the project's text styles from Rootbox_brochure_03.afpub. Use **Import Styles** on the Panel Preferences pop-up menu of the **Text Styles Panel**.

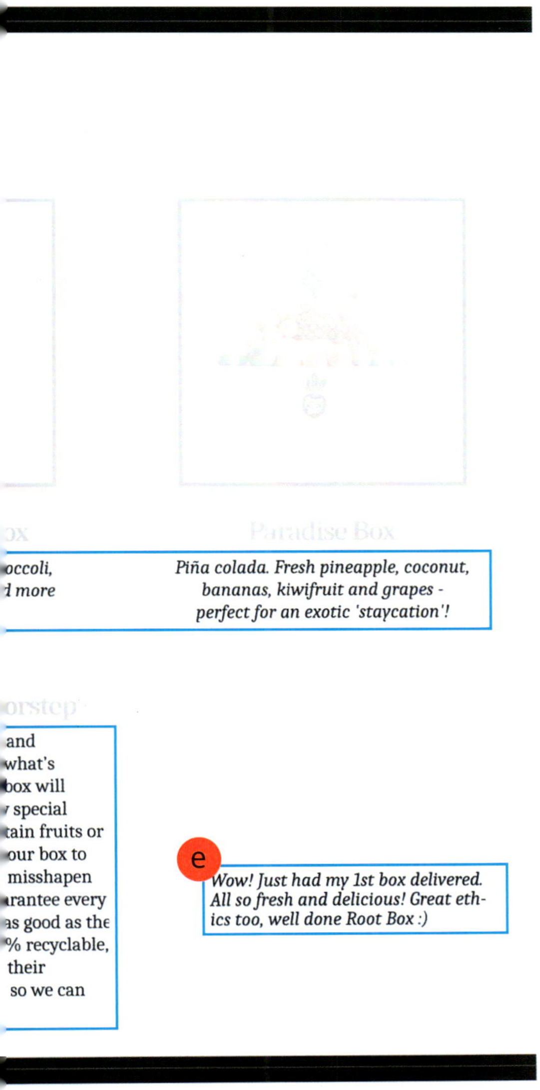

Selected sentence / paragraphs	Editing steps in Text Styles Panel
We'll only send you the freshest.. (a)	Apply *Body* text style and edit to *9.5 pt*. The *Body* style is based on *Base* by default. I increased the **Leading Override** slightly in the text style (**Character > Position and Transform**).
Enjoy a variety of English... *A mix of potatoes, cabbage...* *Pina colada. Fresh pineapple, ...* (b)	Apply *Body* text style then make *Italic* and **Centre Align** from the context toolbar.
Our family has been.. (c)	Create a new style called *Body - Large*, based on Base which should be *11.5 pt*. Change the **Font family** to *[No change]*.
Visit our website (d)	Create a new style called *List*, based on *Body - Large* which should be *12.5 pt Italic*. Change the **Font family** to *[No change]*. Pull in **Tracking** by *-50‰*.
Wow! Just had my 1st box delivered. (e)	Create a new style called *Reviews*, based on *Body - Large* which should be *Italic 9.5 pt*. Change the **Font family** to *[No change]*.
Farm-direct.. Eco-friendly.. Carbon neutral.. (f)	Create a new style called *Body - Alternate*, based on *[No Style]* that uses Special Elite *Regular 9 pt* and **Centre Align** from the context toolbar.

Headings

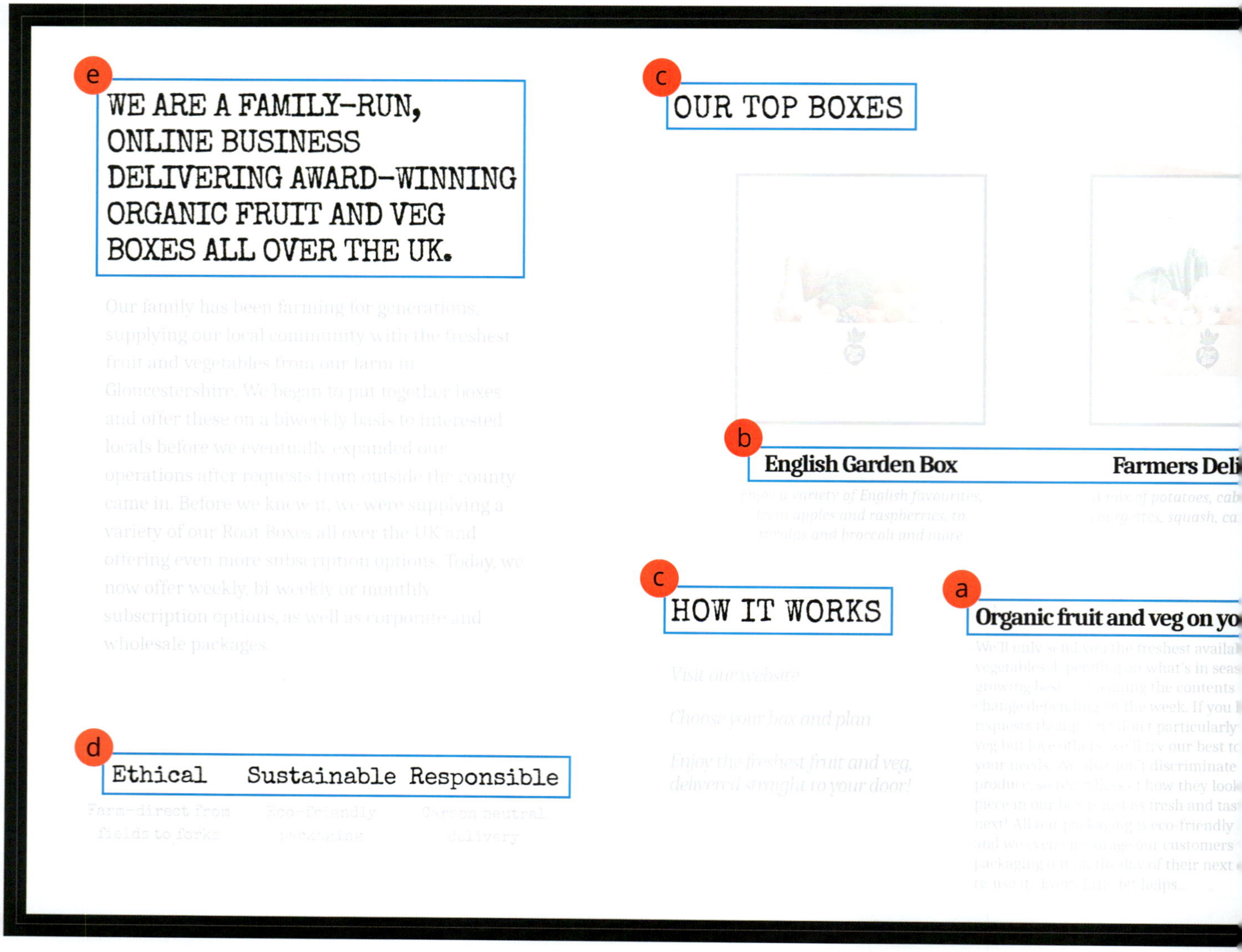
e
WE ARE A FAMILY-RUN, ONLINE BUSINESS DELIVERING AWARD-WINNING ORGANIC FRUIT AND VEG BOXES ALL OVER THE UK.
c
OUR TOP BOXES
b
English Garden Box
c
HOW IT WORKS
a
d
Ethical
Sustainable
Responsible

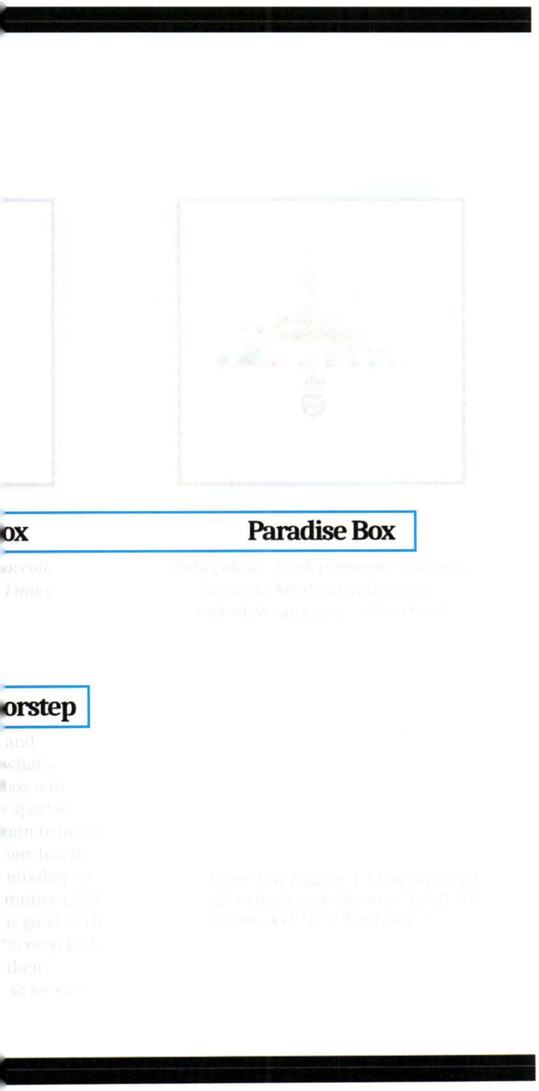

Selected sentence / paragraphs	Editing steps in Text Styles Panel
Organic fruit and veg.. (a)	Create a new style called *Small Heading*, based on *Body* which should be *14 pt Bold*. Change the **Font family** to *[No change]*. Pull in **Tracking** by *-50‰*.
English Garden Box Farmers Delight Box Paradise Box (b)	Apply *Small Heading* style and **Centre Align** from context toolbar.
OUR TOP BOXES HOW IT WORKS (c)	Create a new style called *Heading*, based on *[No Style]* that uses *Special Elite Regular 18 pt* and set **All Caps**.
Ethical Sustainable Responsible (d)	Create a new style called *Smaller Heading*, based on *Heading* which should be *13.5 pt* and **Centre Align** from context toolbar. Change the **Font family** to *[No change]*.
WE ARE A FAMILY-RUN BUSINESS (e)	Create a new style called *INTRO*, based on *Heading*. Tighten **Tracking** to *-50‰* and uncheck **Auto-hyphenation**.

Remove unused text styles via Panel Preferences in the **Text Styles Panel**.

Decorations for headings

Decorations (paragraph rules) are a great way to highlight and underline headings. As they're a property of paragraph text styles, applying decorations to the parent heading style can be made to affect all subordinate headings at once.

1 From the **Text Styles Panel**, double-click the *Heading* style.

2 In the **Paragraph > Decorations** section, check **Enabled**, click the **Fill** icon, then the **Fill** swatch and pick the Yellow global colour from the **Swatches** tab.

The example (below) shows a basic highlighter effect on the text. Decorations can offer other creative possibilities for headings (opposite).

OUR TOP BOXES

OUR TOP BOXES

HOW IT WORKS

Ethical

Sustainable

Responsible

Highlighting extended to frame or column width.

Highlighting including a baseline stroke.

Highlighting with gradient transparency.

Highlighting extended to frame or column width plus extending beyond character cap height and descent.

Highlighting with left vertical stroke.

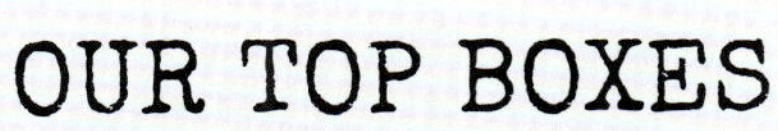

No highlighting with bottom stroke.

Numbering for the list

The list needs to be numbered with number formatting different from the text.

1 On the **Text Styles Panel**, create a new character style called *Bullet* using *Special Elite 20 pt*.

2 Double-click the *List* paragraph style.

3 In the **Paragraph > Bullets and Numbering** section, adjust settings as shown. Importantly, in the **Text** box use **Current Level** (\#) from the drop-down menu plus two spaces.

4 In the **Spacing** section, set **Left indent** to *0.3 in*, then reset **First line indent** back to *0*.

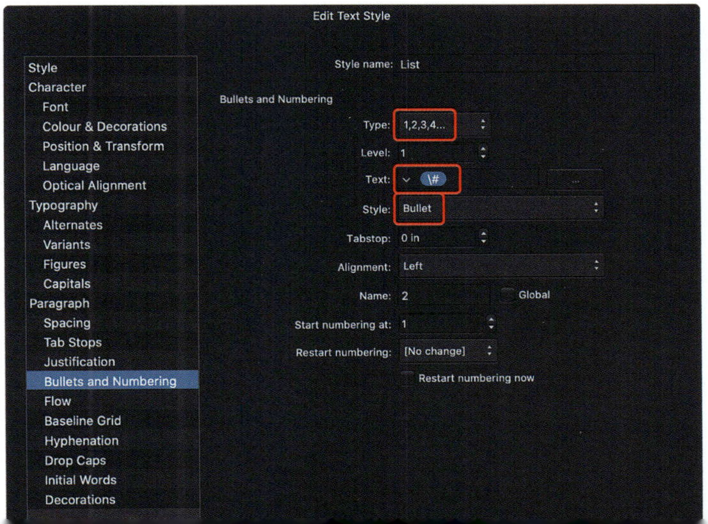

Final Steps

Here's a roundup of how the inner page was finished off.

- Place rootbox-ribeiro-berries.png over the initial body text and apply a **Tight** text wrap using **Show Text Wrap** settings on the **Toolbar**. This helps to attract attention to the main text.

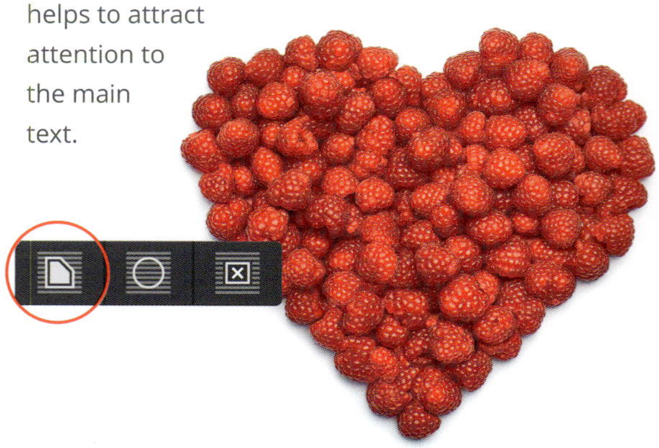

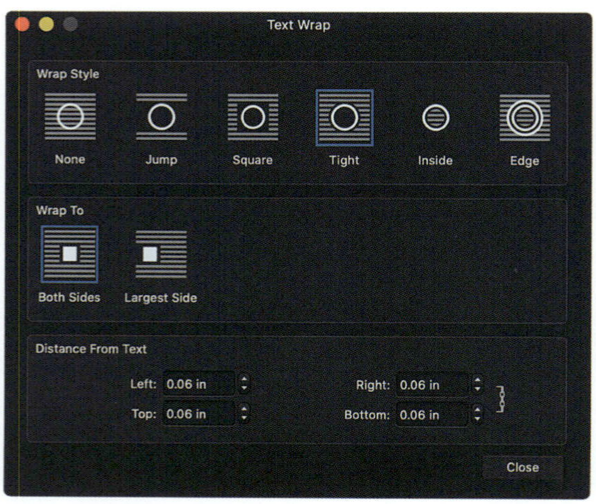

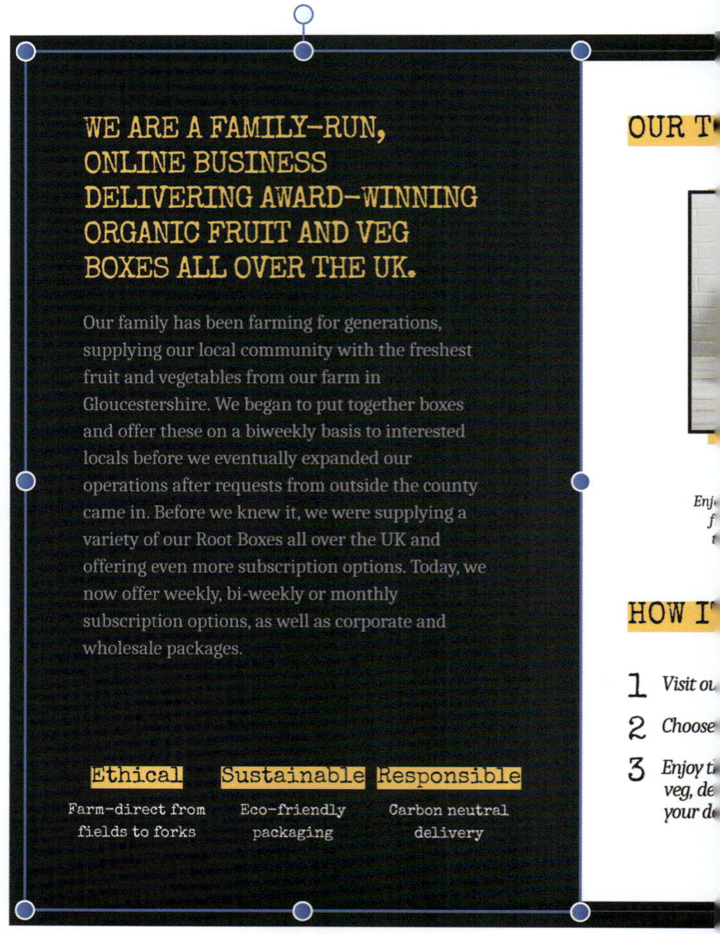

- To add more impact to Panel 1, a contrasting panel using the *Background* global colour was added behind the text. To make the text visible, some character overrides were applied—the yellow *Global Colour 2* to the heading, grey (*CMYK 0,0,0,40*) to the main paragraph and white to Farm-direct, Eco-friendly and Carbon neutral text.

Resource

Rootbox_brochure_04.afpub
rootbox-ribeiro-berries.png

- The overset text needed addressing. To make an extra linked frame, click the frame's rightmost red triangle and drag out another frame to the right as shown in example above.

OUTER PAGE DESIGN (PAGE 1)

The outer page hosts the all-important front, back and flap. The minimalist image-led look was designed to encourage potential readers to pick the brochure up.

Flap

The flap displays a lifestyle image incorporating a product in detail—this is the first panel displayed when opening the brochure and helps the reader imagine the product in their own kitchen.

Adding a lifestyle photo

1 With the **Picture Frame Rectangle Tool**, place a picture frame spanning the Flap panel that is drawn to the bleed edges.

2 Select **File > Place** to add the rootbox-ribeiro-kitchen.jpg file to the frame.

3 Deselect the picture frame.

> We'll look at how to enhance such placed imagery later (p. 206).

Resource
Rootbox_brochure_05.afpub rootbox-ribeiro-kitchen.jpg 170577635.jpg rootbox-ribeiro-overhead.png Root Box Logo.afdesign Root Box LogoType.afdesign

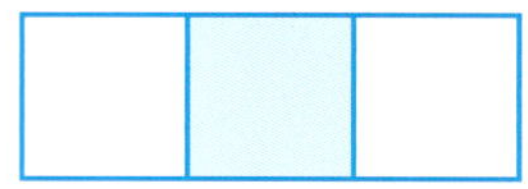

Back cover

Contact details and a small callback logo are to be added in front of a pattern background shared across the back and front covers.

Adding a pattern background

1 Draw another picture frame so it is placed from top-left bleed corner of the back cover to bottom-right bleed corner of the front cover.

2 Add 170577635.jpg to the frame.

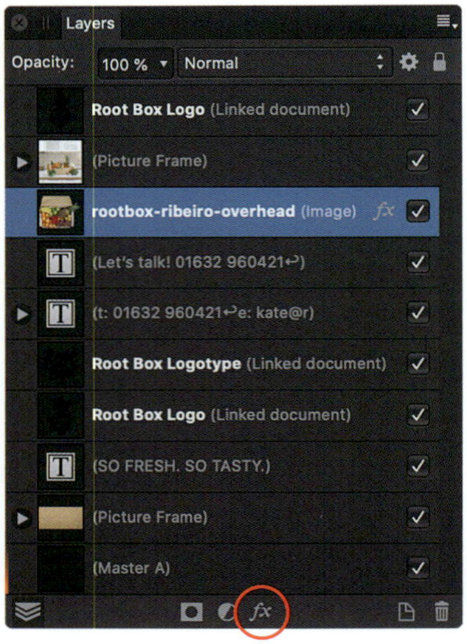

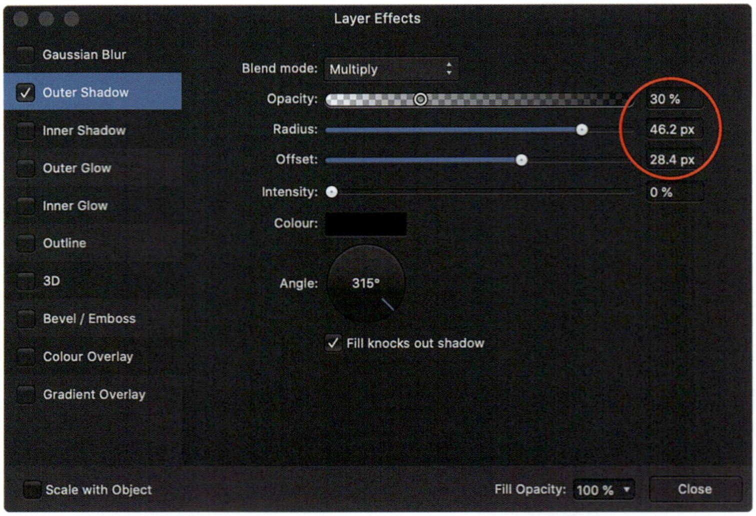

Adding the open box image

1 Place the rootbox-ribeiro-overhead.png image off the page so it doesn't attempt to replace the previously framed image.

2 Reposition it back onto the page so it snaps from the top bleed edge, then resize to over halfway down the panel (a).

3 To 'lift' the image off the page, add an **Outer Shadow** layer effect via the **Layers Panel**, adjusting **Opacity**, **Radius** and **Offset** to suit.

This image is a pre-supplied transparent PNG—the image is cut out and exported from a standalone photo editing app such as Affinity Photo. Later (p. 208), we'll look at time saving in-app cutouts using Publisher's Photo Persona (Affinity Photo owners only).

Contact details

The back cover also hosts 'toned down' contact details including a single telephone number—speaking to a member of the Root Box 'family' will increase trust and reinforce the brand's principles. Social media handles are included too.

1 With the **Frame Text Tool**, add single- and two-column text frames; the latter helps keeps spacing consistent (b).

2 Drag the remaining Let's Talk and social media text from the pasteboard into the respective text frames.

3 Apply the *Body - Alternate* and *Body* text styles to respective frame text. The Let's Talk! paragraph benefits from some contrasting white text; the *Let's Talk!* title and telephone number needed a style override to increase font size to *14.5 pt*, while tighter leading was applied to finish off.

We created a new Pure Black swatch (*CMYK 0,0,0,100*) that was set to **Overprint**. This was applied to all the social media text.

This gives a 'heads up' that overprint has been considered. In reality, any press-ready PDF profile preset chosen at export will have Overprint Black checked so swatch creation is optional.

Adding supporting graphics

- Place the Root Box Logotype.afdesign file next to the contact information. This reinforces the brand.

- Social media icons can be sourced from instagram.com and facebook.com, then copy/pasted inline in your text.

Root
Box
a
b
SO FRESH. SO TASTY.

Front cover

Always on show, the front cover presents the logo along with an enticing tagline. The logo uniquely identifies the company and fosters brand loyalty.

Adding the logo

- Select **File > Place** to add the Root Box Logo.afdesign file centrally on the panel (a).

Tagline

The final text to add to the design is the important tagline supporting the logo. We went big here as the text needed to be readable from afar.

1. Drag a text frame out that spans the front cover (b).
2. Enter the text *SO FRESH. SO TASTY.*
3. Apply a new text style called *Tagline*, based on *Heading* text style, and with *29 pt* font size and centre alignment.
4. Uncheck **Enable Decoration** to inherit the parent yellow decoration.

As a nice touch, try copy and pasting this logo onto the box in the Flap lifestyle photo, adjusting its size to suit. For added realism, shear the image upwards from the right edge handle so it fits the same perspective box as the box.

BRINGING THE DESIGN TOGETHER

We'll now make the pages look more visually unified by applying the same colours to a selection of design elements across both pages—first using an image colour overlay and then by text formatting. A White Balance adjustment can also 'tune' image colours to the rest of the design.

Outer (Page 1)

Applying colour overlays

The pattern background image can be made more striking by recolouring with a bold global colour, in this case teal green. The same yellow used for heading decorations can also be applied to the Root Box logotype.

1 Select the pattern background's picture frame.

2 On the **Layers Panel**, click **Layer Effects**.

3 Check the **Colour Overlay** effect and navigate via the **Colour** swatch to the **Swatches** and **Document** Palette pop-up options.

Resource
Rootbox_brochure_final.afpub

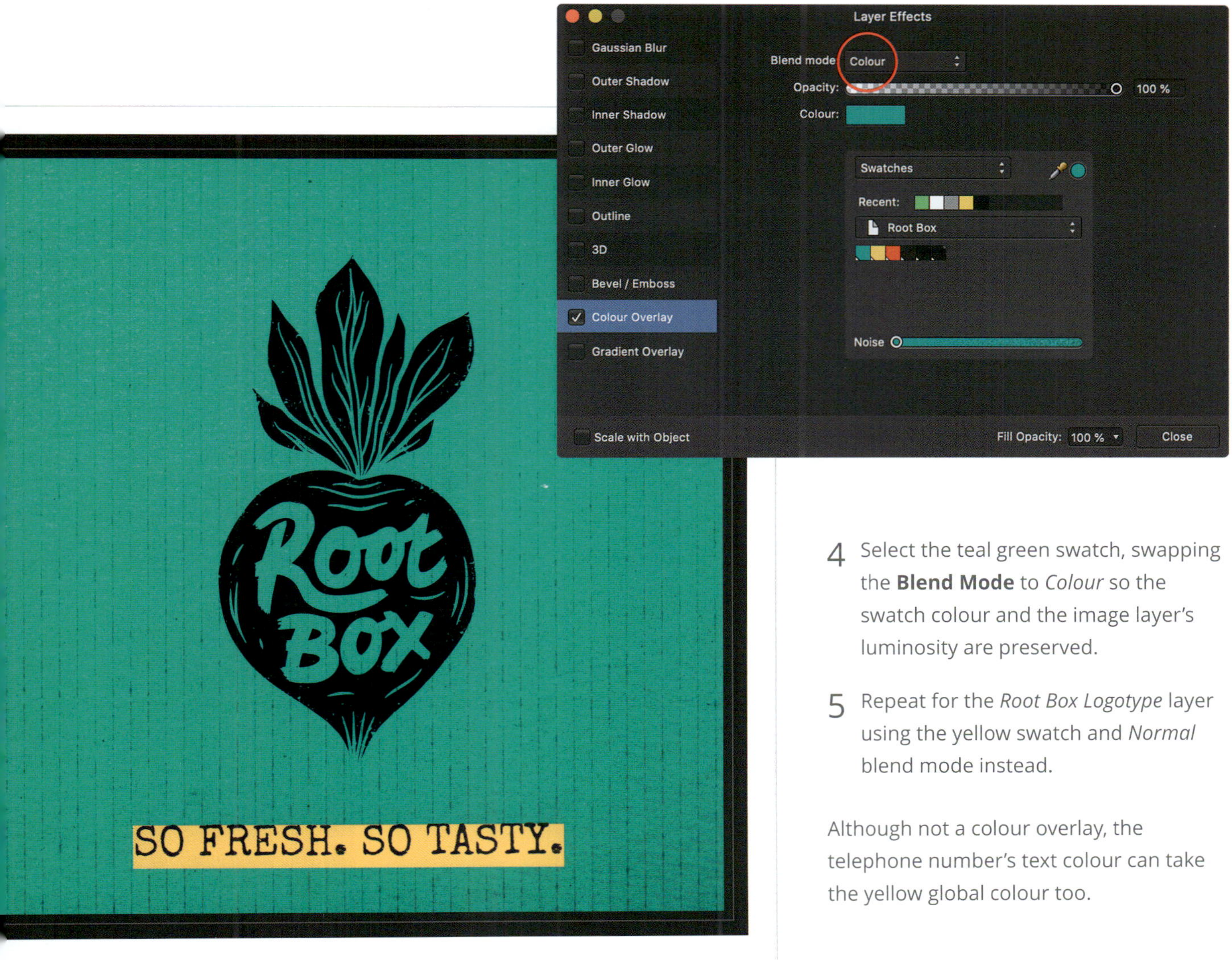

4 Select the teal green swatch, swapping the **Blend Mode** to *Colour* so the swatch colour and the image layer's luminosity are preserved.

5 Repeat for the *Root Box Logotype* layer using the yellow swatch and *Normal* blend mode instead.

Although not a colour overlay, the telephone number's text colour can take the yellow global colour too.

Applying a White Balance adjustment

The lifestyle photo on the flap could benefit from a White Balance adjustment. This 'warms' the photo up so it matches the colour of the adjacent fruit and vegetable box lid.

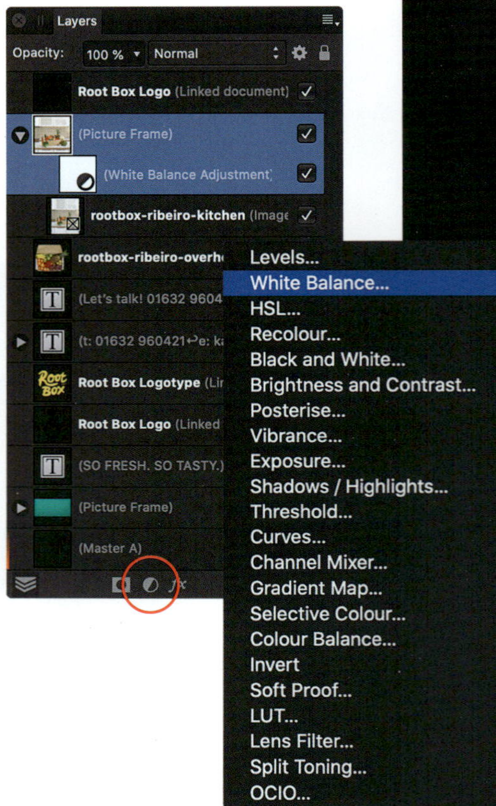

1. On the **Layers Panel**, select the lifestyle photo's picture frame.
2. Click **Adjustments** at the bottom of the panel and choose **White Balance** from the pop-up menu.
3. Adjust the **White Balance** to *5%*.

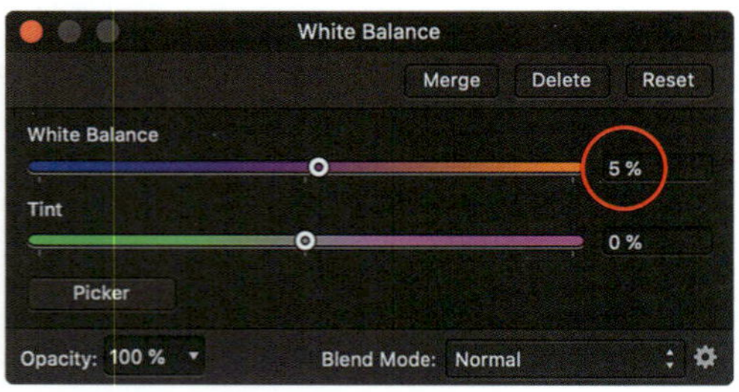

Inner (Page 2)

A couple of small edits completes the main project. Now the teal green background is introduced on the Front Cover, it seemed a good idea to carry this colour to Inner (Page 2)—in this case to the List text colour and review text background.

1. On the **Text Styles Panel**, edit the *List* paragraph style to have a **Text fill** colour of teal green.
2. Revert the *Bullet* character style colour using the *100k* black swatch.

- For the review text, make the text white, and place a callout using the **Callout Rounded Rectangle Tool** behind the text and fill with the teal green colour. Add some yellow stars with the **Star Tool** for effect.

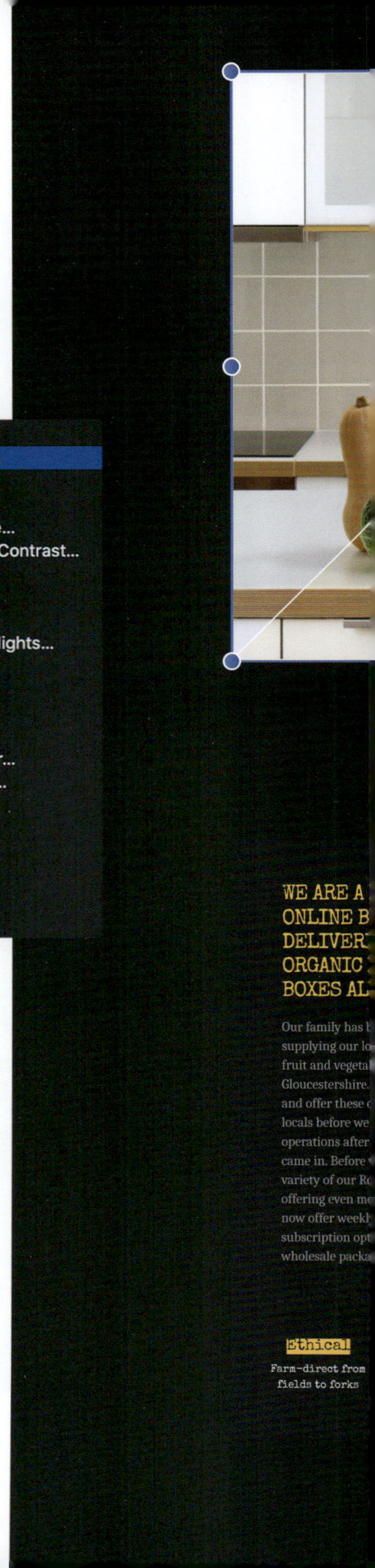

Let's talk! 01632 960421
Ask us about our subscription services, wholesale offering, corporate packages, loyalty scheme and referral bonuses!
Root Box
t: 01632 960421
e: kate@rootbox.website
w: www.rootbox.website
root_box
rootbox.fruit

RD-WINNING
ND VEG
THE UK.
for generations,
ity with the freshest
put together boxes
basis to interested
expanded our
outside the county
we were supplying a
over the UK and
or monthly
OUR TOP BOXES
Farmers Delight Box
A mix of potatoes, cabbage, broccoli, courgettes, squash, carrots and more
Paradise Box
Piña colada. Fresh pineapple, coconut,
HOW IT WORKS
1 Visit our website
2 Choose your box and plan
3 Enjoy the freshest fruit and veg, delivered straight to your door!
Organic fruit and veg on your doorstep
We'll only send you the freshest available fruit and vegetables depending on what's in season and what's growing best — meaning the contents of your box will change depending on the week. If you have any special requests though and don't particularly like certain fruits or veg but love others, we'll try our best to tailor your box to your needs. We also don't discriminate against misshapen produce, so regardless of how they look, we guarantee every piece in our box is just as fresh and tastes just as good as the next!
Wow! Just had my 1st box delivered. All so fresh and delicious! Great ethics too, well done Root Box :)
Root Box

TAKING IMAGES FURTHER WITH STUDIOLINK

If you're also an owner of Affinity Designer and Affinity Photo you'll have direct access to them without leaving Affinity Publisher thanks to **StudioLink**. For the latter, you can access all the power of Photo including live filters, pro selection tools for cutouts and retouch tools. No more external image editing and laborious reimporting cycles for you.

With the main project complete, we'll swap to an alternative resource file and specifically look at enhancing images using the power of Affinity Photo including:

- Cutting out a subject.
- Removing unwanted content.

Cutting out a subject

Earlier in this project (p. 200) we placed an overhead fruit box photo (transparent PNG) which was cut out by an external app. Instead, the box can be cut out using a pixel selection, selection refinement and masking.

> In some circumstances, already cut out PNG images may not always be available. With StudioLink, you resolve this by cutting out in-app while keeping you original image unaffected.

1 Click **Photo Persona** on the **Persona toolbar**.

2 Select the fruit box.

3 With the **Selection Brush Tool** (W), paint inside the box until it is completely enclosed by a flashing 'marching ants' outline.

> Frequent zooming in/out operations and brush resizing work well here. Use [and] keys to size your brush.

Resource
Rootbox_brochure_StudioLink.afpub

4 On the context toolbar, click **Refine**, then drop the **Border width** down to *1%* to improve selection accuracy.

5 Choose to **Output** the selection as *New layer with mask*, then click **Apply**.

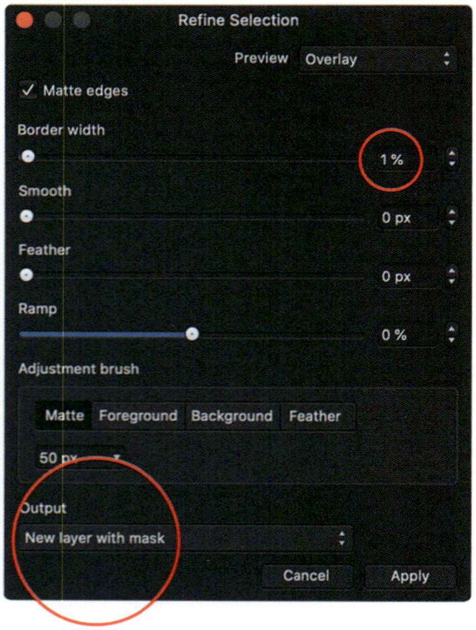

6 You can optionally add the Outer Shadow effect applied in the main project.

Removing unwanted content

The image most in need of work is the high-profile lifestyle shot on the flap. There are several blemishes on the cauliflower, right-hand pear and right-hand garlic bulb that can be made to magically disappear using the Inpainting Brush Tool.

1 On the **Layers Panel**, create a new pixel layer above the image.

2 Select the white triangle on the **Healing Brush Tool** to access and select the **Inpainting Brush Tool** (J) from the flyout.

3 On the context toolbar, set **Current layer & below**. This makes the removal process non-destructive.

4 Brush over imperfections using brush widths slightly larger than the area to be removed.

Remember to switch back to the Publisher Persona once photo editing is complete

EXPORTING AS PDF

The brochure needs to be exported to a high-resolution CMYK PDF file for professional printing.

First we'll preflight check the project, then export all pages, ensuring bleed and printer marks are set on output.

Preflight checking

Affinity Publisher performs live preflight checking for warnings and errors—these generate automatically as they occur.

Fixing preflight errors

1 Locate the bell icon on the bottom **Status bar**. If the bell icon is red or yellow, click it to reveal the **Preflight Panel**. A red colour indicates a higher severity error; yellow a less severe warning; green means no problems.

2 Double-click on the entry to jump to the problem area and resolve.

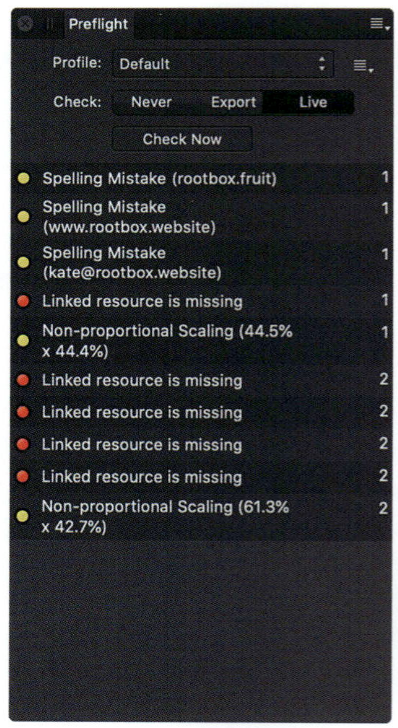

Exporting the file

1. On the **File Menu**, select **Export**.
2. Select the *PDF* icon, and then a **Preset** of *PDF/X-4*.
3. Change **Area** to *All Pages*.
4. To include bleed and printer marks, click **More**, then check **Include bleed** and **Include printers marks**.
5. Click **Export**.
6. Save the file as Root Box Brochure.pdf.

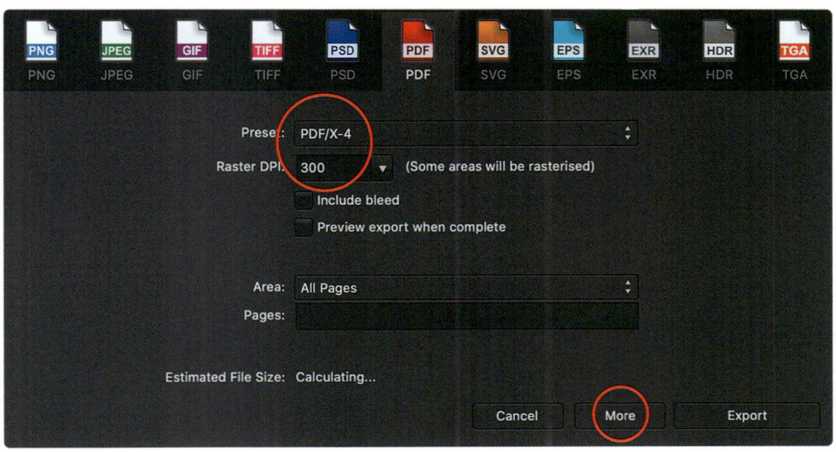

ESH. SO TASTY.
Let's talk! 01832
Ask us about our
corporate packages,
Root Box

2

Spotlight Magazine

Editorial design and templating by *Adam Banks*

Producing a periodical publication is a complex challenge. Learn the steps to success from an experienced designer of newsstand magazines and two times editor of *MacUser*, aimed at creative professionals.

The magazine you'll make in this project is based on our Affinity Spotlight website but is purely an example, not a publication we intend to launch.

Editor's Letter

Hello, readers!

We're proud to bring you the inaugural issue of *Affinity Spotlight*, a celebration of inspirational content created by artists who use Affinity Designer, Photo and Publisher.

Our cover story is an interview with and profile of Eleni Debo, an illustrator working in the Italian Alps who's the winner of a World Illustration Award and a regular contributor to international newspapers and magazines. Eleni talks to us about the artwork that secured her recognition by the judges, her artistic influences, and how Affinity Photo benefits her workflow.

In this issue's tutorial section you'll learn how to create enchanting character art by following the technique of Italian-Australian artist Roberta Burattini, aka Moon Lotus Dreams. From choosing brushes and their settings to adding extra pizazz by considering tonality, noise and reflections, discover how to make figurative art that elicits an emotional response.

The whole team here at Serif is grateful for the support you've given to our apps and work-books – and now this magazine, too. We want to see more of your incredible work created using Affinity apps, so tag your social media posts with *#madeinaffinity* or contact us directly at hello@affinityspotlight.com and your creativity may feature in a future issue or on our website.

Melanie

Melanie Khareghat
Editor

Melanie

BEFORE YOU GET STARTED

Resources

You can get all the resources that are referenced in this project from: https://affin.co/SpotlightMag

Knowledge of Affinity Publisher

To get the most from undertaking this project, you will need to:

- Be familiar with the interface of Affinity Publisher. You can learn more about the interface in the Interface Tour chapter, starting on p. 14.
- Have good core skills. See the skills table below to see which additional aspects of Affinity Publisher you need to be confident with to complete this project:

Pages and Master Pages	p. 82
Design Aids	p. 96
Working With Text	p. 112
Picture Frames	p. 124
Adding Content	p. 130
Text Styles	p. 140

Downloading and Installing fonts

1. Go to https://fonts.google.com (or search online for Google fonts) and download the **Chivo**, **Crimson Pro**[1], **IBM Plex Sans** and **IBM Plex Sans Condensed** families.

2. Open the downloaded font folders and read the OFL.txt file.

3. For *Mac*: ctrl-click the files, select **Open**, then select **Install Font**.
   or:
   For *Windows*: Right-click the downloaded font files and select **Install**.

[1]When installing this font, choose the version in the **static** folder rather than the variable font version.

WHAT IS MAGAZINE DESIGN?

Producing a magazine is different from designing a one-off document. Instead of laying out pages from scratch, you'll use master pages and templates extensively so that you and others can efficiently and consistently produce each issue.

Following some design conventions will help your readers find their way around.

Templates versus layouts

We'll look first at setting up templates as master pages, then laying out publication pages with actual content. In practice, starting a new magazine is a mixture of these processes.

Using existing magazines for inspiration, first rough out some layouts to work out a look and feel, and agree it with your client/collaborators. Based on these, you can start to set up guides, master pages and text styles. This will give you a basis to commission articles and source images. As you lay out the final pages, continue to incorporate your design decisions into your masters and text styles.

> When you finish issue 1, save a copy of the document, tidy up the layouts you're likely to reuse (and create extra masters where appropriate), and you'll have a foundation for future issues.

Magazine Terminology

Magazine designers often use their own lexicon when talking about pages. Here are common terms to help you through this project and beyond.

Slug

Some designers, like myself, use this term to refer to the visual presentation of any small piece of text as a distinct block.

Running head

A section heading that helps the reader to navigate your magazine. It should fit with the overall looks and, despite its position, not dominate other elements.

Headline

The largest text of an article, usually located near the page's top and flowing naturally into the standfirst.

Standfirst

An introduction that bridges the headline and the body copy, typically set at a smaller font size than the former but larger than the latter.

Byline

The position of author (and sometimes illustrator) credits may vary between article types—e.g. in a gutter, in the standfirst, or at the end of body copy.

Folio

This critical element should at least include page numbering. It might also include the publication's name, issue date or number, or a web address.

LOREM IPSUM

Donec semper consequat velit eget ligula mattis faucibus

LOREM IPSUM DOLOR sit amet, consectetur adipiscing elit. Morbi sed neque metus. Donec condimentum, nunc et luctus mollis, dui ante blandit dolor, quis pellentesque ex sem sapien. Praesent luctus odio sem

LOREM IPSUM DOLOR SIT AMET, CONSECTETUR ADIPISCING ELIT

Lorem ipsum dolor sit amet, consectetur adipiscing elit. Morbi sed neque metus. Donec condimentum, nunc et luctus mollis, dui ante blandit dolor, quis pellentesque ex sem ut sapien. Ac pharetra urna vulputate vitae. Aenean in vulputate diam. Maecenas vulputate arcu vitae feugiat porttitor. Vestibulum eleifend aliquet sem eu. Suspendisse porta turpis nec fermentum scelerisque. Integer varius vitae diam ut maximus. Quisque interdum tellus ut turpis porta interdum. Aenean posuere, tellus vel venenatis venenatis, arcu urna molestie tellus, vel suscipit magna turpis eget enim. Maecenas sollicitudin orci sapien, sed sollicitudin risus pharetra vel. Donec semper, sem vel

▾Morbi sed neque metus. Donec condimentum, nunc et luctus mollis, dui ante blandit dolor, quis pellentesque ex sem ut sapien.

scelerisque auctor, risus urna vestibulum turpis, vel viverra orci ante sed enim. Sed ex lorem, lacinia id dapibus at, lacinia eget quam. Cras lacinia egestas tortor, accumsan ornare nibh ornare ut. Etiam ac imperdiet leo. Suspendisse rutrum erat purus, id tempus lorem dapibus et.

Praesent luctus

Class aptent taciti sociosqu ad litora torquent per conubia nostra, per inceptos himenaeos. Aenean ante est, pellentesque nec malesuada et, porttitor ac lorem. Vestibulum interdum sodales erat, a lacinia metus laoreet a. Cras sit amet lacinia mi. Cras non quam sit amet massa molestie pulvinar non non arcu. Cras eu augue a mauris porta rutrum a eget urna. In imperdiet sem justo, eget rutrum lectus luctus ut. Morbi rutrum malesuada tortor, in blandit diam posuere at. Maecenas euismod pulvinar sapien non accumsan. Integer eu tellus eu nulla blandit ullamcorper. In vel placerat sem. In pharetra, sem ut pretium placerat, diam risus mattis nulla, in egestas ex sem eget elit. Vivamus suscipit ut ex vel rhoncus. Integer at fringilla purus, id sodales mauris. Nunc sed porttitor augue.

Pellentesque consequat velit eget ligula mattis faucibus. Ut non mauris convallis, tempus nisi ac, varius magna. Suspendisse bibendum pellentesque hendrerit. Phasellus ultrices et urna nec blandit. Lorem ipsum dolor sit amet, consectetur adipiscing elit. Sed quis diam ut tortor convallis accumsan eget vel elit. In sed convallis nibh.

30 SUMMER 2020 *Spotlight*

Maecenas sollicitudin
Donec semper, sem vel scelerisque auctor, risus urna vestibulum turpis, vel viverra orci ante sed enim. Sed ex lorem, lacinia id dapibus at, lacinia eget quam. Cras lacinia egestas tortor, accumsan ornare nibh ornare ut. Etiam ac imperdiet leo. Suspendisse rutrum erat purus, id tempus lorem dapibus et erat puru.

Class aptent taciti sociosqu ad litora torquent per conubia nostra, per inceptos himenaeos. Aenean ante est, pellentesque nec malesuada et, porttitor ac lorem. Vestibulum interdum sodales erat, a lacinia metus laoreet a. Cras sit amet lacinia mi. Cras non quam sit amet massa molestie pulvinar non non arcu. Cras eu augue a mauris porta rutrum a eget urna. In imperdiet sem justo, eget rutrum lectus luctus ut. Morbi rutrum malesuada tortor, in blandit diam.

Maecenas eusimod
Pulvinar sapien non accumsan. Eu nulla blandit ullamcorper. In vel placerat sem. In pharetra, sem ut pretium placerat, diam risus mattis nulla, in egestas ex sem eget elit. Vivamus suscipit ut ex vel rhoncus. Integer at fringilla purus, id sodales mauris. Nunc sed porttitor augue, non.

Pellentesque consequat velit eget ligula mattis faucibus. Ut non mauris convallis, tempus nisi ac, varius magna. Suspendisse bibendum pellentesque hendrerit. Phasellus ultrices et urna nec blandit. Lorem ipsum dolor sit amet, consectetur adipiscing elit. Sed quis diam ut tortor convallis accumsan eget vel elit. In sed convallis nibh. Nullam a elit magna. Phasellus eget nisi eu odio tempus pretium. Nullam ullamcorper augue in pellentesque sagittis. Cras vitae orci sed neque gravida fermentum. Ut ultrices nisl nisi, vitae euismod elit accumsan sed.

Proin varius turpis at condimentum mattis. Mauris sollicitudin arcu ex, sit amet egestas lectus porttitor in. Nam id condimentum tellus. Donec ac ipsum sapien. Donec efficitur, eros sit amet accumsan dignissim, dui est gravida urna, a blandit tellus mauris sed eros. Duis rutrum dictum nunc, et blandit ante blandit ac. Aenean in nibh libero. Maecenas ornare mi vitae posuere egestas. Aliquam placerat laoreet tortor id finibus. Aenean at sapien cursus augue eleifend dictum non nec est. Sed ultrices gravida purus eu pharetra. Integer elementum massa purus, vel efficitur enim iaculis vel. Nullam et arcu purus. Praesent vehicula non lacus sit amet pulvinar. Curabitur congue turpis nec nibh tincidunt, id egestas velit feugiat. Donec tincidunt volutpat magna ac rutrum. Nullam quis eros quis augue ultricies dignissim. Vestibulum est justo, fermentum id facilisis sed, feugiat ac lacus. Praesent fringilla lorem magna, pellentesque bibendum ante dictum sed. Donec at eros sodales, rutrum felis quis, tincidunt urna. Morbi sed neque metus. Donec condimentum, nunc et luctus mollis, dui ante blandit dolor, quis pellentesque ex sem.

Nullam a elit magna. Phasellus eget nisi eu odio tempus pretium. Nullam ullamcorper augue in pellentesque sagittis. Cras vitae orci sed neque gravida fermentum. Ut ultrices nisl nisi, vitae euismod elit accumsan sed.

Proin varius turpis
Mauris sollicitudin arcu ex, sit amet egestas lectus porttitor in. Nam id condimentum tellus. Donec ac ipsum sapien. Donec efficitur, eros sit amet accumsan dignissim, dui est gravida urna, a blandit tellus mauris sed eros. Donec tincidunt volutpat magna ac rutrum. Duis rutrum dictum nunc, et blandit ante blandit ac. Aenean in nibh libero. Maecenas ornare mi vitae posuere egestas. Aliquam placerat laoreet tortor id finibus. Aenean at sapien cursus augue eleifend dictum non nec est. Sed ultrices gravida purus eu pharetra. Integer elementum massa purus, vel efficitur enim iaculis vel. Donec tincidunt volutpat magna ac rutrum. Nullam quis eros quis augue ultricies dignissim. Vestibulum est justo, fermentum id facilisis sed, feugiat ac lacus. Donec tincidunt volutpat magna ac rutrum. Praesent fringilla lorem magna, pellentesque bibendum ante dictum sed. Donec at eros sodales, rutrum felis quis, tincidunt urna. Lorem ipsum dolor sit amet, consectetur adipiscing elit. Morbi sed neque metus. Donec condimentum, nunc et luctu. Cras eu augue a mauris porta rutrum a eget urna. Sed ultrices gravida purus eu pharetra. Integer elementum massa purus.

▲Lorem ipsum dolor sit amet, consectetur adipiscing elit.

Pellentesque consequat velit eget ligula mattis faucibus. Proin varius turpis at condimentum

Spotlight SUMMER 2020 31

Cross heading

A heading positioned within body copy that indicates what the following paragraphs are about, often in a different font style or slightly larger size.

Column

Body copy is typically split into two or three columns per page, which helps to keep each line of text to a comfortable reading length.

Bastard Column

Bastard columns are used to introduce space into layouts and often contain captions and other supporting info. They are usually narrower than story columns and different in visual style.

Caption

An explanation of an image on the page. Carefully consider whether it's clear to the reader what the caption refers to; an arrow can help.

Boxout

A separated-off area for tangential discussion points outside of the body copy. Larger boxouts often have their own headline and sometimes a standfirst.

DOCUMENT SETUP

Magazines are designed as facing pages (spreads) and are usually printed on a CMYK colour press.

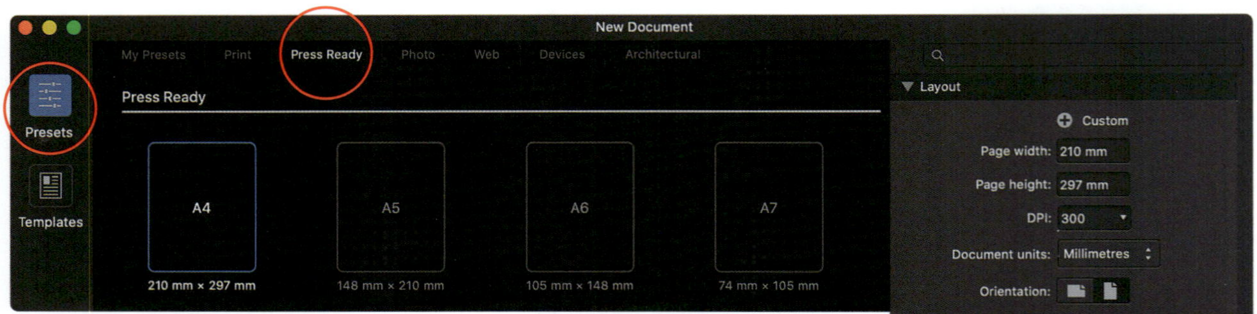

1 Select **File > New** and then the **Press Ready** *A4* preset.

2 Keep most settings on their defaults. Leave **DPI** at *300*, the standard target resolution for images in printed publications.

3 Set **Number of pages** to *3*. Page 1 will be a right-hand page containing the magazine's cover. You'll add more pages later.

4 Set **Colour profile** to match the press: your print partner will advise, but *Coated FOGRA39* is commonly used in the UK and Europe, *US Web Coated (SWOP) v2* in the US. You can change this later.

5 Leave **Bleed** set to *3 mm* all round, which is correct for nearly every press.

6 Click **Create**.

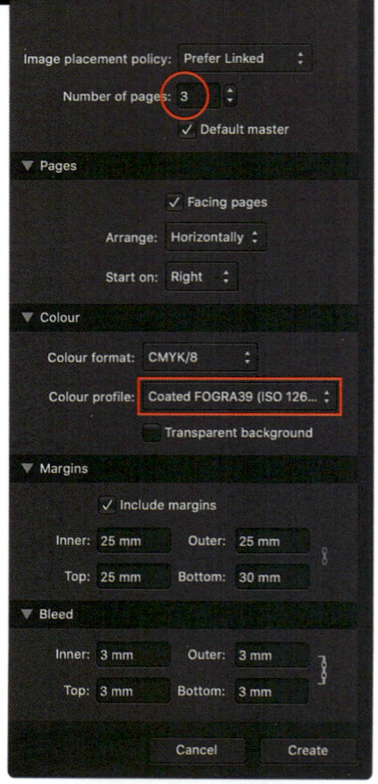

Design to a grid

Every magazine's layout is based on what designers call a 'grid', which isn't Affinity Publisher's document grid feature on its own. Instead, it could be a combination of column guides, ruler guides, and text and picture frames.

By setting up these elements on master pages, you can use your grid as the starting point for each page you create.

Margin conventions

Some magazines have narrow margins—less than half an inch, or just over a centimetre—to maximise the usable space (the 'frame'). For a substantial bound magazine, make the inner margin a little wider so content isn't lost into the spine, as I've done in this project.

Story text will sit between the margins. A taller bottom margin allows a footer to sit below it. A wider top margin lets the page breathe a little and accommodates 'running heads'—titles, often set in a colour or on a slug, that tell the reader which article they're looking at.

INSPIRATION

Drawing the news: an artist's story

ELENI DEBO IS a Belgian illustrator who freelances from the breathtaking Italian Alps. Her work regularly features in international newspapers, books and magazines and she has an incredible talent for distilling complex stories and subject matter into a single thought-provoking image.

Fresh from winning a prestigious World Illustration Award, Eleni talks to us about her *Spotlight* submission piece (created in Affinity Photo), how she got into editorial illustration and why she loves to combine and mix analogue and digital painting in her work.

Firstly, congratulations on winning the professional editorial category in the World Illustration Awards 2019! Could you tell us a bit about your entry and what the award means to you?

Thanks! I submitted 'When to stop', a three page editorial illustration I made for Belgian newspaper *De Morgen* in the wake of the #metoo movement and the viral short story 'Cat Person' by Kirsten Roupenian. The article dealt with the dilemma of how even consensual sex can turn bad, and the taboos involved.

Based on the story of Roupenian, my illustration reads as the story of a sexual experience slowly turning bad. I tried to represent this in the gradual removal of colour and the evolution of soft and flowy to sharp and aggressive shapes. The passage of time and the feeling of movement is suggested by showing fragmented scenes both flowing into and disrupting each other.

Winning the award with this work was a wonderful surprise to me. For the past year I have been setting my sights on new horizons, hoping to attract overseas clients. By participating in the contest, I had hoped to at least catch the eye of a few people involved. Actually winning my category has, aside from a pleasant confidence boost, definitely opened doors for me professionally, and will go a long way towards reaching my goal.

▼Each illustration starts as a sketch on paper or Eleni's iPad before being developed into the final piece

What inspired you to submit this particular illustration?

It's always such a pleasure for me to illustrate for *De Morgen*, as they give me a lot of freedom to work with a subject. So I felt confident to approach this assignment somewhat more experimentally. Despite the deadline, I ended up really having fun working on this illustration, and the end result was exactly as I had wanted it to be. I felt like this illustration represented my abilities, both visually and conceptually, especially given the delicate nature of the subject, and it remains to this day one of my favourite editorial pieces.

Your work regularly appears in international newspapers and magazines. How did you first get into editorial illustration?

When I finished my studies at the academy, I knew I wanted to get involved with editorial illustration and had in particular set my sights on De *Morgen*, as they had a very decently designed newspaper and weren't afraid of experimenting with their visuals. I decided that, while having a part time job in an awesome little letterpress studio, I would spend that first year out of school working on a strong portfolio.

I bought a random newspaper, chose a variety of articles (going from psychological and human interest to economics and politics) and got to work illustrating them. Once I was confident my portfolio was strong enough, I sent them to different potential clients, including the art director of *De Morgen*, making sure to include an honest handwritten note explaining why I wanted to work for them.

De Morgen was actually the first client to contact me upon receiving my portfolio. Our first collaboration was a successful one, and I ended up working for them almost weekly. This kind of exposure turned out to be huge, and very soon other clients started trickling in. Before I knew it, I had enough work on my hands to start working full-time as an illustrator, and things have been trucking along rather pleasantly ever since.

How would you describe your style?

I would say that, for me, the important part of my illustration is the concept, and the style of the illustration is often chosen as a function of how to best represent that idea. That being said, I suppose there are some common factors, stylewise. My work often shows a mix of analogue and digital painting, which does give it a signature noisy/painterly feel. I developed a range of brushes based on my favourite analogue painting techniques to further blend the line between the analogue and the digital.

In terms of content, shadow and light play a big role in my illustrations and are often a determining factor for the mood of the image. Other than that, I've noted people often saying that I have a rather particular use of colour. To be honest, I always felt like I am having a hard time choosing a palette (which is something I could keep going back and forth on for hours, given the opportunity), but perhaps that might just be the exact reason why people find it so particular. Perhaps a classic case of weaknesses becoming strengths.

▲Illustration for the Belgian cycling magazine *Bahamontes*

▲Eleni Debo makes illustrations for a variety of international clients. See more examples of her work at elenidebo.com

When starting a new illustration, do you normally have access to the full article your work will accompany?

It depends. For the daily news, I often just get the six-sentence pitch of the journalist describing the article. So in the same time I'll be illustrating this embryonic article, the journalist will be actually writing it. For weekend publications, or opinion pieces, it does happen that I get the full article or a proof of some sort. In some cases, however, I just get the phone number of the journalist and the message to go find out whatever it is I need to

ILLUSTRATIONS ELENI DEBO INTERVIEW MELANIE KHAREGHAT

30 SUMMER 2020 *Spotlight*

Spotlight SUMMER 2020 31

Resource

Groundwork folder

SET UP COLUMN GUIDES

The **Guides Manager** lets you visualise columns, which are the scaffolding of magazine design.

1 On the **Pages Panel**, double-click *Master A* to edit it.

2 Select **View > Guides Manager**. Set **Margins** as shown.

3 Under **Column Guides**, set **Columns** to *5*.

4 Set the **Gutter** width to *5 mm*.

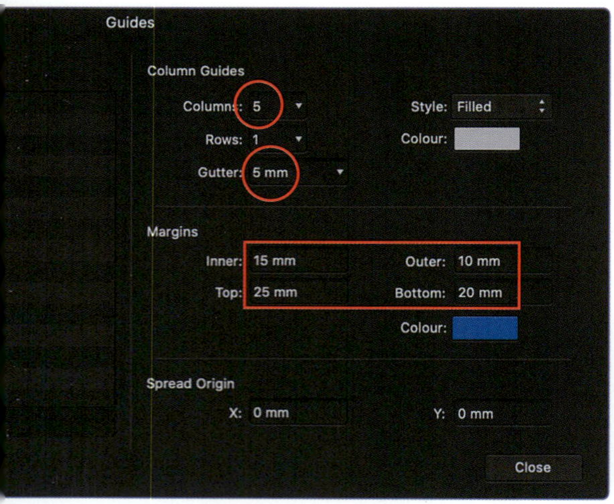

Around 4–5mm is a good starting range for our document's gutter but when setting up a baseline grid and text styles you can review it based on your baseline grid's spacing, which I recommend using as a common value throughout your magazine design.

A three-column grid is practical but can be dull. It's common to use a larger, usually odd number of columns as guides for uneven text frames, as you'll see.

In the project, I've used a five-column grid on some pages and three columns on others.

Experiment with body text

Columns set your design's horizontal rhythm. Vertical spacing should be aligned by a baseline grid that matches the leading of your body text.

Start by working out your body text style.

1. On *Master A*, use the **Frame Text Tool** (T) to draw two text frames, each displaying one text column across two column guides (as shown).
2. Use the left frame's **Text Flow** button to link it to the right frame.
3. Select **Text > Insert Filler Text** and then select the text.
4. On the context toolbar, I've chosen *Crimson Pro* in its *Light* style. I've set **Font Size** to *10.5 pt* and **Paragraph Leading** to *4 mm* (which the app converts to points). Normally I'd start with measurements that resolve to around *8* to *10 pt* for font size and *10* to *12 pt* for leading, and experiment from there.

Your document should look like Document_setup_with_column_guides.afpub.

Notice that the visual size of type varies as you switch fonts, while the leading stays fixed. Adjust leading so there's clear space between lines, but only just.

Leading

Existing magazines can help you decide on leading. Measure between the bottom of the characters (the 'baseline') on one line of text and on the eighth line below, and divide by eight.

Enter the leading value and unit of measurement—e.g. *4 mm*—and Affinity Publisher precisely converts it to points.

Choosing typefaces

Magazines often use one serif and one sans-serif typeface, picked for similar tone and proportions.

There are no hard and fast rules, but the following often applies: a serif for body text; a sans-serif for cross headings; a sans-serif in a bold weight for breakout text like captions; a sans serif in regular weight for additional copy such as boxouts and how-tos; and use your artistic judgement for headlines, standfirsts and other elements.

For serif and sans-serif text you intend to be the same size, such as body and boxout text, adjust their point sizes visually rather than simply setting the same value. Choose font families that include at least italic and bold, and ideally more weights.

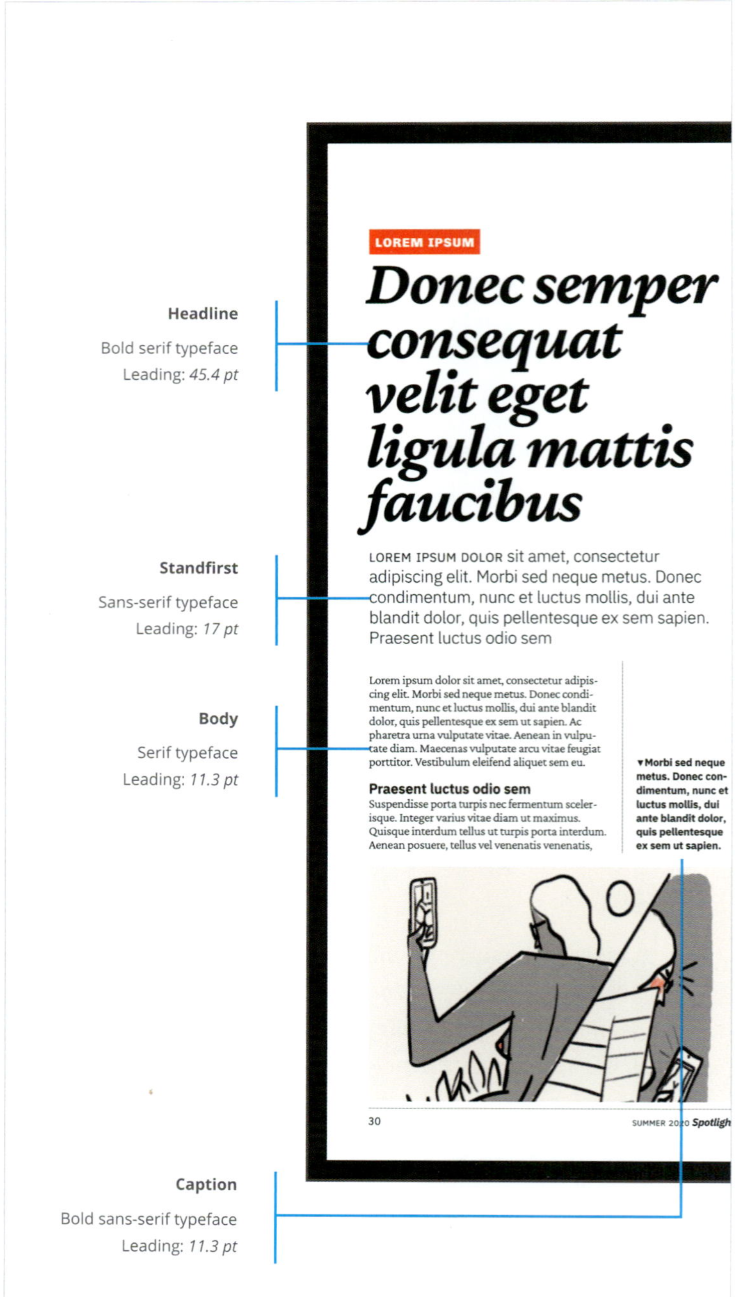

Resource
Baseline_Grid folder

SET UP YOUR BASELINE GRID

When happy with your body text style, apply its leading to the document-wide baseline grid. This ensures lines of text remain vertically aligned in all the columns across each spread, keeping your layouts neat. If you use a background grid (p. 228), do this after you've set it up.

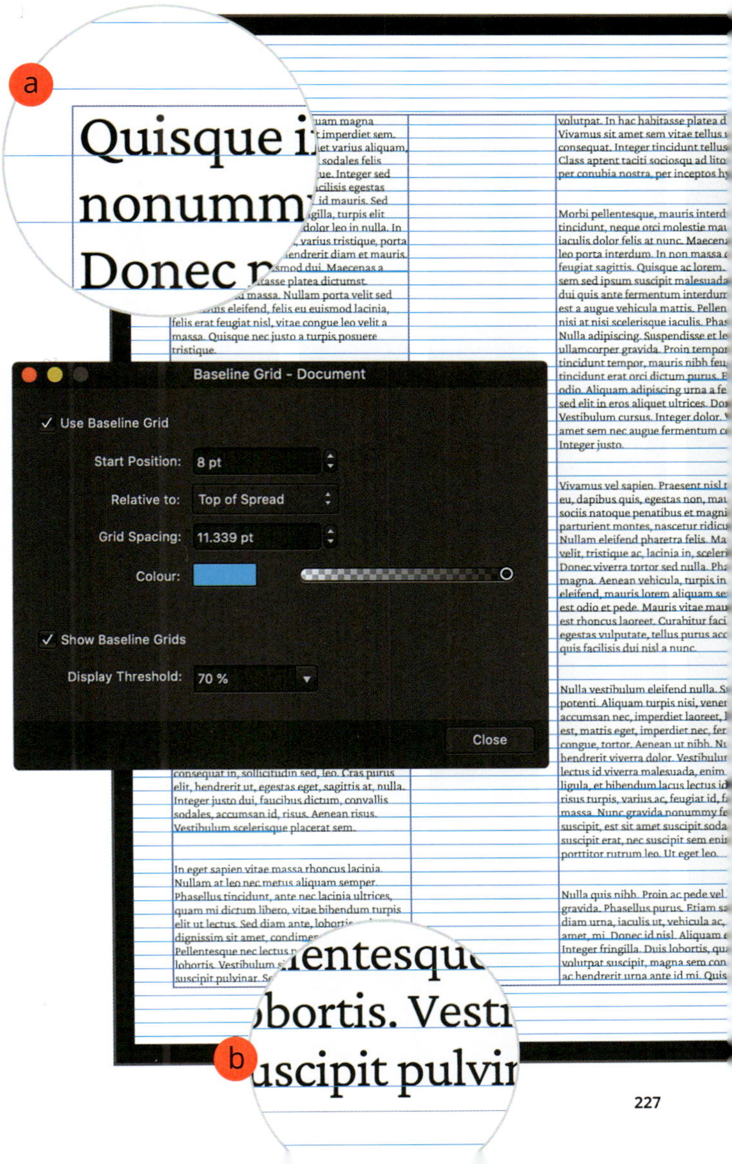

1 In **View > Baseline Grid Manager**, check **Use Baseline Grid** and **Show Baseline Grid**.

2 Set **Grid Spacing** to your leading value. Mine is input as *4 mm* (converted to *11.339 pt*).

3 In **File > Spread Setup**, adjust the top and bottom margins to align with the baseline grid. (The bottom margin includes any discrepancy between your grid and page size—for example, mine is *17 mm* rather than an exact multiple of my grid spacing.)

4 Resize the text frames so that each fills a pair of column guides, like earlier.

Finally, adjust the baseline grid's **Start Position** so text sits evenly between the margins. You are looking for two results:

- The text fills the columns without leaving a blank line at the top or bottom (a).
- The tops of letters in the top row (a) look as far from the top margin as the bottoms of the letters in the bottom row from the bottom margin (b). This also ensures each line of text sits neatly within each row of background grid squares.

Historically, leading is measured in points. When designing pages, however, I want to ensure text aligns with other elements, measured in millimetres in this project's document.

So, I adjust my leading to work out to a round number of millimetres. There's no need to do the maths yourself: enter *4 mm* and the app converts it to Points.

I recommend changing in **Preferences** (User Interface) the number of decimal places displayed for **Points** to *3* so that you see more precise values, but consistently enter values in millimetres to avoid rounding errors accumulating and wrecking your grids. Let the app convert accurately. (Converted values are stored at greater accuracy than shown.)

You can use your baseline grid value as a basis for other spacing too, such as column gutters—which we'll amend in a moment.

Usually the baseline grid should be hidden. Text will continue to be aligned to it but you'll have a clearer view of content and other design aids.

Going further, I like to base my magazine grids on an actual (background) grid, like squared paper, using the same value. This project uses a 4 mm grid.

This makes it even easier to decide how to place and align new objects on pages. By snapping to grid squares, you needn't spend time calculating precise dimensions or positions to keep your layouts neat.

Using a background grid

To set up a grid on your master pages:

1 In **View > Grid and Axis Manager**, select **Basic**, then check **Show grid** and **Show axis editing handles**.

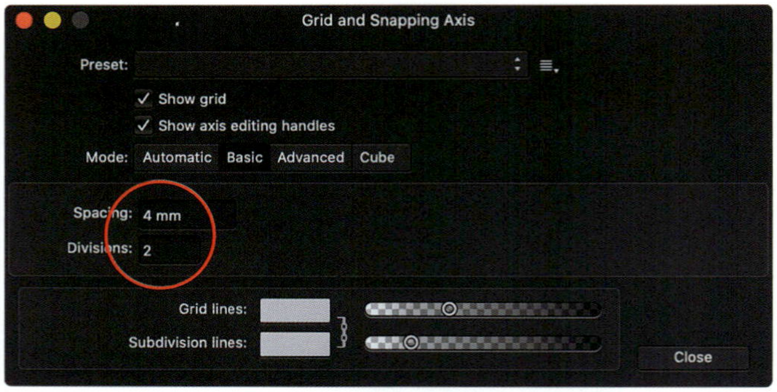

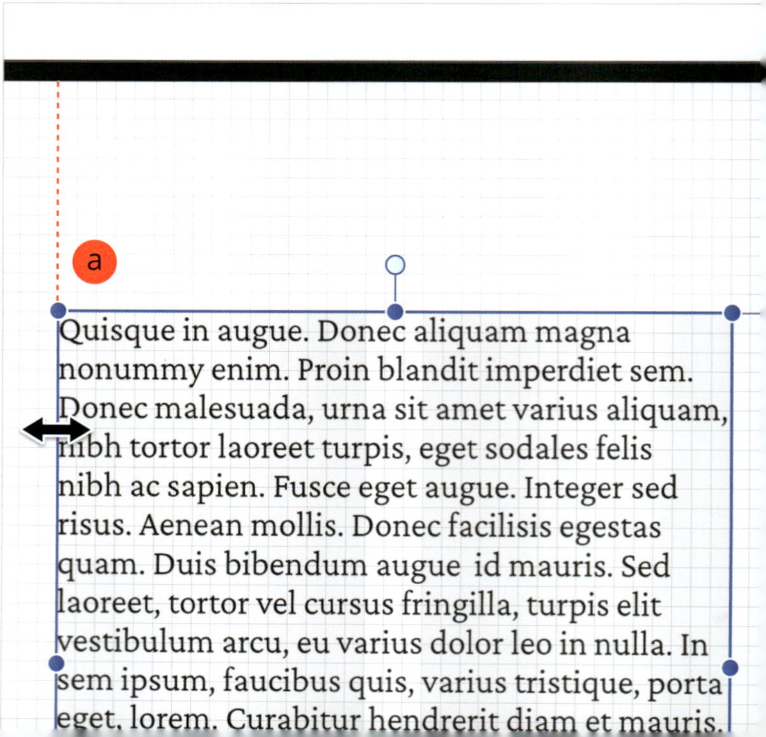

2 Drag the grid origin marker from the top left to the top centre of the spread (c).

3 Match **Spacing** to your baseline grid (*4 mm*). For flexibility, set **Divisions** to *2*.

4 In **View > Snapping Manager**, check **Snap to grid**.

Adjust the master's margins and column guides to fall exactly on background grid lines/subdivisions (as shown), and adjust the text frame to match the margins (a). It helps to temporarily hide the baseline grid during this.

If your column guides are misaligned, try adjusting the inner or outer margin. Mine are now *14 mm* and *12 mm*, respectively.

This is a good time to review your column guides' gutter so the guides align with the grid. I've updated mine to *6 mm*—1.5 times my baseline grid's spacing (b), aligning with my grid subdivisions.

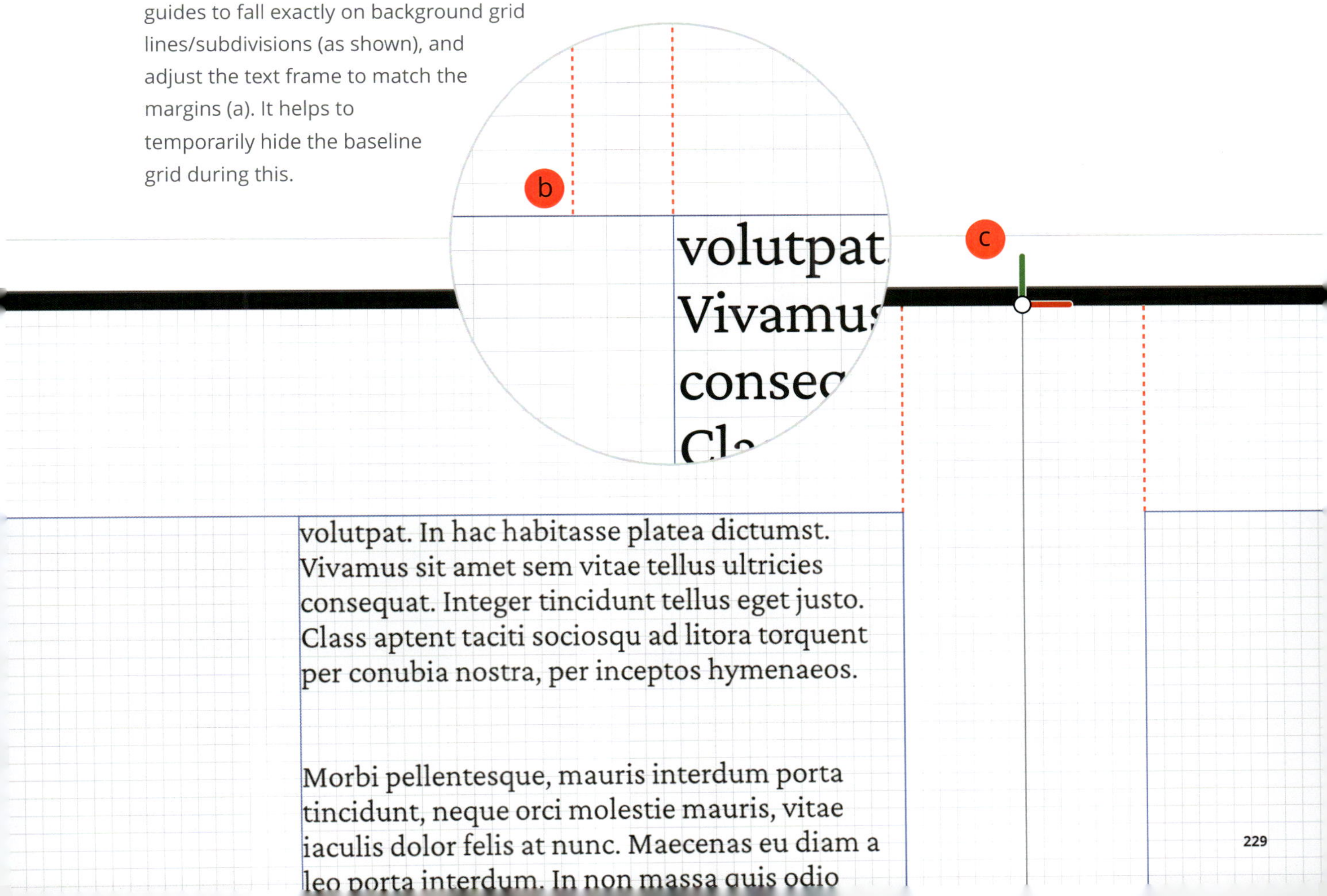

CREATE BODY TEXT STYLES

When laying out magazine pages, you'll apply text styles to quickly turn unformatted text into body text, headlines, captions and other elements.

Start by making two paragraph styles for body text.

1 With the **Frame Text Tool**, ctrl-click (Mac) or right-click (Win) the filler text and select **Expand Field**.

2 Select any word in the text and click **Create Paragraph Style** on the **Text Styles Panel**. The next dialog summarises the word's current styling.

3 For **Style name**, I've used *-SP- Body*.

4 Set a memorable **Keyboard shortcut**. For example, combining multiple modifier keys with 1 for body text, 2 for body text with a first-line indent, and so on.

5 Click **OK**. Now, select only the first paragraph and apply your body style.

6 On the **Paragraph Panel**, set **First Line Indent** to two or three times your baseline grid's spacing.

7 Again, create a paragraph style. Its **Based on** style will be the one created earlier, but this one will include the indent. I've named it *-SP- Body Indent*.

If memorising multiple keyboard shortcuts for text styles is difficult, at least assign one to the **Text Styles Panel** for quick access. This can be done in **Keyboard Shortcuts** preferences, under the *View* category)

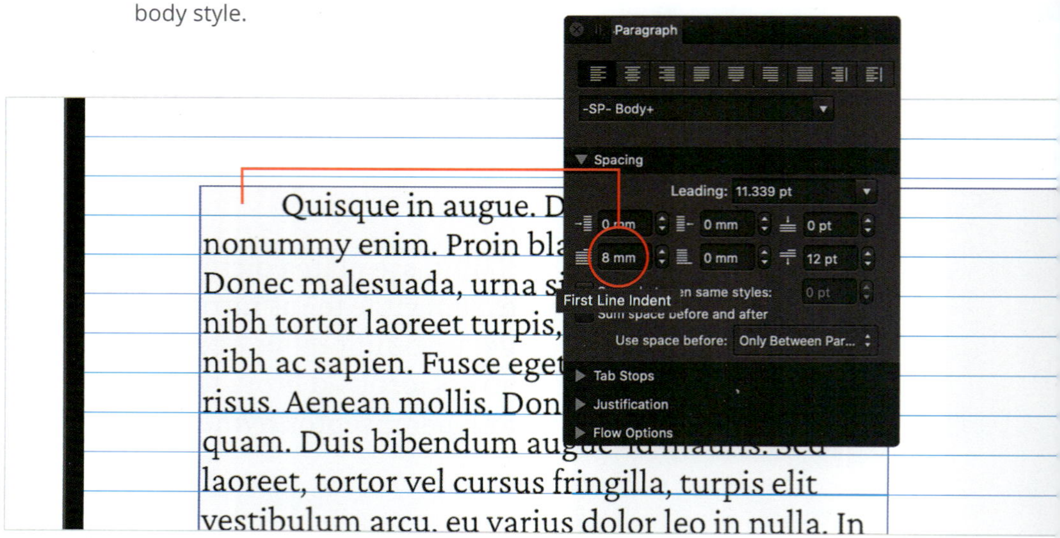

I prefix my style names with an abbreviation of the magazine name to avoid confusion with default or imported styles. Prefixing with punctuation also keeps your styles at the top of the list.

Base styles

Affinity Publisher's default paragraph styles inherit from a group paragraph style called *Base*. If you set your own styles to do the same, any formatting you add to Base is inherited by those styles.

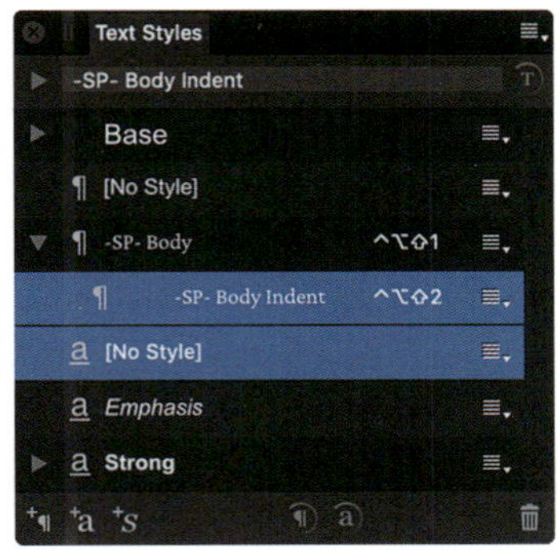

For magazine templates, I recommend you avoid using the default styles with the exception of Base, if you modify it for your own purposes as mentioned.

It's possible that you may want to delete the default styles to tidy up the **Text Styles Panel**. However, don't use **Delete Unused Styles** from the panel's menu: this will remove styles you've set up but not yet applied.

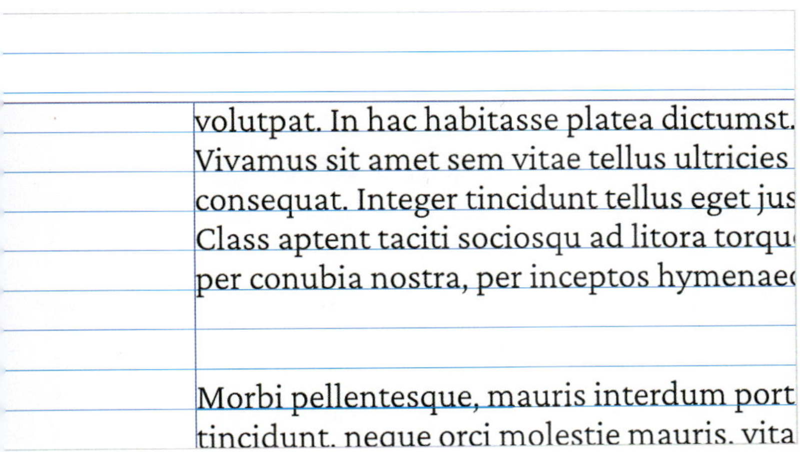

COMPLETE A MASTER PAGE

Resource
Master_Page folder

Your master pages have margins, column guides, a baseline grid, and a dummy text frame.

A footer, or 'folio', usually shows a magazine's name, issue date and a page number. This will appear on nearly every page, so let's set it up on Master A.

1 The large text frame is no longer needed. Delete it.

2 Draw a text frame the width of the space between the left and right margins across the bottom of the left page. Leave at least one empty baseline between the bottom margin and the frame's top.

3 Set the frame to display one column and size it to fill the space between two baselines, as shown.

4 Apply a font size similar to your body text to start. On the context toolbar, select **Left Align**.

5 Place the text insertion point in the frame and select **Text > Insert > Fields > Page Number**.

6 To right-align some text, press the shift+tab keys to add a **Right Indent Tab** character. Type an issue date and the magazine name.

7 Style the page number and other details as you like. This styling is used only here, so you needn't create text styles.

8 Repeat on the right page, reversing item order from left to right.

When you created your document, the default master page (Master A) was applied to the publication pages created then, so they now include your folio.

PLACE EXTERNAL CONTENT

Importing text from Word

I don't recommend pre-styling text in Word, but if you want to, first lay out an example article in Affinity Publisher, using named text styles for all the elements.

Copy and paste all of the text into a blank Word document; the styles are imported too. Delete the text and save as a template for writers/production staff to use. They can format their text in Word using the imported styles before it's placed in your magazine.

I prefer to prepare article text, in Microsoft Word or another text editor, in the default ('Normal') style but otherwise unformatted. In Affinity Publisher, I use **File > Place** to import the text and then apply my text styles.

Word count and copy-fitting

When a magazine commissions a writer, they agree on a word count and fee. This is important to design and budgeting.

Word counts depend on body text size and the balance of words to images. Prepare example articles at lengths that feel right. Place in your design to see how text fits, adding pages or cutting words as necessary. Copy the text back to Microsoft Word to calculate word counts to commission and page allocations.

Don't change font size or spacing to make copy fit. However, an acceptable cheat is to triple-click a line of text and reduce its tracking by 10%—but no more!

How many documents?

When production is divided among a team, it may be more efficient to break articles or sections into separate Affinity Publisher documents. If you alter text styles in one, others can be updated from it using **Text > Text Styles > Import Text Styles**.

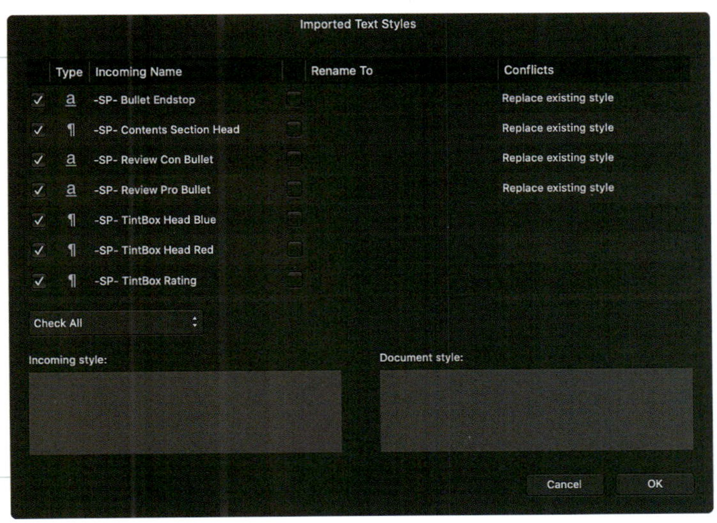

Resource
Feature_Article folder

LAY OUT A FEATURE

Let's lay out your first article, an interview that uses multiple text styles in its body. Continue in the same document.

1. In the **Snapping Manager** (**View Menu**), ensure **Enable snapping**, **Snap to grid**, **Snap to guides** and **Snap to margin** are checked, and **Snap to baseline grid** isn't.

2. Check all the **Show...** options in the top section of the **View menu**.

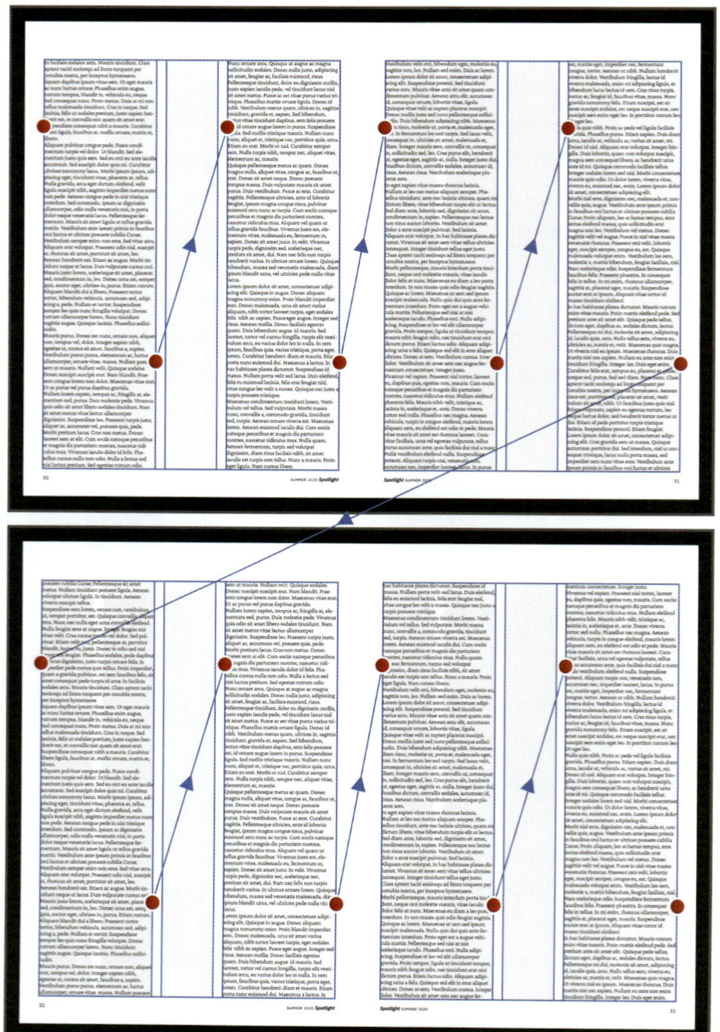

Set up the pages

1. On the **Pages Panel**, double-click *Pages 2,3* to edit them. (Master A is already applied to them.)
2. On the left page, draw two text frames, each two column guides wide (as shown), and another against the middle guide.
3. Repeat this layout on the right page.
4. Insert filler text in the leftmost frame.
5. From left to right, link the wide frames by clicking the blue Text Flow triangle then the next text frame to flow to.
6. Duplicate the spread so there are as many as are allocated on your magazine's page plan—two spreads in our case.
7. Link the first spread's rightmost wide frame to the next one's leftmost.

Add body text and style it

The rest of this project requires more text styles than the two created earlier.

When designing a magazine from scratch, you'll experiment with styles to decide what is needed. To save time here, use **Text > Text Styles > Import Text Styles** to import the styles from magazine_text_styles.afpub.

1 Using the **Frame Text Tool**, select all of the filler text.

2 Use **File > Place** to overwrite the selection with magazine_profile_body.rtf.

3 Apply your indented body text style (*-SP- Body Indent*) to all text.

4 Apply your regular body text style (*-SP- Body*) to the first paragraph.

5 Working through the paragraphs:

- Apply *-SP- BodyBold* to interviewer questions (a)
- Apply *-SP- Body* to the first paragraph after each question (b)
- Remove any extraneous space between paragraphs

Quadruple-click paragraphs to select them, even if discontinuous.

It is your subeditor's role to edit text to fit its allocated space, which ought to be straightforward if the writer has kept to the commissioned word count.

They will also make readability decisions about paragraph breaks, heading positions, widows and orphans (p. 169); and check character styling according to a style guide—such as names of other creative works being italicised.

Add page furniture

In the spaces to the left and right of each page's narrow centre text frame, add **column rules** (lines) (a) to reinforce the pages' visual structure.

1. Reduce the narrow text frame's width by *2 mm* on each side to make room for the column rules.
2. Using the **Pen Tool** (P), click where you want the column rule to start.
3. Hold the shift key (⇧) and click where the column rule will end.
4. Set the stroke to the *Greys* palette's default *Black* and a width of *0.24 pt*.
5. Duplicate the grid line and mirror the duplicate to the column guide's right.
6. Repeat on each of the article's pages.

INSPIRATION

Drawing the news: an artist's story

ELENI DEBO IS a Belgian illustrator who freelances from the breathtaking Italian Alps. Her work regularly features in international newspapers, books and magazines and she has an incredible talent for distilling complex stories and subject matter into a single thought-provoking image.

...award with this work was a wonderful surprise to me. For the past year I have been setting my sights on new horizons, hoping to attract overseas clients. By participating in the contest, I had hoped to at least catch the eye of a few people involved. Actually winning my category has, aside from a pleasant confidence boost, definitely opened doors for me professionally, and will go a long way towards reaching my goal.

What inspired you to submit this particular illustration?
It's always such a pleasure for me to illustrate for *De Morgen*, as they give me a lot of freedom to work with a subject. So I felt confident to approach this assignment somewhat more experimentally. Despite the deadline, I ended up really having fun working on this illustration, and the end result was exactly as I had wanted it to be. I felt like this illustration represented my abilities, both visually and conceptually, especially given the delicate nature of the subject, and it remains to this day one of my favourite editorial pieces.

Your work regularly appears in international newspapers and magazines. How did you first get into editorial illustration?
When I finished my studies at the academy, I knew I wanted to get involved with editorial illustration and had in particular set my sights on De *Morgen*, as they had a very decently designed newspaper and weren't afraid of experimenting with their visuals. I decided that, while having a part time job in an awesome little letterpress studio, I would spend that first year out of school working on a strong portfolio.

I bought a random newspaper, chose a variety of articles (going from psychological and human interest to economics and politics) and got to work illustrating them. Once I was confident my portfolio was strong enough, I sent them to different potential clients, including the art director of *De Morgen*, making sure to include an honest handwritten note explaining why I wanted to work for them.

De Morgen was actually the first client to contact me upon receiving my portfolio. Our first collaboration was a successful one, and I ended up working for them almost weekly. This kind of exposure turned out to be huge, and very soon other clients started trickling in. Before I knew it, I had enough work on my hands to start working full-time as an illustrator, and things have been trucking along rather pleasantly ever since.

How would you describe your style?
I would say that, for me, the important part of my illustration is the concept, and the style of the illustration is often chosen as a function of how to best represent that idea. That being said, I suppose there are some common factors, style-wise. My work often shows a mix of analogue and digital painting, which does give it a signature noisy/painterly feel. I developed a range of brushes based on my favourite analogue painting techniques to further blend the line between the analogue and the digital.

In terms of content, shadow and light play a big role in my illustrations and are often a determining factor for the mood of the image. Other than that, I've noted people often saying that I have a rather particular use of colour. To be honest, I always felt like I am having a hard time choosing a palette (which is something I could keep going back and forth on for hours, given the opportunity), but perhaps that might just be the exact reason why people find it so particular. Perhaps a

30 SUMMER 2020 *Spotlight*

Add a headline and other large text

Let's edit the article's first page to provide an inviting entry point (b).

1. Use the **Frame Text Tool** to draw a text frame across two or more column guides for a headline.
2. With the frame selected, click **Show Text Wrap Settings** on the **Toolbar** and apply the **Square** wrap style.
3. Type *Inspiration* in the frame, press the Return ↲ key, then type *Drawing the news: an artist's story*.
4. Apply *-SP- Slug Sans Caps* to the first line and *-SP- Head x4 Italic* to the rest.

When creating your own headline paragraph style from scratch, set its leading to a multiple of your baseline (hence x4).

classic case of weaknesses becoming strengths.

When starting a new illustration, do you normally have access to the full article your work will accompany?
It depends. For the daily news, I often just get the six-sentence pitch of the journalist describing the article. So in the same time I'll be illustrating this embryonic article, the journalist will be actually writing it. For weekend publications, or opinion pieces, it does happen that I get the full article or a proof of some sort. In some cases, however, I just get the phone number of the journalist and the message to go find out whatever it is I need to know, which often results in a way-too-lengthy, non-billable, but nonetheless pleasant chat.

How do you go about creating your illustrations? Do you prefer to sketch ideas on paper first or work straight on computer?
Generally I start off jotting down my ideas in scraggly looking thumbnail-sized sketches on paper, which honestly would suffice for me to work on. However, given that my thumbnails are usually bordering on illegibility, I tend to sketch the ideas out a bit bigger and neater in order to present them to the client. After getting the approval of the client, I'll start working directly on top of my sketch.

Technology has definitely influenced my process these past few years. When I started, my sketches and finals were mainly analogue. But the fast-paced newspaper work really forced me to develop quicker ways of working, which lead me to working a lot more digitally.

Since I bought the Apple iPad Pro, it has been a lot easier to work completely digitally, from sketch to finish – which can be very handy, since I'm travelling a lot and I can just take all of my work with me. But ideally my process will be a mix of an analogue painted base, which I combine with digital painting, generally going back and forth between the two media during the process until I'm satisfied.

We were delighted to hear that you use Affinity as part of your workflow. How did you discover the apps and what inspired you to start using them?
After having spent countless evenings as a young kid entertaining myself with drawing in MS Paint, discovering a program like Photoshop as a teenager effectively propelled my love for digital painting, even if this was not the primary function of the software. When, years later, my boyfriend introduced me to the launch of this promising new software suite called Affinity – similar to Adobe, but seemingly better and definitely more democratically priced – I quickly fell in love all over again.

Given my familiarity with Photoshop, I was most attracted to switch to Affinity Photo, and although illustration might not be its main focus (as opposed to, say, Designer), I discovered that the software was perfect for my workflow of mixing scanned analogue painting with digital painting. I have been working with the Affinity software for a few years now, and I'm definitely not regretting my decision!

What do you like most about Affinity apps?
Live previews of blending modes and brushes have been a game changer. It has without a doubt greatly improved the speed of my workflow. Other than that, there's Affinity Photo for iPad, which has definitely appealed to my cocooning habits: drawing while sitting on the couch wrapped in a comfy blanket, count me in!

What are your greatest influences and inspirations?
I suppose it's a bit of a mix. There's the amazing black-and-white ink drawings of Tove Jansson, or the expressiveness of the Italian Futurists. Then there's the effective simpleness of the works of Dick Bruna or the downright disarming charm of the drawings of Josef Lada. And of course there are many of my contemporaries like Leonie Bos or Charlotte Dumortier.

My first big inspiration, however, was my mother, who used to show me these amazing drawings she had once done of birds and gnomes. She didn't end up working in the creative field, but definitely had a hand in me ending up in it.

What does a typical working day look like?
I wake up to the sound of my (early-rising) boyfriend preparing breakfast: oatmeal porridge. I'll start working around 8:30, unless I have an early deadline, in which case I'll rise at an ungodly hour and eat breakfast after having finished. I tend to be more productive and focused in the mornings, so this is when any conceptual work or sketching is done. Communication with clients and the actual painting of the finals is reserved for after lunch.

Usually I'll start with a new brief at 9am, go through the research and jot down some ideas in thumbnail sketches. At around half past ten I'll be craving a coffee, and there will usually be a small debate between me and my boyfriend (who also works from home) on who will be the one to make it. We will sit together with our coffee and discuss our projects for the day. Usually this is where I pitch those thumbnail ideas to him to get a feel of which would work best with the client. After having chosen one or more ideas, I'll work those out in a neater sketch and present them to the client.

When lunchtime comes around, and it's a particularly pleasant day, we'll pack a picnic and either hike to the top of the little mountain our village is situated on, or descend from said mountain to the little lake below to have a swim and cool down during the hottest hours of the day. If I'm lucky, by the time I get back behind my computer the client will have reviewed my sketches and I can proceed with finishing the illustration. I usually keep painting until it's finished –

Spotlight SUMMER 2020 31

Strengthen text's left alignment

You may need to nudge the headline's frame left of the margin so large text aligns horizontally with the body copy (b). Aim to align strong elements of the leftmost characters visually to equivalent strokes in body text, with serifs overhanging. For characters that lead with a curve, such as a C, or a weak element, such as a T or J, judge the alignment by eye.

Add a standfirst and pull-quotes

1 Below the headline, add another text frame with the **Square** wrap style to contain a standfirst (intro paragraph) (c).

2 Add magazine_profile_standfirst.rtf to the frame using **File > Place**.

3 Apply the *-SP- Standfirst Sans* paragraph style. In turn, this applies the *-SP- SmallCapsRegular* character style to the initial words.

4 On the **Text Frame Panel**, check **Use Baseline Grid** to override the document-wide one.

5 Enter *6 mm* next to **Grid Spacing**.

6 For **Start position**, how type fits vertically depends on font metrics. Experiment till you find what looks right. I used *4.5 mm*.

When creating a standfirst style with a text size larger than your body text, you may need to make its leading an intermediate size—larger than your baseline grid value would accommodate, but smaller than double it. I used *6 mm* (1.5x).

On the article's third page, repeat this procedure to add a text frame for magazine_profile_pullquote.rtf, styled using *-SP- Pullquote SerifItalic* and its baseline grid starting at *6 mm* and spacing of *8 mm*.

Adjust the height of column rules that intersect the three text frames you just created so they stop short, leaving a gap dictated by your background grid.

Your pages should now look like magazine_profile_structure.afpub, minus the large empty picture frames.

Add your images

For these steps, it's crucial that the background grid is visible and snapping to it is turned on.

1 On the article's first page, use the **Picture Frame Rectangle Tool** (F) to draw a frame from above the right column rule to the bleed area's top-right corner on the right page and about half the page's height.

2 Apply a **Square** text wrap and set **Distance From Text** to your baseline spacing.

3 Place magazine_profile_EleniDebo_Raimondas.jpg in the frame. Position and size the image within the frame as you wish.

4 Repeat for additional picture frames as shown in magazine_profile_completed.afpub.

INSPIRATION

Drawing the news: an artist's story

ELENI DEBO IS a Belgian illustrator who freelances from the breathtaking Italian Alps. Her work regularly features in international newspapers, books and magazines and she has an incredible talent for distilling complex stories and subject matter into a single thought-provoking image.

Fresh from winning a prestigious World Illustration Award, Eleni talks to us about her *Spotlight* submission piece (created in Affinity Photo), how she got into editorial illustration and why she loves to combine and mix analogue and digital painting in her work.

Firstly, congratulations on winning the professional editorial category in the World Illustration Awards 2019! Could you tell us a bit about your entry and what the award means to you?
Thanks! I submitted 'When to stop', a three page editorial illustration I made for Belgian newspaper *De Morgen* in the wake of the #metoo movement and the viral short story 'Cat Person' by Kirsten Roupenian. The article dealt with the dilemma of how even consensual sex can turn bad, and the taboos involved.

Based on the story of Roupenian, my illustration reads as the story of a sexual experience slowly turning bad. I tried to represent this in the gradual removal of colour and the evolution of soft and flowy to sharp and aggressive shapes. The passage of time and the feeling of movement is suggested by showing fragmented scenes both flowing into and disrupting each other.

Winning the award with this work was a wonderful surprise to me. For the past year I have been setting my sights on new horizons, hoping to attract overseas clients. By participating in the contest, I had hoped to at least catch the eye of a few people involved. Actually winning my category has, aside from a pleasant confidence boost, definitely opened doors for me professionally, and will go a long way towards reaching my goal.

What inspired you to submit this particular illustration?
It's always such a pleasure for me to illustrate for *De Morgen*, as they give me a lot of freedom to work with a subject. So I felt confident to approach this assignment somewhat more experimentally. Despite the deadline, I ended up really having fun working on this illustration, and the end result was exactly as I had wanted it to be. I felt like this illustration represented my abilities, both visually and conceptually, especially given the delicate nature of the subject, and it remains to this day one of my favourite editorial pieces.

Your work regularly appears in international newspapers and magazines. How did you first get into editorial illustration?
When I finished my studies at the academy, I knew I wanted to get involved with editorial illustration and had in particular set my sights on De *Morgen*, as they had a very decently designed newspaper and weren't afraid of experimenting with their visuals. I decided that, while having a part time job in an awesome little letterpress studio, I would spend that first year out of school working on a strong portfolio.

I bought a random newspaper, chose a variety of articles (going from psychological and human interest to economics and politics) and got to work illustrating them. Once I was confident my portfolio was strong enough, I sent them to different potential clients, including the art director of *De Morgen*, making sure to include an honest handwritten note explaining why I wanted to work for them.

De Morgen was actually the first client to contact me upon receiving my portfolio. Our first collaboration was a successful one, and I ended up working for them almost weekly. This kind of exposure turned out to be huge, and very soon other clients started trickling in. Before I knew it, I had enough work on my hands to start working full-time as an illustrator, and things have been trucking along rather pleasantly ever since.

How would you describe your style?
I would say that, for me, the important part of my illustration is the concept, and the style of the illustration is often chosen as a function of how to best represent that idea. That being said, I suppose there are some common factors, stylewise. My work often shows a mix of analogue and digital painting, which does give it a signature noisy/painterly feel. I developed a range of brushes based on my favourite analogue painting techniques to further blend the line between the analogue and the digital.

In terms of content, shadow and light play a big role in my illustrations and are often a determining factor for the mood of the image. Other than that, I've noted people often saying that I have a rather particular use of colour. To be honest, I always felt like I am having a hard time choosing a palette (which is something I could keep going back and forth on for hours, given the opportunity), but perhaps that might just be the exact reason why people find it so particular. Perhaps a classic case of weaknesses becoming strengths.

When starting a new illustration, do you normally have access to the full article your work will accompany?
It depends. For the daily news, I often just get the six-sentence pitch of the journalist describing the article. So in the same time I'll be illustrating this embryonic article, the journalist will be actually writing it. For weekend publications, or opinion pieces, it does happen that I get the full article or a proof of some sort. In some cases, however, I just get the phone number of the journalist and the message to go find out whatever it is I need to

30

SUMMER 2020 Spotlight

Spotlight SUMMER 2020

31

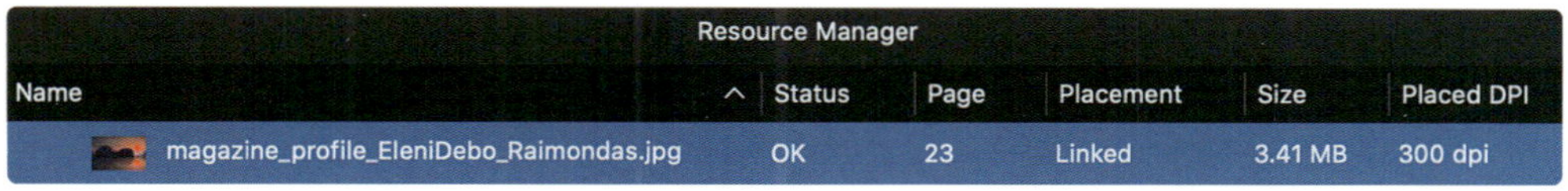

5 Apply a **Tight** text wrap to the picture frame for magazine_profile_EleniDebo_PublicServants.jpg.

6 Click **Back One** on the **Toolbar** to arrange this picture frame's layer behind the affected text frame, so the JPEG's lack of transparent pixels does not cause text to be obscured.

7 Edit the wrap outline (p. 128). It needn't match mine exactly.

8 Adjust the heights of your column rules.

The gap created by a **Tight** wrap outline should again relate to your baseline grid spacing, so all gaps look similar.

and eat breakfast after having finished. I tend to be more productive and focused in the mornings, so this is when any conceptual work or sketching is done. Communication with clients and the actual painting of the finals is reserved for after lunch.

Usually I'll start with a new brief at 9am, go through the research and jot down some ideas in thumbnail sketches. At around half past ten I'll be craving a coffee, and there will usually be a small debate between me and my boyfriend (who also works from home) on who will be the one to make it. We will sit together with our coffee and discuss our projects for the day. Usually this is where I pitch those thumbnail ideas to him to get a feel of which would work best with the client. After having chosen one or more ideas, I'll work those out in a neater sketch and present them to the client.

When lunchtime comes around, and it's a particularly pleasant day, we'll pack a picnic and either hike to the top of the little mountain our village is situated on, or descend from said mountain to the little lake below to have a swim and cool down during the hottest hours of the day. If I'm lucky, by the time I get back behind my computer the client will have reviewed my sketches and I can proceed with finishing the illustration.

I usually keep painting until it's finished – I hate getting interrupted during the process – or if it's a particularly labour-intensive illustration, until I get too hungry. If all goes well, I stop working between 18:00 and 19:00.

After dinner, I spend some time relaxing or meeting up with friends before going to bed and waking up to the sound of my boyfriend making oatmeal porridge. Rinse and repeat.

You've worked for an impressive variety of clients around the world. What have been some of your favourite projects so far?

My work on the book *Shoplifter* by German art and design book publisher Gestalten is definitely way up there on the list. I also very much enjoy working regularly for the beautifully designed Belgian cycling magazine *Bahamontes*, or the American, equally aesthetic but more spiritually

▲ Illustration for the Dutch newspaper *De Volkskrant*

Working for the *New Yorker* or the *New York Times* is of course up there on my list, as illustrating for those iconic covers is probably any editorial illustrator's dream. That being said, I'd love illustrating for any publication that tries to push boundaries with the use of its visuals.

In a more modest aspiration, I've been

Image resolution

When an image on a page is selected, its pixel dimensions and effective resolution are shown on the context toolbar. Only the dpi (dots per inch) figure matters.

If it's under 300 dpi, the image file has insufficient resolution and should be made smaller on the page for professional print quality. For some images, such as computer screenshots, lower dpi is normal, but prepress systems typically give errors below 300 dpi, which you may need to ask your printer to override.

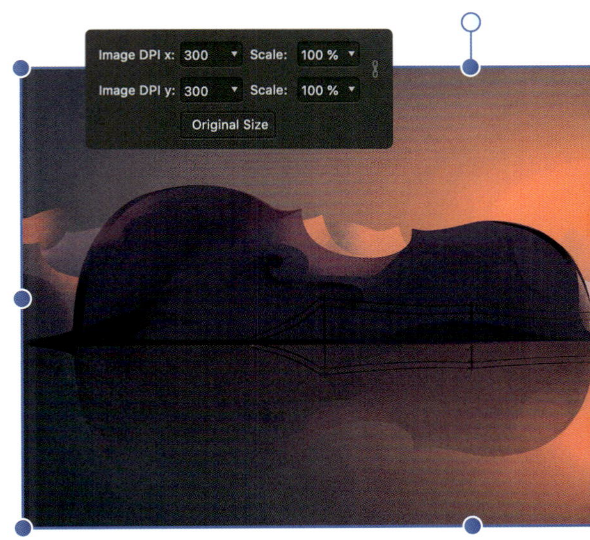

Images provided in this project have reduced resolution for licensing reasons

Final touches

Add credits

1. Copy the credit line (a) from magazine_profile_ captions_credits.rtf and paste it into a new text frame with a height of *4 mm*.
2. Apply the *-SP- Credit* text style.
3. Set the frame to ignore the document's baseline grid and text wraps.
4. Select *Illustrations* and *Interview* and apply the *Bold* font style.
5. Rotate the text frame *90°* left and run it up the left of the first illustration, snapped to the background grid.

> Use the commands in **View > Rotate** to comfortably edit vertical text.

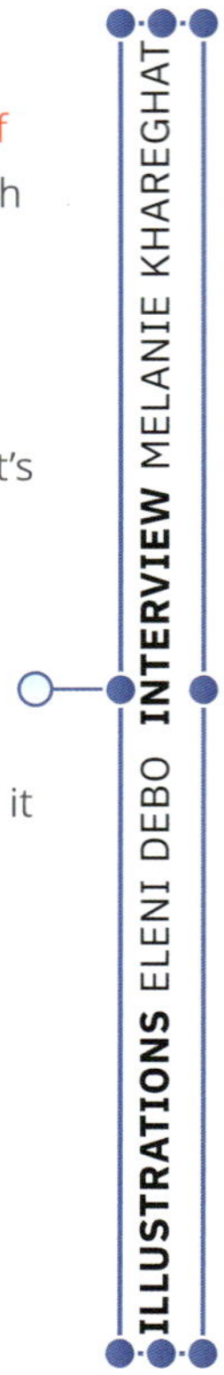

Add captions

Use the text frames in each page's centre column for captions (b). As discussed earlier, make these frames 4 mm narrower than the column guides to increase the gap each side by 2 mm. Duplicate and resize a caption text frame for each picture.

1. Copy each caption from the previous text file and paste into the corresponding text frame.
2. Apply the *-SP- CaptionArrowUp* or *-SP- CaptionArrowDown* text style as appropriate.

> My caption text styles use **Bullets and Numbering** settings to prefix an arrow. Use the **Glyph Browser** to see if a font contains arrows. If not, copy and paste from another font you're licensed to publish. I used Arial.

or daily news, I often just get
e six-sentence pitch describing
e article. The journalist will be
iting it as I'm illustrating it"

tration for
lgian
le magazine
Weekend

We were delighted to hear that you use Affinity as part of your workflow. How did you discover the apps and what inspired you to start using them?
After having spent countless evenings as a young kid entertaining myself with drawing in MS Paint, discovering a program like Photoshop as a teenager effectively propelled my love for digital painting, even if this was not the primary function of the software. When, years later, my boyfriend introduced me to the launch of this promising new software suite called Affinity – similar to Adobe, but seemingly better and definitely more democratically priced – I quickly fell in love all over again.

Given my familiarity with Photoshop, I was most attracted to switch to Affinity Photo, and although illustration might not be its main focus (as opposed to, say, Designer), I discovered that the software was perfect for my workflow of mixing scanned analogue painting with digital painting. I have been working with the Affinity software for a few years now, and I'm definitely not regretting my decision!

What do you like most about Affinity apps?
Live previews of blending modes and brushes have been a game changer. It has without a doubt greatly improved the speed of my workflow. Other than that, there's Affinity Photo for iPad, which has definitely appealed to my cocooning habits: drawing while sitting on the couch wrapped in a comfy blanket, count me in!

What are your greatest influences and inspirations?
I suppose it's a bit of a mix. There's the amazing black-and-white ink drawings of Tove Jansson, or the expressiveness of the Italian Futurists. Then there's the effective simpleness of the works of Dick Bruna or the downright disarming charm of the drawings of Josef Lada. And of course there are many of my contemporaries like Leonie Bos or Charlotte Dumortier.

My first big inspiration, however, was my mother, who used to show me these amazing drawings she had once done of birds and gnomes. She didn't end up working in the creative field, but definitely had a hand in me ending up in it.

What does a typical working day look like?
I wake up to the sound of my (early-rising) boyfriend preparing breakfast: oatmeal porridge. I'll start working around 8:30, unless I have an early deadline, in which case I'll rise at an ungodly hour and eat breakfast after having finished. I tend to be more productive and focused in the mornings, so this is when any conceptual work or sketching is done. Communication with clients and the actual painting of the finals is reserved for after lunch.

Usually I'll start with a new brief at 9am, go through the research and jot down some ideas in thumbnail sketches. At around half past ten I'll be craving a coffee, and there will usually be a small debate between me and my boyfriend (who also works from home) on who will be the one to make it. We will sit together with our coffee and discuss our projects for the day. Usually this is where I pitch those thumbnail ideas to him to get a feel of which would work best with the client. After having chosen one or more ideas, I'll work those out in a neater sketch and present them to the client.

When lunchtime comes around, and it's a particularly pleasant day, we'll pack a picnic and either hike to the top of the little mountain our village is situated on, or descend from said mountain to the little lake below to have a swim and cool down during the hottest hours of the day. If I'm lucky, by the time I get back behind my computer the client will have reviewed my sketches and I can proceed with finishing the illustration.

I usually keep painting until it's finished – I hate getting interrupted during the process – or if ... ularly labour-inte... until I get too... stop work...

SUMMER 2020 **Spotlight**

...ew *Yorker* or the *New York Times* ...e on my list, as illustrating for ... is probably any editorial illus- ...t being said, I'd love illus- ...ication that tries to push ... use of its visuals. ...est aspiration, I've been ...nds on a commission to do ... much fun to make bigge... and I'd love an opportun... interact with an actual envi... of a layout. So if anyone has an ...g around, give me a call! •

33

End marks

Many magazines display an end mark (c) at the end of articles. I've used a bullet (**Text > Insert > Symbols > Bullet**) and created a character style (*-SP- Bullet Endstop*) that applies distinctive italicisation and colour.

Bullets are small in many fonts. Your character style may need to increase the font size and shift the **Baseline** (**Character Panel**) to realign with lower-case text.

Knowing when to finish

You've laid out a professional-looking magazine article, but how do you judge that your layout is finished?

- Use **Preview Mode** to follow the text flow with your eyes. After each column, the reader will look up and to the right, then down that column. Will they find the next column easily?
- Check balance and hierarchy, in terms of contrasts and diagonals, e.g. our first spread has a small image at the bottom left and a large image at the top right.
- Avoid similar elements sitting side by side—image beside image, headline beside headline—unless you're arranging them this way for a reason.
- Check elements that break up the page, like cross headings and pull-quotes, are serving that purpose, not just adding clutter and clashing with others.

Never be afraid to duplicate a finished layout and completely tear it up to see if you missed a better approach.

LAY OUT A TUTORIAL ARTICLE

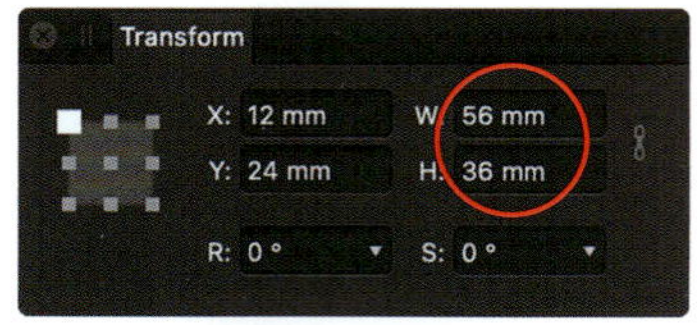

Step-by-step tutorials are common in magazines. Let's set up a grid for one.

1 In your existing document, add a new master page with the default settings.

2 Apply *Master A* to it by dragging. We'll override Master A's column guides and margins.

3 In the **Guides Manager**, set **Columns** and **Rows** to *3* (a nine-steps-per-page grid) and **Gutter** to *8 mm*.

4 Set the bottom margin to *29 mm* to leave room for text frames containing extra information and a pull-quote.

5 In the top-left column 'block', draw a *36 mm* tall picture frame and a text frame below it, with a *4 mm* gap between them.

6 Insert filler text, expand it, then apply the *-SP- Step Sans* paragraph style. Remove any unwanted line breaks.

7 On the **Text Frame Panel**, ensure **Use Baseline Grid** and **Ignore Baseline Grid** are unchecked so the frame does not override the document's baseline grid.

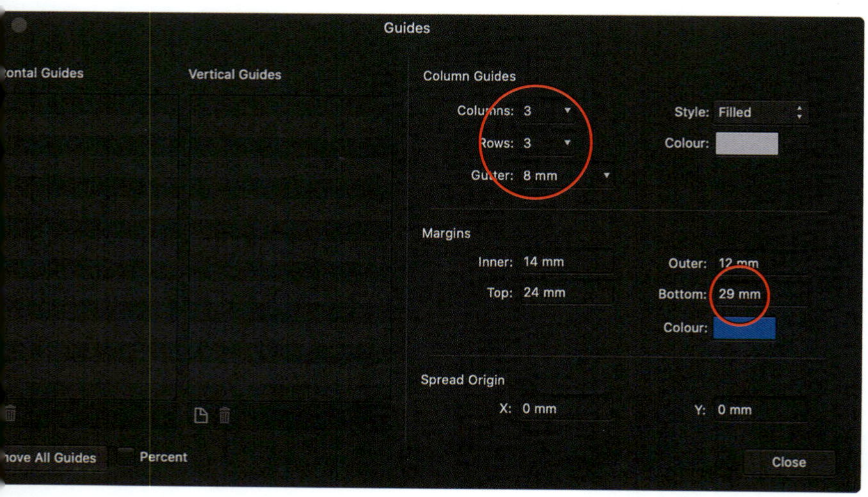

Resource
Tutorial_Article folder

Numbering the steps

1 Type *1* at the start of the filler text and select it.

2 Apply the Chivo Black font at *8.75 pt* and the *-SP- Blue* colour from magazine_palette.afpalette. (Import it using the **Swatches Panel**.)

3 Create a character style from this, called *-SP- Step Number*.

4 Edit the *-SP- Step Sans* paragraph style.

5 Under **Drop Caps**, set the options as shown in the screenshot.

6 Check **Enabled** and click **OK**.

1 Maecenas eu diam a leo porta interdum. In non massa quis odio feugiat sagittis. Quisque ac lorem. Maecenas ut sem sed ipsum suscipit malesuada. Nulla quis dui quis ante fermentum interdum. Proin eget est a augue vehicula mattis. Pellentesque sed nisi at nisi scelerisque iaculis. Phasellus orci. Nulla adipiscing. Suspendisse et leo

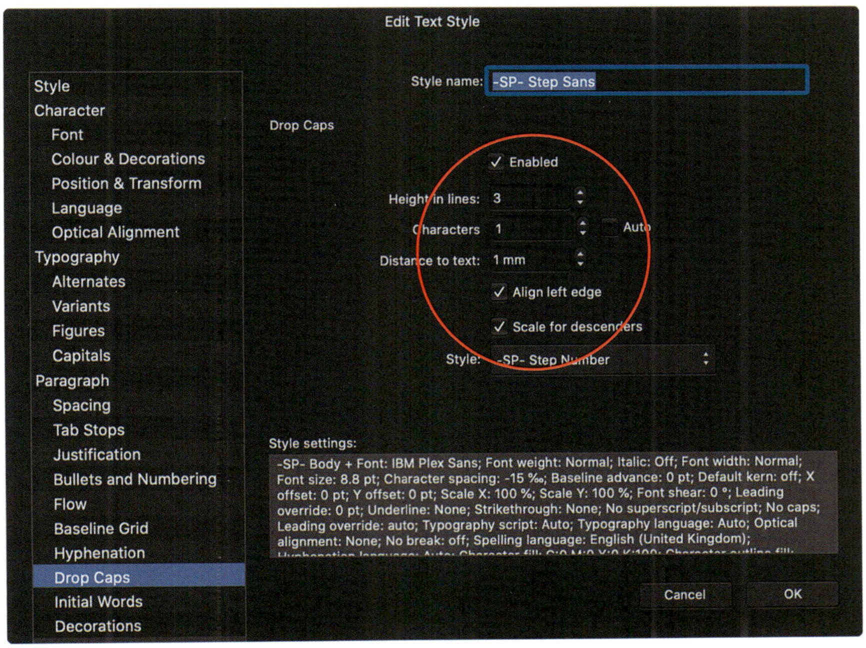

When step numbers reach two digits, simply increase the **Characters** value under **Drop Caps** on the **Paragraph Panel**.

Complete the layout

1 Select the picture and text frame.

2 Copy them to the next guide 'block'.

3 Repeat until the page has nine steps.

Add finishing touches, like for the profile article. I deleted the first two steps to make room for a headline and standfirst, and varied the steps on the right page, adding a larger one to give the spread a focal point. I manually drew horizontal decorative lines akin to the profile article's column rules.

Apply this master to two new facing publication pages. The inherited text and picture frames are placeholders; practice filling them using the provided image and text resources. I set tracking for each step's text to *-15‰* to get it to fit (p. 170).

Your result should look like the pages in magazine_tutorial_completed.afpub. Finish styling the text, using the publication pages in the above .afpub file as a guide.

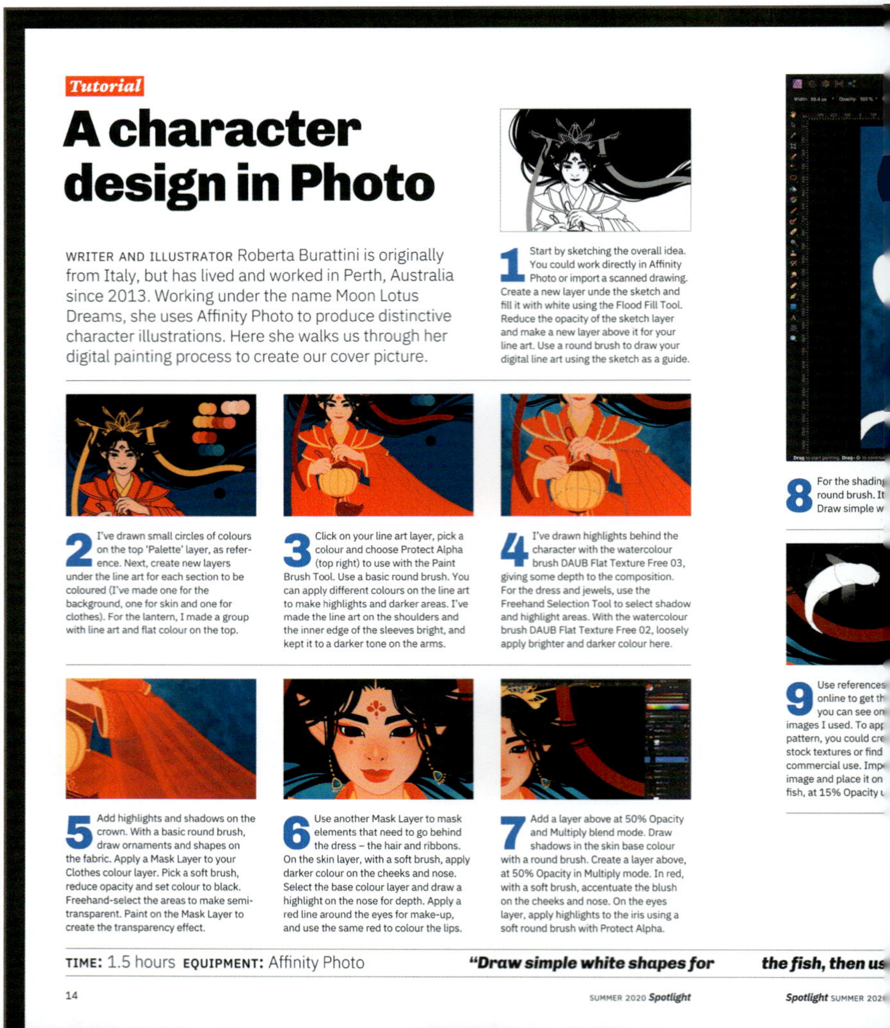
Tutorial

A character design in Photo

WRITER AND ILLUSTRATOR Roberta Burattini is originally from Italy, but has lived and worked in Perth, Australia since 2013. Working under the name Moon Lotus Dreams, she uses Affinity Photo to produce distinctive character illustrations. Here she walks us through her digital painting process to create our cover picture.

1 Start by sketching the overall idea. You could work directly in Affinity Photo or import a scanned drawing. Create a new layer unde the sketch and fill it with white using the Flood Fill Tool. Reduce the opacity of the sketch layer and make a new layer above it for your line art. Use a round brush to draw your digital line art using the sketch as a guide.

2 I've drawn small circles of colours on the top 'Palette' layer, as reference. Next, create new layers under the line art for each section to be coloured (I've made one for the background, one for skin and one for clothes). For the lantern, I made a group with line art and flat colour on the top.

3 Click on your line art layer, pick a colour and choose Protect Alpha (top right) to use with the Paint Brush Tool. Use a basic round brush. You can apply different colours on the line art to make highlights and darker areas. I've made the line art on the shoulders and the inner edge of the sleeves bright, and kept it to a darker tone on the arms.

4 I've drawn highlights behind the character with the watercolour brush DAUB Flat Texture Free 03, giving some depth to the composition. For the dress and jewels, use the Freehand Selection Tool to select shadow and highlight areas. With the watercolour brush DAUB Flat Texture Free 02, loosely apply brighter and darker colour here.

5 Add highlights and shadows on the crown. With a basic round brush, draw ornaments and shapes on the fabric. Apply a Mask Layer to your Clothes colour layer. Pick a soft brush, reduce opacity and set colour to black. Freehand-select the areas to make semi-transparent. Paint on the Mask Layer to create the transparency effect.

6 Use another Mask Layer to mask elements that need to go behind the dress – the hair and ribbons. On the skin layer, with a soft brush, apply darker colour on the cheeks and nose. Select the base colour layer and draw a highlight on the nose for depth. Apply a red line around the eyes for make-up, and use the same red to colour the lips.

7 Add a layer above at 50% Opacity and Multiply blend mode. Draw shadows in the skin base colour with a round brush. Create a layer above, at 50% Opacity in Multiply mode. In red, with a soft brush, accentuate the blush on the cheeks and nose. On the eyes layer, apply highlights to the iris using a soft round brush with Protect Alpha.

8 For the shadin round brush. It Draw simple w

9 Use references online to get th you can see on images I used. To app pattern, you could cre stock textures or find commercial use. Imp image and place it on fish, at 15% Opacity

TIME: 1.5 hours EQUIPMENT: Affinity Photo

"Draw simple white shapes for the fish, then us

14 SUMMER 2020 *Spotlight* | *Spotlight* SUMMER 202

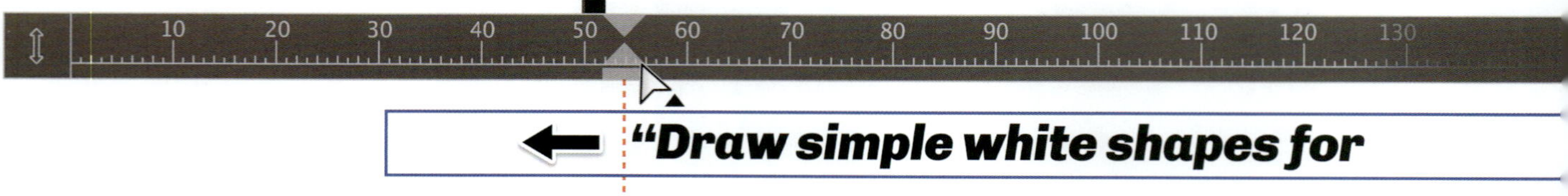

With a thin, stapled document you needn't make allowance for the pull-quote running across the spine, but with a thick, perfect-bound magazine some leeway is required. That means splitting the text to avoid the area.

Positioning involves some guesswork. I inserted a **Right Indent Tab** (**Text > Insert > Spaces and Tabs**) and dragged the text ruler's left indent marker to move the left portion of the text.

Hold the option ⌥ key (Mac) or alt key (Win) to override snapping to the text ruler's notches.

Rather than link the text frames and flow in all the text, you may find it easier to copy step text individually and use **Edit > Paste Without Format** to preserve the style applied at the insertion point in Affinity Publisher.

Reusable assets

Having built a repeating design element (such as a tutorial step), group its objects, select the group and choose **Add from Selection** from a category's menu on the **Assets Panel**.

Now you can drag the element from the Assets Panel onto pages as required.

Select **Embed in current document** from the panel's preferences menu to store assets in your magazine document(s).

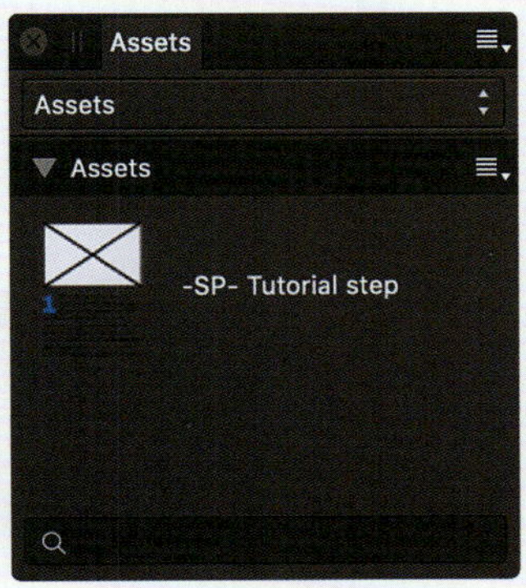

Review_Article folder

LAY OUT A REVIEW PAGE

Many magazines feature product reviews. For this, I applied my five-column master (Master A) to two new publication pages, then copied and adjusted elements from my previous layouts.

Use **Document > Add Pages from File** to append all pages from magazine_review_start.afpub to your document. They contain pre-placed text and image elements you know how to create already. Note the new ones.

- Breaking up the body text are 'cross headings', small subheadings in a sans-serif font slightly larger and bolder than the body. Inspect paragraph style *-SP- Crosshead* to see my choices.
- An italicised and bolder character style, *-SP- Signoff*, is used for the byline text (reviewer's name). This text is right-aligned by inserting a **Right Indent Tab** character before it.

The key visual addition is the text frames with a background colour, or 'tint', and an indent on the centre column guides, for fragmentary info such as product specs, pros and cons, and a rating. Informational text like this will often 'hang' at whatever length is required, rather than filling its column.

1 There's already a one-column text frame on the left page's centre column guide. I've made it *4 mm* wider than the guide as we won't add column rules here.

2 Select the frame. It has no fill colour as we'll use a paragraph decoration to fill behind the text, which ensures the background height automatically matches the number of lines. So, you won't have to adjust the frame's height wherever this effect is used.

3 Apply the *-SP- TintBox Sans* paragraph style to the frame.

4 Open magazine_review_left_box.rtf. Retype its contents in the frame. The blue will expand with the text.

5 Apply the *-SP- TintBox Head Blue* paragraph style to the first line, *Bold* to subheadings, and other local formatting as you like.

6 On the **Text Frame Panel**, check **Ignore Text Wraps**. Set all **Insets** to *4 mm* (our baseline grid spacing).

Key info

Price
From £799
Tested: £1,399 with Intel Core i5, 16GB memory, 256GB SSD

Display
12.3-inch 10-point touchscreen with 2736x1824 pixels

Connectivity
Wi-Fi 6, Bluetooth 5.0, 1x USB-A, 1x USB-C, 3.5mm headphone jack, microSDXC reader, Surface Connect port, Surface Type Cover port

The blue 'fill' comes from *-SP- TintBox Sans*. Edit it and select **Decorations** under **Paragraph** to fill the frame background with blue. The settings put a band of colour behind each line of text, forming a block. The text frame's insets have been subtracted from each **Indent** value to fill the inset area with colour too.

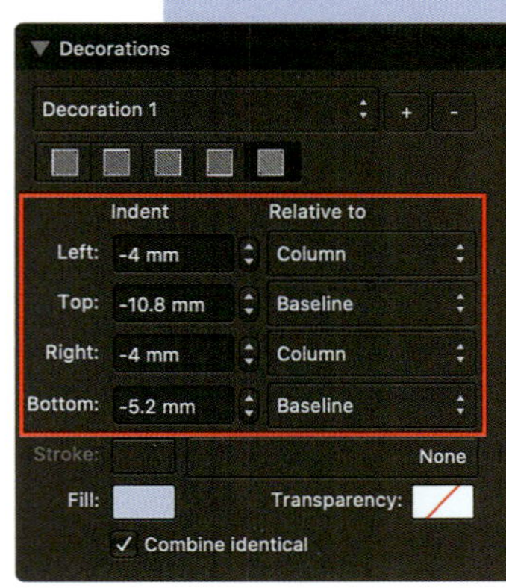

You may need to align the fill vertically to the page's grid (or any horizontal guides) by adjusting **Top** and **Bottom**, adding as much to one as you subtract from the other. If you use a larger font size for the first line, it might jump down to the next baseline, bringing the fill with it. If so, subtract your baseline grid value from **Top** to fill in the top line.

To ensure black text is legible against your coloured background, keep the background's total CMYK value under 50%. Or, use white text on a darker colour.

Creating a star rating

The equivalent text frame on the review's right page uses a few different styles (*-SP- TintBox Head Red*, *-SP- TintBox Reviews Pro* and *-SP- TintBox Reviews Con*). Apply the procedure to the text from magazine_review_right_box.rtf.

There's a new element to add here, a star rating that you'll recreate.

1 Make the layer named *Star* visible. I drew this shape with the **Star Tool** and used **Layer > Convert to Curves** to refine it.

2 Hold option ⌥ + shift ⇧ (Mac) or alt + shift (Win) and drag the star right to make an aligned copy.

3 Press cmd ⌘ + J (Mac) or ctrl + J (Win). Repeat till you have a row of five stars.

4 Group the stars and scale the group to fit the centre column's text frame.

5 Cut the group, place the insertion point on an empty line in the text frame and paste. This inline graphic will move as text is added or deleted.

Change the stars' fill colours to create ratings out of five as needed.

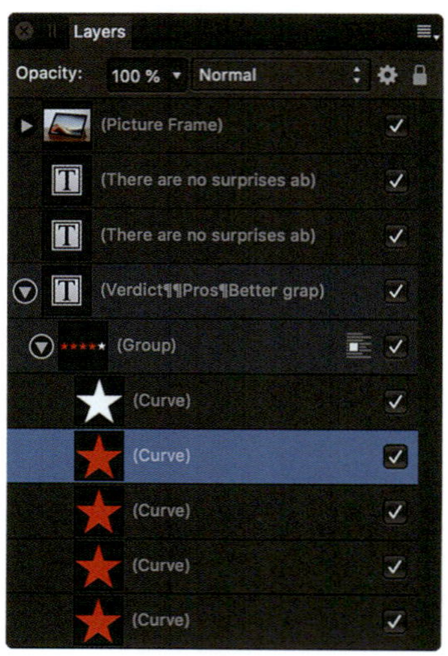

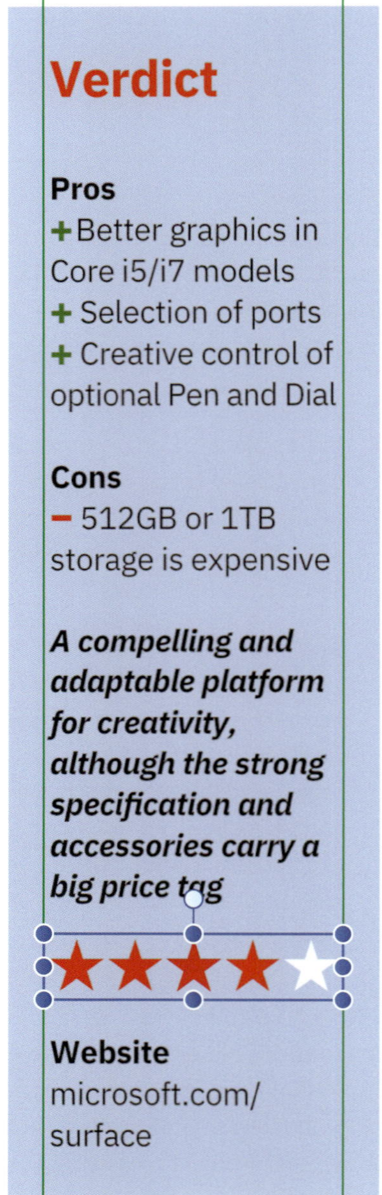

Decorating running heads

The styling of the 'Review' slug is incomplete compared to earlier articles. There should be a coloured bar (in red) that extends only to the text's length, with some breathing space all around the lettering.

1 Select the word and set its **Font Colour** to *White* (*CMYK 0,0,0,0*).

2 Under **Decorations** on the **Paragraph Panel**, select the **Fill** position, and set **Fill** colour to the red swatch imported earlier (p. 248).

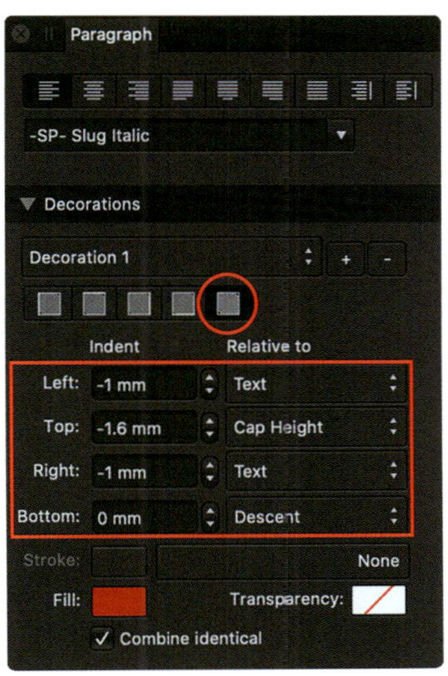

3 For the **Left** and **Right** indents, select *Text* under **Relative to**.

4 For the **Top** indent, select **Cap Height** (or **Ascent**).

5 For the **Bottom** indent, use **Descent** (or **Baseline**).

6 Adjust the indent values so there's comfortable space around the text.

You can compare my indents in the *-SP Slug Italic-* and *-SP- Slug Sans Caps* paragraph styles. (When a headline is italicised the non-italic slug is intended to be used for contrast, and vice versa.)

If these styles didn't exist, you'd create them from your styled text at this point.

Mixing colours

- When picking colours for objects like slugs and tint boxes, avoid CMYK ink values very close to 0% or 100%, which print unpredictably.
- Don't exceed 300% in total across all four inks.
- For a solidly printed colour, include 100% of at least one ink. Most text and fine rules should always be set in 100% K only. Publisher will overprint black by default on PDF CMYK exports.
- If you arrange with the printer to use a spot colour, an extra ink that adds a colour or effect outside the CMYK range, select it from a PANTONE® palette and check **Spot** when adding it as a global colour.
- When applying a colour, use **Add Global Colour** from the **Swatches Panel**'s preferences to save it in your document, and always apply global colours to objects. Then you can easily change colours throughout your magazine.

Resource
Welcome_Page folder

LAY OUT A WELCOME PAGE

Many magazines include a welcome page showing a letter from the editor, summarising contents or giving an opinion.

This may be accompanied by a masthead, or 'flannel panel', showing publisher and staff details and the 'imprint', a statement of the name and address of the printer —legally required in the UK—and other legal notices.

I've divided a page based on my five-column grid into two unequal parts. The welcome letter is in the larger part. It uses a larger font size than our usual body text and so overrides the document's baseline grid with appropriate spacing to avoid large gaps between lines.

Using **Document > Add Pages from File**, insert all pages from magazine_welcome_start.afpub after page 1 of your document.

Adding a staff list

1 Use the **Frame Text Tool** to put the insertion point in the empty text frame on the right and select the *-SP- Staff List* paragraph style.

2 Type the first job title, press the Tab key, type the incumbent's name and press the Return ↲ key.

3 Repeat step 2 to finish your first block of staff details.

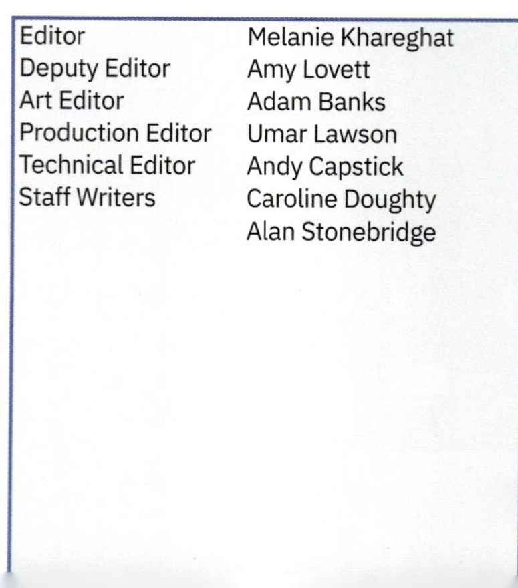

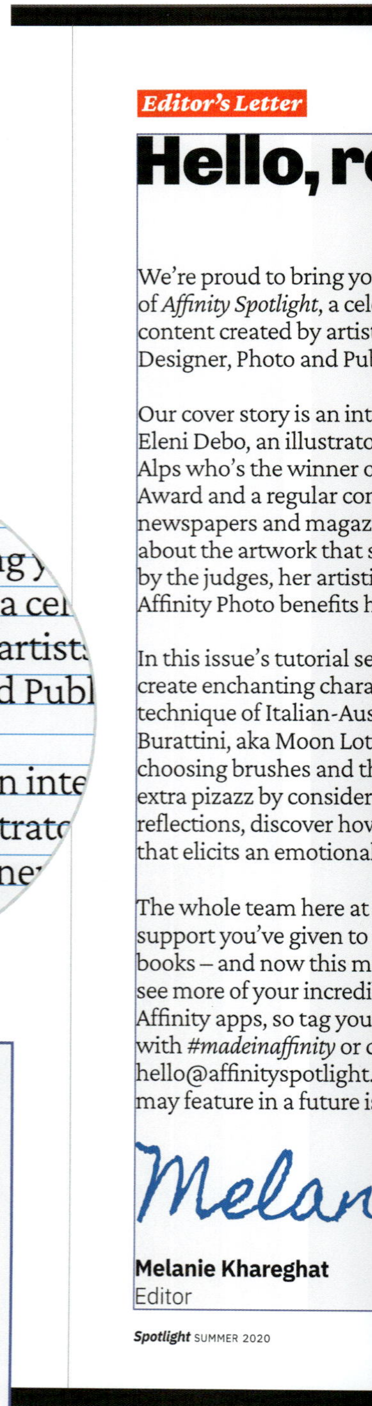

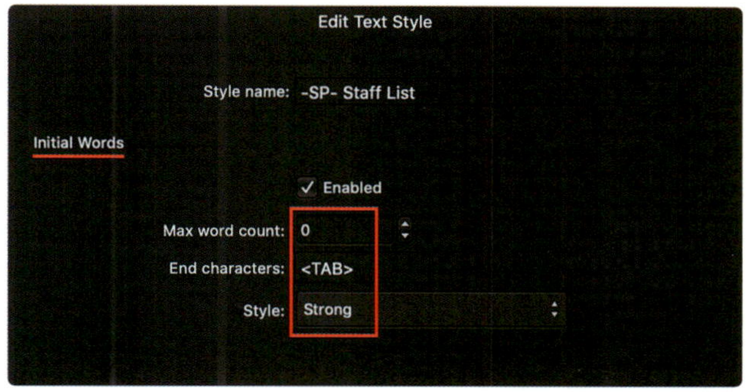

4 Copy a tab character from between a title/name pair. (Use **Text > Show Special Characters** to do this more easily.)

5 Edit the *-SP- Staff List* style. Under **Initial Words**, paste the tab character over the default **End characters**.

6 Set **Max word count** to *0*.

7 Set **Style** to *Strong* so job titles are emboldened but names aren't. To use additional formatting, make a character style and apply it instead.

8 Check **Enabled** and click **OK**.

9 Select **View > Show Text Ruler**. On the text frame's ruler, click to place a tab stop. All of the names align to the tab stop; drag it to a position that looks good.

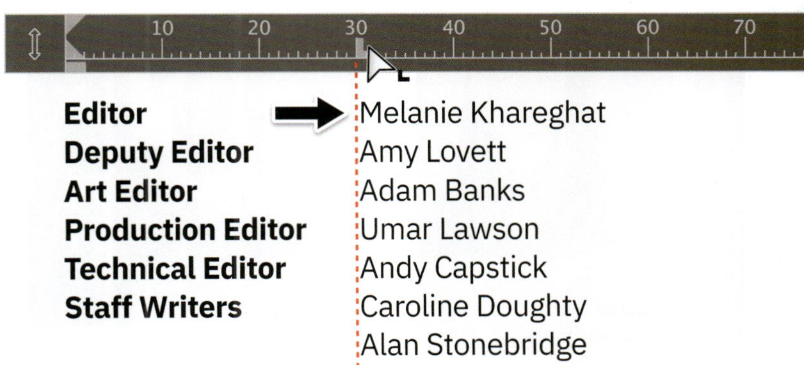

Adding headshot photos

For a human touch, add headshot photos of key staff.

1 Above the staff list, draw two *32 mm* by *36 mm* picture frames.

2 Select the left frame, then select **File > Place** and choose magazine_staff_pics_amy.jpg. Scale/position the image similar to the example below the letter.

3 Effects can make photos shot in non-matching conditions look consistent. Select the picture frame you just populated and press cmd ⌘ + J (Mac)/ ctrl + J (Win) to duplicate it.

4 Double-click the copy and press Backspace to remove the image. With the copy selected, use the **Swatches Panel** to apply our document palette's *-SP- Blue*.

5 On the **Toolbar**, select **Back One**.

6 On the **Layers Panel**, set the populated picture frame's blend mode to *Linear Light*.

7 These photos have a near-white background, so I clicked the cogwheel and dragged the **Source Layer Ranges**' right (**Out**) handle to *80%*, so the other frame's colour fills in.

8 To restore detail and flesh tone, duplicate the populated picture frame again and set the new copy's blend mode to *Darken*.

Repeat for the other picture frame and magazine_staff_pics_umar.jpg. Remember, you can use **Edit > Copy** and **Edit > Paste Style** to replicate effects from one object to another.

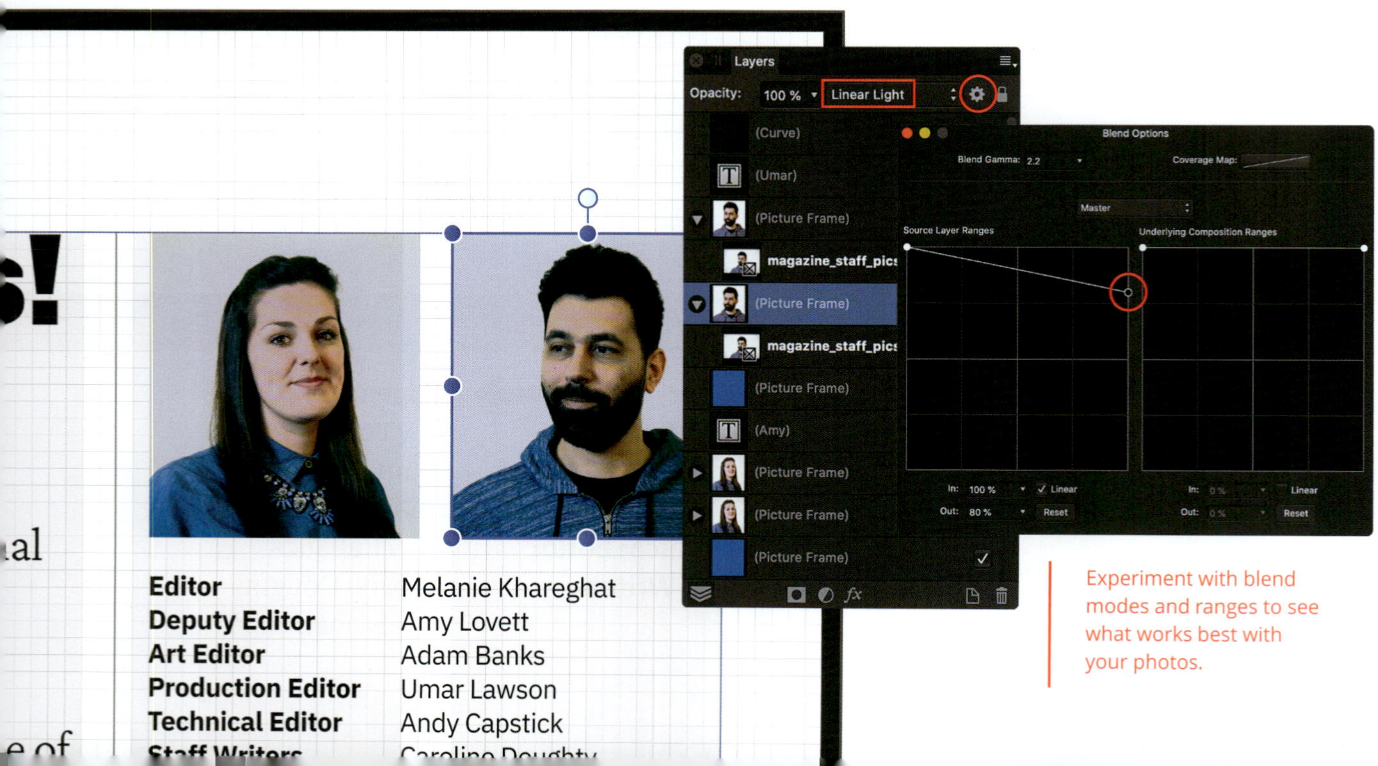

Experiment with blend modes and ranges to see what works best with your photos.

The name tags are implemented using paragraph decorations, like with section slugs (p. 249), though via the **Paragraph Panel** rather than using a text style.

LAY OUT A CONTENTS PAGE

Resource
Contents_Page folder

INSIDE

Contents

▲Learn more about this cycling illustration and other work by Eleni Debo on p. XX.

Regulars

Editor's Letter 3
Lorem ipsum dolor sit amet, adipiscum veletor

Back page 62
Ipsum dolor sit amet, lorem adipiscum veletor

News & Updates

Update your power tools 8
Biggest-ever Affinity updates bring extensive and powerful new features to desktop and tablet

New Affinity beta versions released 9
Take part in testing new features and contribute to the development of Affinity software

Learning

Artboards demystified 12
Make your workflow more effective with this in-depth explanation of a key Affinity Designer feature

A character design in Photo 14
Illustrator Moon Lotus Dreams walks us through her digital painting process in Affinity Designer

Remove haze from photos 16
Disappointed by haze dampening your scene? Affinity Photo's Haze Removal filter will fix things.

Understanding clipping in Affinity apps 20
Explore this fundamental design technique

Spotlight
Summer 2020

Inspiration

Juan Manuel Tastzian 24
A software engineer and car enthusiast's creative journey into vector illustration with Affinity Designer

Nick Liefhebber 28
Discover the inspirations of this Dutch designer's dynamic, colour-rich illustrated worlds

Eleni Debo 30
The widely published illustrator tells us about her career, methods and work-life balance

12 tips for pitching a project to photo editors 34
Esteemed photographers and editors give their insights on how to successfully pitch a project

Reviews

Surface Pro 7 38
Is Microsoft's new tablet your perfect mobile creative partner?

Behind the Scenes

Sami Hobbs 40
Exploring body-positive fashion photography with a New York-based freelance photographer

Brett Stebbins 42
Why Affinity Designer was his tool of choice for redesigning the 176 tiles of board game Suburbia

Chris Patmore 45
The story behind martial arts magazine Wing Chun Illustrated's switch to Publisher from its 50th issue

2

SUMMER 2020 *Spotlight*

Affinity Publisher's **Table of Contents** feature is unlikely to be a time-saver for magazines; it's usually simpler to type section headings, page numbers, and article titles and descriptions manually—usually on press day as you won't want to move articles around by then.

For fast working, set up paragraph styles for use exclusively on this page, even if visually identical to styles used elsewhere. We'll use the **Next style** setting to automatically switch between article title and description styles.

Insert all pages from magazine_contents_start.afpub after page 3 of your document. In the new pages' leftmost text frame, I've already typed a section name and the title and description of that section's first article.

1 Create paragraph styles from each item, named as shown in the table.

2 With the basic styles created, edit them in turn and set their **Next style** as shown in the table.

Item	Paragraph style name	Next style
Section name	-SP- Contents Section Head	-SP- Contents Bold
Article title	-SP- Contents Bold	-SP- Contents Body
Article description	-SP- Contents Body	-SP- Contents Bold

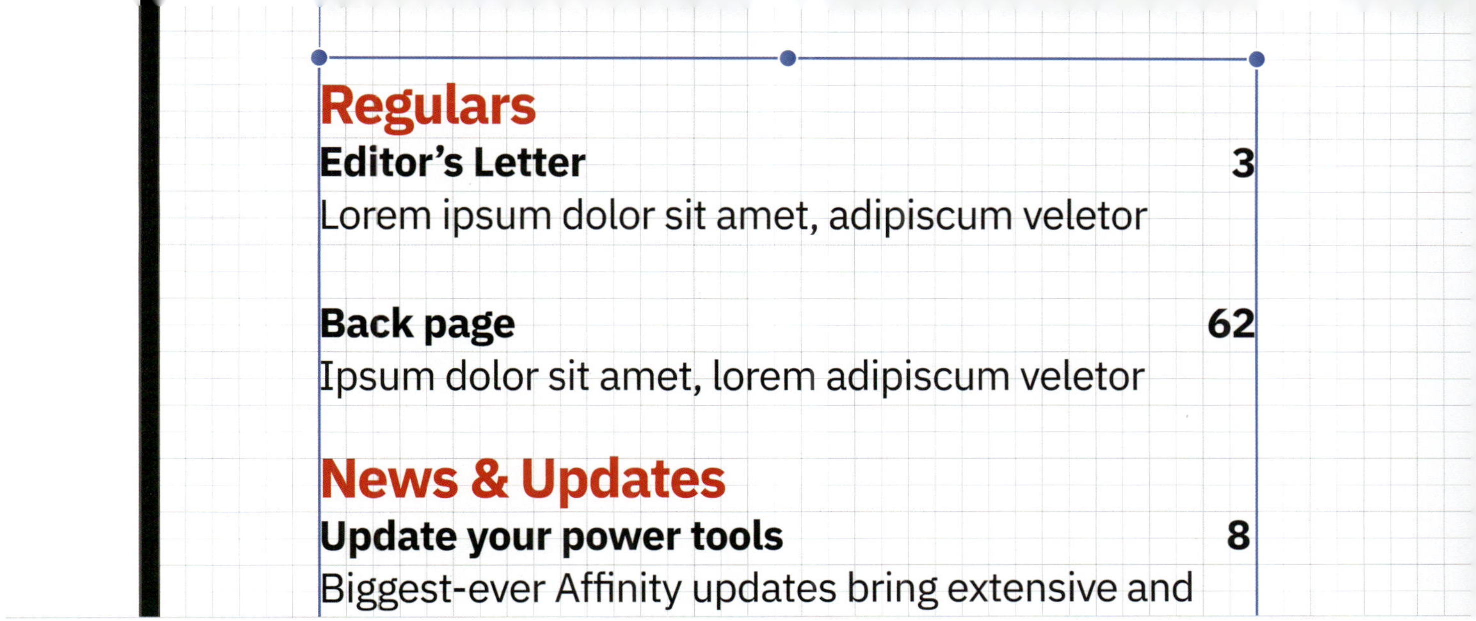
Regulars
Editor's Letter 3
Lorem ipsum dolor sit amet, adipiscum veletor

Back page 62
Ipsum dolor sit amet, lorem adipiscum veletor

News & Updates
Update your power tools 8
Biggest-ever Affinity updates bring extensive and

3 With the **Frame Text Tool**, click after the article description, then press the Return ↵ key.

4 Type an article title.

5 Select **Text** > **Insert** > **Spaces and Tabs** > **Right Indent Tab**.

6 Type the article's starting page number, then press the Return ↵ key.

7 Type a description. Press the shift+Return (⇧ + ↵) keys and then the Return (↵) key to leave a blank line.

8 If the section contains more articles, repeat steps 4 through to 7.

9 When the section's contents are complete, press Return once again and select the *-SP- Contents Section Head* paragraph style on the context toolbar.

10 Type the next section's name and press Return.

11 Repeat from step 4 until your contents page looks more like magazine_contents_completed.afpub.

The **Next style** setting won't affect placed or pasted text.

Sections

When laying out multiple articles in one document, or if you need to leave space for an advertising page within an article, you may need to skip page numbers using the **Section Manager**.

By naming sections, their names can be used on pages with **Insert** > **Fields** > **Section Name**—ideal for running heads on master pages.

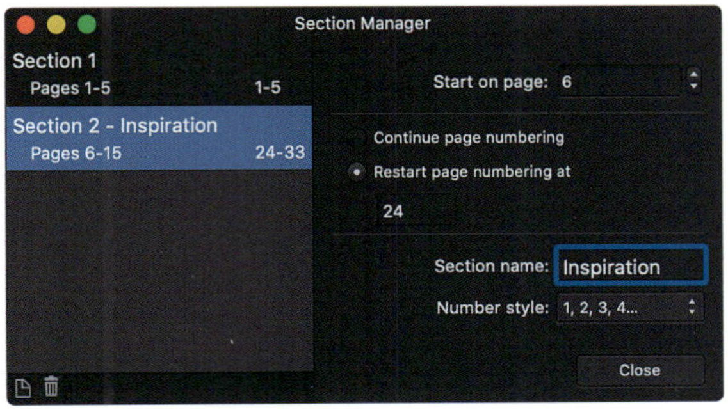

Resource

PDF_Advert folder

PLACE A PDF ADVERTISEMENT

You might sell advertising space in your magazine, often as a full single page or double-page spread. You might sell smaller spaces as well, such as half pages, quarter pages, or custom spaces within your editorial design.

Adverts are usually provided as PDF files. You'd normally pass the PDF for a full-page advert directly to the printer.

Those that are smaller than a page are easily placed alongside other content in your Affinity Publisher document.

1. On Page 3, select and delete all the flannel panel's objects and the hand-drawn column rule.

2. Select **File > Place** and choose Outdoor_Heritage_Advert.pdf.

3. Starting at the top-right bleed corner, drag left and down to the bottom bleed edge.

4. The ad is backwards, so select **Layer > Transform > Flip Horizontal**.

Affinity Publisher's default behaviour when a placing a PDF is *Passthrough*, which attempts to maintain the PDF's appearance all the way through to the export of your publication.

For this to succeed, the PDF must match the colour space and PDF version used by your Affinity Publisher document, so provide those specifications to advertisers.

If mismatched, Affinity Publisher will fall back on the *Interpret* option, which may result in visual changes to the advert, such as font substitution.

Confirm which option is applied to an individual placed PDF by selecting it and inspecting the **PDF Passthrough** setting on the context toolbar. Use the **PDF Passthrough** settings of the selected profile on the **Preflight Panel** to be warned about mismatches throughout your document.

I have undone these changes to restore the flannel panel.

LAY OUT A COVER

Cover design is a discipline all of its own, but a good starting point is a full-bleed image with your masthead (title) and cover lines (other text) over it, teasing your top articles. Use **Document > Add Pages from File** to replace page 1 of your document with the ready-made magazine_cover_completed.afpub.

Our masthead is based on an existing brand design, but if you're coming up with one for your magazine from scratch, use the **Artistic Text Tool** to typeset and size it. If necessary, use **Layer > Convert to Curves** in order to reshape characters if needed.

It's usually safest to apply **No Style** to cover lines and style them from scratch, because you'll resize, space and colour them to fit around an image. Other than (mostly) using the same fonts as other magazine pages, there's no reason why cover lines should reuse your existing text styles.

If your magazine will be sold in retail stores, your newstrade contact will advise on barcodes, including size and position, which you'll need to include along with the issue date and price.

PREPARE FOR PRESS

Affinity Publisher's **Preflight Panel** picks up small mistakes that could slip through into print or throw up errors at the printer. Most issues will be spelling mistakes, which your subeditor will fix. Other common errors (red) and warnings (yellow) are:

Overflowing text frame

Before cutting words to fit, check there is not just a stray paragraph break at the end, and that affected text frames and their contents have not been accidentally resized.

Non-proportional Scaling

Unless an image is intentionally distorted, select it, click its dimensions on the context toolbar, uncheck Scale's lock and even up. Check that the image still fills the intended area.

Bleed Hazard

An object overlaps the page edge by less than the Bleed settings in Document Setup; move or resize it to reach the bleed guide or to sit well within the page.

Placed image DPI too low

Make the image smaller on the page or get a higher-resolution file. It's usually okay if resolution is too high, but it may reduce sharpness and some printing presses will flag it.

Linked resource is missing

Use **Document > Resource Manager** to check all placed images are available; any that are missing will appear low quality in your PDF.

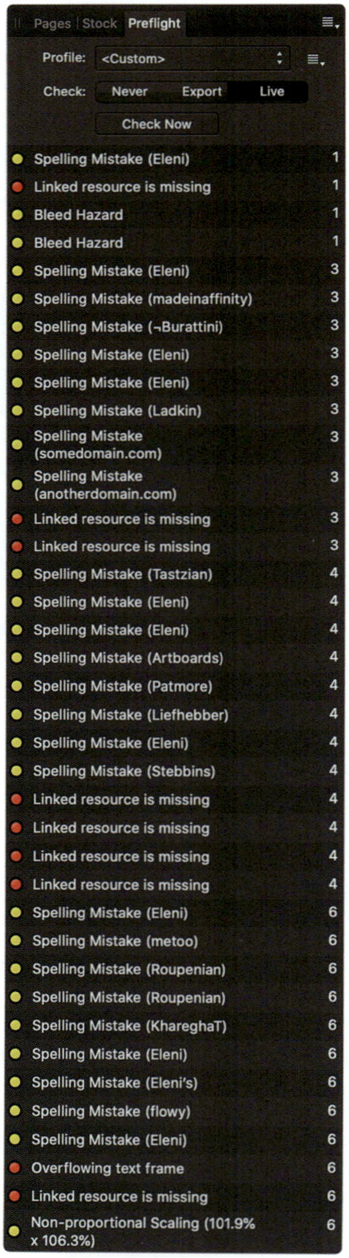

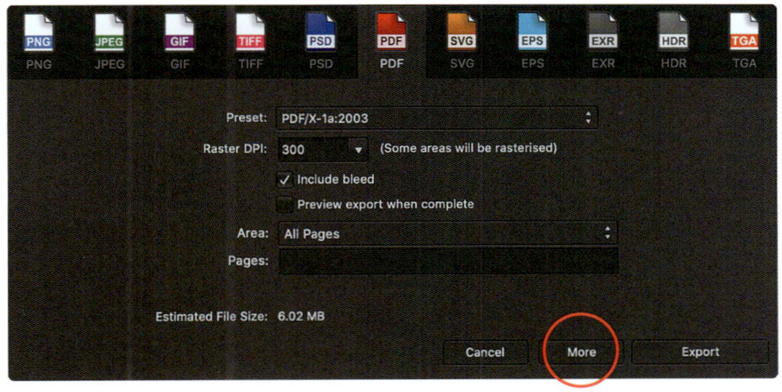

Export to PDF

Commercial printers require pages to be supplied as PDF files.

1 Select **File > Export**. Deal with any preflight warning prompts.

2 Select **PDF**, then the **Preset** called *PDF/X-1a:2003* and check **Include bleed**.

3 For press, set **Area** to *All Pages*, not *All Spreads*. The printer will rearrange the pages on press, so facing pages won't print together.

4 Click **More**. Your printer may advise a PDF-X standard (**Compatibility**).

Leave other options alone unless advised otherwise by your commercial printer, but check **Include printers marks** as many printers require these; ask yours.

5 Ask your printer whether they want to receive the whole publication as one PDF or in smaller sections. Set **Pages** appropriately and repeat the export for each page if necessary; Affinity Publisher will maintain the same settings.

6 Click **Export**.

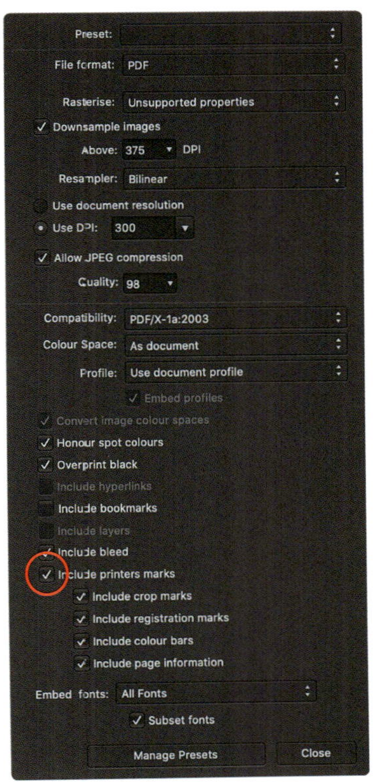

Advanced PDF colour options

It's important that you discuss with your printer which PDF profile and other specifications your print job requires, as this affects your PDF export settings. In **More**, I would do the following.

- Tick **Convert image colour spaces** so that placed resources are converted to this document's CMYK profile. This makes it unnecessary to pre-convert photos to CMYK in another app, and I wouldn't do so.
- Photos usually contain a colour profile from their source, such as a digital camera. If you edit them before placing in Affinity Publisher, either preserve this profile when saving, or save with a working profile such as Adobe RGB, a larger colour space than sRGB.
- Only check **Honour spot colours** if you've used spot colours in your document and arranged for them to be used on press.

WHERE TO GO FROM HERE

The page layouts and grids you've made are a sufficient basis for at least the first issue of a new title, providing formats for regular pages and enough elements to mix and match in additional layouts.

There's a Silicon Valley saying that starting a company is like building a plane while flying it. Designing a magazine is very much like that. As you lay out real content, you'll find flaws in your initial text formatting and limitations in your grids. Don't be afraid to fix them! Changing already-designed pages takes some extra work and careful checking, but by using master pages and text styles you can achieve consistency.

Reusing layouts

After publishing your first issue, consider which layouts to keep as future starting points, removing pics and adding filler text. Not everything needs to be a master page: you can reuse publication pages via **Document > Add Pages from File**.

Template files

Turn regular pages, such as Welcome, Contents and tutorial layouts, into template files (**File > Export as Template**), or one template if you're working solo on one document (p. 219).

Select **File > New**, then **Templates**, click **Add Folder** and pick the place where you've stored the templates to make them available on the **New Document** dialog.

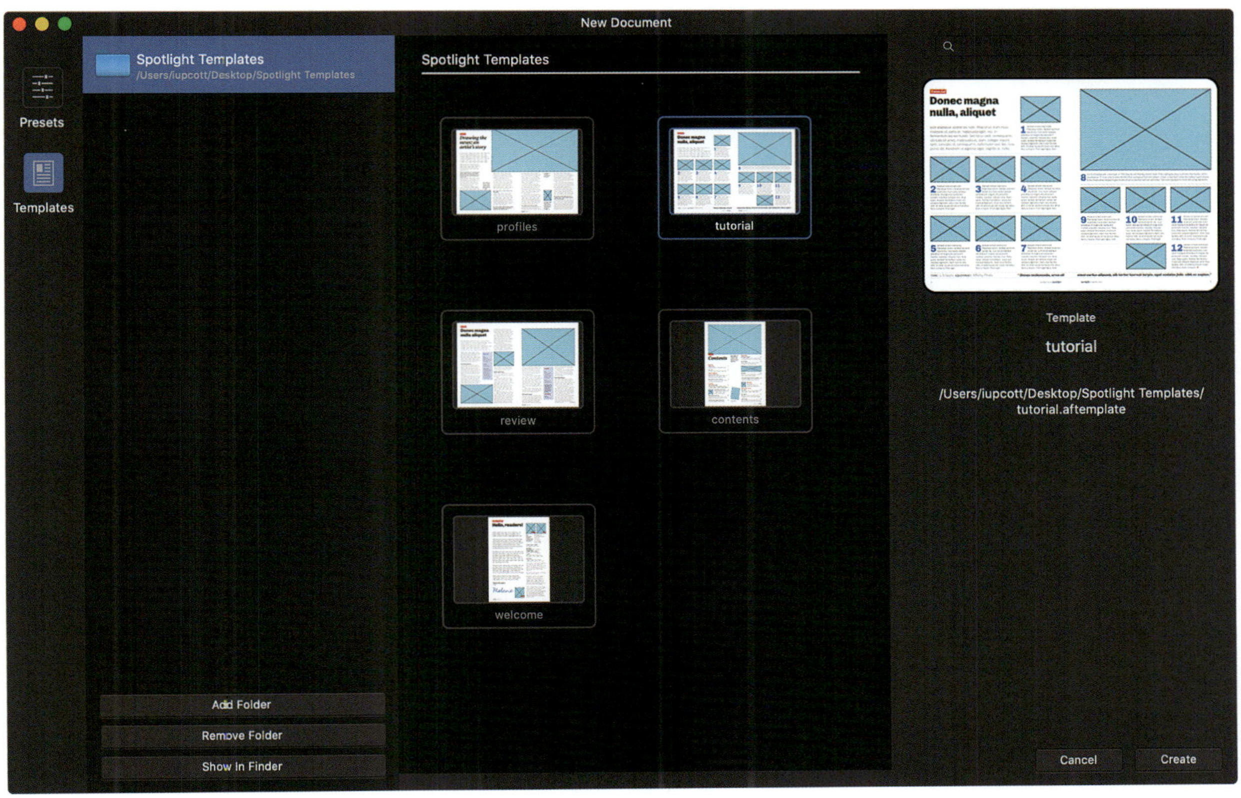

SPOTLIGHT
Your creative quarterly • Summer 2020
COVER ART BY MOON LOTUS DREAMS
Eleni Debo
Behind the scenes with the award-winning illustrator
Microsoft Surface Pro
The best tablet yet for art?
Look and feel
CHARACTER DESIGN
STEP BY STEP
Mac Pro
Living with the quickest Apple ever
ON TEST
Photo apps
iPad cases
Laptop bags
Issue 1 £5.99

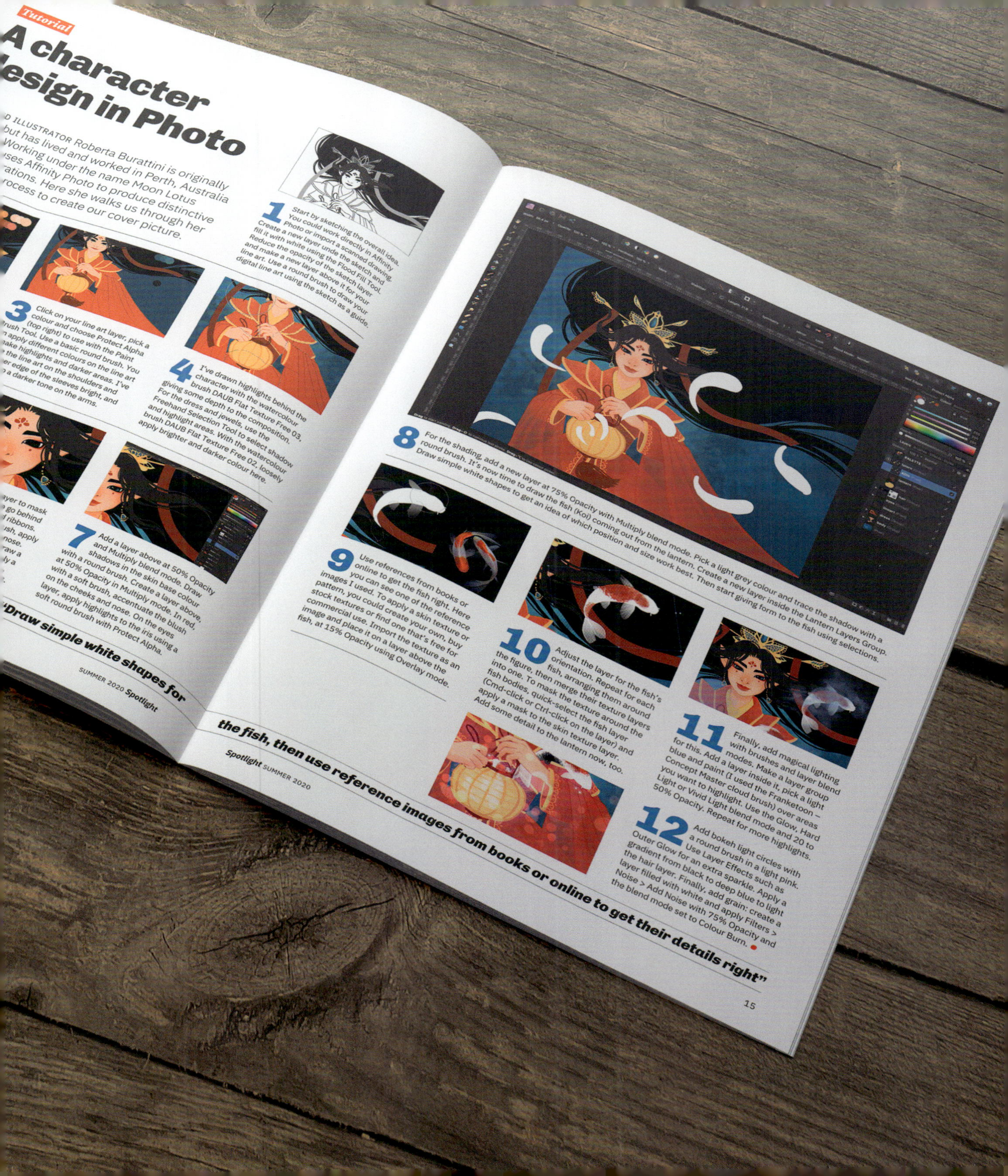

Tutorial

A character [d]esign in Photo

[…]D ILLUSTRATOR Roberta Burattini is originally […]but has lived and worked in Perth, Australia […] Working under the name Moon Lotus […]uses Affinity Photo to produce distinctive […]rations. Here she walks us through her […]rocess to create our cover picture.

1 Start by sketching the overall idea. You could work directly in Affinity Photo or import a scanned drawing. Create a new layer unde the sketch and fill it with white using the Flood Fill Tool. Reduce the opacity of the sketch layer and make a new layer above it for your line art. Use a round brush to draw your digital line art using the sketch as a guide.

3 Click on your line art layer, pick a colour and choose Protect Alpha (top right) to use with the Paint […]rush Tool. Use a basic round brush. You […]n apply different colours on the line art […]make highlights and darker areas. I've […] the line art on the shoulders and […]er edge of the sleeves bright, and […] a darker tone on the arms.

4 I've drawn highlights behind the character with the watercolour brush DAUB Flat Texture Free 03, giving some depth to the composition. For the dress and jewels, use the Freehand Selection Tool to select shadow and highlight areas. With the watercolour brush DAUB Flat Texture Free 02, loosely apply brighter and darker colour here.

[…]ayer to mask […] go behind […]d ribbons. […]ush, apply […]nose. […]raw a […]ly a

7 Add a layer above at 50% Opacity and Multiply blend mode. Draw shadows in the skin base colour with a round brush. Create a layer above, at 50% Opacity in Multiply mode. In red, with a soft brush, accentuate the blush on the cheeks and nose. On the eyes layer, apply highlights to the iris using a soft round brush with Protect Alpha.

8 For the shading, add a new layer at 75% Opacity with Multiply blend mode. Pick a light grey colour and trace the shadow with a round brush. It's now time to draw the fish (Koi) coming out from the lantern. Create a new layer inside the Lantern Layers Group. Draw simple white shapes to get an idea of which position and size work best. Then start giving form to the fish using selections.

9 Use references from books or online to get the fish right. Here you can see one of the reference images I used. To apply a skin texture or pattern, you could create your own, buy stock textures or find one that's free for commercial use. Import the texture as an image and place it on a layer above the fish, at 15% Opacity using Overlay mode.

10 Adjust the layer for the fish's orientation. Repeat for each fish, arranging them around the figure, then merge their texture layers into one. To mask the texture around the fish bodies, quick-select the fish layer (Cmd-click or Ctrl-click on the layer) and apply a mask to the skin texture layer. Add some detail to the lantern now, too.

11 Finally, add magical lighting with brushes and layer blend modes. Make a layer group for this. Add a layer inside it, pick a light blue and paint (I used the Franketoon – Concept Master cloud brush) over areas you want to highlight. Use the Glow, Hard Light or Vivid Light blend mode and 20 to 50% Opacity. Repeat for more highlights.

12 Add bokeh light circles with a round brush in a light pink. Use Layer Effects such as Outer Glow for an extra sparkle. Apply a gradient from black to deep blue to light the hair layer. Finally, add grain: create a layer filled with white and apply Filters > Noise > Add Noise with 75% Opacity and the blend mode set to Colour Burn.

"Draw simple white shapes for the fish, then use reference images from books or online to get their details right"

3

Fashionista Lookbooks

Publish digital and pro print lookbooks for fashion collections

In this project, we'll look at several image-led lookbook designs and explore the benefits of precise layout, picture frames and captioning.

KOMODO
aurélie.
Discover Elodie Bisset's summer collection
JON VAN
THE JON VAN SPRING SUMMER PREVIEW IS HERE MEETS MODERN CHIC IN MENSWEAR JV'S LATEST WOMENSWEAR COLLECTION.

BEFORE YOU GET STARTED

Resources

You can get all the resources that are referenced in this project from: https://affin.co/Fashionista

Knowledge of Affinity Publisher

To get the most from undertaking this project, you will need to:

- Be familiar with the interface of Affinity Publisher. You can learn more about the interface in the Interface Tour chapter, starting on p. 14.
- Have good core skills. See the skills table below to see which additional aspects of Affinity Publisher you need to be confident with to complete this project:

INTRODUCTION

Lookbooks are essentially fashion photos brought together to display a specific fashion designer's latest collection of clothes. They're also the perfect type of publication to show off any kind of related imagery, so you can use the techniques here to create your own photo book, photo album or portfolios instead.

In this project, we'll focus on laying out picture frames and presenting image and text content in interesting and creative ways. This is all about being strongly image-led and unashamedly minimalist.

The collections of three highly respected and hugely imaginary top designers/fashion houses are presented in separate lookbook projects and template files. We'll look at the following collections: **Aurélie**, **Jon Van** and **Komodo**.

Templates

The resources in this project are Affinity Publisher templates that you can populate with your own sourced imagery. The templates are designed in greyscale and packed with placeholder picture frames, already perfectly sized and positioned as shown in this workbook.

> Templates are created by exporting your publication as a template using **File > Export as Template**.

DOCUMENT SETUP

Let's first set up a facing-pages CMYK document of eight pages and then increase inner margins, making the margins mirrored.

The intention is to produce digital and print-ready artwork so keeping to a CMYK colour workspace means you'll get similar colour results with both PDF outputs.

1 Select **File > New**.

2 With **Presets** selected, choose the **Press Ready** preset category from the top of the dialog.

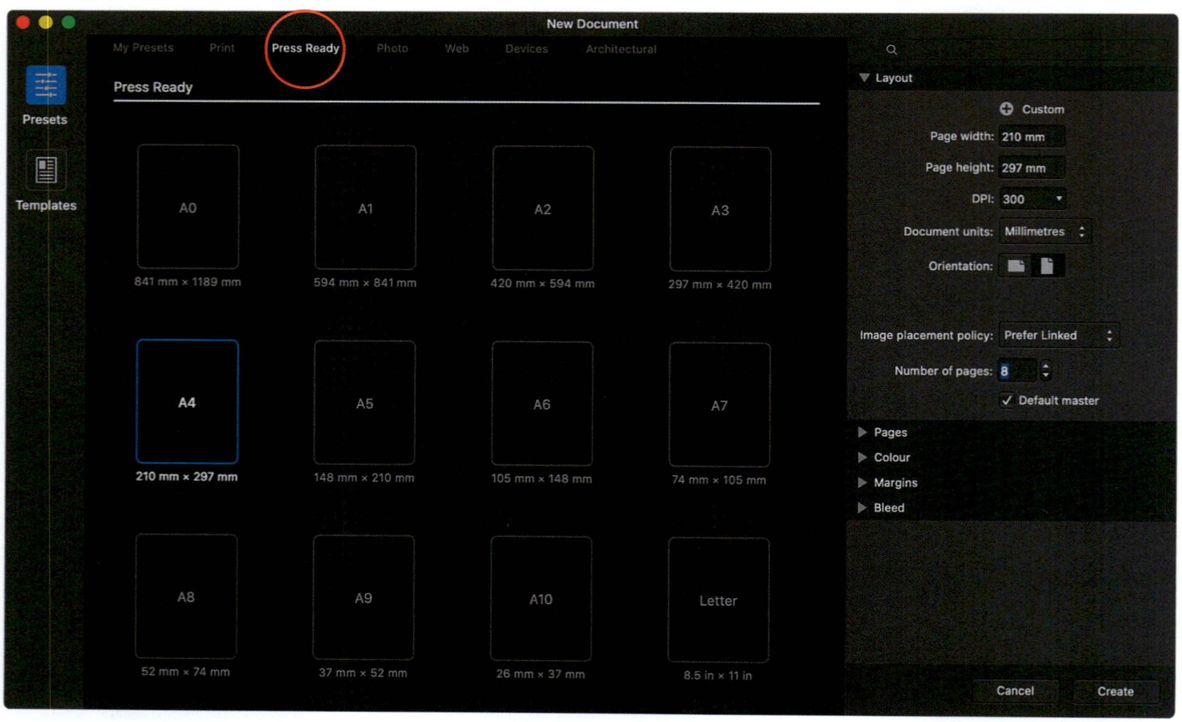

3 Choose the *A4* thumbnail to set up a CMYK colour space.

4 From the right-hand Settings pane (**Pages**), ensure **Facing pages** is checked.

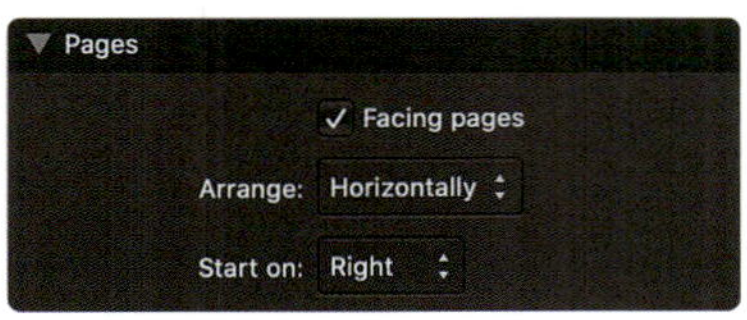

Mirroring margins

- From the Settings pane (**Margins**), set an **Inner** margin of *20 mm* and alter all remaining margin values to *10 mm*.

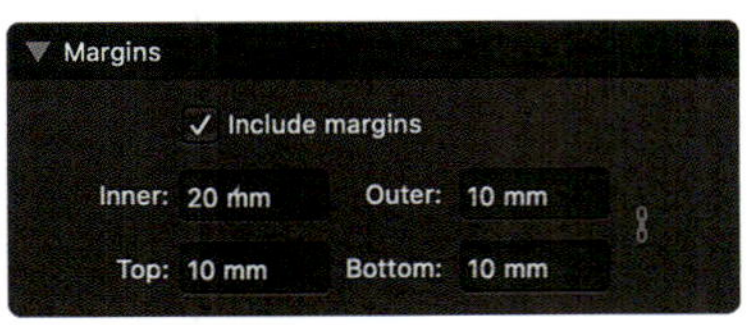

On facing-page spreads, setting a larger Inner Margin provides balance across the spread and can prevent imagery and text being lost from view in the spine.

SNAPPING

The projects rely on snapping a lot. This lets your picture frames and text captions align perfectly to margins, page midpoints, margin midpoints or other objects. This approach is instead of applying fixed grids or ruler guides so it's fundamentally simpler in terms of alignment aids.

Enabling snapping

- On the **Toolbar**, ensure **Snapping** is enabled. This is enabled by default.

Understanding page and margin snapping

By default, you'll be able to snap objects to the page edge, bleed and margins. Less obvious is the ability to snap objects to the page midpoint.

- With the **Picture Frame Rectangle Tool** (F) active, move the + cursor to half way down the right margin. The green vertical dynamic guide that displays is snapping to the right margin, while the horizontal red dynamic guide is snapping to vertical page midpoint.

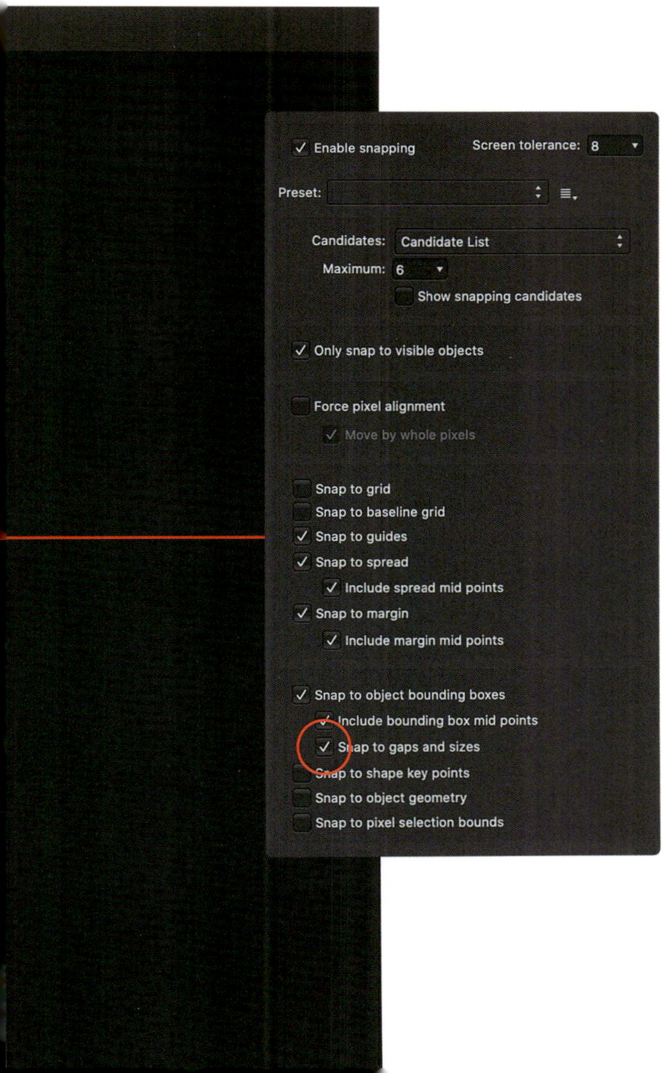

With identical margin values, page and margin midpoint snapping gives the same outcome but for offset margins (e.g., mirrored) you'll get two snapping points—to page midpoint and to an offset margin midpoint (calculated as the distance between margins not the page edges).

When you enable snapping, a series of snapping behaviours are switched on by default. These are shown by clicking the **Snapping** drop-down arrow.

In the example, the snapping behaviour you can see is because **Snap to spread** and **Snap to margin** are checked, as well as their **Include spread mid points** and **Include margin mid points** settings.

We'll cover snapping in more detail as we place picture frames and text frames in later sections. In preparation, **Snap to gaps and sizes** can also be checked.

Resource
Jonvan - Lookbook.aftemplate

USING PICTURE FRAMES

Picture frames are used instead of adding images directly on the page. This is for two reasons:

- The frame's shape and dimensions are integral to the page design and are more important than those of the image.
- Images can be scaled and positioned within the frame to get the right composition and content displayed.

Adding picture frames

Square and rectangular picture frames can be placed on the page.

1 Select the **Picture Frame Rectangle Tool**.

2 Drag from a margin or bleed edge to the centre of the page, margin midpoint or opposite margin.

In the example, a square picture frame is being drawn by dragging from the right page midpoint downwards and to the left, then snapping to the green margin midpoint guide.

> Default snapping will make margins, margin midpoints or other picture frames magnetic.

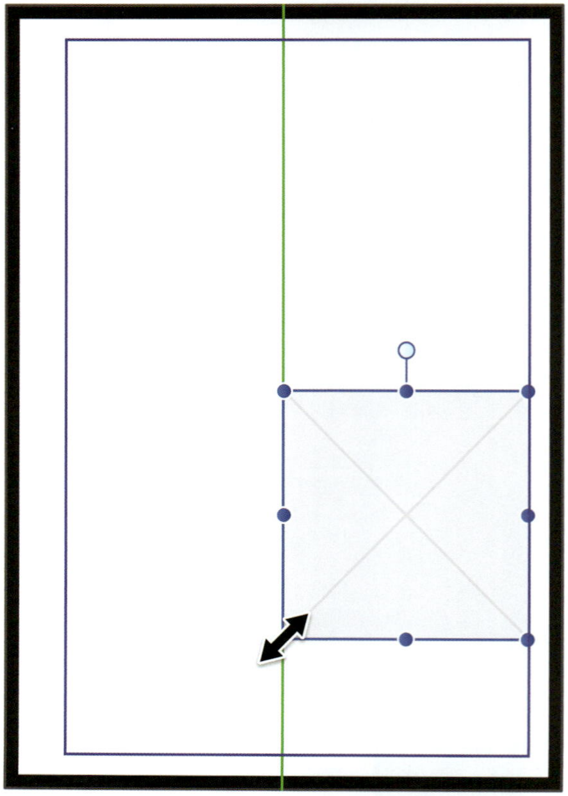

You can snap as you draw or when you reposition the picture frame on the page. For the former, as you drag you can scale about the initial 'snapped' midpoint (a) using both the ctrl key (Mac) or the right mouse button (Win); additionally, the picture frame will be constrained to a square.

The red guide indicates the top/ bottom page midpoint.

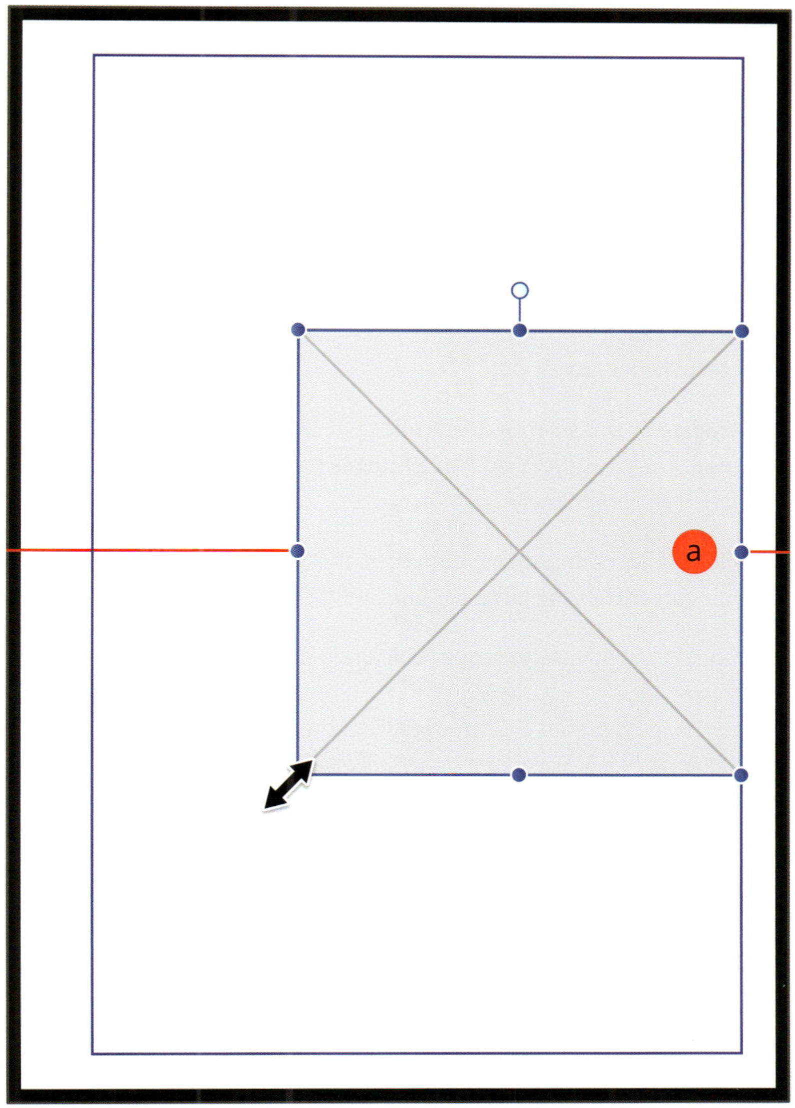

Adding images to picture frames

Picture frames can be populated by placing images within them.

1 Select **File > Place**.

2 Navigate to and select multiple images, then click **Open**. The now displayed **Place Images Panel** is loaded with your images.

3 Select a chosen thumbnail from the panel then hover your cursor over the picture frame and click.

4 Repeat to populate subsequent picture frames.

As each image is placed it is removed from the panel. Once all images are placed the panel will disappear.

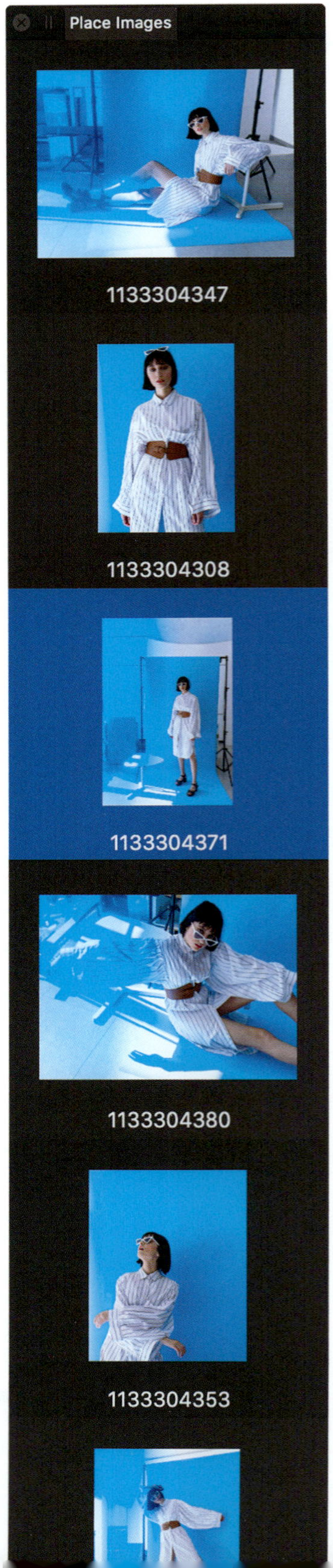

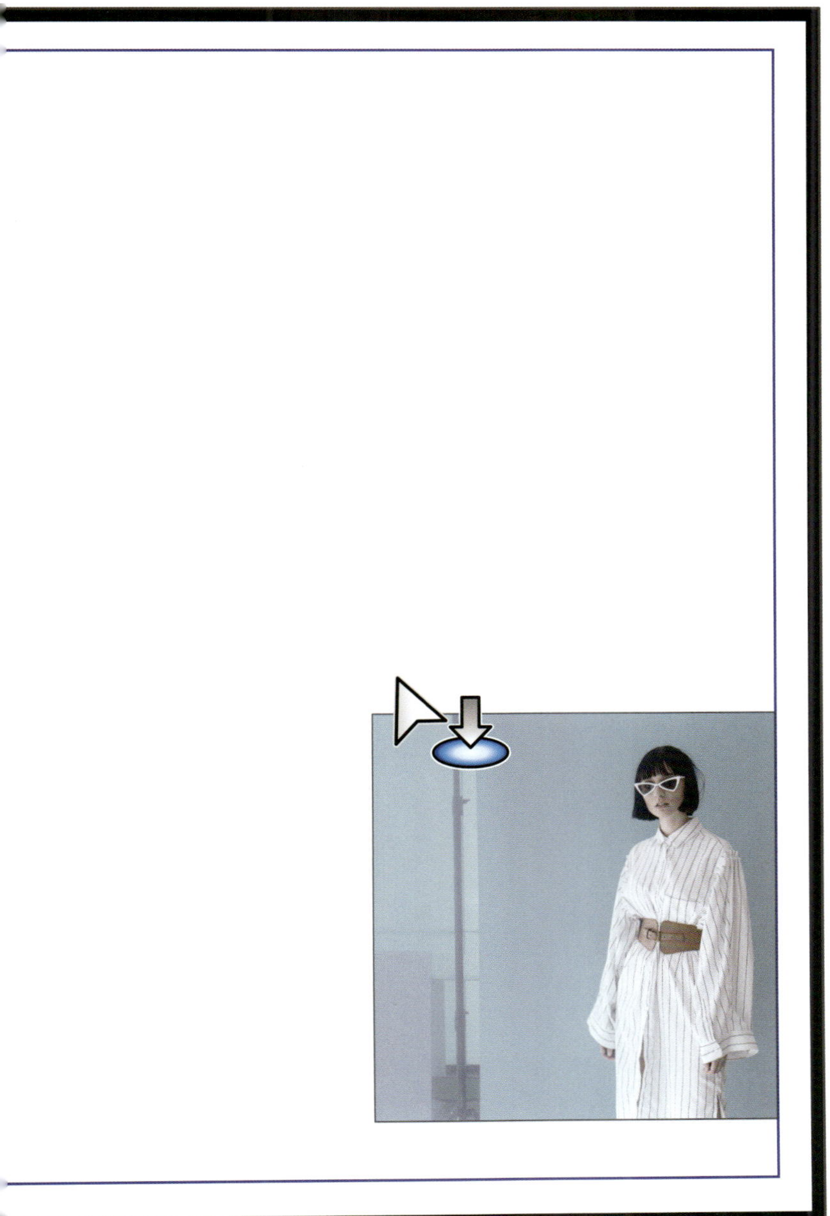

Use the Stock Panel to access royalty-free Unsplash, Pexels and Pixabay imagery—simply drag and drop directly onto a chosen picture frame.

Scaling and repositioning framed images

By default, your newly framed images will be scaled to maximum fit—typically areas around the image are hidden to fully fit the image to frame. Images are also centred and reduced (or increased) in size to fit to the frame size. Often, this is unsatisfactory as no account is taken of the image's composition or subject matter.

Let's take a look at how custom scaling can help this by improving composition, balance and adding interest to the image.

Scaling

Scale to Max fit (Default)
Areas above and below the image are lost in the frame to make the image fit. The model also appears lost in the frame due to the distracting Studio backdrop behind her.

Scale using slider
As shown opposite, scaling up makes most of the backdrop hidden, with more focus on the model and clothing. As the model is already positioned slightly off centre, increasing the scaling will nicely present her offset in the frame—the remaining backdrop frame also offers balance. No image repositioning was needed here.

Repositioning

Positional control lets you move your image around the picture frame while the frame remains static—this is especially important for compositional reasons.

Scale to Max fit (Default)

On this different shot of the same model, by default, part of the model's face is lost inside the frame.

Repositioning using Position control

Dragging left using the multi-arrow Position control repositions the image in the frame—the model is perfectly positioned and backdrop equipment is now hidden. No scaling is needed.

Press the shift key (⇧) to constrain repositioning to horizontal, vertical or diagonal. If needed, the alt key disables snapping as you drag.

Scale/reposition images independently

Absolute control of image scaling and positioning is possible by selecting the image and manipulating it independently of its frame.

Scale to Max fit (Default)

In this shot, the image is in an irregularly shaped picture frame, so it seems oddly balanced with dead space to the model's left.

To temporarily view the image unframed, which may aid repositioning, press the alt key and click on an image's layer thumbnail; press the Esc key to cancel.

Switch off clipping to canvas (use \ key) to view image areas that extend off the page.

Scale and move

Double-click the picture frame to select the image then, with the **Move Tool**, scale it up from its top-right corner handle; reposition slightly to the right. The model is balanced in the frame.

To resize from centre, press the cmd ⌘ key (Mac) or ctrl key (Win) when dragging a corner handle.

Framed images are simply child objects clipped within a picture frame. In the **Layers Panel** you'll see the image nested within an expanded picture frame entry.

Resource
Aurelie - Lookbook.aftemplate

TEXT

An important characteristic of text in these lookbook projects is that it is unstyled, i.e. no character or paragraph text styles are applied. This may contradict with Page Design Principles (p. 151), but the limited text used in these smaller projects means it is eminently controllable using local formatting instead.

For the Aurelie project, the Georgia typeface is used throughout with bold and italic applied as appropriate.

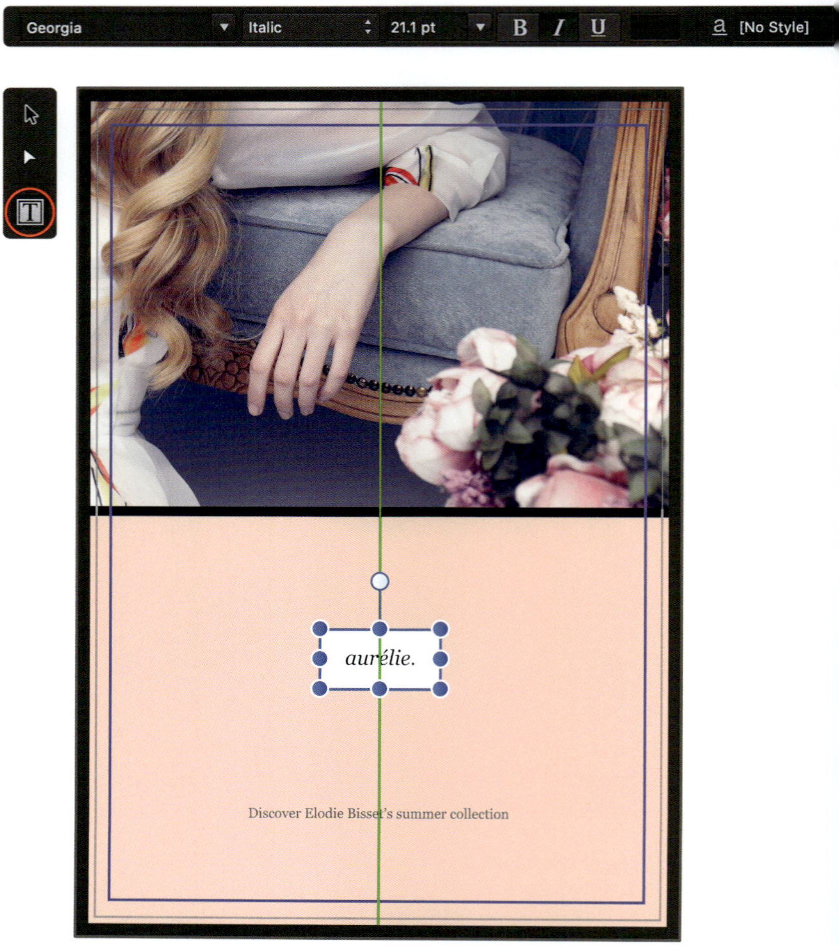

Title and headings

By design, these are relatively subdued in terms of font size. The title is strengthened by using a contrasting lighter background rectangle.

Creating title and headings

- With the **Artistic Text Tool** active, adjust context toolbar settings, drag to size your artistic text then begin typing.

Text snapping

For accurate placement, reposition your artistic text to snap to page midpoint so its positioned centrally. If needed, snap to left edges of text frames on other pages once drawn.

Body text

Text is added sparingly to describe the fashion collection in single or two-column text frames.

Creating body text

1 With the **Frame Text Tool** active, set your preferred text settings from the context toolbar.

2 Drag across the page and begin typing in the text frame.

Note that another use of text is for Captioning (p. 286).

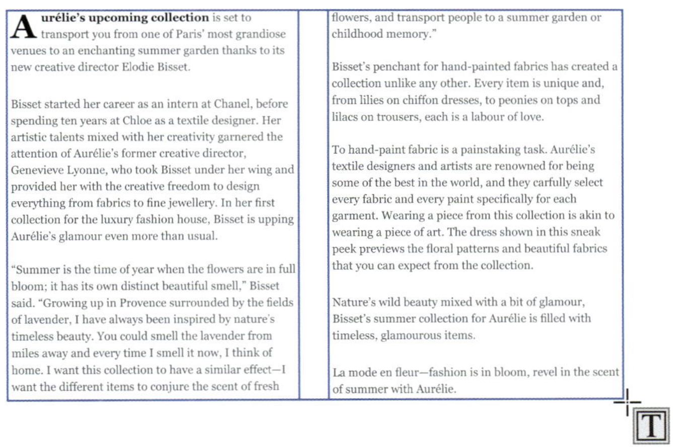

REPEATING PANELS AND STROKES

Let's look at several interesting features of the Aurelie project:

- Repeating panels: these add colour, visual interest and focus to otherwise white pages.
- Global colours: you can swap all panel colours for another sampled colour in one click.
- Colour sampling: this harmonises panels with images.
- Repeating strokes: these add a strong visual theme that connects pages.

Adding panels and strokes

- For a *panel*: With the **Rectangle Tool**, drag across the page or two-page spread from bottom-left bleed corner to page midpoint. Give the panel's fill a placeholder grey colour.
- For a *stroke*: With the **Pen Tool**, click at each end of the spread at page margin midpoints and apply a stroke width.

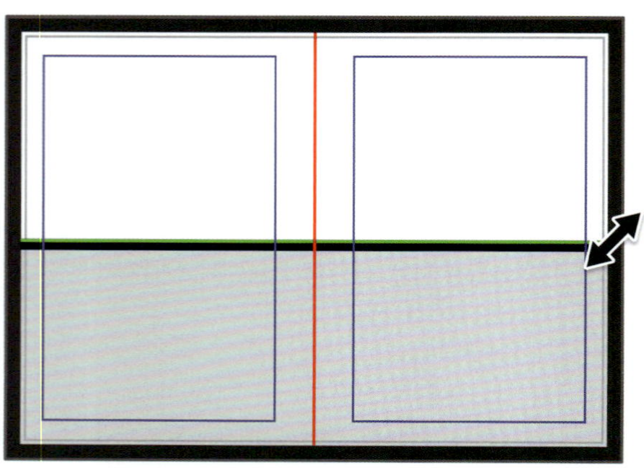

Global colours and sampling

Global colours are linked colours which means they can be swapped for another colour at a later date—all instances of the original colour are updated to the new one simultaneously.

In the Aurelie project, the coloured panels and strokes can take global colours and be updated using colour sampling.

Creating and applying global colours

1 On the **Swatches Panel**, go to **Panel Preferences** and select **Add Global Colour**.

2 Choose a name and colour from the dialog (e.g., Global Colour 1 and blue), then click **Add**. A new Document Palette will contain the swatch.

3 Repeat for a second global colour (i.e., Global Colour 2 and 100K black).

4 Select the panels and apply the first colour as fill.

5 Select straight lines and unfilled rectangles and apply the second colour as a stroke colour.

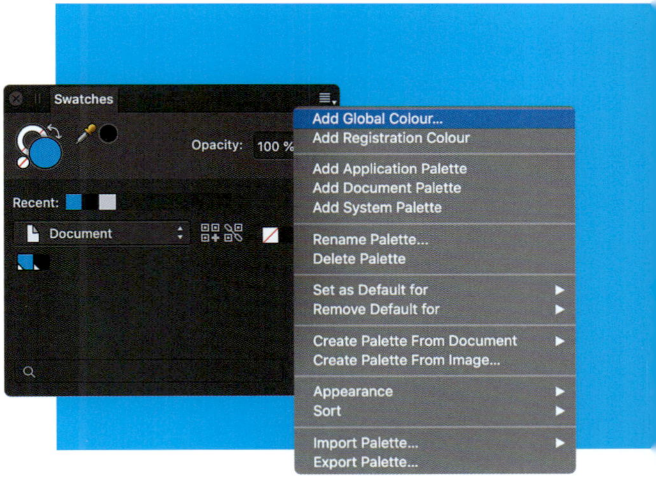

Updating panel colours using sampling

1 On the **Swatches Panel**, right click the first swatch (Global Colour 1) and select **Edit Fill**.

2 Using the colour picker (pipette), drag over a colour on an image and release.

3 Click the circular 'picked up' colour swatch to update all colour instances simultaneously.

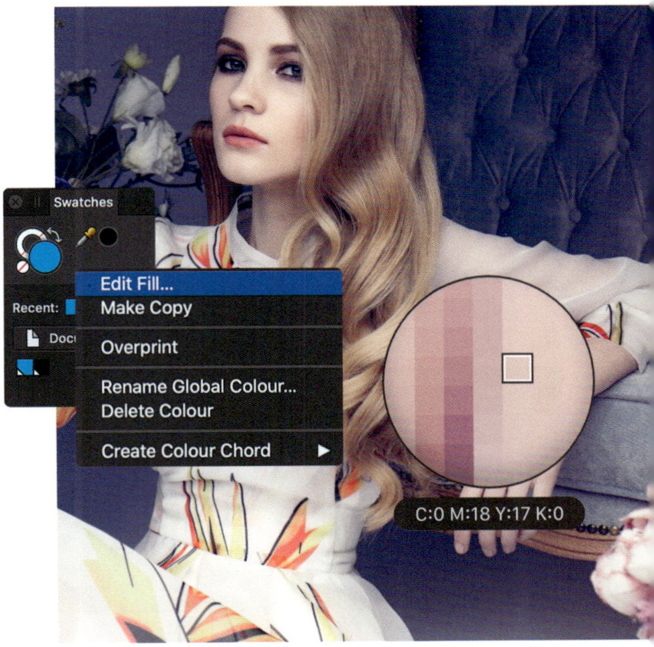

Try colour sampling a colour which is common to model images, e.g. skin tones. This creates document-wide colour harmony.

Resource
Komodo - Lookbook.aftemplate

HYPERLINKS

As the lookbooks are also to be offered digitally, hyperlinks can be added to contact information so the reader can make contact directly.

We'll set up an email contact but you could hyperlink to a website (URL) or link to another part of the document (Page or Anchor).

Hyperlinks will only become clickable once you've output your project to a digital PDF file.

Adding hyperlinks

1 Select the text you want to hyperlink.

2 From the **Text** menu, click **Interactive** and then select **Insert Hyperlink**.

3 From the **Hyperlink Type** pop-up menu, choose *Email*.

4 Enter an email address in the **Email** box.

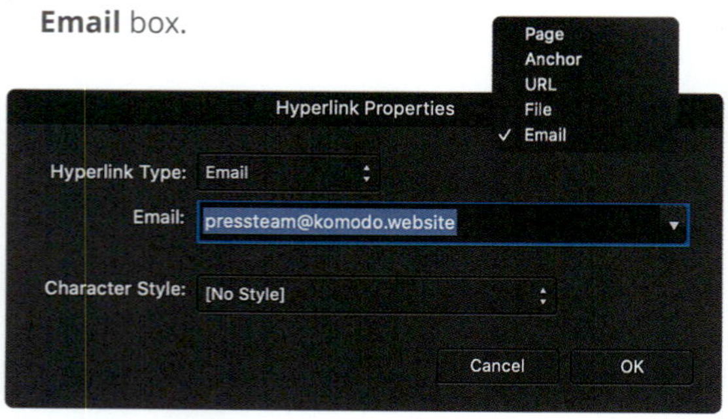

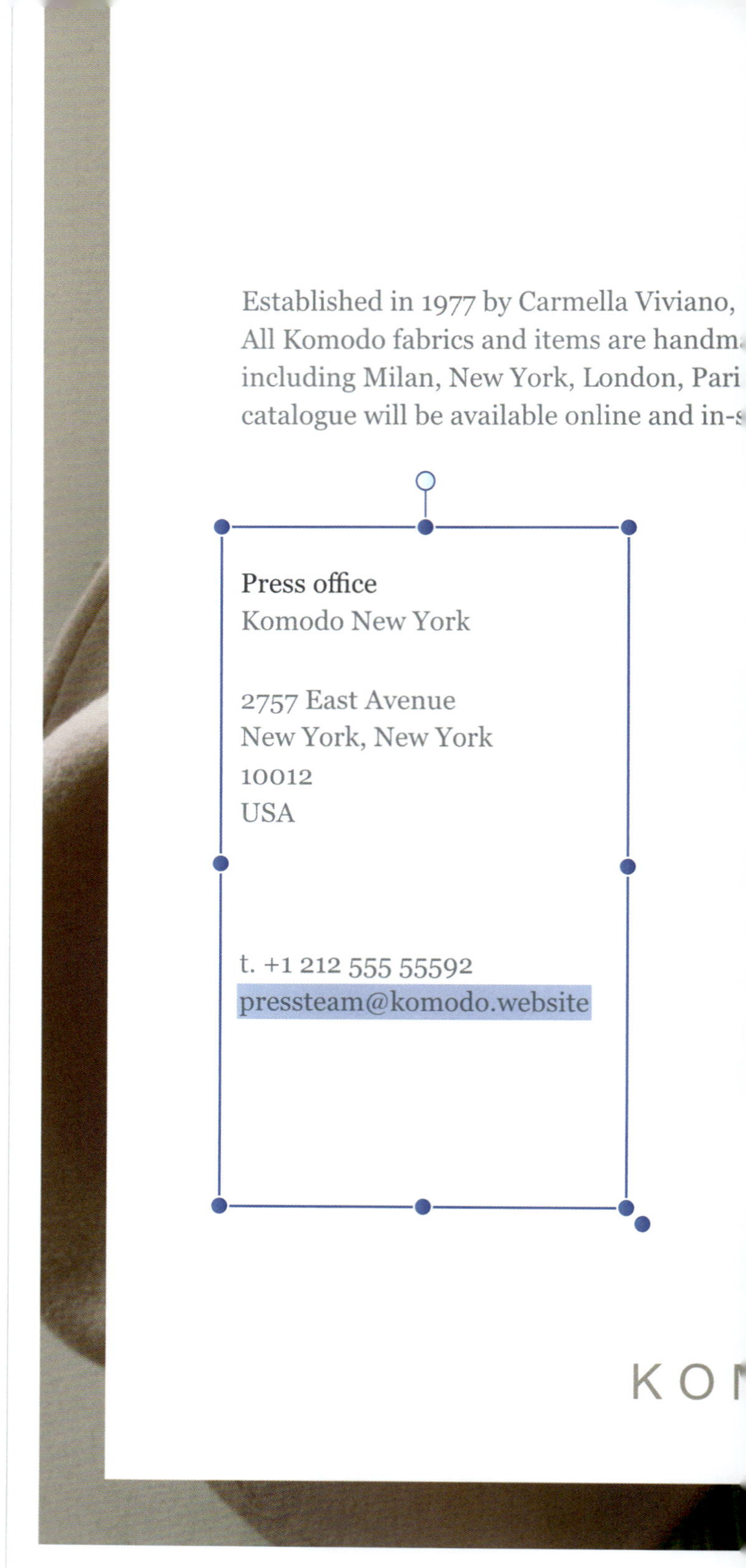

Managing hyperlinks

Once you've added hyperlinks, you can manage all added hyperlinks from one location by using the **Hyperlinks Panel**.

- From the **View** menu, select **Studio > Hyperlinks**.

Any listed hyperlink can be double-clicked to edit its hyperlink properties. You can also jump to a hyperlink's source text at its page location.

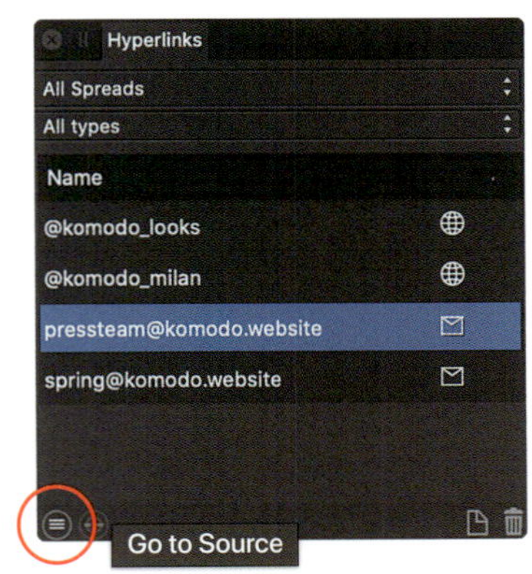

Resource

Jonvan - Lookbook.aftemplate
Aurelie - Lookbook.aftemplate
Komodo - Lookbook.aftemplate

CAPTIONING

Most lookbooks need caption text to support imagery. In the case of fashion lookbooks, each caption could describe the fashion item, collection name, item description or credits.

Technically, these captions are just simple text frames containing locally formatted and unstyled frame text. The interesting aspect of captioning is how versatile snapping and alignment of caption text can be.

Creating caption text

1 With the **Frame Text Tool**, draw out a text frame, type your caption text.

2 Format your caption text using the context toolbar.

Aligning captions

Vertically align text to bottom of text frame. Additional text will fill the text frame given enough frame height.

When placing captions, use dynamic guides to snap to consistent distances both vertically and horizontally. Enable **Snap to gaps and sizes** (p. 271) to do this; distances will be shown.

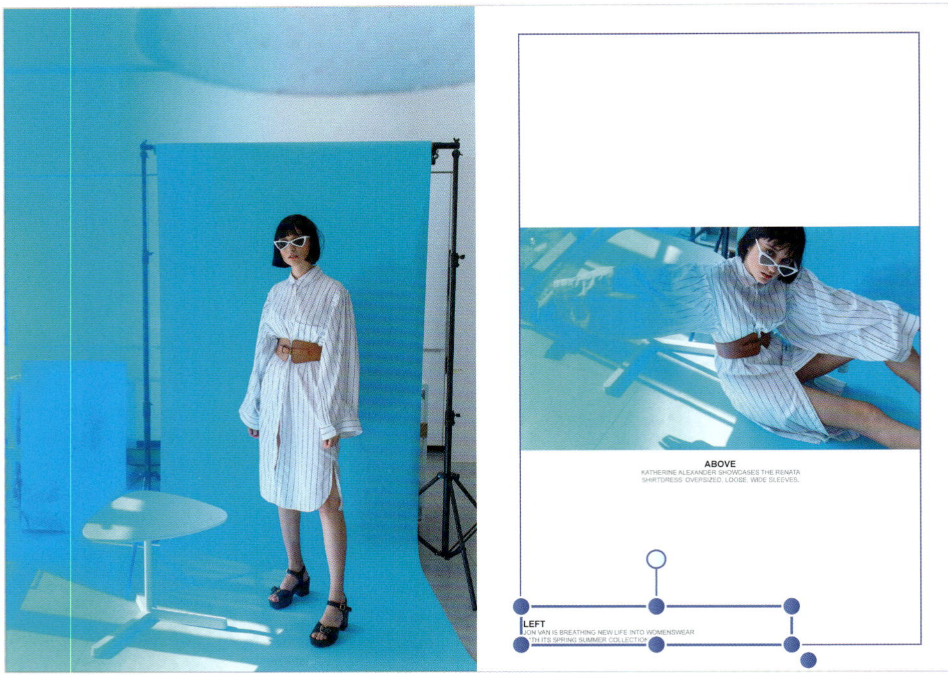

Vertically align text to bottom margin. Additional text will never be lost given enough frame height.

Right align to existing picture frame. Double-click bottom centre handle to remove extra vertical spacing, then reposition text frame to a consistent vertical distance from picture frame using measurement guides.

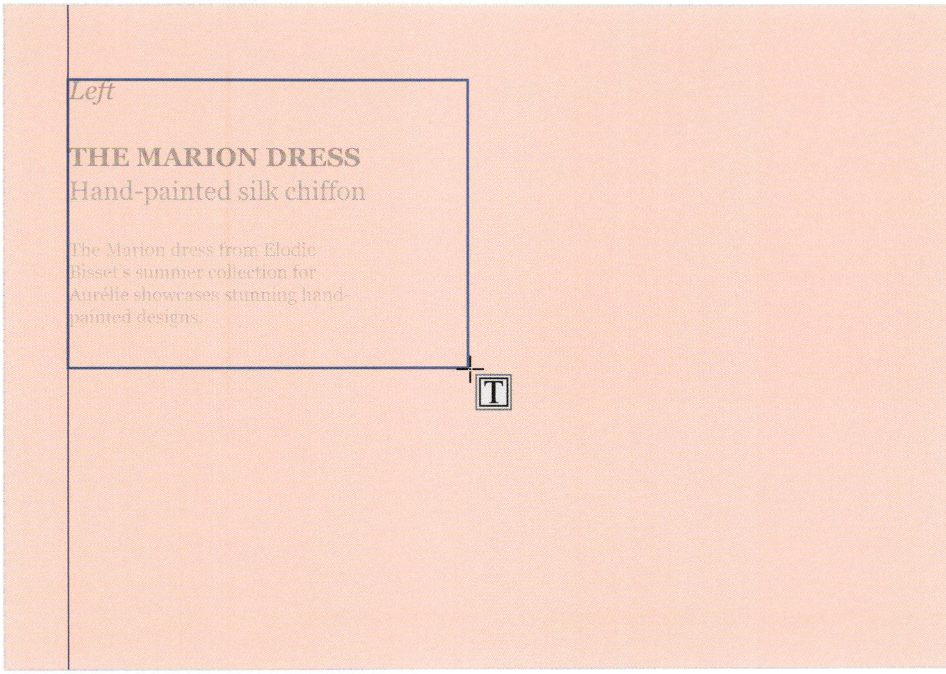

Use existing margins to draw caption text frames out from.

Use text frame insets to set consistent 'in-frame' distances between picture frames and caption text. Use the **Text Frame Panel** for this (switch on via **View > Studio**).

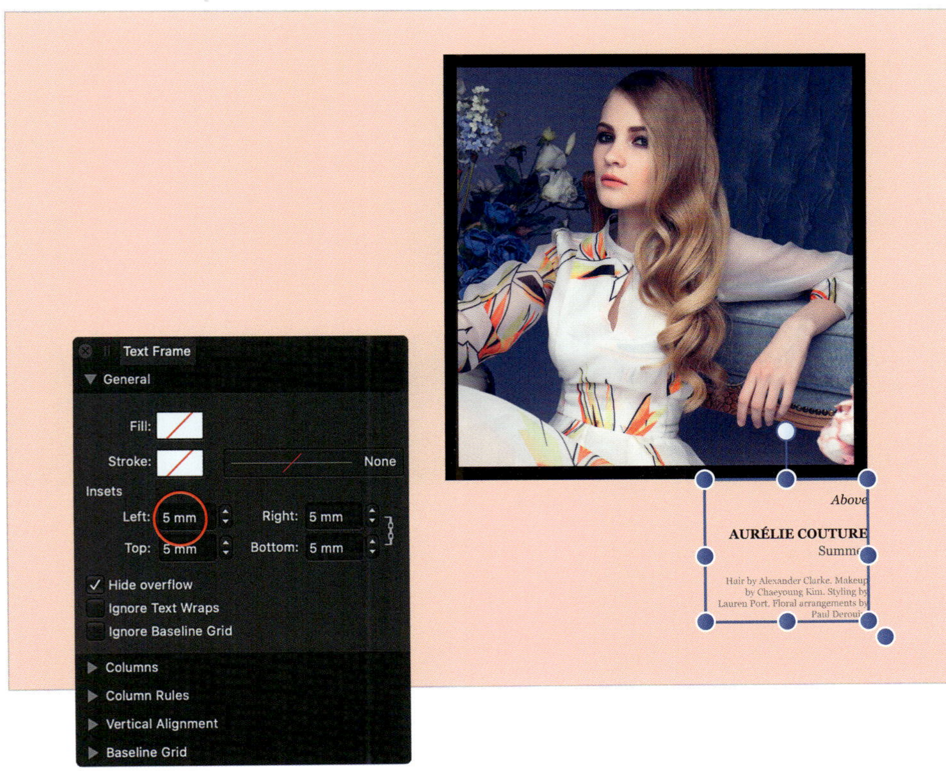

Size the height of caption text frames to be the same, then snap to bottom page edge.

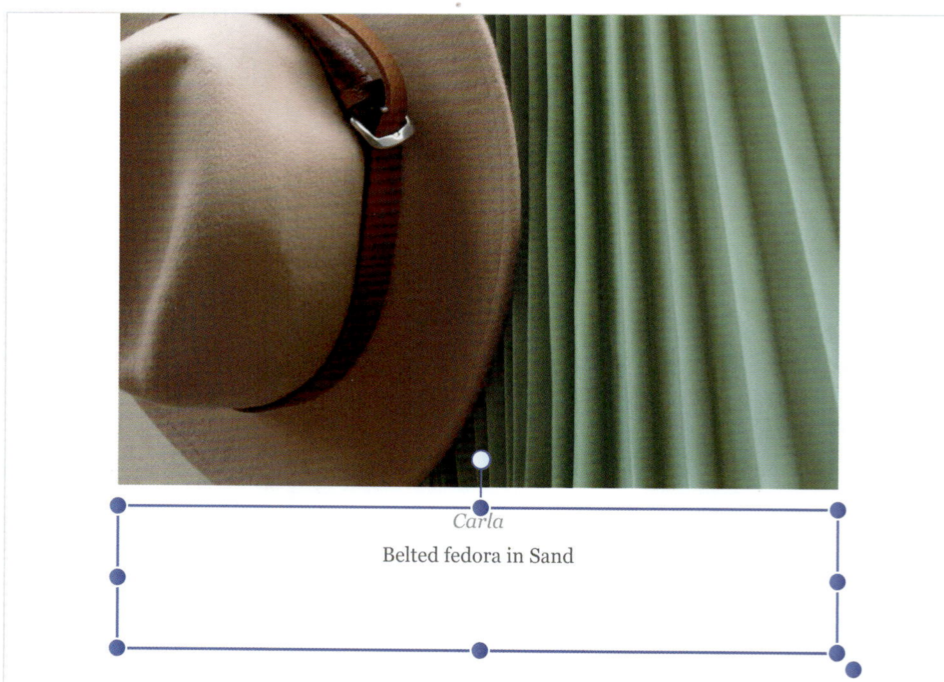

Size the width of caption text frames to match picture frame width and align caption text to horizontal centre.

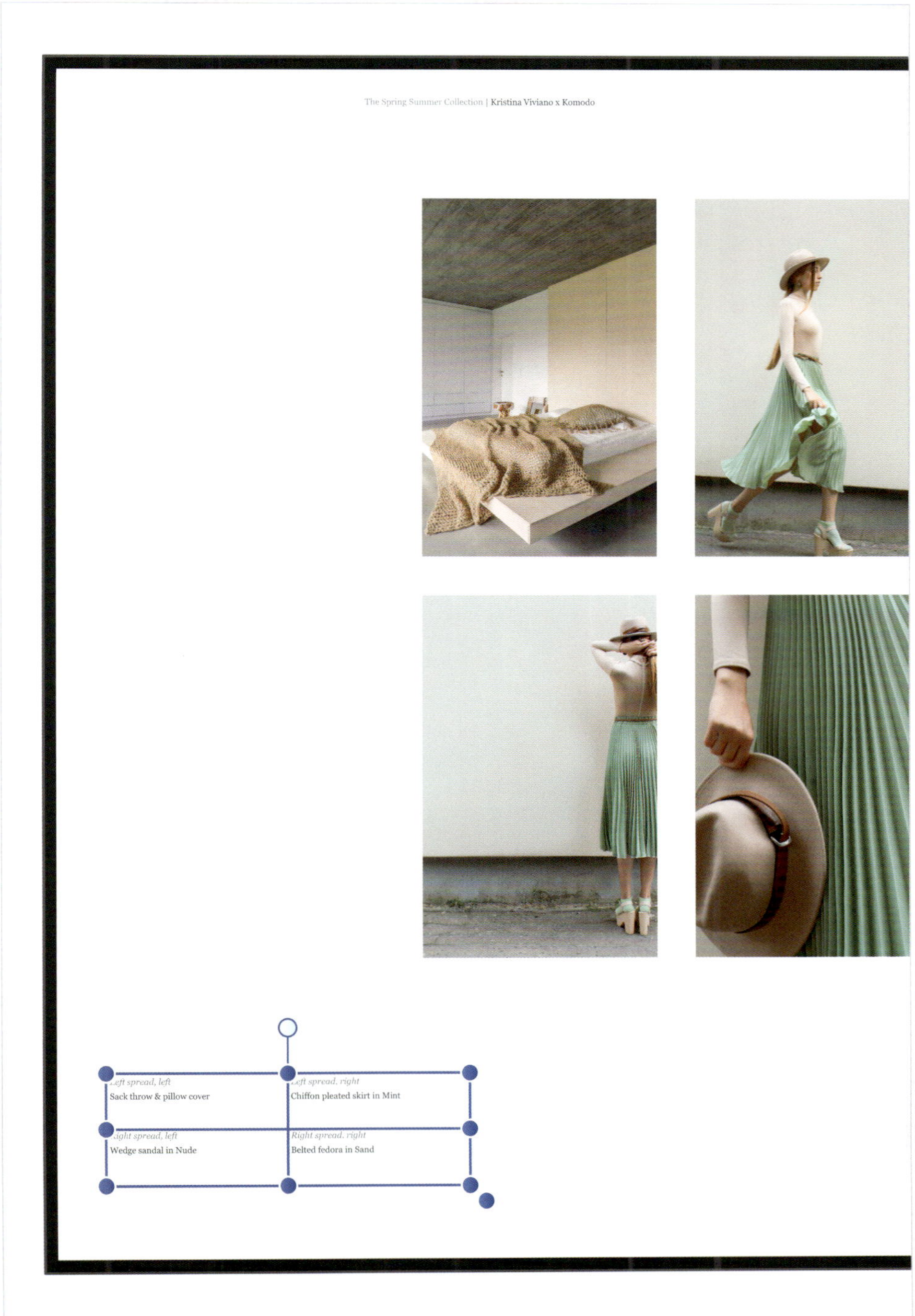

Arrange caption text frames into blocks to spatially mimic the arrangement of imagery.

Resource
Picture Frame Captions.afassets

> *Constraints control how a contained 'child' frame is resized, repositioned or anchored within its containing object, e.g. group.*

Captioning with intelligent anchoring

Caption text can be anchored to stop it from being incorrectly repositioned as you resize its referenced picture frame. Anchoring is possible by using **constraints**.

Captions can be included alongside a picture frame or be an overlay (over the picture). You'll see both examples in the above resource—you can import and experiment with the picture frame captions.

Top & Bottom banner from the Pop category Picture Frame Captions assets

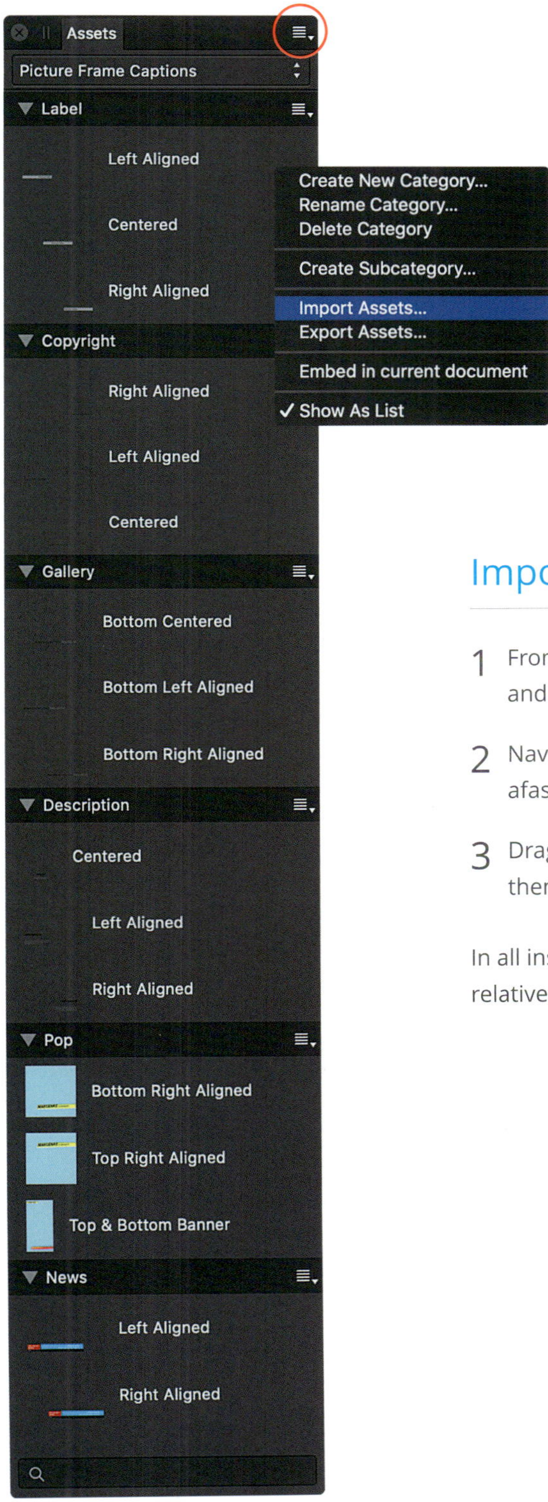

Importing picture frame captions

1 From the **Assets Panel**, click **Panel Preferences** and choose **Import Assets**.

2 Navigate to the downloaded resource, select the afassets file and click **Open**.

3 Drag any picture frame assets onto your page and then resize it from a corner handle.

In all instances, the caption text always retains its relative position to its picture frame.

Creating a group

Captioning with anchoring relies on the picture frame and caption text being grouped. The group acts as a container such that the frame and text edges can be anchored to the group container in different directions.

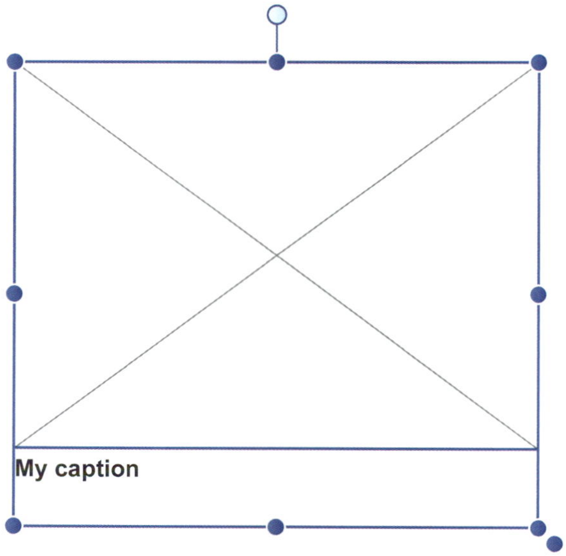

1 With the **Picture Frame Rectangle Tool**, draw out a picture frame.

2 With the **Frame Text Tool**, draw out a text frame, type some caption text, then position and size the frame so it snaps to the bottom of the picture frame.

3 Format your caption text using the context toolbar.

4 Select the picture frame and caption text frame, and from the **Layer Menu**, select **Group**.

Applying constraints

Now both caption text and picture frame are contained within a group, constraints can be applied to each using the **Constraints Panel**.

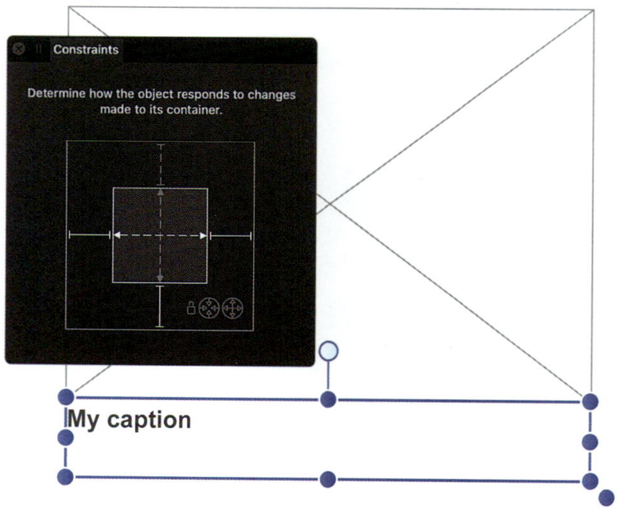

1 Double-click the caption text to select it within the group.

2 Go to **View** > **Studio** > **Constraints**.

3 From the **Constraints Panel**, click the dashed lines between the inner and outer square to anchor to left, right and bottom of the group—they become solid lines. The inner square represents the contained caption text, and the outer square the containing group.

4 Click the arrows within the inner square to prevent vertical scaling of the caption text frame and anchoring horizontally.

For the selected picture frame, configure the panel as shown. This allows scaling and anchoring of the picture frame within the group 'container'.

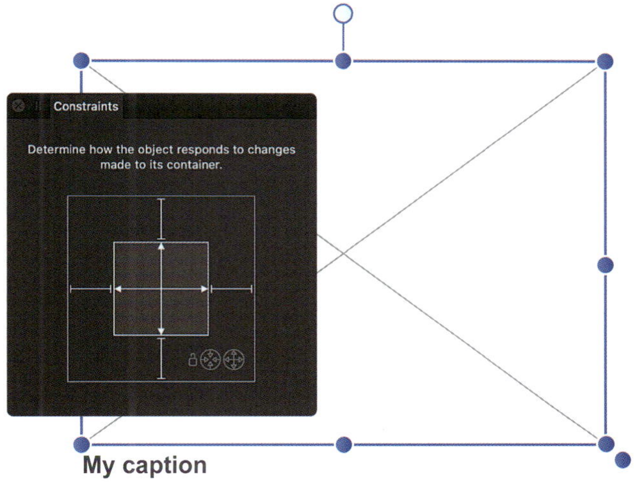

After applying constraints, the group will be automatically renamed to 'Constraints group' to indicate constraints are in place. Keeping caption text in text frames ensures that text will never scale.

Applying caption background colour, insets and vertical alignment

1 With caption text frame selected, click **Text Frame** on the context toolbar.

2 On the now displayed **Text Frame Panel**, click the **Fill** swatch and set a background colour for the entire caption text frame.

- Enter **Insets** values to add buffer space between text frame edge and caption text.
- In the **Vertical Position** section, choose an alignment option, e.g. Centre Align.

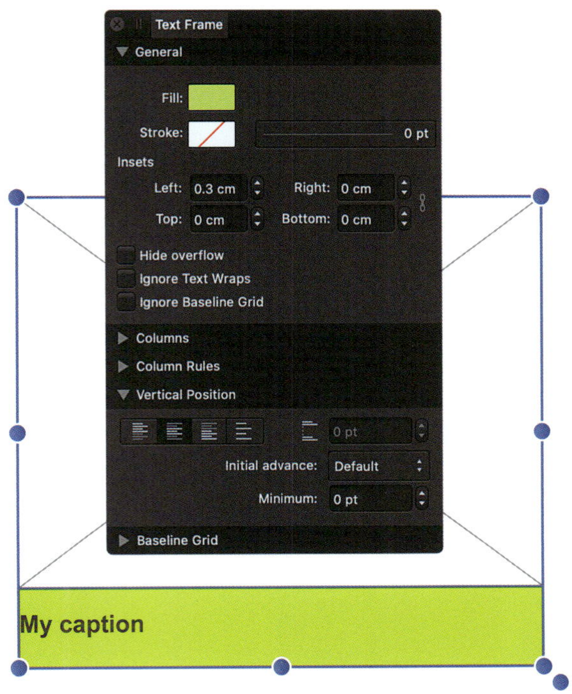

If you now try resizing the group you'll see that the text caption will always retain its correct size and position in relation to the picture frame.

Resource

Smart pages - Lookbook.afpub

SMART MASTER PAGES

For publications that are based on master pages, the smart master page feature lets you retain any edited 'master' content if you swap out the master page for another.

In a practical sense you'll never lose copy or populated picture frames—they'll be kept on your page ready for further editing or layout.

While this is smart in itself, the real intelligence comes when providing a range of master page variants offering different frame layouts. By swapping these master pages in and out, you have a choice of layouts that can be demonstrated in a powerful way. Frames will reposition according to the new master automatically.

In this project, a spread (p. 4-5) of the Komodo Lookbook can demonstrate this smart master page intelligence.

How does it work?

1 Create a master page with placeholder text frames and picture frames. Uniquely name them in the **Layers Panel**.

2 Assign the master page to the publication page and add content to the frames.

3 On the **Pages Panel**, duplicate the master page several times, then create different master page layouts for each master page.

4 Drag each master page thumbnail onto the publication spread in turn.

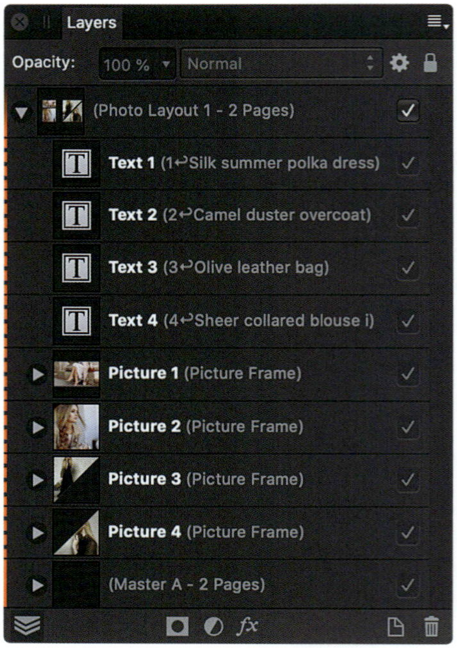

Identical object naming across Photo Layout master pages

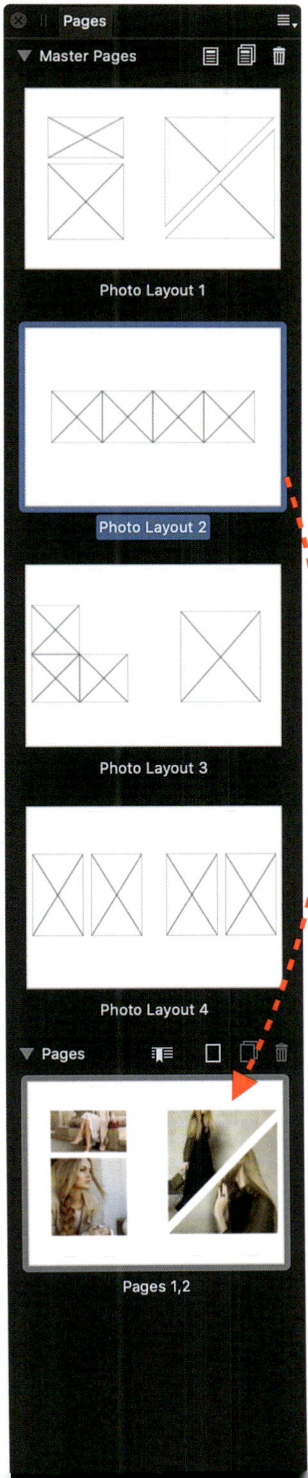
Pages
Master Pages
Photo Layout 1
Photo Layout 2
Photo Layout 3
Photo Layout 4
Pages
Pages 1,2

RIGHT
LEFT
ABOVE
JON VAN
THE JON VAN SPRING SUMMER PREVIEW IS HERE
MENSWEAR MEETS MODERN CHIC IN JV'S LATEST WOMENSWEAR COLLECTION

Awaken your wardrobe with Komodo
and daring to light and chic; the collection
woman. Get the look this January.
ie.
Bisset's summer collection
Above
AURÉLIE COUTURE
Summer

4

Skills On Show CV/Résumé

Designing a CV/Résumé by Rosa Maglione

Rosa Maglione, a respected US-based designer and user advocate looks at how guides, text styles, appealing fonts, accent colours and text frame positioning can create CV/résumé designs that will catch and hold a recruiter's attention.

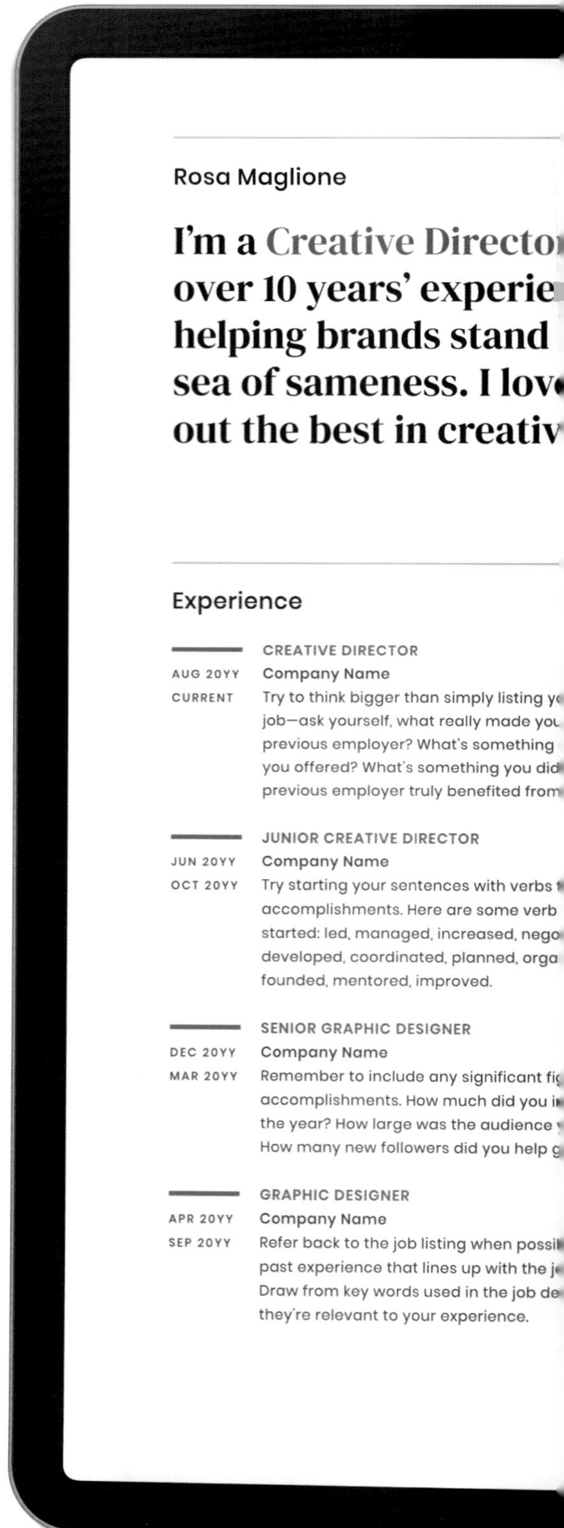

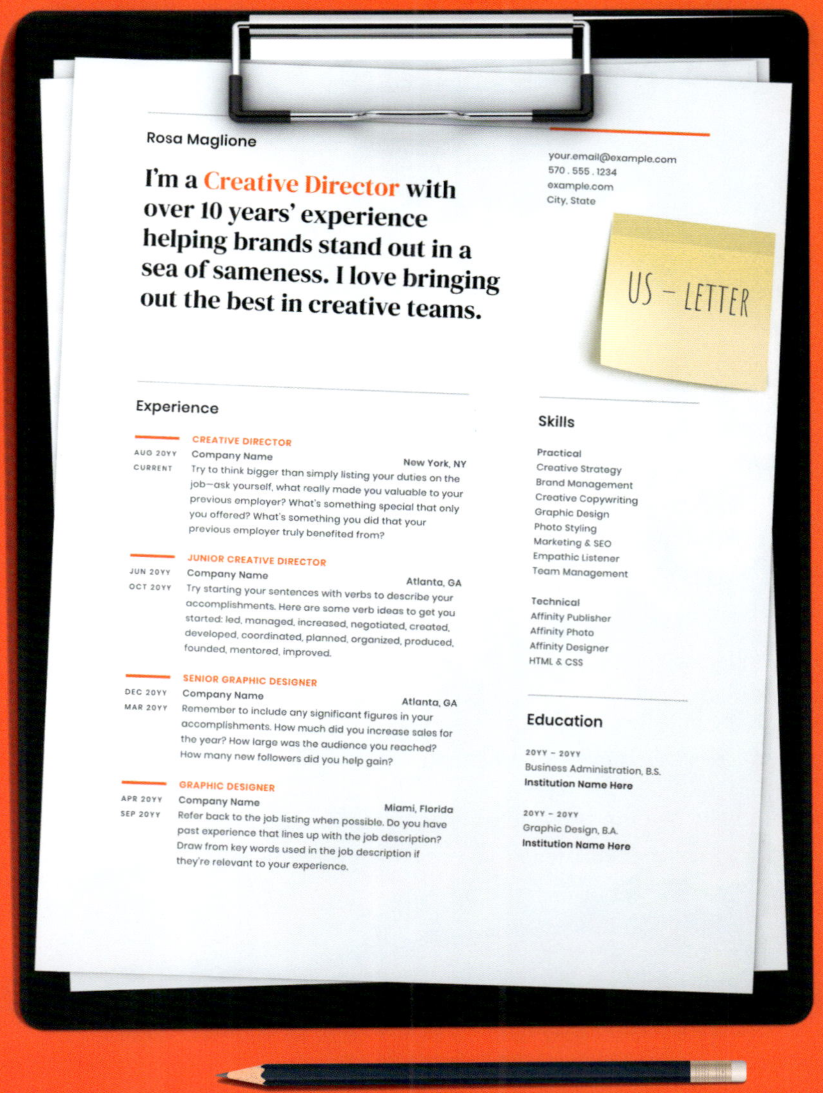
Rosa Maglione
I'm a Creative Director with over 10 years' experience helping brands stand out in a sea of sameness. I love bringing out the best in creative teams.
your.email@example.com
570 . 555 . 1234
example.com
City, State
US – LETTER
Experience
CREATIVE DIRECTOR
AUG 20YY
CURRENT
Company Name
New York, NY
Try to think bigger than simply listing your duties on the job—ask yourself, what really made you valuable to your previous employer? What's something special that only you offered? What's something you did that your previous employer truly benefited from?
JUNIOR CREATIVE DIRECTOR
JUN 20YY
OCT 20YY
Company Name
Atlanta, GA
Try starting your sentences with verbs to describe your accomplishments. Here are some verb ideas to get you started: led, managed, increased, negotiated, created, developed, coordinated, planned, organized, produced, founded, mentored, improved.
SENIOR GRAPHIC DESIGNER
DEC 20YY
MAR 20YY
Company Name
Atlanta, GA
Remember to include any significant figures in your accomplishments. How much did you increase sales for the year? How large was the audience you reached? How many new followers did you help gain?
GRAPHIC DESIGNER
APR 20YY
SEP 20YY
Company Name
Miami, Florida
Refer back to the job listing when possible. Do you have past experience that lines up with the job description? Draw from key words used in the job description if they're relevant to your experience.
Skills
Practical
Creative Strategy
Brand Management
Creative Copywriting
Graphic Design
Photo Styling
Marketing & SEO
Empathic Listener
Team Management
Technical
Affinity Publisher
Affinity Photo
Affinity Designer
HTML & CSS
Education
20YY – 20YY
Business Administration, B.S.
Institution Name Here
20YY – 20YY
Graphic Design, B.A.
Institution Name Here

BEFORE YOU GET STARTED

Resources

You can get all the resources that are referenced in this project from: https://affin.co/SkillsOnShow

In the resources, you'll find both résumé (US letter) and CV (A4) final versions for this project—intermediate project files will be based on the US résumé version only.

Knowledge of Affinity Publisher

To get the most from undertaking this project, you will need to:

- Be familiar with the interface of Affinity Publisher. You can learn more about the interface in the Interface Tour chapter, starting on p. 14.
- Have good core skills. See the skills table below to see which additional aspects of Affinity Publisher you need to be confident with to complete this project:

Working with Text	p. 112
Text Styles	p. 140

For CVs, you are the "brand" and the employer is the "customer".

INTRODUCTION

When tackling a new CV design, I treat it just as I would any branding project for a client.

It should reflect who you are, what you value, and the type of employer you want to attract. If done right, your CV can help you attract a company that speaks your language. The employer gets someone who is a great fit, and you land a job you love. It's a win-win situation.

STARTING THE DESIGN PROCESS

Put yourself in a recruiter's shoes for a moment. They've been looking at CVs all morning and, for the most part, every CV they've seen looks the same.

Your CV should stop a recruiter in their tracks and catch their attention just long enough for them to keep reading.

In this project, styling text and typographical hierarchy will play a crucial part in creating a CV design that's legible, readable, and quickly scannable. The recruiter will thank you later.

Resource

Skills_on_show_1.afpub
rosa_text.rtf

DOCUMENT SETUP

When deciding on the document setup for your design, consider the intended final output of your CV. Will it be printed? Will it be emailed or uploaded?

The CV layout we'll be designing is versatile enough to suit both desktop print and digital (web) outputs. Let's get to work.

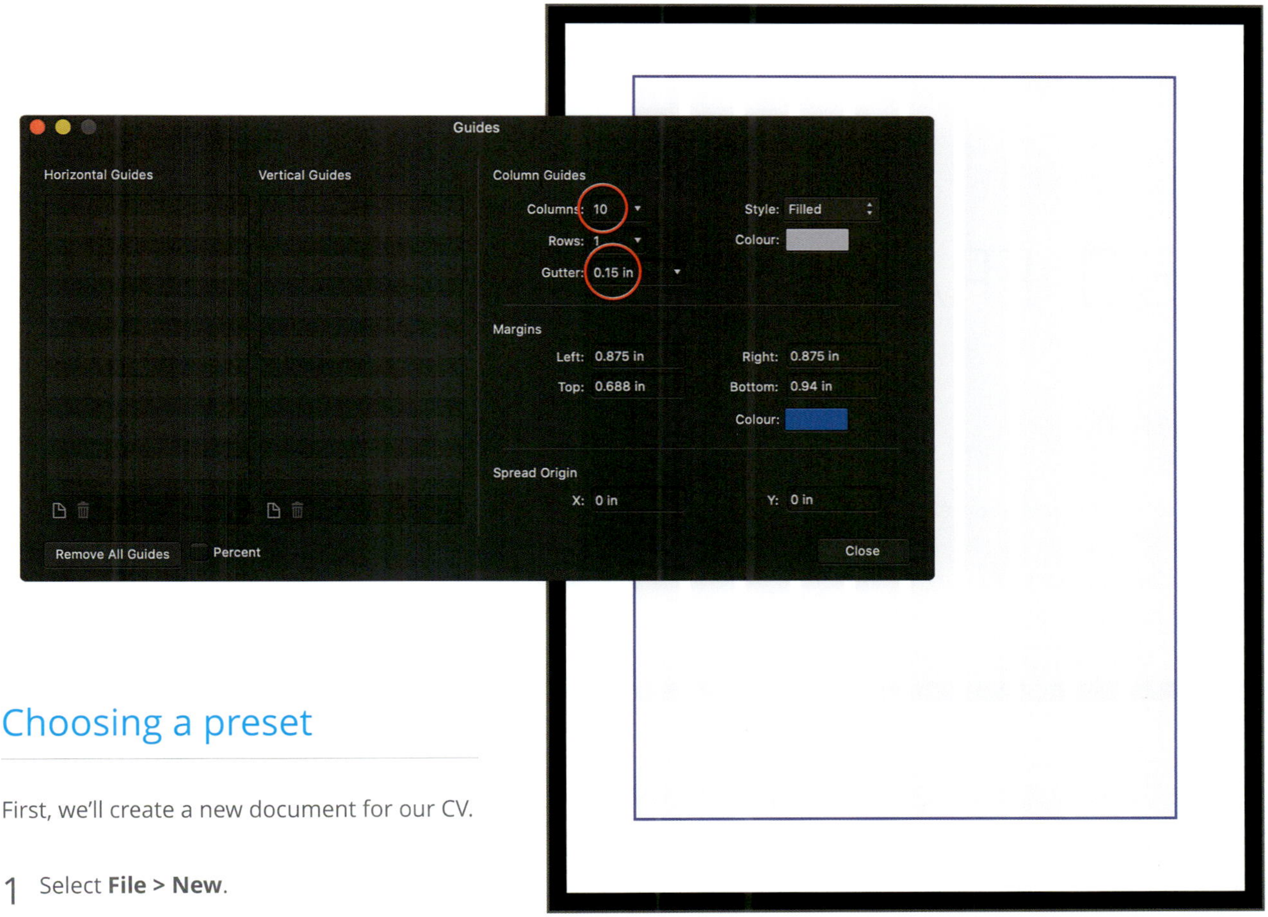

Choosing a preset

First, we'll create a new document for our CV.

1 Select **File > New**.

2 From the dialog, ensure **Presets** and **Print** are selected, then choose the *Letter* thumbnail. This sets up an RGB colour space intended for desktop printing and digital (web) delivery.

3 In the **Layout** and **Pages** sections, uncheck **Default master** and **Facing pages**, respectively, as only a single unmastered page is needed.

4 Adjust the **Margins** settings as shown.

Column guides

Column guides are a good way to neaten up the presentation of text on your CV. Text frames will snap to and horizontally align with vertical column guide edges.

Adding column guides

1 Go to **View > Guides Manager**.

2 Under **Column Guides**, set **Columns** to *10*, and **Gutter** to *0.15 in*.

TEXT FRAMES

General

When you first create your text frames, it's best to keep it simple by using plain unformatted text.

To start off with, we'll just roughly line up the text frames against the column guides. We'll adjust their placement further once we have all of our text styles in place.

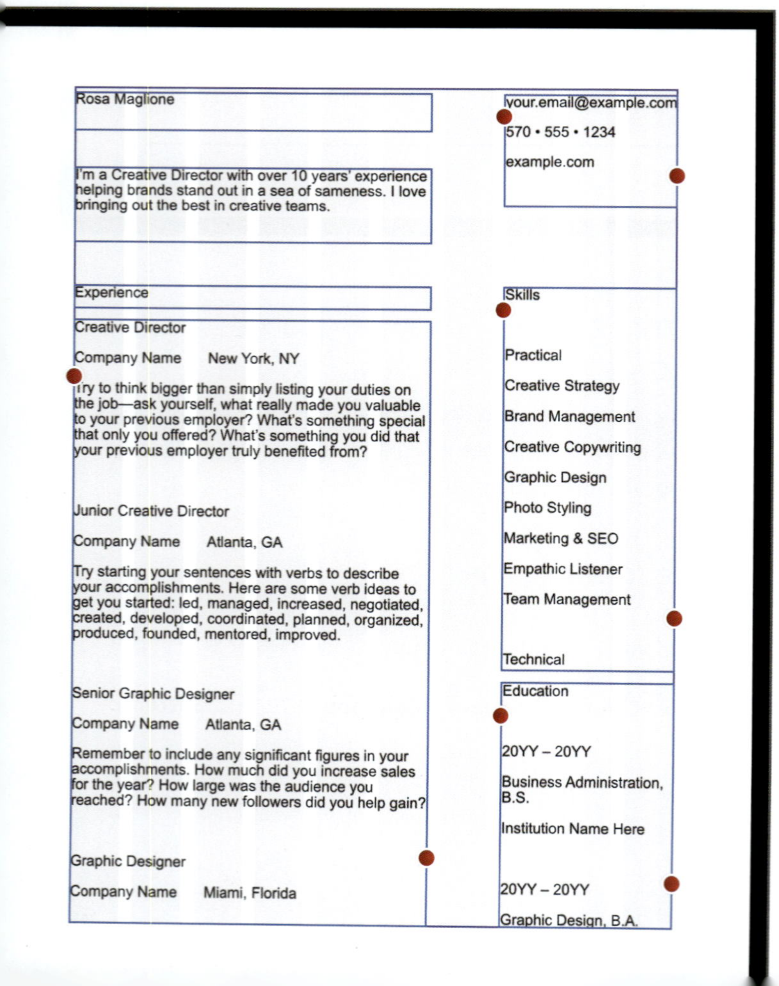

Creating text frames

1. With the **Frame Text Tool** active, lay out your text frames, ensuring they snap to column guides.
2. Type or paste your text into the text frames. Alternatively, copy and paste the sample text from the rosa_text.rtf file.

Don't worry about the red dots indicating overset text—we'll fix text formatting next.

> Use **Edit > Paste Without Format** if you're copying text into Publisher from another document; this avoids carrying over any unnecessary formatting.

Resource
Skills_on_show_02.afpub

STYLING THE BODY

Setting up text styles works well even on smaller projects, allowing you to make changes to all of your same-styled text later in one operation.

Body font

When deciding on a body font, it's important to consider what's easy to read and what looks right for your CV. As a rule of thumb, it's generally considered best to use sans-serif fonts for files that will be viewed on a screen, and serif fonts for a printed document.

The vast majority of CVs are more likely to be viewed on a screen rather than read on paper, so we've gone for Poppins, a versatile sans-serif font that's appealing and professional.

Downloading and installing fonts

1 Go to https://fonts.google.com (or search online for *Google fonts*) and download the **Poppins** family.

2 Open the downloaded zip file and open and read the OFL.txt file.

3 For *Mac*: ctrl-click the downloaded font files and select **Install font**.
or:
For *Windows*: Right-click the downloaded font files and select **Install**.

While visiting Google fonts, download and install the DM Serif Display font family—we'll use this later in the project.

I chose a shade of grey (Black 70%) for the text instead of Black as I can play with contrast to help differentiate darker heading text later.

Body formatting

For our body text, we're going to format it before saving it as a text style.

1 Select all text frames using **Select > Select All**.

2 On the **Character Panel**, format the text as shown. The **Tracking** increase by *30‰* increases the letter spacing uniformly; the characters are more spread out.

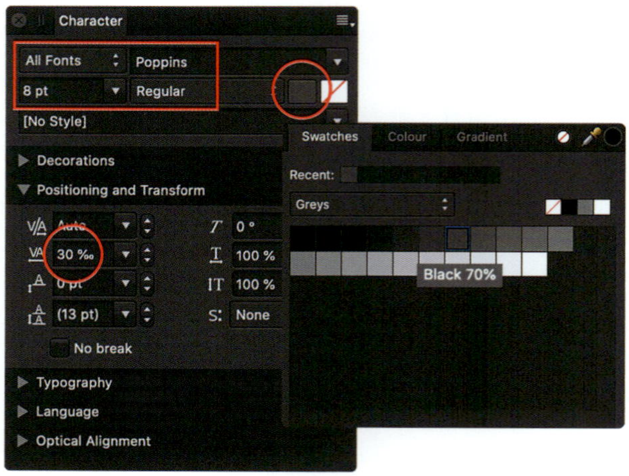

Saving as a base text style

I like to save the body formatting to a Base text style so that it's automatically applied to future 'inheriting' text styles by default.

1 With your text selected, go to the **Text Styles Panel**.

2 Click on the *Base* paragraph style's Options menu.

3 Select **Update "Base"**.

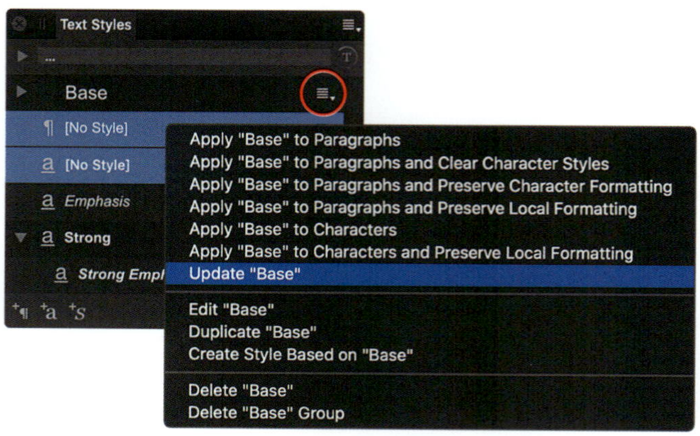

Using the Body text style

Let's now apply and edit the *Body* text style. Remember that the style inherits styling from *Base* by default, but we want to set a font size and leading just for Body as an override.

1 Using the **Text Styles Panel**, apply the *Body* text style to all selected text frames.

2 Double-click the *Body* style entry, then:

- From the **Character > Font** section, set a **Font Size** of *8 pt*.
- From the **Paragraph > Spacing** section, set **Leading** to *Exactly 13 pt* and check **Space between same styles**.

Adding leading will help with legibility and readability.

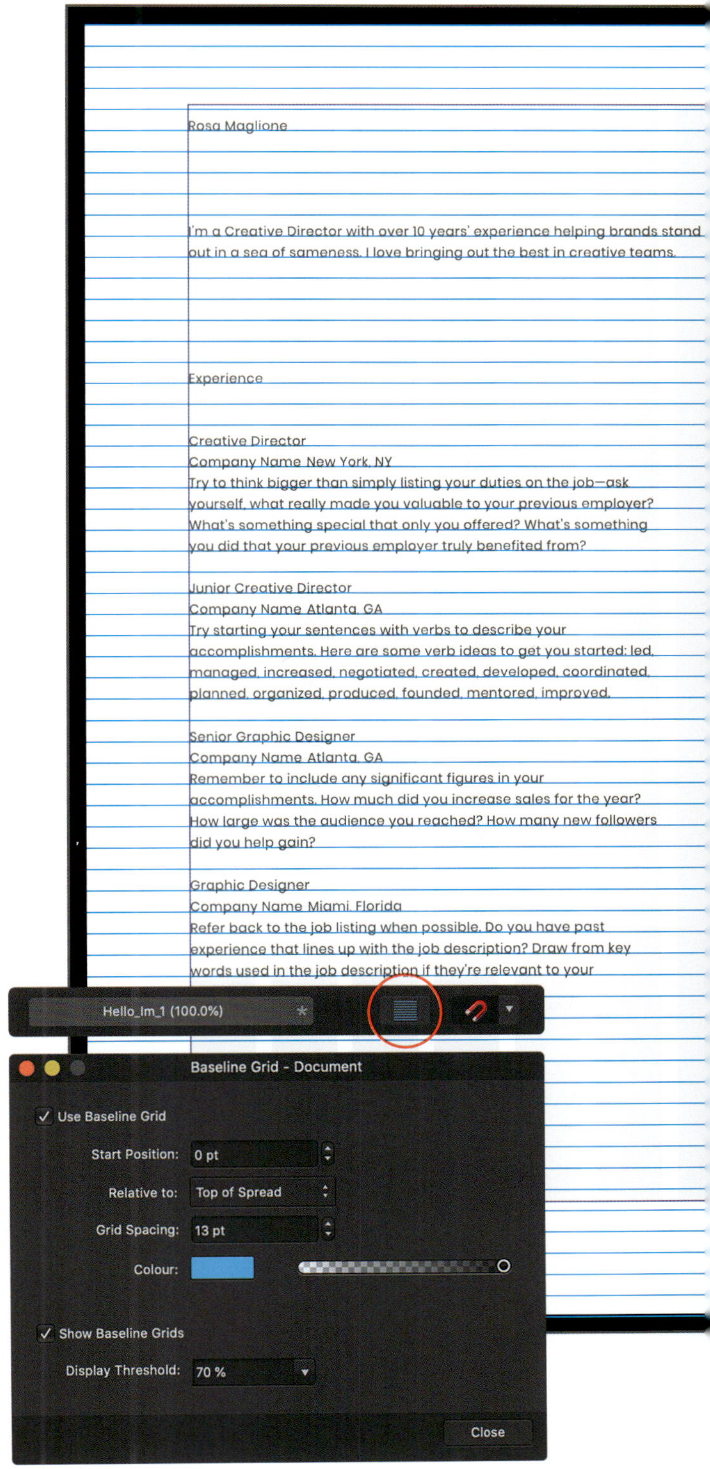

Baseline grid

Now that the body copy is styled, we can set the baseline grid to match the leading we've applied.

1 On the **Toolbar**, click **Show Baseline Grid Manager**.

2 Check **Use Baseline Grid** and set a **Grid spacing** of *13 pt*, making it **Relative to** the *Top of Spread*.

Check Show baseline grids to check baseline alignment.

STYLING THE HEADINGS

Using the **Text Styles Panel** exclusively, let's edit and create paragraph styles for headings so they stand out against the body text.

Double-click a style to edit; click **Create Paragraph Style** for a new style. While styling the frame text, the text frames need to be resized and repositioned as I go to accommodate the larger text, especially the main tagline.

Categories

This text should be clear, concise and easy to skim read. A darker colour and a larger font size will distinguish the headings from our body text.

Heading 2 edits

- **Character > Font:**
  Font weight *Medium*
  Font size *12.5 pt*
- **Character > Colour & Decorations:**
  Text fill *Black*
- **Character > Position & Transform:**
  Tracking *25‰*

Previous job titles

These need to be semibold and draw immediate interest in the text frame. Something in all caps with wide letter spacing was appropriate.

Heading 3 creation

- **Character > Font:**
  Font weight *Semi-bold*
  Font size [No change]
- **Character > Position & Transform:**
  Tracking *60‰*
- **Typography > Capitals:**
  All caps checked
- **Paragraph > Spacing:**
  Space after *0 pt*

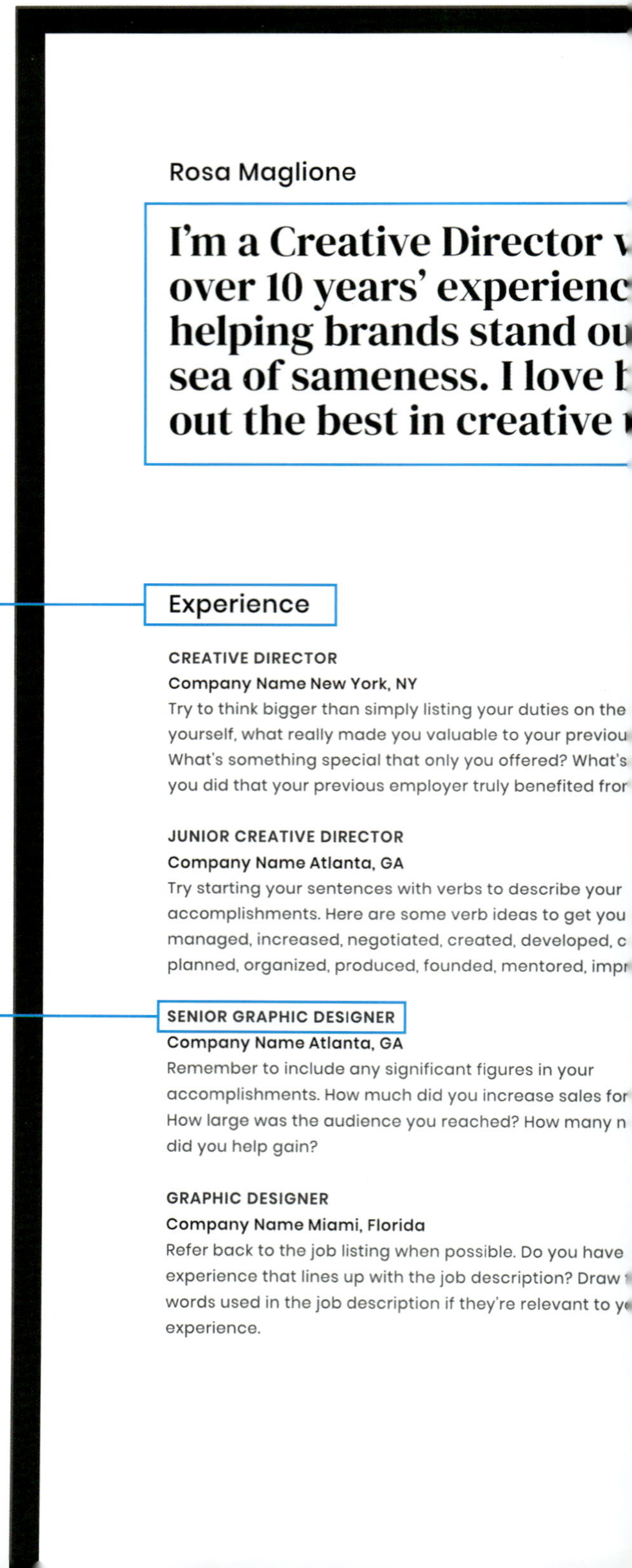

Rosa Maglione

I'm a Creative Director w
over 10 years' experienc
helping brands stand ou
sea of sameness. I love b
out the best in creative t

Experience

CREATIVE DIRECTOR
Company Name New York, NY
Try to think bigger than simply listing your duties on the
yourself, what really made you valuable to your previou
What's something special that only you offered? What's
you did that your previous employer truly benefited fror

JUNIOR CREATIVE DIRECTOR
Company Name Atlanta, GA
Try starting your sentences with verbs to describe your
accomplishments. Here are some verb ideas to get you
managed, increased, negotiated, created, developed, c
planned, organized, produced, founded, mentored, impr

SENIOR GRAPHIC DESIGNER
Company Name Atlanta, GA
Remember to include any significant figures in your
accomplishments. How much did you increase sales for
How large was the audience you reached? How many n
did you help gain?

GRAPHIC DESIGNER
Company Name Miami, Florida
Refer back to the job listing when possible. Do you have
experience that lines up with the job description? Draw
words used in the job description if they're relevant to y
experience.

Resource
Skills_on_show_03.afpub

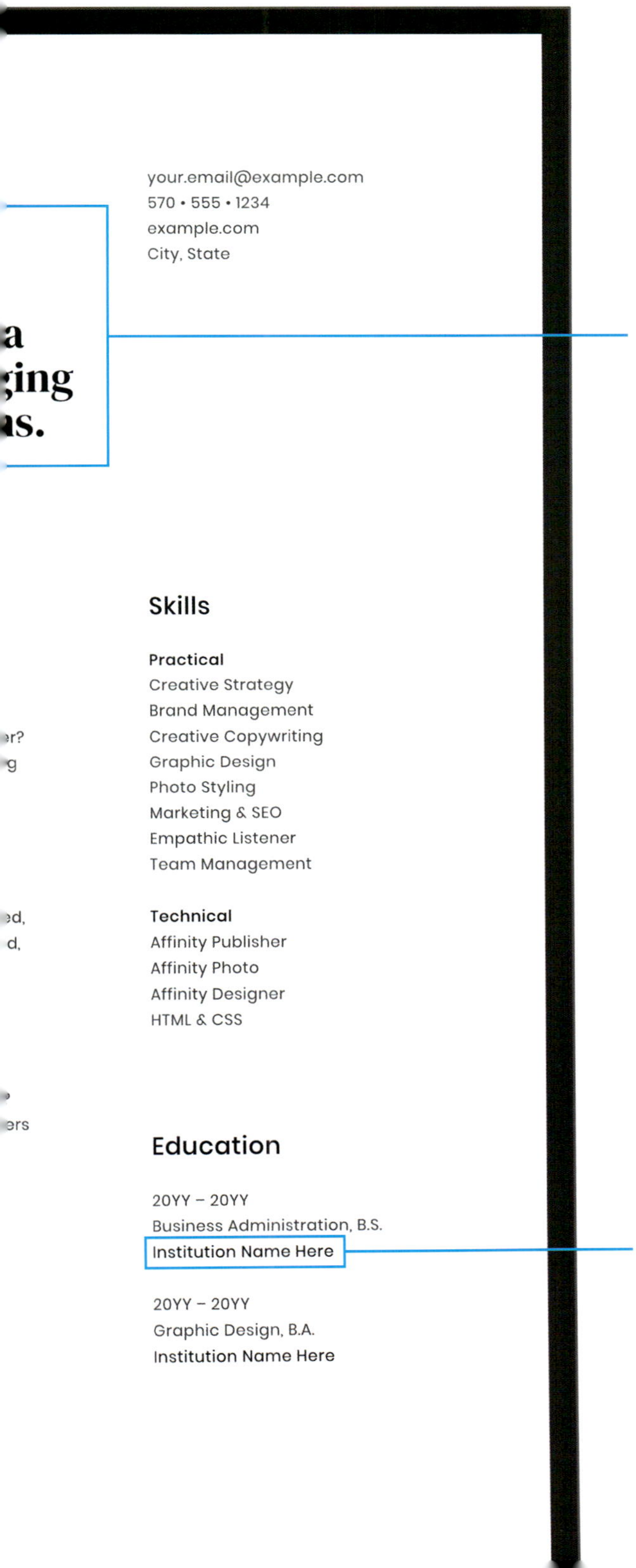
your.email@example.com
570 • 555 • 1234
example.com
City, State

Skills

Practical
Creative Strategy
Brand Management
Creative Copywriting
Graphic Design
Photo Styling
Marketing & SEO
Empathic Listener
Team Management

Technical
Affinity Publisher
Affinity Photo
Affinity Designer
HTML & CSS

Education

20YY – 20YY
Business Administration, B.S.
Institution Name Here

20YY – 20YY
Graphic Design, B.A.
Institution Name Here

CV tagline

In my experience, the upper section of the CV gets the most attention. Visually, this should be the most eye-catching text that appears on the page. A clear hierarchy on the page also makes it easy for someone to scan. The tagline gives a great opportunity to show some of your personality while you've got their attention.

I used 26 pt leading because it's a multiple of 13, which is the baseline measurement, so the tagline aligns with our baseline grid. A bold serif typeface for the tagline creates contrast with the rest of the text and creates a strong focal point for the recruiter's eye. For independent leading control I switched off the style's baseline grid.

Heading 1 edits

- **Character > Font:**
  Font family *DM Serif Display*
  Font size *22 pt*
- **Character > Colour & Decorations:**
  Text fill *Black*
- **Character > Position & Transform:**
  Tracking *5‰*
- **Paragraph > Spacing:**
  Alignment *Left*
  Leading *Exactly 26 pt*
- **Paragraph > Baseline Grid:**
  Align to Baseline grid unchecked

Company names/locations, Skills subcategories and institution names

Click **Create Paragraph Style**, name it Heading 4 and base it on the *Body* style. These are given a higher importance than body text by using a Black text fill and Medium font weight.

Heading 4 creation

- **Character > Font:**
  Font weight *Medium*
  Font size [No change]
- **Character > Colour & Decorations:**
  Text fill *Black*
- **Character > Position & Transform:**
  Tracking *40‰*
- **Paragraph > Spacing:**
  Space after *0 pt*

Adding and styling the dates

After some general text frame repositioning I wanted to address a missing element in the design—the employment dates in the *Experience* section.

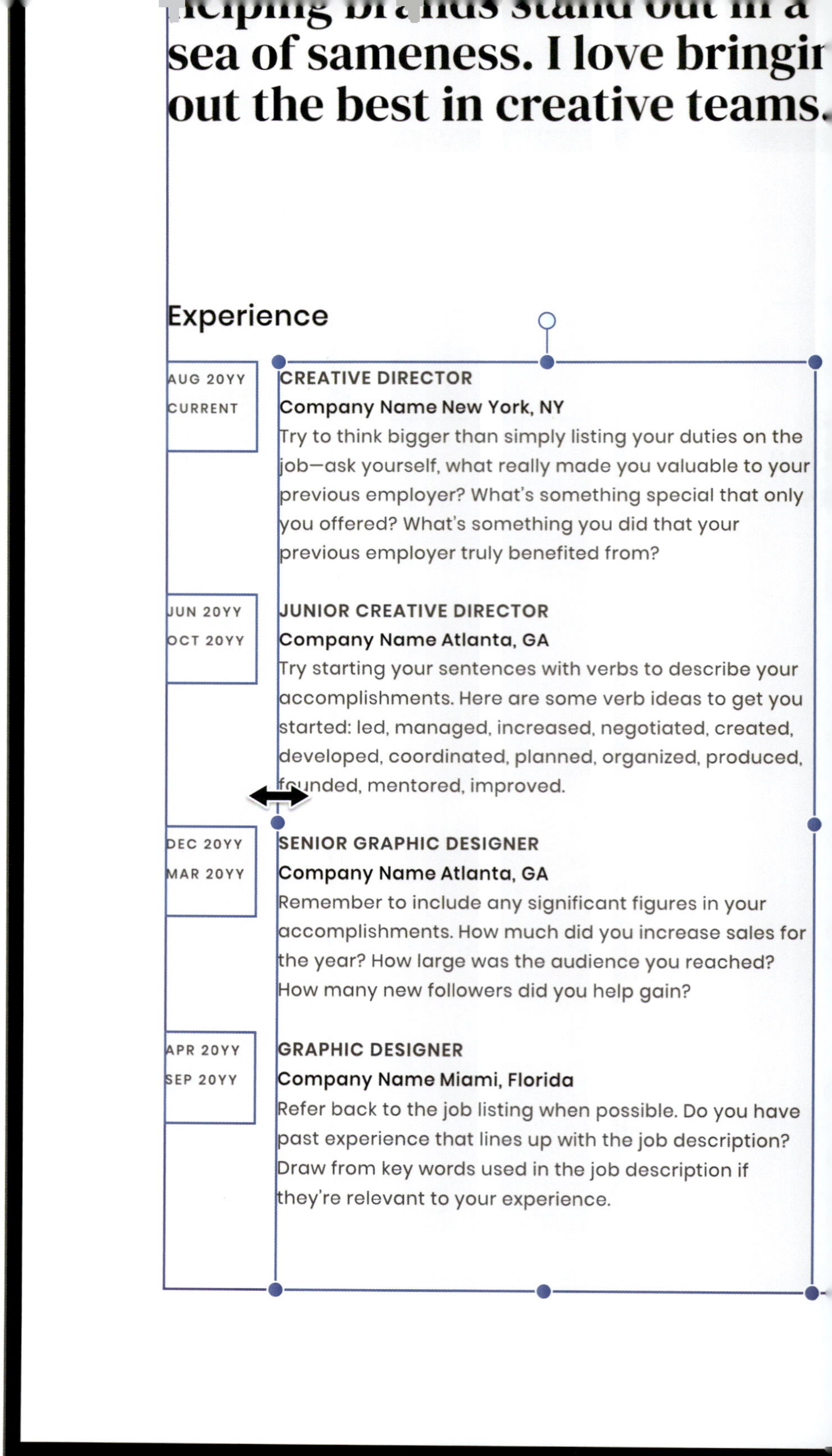

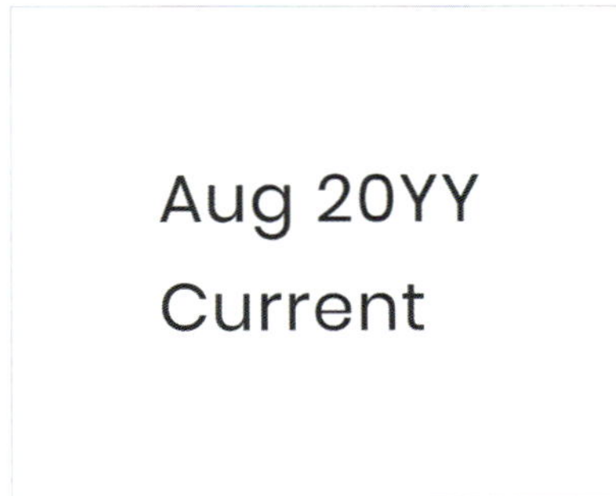

Before

After

Making room for new text frames

1 Drag the left edge of the *Experience* text frame inward by one column to reduce its width. This will clear some space for the dates.

2 Create new text frames to the left of each job position.

3 Add text as shown.

Try to leave a gutter's width of space between your text frames so they don't feel too cramped.

> Although I didn't use the feature, I could have pinned (anchored) the dates to the job positions using the **Toolbar**'s **Float with Text** option. This would automatically reposition dates as your job position text reflows during editing.

Styling the dates

1 Select a date text frame.

2 Click **Create Paragraph Style** and apply these settings:

- **Style:**
  Style name Dates
  Based on Body
- **Character > Font:**
  Font weight *Medium*
  Font size *6 pt*
- **Character > Colour & Decorations:**
  Text fill *70% Black*
- **Character > Position & Transform:**
  Tracking *140‰*
- **Typography > Capitals:**
  All caps checked

3 Apply this text style to the rest of the date text frames, and the dates in the *Education* section. I experimented with font size, case sensitivity and tracking in the Education section too.

ACCENT COLOURS AND DECORATIONS

Accent colours

Let's create an accent colour as a global swatch so it can be updated globally across text. We'll use this colour to add emphasis to certain elements of the CV.

Creating a global colour

1 Go to the **Swatches Panel**.

2 From the Panel Preferences, select **Add Global Colour**.

3 Name your new colour *Accent Color* and adjust the colour settings.

4 Click **Add** to create your global colour in a newly created document palette.

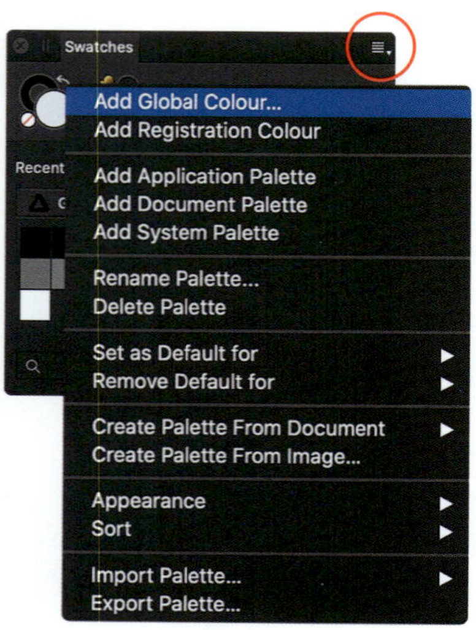

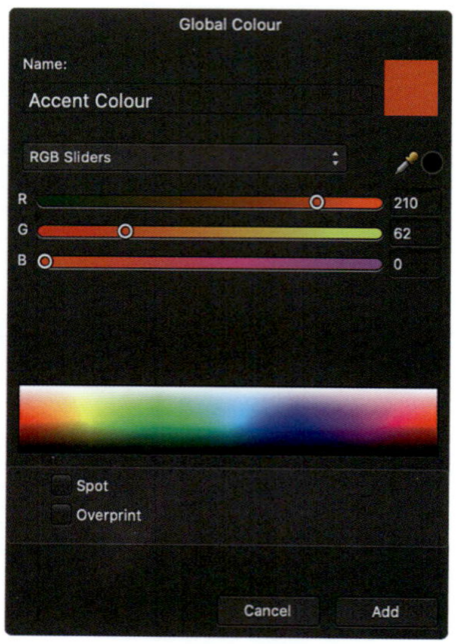

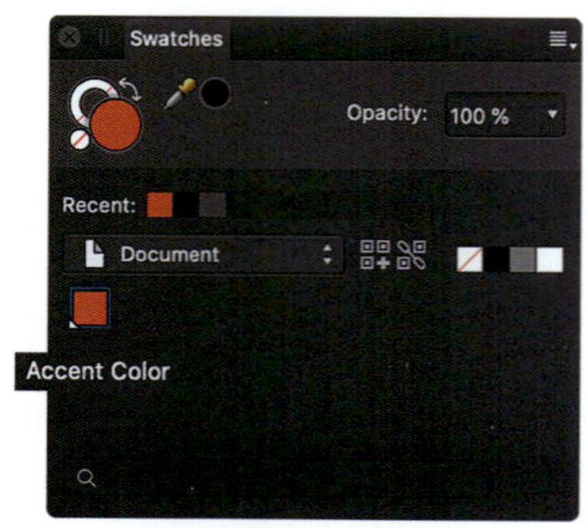

You can identify global colour swatches by the white triangle in the bottom left corner of a swatch.

Resource
Skills_on_show_04.afpub

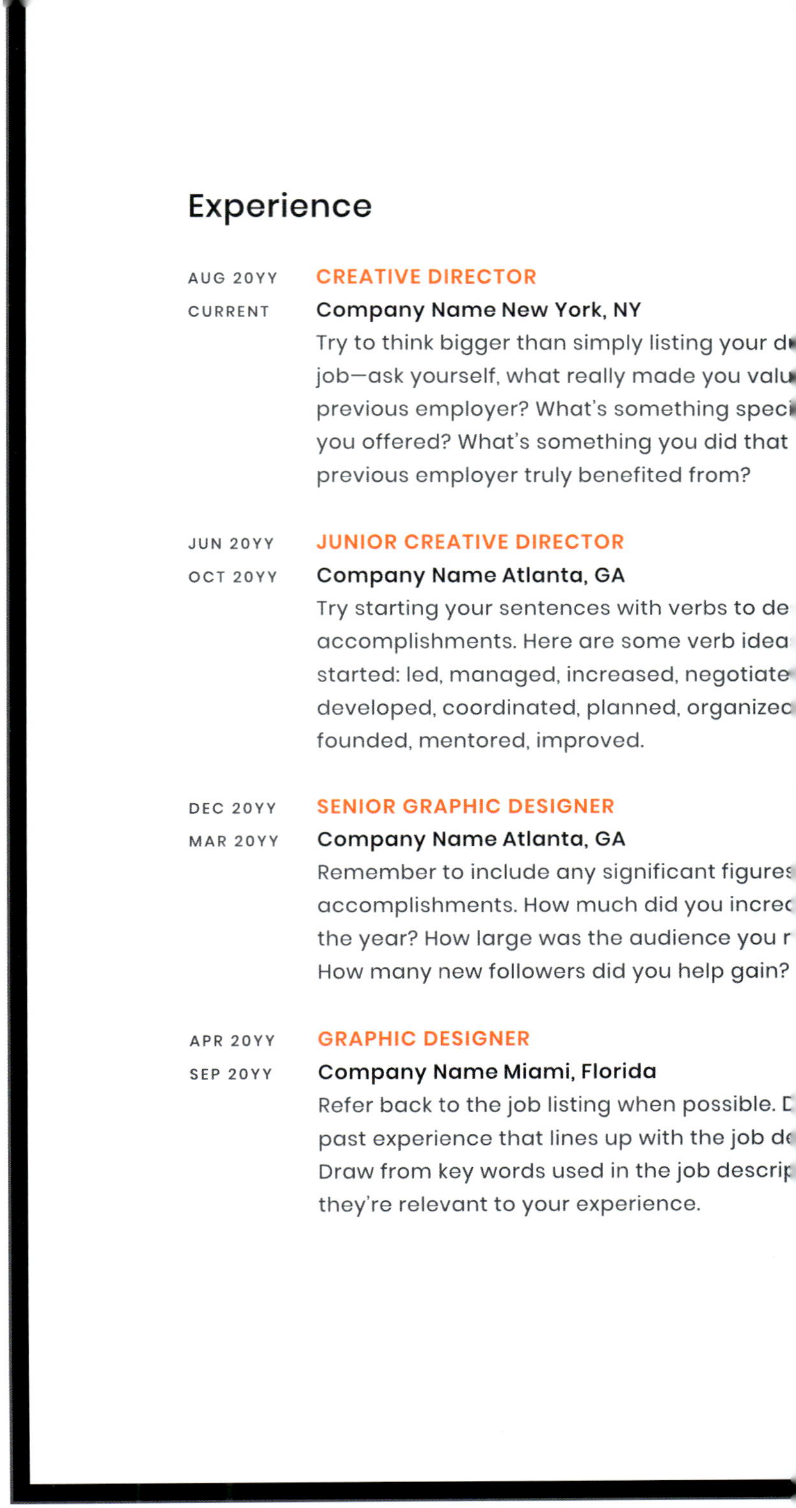

Experience

AUG 20YY
CURRENT

CREATIVE DIRECTOR
Company Name New York, NY
Try to think bigger than simply listing your d
job—ask yourself, what really made you valu
previous employer? What's something speci
you offered? What's something you did that
previous employer truly benefited from?

JUN 20YY
OCT 20YY

JUNIOR CREATIVE DIRECTOR
Company Name Atlanta, GA
Try starting your sentences with verbs to de
accomplishments. Here are some verb idea
started: led, managed, increased, negotiate
developed, coordinated, planned, organized
founded, mentored, improved.

DEC 20YY
MAR 20YY

SENIOR GRAPHIC DESIGNER
Company Name Atlanta, GA
Remember to include any significant figures
accomplishments. How much did you increa
the year? How large was the audience you r
How many new followers did you help gain?

APR 20YY
SEP 20YY

GRAPHIC DESIGNER
Company Name Miami, Florida
Refer back to the job listing when possible. D
past experience that lines up with the job de
Draw from key words used in the job descrip
they're relevant to your experience.

Applying the global colour

Time to try out our new colour on some text.

1 Select all job titles using the cmd ⌘ key (Mac) or ctrl key (Win).

2 On the **Swatches Panel**, select the *Accent Color* global swatch.

> *Adding emphasis to job positions allows the hiring manager to be able to quickly glance at previous roles.*

Applying heading decorations

Now we'll add a horizontal decoration (rule) above the headings so each section is visually anchored.

Adding decorations to a text style

From here, we're going to add some decorations, and tweak the indent settings to space them out a little better. We want our decoration to complement our heading text, not overshadow it, so we'll alter the colour slightly to give it a more faded impression.

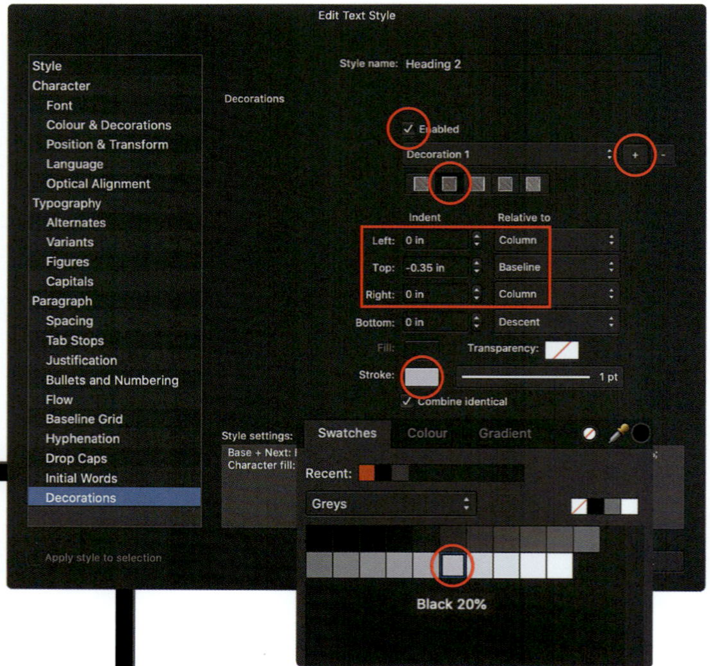

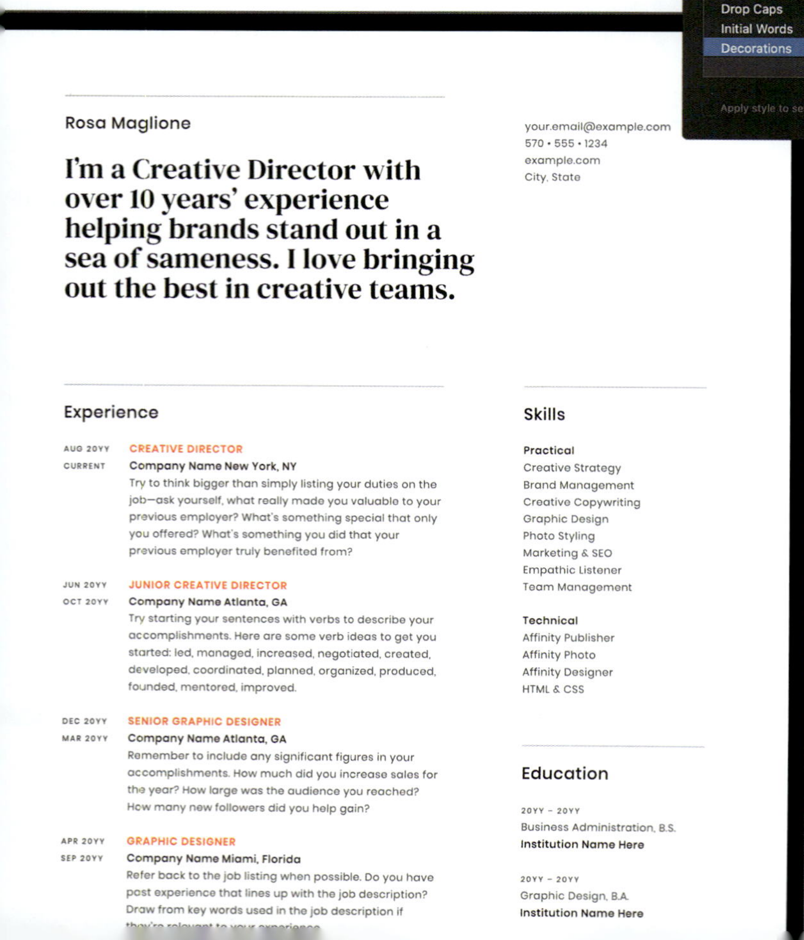

Rosa Maglione

I'm a Creative Director with over 10 years' experience helping brands stand out in a sea of sameness. I love bringing out the best in creative teams.

your.email@example.com
570 • 555 • 1234
example.com
City, State

Experience

AUG 20YY – CURRENT
CREATIVE DIRECTOR
Company Name New York, NY
Try to think bigger than simply listing your duties on the job—ask yourself, what really made you valuable to your previous employer? What's something special that only you offered? What's something you did that your previous employer truly benefited from?

JUN 20YY – OCT 20YY
JUNIOR CREATIVE DIRECTOR
Company Name Atlanta, GA
Try starting your sentences with verbs to describe your accomplishments. Here are some verb ideas to get you started: led, managed, increased, negotiated, created, developed, coordinated, planned, organized, produced, founded, mentored, improved.

DEC 20YY – MAR 20YY
SENIOR GRAPHIC DESIGNER
Company Name Atlanta, GA
Remember to include any significant figures in your accomplishments. How much did you increase sales for the year? How large was the audience you reached? How many new followers did you help gain?

APR 20YY – SEP 20YY
GRAPHIC DESIGNER
Company Name Miami, Florida
Refer back to the job listing when possible. Do you have past experience that lines up with the job description? Draw from key words used in the job description if

Skills

Practical
Creative Strategy
Brand Management
Creative Copywriting
Graphic Design
Photo Styling
Marketing & SEO
Empathic Listener
Team Management

Technical
Affinity Publisher
Affinity Photo
Affinity Designer
HTML & CSS

Education

20YY – 20YY
Business Administration, B.S.
Institution Name Here

20YY – 20YY
Graphic Design, B.A.
Institution Name Here

- On the **Text Styles Panel**, double-click the *Heading 2* style entry and set the following:

- **Paragraph > Decorations:**
  Check **Enabled**
  Enable **Top** border icon

  Left and **Right** indents **Relative to** *Column*
  Top indent *-0.35* in **Relative To** *Baseline*

  Stroke Colour *Black 20%*
  (from **Swatches** tab)

Removing individual decorations

Let's remove the unwanted top border applied to the person's name.

1 Highlight the text *Rosa Maglione*.

2 Go to the **Paragraph Panel**'s **Decorations** section.

3 Click the **Top** border icon to disable it.

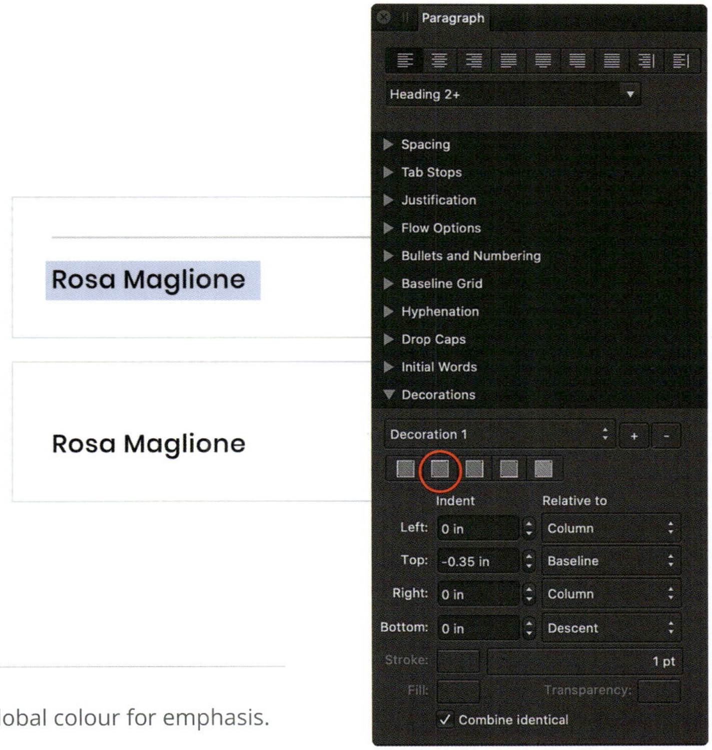

Decorating the dates

Let's add a decoration above each date using our global colour for emphasis.

1 Click **Create Paragraph Style**, naming it *Dates (Line Above)* and adjust settings:

- **Style:**
  Based on *Dates*
  Next style *Dates*

- **Paragraph > Spacing:**
  Space after *0 pt*

- **Paragraph > Decorations:**
  check **Enabled**
  Enable **Top** border icon
  Left and **Right** indents **Relative to** *Column*.
  Top indent *-0.16 in* **Relative To** *Cap Height*
  Click on the **Stroke** colour. From the **Swatches** tab, select the *Accent Color* swatch and boost the stroke width to *2.5 pt*.

2 Select the first line of each date, and apply the *Dates (Line Above)* style.

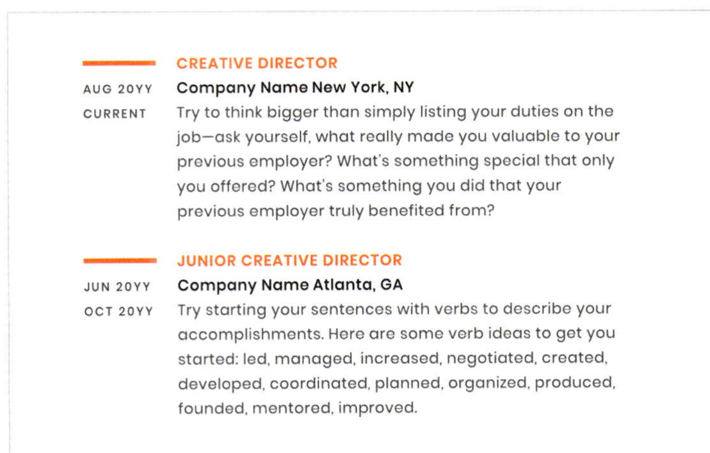

To align decorations with the job position, select all date text frames with the shift key (⇧), and drag them downwards.

Keeping the key pressed during repositioning will constrain the movement horizontally.

Resource
Skills_on_show_final.afpub

THE FINISHING TOUCHES

Offsetting text using right indent tabs

Let's offset the job locations away from the company names by aligning them to the right edge of the text frame. Instead of a complicated tab setup I used a simple right indent tab.

Inserting a right indent tab

1 Place the caret before the location text (*New York, Atlanta, Miami*).

2 Insert using **Text > Insert > Spaces and Tabs > Right Indent Tab**.

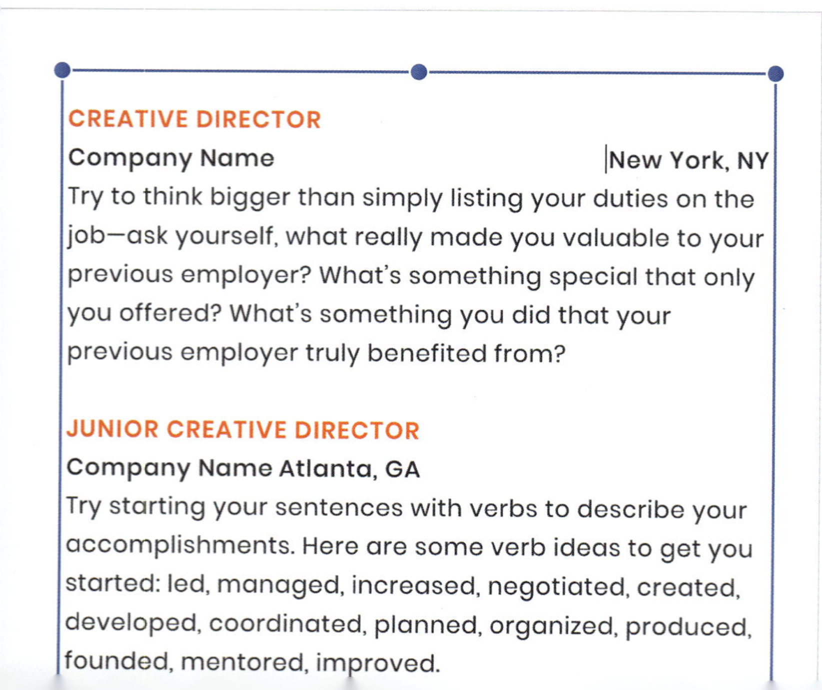

Adding a character style

Let's call out some words in the tagline in our accent colour (a) opposite.

1 In the tagline, select the *Creative Director* text.

2 On the **Swatches Panel**, select the *Accent Color* global swatch.

3 Create a character style called *Accent Color* by selecting the **New Style** option on the context toolbar's **Character Style** pop-up menu. We can reuse this style again easily.

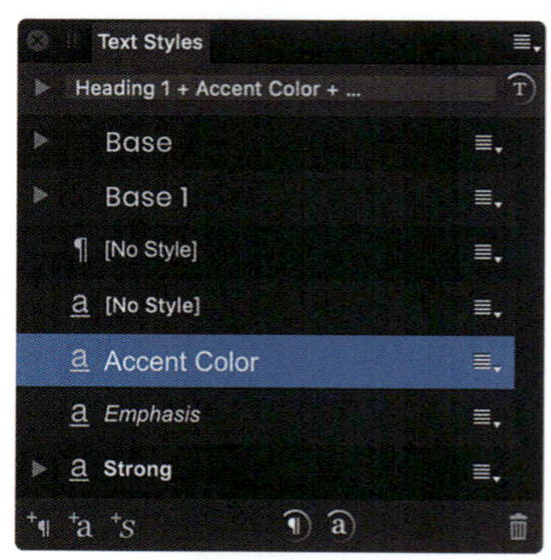

Header details

To embellish the header a little more, we'll use the **Pen Tool** to create lines that go across the top of the CV (b) in the same style as the line we used for the CV categories and dates.

Setting up the Pen Tool

1. Deselect all text frames.
2. Select the **Pen Tool** (P).
3. On the context toolbar, choose a **Fill** of none and a **Stroke** colour of *20% Black*.
4. Click the width option labelled *None*, setting a width of *1 pt* and the line **Cap** to be a **Butt Cap**.

Adding a straight line

1. Using the **Pen Tool**, click at one end of your top margin and then the other. Use the shift key (⇧) to constrain to horizontal.
2. Press the Esc key, then draw another line over just the contact details, adjusting the **Stroke** colour to use *Accent Color* and a width of *2.5 pt*.

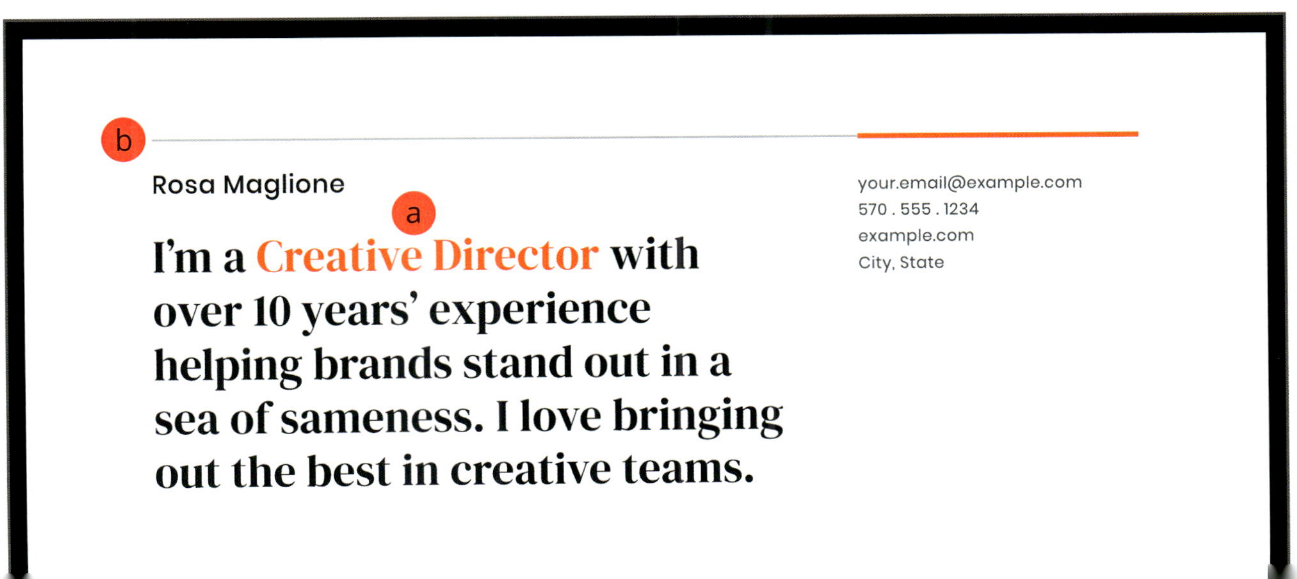

PRINTING & EXPORTING

Printing at home

Setting up a file to print

1. Go to **File > Print**.
2. Select your desktop printer from the list.
3. Click **Show Details** (Mac only). Choose a **Paper Size** that matches the size of your document, e.g. US Letter.
4. Set the **Scale** to *100%*.

> *Running a print test is important to make sure your text is legible and your composition makes sense. I find I always need to make adjustments to my design after seeing it printed on paper. This will also ensure that there are no issues if your potential employer decides to print it too.*

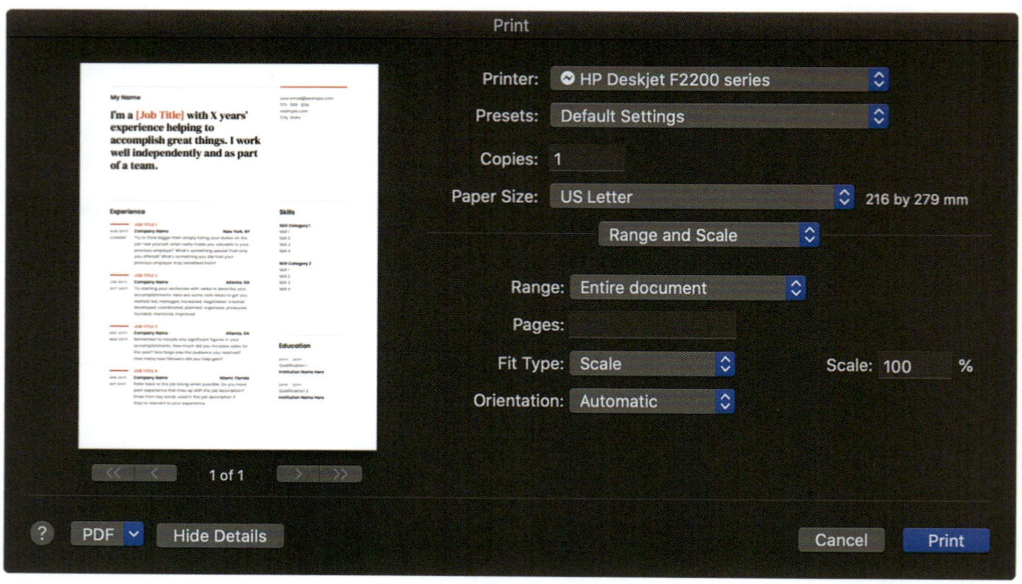

Exporting to PDF

Plenty of employers may prefer a digital copy of your CV instead. In this case, we'll create a screen-ready PDF from our file.

Exporting as a PDF file

1. Go to **File > Export**.
2. Select the **PDF** format option.
3. Choose a **Preset** of *PDF (digital – small size)*. This produces a PDF (RGB 72 DPI) of small file size that is ideal for screen viewing.

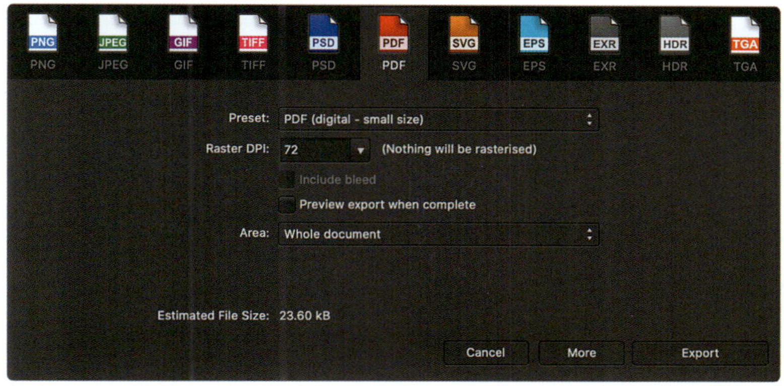

Exporting as a template

It's also possible to save your CV as a template for reuse at a later point.

1. Go to **File > Export as Template**.
2. Enter a file name for your .aftemplate file and click **Save**.

Templates can be made to appear in the **New Document** dialog by specifying the template's folder location there.

> We've also supplied templates (English and US versions) in our resources from which you can develop your own CV/Résumé.

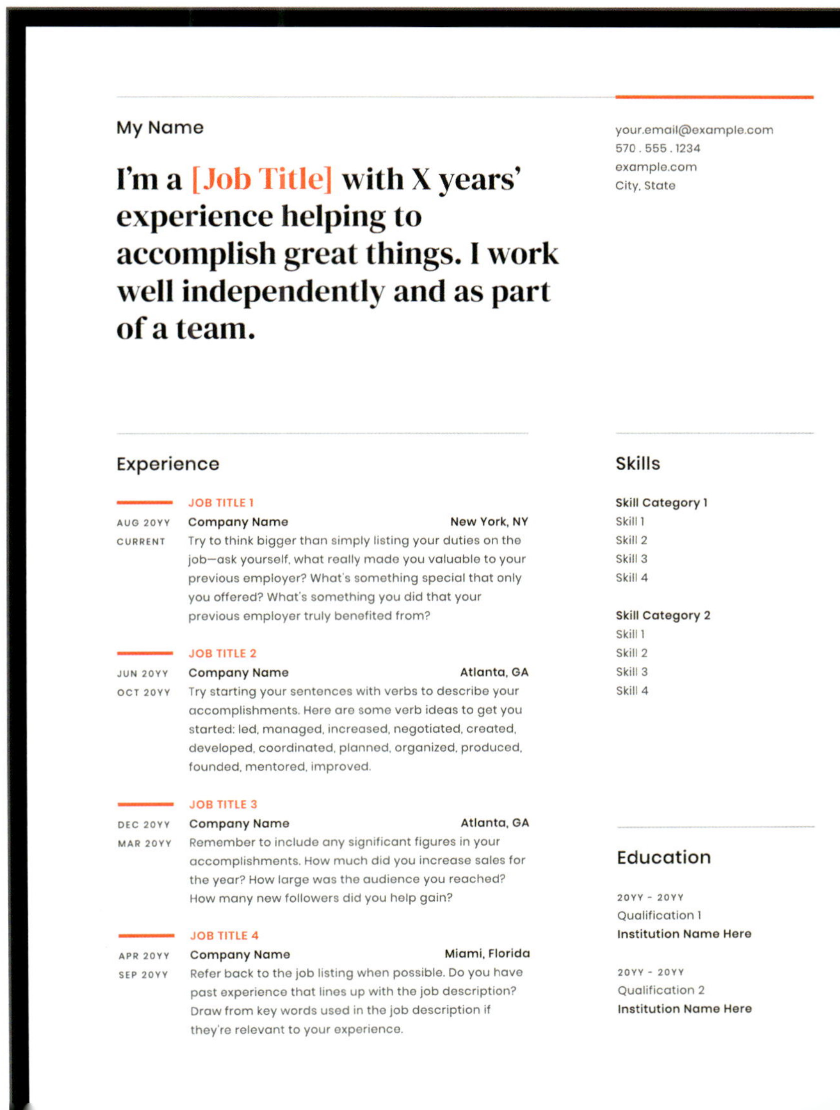

Rosa Maglione

your.email@example
570 . 555 . 1234
example.com
City, State

I'm a Creative Director with over 10 years' experience helping brands stand out in a sea of sameness. I love bringing out the best in creative teams.

Experience

CREATIVE DIRECTOR

AUG 20YY
CURRENT

Company Name New York, NY

Try to think bigger than simply listing your duties on the job—ask yourself, what really made you valuable to your previous employer? What's something special that only you offered? What's something you did that your previous employer truly benefited from?

JUNIOR CREATIVE DIRECTOR

JUN 20YY
OCT 20YY

Company Name Atlanta, GA

Try starting your sentences with verbs to describe your accomplishments. Here are some verb ideas to get you started: led, managed, increased, negotiated, created, developed, coordinated, planned, organized, produced, founded, mentored, improved.

SENIOR GRAPHIC DESIGNER

DEC 20YY
MAR 20YY

Company Name Atlanta, GA

Remember to include any significant figures in your accomplishments. How much did you increase sales for the year? How large was the audience you reached? How many new followers did you help gain?

GRAPHIC DESIGNER

APR 20YY
SEP 20YY

Company Name Miami, Florida

Refer back to the job listing when possible. Do you have past experience that lines up with the job description? Draw from key words used in the job description if they're relevant to your experience.

Skills

Practical
Creative Strategy
Brand Management
Creative Copywriting
Graphic Design
Photo Styling
Marketing & SEO
Empathic Listener
Team Management

Technical
Affinity Publisher
Affinity Photo
Affinity Designer
HTML & CSS

Education

20YY – 20YY
Business Administration, B.S.
Institution Name Here

20YY – 20YY
Graphic Design, B.A.
Institution Name Here

your.email@example.com
570 . 555 . 1234
example.com
City, State
Rosa Maglione
I'm a Creative Director with over 10 years' experience helping brands stand out in a sea of sameness. I love bringing out the best in creative teams.
Skills
Practical
Creative Strategy
Brand Management
Creative Copywriting
Creative Design
Graphic Design
Photo Styling
Marketing & SEO
Empathic Listener
Team Management
Technical
Affinity Publisher
Affinity Photo
Affinity Designer
HTML & CSS
Experience
AUG 20YY
CURRENT
CREATIVE DIRECTOR
Company Name
New York, NY
Try to think bigger than simply listing your duties on the job—ask yourself, what really made you valuable to your previous employer? What's something special that only you offered? What's something you did that your previous employer truly benefited from?
JUN 20YY
OCT 20YY
JUNIOR CREATIVE DIRECTOR
Company Name
Atlanta, GA
Try starting your sentences with verbs to describe your accomplishments. Here are some verb ideas to get you started: led, managed, increased, negotiated, created, developed, coordinated, planned, organized, produced, founded, mentored, improved.
DEC 20YY
MAR 20YY
SENIOR GRAPHIC DESIGNER
Company Name
Atlanta, GA
Remember to include any significant figures in your accomplishments. How much did you increase sales for the year? How large was the audience you reached? How many new followers did you help gain?
APR 20YY
SEP 20YY
GRAPHIC DESIGNER
Company Name
Miami, Florida
Refer back to the job listing when possible. Do you have past experience that lines up with the job description? Draw from key words used in the job description if they're relevant to your experience.
Education
20YY – 20YY
Business Administration, B.S.
Institution Name Here
20YY – 20YY
Graphic Design, B.A.
Institution Name Here

CHAPTER 5

Creative Projects

In this chapter, some classic publishing techniques used in book creation are explored, including autoflowing text, and generating tables of contents and indexes. Single page design for covers and posters offer a contrasting approach.

The emphasis here is on creative page design and how it can be applied across many pages or just a single page equally.

1

Alice's Adventures in Wonderland Book

Revisiting the classic children's book

Learn how to assemble a book to professional print standard—from the import of the main story to press-ready PDF publishing. Use the text from the original classic book "Alice's Adventures in Wonderland" by Lewis Carroll alongside sumptuous illustrations by Steve Simpson (for personal use only).

Plus, the subsequent project in this chapter looks at creating the accompanying cover for this book.

A CAUCUS RACE
III
AND A
CHAPTER III.
A Caucus-Race and a Long Tale
They were indeed a queer-looking party that assembled on the
bank — the birds with draggled feathers, the animals with their
fur clinging close to them, and all dripping wet, cross, and uncom-
fortable.
The first question of course was, how to get dry again: they had
consultation about this, and after a few minutes it seemed qu
natural to Alice to find herself talking familiarly with them,
she had known them all her life. Indeed, she had quite a long
gument with the Lory, who at last turned sulky, and would
say, 'I am older than you, and must know better'; and this Al
would not allow without knowing how old it was, and,
Lory positively refused to tell its age, there was no

BEFORE YOU GET STARTED

Resources

You can get all the resources that are referenced in this project from: https://affin.co/AAIWBook

Knowledge of Affinity Publisher

To get the most from undertaking this project, you will need to:

- Be familiar with the interface of Affinity Publisher. You can learn more about the interface in the Interface Tour chapter, starting on p. 14.
- Have good core skills. See the skills table below to see which additional aspects of Affinity Publisher you need to be confident with to complete this project:

Pages and Master Pages	p. 82
Working with Text	p. 112
Picture Frames	p. 124
Text Styles	p. 140

INTRODUCTION

Putting a book together might seem quite daunting but with a step-by-step approach and some understanding of Affinity Publisher's capabilities you can create your very own classic book.

DOCUMENT SETUP

Let's set up our book.

1 Select **File > New**.

2 On the dialog, ensure **Presets** and **Press Ready** are selected, then choose the *A4* thumbnail to set up a CMYK colour space ready for professional printing.

3 In the right-hand Settings pane (**Layout**), set a **Page width** of *127 mm* and **Page height** of *200 mm*. Set the **Image placement policy** to *Prefer Embedded* to store illustrations in the document.

4 In the **Pages** section, ensure **Facing pages** is checked so the book will have a left and right two-page spread format.

5 Adjust the remaining **Margins** and **Bleed** settings as shown.

6 Click **Create**.

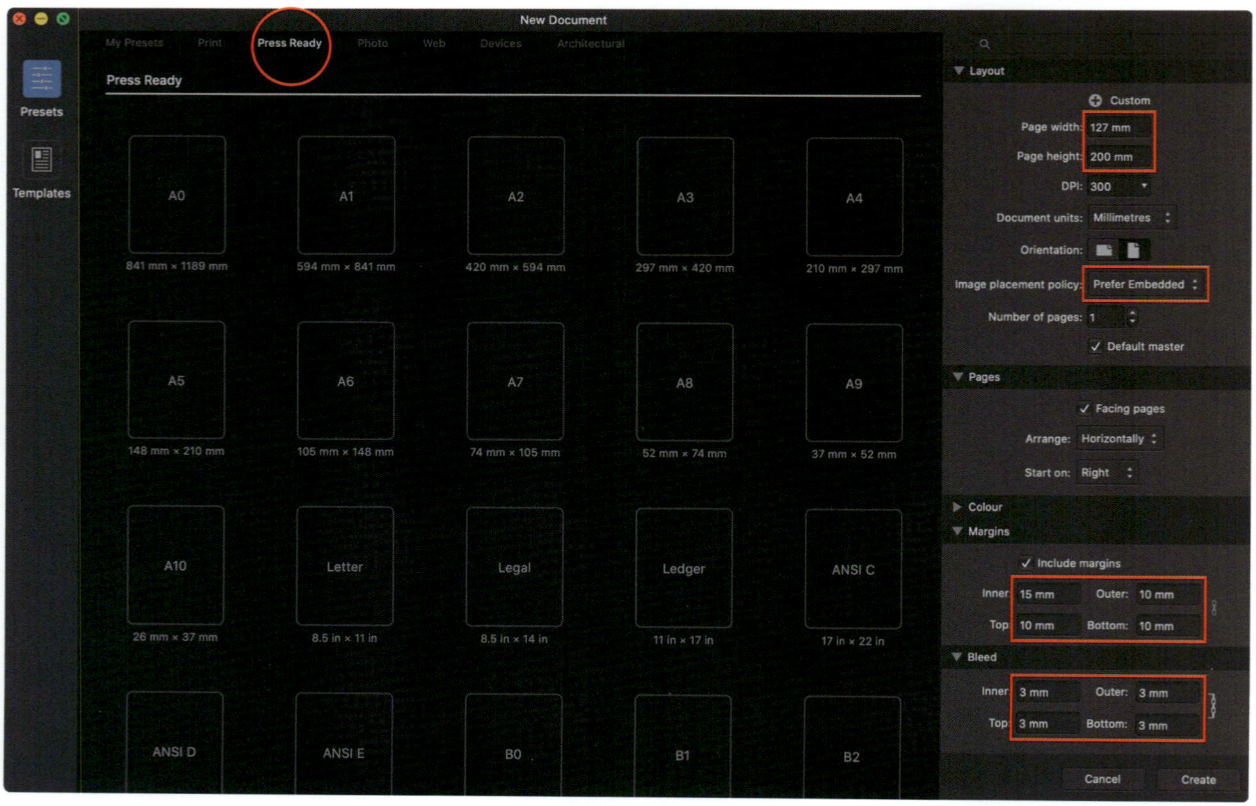

Resource

Alices Adventures in Wonderland.docx

IMPORTING THE STORY

Setting up the initial text frame

- With the **Frame Text Tool** (T) active, drag from the top-left margin corner to the bottom-right margin corner and release. Default snapping makes the new text frame 'magnetise' to the margins.

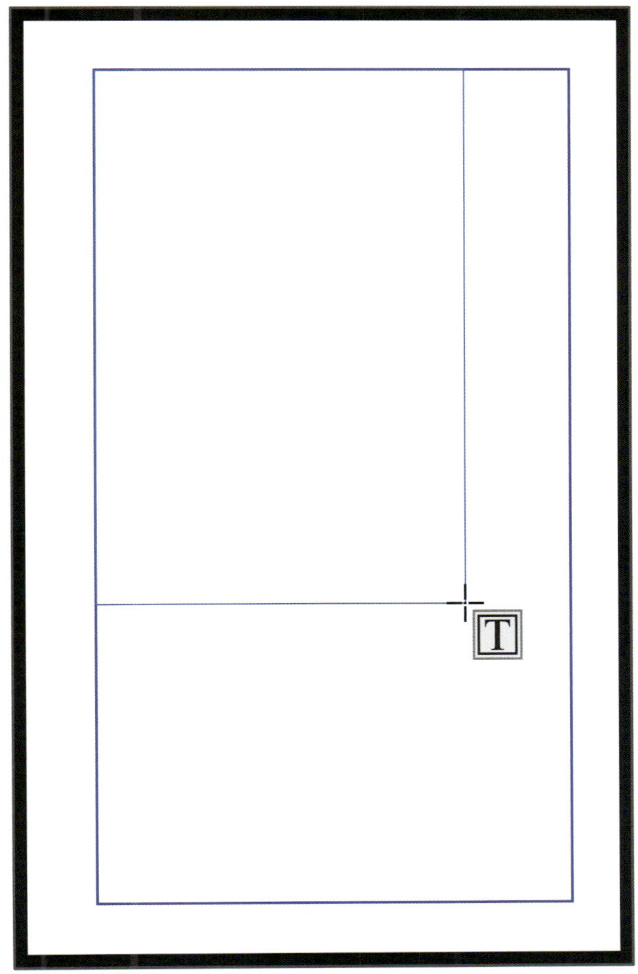

Importing the story text

1 Select the text frame.

2 Select **File > Place**.

3 Navigate to the downloaded Word .docx file, select it and click **Open**.

Imported text will populate the text frame but will only show a small portion of the entire story, with the remainder overflowing the text frame and being hidden. This is called overset text.

CHOOSING YOUR FONTS

This is the right time to consider your choice of fonts. We'll use heading and body text styles based on sans-serif and serif fonts, respectively, giving contrasting font combinations from separate font families.

- **Heading 1**
  Muli was chosen as a modern minimalist **sans-serif** font.

- **Heading 2** and **Body text**
  Crimson Pro font was chosen as a very readable **serif** font—it has a contemporary look but still retains traditional Garamond-like qualities. It also works as a heading.

Downloading and Installing fonts

1 Go to https:/fonts.google.com/ (or search online for Google fonts) and download the **Muli** and **Crimson Pro** family.

2 Open the downloaded font folders and read the OFL.txt file.

3 Open the static sub-folders and select all the files.

4 For *Mac*: ctrl-click the downloaded font files and select **Install font**.
or:
For *Windows*: Right-click the downloaded font files and select **Install**.

Resource
alices_adventures_in_wonderland_01.afpub

TEXT STYLES

When the Word document was placed, several character and paragraph text styles were imported. With the **Frame Text Tool** active, you can see these text styles in **Character Style** and **Paragraph Style** pop-up menus on the context toolbar.

In this project, we want to keep these imported text styles but edit them to use our newly installed fonts and fine-tune text styling.

> The main objective here is to finalise text styling in advance of rolling out the rest of the story.

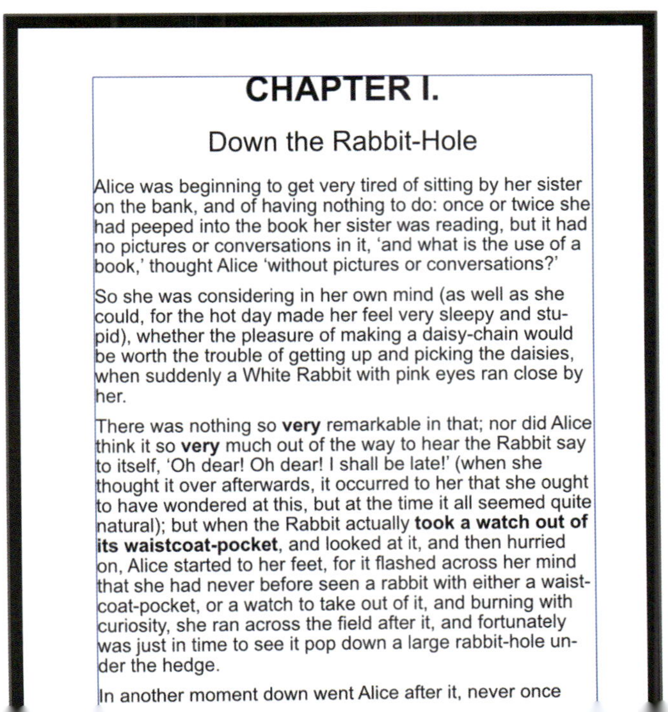

CHAPTER I.

Down the Rabbit-Hole

Alice was beginning to get very tired of sitting by her sister on the bank, and of having nothing to do: once or twice she had peeped into the book her sister was reading, but it had no pictures or conversations in it, 'and what is the use of a book,' thought Alice 'without pictures or conversations?'

So she was considering in her own mind (as well as she could, for the hot day made her feel very sleepy and stupid), whether the pleasure of making a daisy-chain would be worth the trouble of getting up and picking the daisies, when suddenly a White Rabbit with pink eyes ran close by her.

There was nothing so **very** remarkable in that; nor did Alice think it so **very** much out of the way to hear the Rabbit say to itself, 'Oh dear! Oh dear! I shall be late!' (when she thought it over afterwards, it occurred to her that she ought to have wondered at this, but at the time it all seemed quite natural); but when the Rabbit actually **took a watch out of its waistcoat-pocket**, and looked at it, and then hurried on, Alice started to her feet, for it flashed across her mind that she had never before seen a rabbit with either a waistcoat-pocket, or a watch to take out of it, and burning with curiosity, she ran across the field after it, and fortunately was just in time to see it pop down a large rabbit-hole under the hedge.

In another moment down went Alice after it, never once

Editing paragraph styles

1. With the **Frame Text Tool** active, select the chapter heading text 'CHAPTER I.'.

2. On the context toolbar, select the newly installed Muli font from the **Font Family** pop-up menu and set a **Font Style** of *Black* and **Font Size** of *9 pt*.

3. Click **Update Paragraph Style** to update *Heading 1 – Alice* text style to that of the chapter heading text.

4. Repeat for *Heading 2 – Alice* and *Body text – Alice* setting **Font Family** to *Crimson Pro* and **Font Style** to *Regular*, then set a **Font Size** of *20 pt* and *11 pt*, respectively. Update both styles as in step 3.

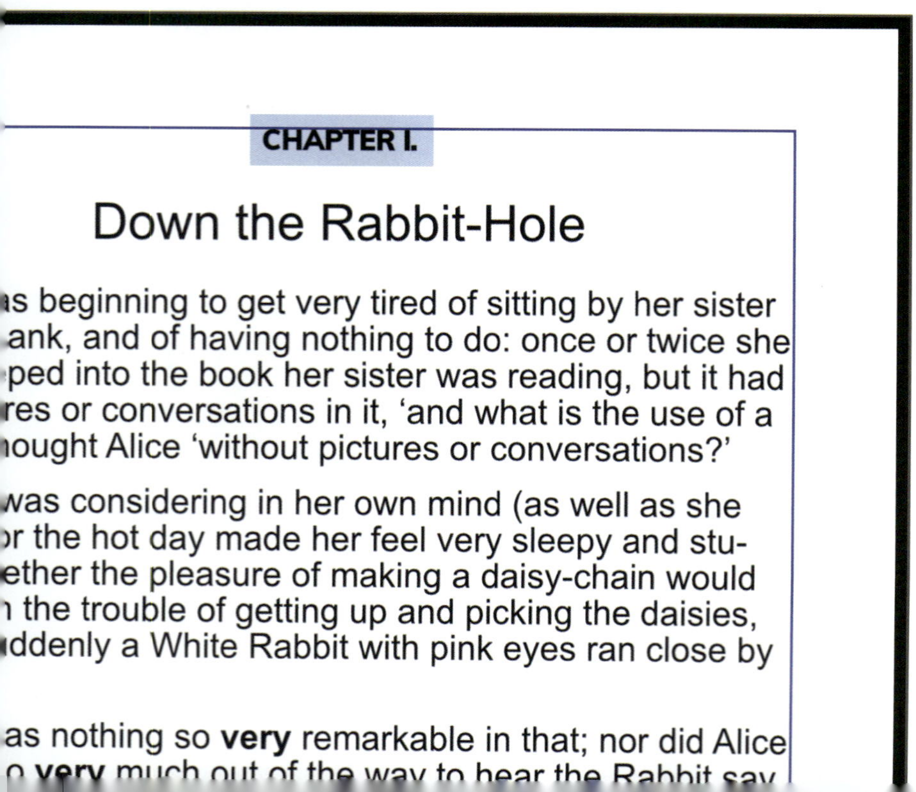

Use the **Recent** tab on the **Font Family** pop-up menu to quickly access your previously used font again.

Editing character styles

For *Emphasis – Alice* and *Small Caps – Alice*:

1. In the third paragraph, select the first instance of the text 'very'.

2. On the context toolbar, select the newly installed Crimson Pro font from the font pop-up menu and change **Font Style** from *Bold* to *Italic*.

3. Click **Update Character Style** to update the *Emphasis – Alice* text style.

4. Repeat for the text 'ORANGE MARMALADE' in the sixth paragraph, again choosing the Crimson Pro font this updates the *Small Caps - Alice* style. Update this style as in step 3.

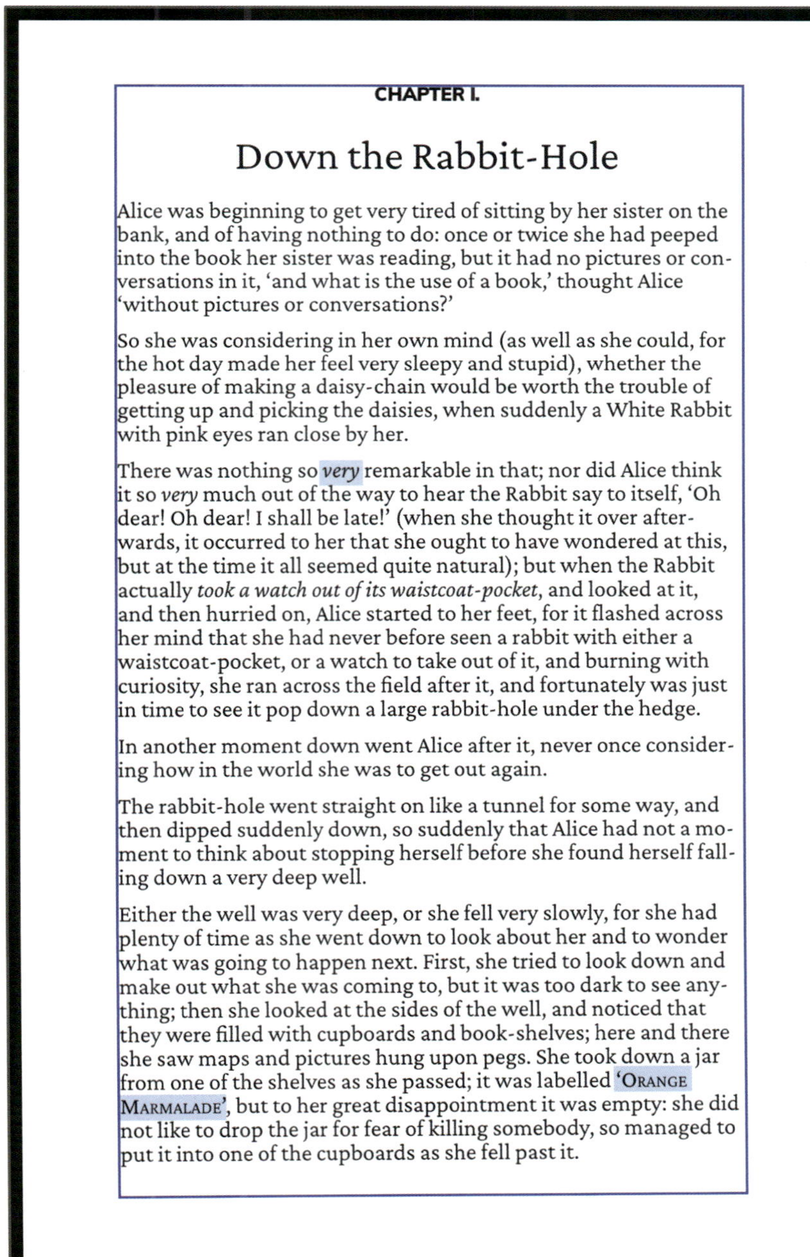

CHAPTER I.

Down the Rabbit-Hole

Alice was beginning to get very tired of sitting by her sister on the bank, and of having nothing to do: once or twice she had peeped into the book her sister was reading, but it had no pictures or conversations in it, 'and what is the use of a book,' thought Alice 'without pictures or conversations?'

So she was considering in her own mind (as well as she could, for the hot day made her feel very sleepy and stupid), whether the pleasure of making a daisy-chain would be worth the trouble of getting up and picking the daisies, when suddenly a White Rabbit with pink eyes ran close by her.

There was nothing so *very* remarkable in that; nor did Alice think it so *very* much out of the way to hear the Rabbit say to itself, 'Oh dear! Oh dear! I shall be late!' (when she thought it over afterwards, it occurred to her that she ought to have wondered at this, but at the time it all seemed quite natural); but when the Rabbit actually *took a watch out of its waistcoat-pocket*, and looked at it, and then hurried on, Alice started to her feet, for it flashed across her mind that she had never before seen a rabbit with either a waistcoat-pocket, or a watch to take out of it, and burning with curiosity, she ran across the field after it, and fortunately was just in time to see it pop down a large rabbit-hole under the hedge.

In another moment down went Alice after it, never once considering how in the world she was to get out again.

The rabbit-hole went straight on like a tunnel for some way, and then dipped suddenly down, so suddenly that Alice had not a moment to think about stopping herself before she found herself falling down a very deep well.

Either the well was very deep, or she fell very slowly, for she had plenty of time as she went down to look about her and to wonder what was going to happen next. First, she tried to look down and make out what she was coming to, but it was too dark to see anything; then she looked at the sides of the well, and noticed that they were filled with cupboards and book-shelves; here and there she saw maps and pictures hung upon pegs. She took down a jar from one of the shelves as she passed; it was labelled 'ORANGE MARMALADE', but to her great disappointment it was empty: she did not like to drop the jar for fear of killing somebody, so managed to put it into one of the cupboards as she fell past it.

Heading spacings and page breaks

The project requires that the main heading (*Heading 1 - Alice*) always appears approximately two-thirds of the way down on a right-facing spread. As this will be document-wide, an adjustment to the text style can be made.

Applying spacing and heading page break

1. On the **Text Styles Panel**, double-click the *Heading 1 - Alice* entry.
2. Adjust the settings in the **Edit Text Style** dialog to alter tracking, spacing and flow.

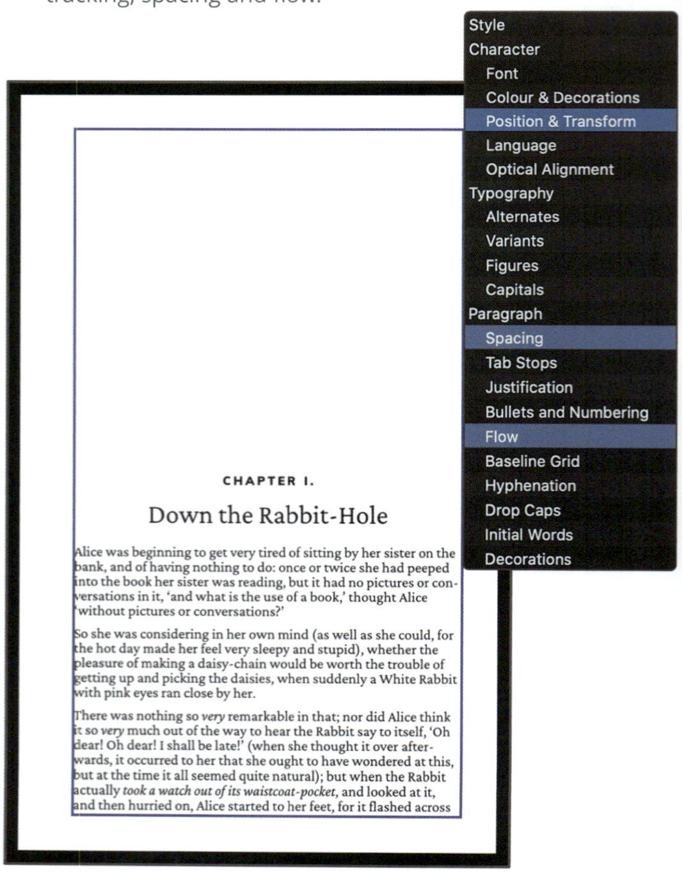

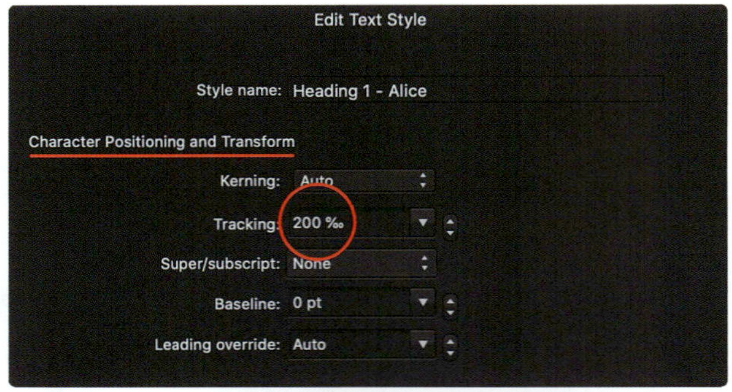

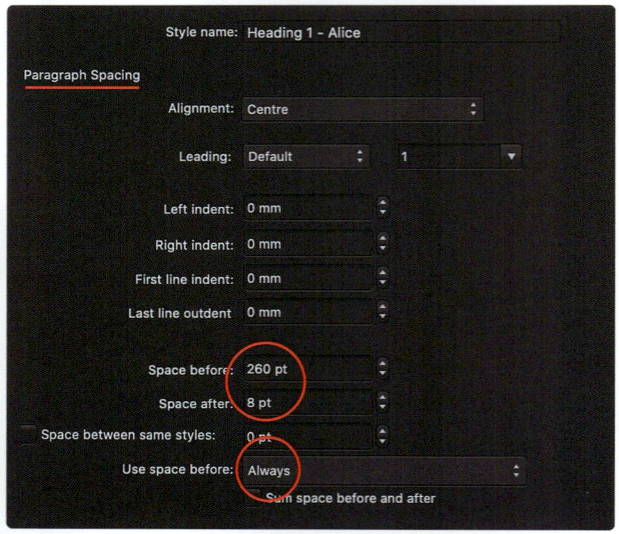

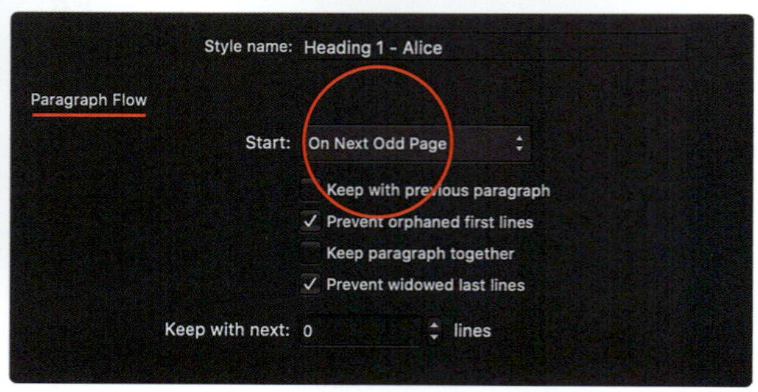

For *Heading 2 - Alice*, just make adjustment to the **Paragraph > Spacing** section, setting **Space before** to *0 pt* and **Space after** to *14 pt*.

BASELINE GRID

A baseline grid makes your body text baselines vertically align to other body text baselines across columns or spreads.

In this project, the grid can be applied to our initial text frame—all future linked text frames will adopt the same grid settings so text baselines will automatically align across all facing page spreads.

Applying a text frame baseline grid

1. Select the text frame.
2. On the context toolbar, click **Text Frame** to display the **Text Frame Panel**.
3. Check **Use Baseline Grid** in the **Baseline Grid** section, and set a **Grid Spacing** of *14 pt*.
4. (Optional) Make the grid visible via **View > Show Baseline Grid**. It shows as equally spaced blue horizonal lines.

Watch for the text baselines reposition themselves as you apply the baseline grid.

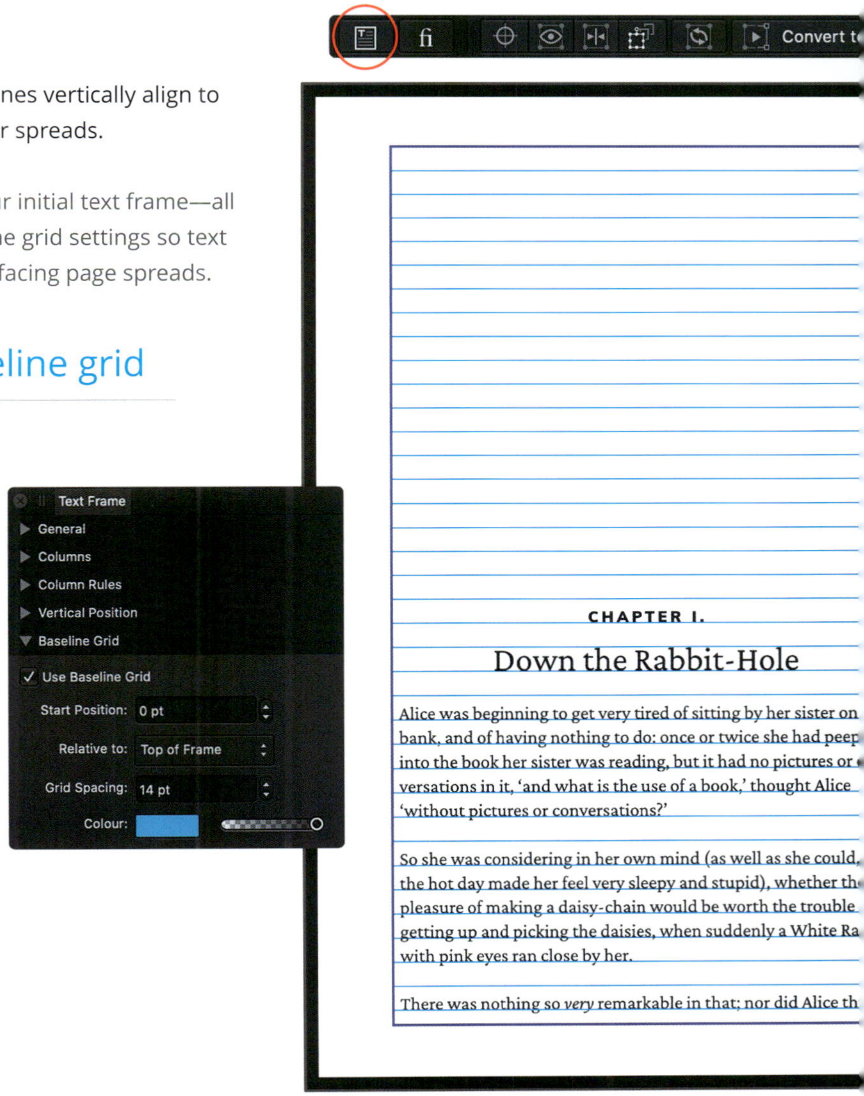

Resource
alices_adventures_in_wonderland_02.afpub

AUTOFLOW

With text styling now taken care of, the powerful and time-saving Autoflow feature can be used to 'roll out' the remaining story, creating new pages with text frames automatically until all the story text is laid out.

Autoflowing to new pages

- With the shift key (⇧) pressed, click the red triangle which indicates overset (overflowing) text.

The story remains connected within the series of text frames—each frame identically sized and positioned per page.

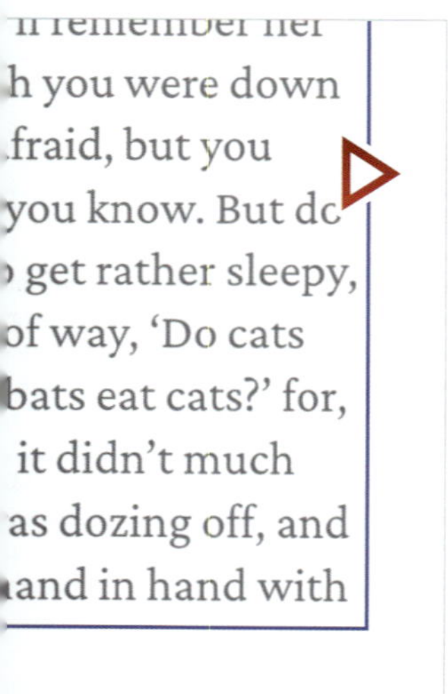

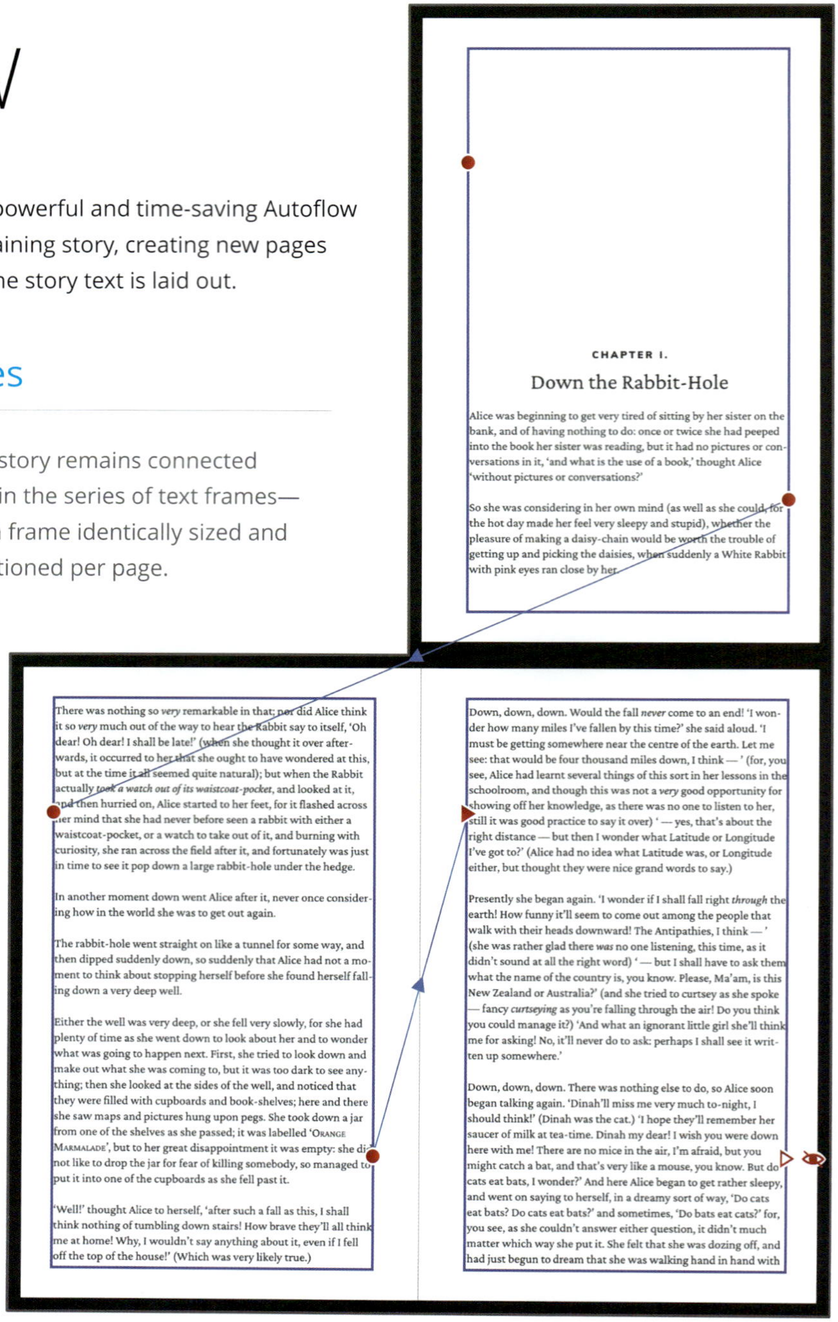

The baseline grid keeps the text vertically aligned across text frames on any facing page spread.

Further Text Style edits

Now that all the text is flowing out to all pages, text for lyrics and poems needs to be located and updated to use the new Crimson Pro font. We'll also fine tune the automatic hyphenation applied to the body text style.

Searching for a used paragraph style

1 Switch on the **Find and Replace Panel** (via **View > Studio**).

2 In the Find section, click the **Formatting** cog icon, then select *Lyrics and poems – Alice* from the **Paragraph Style** flyout.

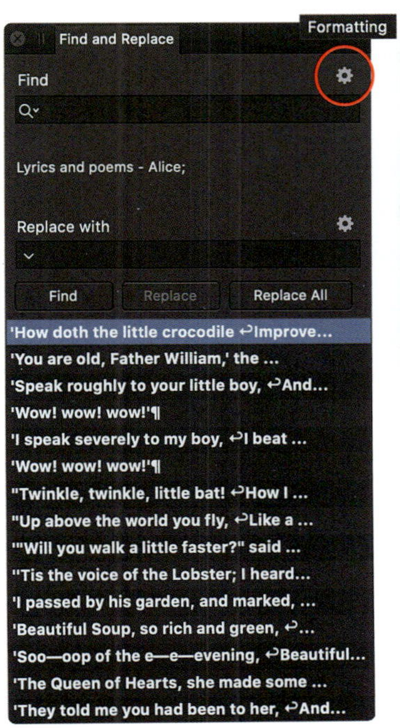

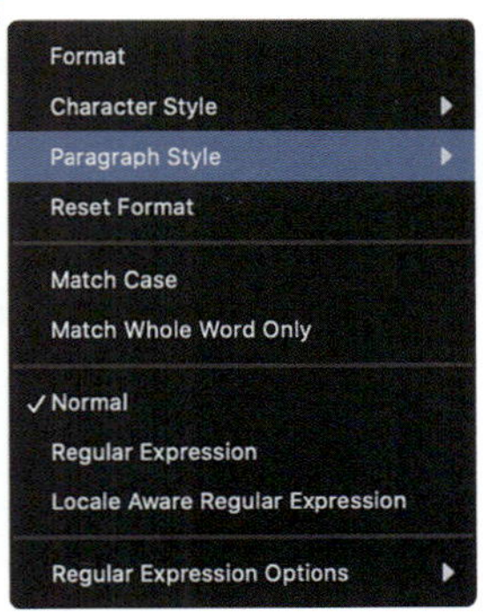

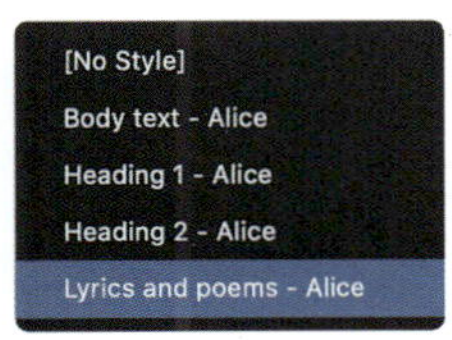

3 Click **Find**.

4 On the context toolbar, apply the Crimson Pro font then update the *Lyrics and poems – Alice* paragraph style. See Editing paragraph styles on p. 334.

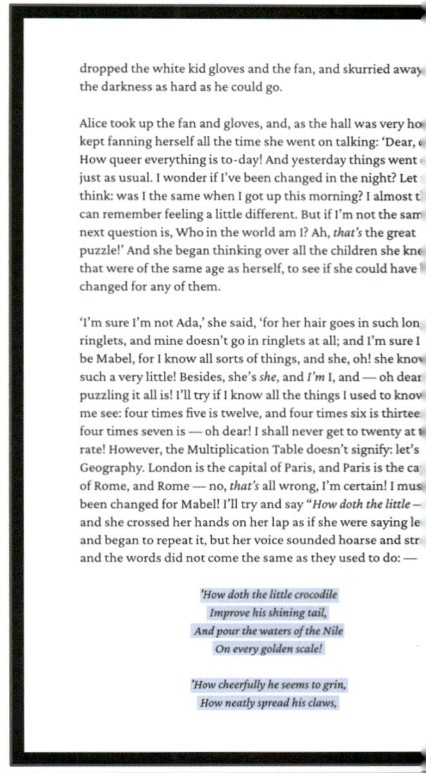

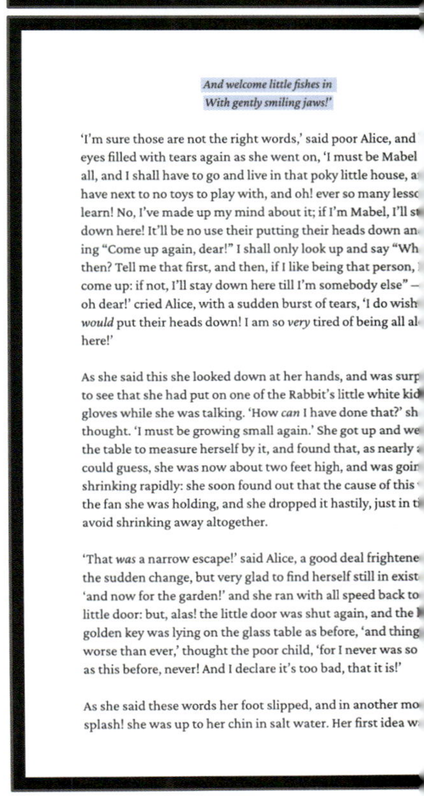

PAGE NUMBERS

At document setup (p. 330), a master page spread was created by default. Adding page number fields to this page's footer will apply page numbering automatically across all your pages.

Adding page numbers to master page

1 On the **Pages Panel**, reveal the **Master Pages** window by clicking its label, then double-click the *Master A* thumbnail.

2 With the **Frame Text Tool**, draw a text frame on the left spread, starting at the bottom-left corner of the margin and finishing *7 mm* below the bottom-right corner of the margin.

3 Click in the frame to add a page number field (shown as a # symbol) via **Text > Insert > Fields > Page Number**.

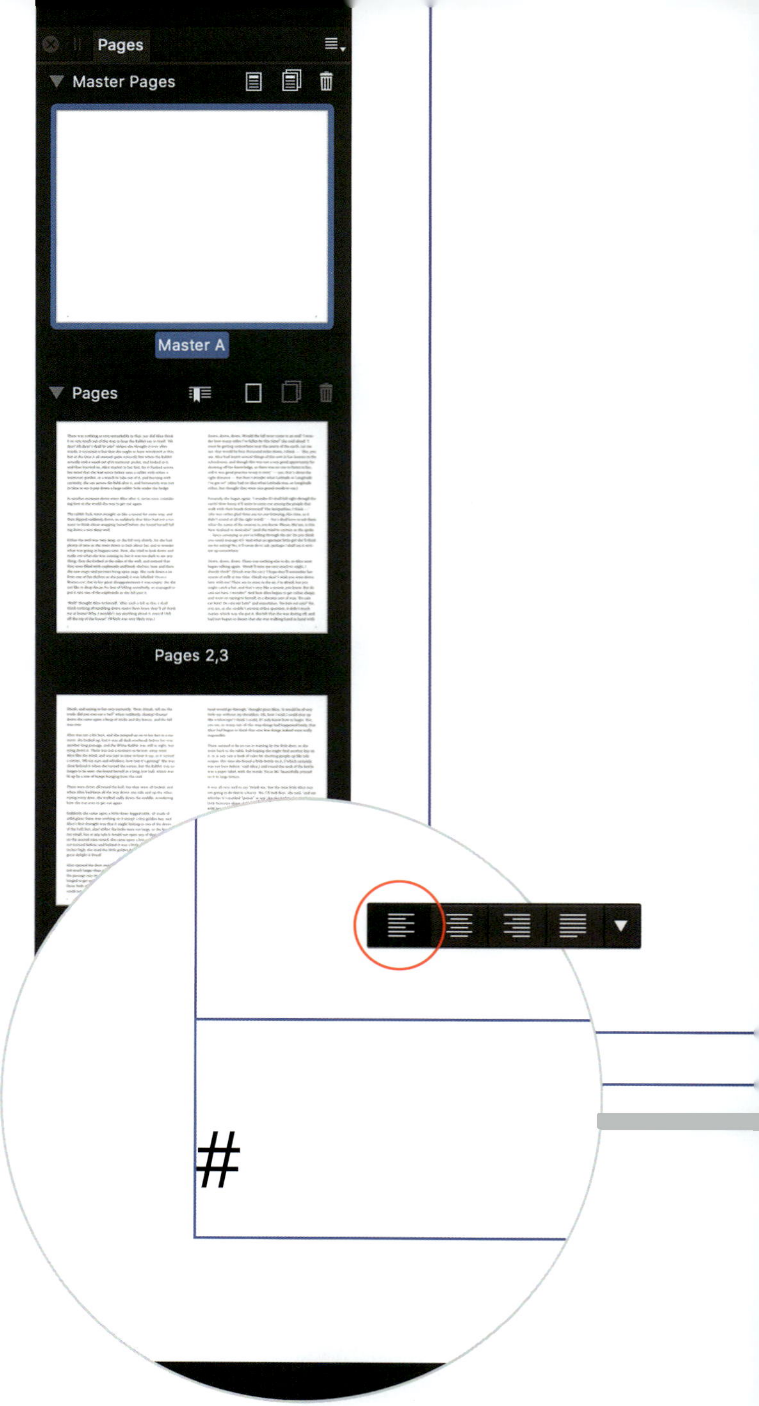

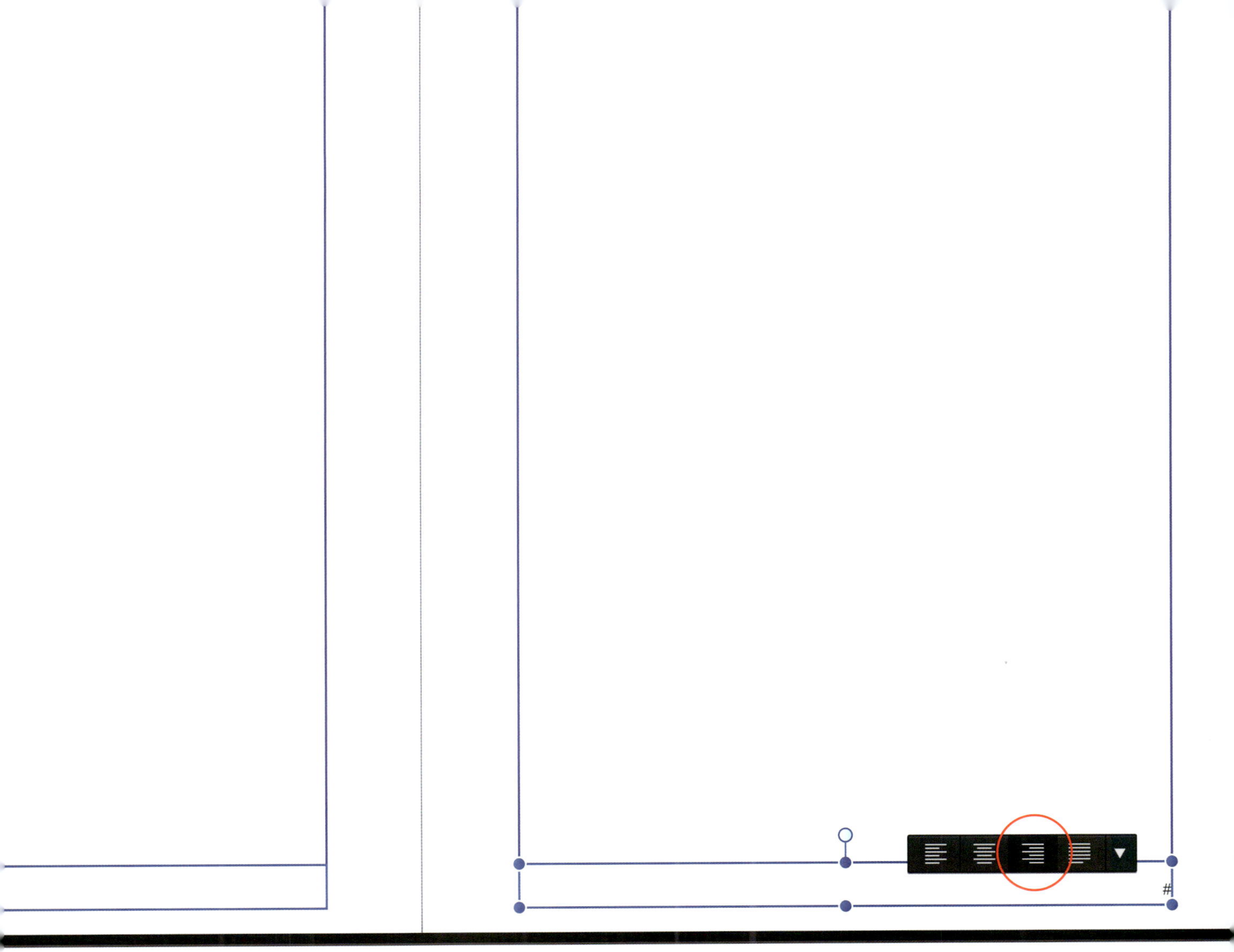

4 Double click the unstyled field and set a font and font size to *Crimson Pro* and *7 pt*.

5 Mirror a copy of the text frame to the right spread by selecting and dragging with the cmd ⌘ key (Mac) or ctrl key (Win) pressed.

6 On the copied text frame, set the Page number field to **Right Align** from the context toolbar.

Your pages will now be automatically numbered.

Resource

alices_adventures_in_wonderland_03.afpub
alice_chapter_I-drinkme.png

IMAGES

This project introduces some beautiful illustrations, mainly for inclusion at chapter starts. Let's look at how you can:

- Place the imagery.
- Wrap text around images.
- Pin images to keep them with their referencing text.

Text wrapping

Text will wrap around any vector object's outline. However, for non-transparent images (JPGs, GIFs, 24-bit PNGs and more), text will only wrap around their rectangular outlines.

For transparent PNGs, created by exporting a selected portion of a design without its background, text will wrap around the image's 'contents' outline instead of its rectangular outline.

Applying text wrap

1. On Page 5, select **File > Place**.
2. Navigate to, then select alice_chapter_I-drinkme.png and click **Open**.
3. Drag over the text frame so text will initially be overlapped.
4. On the top **Toolbar**, click **Show Text Wrap Settings** (a).
5. Choose a **Wrap Style** of *Tight*, wrap to *Largest Side* and adjust **Distance from Text** values so more space appears around the image.

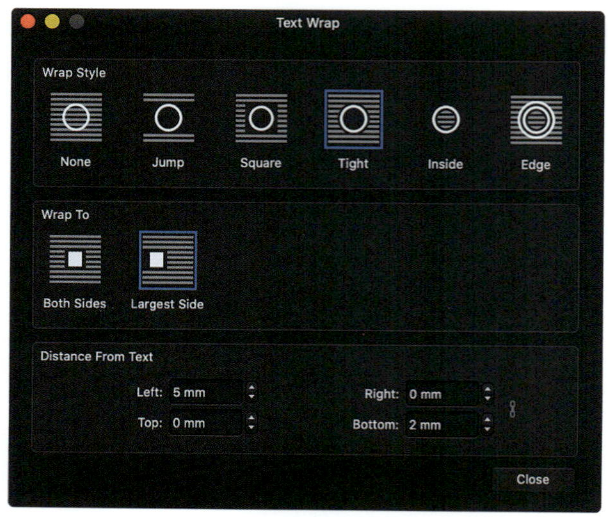

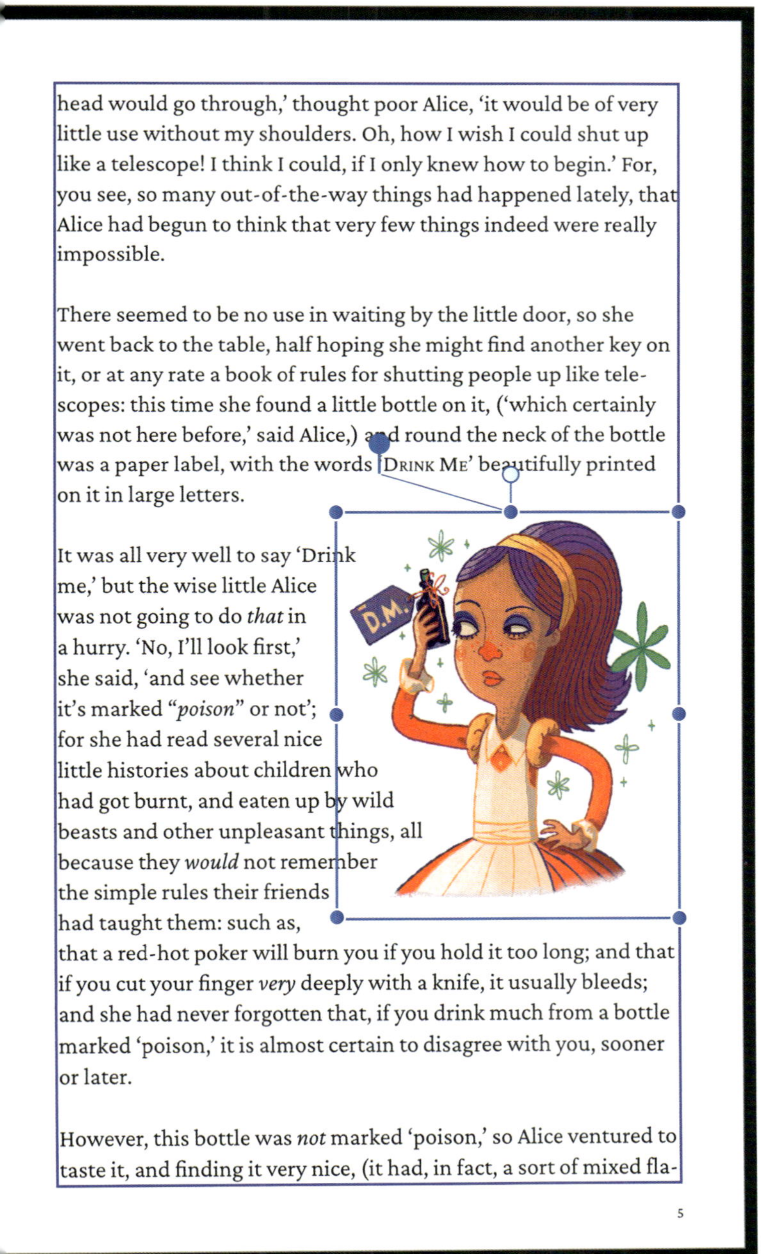
head would go through,' thought poor Alice, 'it would be of very little use without my shoulders. Oh, how I wish I could shut up like a telescope! I think I could, if I only knew how to begin.' For, you see, so many out-of-the-way things had happened lately, that Alice had begun to think that very few things indeed were really impossible.

There seemed to be no use in waiting by the little door, so she went back to the table, half hoping she might find another key on it, or at any rate a book of rules for shutting people up like telescopes: this time she found a little bottle on it, ('which certainly was not here before,' said Alice,) and round the neck of the bottle was a paper label, with the words 'DRINK ME' beautifully printed on it in large letters.

It was all very well to say 'Drink me,' but the wise little Alice was not going to do *that* in a hurry. 'No, I'll look first,' she said, 'and see whether it's marked "*poison*" or not'; for she had read several nice little histories about children who had got burnt, and eaten up by wild beasts and other unpleasant things, all because they *would* not remember the simple rules their friends had taught them: such as, that a red-hot poker will burn you if you hold it too long; and that if you cut your finger *very* deeply with a knife, it usually bleeds; and she had never forgotten that, if you drink much from a bottle marked 'poison,' it is almost certain to disagree with you, sooner or later.

However, this bottle was *not* marked 'poison,' so Alice ventured to taste it, and finding it very nice, (it had, in fact, a sort of mixed fla-

5

Pinning images

It makes sense to keep a supporting image close to its referencing text. By pinning (anchoring) the image to that text, the image will move relative to the text if it reflows so it never becomes out of position.

Two types of pinning are possible in Affinity Publisher—floating and inline.

Floating a pinned image

1. Select the drinkme image.
2. On the top **Toolbar**, click **Float With Text** (b).
3. Move the solid blue pin to before the referencing text, i.e. the DRINK ME text.

Now try adding a few extra paragraphs anywhere before the pin—the image will move relative to the reflowing text. Remember to undo your temporary edits after testing this!

For advanced horizontal and vertical image alignment when pinning, switch on the **Pinning Panel** via **View > Studio**.

Resource
alice_chapter_IX-gryphon.png, alice_chapter_XII-packofcards.png

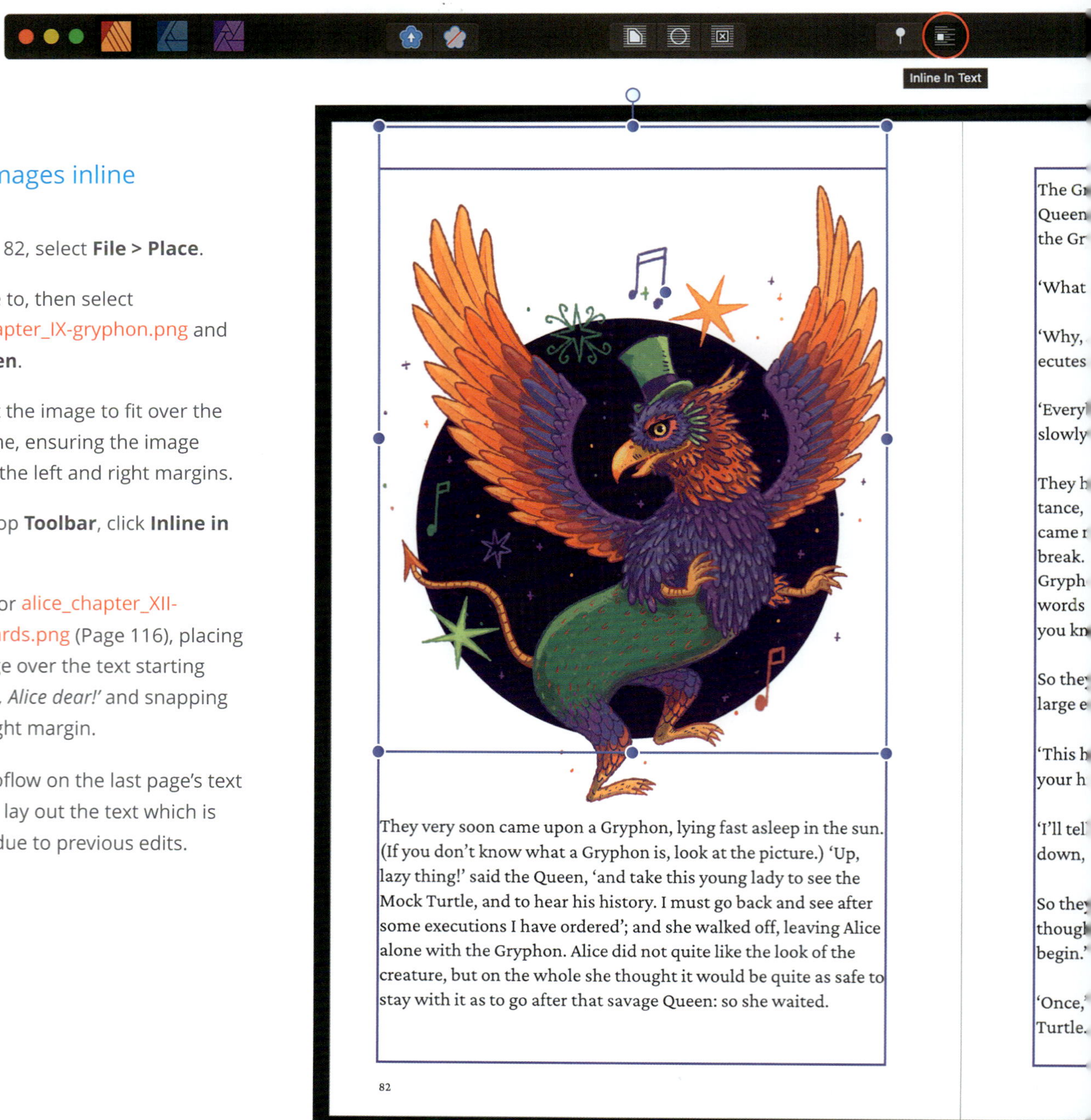

Making images inline

1. On Page 82, select **File > Place**.
2. Navigate to, then select alice_chapter_IX-gryphon.png and click **Open**.
3. Drag out the image to fit over the text frame, ensuring the image touches the left and right margins.
4. On the top **Toolbar**, click **Inline in Text**.
5. Repeat for alice_chapter_XII-packofcards.png (Page 116), placing the image over the text starting *'Wake up, Alice dear!'* and snapping to the right margin.
6. Use Autoflow on the last page's text frame to lay out the text which is overset due to previous edits.

Resource
alice_chapter_I.png to alice_chapter_XI.png

Adding chapter images

Add chapter images at the suggested project page number in the table.

1. At your chosen page, select **File > Place**.
2. Navigate to, then select the image and click **Open**.
3. Drag out the image across the page, using the reference notes as placement guides.

Project page number	Image name
1	alice_chapter_I.png[1] *(Down the Rabbit Hole)*
8-9	alice_chapter_II.png[2] *(The Pool of Tears)*
16	alice_chapter_III.png[3] *(A Caucus-Race and a Long Tale)*
25	alice_chapter_IV.png[1] *(The Rabbit Sends in a Little Bill)*
34	alice_chapter_V.png[3] *(Advice from a caterpillar)*
45	alice_chapter_VI.png[3] *(Pig and Pepper)*
55	alice_chapter_VII.png[1] *(A Mad Tea Party)*
66	alice_chapter_VIII.png[3] *(The Queen's Croquet-Ground)*
77	alice_chapter_IX.png[1] *(Have You Seen the Mock Turtle?)*
88	alice_chapter_X.png[4] *(Lobster Quadrille)*
98	alice_chapter_XI.png[3] *(Who Stole the Tarts?)*
108	alice_chapter_XII.png[4] *(Alice's Evidence)*

[1] Placed right spread within left/right margin; image bottom snapped to vertical page centre.

[2] Transparent PNG, placed cross spread to bleed edge

[3] Placed left spread within left/right margin and centred vertically.

[4] Placed left spread, snapped within margins.

Resource
alices_adventures_in_wonderland_04.afpub

TABLE OF CONTENTS

Adding a table of contents is fairly straightforward. By ignoring the Heading 1 paragraph style (the chapter number) and instead basing our table of contents on the *Heading 2 - Alice* paragraph style only (the important chapter names) we can create a basic table of contents.

Firstly, as with any publication with a Table of Contents, some provision needs to be made for placing it. Secondly, the Table of Contents has to be generated and formatted appropriately.

Adding a table of contents page

1 On the **Pages Panel**, ctrl-click (Mac) or right-click (Win) the *Page 1* thumbnail and select **Add Pages**.

2 Set **Number of Pages** to *4* and **Insert** to *Before*.

3 Click **OK**.

4 Double-click the *Pages 2, 3* thumbnail, and drag out a text frame on Page 3 that snaps to all page margins.

Additional pages are added to also accommodate an inner book title page (p. 355) and to maintain the correct spread arrangement.

Generating the table of contents

1 Using the **Frame Text Tool**, place a caret inside the newly created text frame.

2 On the **Text Menu**, select **Table of Contents > Insert Table of Contents.**

For the moment, the frame contains entries from all heading paragraph styles but you can limit the TOC to just the *Heading 2 – Alice style*.

- On the now displayed **Table of Contents Panel**, uncheck the boxes preceding checked styles except for *Heading 2 – Alice*.

Applying numbering to Table of Contents entries

1 On the **Text Styles Panel**, double-click the *TOC 1: Heading 2 – Alice* style.

2 Adjust the settings as shown (opposite).

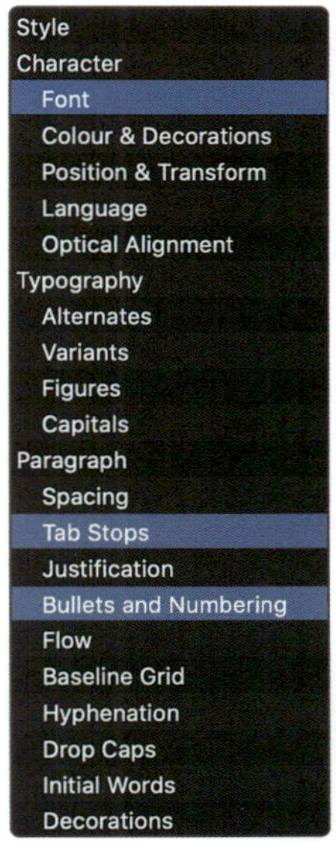

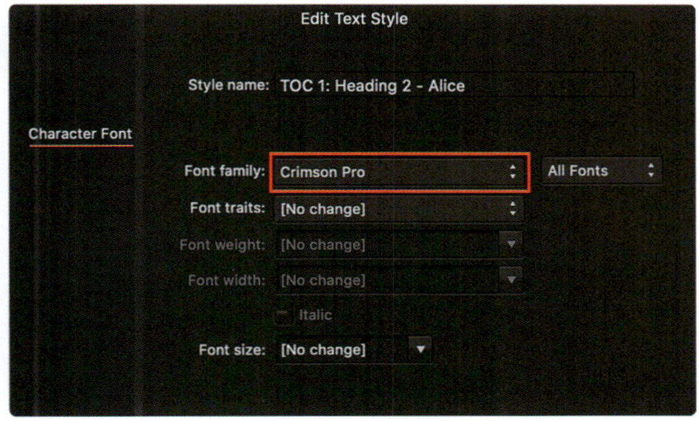

The Table of Contents style replicates the use of Roman numerals in each chapter's *Heading 1 - Alice* style. The tabs and tab leaders help to keep chapter names distinct from chapter and page numbering.

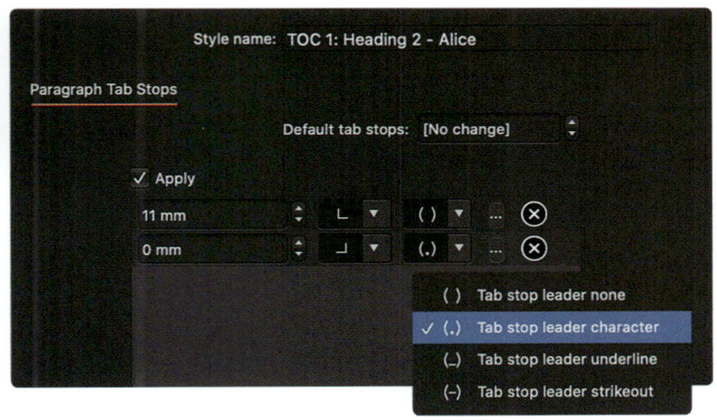

Let's finish off by making the text frame height shorter to accommodate a Contents title (20 pt Crimson Pro Regular font) in its own created text frame.

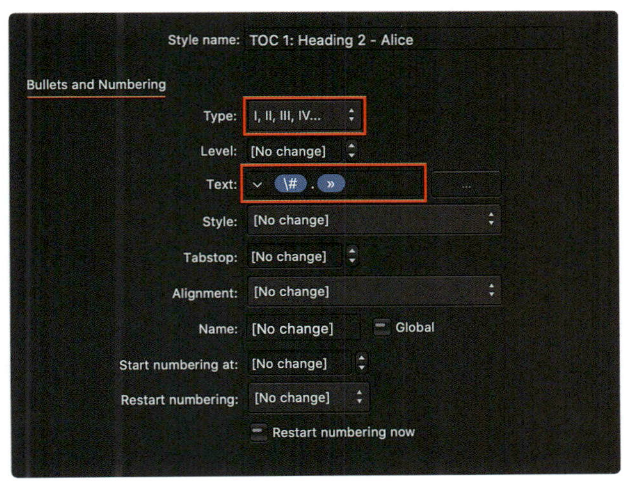

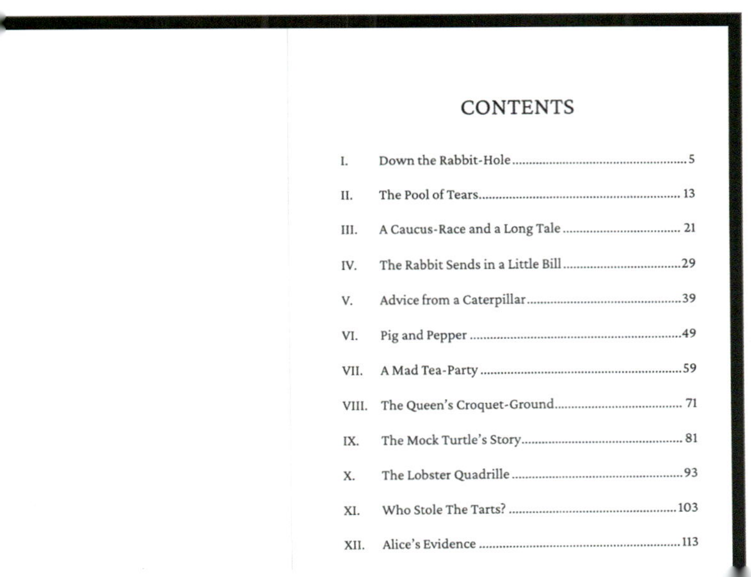

Resource
alices_adventures_in_wonderland_05.afpub

SECTIONS

With page numbers already added (p. 340) you can additionally include chapter names on each page's footer. This is possible by creating sections per chapter and adding a section name field to your master page.

Adding sections

1 On the **Pages Panel**, ctrl-click (Mac) or right-click (Win) each chapter start page thumbnail and select **Start New Section**. Start from the *Page 4,5* thumbnail (ensure only the right spread, Page 5, is right-clicked).

2 On the **Section Manager**, enter a **Section name** (i.e., the chapter name) for the new section.

3 Repeat for each chapter start using the appropriate chapter names.

> Double-click the panel thumbnail's page numbers to jump to the spread—from there you can copy and paste the on-page chapter name to the **Section name** field.

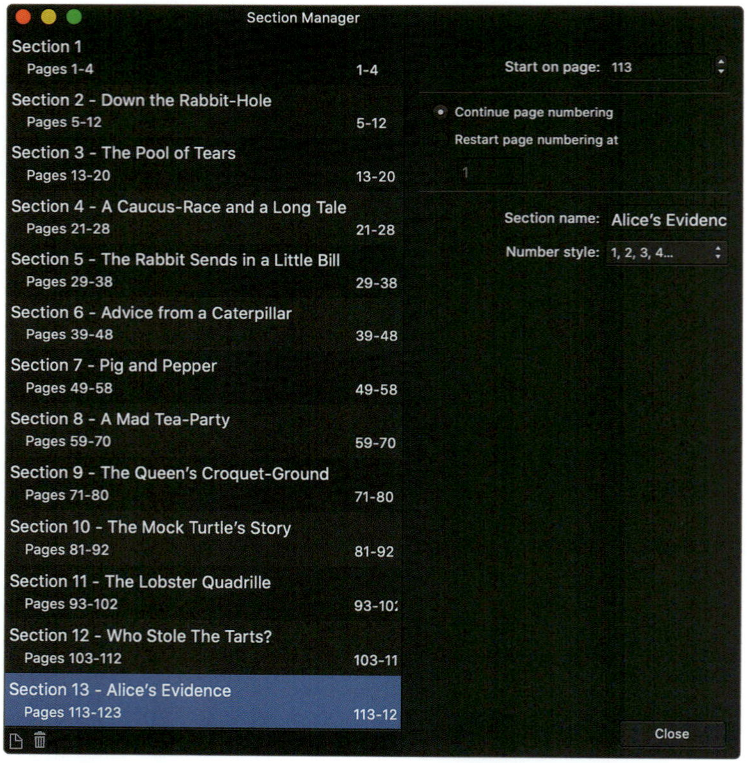

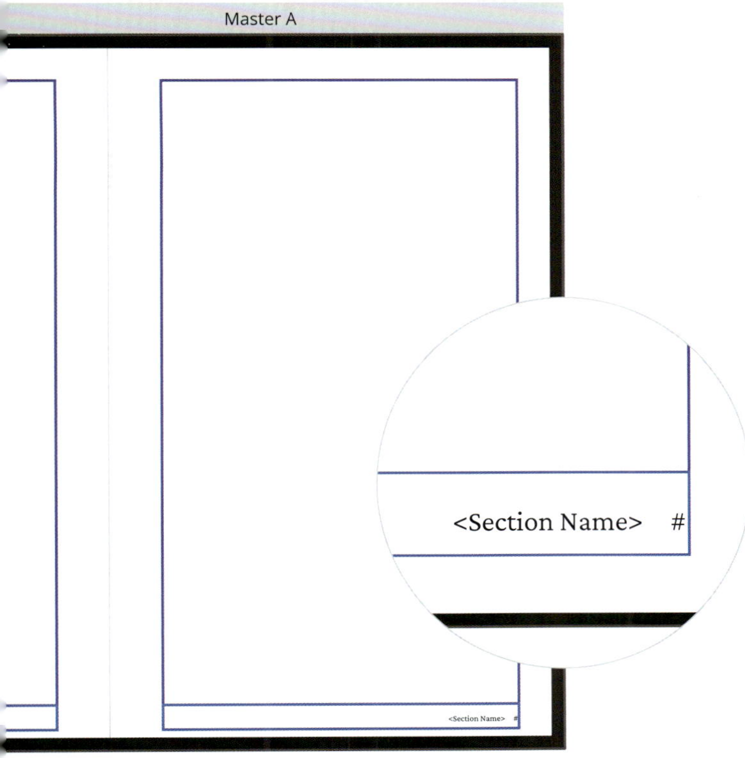

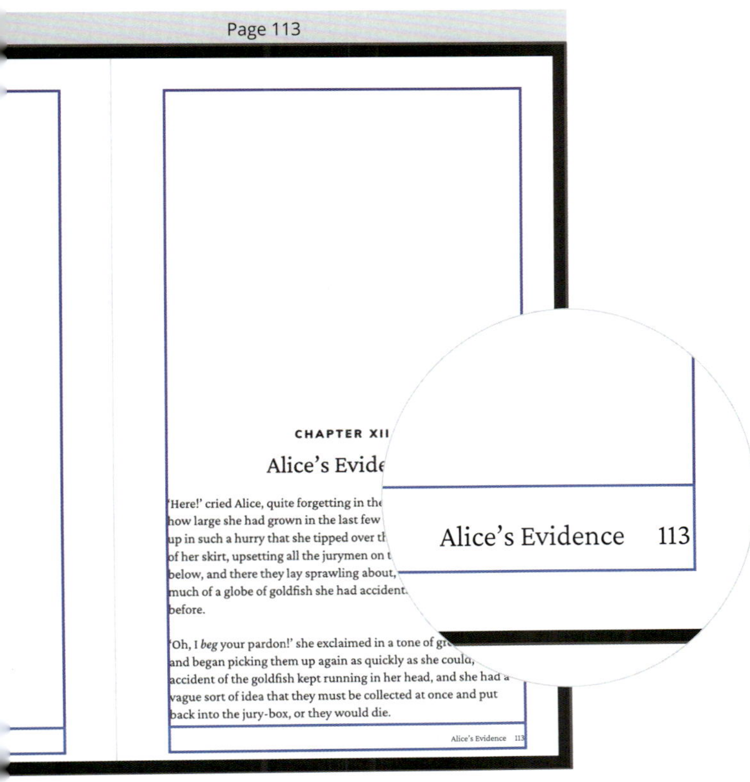

Adding chapter names

1 On the **Pages Panel**, double-click the *Master A* thumbnail in the Master Pages window.

2 In the right facing page footer, click before the page number field and select **Text > Insert > Fields > Section Name**. Apply a *7 pt* Crimson Pro font to the new field.

3 Add an Em space between fields using **Text > Insert > Spaces and Tabs > Em Space**.

Resource
alices_adventures_in_wonderland_06.afpub shapetext_alice.afdesign booktitle_alice.svg

FINAL TOUCHES

The project is nearing completion but some essential work and fine tuning are needed, including some unusual but fun text formatting.

Shape text

One page's text in the book needs to look as if it is contained within a tail shape to fit with the story. To achieve this, the affected text can be made into shape text that flows inside a previously drawn shape.

Drawing a shape

1 On Page 25, insert two page breaks at the start of the paragraph beginning "Fury said to a mouse, that he met..." via **Text > Insert > Breaks**.

2 On Page 26, with the **Pen Tool** active and **Smart Mode** enabled on its context toolbar (below), click repeatedly on the page to form a shape outline, remembering to click on the initial node to close the shape. If needed, press the cmd ⌘ key (Mac) or ctrl Key (Win) to reshape as you draw.

3 On Page 27, select the **Frame Text Tool**, then triple-click the paragraph beginning " 'Fury said to a mouse, ..." then choose **Edit > Cut**.

4 Select the shape in the **Layers Panel**, and with the **Frame Text Tool** active, hover over the shape so the shape text cursor appears, then click for an insertion point.

5 Paste the copied text using **Edit > Paste**, then from the context toolbar, centre the paragraph using **Centre Align**.

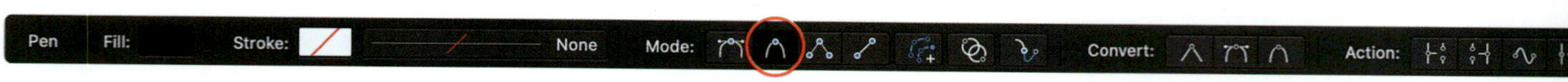

Ensure your shaped text frame is not using a baseline grid on the **Text Frame Panel**.

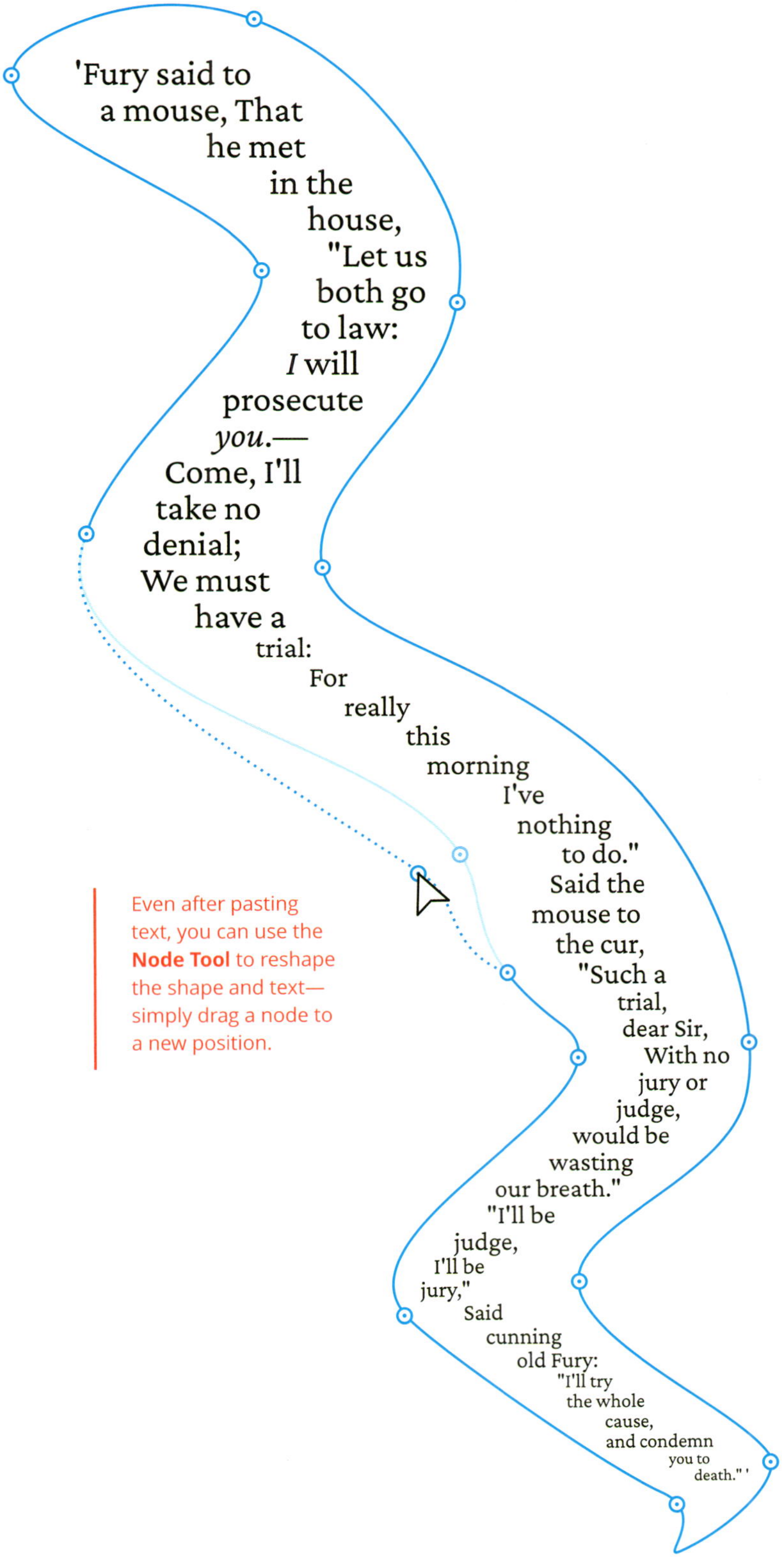

Even after pasting text, you can use the **Node Tool** to reshape the shape and text—simply drag a node to a new position.

Don't worry if you're having trouble drawing your shape outline. As an alternative, we've supplied shapetext_alice.afdesign *in your resources that can be placed instead of creating the shape text from scratch.*

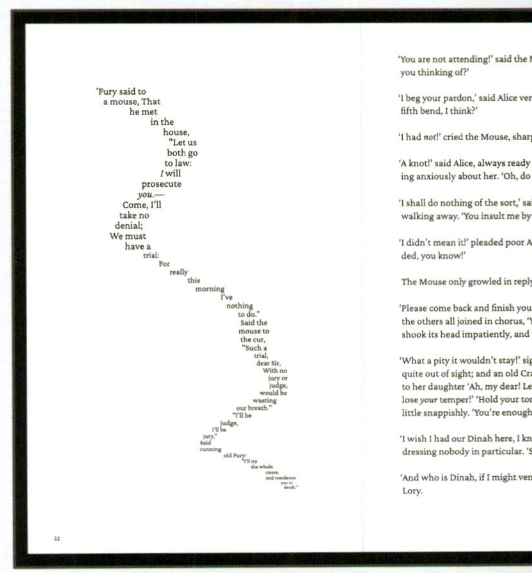

Hanging punctuation/ optical alignment

Punctuation marks, dashes or capitalised words appearing at the start of lines can give an unwanted jagged appearance as your eye scans vertically down the left edge of your frame text. This can be fixed by using optical alignment.

Applying optical alignment

1 On the **Text Styles Panel**, double-click the *Body text - Alice* entry.

2 In **Character > Optical Alignment**, select **Type** to be *Manual*.

As punctuation marks appear in the default manual list by default, punctuation will be presented outside the text frame, e.g. at the start of the 'As wet as ever,' paragraph.

If you notice that ATWY capital letters at the start of lines are outdented slightly after optical alignment, this can be fixed by editing the ATWY entry to have a **Left** setting of *0%* (not *20%*).

Before optical alignment

The Mouse did not notice this question, but hurriedly went on, — found it advisable to go with Edgar Atheling to meet William and offer him the crown.

'As wet as ever,' said Alice in a melancholy tone: 'it doesn't seem to dry me at all.'

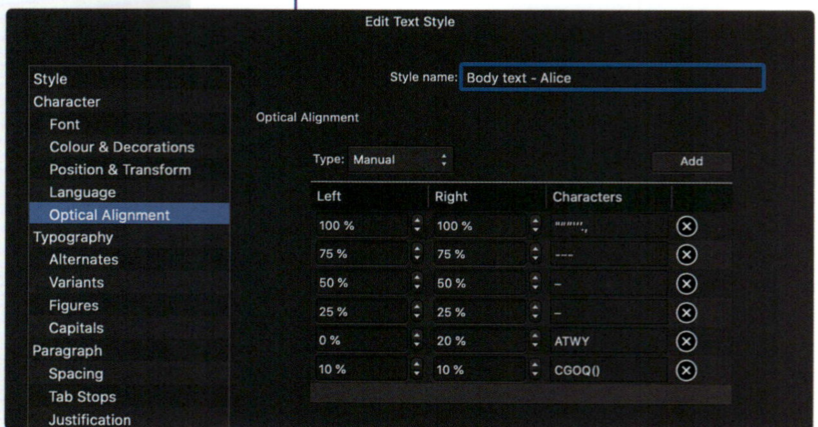

After optical alignment

The Mouse did not notice this question, but hurriedly went on, — found it advisable to go with Edgar Atheling to meet William and offer him the crown.

'As wet as ever,' said Alice in a melancholy tone: 'it doesn't seem to dry me at all.'

Disabling page numbering

Some final edits are required before export. The starting pages of the book and the verso chapter starts need their page numbers removed. We can manipulate master pages to fix this quickly.

For initial pages:

1 On the **Pages Panel**, press the cmd ⌘ key (Mac) or ctrl key (Win) and select *Page 1* and *Page 2,3* thumbnails.

2 Ctrl-click (Mac) or right-click (Win) any selected thumbnail and select **Clear Masters**.

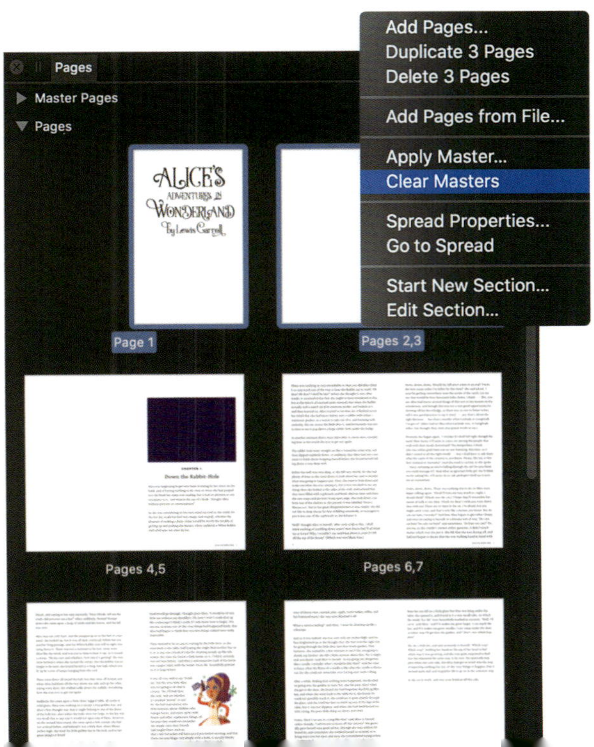

For the verso chapter starts:

1 On the **Pages Panel**, right-click the *Master A* thumbnail in the **Master Pages** window and select **Duplicate**.

2 Double-click the created *Master B* thumbnail and delete the verso footer page number field (shown as #). This is the left page of the spead.

3 On the **Pages** window, press the cmd ⌘ key (Mac) or ctrl key (Win) and click the Page number labels (e.g., Pages *4,5*, then *12,13*, etc.) for each chapter start spread.

4 Ctrl-click (Mac) or right-click (Win) any selected thumbnail and choose **Apply Master**.

5 In the dialog, change **Apply Master** to be *Master B* and set **Content** to *Clear* (this ensures previous master page content is removed).

6 Click **OK**.

Ensure **Replace Existing** is checked to prevent multiple master pages from being applied.

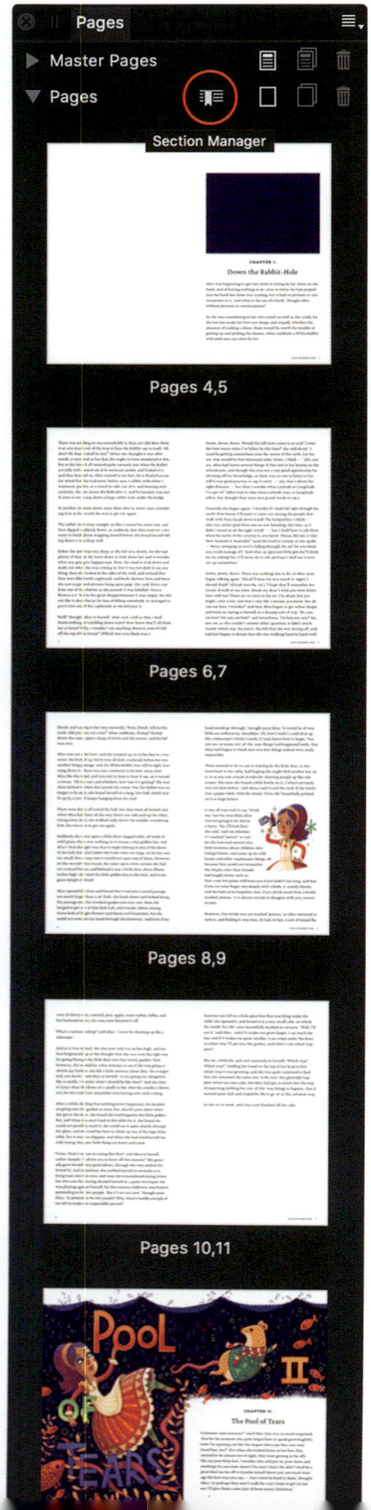

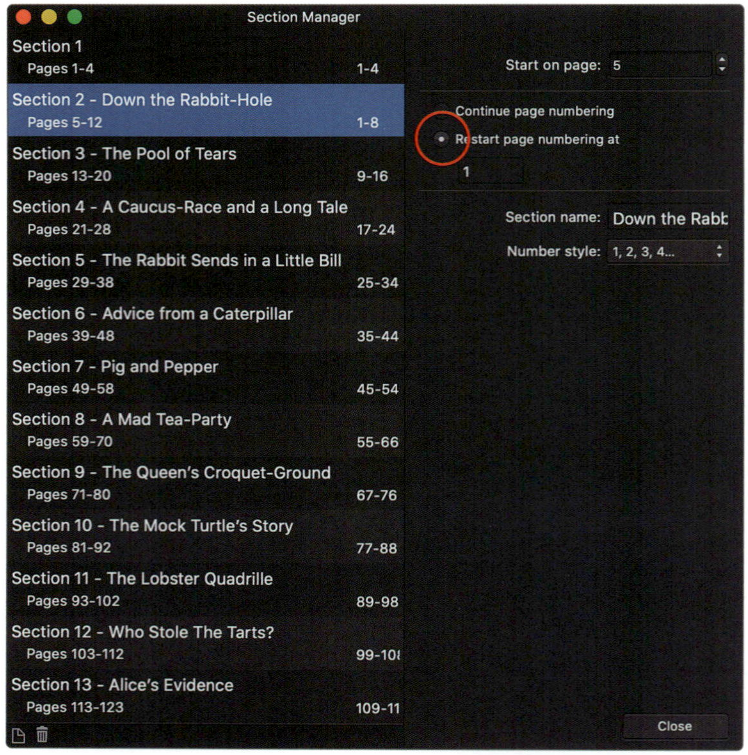

Restarting first chapter numbering

The first four pages are now unnumbered, so numbering can be restarted from Chapter 1 to follow usual book page numbering convention.

1 On the **Pages Panel**, click **Section Manager**.

2 Select the Section 2 entry and enable **Restart page numbering at**, ensuring the number *1* is set.

Book title page

The empty first page is reserved for an internal book title. The design on this page is identical to that used on the book cover (see next project; p. 362)—this ties the cover and contents together nicely from a creative perspective.

All that's needed is to place an SVG exported from the book cover project.

1 With Page 1 displayed, select **File > Place**.

2 Navigate to, then select booktitle_alice.svg and click **Open**.

3 Drag the cursor from the left margin downwards to the right to snap to the right margin. Reposition the image so its bottom edge snaps to the the middle of the page.

Resource

alices_adventures_in_wonderland_07.afpub

INDEXING

While most books of this type don't offer an index at the end of the book, we'll add one so we can easily jump to our favourite characters and events.

Like the Table of Contents, pages have to be set aside for the index to be placed. Traditionally, an index is placed at the very end of the publication—so it's easy to reference from.

Also, like the Table of Contents, the index is generated from the content of the book and placed on a set aside page. However, indexes are generated from index marks (i.e., inline references) inserted into text that is to be referenced to in the index, rather than generated from paragraph text styles.

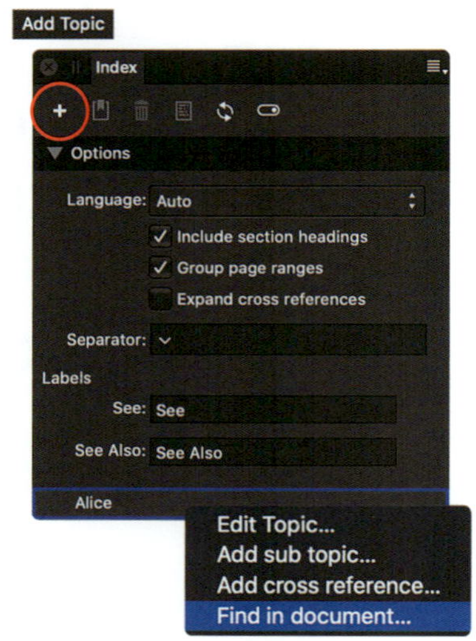

Adding index marks

Let's insert index marks at the text locations in the book where the characters and events are first referenced. This can all be done via the **Index Panel**.

1 Switch on the **Index Panel** via **View > Studio**.

2 Click **Add Topic**, enter your favourite character as **Topic Name** (e.g., Alice) and click **OK**.

3 Ctrl-click (Mac) or right-click (Win) the new topic entry and choose **Find in document**.

4 From the search results, check the first entry so it's included in the index and click **Done**.

5 Repeat for other characters and events.

Index marks will have been inserted into the book copy. Alternatively, you can scan through the book and select text, choosing **Text > Index > Insert Index Mark** to add one.

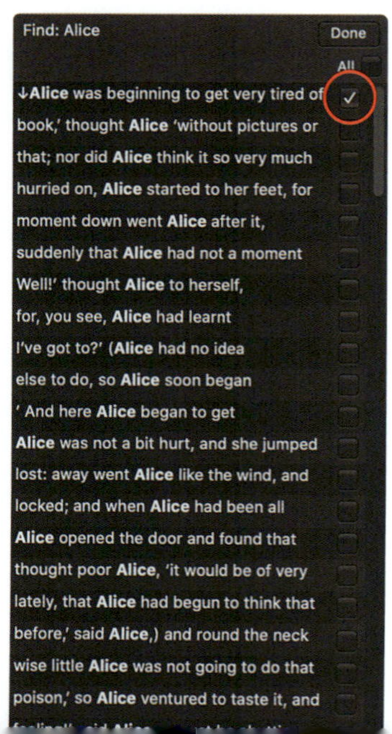

Generating the Index

1. On the last recto blank page, drag out a text frame that snaps to all page margins, leaving room for a separate text frame for the INDEX heading.
2. For a shorter index, uncheck **Include section headings** and tighten the space between entries and page numbers by using, as a **Separator**, a comma and En space (from drop-down).
3. With frame selected, click **Insert Index** on the **Index Panel**.
4. On the context toolbar, change the text frame **Columns** to *2*.
5. Edit the index-specific text styles applied to fit with the content.

Instead of 'same level' index entries, consider creating parent Topic Names, e.g. the word Characters, and then making your actual character names all display under that parent entry.

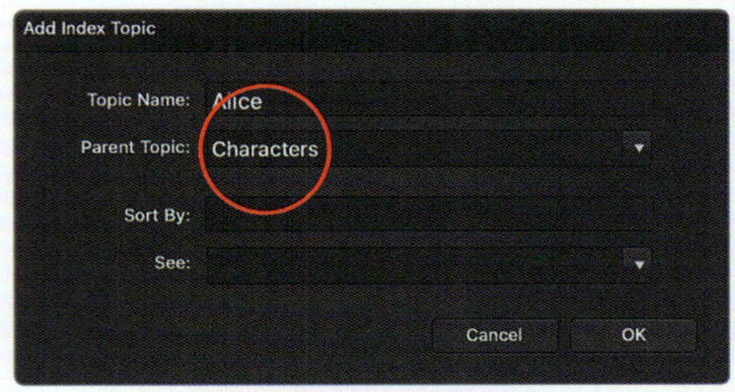

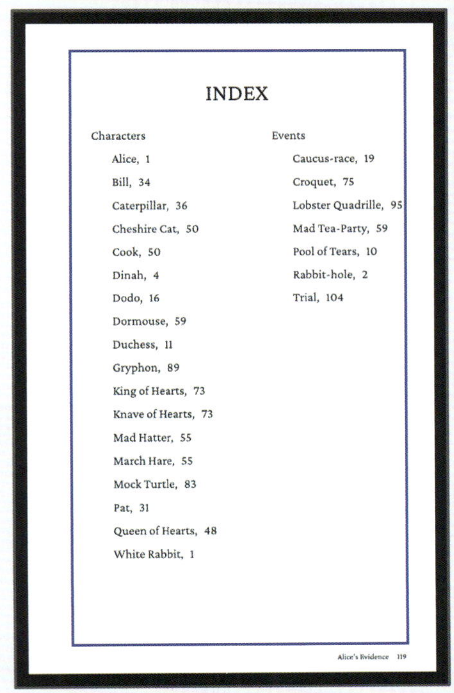

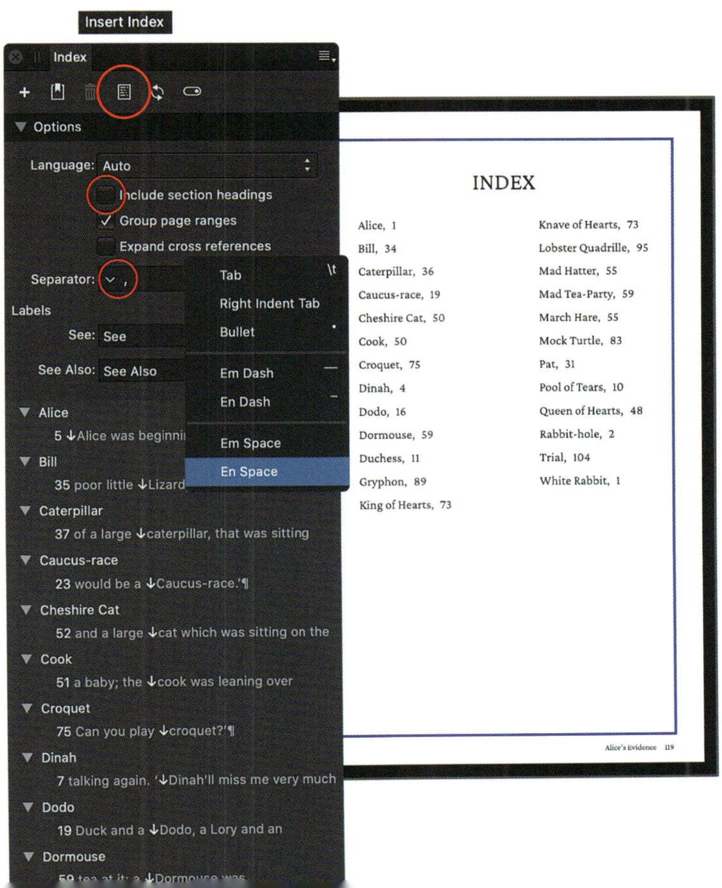

Resource
alices_adventures_in_wonderland_08.afpub

EXPORTING AS PRESS-READY PDF

Let's export as CMYK PDF but it's important to first check the project using the **Preflight Panel**, then make necessary edits to resolve warnings and errors as required.

Preflight checking

By default, Affinity Publisher performs live preflight checks, i.e. publishing warnings and errors are generated automatically as they occur.

The bell indicator on the status bar shows different preflight statuses; green for no preflight issues; yellow for a preflight warning; and red for a higher severity preflight error.

As the document's page numbering was restarted at Chapter 1, this created a single preflight error that prompts to update the now out-of-date Table of Contents page.

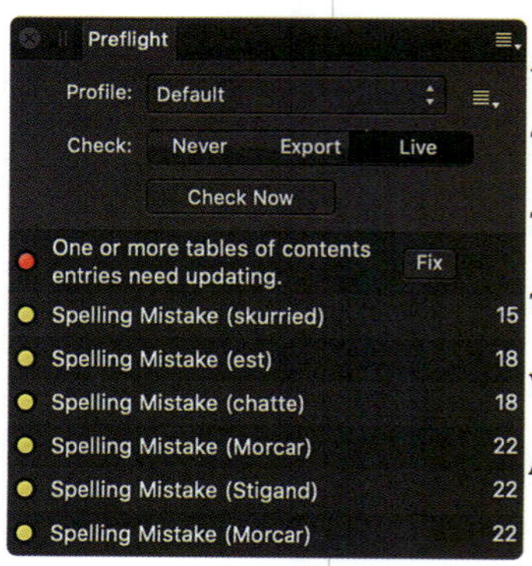

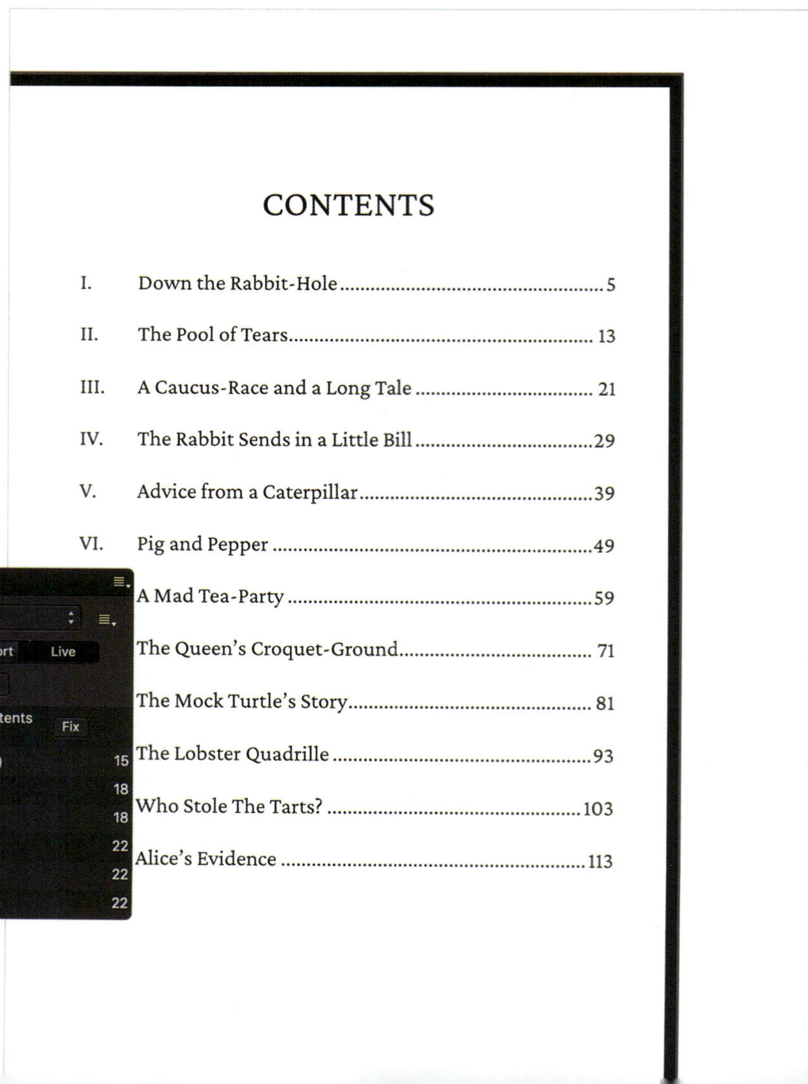

CONTENTS

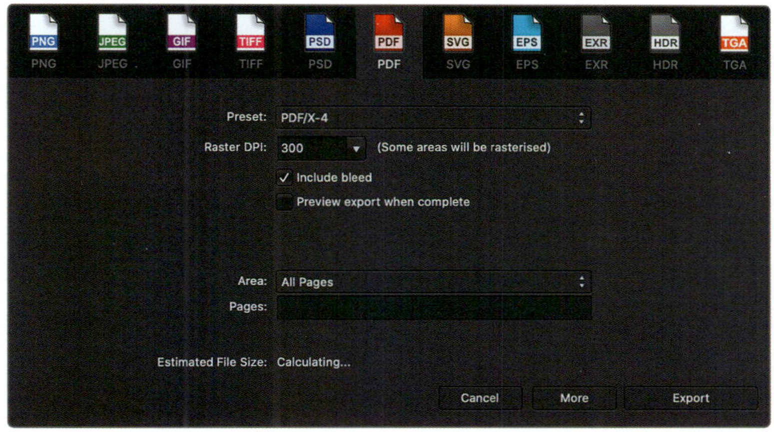

Exporting to PDF

High-resolution CMYK PDF is the recommended file format for sharing your artwork with professional printers.

1. On the **File Menu**, select **Export**.
2. On the dialog, select **PDF**, then set the **Preset** to *PDF/X-4*.
3. Check **Include bleed** and set the **Area** to *All Pages*.
4. To include printers marks, click **More**, check **Include printers marks** then click **Close** in the secondary dialog.
5. Click **Export**.
6. Save the file as 'alice-book', navigate to a folder of your choice and click **Save**.

Fixing preflight errors

1. Click the red bell icon to display the **Preflight Panel**.
2. (Optional) On the **Pages Panel**, jump to Page 3.
3. Click **Fix** on the generated Table of Contents error entry to update the Table of Contents automatically in-panel. You'll see the page numbers on the page update.
4. If you've introduced other preflight issues if you've followed this tutorial, simply double-click a preflight entry to jump to the offending object and resolve the issue.

By default, spelling warnings (in yellow) will be generated. In this project, many such warnings are generated because of some unusual words and character names—an example that warnings don't always need to be resolved. Yellow warnings should still be closely reviewed before resolution as for red errors.

A
AND A
LONG
TAIL

CUCUS
III
CHAPTER III.
A Caucus-Race and a Long Tale
They were indeed a queer-looking party that assembled on the bank — the birds with draggled feathers, the animals with their fur clinging close to them, and all dripping wet, cross, and uncomfortable.
The first question of course was, how to get dry again: they had
consultation about this, and after a few minutes it seemed
natural to Alice to find herself talking familiarly with them,
she had known them all her life. Indeed, she had quite a
gument with the Lory, who at last turned sulky, and would
say, 'I am older than you, and must know better'; and this
ould not allow without knowing how old it was, and,
positively refused to tell its age, there was no

2

Alice's Adventures in Wonderland Cover

Design an eye-catching book cover rich in typographic enhancements

Let's challenge the saying "You can't judge a book by its cover" by designing a cover that suggests the highly creative content we created in the previous Alice's Adventures in Wonderland book project.

ALICE'S
ADVENTURES IN
WONDERLAND
By Lewis Carroll
Illustrated by
Steve Simpson

BEFORE YOU GET STARTED

Resources

You can get all the resources that are referenced in this project from:
https://affin.co/AAIWCover

Knowledge of Affinity Publisher

To get the most from undertaking this project, you will need to be familiar with the interface of Affinity Publisher. You can learn more about the interface in the Interface Tour chapter, starting on p. 14.

INTRODUCTION

In this project we'll create book cover artwork to accompany the Alice's Adventures in Wonderland book contents.

The project focuses on several key aspects of cover design.

- Getting the book cover dimensions to match those of the book contents with consideration to spine width.
- Creating a design that incorporates front and back covers, plus the spine.
- Using typography to alter title text characters in powerfully creative ways.

Steve Simpson

Renowned illustrator, Steve Simpson, created all the illustrations for our Alice's Adventures in Wonderland projects for this workbook in Affinity Designer for iPad.

Steve's characteristically playful illustration style has roots in the Arts & Crafts movement and folk art, making him the ideal person to illustrate this children's classic.

"It was a real pleasure to work on these illustrations. I was introduced to Alice's Adventures in Wonderland at an early age, growing up just a few miles down the road from Lewis Carroll's birthplace, and over the years I've collected several vintage illustrated copies of the book. I'm most happy when I can combine illustration with hand lettering and perhaps this was the perfect project to do that."

CHOOSING A SPINE WIDTH

Before getting started, a wrap-around 'front-back' cover design must be planned with the spine width in mind. Several factors need to be considered—the number of pages you envisage and the paper stock used (paper thickness and weight).

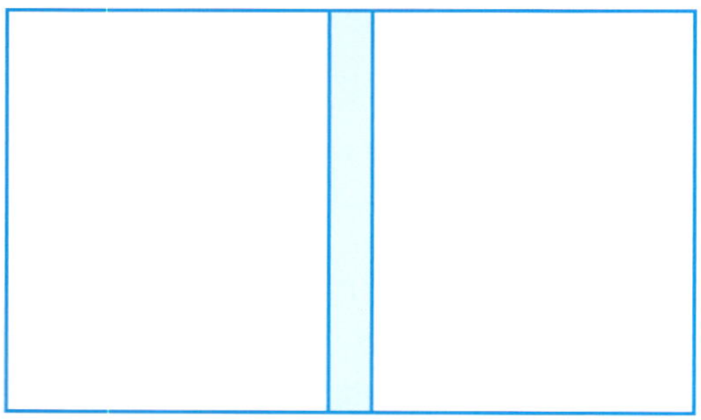

Leave the exact spine width calculation to a printing professional—they can propose paper stock appropriate to the project and then recommend a spine width from your proposed page count. Double-check with your printer on bleed settings for cover and book contents at the time too.

If you don't have a printing contact already set up, you can take advantage of online spine width calculators that will get an approximate spine width value until you confirm the correct values.

Paper stock

In this project, we were able to decide on a page count as the book contents were designed first (p. 326). We then physically viewed and chose some paper stock with the help of our print partners.

70gsm Uncoated
80gsm Uncoated
90gsm Matt
100gsm Uncoated
100gsm Matt
115gsm Silk (coated)[1]
115gsm Gloss (coated)
120gsm Uncoated
130gsm Silk (coated)
135gsm Silk (coated)
135gsm Gloss (coated)
170gsm Silk (coated)
170gsm Gloss (coated)
250gsm
300gsm

50# White Smooth Offset
60# White Smooth Offset
60# White Uncoated
60# Cream Uncoated
50# Natural Smooth Offset
70# White Smooth Offset
80# White Gloss Text
80# White Coated
100# Satin
100# Gloss

[1] Indicates the chosen item.
gsm = grams per square metre.

CHOOSING CONTENTS AND COVER STOCK

Although papers are measured by their weight (e.g., 115 gsm) they also vary in their thickness (and opacity). Correctly calculated spine values should take this into account.

Paper stock considerations

For contents:

- **Reproduction of illustrations**
  These are best presented on a coated stock to reproduce them to their best quality.
- **Ease of reading**
  Too glossy a paper stock can produce glare from light reflections.
- **Weight/Thickness/Opacity**
  For thicker books, this may be a big issue for cost and handling. Practically, too thin a paper stock may make illustrations show through the 'semi-transparent' pages.

For cover and binding:

- **Hardback vs softback**
  This choice sends a message to the buyer. The former suggests a prestigious high-end offering; the latter, a more practical less-expensive one.
- **Cover thickness/material**
  The cover needs to protect the book contents, give strength and prolong the book's lifetime.
- **Matching stock**
  Choose coated or uncoated depending on the coating used for the book contents.
- **Stitch or bind?**
  The options depend on page count and text weight; higher page counts/weights would require binding.

Spine width calculation

Finalised book page count	124
Paper stock Silk (coated) called *Chorus Silk* (this was the paper stock product name)	115 gsm
Calculated spine width*	7 mm

* Excludes cover: 300 gsm gloss film laminate

DOCUMENT SETUP

The cover design needs to be sized to accommodate not just the front cover but the spine and back cover too. It also needs to fit with the book content's dimensions, i.e. *127 mm* (W) x *200 mm* (H).

1 Select **File > New**.

2 From the dialog, ensure **Presets** and **Press Ready** are selected, then choose the *A4* thumbnail to set up a CMYK colour space.

3 In the right-hand Settings pane (**Layout**), set a **Page width** and **Page height** of *261 mm* and *200 mm*, respectively.

4 Uncheck **Default master** and **Facing pages** as we're creating a single page layout—a master page and two-page spread layout are not needed.

5 Reduce the remaining **Margins** values to *5 mm* to set a safe zone and keep the default **Bleed** settings as shown.

6 Click **Create**.

Ensure your cover dimensions match those of your book content.

ADDING THE BACKGROUND ARTWORK

Steve Simpson, our Illustrator, carried on the illustration style from the book illustrations (p. 342) to the cover artwork—creating a highly decorative background graphic.

Adding the background artwork

1 Select **File > Place**.

2 Navigate to, then select artwork_alicecover.jpg and click **Open**.

3 Drag the cursor from the top-left bleed-edge corner to bottom-right bleed-edge corner, ensuring the image snaps into place.

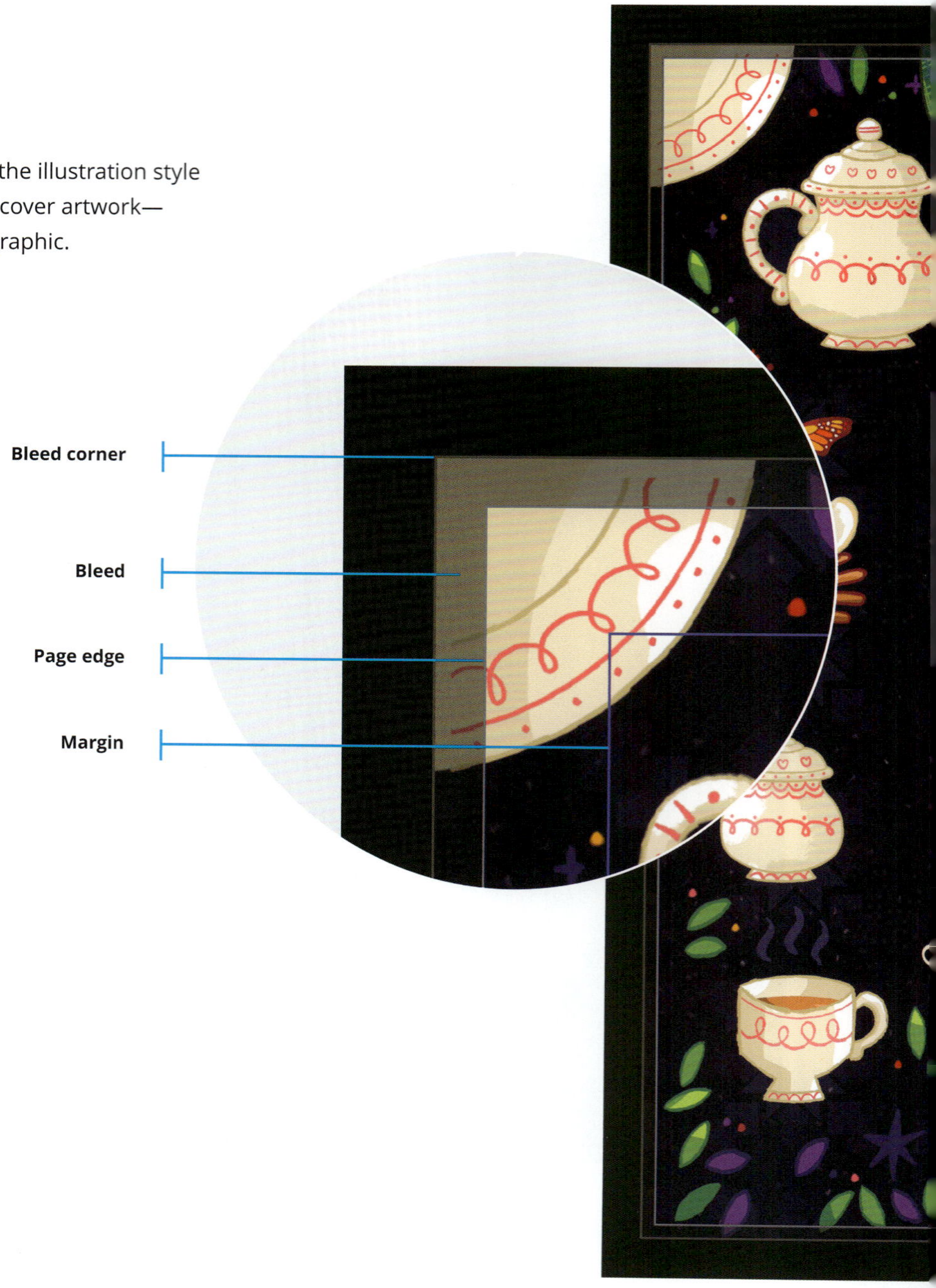

Resource

Alices_adventures_in_wonderland_cover_01.afpub
artwork_alicecover.jpg

ADDING TITLE TEXT

The cover artwork has been designed to accommodate the book title text in the dark central area on the front cover.

We'll add some artistic text to this area shortly, but first let's set the font properties in advance of this.

Setting font size and colour

- With the **Artistic Text Tool** active, choose the Wallington Pro font and a font colour sampled from an area of the background artwork.

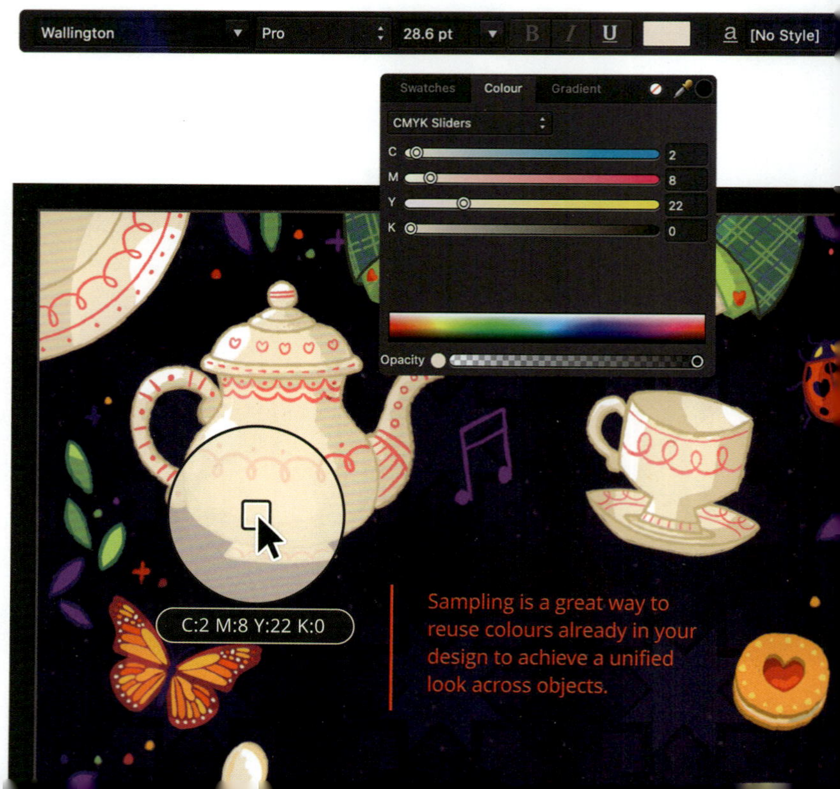

About the Wallington Pro Typeface

Wallington Pro is a decorative serif typeface with beautiful vintage and elegant curves—a perfect choice for our cover title text. It takes advantage of OpenType features and includes special characters that allow you to mix and match letters to fit your design.

The Wallington Pro typeface has been licensed from the incredible Zeune Type Foundry for commercial use for all purchasers of the Affinity Publisher Workbook.

Downloading and installing Wallington Pro

1 Go to https://affin.co/WallingtonPro and follow the basket/checkout instructions.

2 For *Mac*: ctrl-click the downloaded font files and select **Install font**.
or:
For *Windows*: Right-click the downloaded font files and select **Install**.

Resource
Alices_adventures_in_wonderland_cover_02.afpub

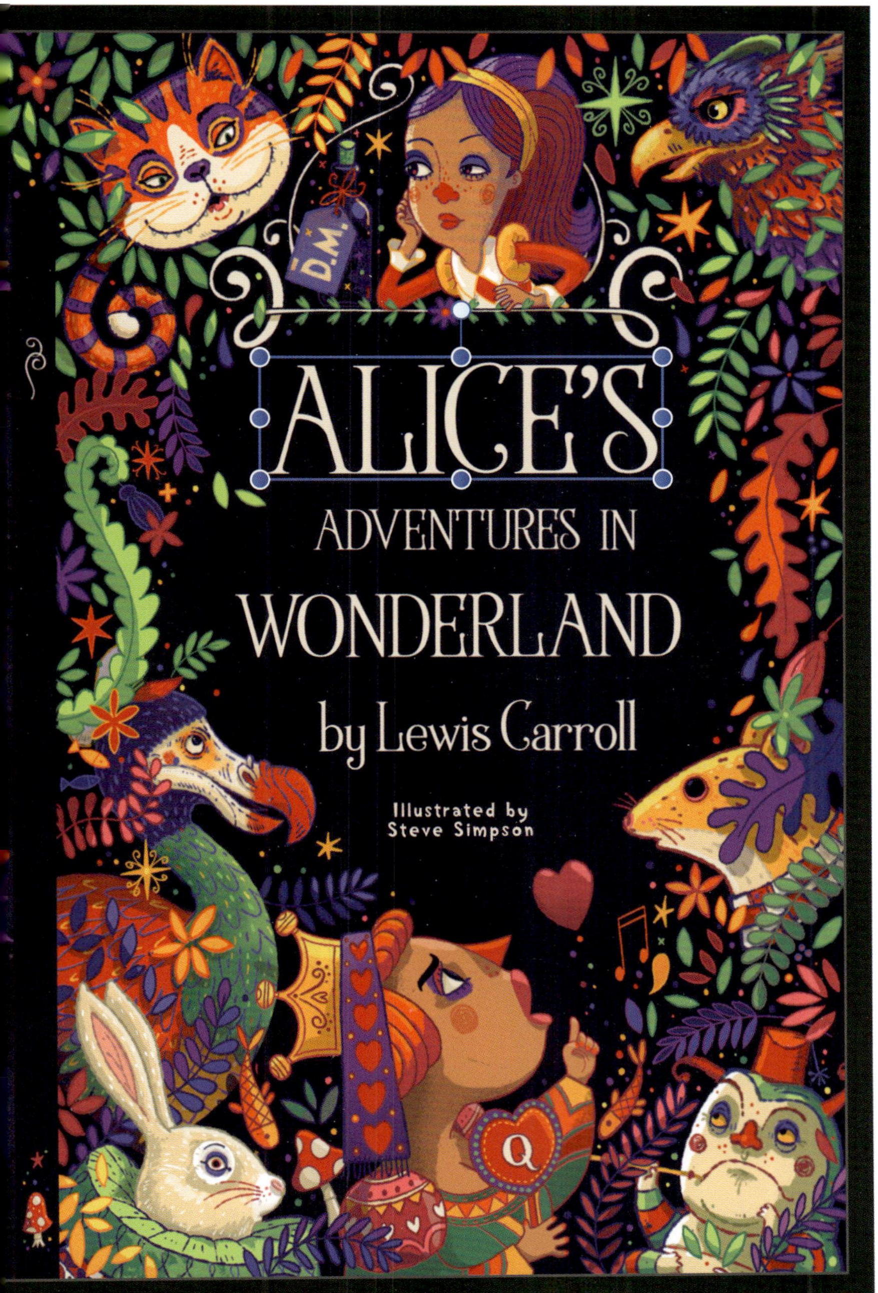

Adding artistic text

- Drag out the cursor to your preferred text size and type ALICE'S. Repeat for each word to complete the title as separate text objects. Add the credit for the illustrator too.

If the font sizes aren't quite right it's easy to resize from the selected text's corner handle. This makes use of artistic text's inherent scalability.

In terms of alignment and distribution, there's no fixed rule applied here—introducing typographic enhancements later may negate any fine positioning. For alignment, let your eyes be the judge; also set a font size for each title word that befits that text's importance to the title.

Credit text

As you'd expect, an illustration-rich book design needs to acknowledge the illustrator in a prominent position. We picked a font called *Nincompoop* from https://creativemarket.com and added *Illustrated by Steve Simpson* under the title—this made the text distinct from the title. The text was converted to curves using **Layer > Convert To Curves**.

Resource
Alices_adventures_in_wonderland_cover_03.afpub

TYPOGRAPHIC TITLE STYLING

With the book title now using our preferred font we can now explore why this font was chosen.

In typography, each character in a font can potentially offer a choice of character designs beyond what is possible by simply typing. These choices are dependent on how the font was designed by the Font Designer.

In this project, our chosen Wallington Pro font has a rich variety of alternate characters to choose from. Let's swap our 'default' title characters for some exciting alternatives to give the text a much more decorative and attractive look.

Applying typographic styling

1 With **Artistic Text Tool** active, select the first letter *A* in the word *ALICE'S*.

2 On the **Character Panel**, select the ellipsis (...) from the **Typography** section (or use **Text > Show Typography**).

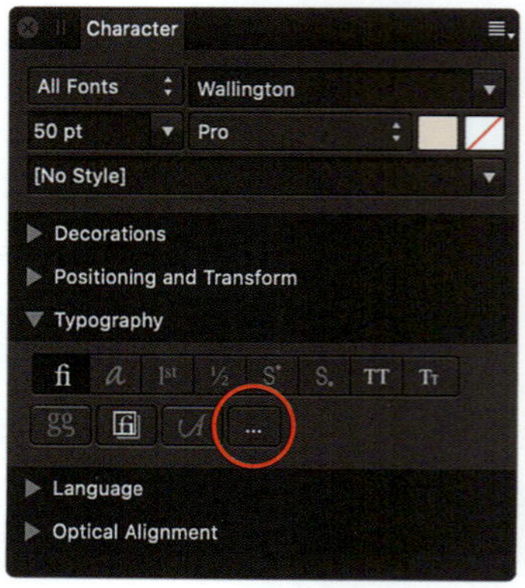

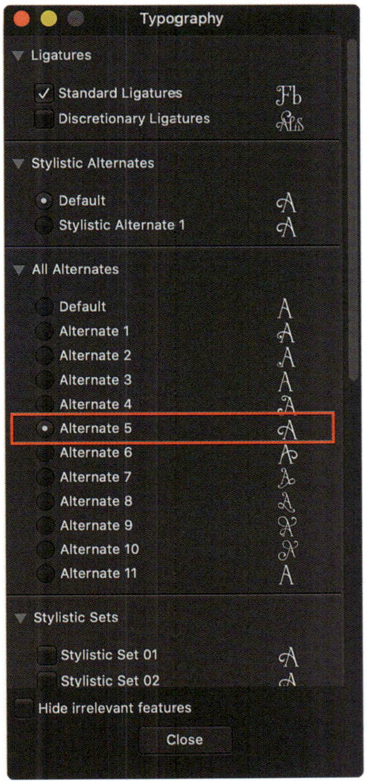

3 Enable each **Alternate** option in turn; the *Alternate 5* option was eventually chosen in this project.

4 Repeat for other characters in the title.

> Avoid applying an alternate to entire words and paragraphs—some characters may have more suitable alternates than others.

Be creative
Let your alternate character extend into the empty space around it

Use discretionary ligatures
These combine characters into a single graceful design using a 'spanning' ligature

Explore a specific character's typography
A character might offer a much more appropriate alternate. The example shown suggests a diamond playing card suit.

Edit sparingly
Choose characters to edit with thought—experimenting with the first and last characters in a word is popular. Individual characters within the word are also good candidates

Using the **Character Panel**, you can still apply text formatting in combination with alternates.

- Use **Baseline** shifts on apostrophes (circled opposite)
- Increase **Font Size** on already upper-case first characters
- Make fine **Tracking** adjustments to readjust characters after using alternates

Alternates and Ligatures explained

Alternates, as its name suggests, offer an alternative character to replace the current one.

Standard Ligatures bring two letter pairs together to give the appearance of a single character. This is for practical reasons—maybe the characters would otherwise look clumsy together or less appealing to the eye.

Discretionary Ligatures are perfect for a more decorative approach but still merge letter pairs into a single design.

> Depending on your chosen font's design, combining a standard or discretionary ligature with a particular alternate can offer some exciting typographic choices.

Resource
Alices_adventures_in_wonderland_cover_04.afpub backcovertext_alicecover.docx

SUPPORTING TEXT

As we're designing a wrap-around cover, additional text needs to be added to the project—the spine text and the back cover text.

For different reasons, these often undervalued elements of any cover serve an important role—the spine text to make the book identifiable when placed on a book shelf; the back cover text to draw the potential book buyer into making the purchase.

In terms of the technical aspects, the text pretty much follows the same design ideas as the title text, perhaps with fewer typographic enhancements.

Spine text

If you're designing vertical text, such as book spine text, you can temporarily rotate the Document View for easier text input and editing.

Rotating your view

- On the **View Menu**, select **Rotate > Rotate Left** (or right-click the Document View).

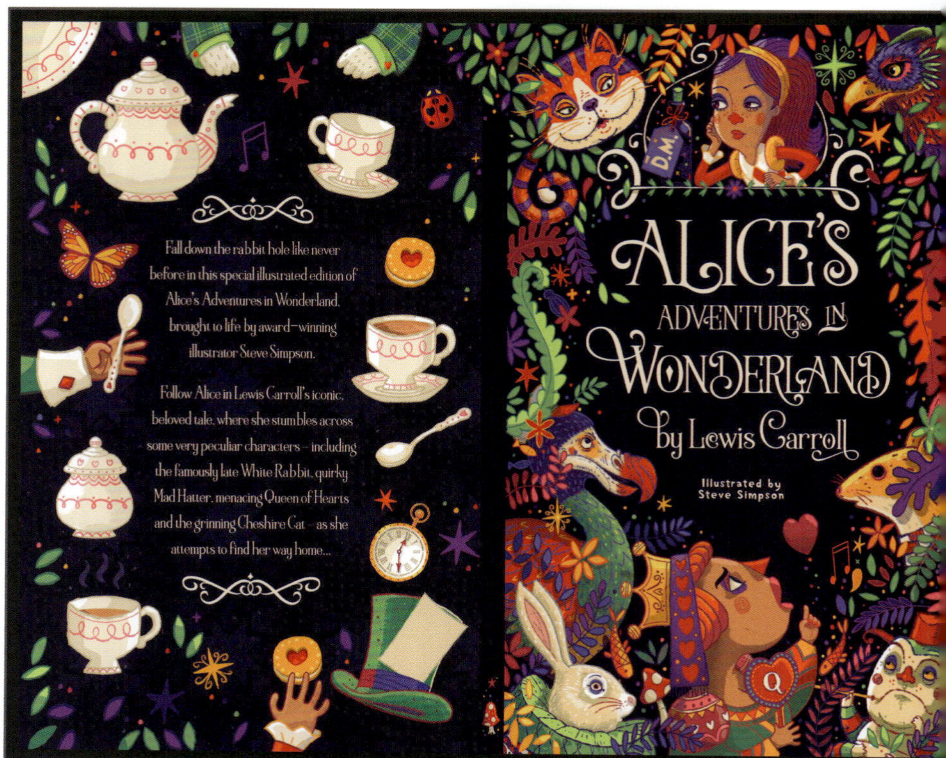

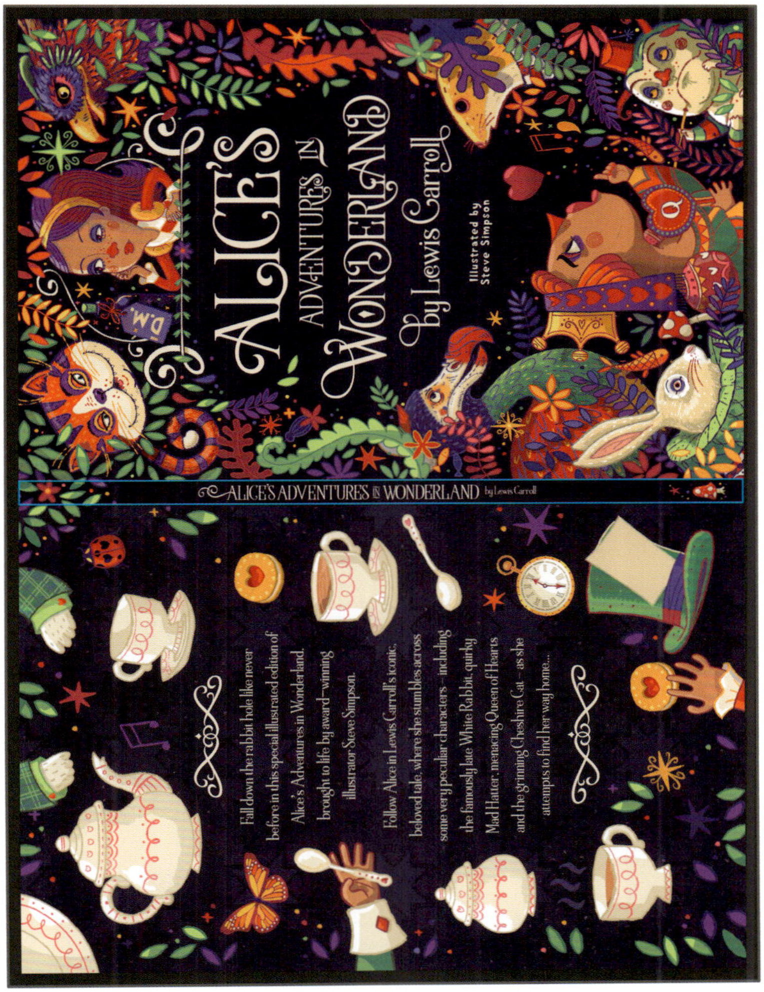

Adding spine text

1. Once rotated, enter the title and author name text with the **Artistic Text Tool** using Wallington Pro font.
2. As you're typing, rotate the text using **Rotate Clockwise** on the **Toolbar**, then make it align centre vertically; the author name in a reduced font size will then centre nicely.
3. Use a discretionary ligature on the word *IN*.

Select **View > Rotate > Reset Rotation** to revert rotation when finished.

Back cover text

The longest passage of text used is for the back cover. This should enticingly describe the book's story. In terms of design, this is superficially just two paragraphs of text added to a text frame, but there are some interesting ligature control and leading override techniques also being used here.

Adding back cover text

1 With nothing selected, choose **File > Place**.

2 Navigate to the backcovertext_alicecover.docx file, select it and click **Open**.

3 Drag out the text's frame in the available free space on the back cover.

4 The text will be using the same font from the docx file (the same as the spine text). Give it the same colour as previous text, make it **Centre Align** using the context toolbar and drop the **Font Size** to *10 pt*.

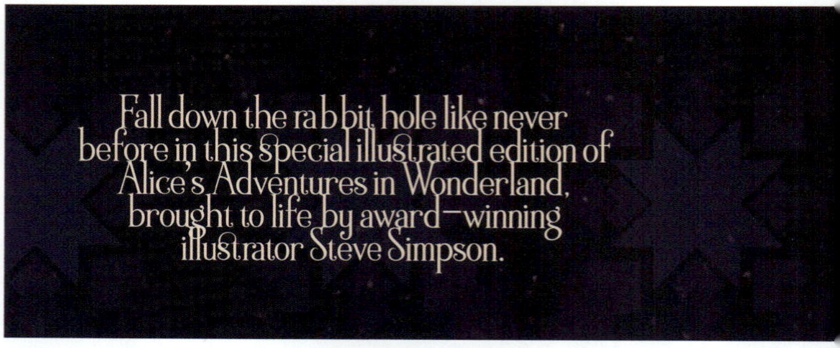

Overriding leading

With the text looking too tight vertically—due to default paragraph leading—a character-level leading override can be applied to both selected paragraphs.

On the **Character Panel** (**Positioning and Transform**), adjust the **Leading Override** to be *20 pt*.

To prevent hyphenation being unnecessarily applied, you can switch hyphenation off on the **Character Panel** (Language section) by setting **Hyphenation** to *None*.

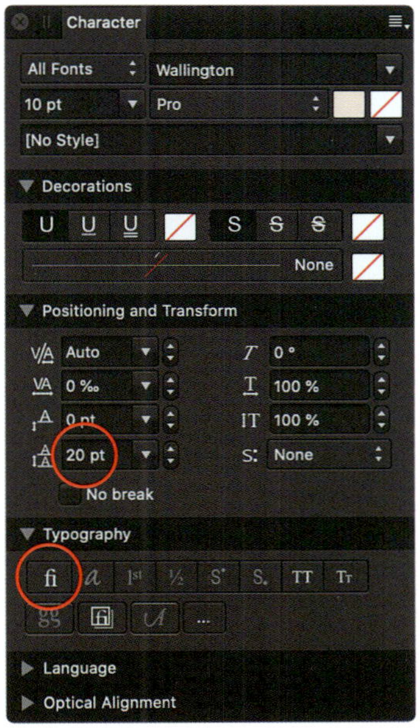

Switching off ligatures

As a general rule, body text should not be embellished so that readability is enhanced. To allow this, you can switch off ligatures normally applied to characters by default.

1 Select both paragraphs.

2 On the **Character Panel**, uncheck **Standard Ligatures** from the **Typography** section.

No other typographic formatting, i.e. Alternates or Stylistic Sets, was used.

FINAL TOUCHES

With the typographic work out of the way, there's one small task left to do.

ISBN numbers and barcodes

You may want to allocate an International Standard Book Number (ISBN) to your book. This is a 13-digit number which uniquely identifies your book to aid its listing, ordering, stock control and physical distribution (especially via Amazon). The number is allocated to you and registered via Nielson Book Agency (nielsenbook.co.uk).

Generating a barcode

Once registered and in possession of an ISBN number, you can use one of many online ISBN barcode generators to produce a barcode based on that ISBN number.

ISBN 9781909581050

9 781909 581050

This project uses a dummy ISBN number and barcode.

Resource
Alices_adventures_in_wonderland_cover_final.afpub barcode_alicecover.svg

Adding a barcode

With many book covers, the ISBN barcode is typically placed on the back cover.

In this project, as a nice touch we generated our sample ISBN barcode graphic and our Illustrator incorporated it into the Mad Hatter's hat.

1 Select **File > Place**.

2 Navigate to, then select barcode_alicecover.svg and click **Open**.

3 Hover then drag the cursor out over the hat design.

4 From the graphic's top rotation handle, drag to the left to rotate the graphic.

5 Fine-tune scaling via corner handles and reposition if needed.

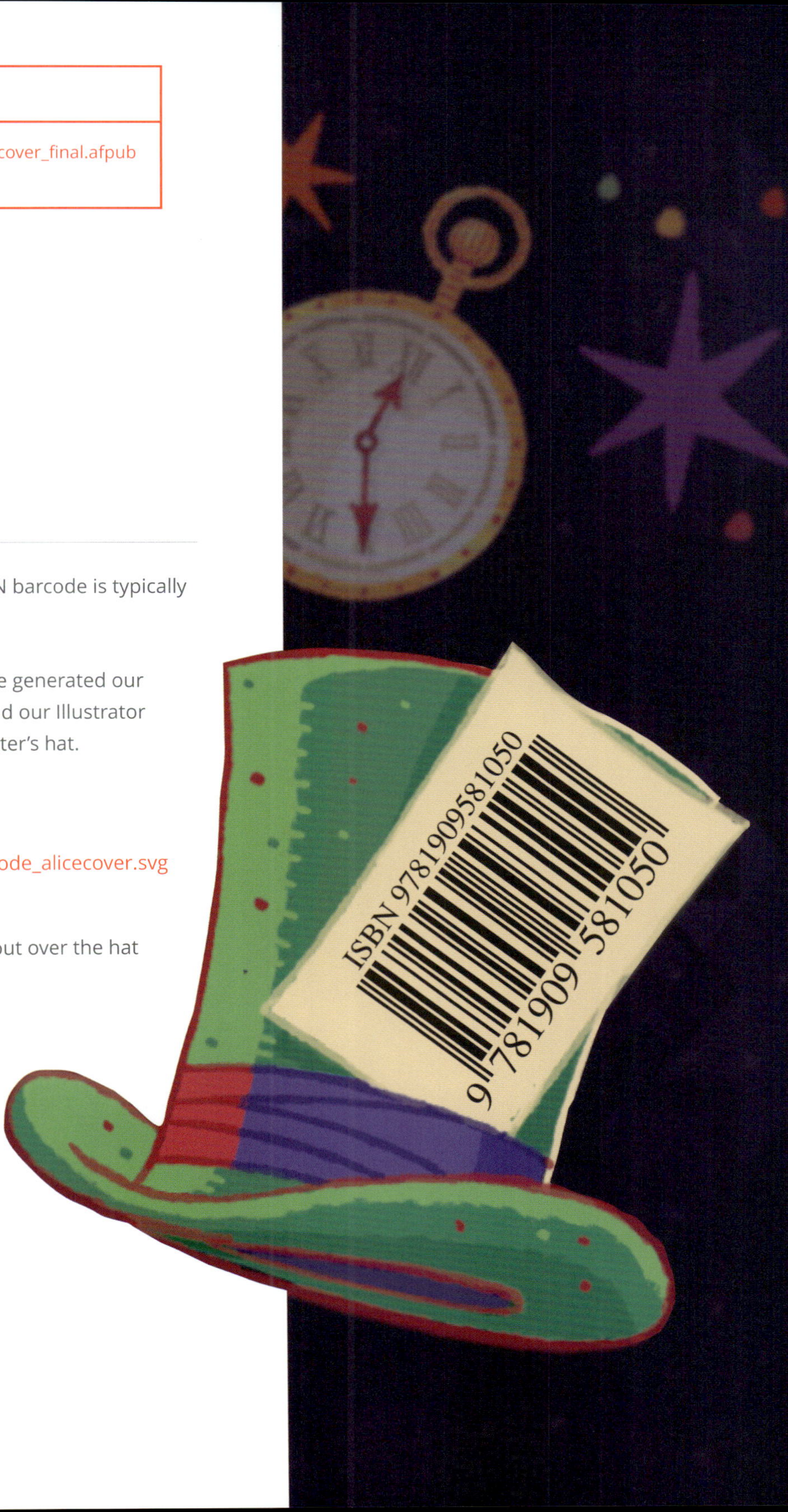

EXPORTING

With the design now complete you can export it using the same procedure and settings described for the main book contents on p. 358

ALICE'S
ADVENTURES IN
WONDERLAND
by Lewis Carroll
Illustrated by
Steve Simpson

3

Bijou Film Festival Poster

Create a print-ready large-format poster for a local short-film festival

Creating a single page design such as a poster creates its own challenges. In this project, we'll look at making an impact using a large-format design with a strong focal point.

JOV | iFederations | East Institute of Films
22ND
BIJOU
Bijou
Short
Film
Festival
/ animation
/ documentary
/ live action
october 3-9
Short Film Council
RUNNING TIME
venue
Gotham South Campus
Godmanchester, UK
talks
From 13:00
Esther Feldman
Donald J Cornwell
Dan Platts
Tammy Rogers
Amanda Allan
screenings
From 19:00
(Amy L Dior)
Tucked In
(Ben Gunn)
Clapping Hands
(Amy Schumacher)
Wolves
(Edward Zenidr)
The Mark
(Amanda Allan)
Reaccuring
(Terence Larkin)
Sound From The Sun
(William Sean Twaid)
Count to Ten
(Donald J Cornwell)
Polaroids
(Amida Khan)
Everyday
(Esther Feldman)
Just Walk On In
Charles Upcott)
Love Under Will
(Savid Mohammed)
Ready For Nothing

BEFORE YOU GET STARTED

Resources

You can get all the resources that are referenced in this project from: https://affin.co/BijouPoster

Knowledge of Affinity Publisher

To get the most from undertaking this project, you will need to:

- Be familiar with the interface of Affinity Publisher. You can learn more about the interface in the Interface Tour chapter, starting on p. 14.
- Have good core skills. See the skills table below to see which additional aspects of Affinity Publisher you need to be confident with to complete this project:

Working with Text	p. 112
Picture Frames	p. 124
Adding Content	p. 130

INTRODUCTION

When making a poster, it's not always easy to know where to start. Think about your audience. What are they looking for? What's the aim of our poster? Knowing your audience is key to designing a poster that works.

In this project, we'll assume we're working with a client to establish a client brief. This will help to understand the target audience which will influence the poster's design.

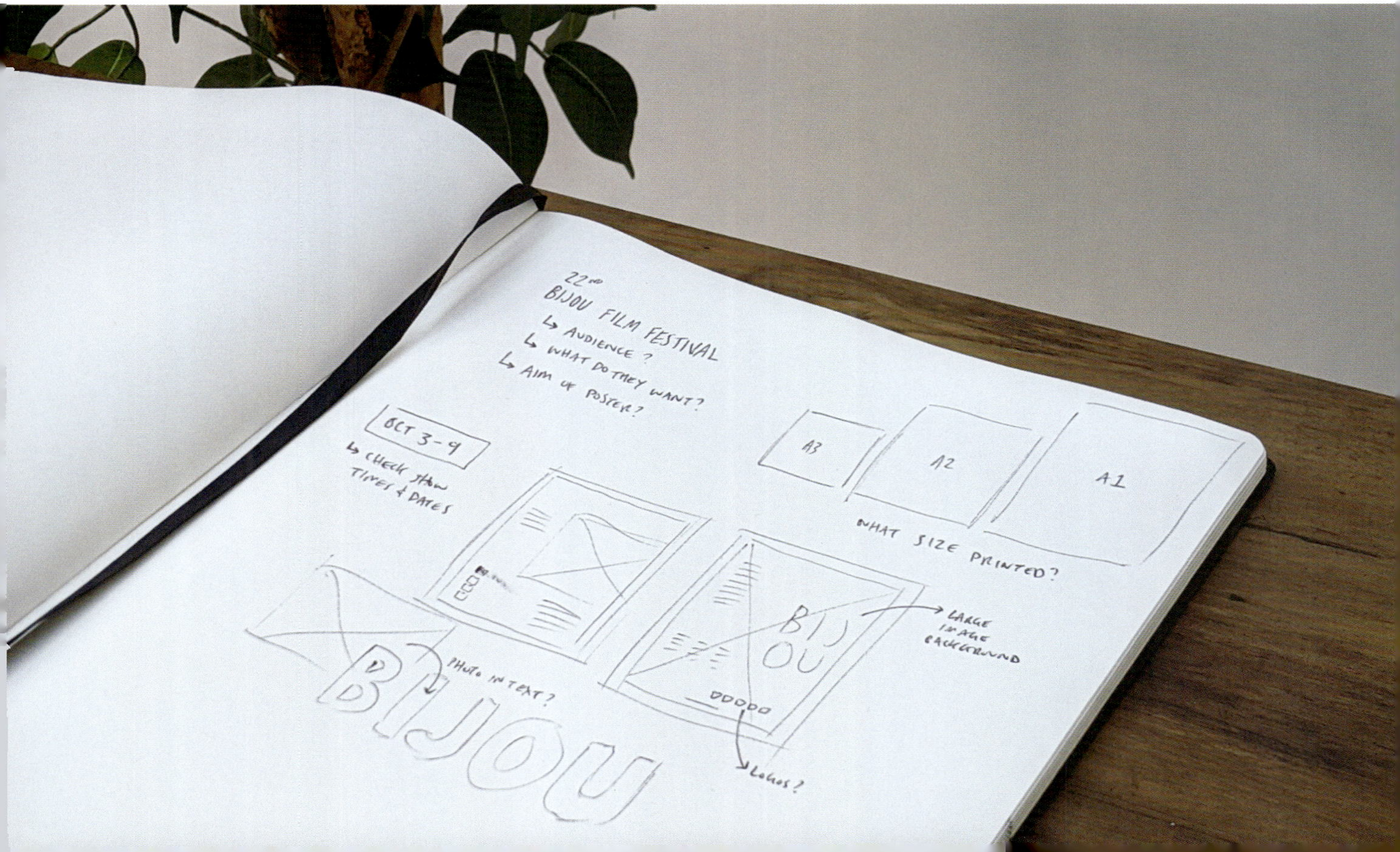

CLIENT BRIEF

By the end of your kick-off meeting with your client, it's vital that you have both agreed on a brief for your project. This should outline exactly what is needed and aim to reduce miscommunication and lost time.

Once you have a brief and an insight into what your client is looking for, you can begin the design process.

Six key questions to ask your client

1 What is the purpose/objective/context of the project?

2 What are the deliverables for the project?

3 Are there specific design do's and don'ts?

4 What existing designs do you like and dislike?

5 Who is the main point of contact and who is the decision maker on the project?

6 What are the timescales and budget for the project?

STARTING THE PROCESS

In this project, the fictional Bijou Film Festival is set to take place in a local entertainment campus.

Name:	Bijou Film Festival
Client Details:	Local festival organisation committee based in Misterham, UK. The festival runs annually, with a growing respect in art and cultural circles nationally.
Your Brief:	To design a high-quality poster that will attract attention at already busy locations. Its strong visual impact should be supported by show times, dates and sponsorship logos.

When working on a commission, it's important to **keep the client's requirements in mind**, while taking an open and flexible approach to your own working.

Think about how you want to **present your information**. It may be tempting to try to cram details into your poster, but simplicity is key when it comes to your design and your copy.

Sketch out poster ideas on paper to help you mentally organise what you want to share with your client without the constraints of sitting at your computer.

Keep it simple and **let your ideas flow** as you work. If you're looking for inspiration, there are many poster designs online that make great use of spacing, colour, image placement and styling choices. You could browse through existing designs and have a play with some poster templates before you get to work on your design.

Ultimately, the **poster should be both informative and eye-catching**, drawing attention in all the right ways and emphasising the poster's main message.

DOCUMENT SETUP

Choosing a poster size

Posters come in all shapes and sizes. Choosing the right size will ultimately come down to where it is going to be displayed and the page size standards appropriate to your country.

For this festival, the client was offered various size options in consultation with the client's professional printer partner. After reviewing a few sizes, the client wanted to keep to the more popular A Series page sizes, in particular the A2 page size for the poster.

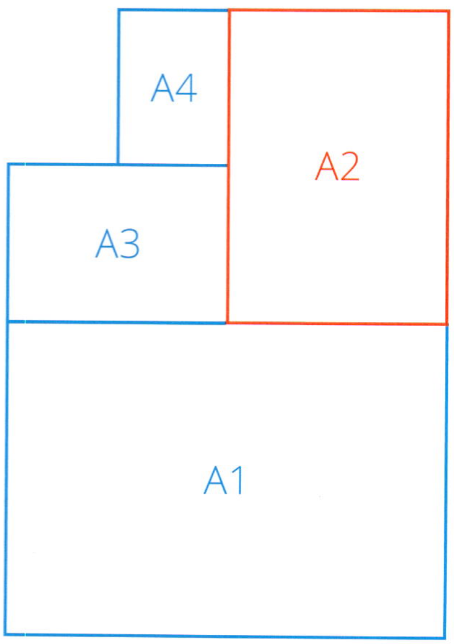

UK Billboard	Dimensions
1 Sheet Poster (Double Crown)	20" x 30"
2 Sheet Poster (Quad)	30" x 40"
4 Sheet Poster (Bus Stop)	40" x 60"

A Series	Dimensions
A0	841 mm x 1189 mm
A1	594 mm x 841 mm
A2	420 mm x 594 mm
A3	297 mm x 420 mm
A4	210 mm x 297 mm

US	Dimensions
3 Sheet	41" x 81"
1 Sheet	27" x 40"
Large Poster	24" x 36"
Medium Poster	18" x 24"
Small Poster (Ledger ANSI B)	11" x 17"

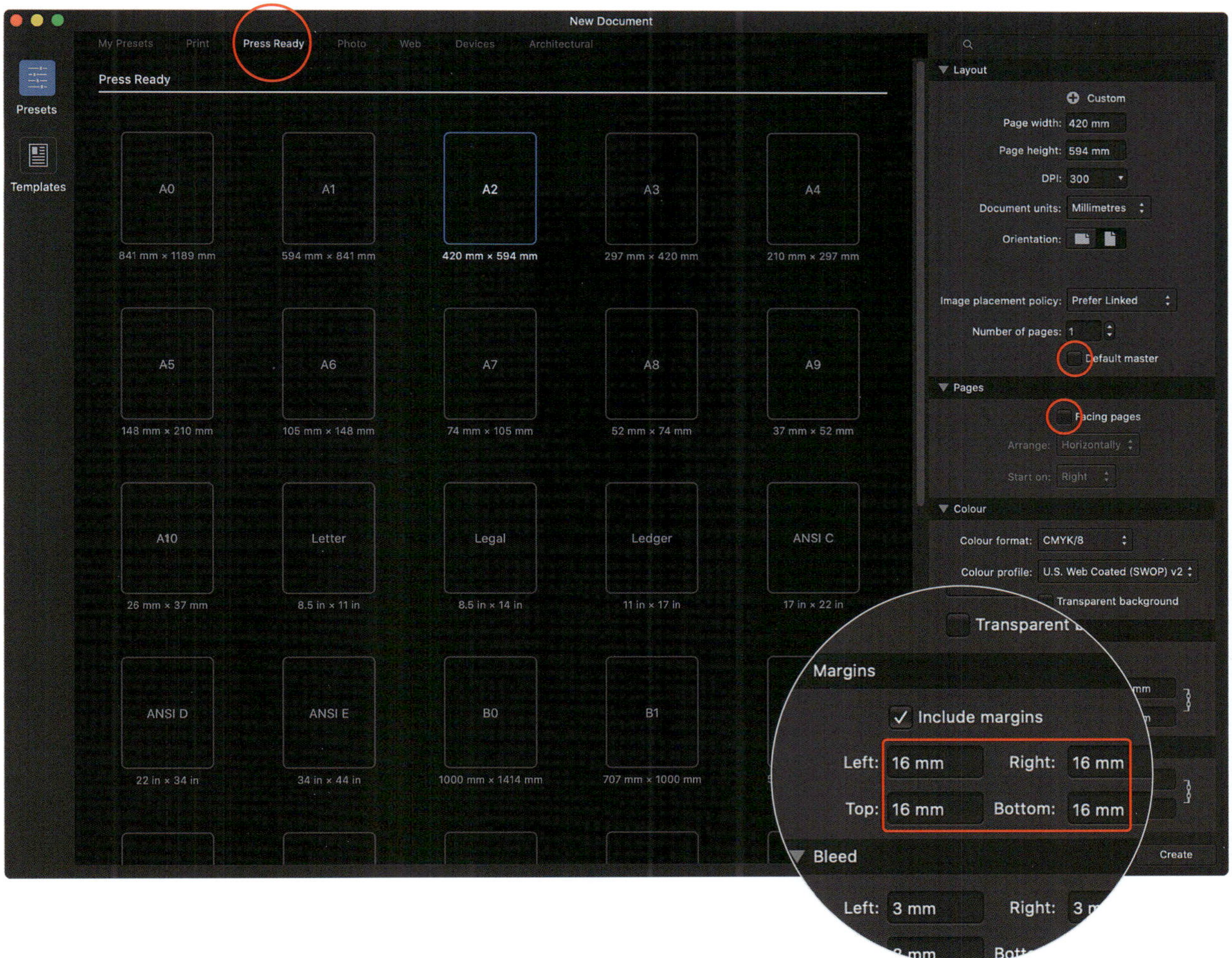

Creating an A2 poster

Let's set up a CMYK document for our poster.

The intention is to produce a print-ready poster so keeping to a CMYK colour workspace means the delivered artwork is ready for professional litho printing.

1 Select **File > New**.

2 With **Presets** selected, choose the **Press Ready** preset category from the top of the dialog.

3 Choose the *A2* thumbnail to set the document's size.

4 On the right-hand Settings pane, adjust key values as shown in dialog above.

5 Click **Create**.

Choosing a preset from the Press Ready category automatically sets the page dimensions, a CMYK colour space and a 3-mm bleed. The settings above are shown as Custom because we've overriden the original values as indicated.

Resource
Bijou_poster_01.afpub

GUIDES AND SNAPPING

Combining added ruler guides with snapping helps you to position your poster content accurately on the page.

Enabling guides

For this poster, we've set up a single ruler guide on the left side of the page to align our page content.

- Ensure you have rulers displayed (**View > Show Rulers**) and then drag a vertical guide from the left ruler to *30 mm*.

Use **View > Guides Manager** to be millimetre accurate.

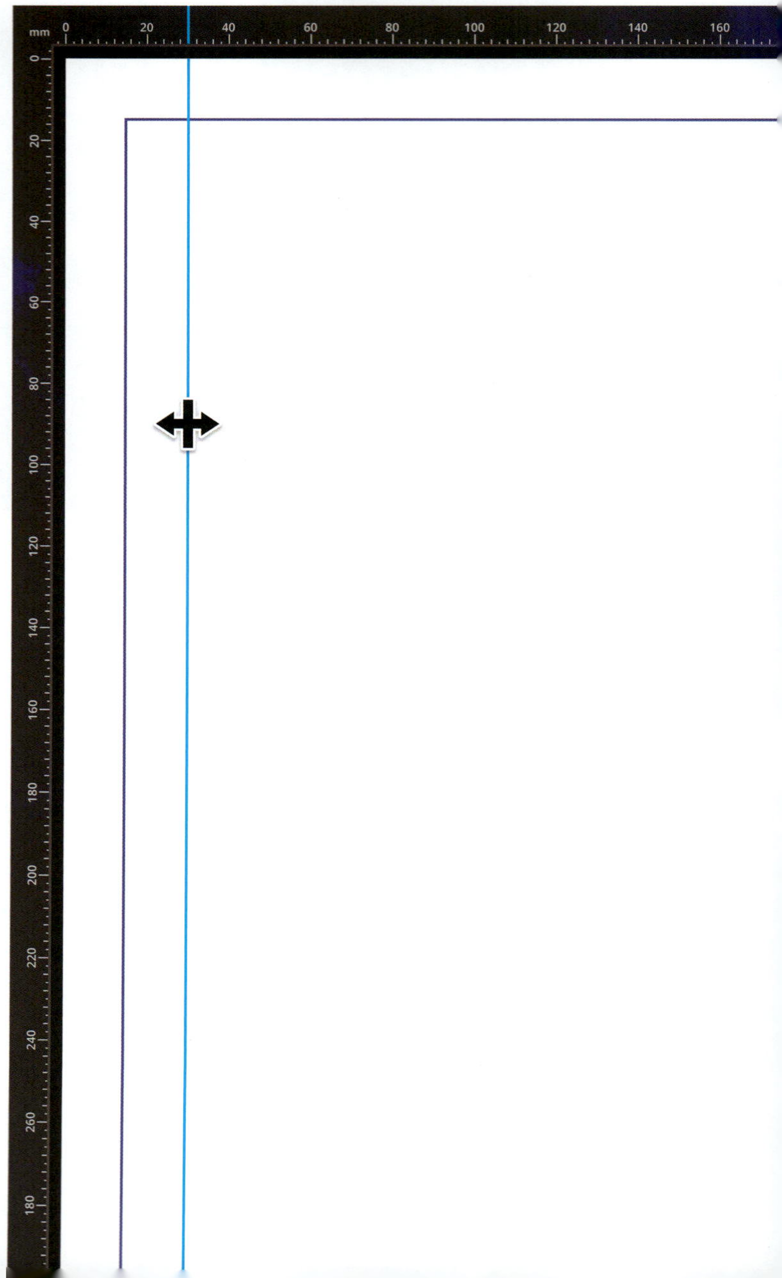

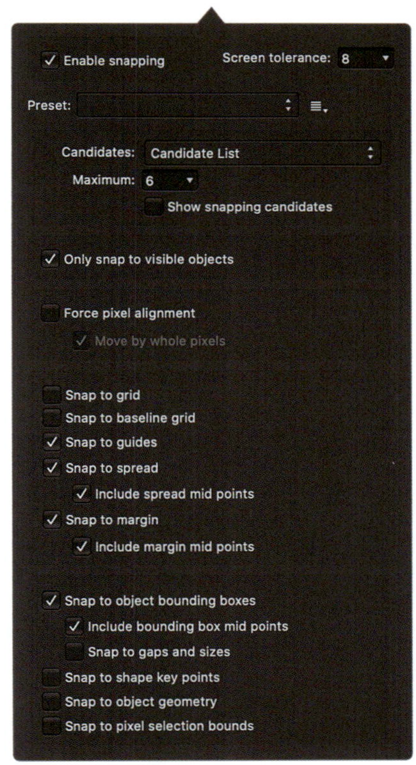

Snapping

- On the **Toolbar**, ensure **Snapping** is enabled (this is the default).

This will let you snap your text frame or artistic text to your added guide, but also to margins or text frame edges for accurate placement. You can snap both horizontally and vertically.

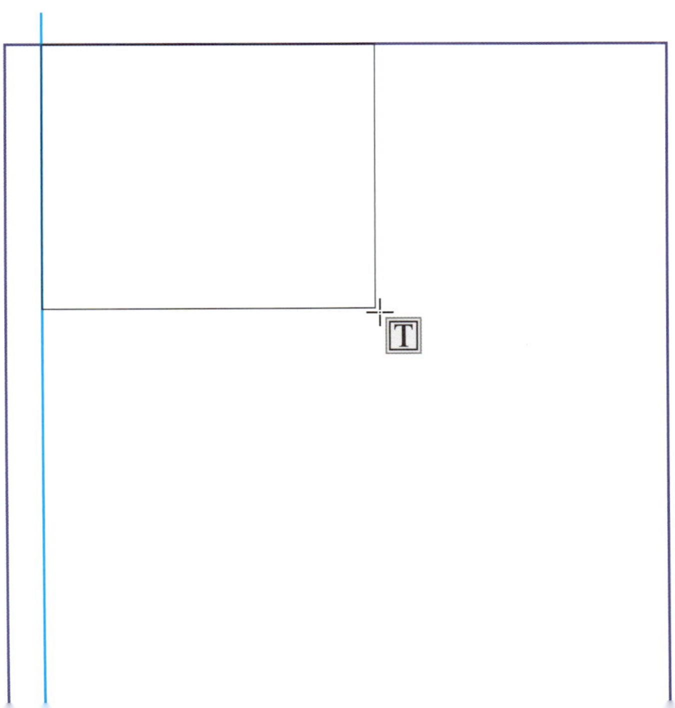

Resource
Bijou_poster_02.afpub Bijou_model.jpg

BACKGROUND IMAGE

Background imagery sets the scene for your poster. You'll need a high-quality graphic that is going to work at your intended print size.

For this poster, we have used a framed picture instead of adding a picture directly to the page; this allows the framed image to be scaled and positioned within the picture frame to get the right composition.

Adding the picture frame

1 Select the **Picture Frame Rectangle Tool** (F).

2 Drag from the top-left bleed corner to the bottom-right bleed corner of the page and release. The picture frame spans beyond the page edges.

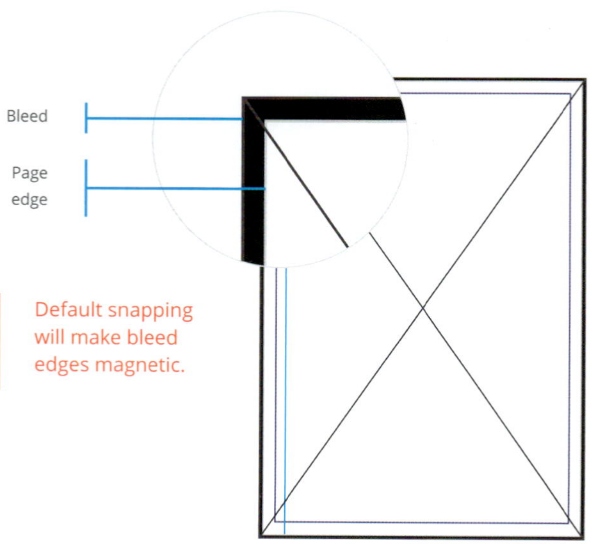

Default snapping will make bleed edges magnetic.

Adding an image to the picture frame

1 With the picture frame selected, choose **File > Place**.

2 Navigate to the bijou_model.jpg* file, then click **Open**.

*In your resource files, we've provided a different royalty-free image to that shown in this project. The image's composition will offer the same results.

As the linked image is landscape oriented and scaled to maximum fit in the frame, areas to the left and right of the image are hidden under the frame. These can be revealed to improve image composition.

Adjusting image composition

1 Double-click the picture frame to select the framed image.

2 With the shift key (⇧) pressed (this constrains the image horizontally), drag the image to the left.

Colour choice

Your colour palette sets the mood of your whole design. Bold and flashy isn't always good—bright contrasting colours might go well on a poster for an upcoming rock concert, but a nature walk poster might call for something a bit calmer and earthier. Be sure to keep the subject matter in mind when you're choosing colours for your poster, and don't be afraid to experiment with a few different ideas.

For this poster, we're looking to set the mood using a coloured thick frame border followed by a matching colour 'image' wash. The poster text will adopt the border colour in due course.

We'll first create colours as global colours—these let you change the colour across your design at a later time in one operation (p. 418).

Creating global CMYK colours

1 On the **Swatches Panel**, click **Panel Preferences**, then select **Add Global Colour**.

2 In the dialog's HSL Colour Wheel pop-up menu, choose **CMYK Sliders**.

3 Create a CMYK colour *30,0,0,0*, then click **Add**.

4 Repeat for a second darker colour (*CMYK 48,0,0,64*).

Adding a coloured picture frame border

1 Select the picture frame.

2 On the **Stroke Panel**, set a stroke **Width** of *54 pt* and enable **Align Stroke to Inside**. Check **Scale with Object** for later project resizing.

3 On the **Swatches Panel**, click the Stroke Colour Selector and choose the darker global colour swatch from the Document Palette.

These colour choices are similar to those present in the image. Another option would be to sample colour directly from the image using the **Colour Picker Tool**.

Stroke
Style:
Width:
54 pt
Cap:
Join:
Mitre: 1.5
Align:
Order:
Scale with object
Start:
100 %
End:
100 %
Properties...
Pressure:
Swatches
Opacity: 100 %
Recent:
Document
Add Global Colour...
Add Registration Colour
Add Application Palette
Add Document Palette
Add System Palette
Rename Palette...
Delete Palette
Set as Default for
Remove Default for
Create Palette From Document
Create Palette From Image...
Appearance
Sort
Import Palette...
Export Palette...

Applying adjustments

A background image injects personality into a poster, but it can also make the design too busy and obscure parts of the text. To ensure our background image blends with the planned text content, let's apply some colour adjustments.

Gradient Map adjustment

The **Gradient Map** adjustment allows you to recolour the frame and image by mapping their greyscale ranges to a colour gradient, in this case our two chosen global colours.

1. Select the picture frame.
2. On the bottom of the **Layers Panel**, click **Adjustments** and select **Gradient Map** from the pop-up menu.
3. Edit the colour gradient spectrum in the dialog by manipulating the circular stops on the gradient:
    - Delete the unwanted middle stop using **Delete**.
    - Select the left end point and click the **Colour** swatch beneath the spectrum. On the top pop-up menu, choose **Swatches**, then **Document**—choose the darker global colour from the Document Palette. Repeat for the right-hand end point, choosing the lighter global colour.

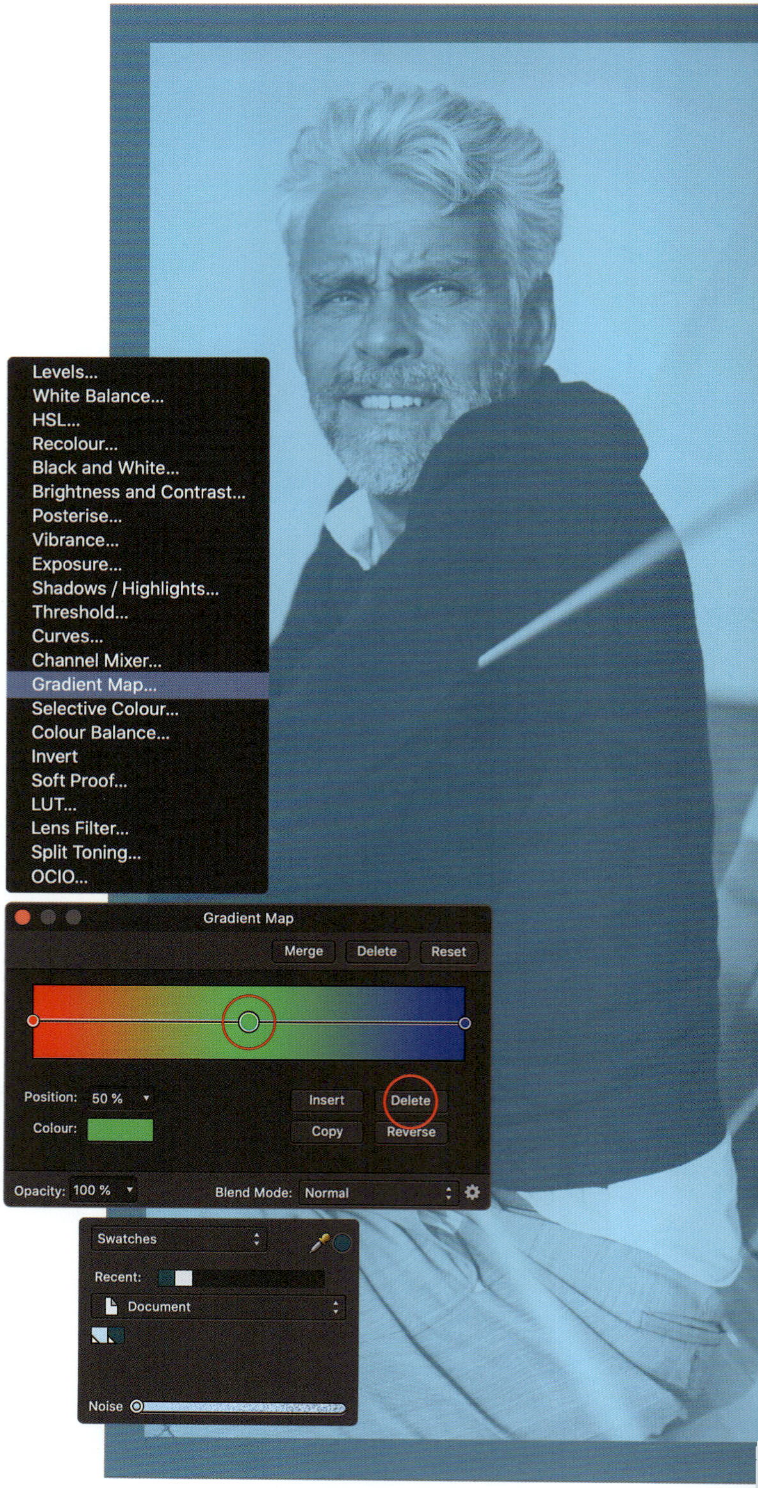

HSL adjustment

By applying an **HSL** adjustment, we can pull down the lightness of the image, which seems overly bright.

1 Double-click the picture frame to select the framed image.

2 On the **Layers Panel**, click **Adjustments** and select **HSL** from the pop-up menu.

3 Decrease **Luminosity Shift** to *-50%*.

Gradient Map and HSL adjustments will be clipped to picture frame and image, respectively.

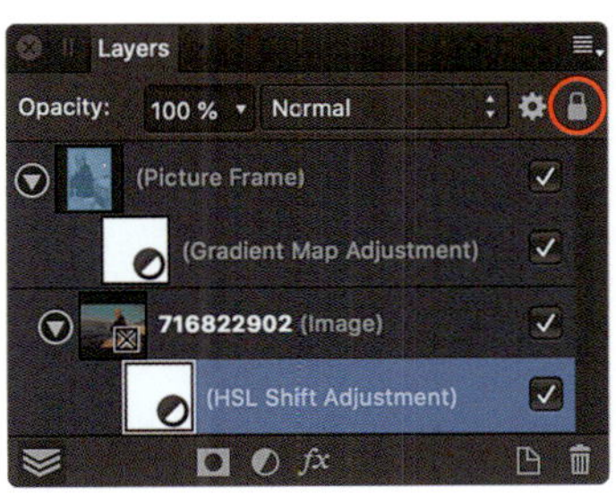

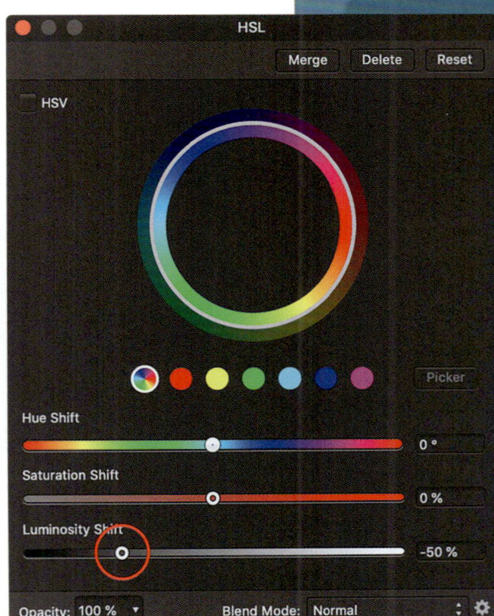

With picture frame and image finished, protect them in the Layers Panel by clicking the Lock symbol.

Resource
Bijou_poster_03.afpub

POSTER TEXT

Downloading and installing fonts

1 Go to https://fonts.google.com/ (or search online for Google fonts) and download the **Istok Web** family.

2 Open the downloaded zip file and open and read the OFL.txt file.

3 For *Mac*: ctrl-click the downloaded font files and select **Install font**.
or:
For *Windows*: Right-click the downloaded font files and select **Install**.

General

When it comes to poster text, less is more. It's easy to get carried away by including as much detail as possible but try to keep to just the key details.

You should also be thinking about whether important text can be read at distance—you may have only one chance to grab someone's attention!

Creating poster text

Using a single typeface with varied weights creates a visual hierarchy for the poster. Text size should match the text's level of importance, with key information like dates and headings set at a larger size.

1 With the **Frame Text Tool** (T) active, set your preferred text settings (font family, style, size, trait and light-blue global colour) from the Frame Text context toolbar (opposite).

2 Drag across the page and begin typing in the text frame, adjusting font size and font style as you go.

3 Repeat for additional text frames.

The 22ND text is actually Artistic text with no fill and a light blue stroke. The **Tracking** (**Character Panel**) is tightened to *-25%*.

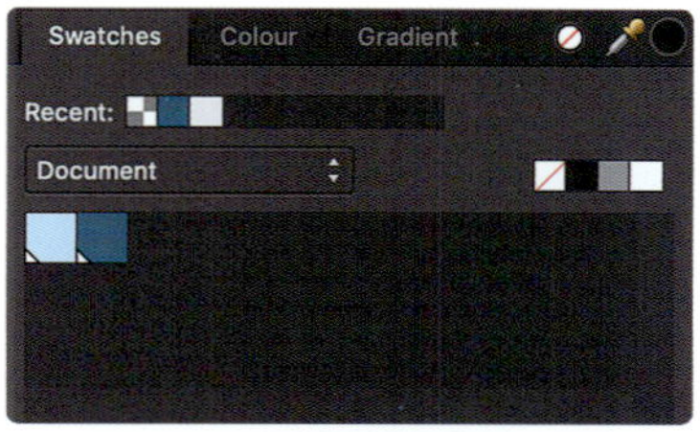

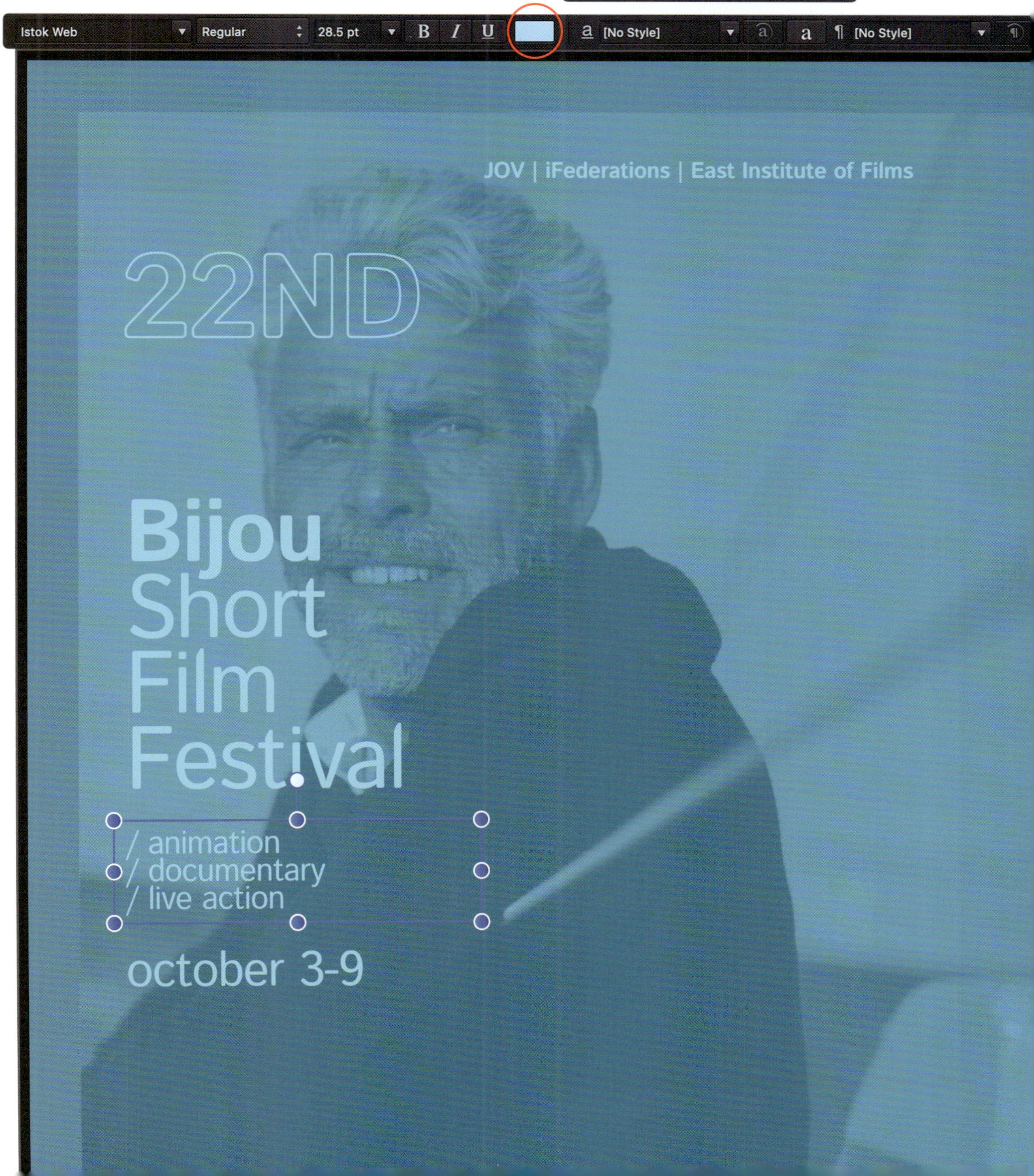

Title

Your title needs to grab your reader's attention, making them want to read more.

First, we'll create a small version of the title text to keep the title design manageable, before scaling up the finished title to fill the page—let's go big on the font size here!

Creating title text

1 With the **Frame Text Tool** active, adjust the context toolbar settings.

2 Drag out a roughly square text frame to accommodate your title text, then type *BIJOU*.

Fine-tuning the title text

The text now needs to run onto a second line.

- Drag the edge handle on the left edge of the text frame inwards until the characters *OU* begin a new line.

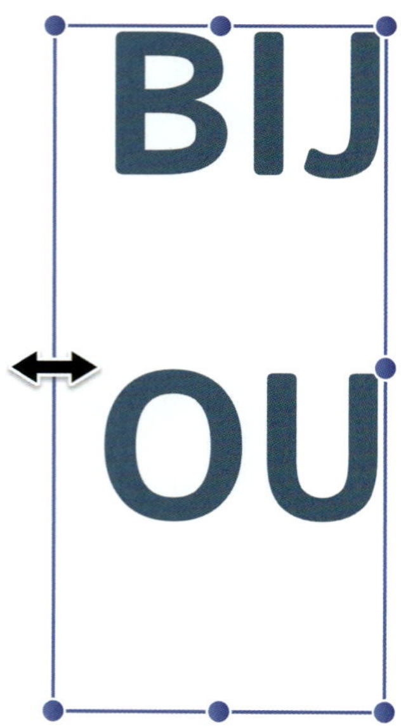

Additionally, leading and tracking helps to tighten up the title, adding a little more symmetry to the title design.

1 Select all the text.

2 On the **Character Panel** (Positioning and Transform), use the **Leading Override** down arrow to tighten the distance between baselines. Let your eye be the judge.

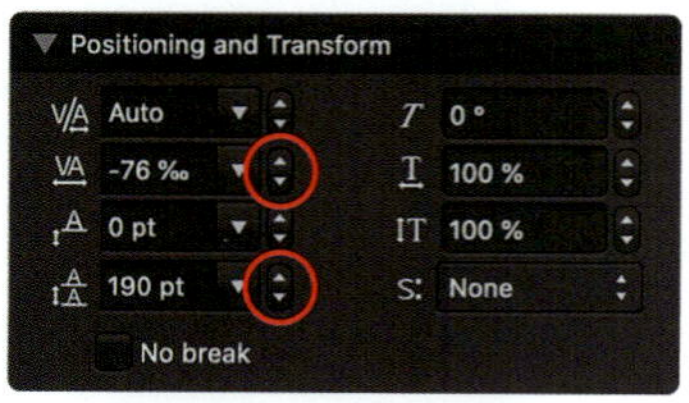

3 Tighten **Tracking**, using its down arrow, so the letters *I* and the left stem of *U* are horizontally aligned. Make another **Tracking** adjustment to 'tighten' the selected letter *B* so the letter's right edge aligns vertically with the right edge of letter *O*.

Try reducing the text frame's dimensions to automatically fit its text content—this makes scaling more controllable. Simply double-click the bottom edge handle, followed by the left edge handle.

Scaling up the title text

- Drag the outer bottom-right corner handle of the text frame outwards.

With a little repositioning the title is complete.

FILM SCHEDULE TABLE

A table is the perfect way to organise key event information like a festival film schedule that details the venue location and timetable.

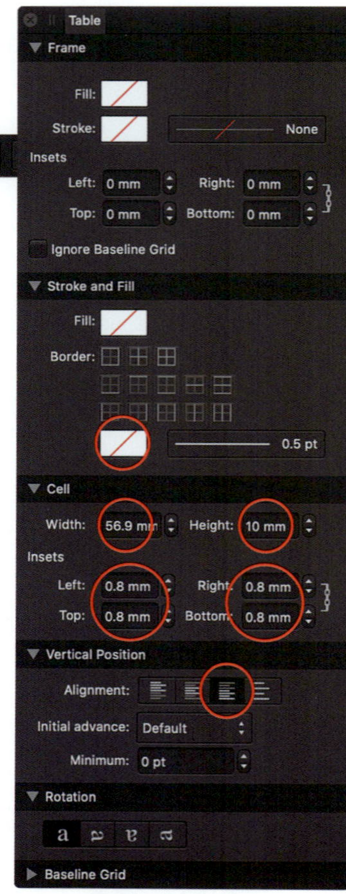

Creating a basic table

1 With the **Table Tool** (T) selected, drag out a new table below the title text —a readout of table dimensions and column/row count helps you plan your table structure. Go for a 4-column, 13-row table structure.

2 On the context toolbar, select **Table** to display the **Table Panel**.

3 The **Table Panel** lets you format your table before, after or while adding text. Adjust settings as shown.

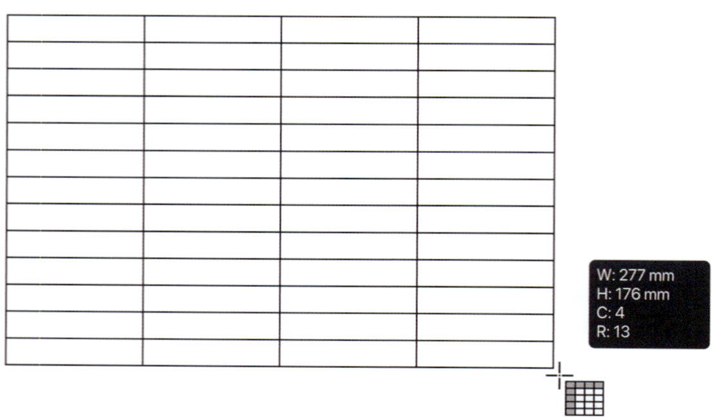

Table Design Tips

Instead of adding text content before or during table design, you could plan and design your table first. This lets you focus on the table look first and the text content later.

In this project, these tips are appropriate to this design but they could be applied to your own table designs.

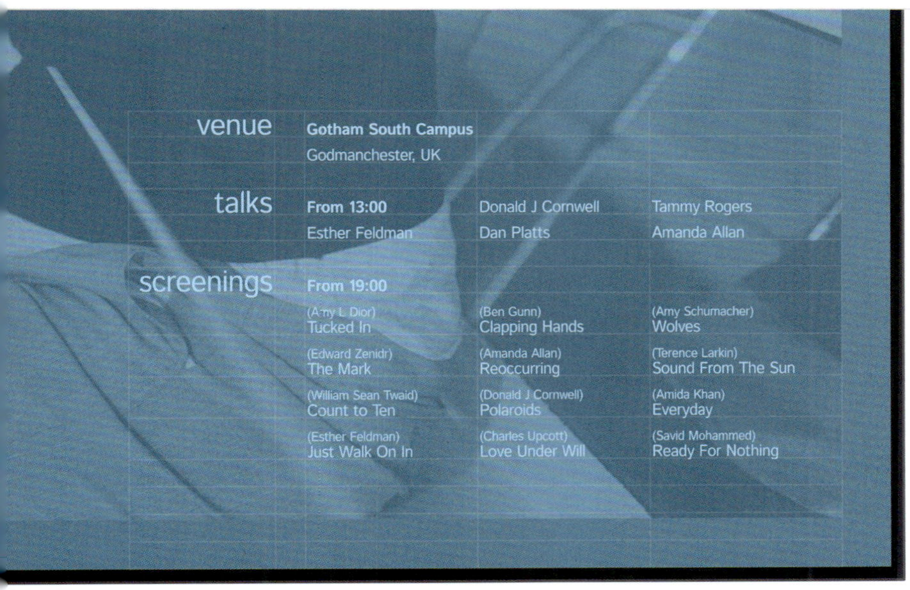

- Set up a basic table to accommodate your source data.
- Add placeholder table text temporarily while designing the table (e.g., 10 crosses, xxxxxxxxxx).
- Vertically align cell text to bottom, using bottom cell border as a text 'baseline'.
- Set a generous and uniform column width and row height for consistency. In this table, the latter avoids setting more complex paragraph leading and inter-paragraph spacing.
- Apply uniform text formatting (font size, font style, font colour, apply fill).
- Apply text formatting to first columns (e.g., increase font size and/or bold, align right, apply fill). This draws the eye to these 'headings', emphasising the venue and event times.
- Edit uniform table cell borders. In this project, these are removed so the traditional rectangular table appearance is deliberately lost.
- Add 'buffer' columns or rows as padding. In this poster, it helps separate festival event categories from talk/film titles. Adjust column widths and row heights by dragging header dividers—use shift key (⇧) while dragging to honour other column/row widths.

Resource
Bijou_poster_04.afpub

CLIPPING IMAGES TO TITLES

Clipping an image to an object restricts the image's visibility to just within the object's outline.

In this project, we'll target the title text for clipping to a framed image.

Targeting title text for clipping

1 Select the title text.

2 On the **Toolbar**, select **Insert inside the selection**.

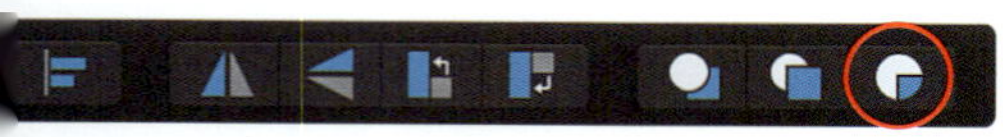

Adding a clipped picture frame and image

1 Select the **Picture Frame Rectangle Tool**.

2 Drag the cursor out from the left margin to the right page edge so the drawn picture frame is covering all of the title text.

3 Select **File > Place**.

4 Navigate to an image of your choice, then click **Open**.

Positioning your framed image

By default, your newly framed image will be scaled to maximum fit within the picture frame. Unfortunately, the main character's face is badly obscured—let's reposition the image to resolve this and improve the composition.

1 Double-click the picture frame to select the image.

2 With the shift key (⇧) pressed, drag the image to the right so the face appears centred to the letter *I*.

INTRODUCING LOGO GRAPHICS

Resource

Bijou_poster_05.afpub
short-film-council_exported logo.svg
Fly Free_LOGO.eps
RunningTimeLogo.svg
European-screen-committee_final.psd
estel-logo-white.afdesign

For our design, we've requested third-party logo graphics from external sponsors to sit alongside our own Estell logo on the poster. We've specifically asked for vectors and project files (not bitmaps), as we want to recolour the logos with our lighter global colour, in keeping with the rest of the poster.

Placing multiple logos one-by-one

1 Select the **Place Image Tool**.

2 Navigate to and select all the resource files (except the .afpub file), then click **Open**.

3 On the temporary **Place Images Panel**, select a graphic and drag from the vertical guide to place; repeat for the others, ensuring they snap to the same widths (except the Estell graphic)

Arranging the logos

The logos should be small enough not to distract from the main design, but large enough to be noticed. Also, using alignment options lets you centre and vertically space the graphics evenly.

- To *scale*: With the shift key (⇧) pressed, select all the graphics and resize using the bottom-right corner handle. The aspect ratio will be maintained.

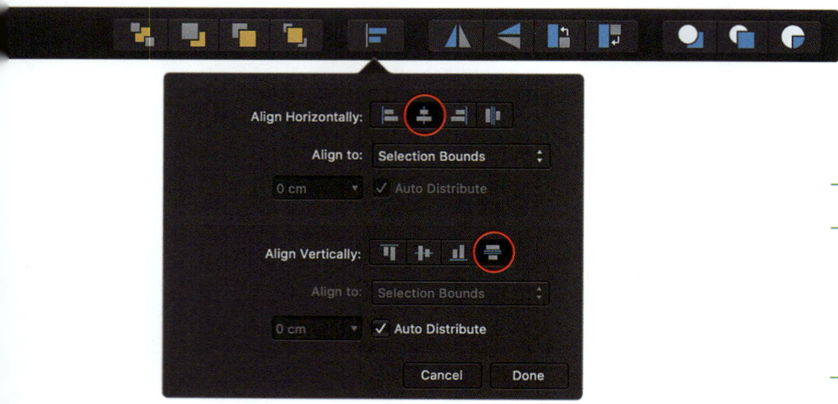

- To *align and space evenly*: On the **Toolbar**, select **Alignment** and click **Align Centre** then **Space Vertically**.

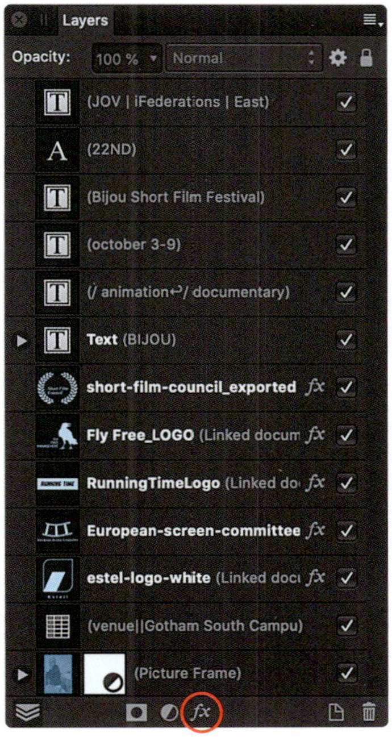

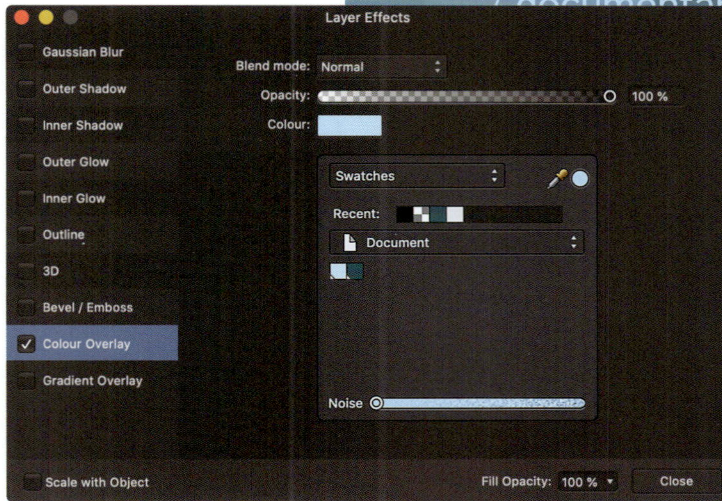

Colouring the logos

For this project, the logos should adopt the same global colour that was used for the poster text. This makes the images fit with the overall colour scheme.

1. Select all the logo images.
2. On the **Layers Panel**, click **Layer Effects**.
3. Check the **Colour Overlay** effect and navigate via the **Colour** swatch to the **Swatches** and **Document** Palette pop-up options.
4. Select the first lighter coloured global colour.

Resource
Bijou_poster_06.afpub

ADDING EXTRA IMPACT

Adding additional shapes, lines and textures is a great way to add impact to your project. Where they're placed can determine or influence focal points, add symmetry or simply add an aesthetic suitable to your design's theme.

In this project, we've subtly introduced a couple of objects for these reasons.

- **Vertical edge:** (a)
  A thin white rectangle helps keep the focal point on the centre of the page while 'lifting' the design off the page slightly.

- **Circle grids:** (b)
  Adds symmetry and balance to the design in what would otherwise be a blank area of the background.

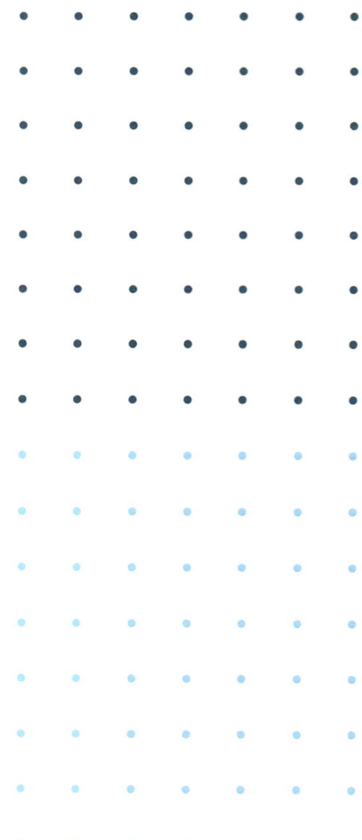

a
b
JOV | iFederations | East Institute of Films
22ND
BIJOU
Bijou
Short
Film
Festival
/ animation
/ documentary
/ live action
october 3-9
Short Film Council
FLY FREE MANAGEMENT
RUNNING TIME
European Screen Committee
venue
Gotham South Campus
Godmanchester, UK
talks
From 13:00
Esther Feldman
Donald J Cornwell
Dan Platts
Tammy Rogers
Amanda Allan
screenings
From 19:00
(Amy L Dior)
Tucked In
(Ben Gunn)
Clapping Hands
(Amy Schumacher)
Wolves
(Edward Zenidr)
The Mark
(Amanda Allan)
Reoccurring
(Terence Larkin)
Sound From The Sun
(William Sean Twaid)
Count to Ten
(Donald J Cornwell)
Polaroids
(Amida Khan)
Everyday
(Esther Feldman)
Just Walk On In
(Charles Upcott)
Love Under Will
(Savid Mohammed)
Ready For Nothing

CLIENT REVIEW

Following a review of the design so far with the client we looked into:

- Different colour choices (which could demo easily)
- Different sizing options
- Poster design variants

Colour choices

As the poster had been designed exclusively using two global colours, we were able to quickly transform the poster's look by editing just these colours.

Editing global colours

- On the **Swatches Panel**, right-click either colour swatch and choose **Edit Fill**.

> *Colour changes can dramatically change the mood of the poster.*

Resizing posters

One of the benefits of using the A series of page sizes is the ability to rescale page objects to different print sizes while keeping aspect ratios and relative object positioning the same whether A1, A2, or A3 size, etc.

For our final poster design, we will be scaling up from A2 to A1.

1 Go to **File > Spread Setup**.

2 On the **Dimensions** tab, select *A1* from the **Page Preset** menu.

3 Jump to the **Scaling** tab, and select **Rescale**.

4 Click **OK**.

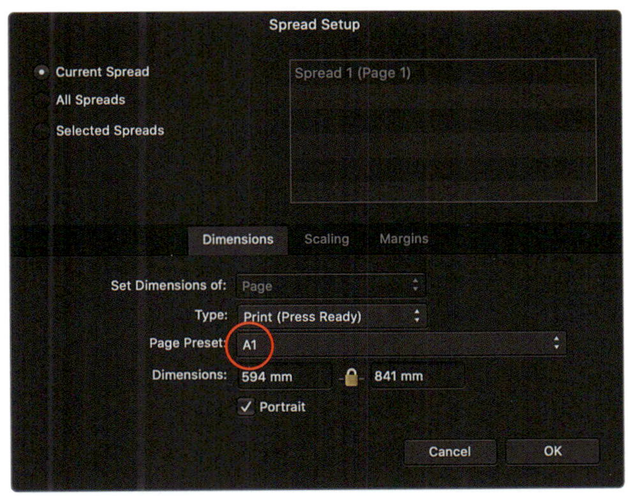

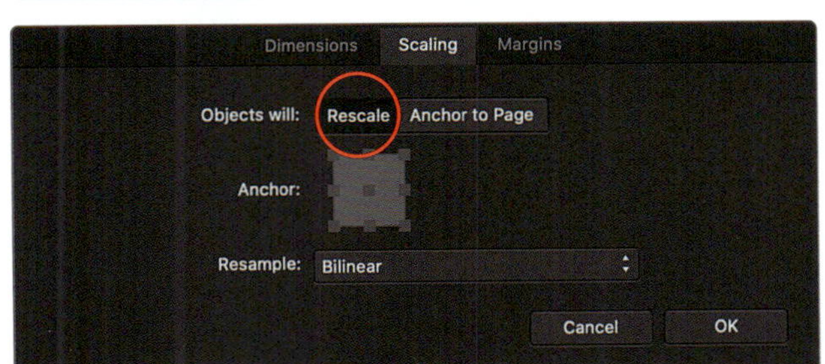

Poster design variants

Designing some poster variants offers the client a choice of designs at review stage. In this project, the base design remained unchanged, but a couple of alternative ideas were suggested for presenting the male model.

- A series of rectangles of varying heights and widths in place of title text to give the poster a scattered broken look.

  Uneven spacing between the rectangles makes the design more eye-catching. This is perfect for a poster that needs to demand attention.

- A stylish logomark used in the place of title text. If you want to reinforce your brand or catch a reader's eye with an identifying design, then a logo graphic is the obvious choice.

JOV | iFederations | East Institute of Films
22ND
BIJOU
Bijou
Short
Film
Festival
/ animation
/ documentary
/ live action
october 3-9
Short Film Council
RUNNING TIME
venue
Gotham South Campus
Godmanchester, UK
talks
From 13:00
Esther Feldman
Donald J Cornwell
Dan Platts
Tammy Rogers
Amanda Allan
screenings
From 19:00
(Amy L Dior)
Tucked In
The Mark
Count to Ten
(Esther Feldman)
Just Walk On In
(Ben Gunn)
Clapping Hands
(Amanda Allan)
Reaccuring
(Donald J Cornwell)
Polaroids
Charles Upcott)
Love Under Will
(Amy Schumacher)
Wolves
(Terence Larkin)
Sound From The Sun
(Amida Khan)
Everyday
(Savid Mohammed)
Ready For Nothing

CHAPTER 6

Corporate Publishing Projects

This chapter explores the world of corporate publishing and how branding can be communicated throughout a company so its identity and message are clear to its stakeholders and customers.

As well as a short introduction to the branding approach of a fictitious architectural company, KB/A, we'll look at how its brand is carried over to its stationery and an annual report—all driven by an overarching brand guide.

KB/A ARCHITECTS —AN INTRODUCTION

About Branding

Pairing a business's ideals and aesthetic to create a brand or identity can feel daunting, but a bit of careful planning allows you to break this big task down into smaller, more manageable parts.

In this chapter, a brand guide project will help you create the smaller portions of the bigger picture and enable you to methodically piece together your brand that will translate to design, marketing, communication and human resources, making the company's strategy visible to all audiences.

Brief

Establishing a Feel for the Company

The core idea of a brand is everything the company does. You need to creatively consider where the company started from, where it is at present and where it plans to be in the future.

Sometimes a client knows exactly what they want and will be happy to guide the process with as much detail as possible. Other times there will be blockers that require clear communication from both sides to ensure the end product is viable.

Building the Brand

So, we know the brand has to communicate the ethos of the company as well as its roots and what it will hopefully transform into. We can facilitate this by using some recognised techniques.

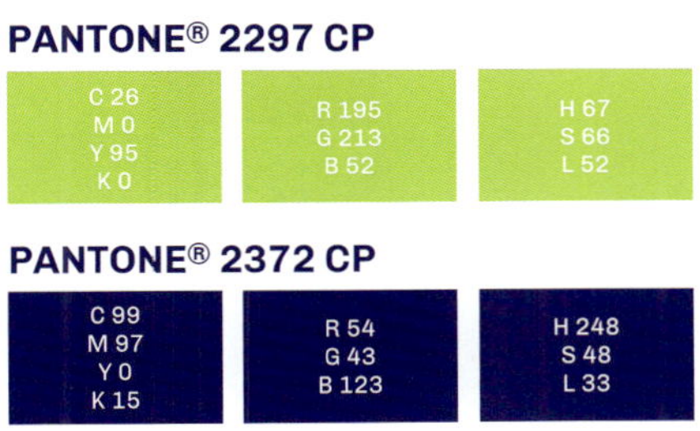

Swatches - primary and secondary

Logo in primary and secondary swatches

Chivo Light 22pt. **Chivo Bold 22pt.**
Chivo Reg. 22pt. *Chivo Italic 22pt.*

Font styling and attributes

The fun part is distilling all this information into more familiar design aspects such as colour, logos and type style that are agreed upon and approved.

Colour

This is about establishing an approved colour set that embodies the brand and what it represents.

Logos

This is the number one identifier for a company. Seen across all aspects of the marketing collateral, they're very powerful—both as a trigger for the market and a company standard (the military kind) for the organisation itself.

Type styles

Text styling, incorporating typeface, font sizing and attributes, decides the voice of the brand as much as a block of colour or a beautifully designed logo.

Colour, logo design and type styles ultimately come together to form a cohesive and strong representation of a company's brand.

Deliverables

This simply means the development of print and digital documentation essential for the company's communication with its partners and customers.

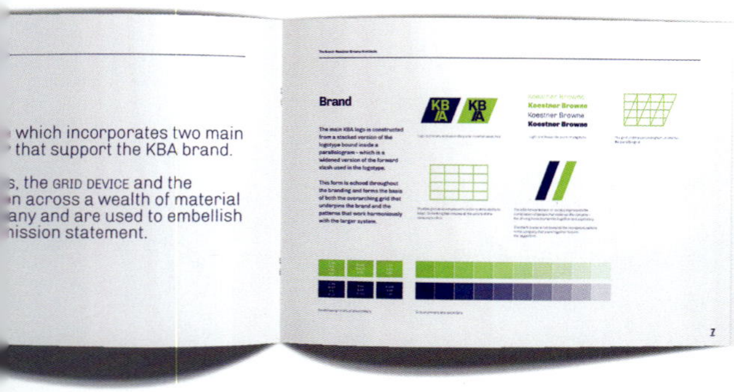

Brand Guide

This document will facilitate all aspects of the company's branding and overall aesthetic within one package. It's an opportunity to give a clear, short and imaginative story of the company itself whilst presenting the user with the branding tools to create inspiring marketing material and other pieces of work.

All deliverables maintain the agreed branding according to the Brand Guide.

Stationery

Stationery ties in branding and aesthetics in a selection of commercially manufactured writing materials. The stationery used by a company will vary slightly depending on the nature of the company itself. For example, a company with a solely online presence may well use a letterhead and company envelope for its communications, whilst another with a focus on a personable approach might have letterheads, business cards, and compliment slips to accompany packages. So it's a good idea to pin down what would benefit a client for their day-to-day needs.

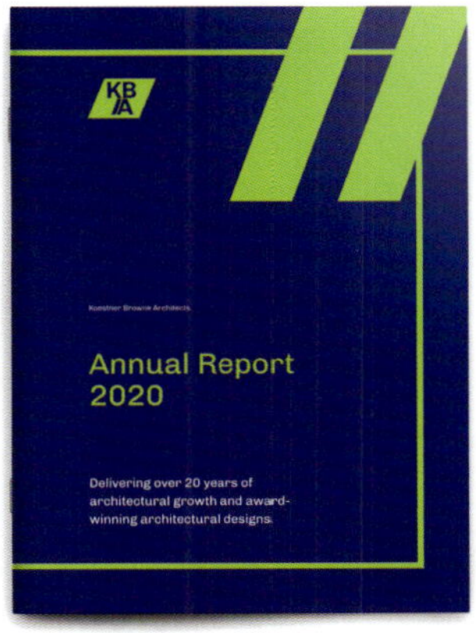

Annual Report

This is a summary of the company's fiscal year and a culmination of all its positive achievements. It typically comprises data-driven imagery, e.g. infographics, charts, and graphs, along with mission statements and typographic elements. It's a good place to marry up the insight (possibly from audits) from different departments, e.g. marketing, management, trustees or development.

The report is also an opportunity to translate a company's vast amount of written details into something a bit more dynamic and visually appealing.

Organising Your Assets and Deliverables

Once you have all your brand assets (colours, logos, etc.), you're in a good place to start laying them down in the Brand Guide, then putting them into practice in your deliverables.

An important part of the exercise involves forming a folder structure that links your logos to your deliverables—if the logos change, e.g., due to brand redesign, you'll get the very latest versions just as other colleagues would, avoiding out-of-date ones tarnishing the brand.

For this chapter, we've kept the projects modular, but the linkage to logos is demonstrated as is the use of imported common colour palettes and type styles.

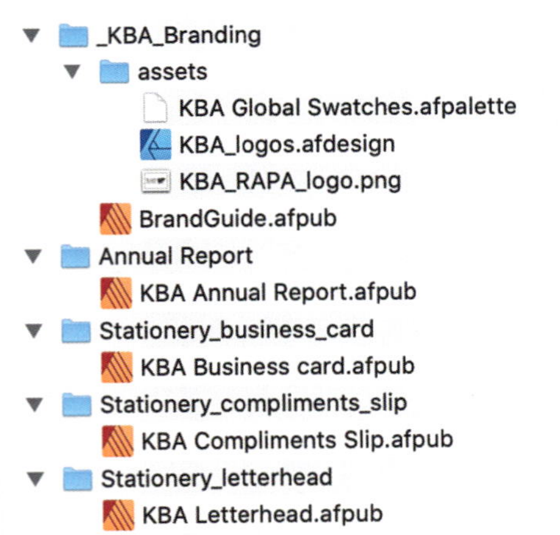

1

KB/A Brand Guide

Communicating a company brand by James Bates

This project looks at creating a brand guide for KB/A Architects that covers branding information, the brand story and how brand-approved assets such as logos and colour palettes can be practically adopted and demonstrated.

KB
/A
Koestner Browne Architects - Brand Guide
A visual language wh
pieces of imagery tha
These two devices, th
SOLIDUS can be seen ac
used by the company a
the overarching missi
6
Koestner Browne Architects
10
Typography
Chivo is a grotesque Sans Serif typeface family.
Chosen for its strength across the board as a font family, it is ideal for highlights and headlines whilst performing elegantly when used in the lighter weights for continuous reading.
Its design details make it an indispensable ally for KBA where we often require a seamless interaction of light and heavy typographic treatments within our marketing collateral.
Chivo Light 22pt.
ABCDEFGHIJKLMNOPQRSTUVWXYZ
abcdefghijklmnopqrstuvwxyz
1234567890.,/?!()
Chivo Reg. 22pt.
ABCDEFGHIJKLMNOPQRSTUVWXYZ
abcdefghijklmnopqrstuvwxyz
1234567890.,/?!()

BEFORE YOU GET STARTED

Resources

You can get all the resources that are referenced in this project from: https://affin.co/KBABrandGuide

Knowledge of Affinity Publisher

To get the most from undertaking this project, you will need to:

- Be familiar with the interface of Affinity Publisher. You can learn more about the interface in the Interface Tour chapter, starting on p. 14.
- Have good core skills. See the skills table below to see which additional aspects of Affinity Publisher you need to be confident with to complete this project:

Pages and Master Pages	p. 82
Working with Text	p. 112
Picture Frames	p. 124
Adding Content	p. 130

> *Think of the guide as a kind of story. It should flow and give a clear picture of the brand and the company.*

INTRODUCTION

Before you lay down the initial pages in any working document and before you start any multipage document over two pages, it's good practice to sketch out the pagination by hand. At any stage of the design process it pays to move away from the screen for a short while. This way you can see the project from a different perspective and discover any pages that need reshuffling or reworking.

In this project, once you have a plan to put together for the Brand Guide, it's time to lay out all the sections and arrange them in an order which reads well.

Font choice

As part of the branding process, Chivo was chosen as the main company typeface. It has four weight variants, plus matching italics. Which gives the user a great deal of flexibility when applying copy at different levels. Its solidness and balanced form give Chivo both elegance and practicality.

Downloading and installing fonts

1 Go to https://fonts.google.com (or search online for *Google fonts*) and download the **Chivo** family.

2 Open the downloaded zip file and open and read the OFL.txt file.

3 For *Mac*: ctrl-click the downloaded font files and select **Install font**.
or:
For *Windows*: Right-click the downloaded font files and select **Install**.

Chivo-Light.ttf

Chivo

Chivo-Regular.ttf

Chivo

Chivo-Bold.ttf

Chivo

Chivo-Black.ttf

Chivo

Resource

KBA_brand_guide_setup.afpub

DOCUMENT SETUP

Now for creating the skeleton of the document. After document setup, we'll add more master/publication pages, edit our master page for page numbering and column guides, then add paragraph styles and initial placement of content.

1 Select **File > New**.

2 On the dialog, ensure **Presets** and **Press Ready** are selected, then choose the *A4* thumbnail.

3 In the **Layout** section, set the **Orientation** to *Landscape* and **Image placement policy** to *Prefer Linked*; I unchecked **Default master** as I wanted to add masters later.

The other default settings will ensure a facing-pages CMYK document with a 3 *mm* bleed (not shown) is created for professional printing.

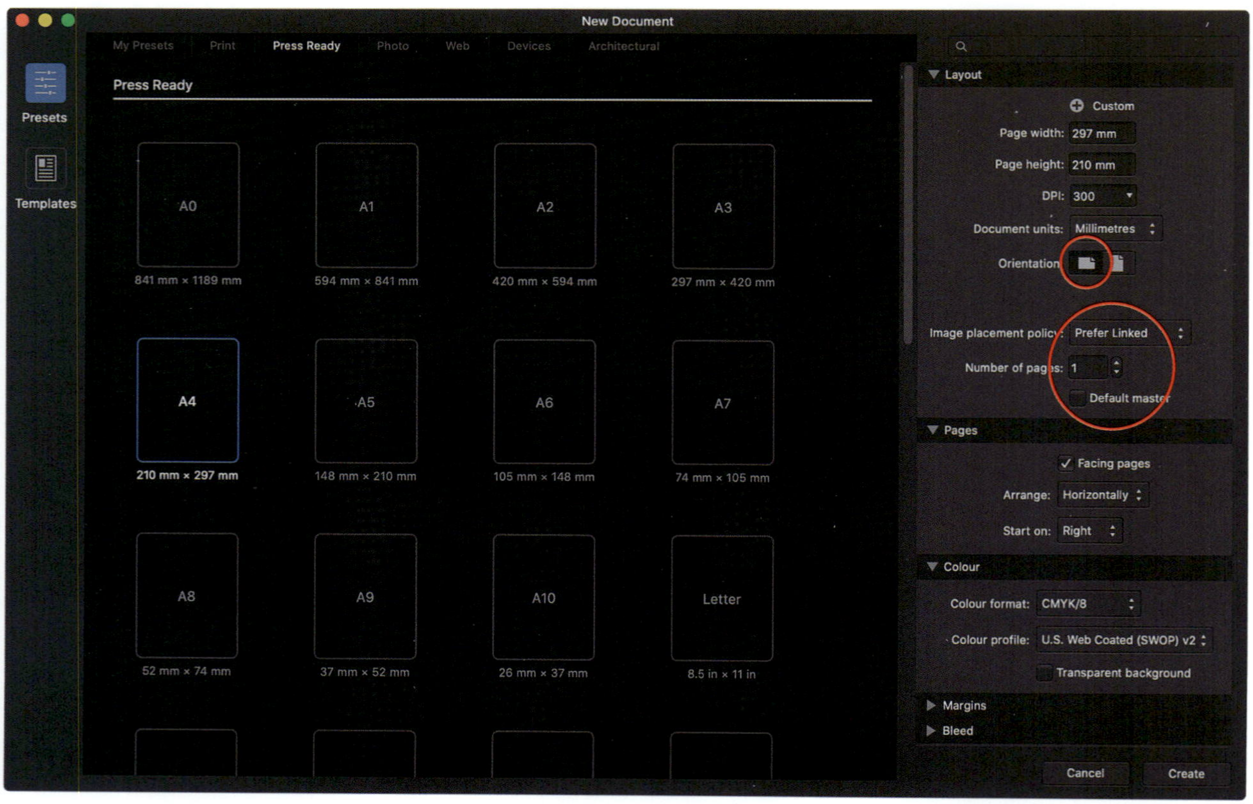

Master A

Master B

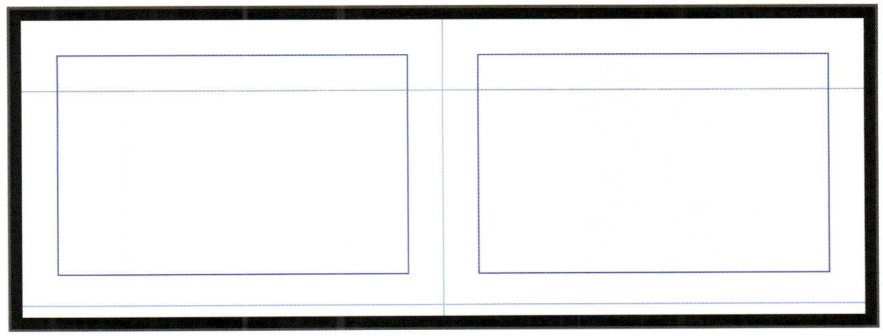

Creating master pages

The main thing when adding master pages was to create a degree of flexibility with the column guides to offer varied layouts.

1 On the **Pages Panel**, click **Add Master**.

2 On the dialog, add a single master page (*Master A*) by enabling **Single**.

3 Repeat to add a facing page master (*Master B*) by enabling **Facing**, then add another single one (*Master C*).

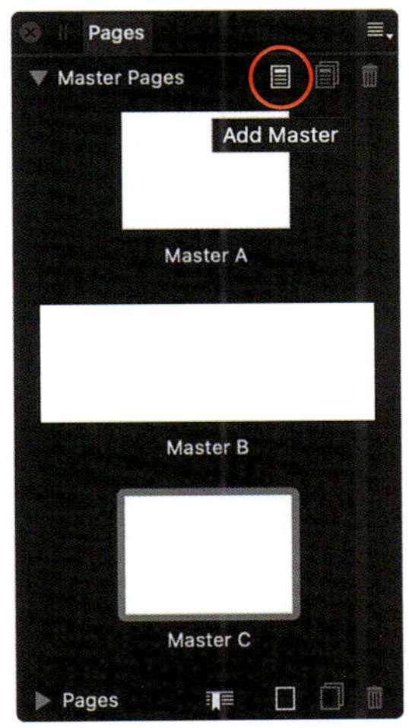

Master C

Adding column guides to masters

1 On the **Pages Panel**, double-click *Master B.*

2 On the **View Menu**, select **Guides Manager** and set **Columns** to *4*; for *Master C*, set **Columns** to *8*.

Four columns were perfect for general use, but the finer 'doubled up' column guides were useful for more flexibility on specific pages.

Adding guides to masters

Guides are great for setting hanglines and baselines on which to snap text frames.

- For *Master B* and *Master C*, use the **Guides Manager** to set a horizontal 'hangline' guide about a quarter of the way down (*50 mm*) each page; a lower guide (*202 mm*) was also added to position page numbering accurately.

With **View > Show Rulers** enabled, you can drag from rulers to set page midpoint guides easily.

Adding page numbering to masters

Master pages will also provide the means to implement page numbering which we'll use for our main facing-page spreads.

1 Double-click *Master B*.

2 Create a text frame in each bottom corner.

3 On the **Text Menu**, select **Insert > Fields > Page Number**.

4 The # page number field was formatted with Chivo Black Bold *16 pt* (Underline) and *Blue* brand colour.

5 On the context toobar, make the field **Align Right** horizontally and **Align Bottom** vertically.

6 Along the top margins, text frames were added for placeholder *Page name* text—I used Chivo Bold *6 pt* text in *Blue* and saved as a new character style called *Small Header*. Margin-wide straight *Blue* lines were drawn with the **Pen Tool**.

For page numbers, ensure text frames are mirrored in identical positions on opposing sides of the spread. For *Master C*, copy and paste just the right-hand page header from *Master B*.

> Adding the # field will auto-populate the page number on the publication pages that have been connected to the master page.

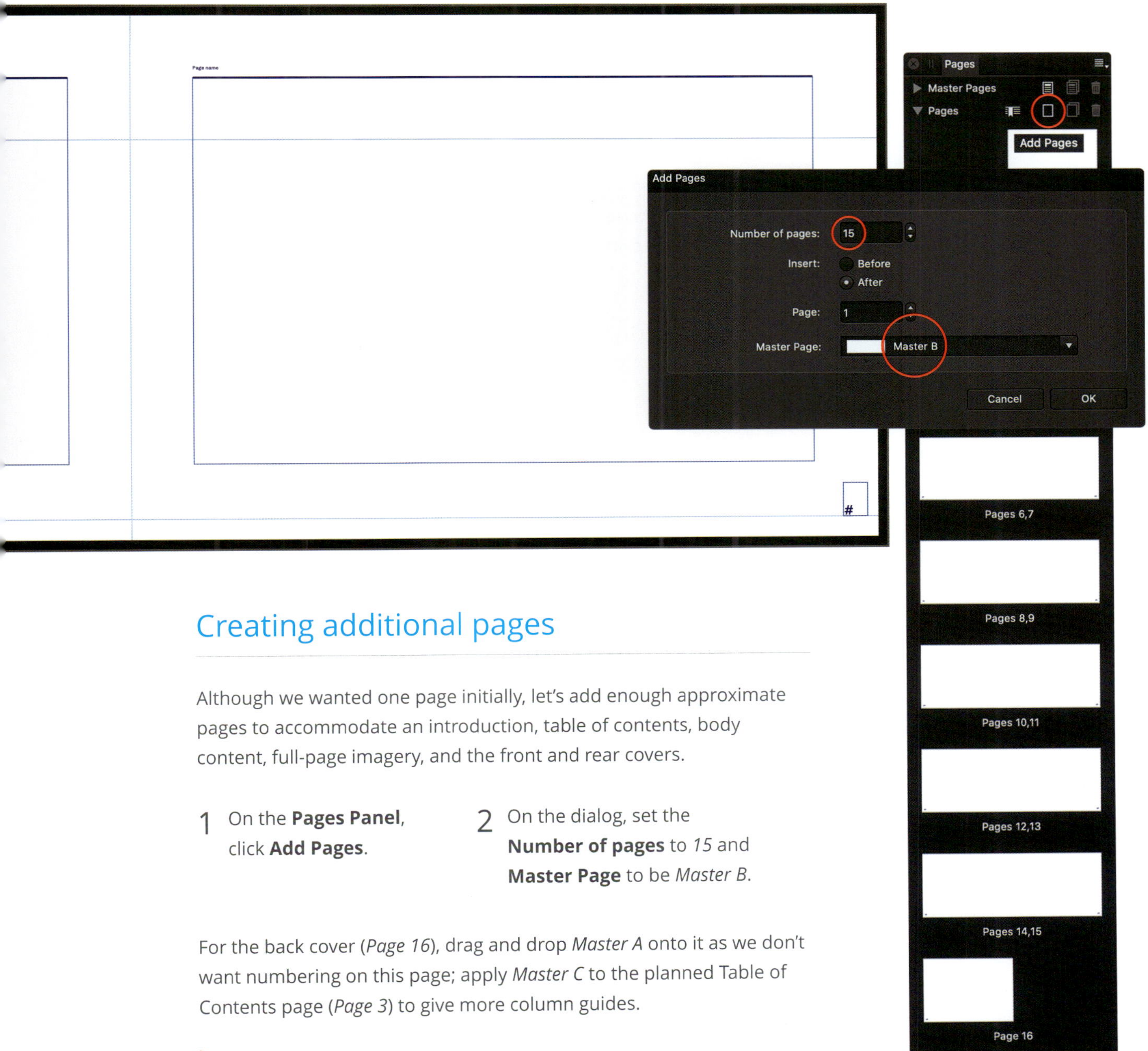

Creating additional pages

Although we wanted one page initially, let's add enough approximate pages to accommodate an introduction, table of contents, body content, full-page imagery, and the front and rear covers.

1 On the **Pages Panel**, click **Add Pages**.

2 On the dialog, set the **Number of pages** to *15* and **Master Page** to be *Master B*.

For the back cover (*Page 16*), drag and drop *Master A* onto it as we don't want numbering on this page; apply *Master C* to the planned Table of Contents page (*Page 3*) to give more column guides.

For professional printing, make the page count a multiple of four, otherwise when imposed there will be an anomaly with the 'leaves' (the piece of paper that is printed on and turned into pages when folded).

BRAND COLOURS

An important output from the branding process is an approved colour set. Once done, the Brand Guide can be used to demonstrate and provide an actual importable colour palette for use in other deliverables.

In Affinity Publisher, these colours can be made global which lets you change the entire colour scheme of a project from a single colour swatch, which is very useful in the case of a rebrand.

Creating brand global colours

Let's set up some global swatches in our company's brand colours chosen from the *PANTONE® Color Bridge Coated V4* palette available within Affinity Publisher:

Green:
PANTONE® 2297 CP
(CMYK 26,0,95,0)

Blue:
PANTONE® 2372 CP
(CMYK 99,97,0,15)

Adding the first global swatch

1 On the **Swatches Panel**, click the pop-up menu and navigate to the *PANTONE® Color Bridge Coated V4* category.

2 In the search box, type *2297 CP* and click the displayed swatch. Clear the search box to reveal a newly created document palette containing your new global colour.

3 Right-click the swatch and choose **Rename Global Colour** to rename to *Green*.

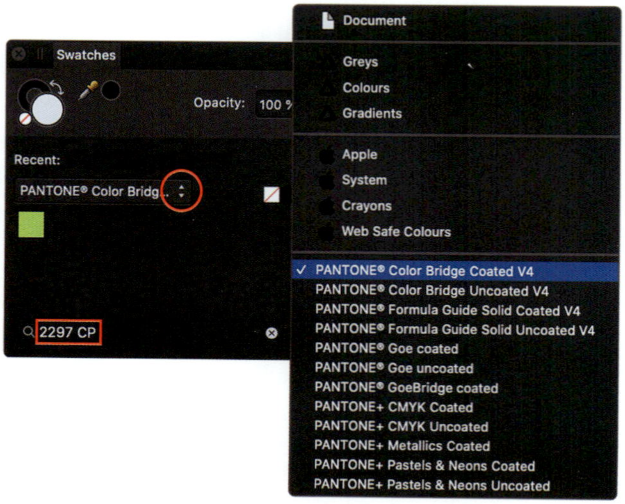

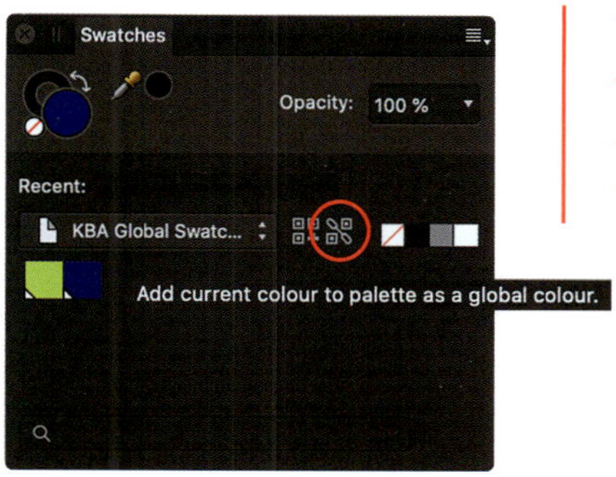

You can distinguish global colour swatches by the white triangle in the bottom-left corner of the swatch.

4 Repeat the search process for PANTONE® 2372 CP, but then navigate to the document palette via the pop-up menu, then click **Add current colour to palette as a global colour**. Clearing the search box reveals both global colours; you can rename the second colour to be *Blue*.

5 Rename the palette to *KBA Global Swatches* via Panel Preferences and select **Rename Palette**.

Even though you've renamed the colours, you can check their original PANTONE names anytime by selecting the **Colour Panel**.

Exporting the palette

Now the *KBA Global Swatches* palette is created the colours can be used to visually demonstrate its brand use in the brand guide itself. You're also able to distribute the palette as a standalone Affinity palette file (.afpalette) so other KB/A deliverables (e.g., office stationery and annual reports) can adopt the brand colours.

- On the **Swatches Panel**, go to Panel Preferences and select **Export Palette**.

PANTONE® colours for accurate colour management

PANTONE® spot colours belong to a standardised PANTONE® Matching System that is used by designers and print companies to ensure absolute colour accuracy* from design to print.

In Affinity Publisher, the **Swatches Panel** hosts over 10 PANTONE® palettes from which to search (by PANTONE number) as referenced in physical PANTONE guide sets. Each palette corresponds to an equivalent physical guide set which your print company will use for reference.

Typically, a customer would first review PANTONE guides and decide on colour choice in consultation with their print company. After this, the colours can be chosen from in-app PANTONE palettes and then applied in design. This workbook's chapter dividers use PANTONE® 171 C.

* assumes colour management and screen calibration is in place.

Resource

KBA_brand_guide_1.afpub
KBA_logos.afdesign

FRONT COVER

The front cover (Page 1) presents a brand grid logo on a blue background.

1 Using the **Rectangle Tool**, draw a box that will cover the whole page, extending to each bleed corner.

2 On the **Swatches Panel**, select the *Blue* brand colour as background from the *KBA Global Swatches* document palette.

3 Go to **File > Place**, locate the KBA_logos.afdesign file and open it.

4 Press the cmd ⌘ key (Mac) or ctrl key (Win), then hover over the centre of the page. When you see intersecting red and green snapping guides, drag out to size the first artboard from the document from its centre.

5 Using the context toolbar's **Artboard** option, swap the artboard to the one you want, i.e. *KBA Grid Logo Green*. Resize if needed.

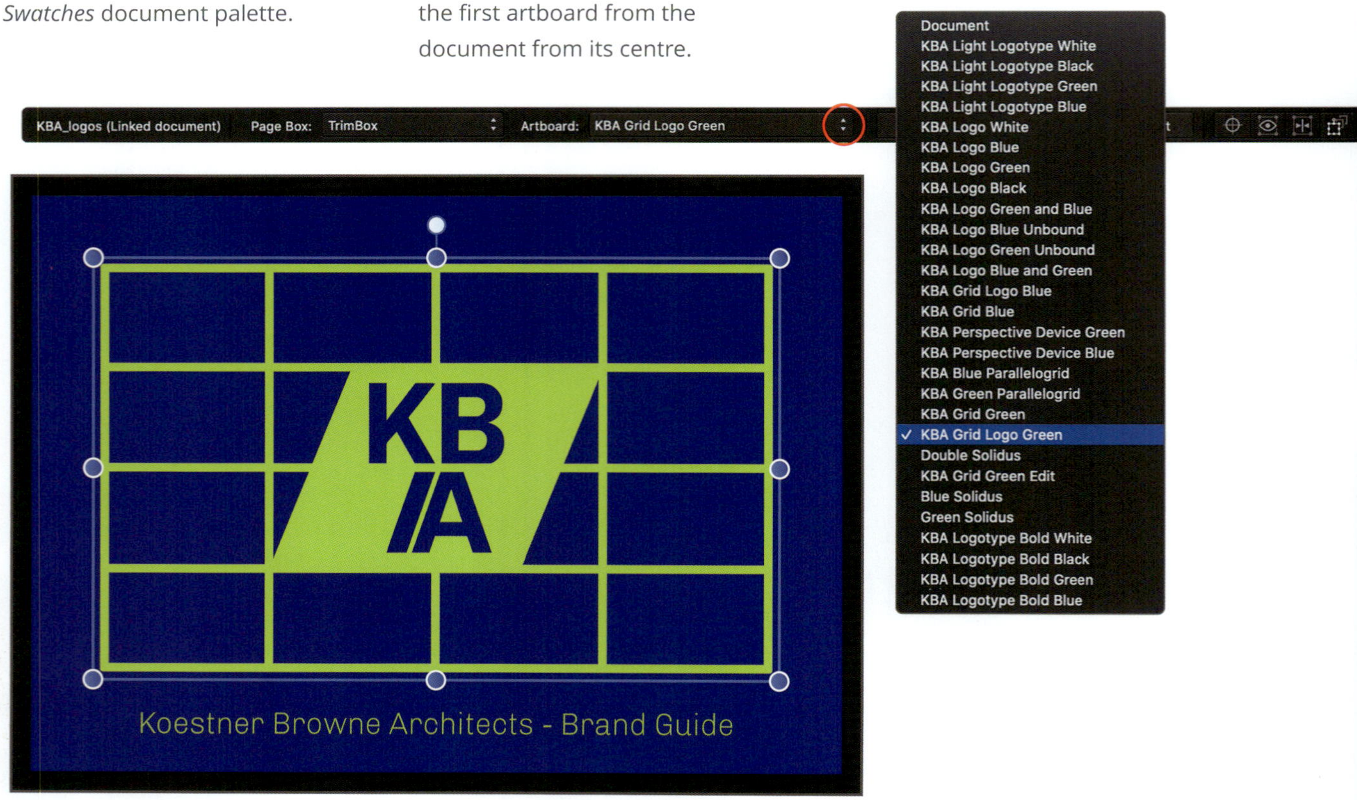

Placing document vs images

Affinity documents can be linked to and placed inside other Affinity documents. This is powerful because:

1. You're so much more efficient as you never need to repeatedly export and import raster graphics from your design document again.
2. When placing Affinity Designer documents containing artboards, you can target a specific artboard to be displayed. For example, on the front cover, and later in the Brand Guide, we're showing a 'live' brand-approved logo variant *KBA Grid Logo Green*.
3. Linking is advantageous because if the original document changes, you'll be prompted to update to the latest version.

KBA_logos.afdesign

FULL PAGE PHOTO AND CONTENTS

Page 2 operates as a filler page, so it's as simple as using the **Picture Frame Rectangle Tool** and **Place Image Tool** to draw a picture frame and populate it.

Page 3 is the contents page. This page utilises the Table of Contents feature that will generate the table of contents from headings on completed pages—we'll look at this, and its text styling, later on p. 454.

First, let's clear out the pre-supplied text styles, then create and apply our own paragraph style for just the heading.

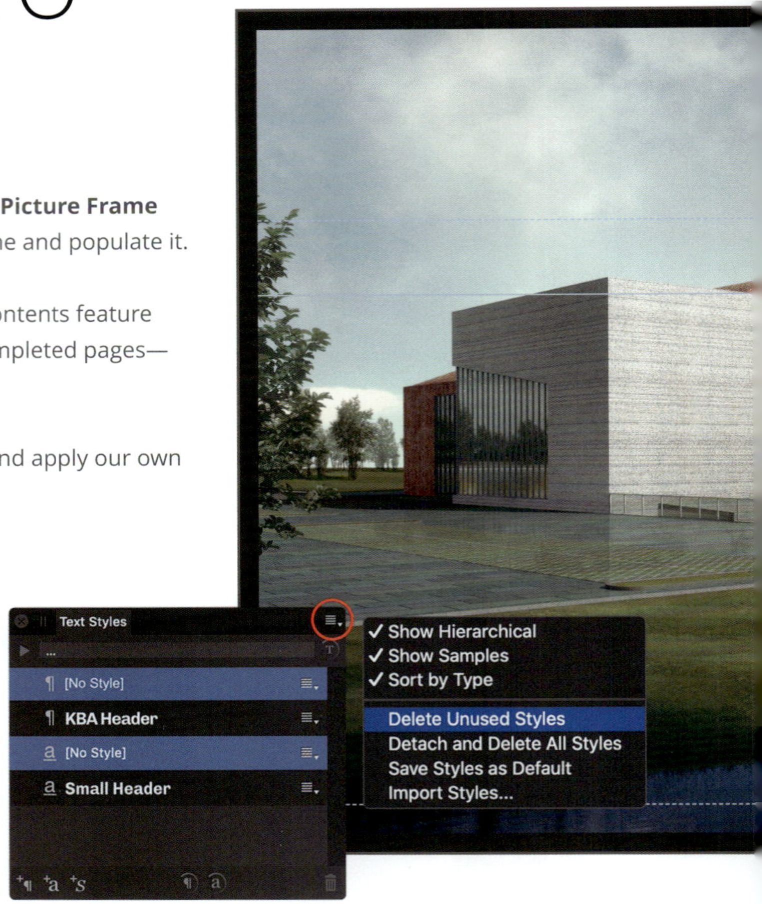

Removing pre-supplied text styles

- On the **Text Styles Panel**, go to Panel Preferences and select **Delete Unused Styles**.

Creating text styles

- The Contents heading (a) is styled by setting the text to Chivo Bold *24 pt* in our *Blue* brand colour and creating the paragraph style *KBA Header* on the context toolbar; use the **Paragraph Style** pop-up menu, then select **New Style**; I also used looser tracking and a leading override.
- The text frame (b) showing the *Page name* text can be overwritten with this page's name *Contents - Koestner Brown Architects* by typing. We're locally editing *Master C*'s placeholder text here. I'll take this approach for all later pages too.
- An empty text frame was created for populating with the table of contents later; this snapped neatly across three column guides and to a hangline guide I added in advance.

Resource
KBA_brand_guide_2&3.afpub

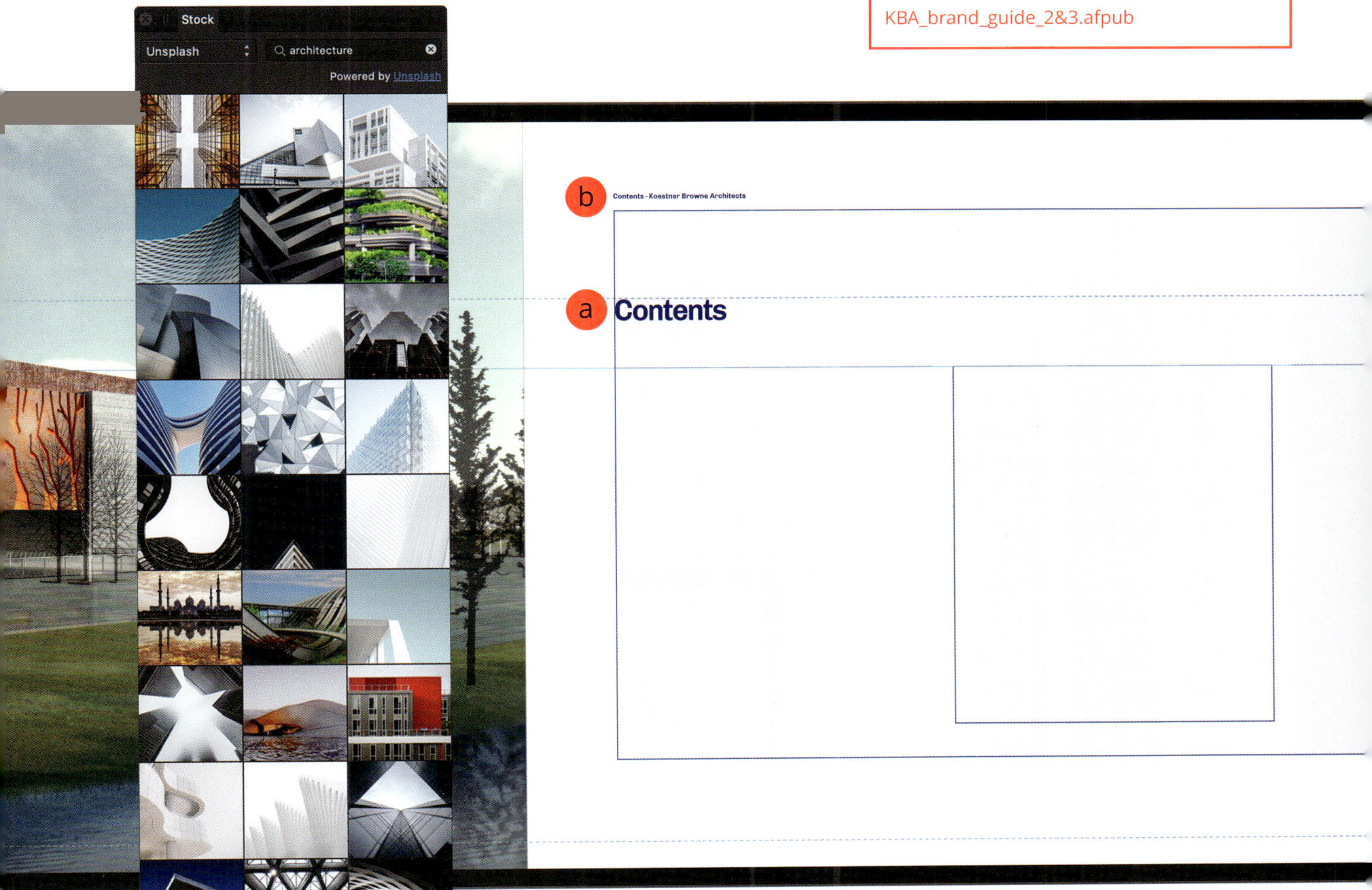

Sourcing your own imagery

The supplied resources exclude stock imagery so you can use your own stock images for this page, and for subsequent pages, as well as for your own projects.

Use the **Stock Panel** to access royalty-free UnSplash, Pexels and Pixabay imagery—simply drag and drop directly onto a chosen picture frame.

ABOUT AND FULL PAGE PHOTO

Resource
KBA_brand_guide_4&5.afpub KBA_logos.afdesign

The About page (Page 4) focuses on using column guides to accurately layout picture frames, text frames and placed documents.

- Using the column guides to snap to, two added picture frames in the first column can accommodate appropriate imagery, e.g. two profile pictures of Koestner and Browne (a).
- Draw a text frame across the other three columns with the same column count and gutter width as the column guides, then populate with copy. Set the text as Chivo Regular *10 pt* and save as a new paragraph style called *KBA Body Copy*; I applied a **Leading Override** of *14 pt* to spread the body copy out vertically a little more (b).
- Add extra details such as the *KBA Perspective Device Blue*, *KBA Logo Blue* and *KBA Blue Parallelogrid* logos. These were placed via **File > Place** from the KBA_logos.afdesign file as before, choosing the correct artboard (c).

> Use lorem placeholder initially (**Text > Insert Filler Text**), that way you don't get distracted with resetting type in the early stages.

For Page 5, a full-page framed image was used as for Page 2 which was recoloured using the *Blue* brand colour to fit with branding. Set the selected image to *K Only* before applying the *Blue* spot colour from the **Swatches Panel**—this will only output to a single spot plate loaded with the Blue PANTONE® colour during printing. No C, M or Y plates will be used; the K plate is overwritten so only the spot colour is used.

BRANDING INTRO AND MAIN BRAND PAGE

Resource
KBA_brand_guide_6&7.afpub KBA_logos.afdesign

Page 6 is an introduction to the core branding section. Its frame text is a quote which was given the *KBA Quote* paragraph style (Chivo Light *31.5 pt*) with a character style called *KBA Small Caps* applied only to the GRID DEVICE and SOLIDUS text; Small caps are set on the **Text Styles Panel** (**Typography > Capitals**).

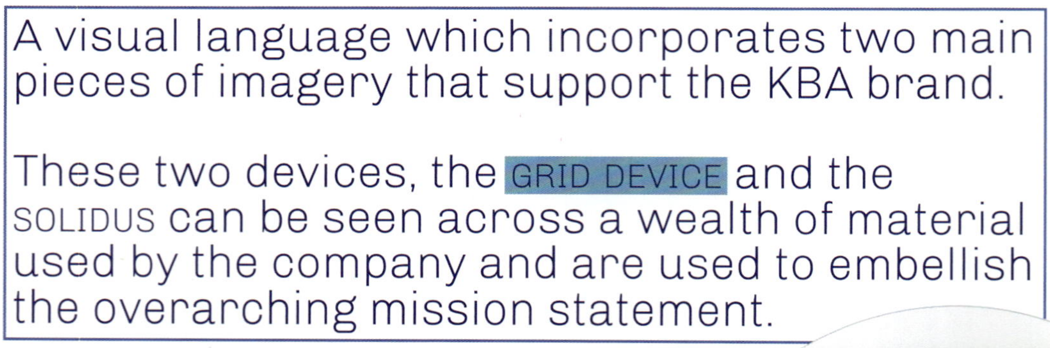
A visual language which incorporates two main pieces of imagery that support the KBA brand.

These two devices, the GRID DEVICE and the SOLIDUS can be seen across a wealth of material used by the company and are used to embellish the overarching mission statement.

The opposite page, Page 7, is the main brand page which presents branding assets for use.

- Place the assets (a) from KBA_logos.afdesign artboards using the column guides for placement. These all have small descriptors set to Chivo Light *6 pt*—they were saved as the *KBA Small Copy* paragraph style for repeated use.

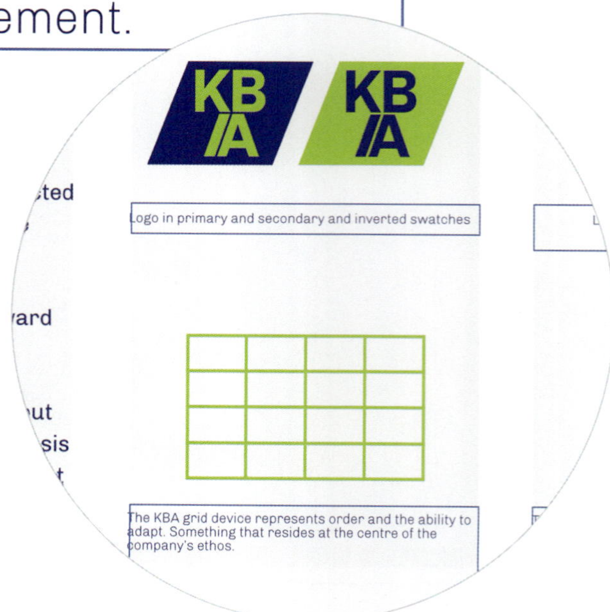

Colour plays a key part in the branding process so approved swatches and tints are also presented and described in support of branding imagery.

- The swatches (b) are drawn as three pairs of rectangles, adding the CMYK, RGB and HSL values for blue and green colours. Draw the text frames the same size as rectangles and centre and vertically align text via the context toolbar.
- To make the ten tints (c), create a rectangle, then with the **Move Tool** active, press the cmd ⌘ key (Mac) or ctrl key (Win) and drag to duplicate it to the right, then press cmd ⌘ + J (Mac) or ctrl + J (Win) eight times to power duplicate. Apply the brand colours then decrease the tint percentage per swatch when the **Colour Panel**'s Preferences has **Tint** checked.

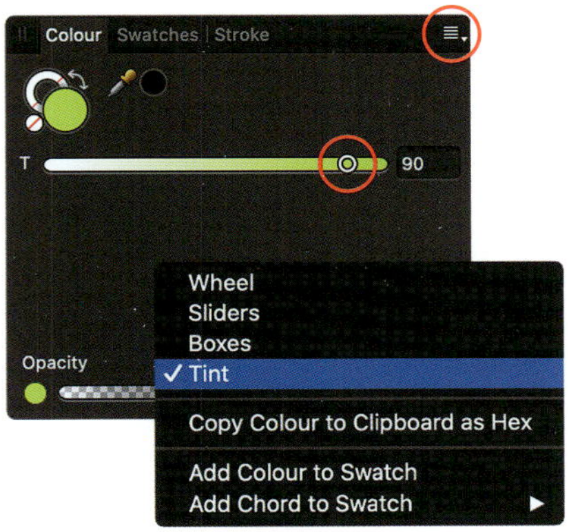

BRAND LOGO USAGE AND ARTWORK

Resource

KBA_brand_guide_8&9.afpub
KBA_logos.afdesign

Page 8 gives a very basic overview of how to use the company logo correctly. This approach can be used for almost any brand guide as fundamental dos and dont's.

Several versions of the logo have been placed as before.

- (a) Two *KBA Logo Green and Blue* logos are set inside a grid to illustrate their correct placement alongside third party logos or secondary imagery. Although these devices can vary stylistically from case to case, the premise is the same—the logo's dimensions are halved, and this measurement is used to set a 'safe' distance from which objects can be placed without interfering with the logos impact. In this case, a fictional logo has been produced as an example for reference.
- (b) The second set of logos has been created to show that no colour adjustments can be made to the logos. In this case, changing either logo's blue or green swatch colours or the incorrect application of a gradient.
- (c) The logo's overall shape should be retained and should not be transformed by squashing, skewing or flipping.

a

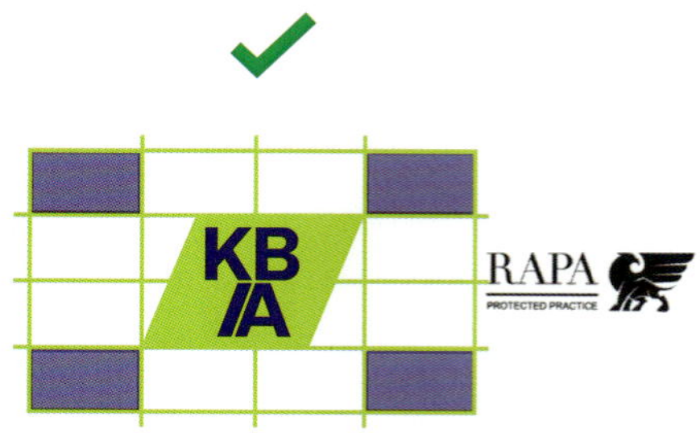

'RAPA' logo spaced correctly alongside KBA

b

c

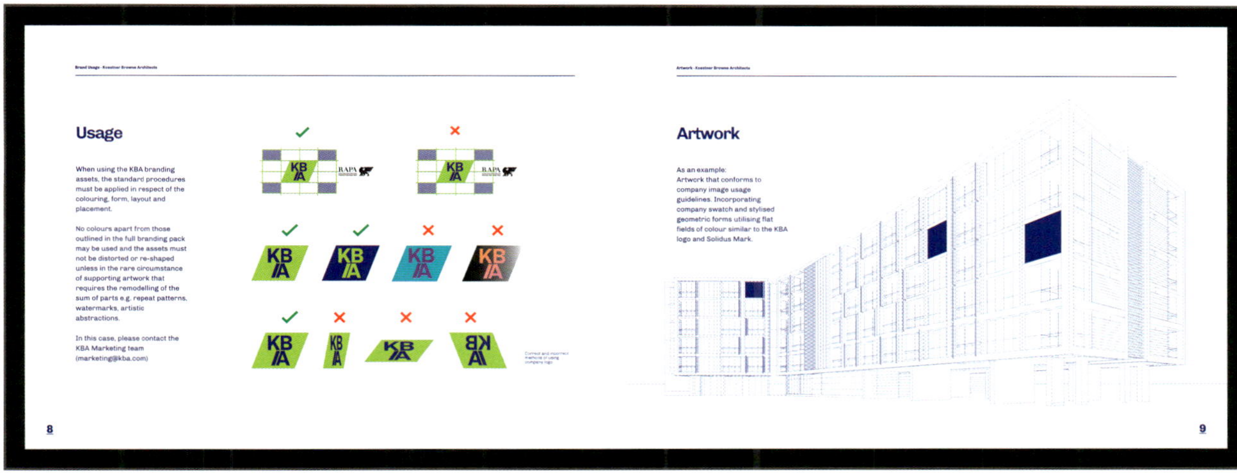

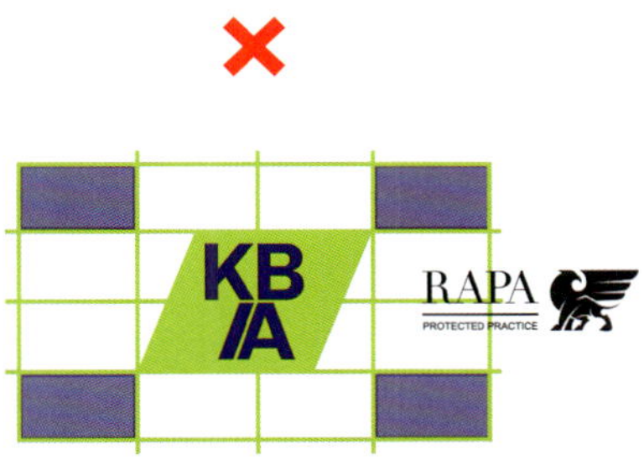

'RAPA' logo spaced incorrectly alongside KBA

Page 9 addresses the matter of supported artwork. In this case it's more of a direction than a pre-defined collection of artworks with the intention that the company will add or commission more and more stylised imagery as it grows.

- The example on Page 9 was traced using the **Pen Tool** which has identical power and accuracy in Affinity Publisher as its counterpart in Affinity Designer, Affinity's graphic design app. The line art used the same *Blue* global colour for the polygons' fill to keep on brand.

Resource

KBA_brand_guide_10&11.afpub

MORE ARTWORK AND TYPOGRAPHY

Page 10 hosts the second page of example artwork. This was made by placing a stock image in a picture frame then drawing two grid devices over the image to suggest building framework.

- **Perspective grid device**: Trace the outline of the window section in the image with the **Pen Tool** so it looks similar to the perspective device shown on p. 444. When all the lines were in place, the individual lines were expanded and filled with the *Green* brand colour.
- **Rectangle grid device**: This was a simple rectangle with two extra vertical lines and three horizontal lines that was sourced from the parallelogrid device (p. 444).

Page 11 hosts a two-column text frame to showcase approved font usage in four standard weights—the fonts and weights themselves were used to illustrate this. The frame was placed so it floats across two-thirds of the layout width.

Chivo Light 22pt.

ABCDEFGHIJKLMNOPQRSTUVWXYZ
abcdefghijklmnopqrstuvwxyz
1234567890,./?!()

Chivo Bold 22pt.

ABCDEFGHIJKLMNOPQRSTUVWXYZ
abcdefghijklmnopqrstuvwxyz
1234567890,./?!()

Chivo Reg. 22pt.

ABCDEFGHIJKLMNOPQRSTUVWXYZ
abcdefghijklmnopqrstuvwxyz
1234567890,./?!()

Chivo Italic 22pt.

ABCDEFGHIJKLMNOPQRSTUVWXYZ
abcdefghijklmnopqrstuvwxyz
1234567890,./?!()

StudioLink

In-app mixed-discipline working

If you have Affinity Designer and Affinity Photo installed, you can use the respective Persona's **Expand Stroke** feature and **Perspective Tool** to apply a perspective effect to rectangular grids such as the Rectangle grid device.

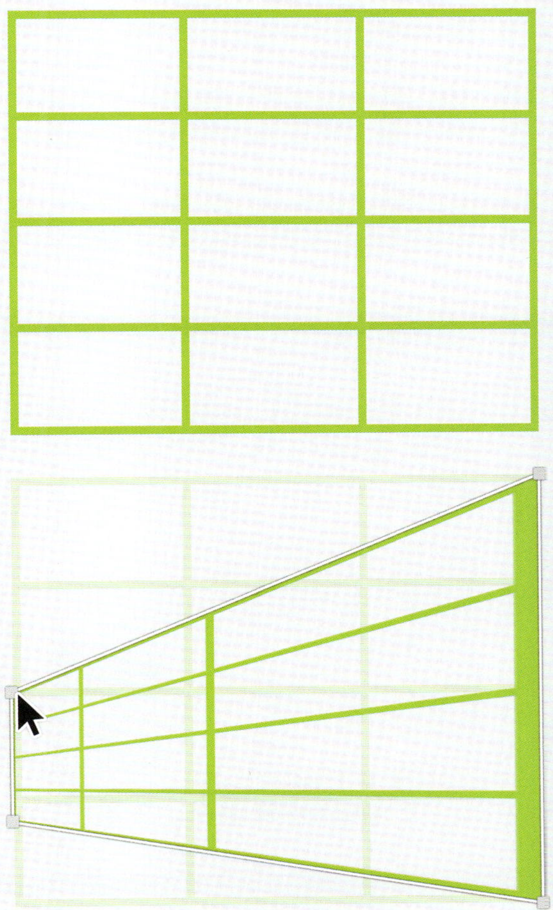

STATIONERY MOCKUPS AND IMAGE USAGE/ TREATMENT

Resource
KBA_brand_guide_12&13.afpub KBA_logos.afdesign

Brand guides communicate brand usage and the approved use of logos, colour and fonts. They can also be used to demonstrate this brand usage by using real business deliverables as examples.

Page 12 shows mockups from the KB/A Stationery project (p. 460) such as KB/A Business Card, KB/A Letterhead and KB/A Compliments Slip. This is a single mockup image—the equivalent placed documents are not required. *Master B* layer was moved to the top of the **Layers Panel** to expose header/ page number.

On Page 13 the guide deals with the correct approach to handling imagery. A basic text frame presents a bulleted list while the two logos at the bottom are a placed linked logo from a KBA_logos.afdesign artboard and a PNG file. I applied *Master C* to suppress the page number; on Page 12 this is hidden by imagery.

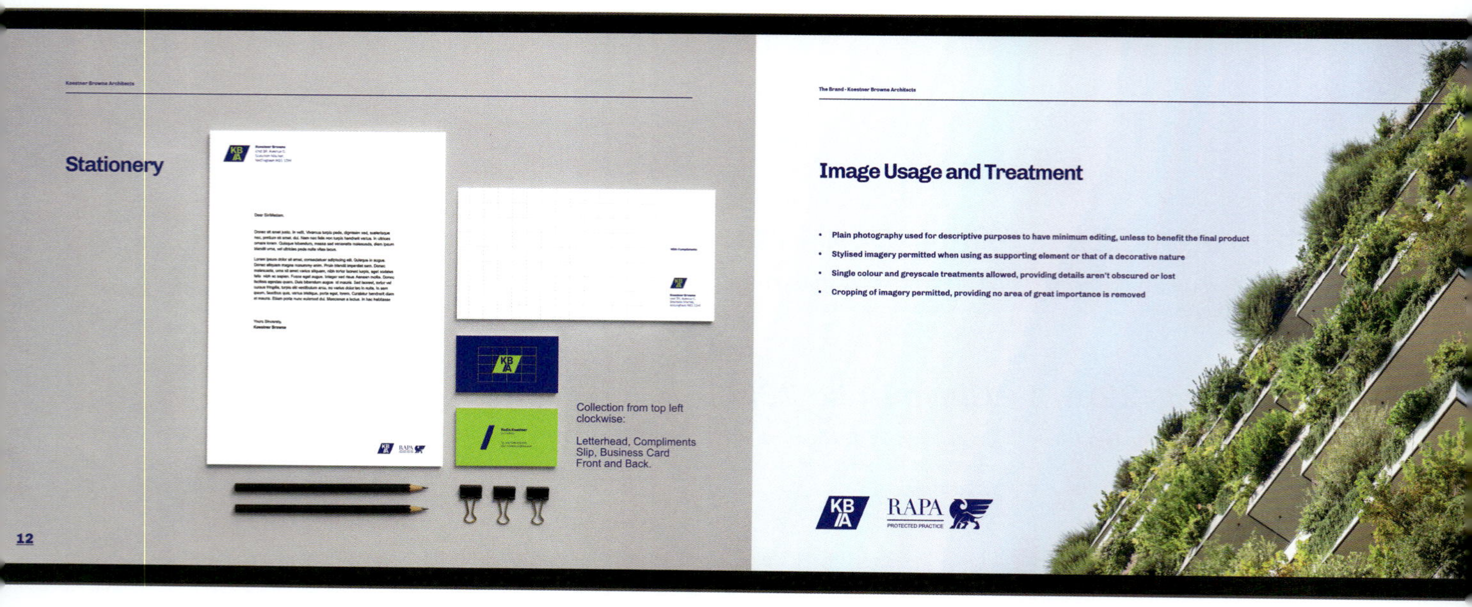

Resource
KBA_brand_guide_14&15.afpub

ARTWORK AND DESKTOP/MOBILE SCREEN MOCKUPS

On Page 14, we added brand-coloured overlay artwork to the framed image as done on Page 9. Tweaked forms of the Solidus Mark were added to the walls of the structure to reinforce brand identity. Like Page 12, *Master B* layer was moved to the front.

- Use the **Pen Tool** to draw out polygons (click to create each corner) and fill using the Blue and Green brand colours.

Page 15 hosts a set of devices which can be added to screen mockups and which stress that the KB/A branding exercise extends to web and mobile page development. Using stock computer imagery, the examples introduce drawn vector devices such as backgrounds, icons and buttons that use the approved blue and green brand colours. *Master C* was again used to suppress the page number.

BACK COVER

For Page 16, follow the steps as for the front cover but for the placed document, swap to the *KBA Grid Green Edit* artboard in the KBA_logos.afdesign file, then add a *KBA Logo Green Unbound* artboard for the logo. All that's left is to create a small text frame with the **Frame Text Tool** for the company URL.

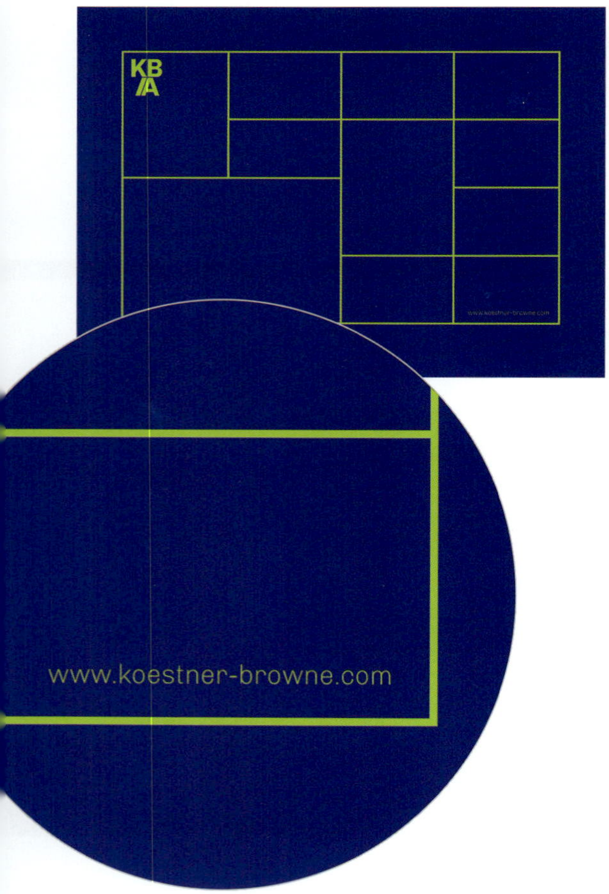

FINISHING OFF

Table of Contents

Very early in the project (p. 442) we created an empty text frame for a table of contents. With the guide complete the table of contents can be generated in that text frame.

1. On Page 3, select the empty text frame with the **Frame Text Tool**.
2. Go to **View > Studio > Table of Contents**.
3. On the panel, select **Insert** to generate the table of contents, then check the **Style Name** called *KBA Header* to include our main headings.

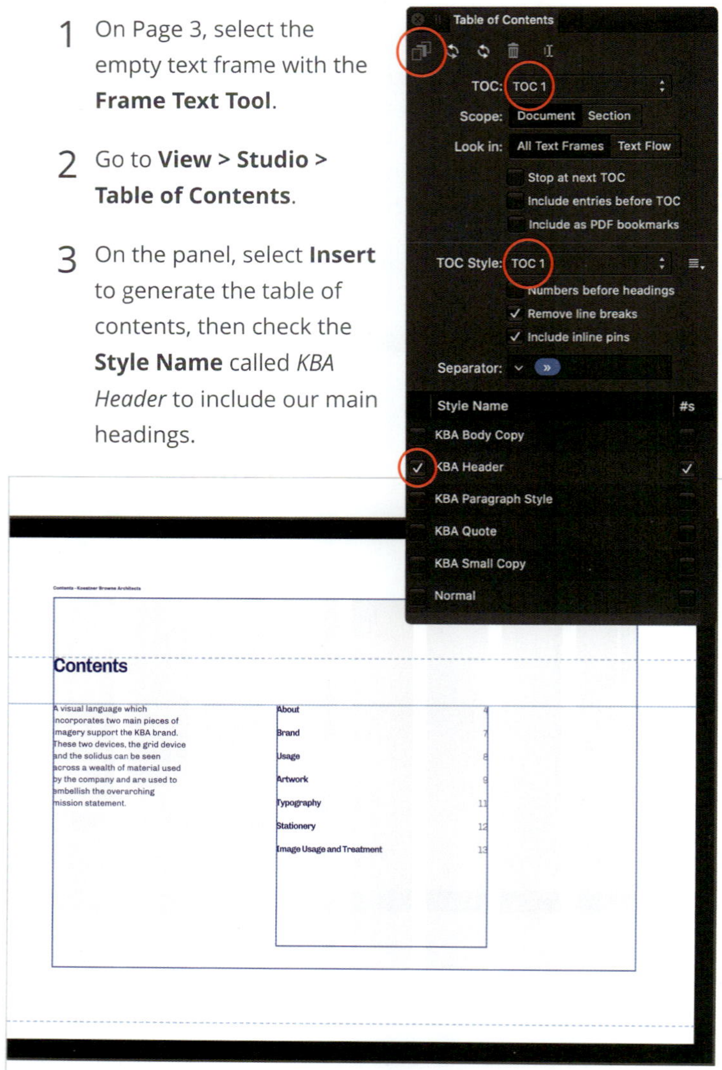

Resource
KBA_brand_guide_final.afpub KBA_logos.afdesign

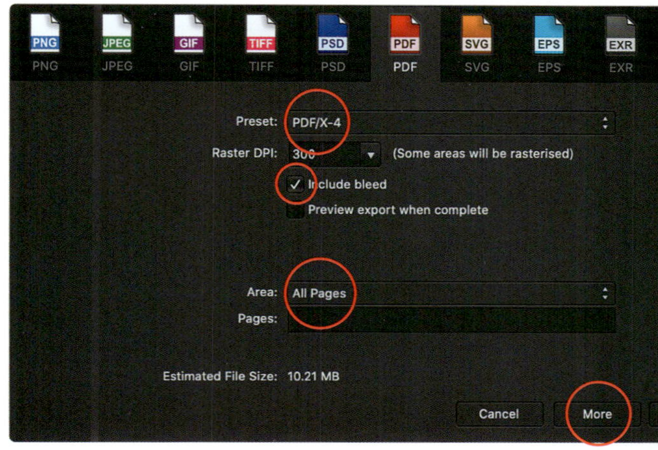

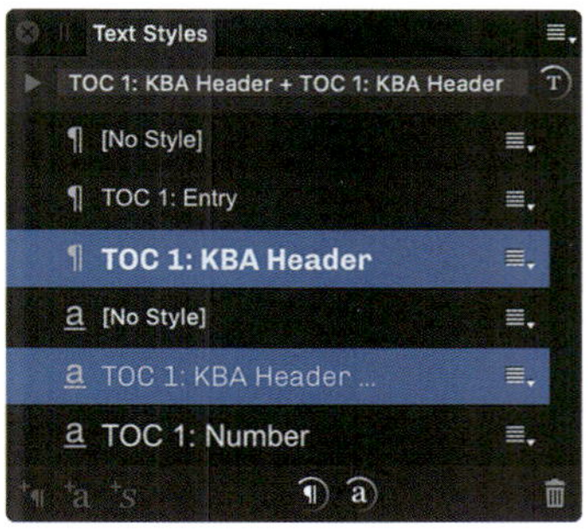

4 On the **Text Styles Panel**, style up the *TOC1: KBA Header* and *TOC1: KBA Header Number* text styles to have Chivo Bold and Chivo Light fonts at *11 pt* in the *Blue* brand colour.

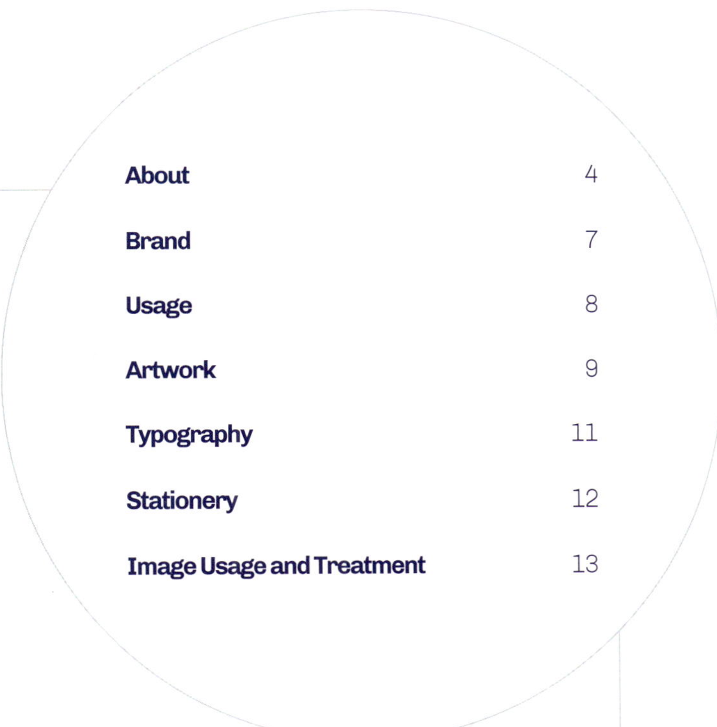

Exporting to PDF

The project is set up for high-resolution CMYK professional PDF printing but we can also choose to output to a screen PDF version.

For high-resolution print-ready PDFs

1 On the **File** menu, select **Export**.

2 On the pop-up dialog, select **PDF**, set the **Preset** to *PDF/X-4* and check **Include bleed**.

3 Set the **Area** to *All Pages*.

4 To include printers marks, click **More**, check **Include printers marks** then click **Close** in the secondary dialog.

5 Click **Export**.

6 Name the file *KBA_brand_guide.pdf*, navigate to a folder of your choice and click **Save**.

For screen-ready PDFs

- As for print-ready PDFs but swap the **Preset** to *PDF (digital - high quality)*. Note that there are no bleed or printers marks set; the project will output to an RGB colour space instead of a CMYK one.

PACKAGING

The Save as Package feature allows you to gather together all the resources that you've used in a publication, including fonts and linked images, for easy transfer to another computer that doesn't have access to those files. Packaging ensures the project is guaranteed to open on any computer and the project will always look the same.

A special package file is created which can be opened and extracted at a later date and will preserve the file links. This method allows you to continue work on the publication, without worrying whether you've overlooked supporting resources.

Saving as a package

1 Go to **File > Save as Package**.

2 On the dialog, review the fonts and linked images that will be packaged, then click **OK**.

3 Choose or create an empty destination folder, then click **Package**.

In the new folder, you'll be creating an .afpackage file with Fonts and Files folders whose collected files are taken from their original folder locations, e.g. system font folder for fonts.

> This folder can be zipped by the user if desired, then transferred to another computer. Affinity Publisher does not do this archiving due to potential font licensing issues—the user must take responsibility for redistributing copyrighted fonts.

Opening a package

1. Place your package file in your preferred folder location.
2. In Affinity Publisher, go to **File > Open**.
3. Browse to the afpackage file, select it, and click **Open**.
4. On the dialog, review the **Summary** details, plus the **Fonts** and **Files** listings that make up the package. You can choose which resources to exclude at this point.
5. Once a package is opened it cannot be saved so the original package isn't overwritten. Instead, you can use **File > Save As** or use **File > Save As Package** to save alongside your original package file.

Font management

On unpackaging, fonts are installed privately for the app by default, and are invisible to other apps (including font management apps). Exporting and printing is possible.

If the font is not available on the target computer, the dialog's **Fonts** category will show the font(s) as *Missing*; the option to **Install** is automatically checked to allow private installation only.

If you want to continue editing but the font is not installed on the target computer, then you have to install the font independently of the app.

Remember to unzip the archived package if needed.

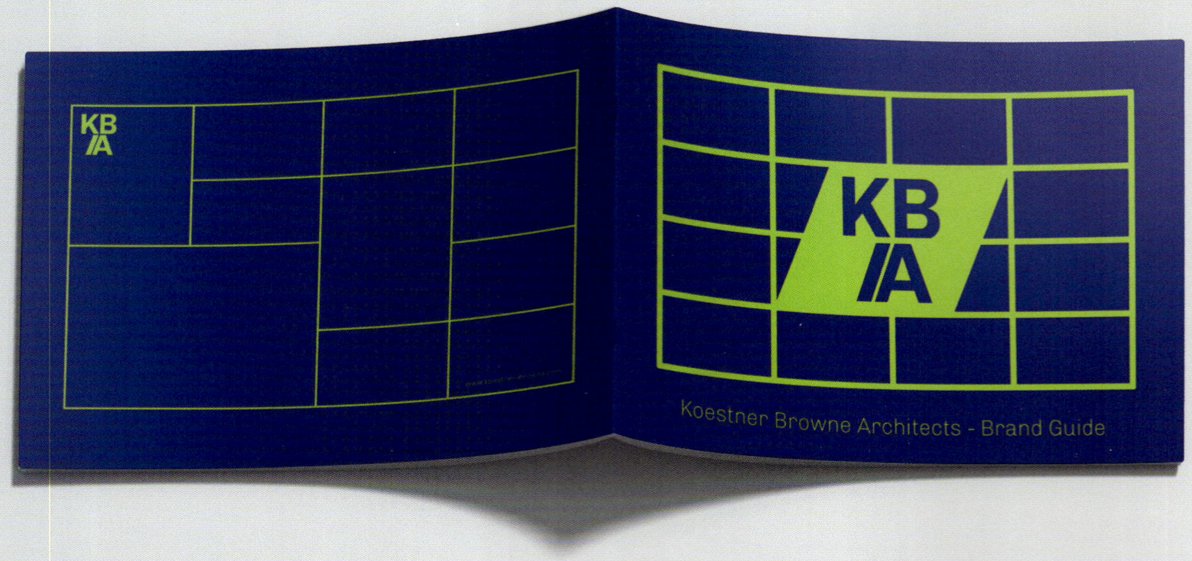
KB/A
KB/A
Koestner Browne Architects - Brand Guide

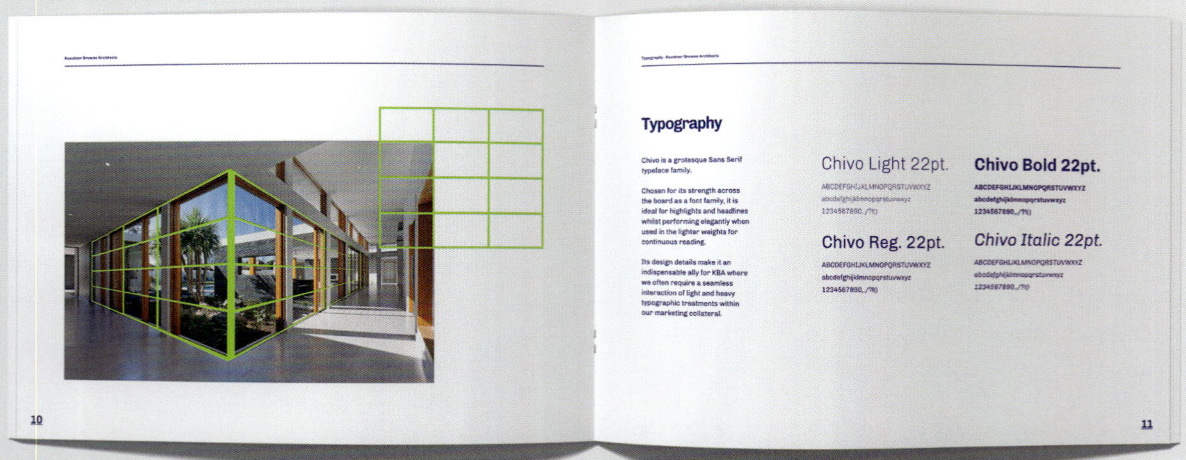
Typography
Chivo is a grotesque Sans Serif typeface family.
Chosen for its strength across the board as a font family, it is ideal for highlights and headlines whilst performing elegantly when used in the lighter weights for continuous reading.
Its design details make it an indispensable ally for KBA where we often require a seamless interaction of light and heavy typographic treatments within our marketing collateral.
Chivo Light 22pt.
ABCDEFGHIJKLMNOPQRSTUVWXYZ
abcdefghijklmnopqrstuvwxyz
1234567890.,/?!()
Chivo Bold 22pt.
ABCDEFGHIJKLMNOPQRSTUVWXYZ
abcdefghijklmnopqrstuvwxyz
1234567890.,/?!()
Chivo Reg. 22pt.
ABCDEFGHIJKLMNOPQRSTUVWXYZ
abcdefghijklmnopqrstuvwxyz
1234567890.,/?!()
Chivo Italic 22pt.
ABCDEFGHIJKLMNOPQRSTUVWXYZ
abcdefghijklmnopqrstuvwxyz
1234567890.,/?!()
10
11

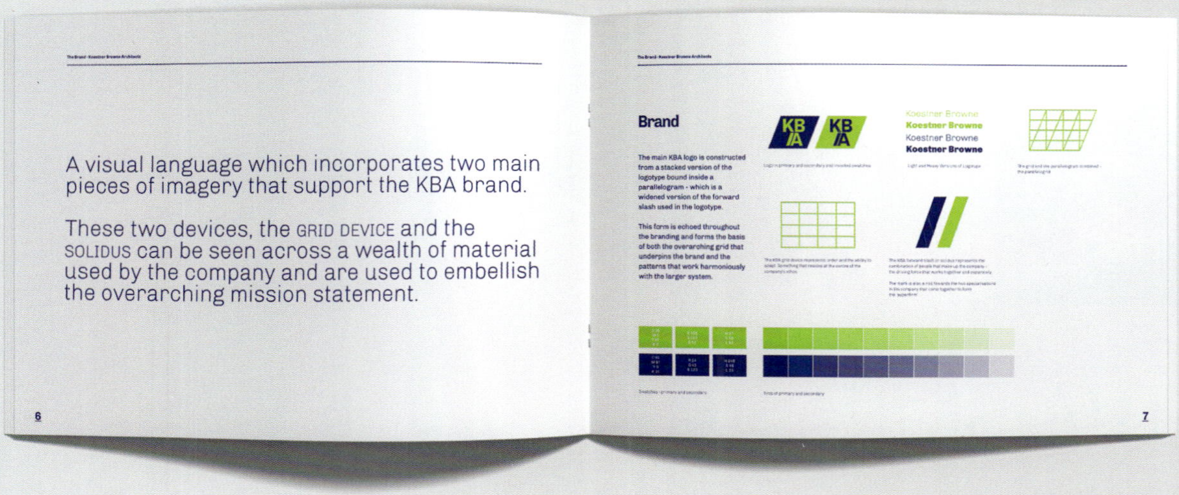

The Brand · Koestner Browne Architects
A visual language which incorporates two main pieces of imagery that support the KBA brand.
These two devices, the GRID DEVICE and the SOLIDUS can be seen across a wealth of material used by the company and are used to embellish the overarching mission statement.
6
Brand
The main KBA logo is constructed from a stacked version of the logotype bound inside a parallelogram - which is a widened version of the forward slash used in the logotype.
This form is echoed throughout the branding and forms the basis of both the overarching grid that underpins the brand and the patterns that work harmoniously with the larger system.
KB/A
Koestner Browne
Koestner Browne
Koestner Browne
Koestner Browne
7

About · Koestner Browne Architects
About
Koestner Browne Architects is one of the UK's leading architecture firms, founded by Nadia Koestner and Alexandra Browne in 1999. Over the past twenty years, the team has grown from two to more than fifty members of staff, all specialising in a range of disciplines and industries, including heritage, corporate and hospitality.
Koestner Browne specialises in both heritage and modern projects, with expert teams in each field. Alexandra Browne's background is in the development and preservation of heritage sites, while Nadia Koestner's lies in sustainable and environmental engineering. The company's mission is to create a super firm that puts placemaking at the forefront, through large projects that work sympathetically with local ecosystems.
Koestner Browne is headquartered in Nottingham city centre, with offices in London and Durham. The team hopes to expand into Scotland in the near future.
KB/A
4

2

KB/A Stationery

Creating brand-aware stationery by James Bates

Stationery can come in many forms, each providing a unique and interesting challenge as a handheld piece of your company's brand.

In this project, we'll look at designing three pieces of stationery, taking into consideration how elements of company branding, established in the previous KB/A Brand Guide project, can be brought together and used effectively in documents of different sizes and styles.

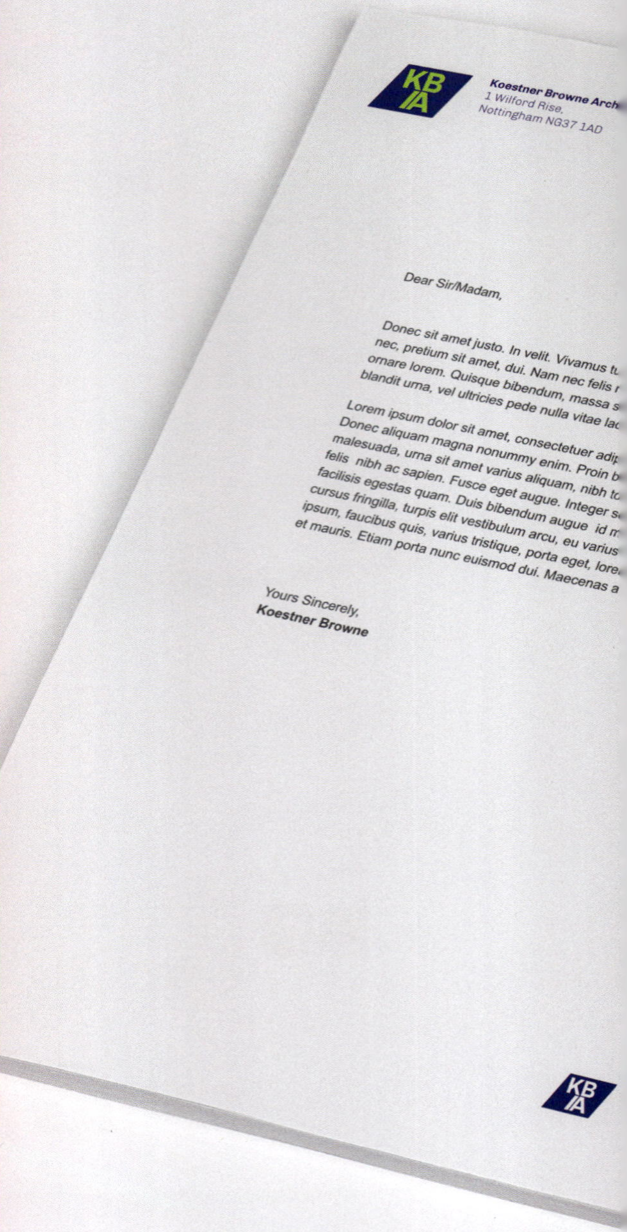

With Compliments
KB/A
Koestner Browne Architects
1 Wilford Rise,
Nottingham NG37 1AD
KB/A
Nadia Koestner
Co-Founder
Tel: +44 1632 960421
Mail: n.koestner@kba.com

BEFORE YOU GET STARTED

Resources

You can get all the resources that are referenced in this project from: https://affin.co/KBAStationery

Knowledge of Affinity Publisher

To get the most from undertaking this project, you will need to:

- Be familiar with the interface of Affinity Publisher. You can learn more about the interface in the Interface Tour chapter, starting on p. 14.
- Have good core skills. See the skills table below to see which additional aspects of Affinity Publisher you need to be confident with to complete this project:

Design Aids	p. 96
Working with Text	p. 112
Adding Content	p. 130

INTRODUCTION

For this project, we will be designing three pieces of stationery for our brand:

- KB/A business card
- KB/A letterhead
- KB/A compliments slip

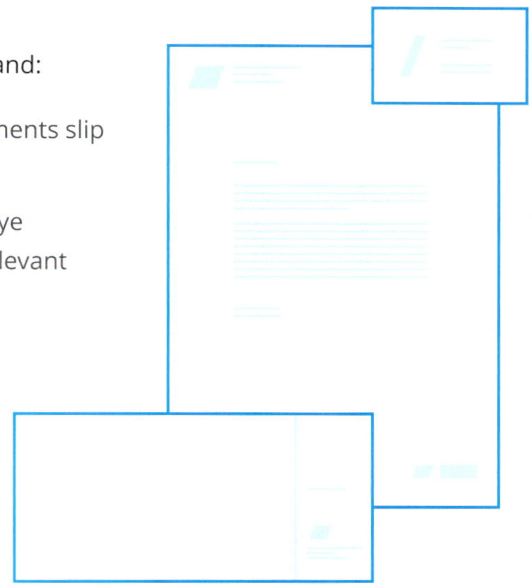

Stationery designs should be smart, professional and draw the reader's eye to important information without overwhelming them with too many irrelevant side details.

The three designs also focus on introducing company brand logos presented in the previous KB/A Brand Guide project (p. 430), while taking into account the page structure and limitations of each piece of stationery we're working with.

STARTING THE DESIGN PROCESS

When you first begin designing, keep in mind the physical dimensions you intend to print for. You'll want to take any size limitations into consideration when planning out where you want your copy and branding to fit.

Think about the most important details you want to include, and where they should sit. For example, letterhead should leave a good amount of white space centrally on the page—a business card, on the other hand, doesn't need this.

Remember to adhere to your company branding guidelines throughout the design process—stick to correct logo use, brand colours and text styling from company branding materials we've already produced. Keeping a consistent look and feel for each piece of stationery really makes it collectively feel like a set, strengthening your company's image.

Resource
KBA_business_card.afpub

BUSINESS CARD

Your business card is a handheld extension of your company and visually reinforces your brand. Your design should stand out visually, without detracting from key contact details. Although the canvas size is minimal, you still have plenty of opportunities to get creative with the space you have, but don't overcomplicate things by introducing too much detail.

We'll be creating a double-sided business card, with the document's first page forming the front side of the business card, showcasing our company logo, and the second page forming the reverse side, which will contain contact details.

The pages uses different plain backgrounds and variants of our company logo, all designed in our company's brand colours.

Document setup

When it comes to business cards, one size doesn't always fit all, so be sure to check your country's standard business card sizes with your printer when deciding on your document's dimensions. For this design, we'll use a dedicated preset for a quick setup.

1 Select **File > New**.

2 On the dialog, ensure **Presets** and **Press Ready** are selected, then choose the *Business Card* thumbnail (scroll down for this). This sets up a CMYK colour space intended for professional printing.

Master page and facing page settings were unchecked as we don't need these for this simple project.

3 In the **Layout** section, set the **Image placement policy** to *Prefer Linked* and the **Number of pages** to *2*.

4 In the **Bleed** section, ensure all **Bleed** settings are set to *3 mm.*

5 Click **Create**.

Resource
KBA Global Swatches.afpalette KBA_logos.afdesign

Importing brand colours

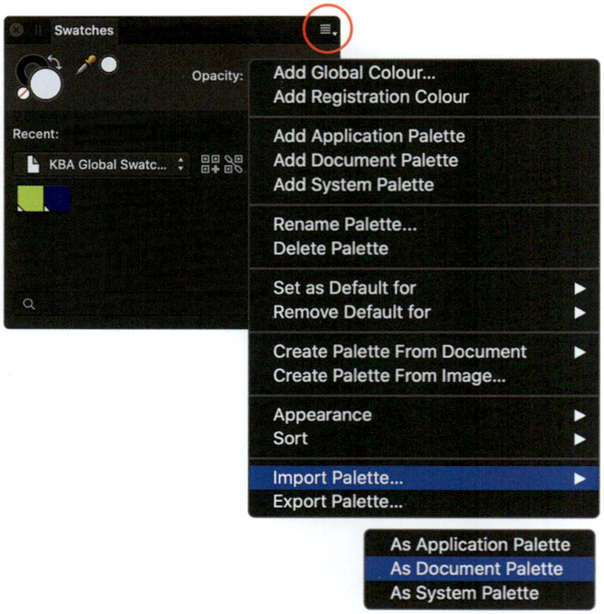

The Brand Guide project looked at creating a colour palette containing approved brand PANTONE® colours. For the business card and other stationery deliverables, we can import and use this palette to apply to objects.

1 On the **Swatches Panel**, click Panel Preferences and choose **Import Palette > As Document Palette** on the pop-up menu.

2 Navigate to the KBA Global Swatches.afpalette file and open it.

3 A new document palette called *KBA Global Swatches* is added to the panel; this contains a *Blue* and *Green* brand colour.

Creating backgrounds

1 Using the **Rectangle Tool** (M), drag a rectangle out across Page 1 so it snaps into opposing bleed edge corners.

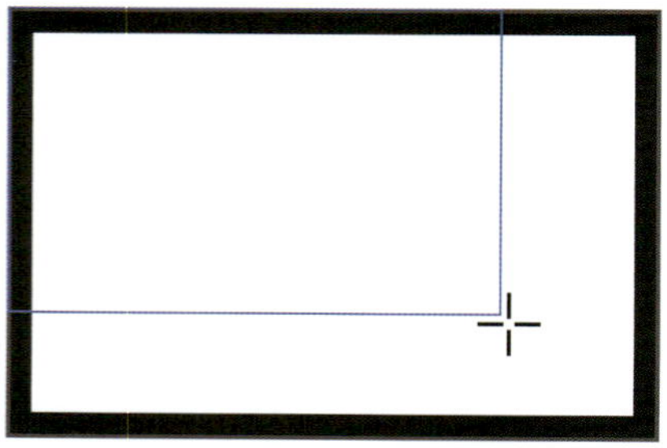

2 Repeat this process for the second page.

3 On the **Swatches Panel**, apply the *Blue* and *Green* swatches to each background rectangle on respective pages.

Placing the company logo

The business card front (Page 1) uses a minimalist version of the company logo: a bold grid pattern with the logo nested inside.

1 Display *Page 1*.

2 Go to **File > Place**.

3 Navigate to the KBA_logos.afdesign file and open it.

4 Press the cmd ⌘ key (Mac) or ctrl key (Win), then hover over the centre of the page. When you see intersecting red and green snapping guides, drag out to size the first artboard from the centre of the document.

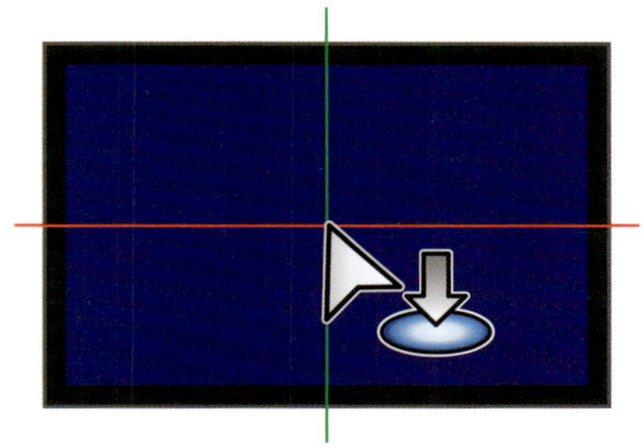

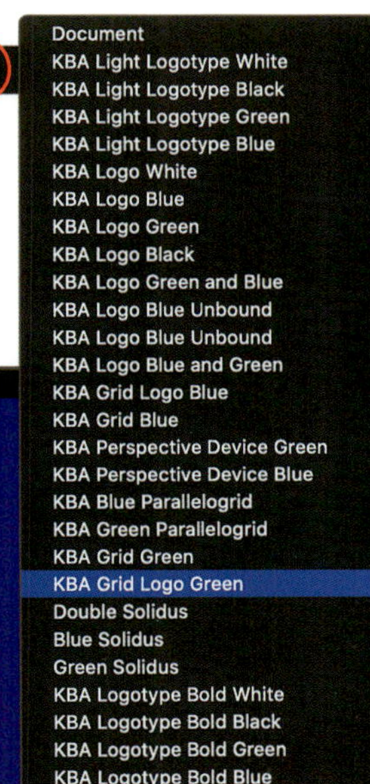

5 Using the context toolbar's **Artboard** option, swap the artboard to the one you want, i.e. *KBA Grid Logo Green*.

6 Resize the logo from centre by dragging from any corner handle with the cmd ⌘ key (Mac) or ctrl key (Win) pressed.

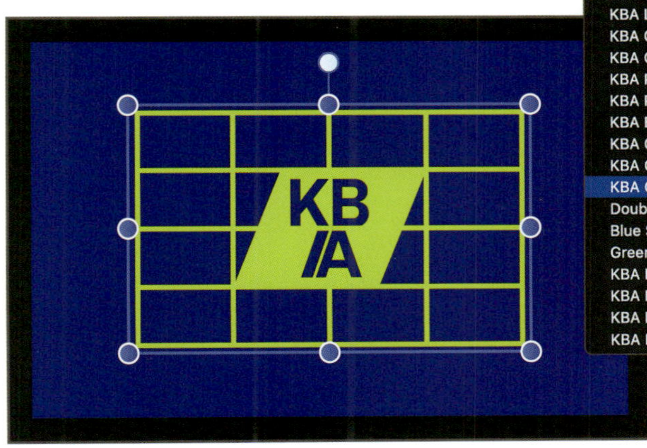

We're using a linked Affinity Designer document with 27 artboards. When placed, the most up to date logo variant will be used so you'll also always conform to the latest brand guidelines.

Contact details

There is plenty of room for flexibility in how your business card can be displayed, but it's important that it attracts attention, is easy to read and focuses on only the most important information.

Downloading and installing fonts

1 Go to https://fonts.google.com (or search online for *Google fonts*) and download the **Chivo** family.

2 Open the downloaded zip file and open and read the OFL.txt file.

3 For *Mac*: ctrl-click the downloaded font files and select **Install font**.
or:
For *Windows*: Right-click the downloaded font files and select **Install**.

Creating body text

Let's add some text to the other side (*Page 2*) of our business card.

1 With the **Frame Text Tool** (T) active, set your preferred text settings on the context toolbar.

2 Drag across the approximate centre of the page and type into the text frame, using shift-Return (⇧↵) as line breaks.

Colouring text using the *Blue* global colour swatch continues the brand colour use and keeps consistency.

Emphasising contact details

Let's use different font sizes and weights to emphasise the person's name in our text.

1 Select the name.

2 On the context toolbar, increase the **Font Size** so it is slightly larger than the rest of the body text and apply the *Bold* **Font Style**.

Adding the Solidus mark

For the second page of our business card, we'll align a placed Solidus mark to sit beside our copy.

1 Deselect the text frame, then go to **File > Place**.

2 Select the KBA_logos.afdesign file as before but place the artboard containing the *Blue Solidus* mark next to your copy. Drag and resize so it snaps to the left of the body text frame.

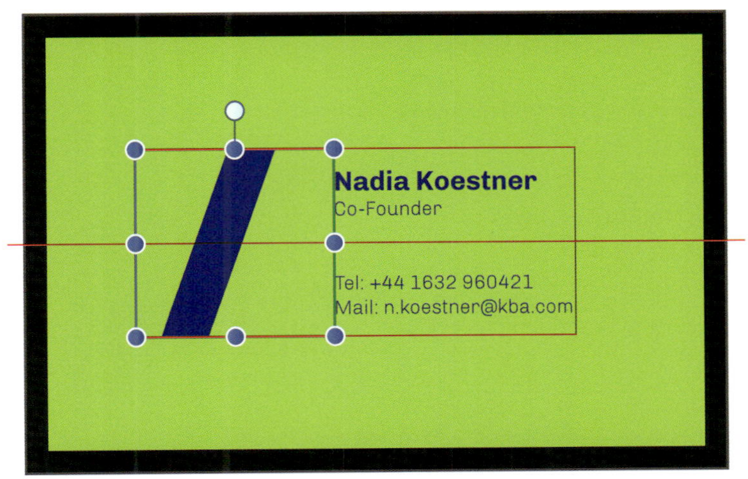

Resource

KBA_letterhead.afpub
KBA_logos.afdesign
KBA_RAPA_logo.png

LETTERHEAD

Using a custom letterhead featuring your company logo and brand colours lends a sleek, professional look to your company letters.

When designing, it's important to leave a good amount of white space for the content of the letter and to use a logo design that's not too overstated or distracting. We're aiming for a letterhead design that's simple, striking and elegant.

Koestner Browne Architects
1 Wilford Rise,
Nottingham NG37 1AD

Dear Sir/Madam,

Donec sit amet justo. In velit. Vivamus turpis pede, dignissim sed, scelerisque nec, pretium sit amet, dui. Nam nec felis non turpis hendrerit varius. In ultrices ornare lorem. Quisque bibendum, massa sed venenatis malesuada, diam ipsum blandit urna, vel ultricies pede nulla vitae lacus.

Lorem ipsum dolor sit amet, consectetuer adipiscing elit. Quisque in augue. Donec aliquam magna nonummy enim. Proin blandit imperdiet sem. Donec malesuada, urna sit amet varius aliquam, nibh tortor laoreet turpis, eget sodales felis nibh ac sapien. Fusce eget augue. Integer sed risus. Aenean mollis. Donec facilisis egestas quam. Duis bibendum augue id mauris. Sed laoreet, tortor vel cursus fringilla, turpis elit vestibulum arcu, eu varius dolor leo in nulla. In sem ipsum, faucibus quis, varius tristique, porta eget, lorem. Curabitur hendrerit diam et mauris. Etiam porta nunc euismod dui. Maecenas a lectus. In hac habitasse

Yours Sincerely,
Koestner Browne

Document setup

Repeat the document setup as described for the business card (p. 465), except for choosing the *A4* preset (**Orientation** set to *Portrait*) and the **Number of pages** to be *1*.

You'll also need to import the brand colour palette as described on p. 466.

Adding address details (a)

1 With the **Frame Text Tool** active, set your preferred text settings on the context toolbar. The Blue global colour adds additional emphasis.

2 Drag across the page in the top-left corner and begin typing the address in the text frame.

3 Give the company name a **Bold** style.

Koestner Browne Architects
1 Wilford Rise,
Nottingham NG37 1AD

Placing the company logo (b)

For our letterhead, we'll follow the same process as placing logos onto the business card. A two-colour version of the company logo was used that blends in with the address text colour, for a clean, professional look.

1 Go to **File > Place**.

2 Using the KBA_logos.afdesign file as before (p. 467), select the **Artboard** called *KBA Logo Blue and Green* on the context toolbar once placed.

3 Move the logo so it snaps in alignment with the top of the address text frame.

Be sure to leave a reasonable amount of white space between the two so the page doesn't feel too crowded.

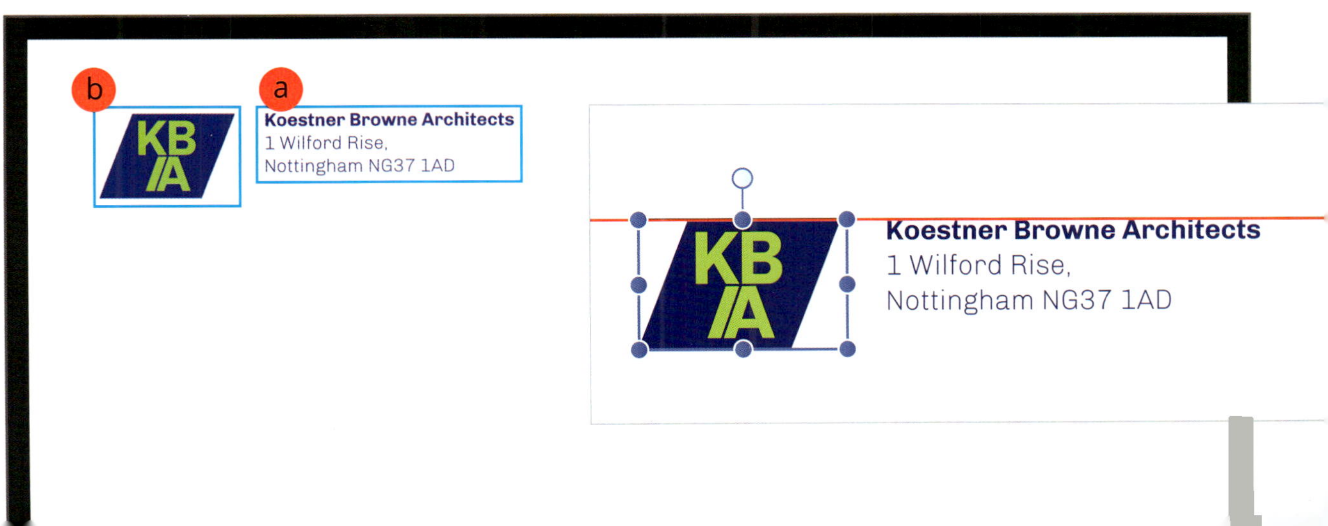

Adding footer logos

For the letterhead's footer section, let's introduce another company branded logo: a flat blue colour version of the already placed KB/A logo, plus a third-party RAPA logo (as a PNG file).

Adding a secondary KB/A logo (c)

1. Go to **File > Place**.
2. Using the KBA_logos.afdesign file, select the **Artboard** called *KBA Logo Blue* on the context toolbar once placed.

Adding a third-party graphic (d)

1. Go to **File > Place**.
2. Navigate to the KBA_RAPA_logo.png file, open it and place it to be aligned vertical centre with the KB/A logo.

KB
/A

RAPA
PROTECTED PRACTICE

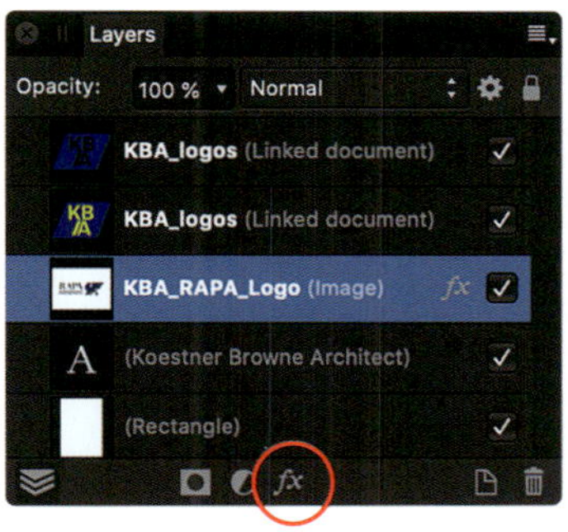

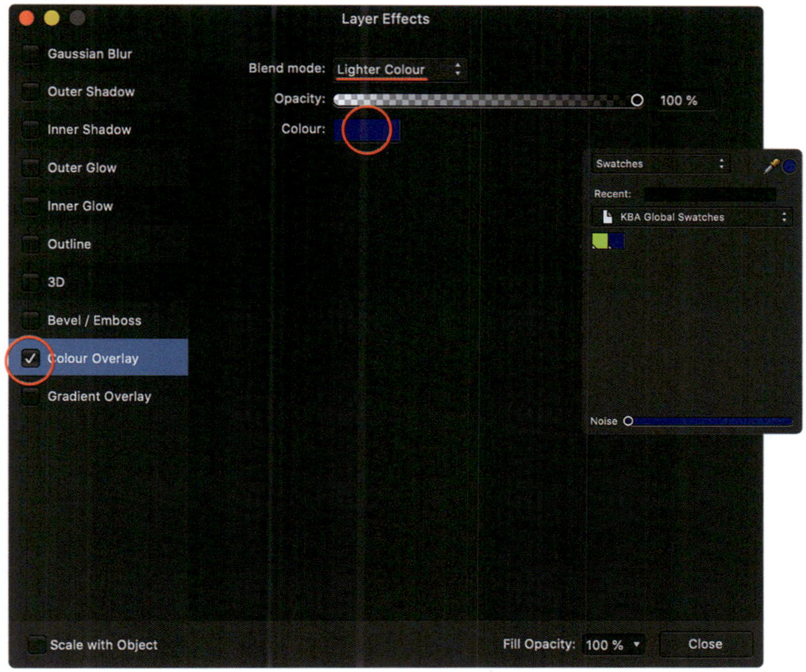

Applying brand colours to third-party graphic

It's likely that introducing third-party graphics will clash with your brand colours. With your third party's permission, you can recolour their logo to keep colours on brand.

1. Select the placed third-party graphic.
2. On the **Layers Panel**, click **Layer Effects**.
3. Check the **Colour Overlay** effect and navigate via the **Colour** swatch to the **Swatches** and **Document Palette** pop-up options.
4. Select the *Blue* swatch, swapping the **Blend Mode** to *Lighter Colour* so the highest colour values from both the base and blend colour will be used.

Resource

KBA_compliments_slip.afpub
KBA_logos.afdesign

COMPLIMENTS SLIP

Compliments slips are generally enclosed with documents or products requested by a customer. They can also be used as a thank you note, an apology, and serve an additional promotional function as they contain contact details that can be used to get in touch with your company.

Your compliments slip should be simplistic and make effective use of a large amount of white space.

Document setup

Repeat the Document setup described for the business card (p. 465), except for choosing the *Dimension Lengthwise* preset, set **Orientation** to *Landscape* and the **Number of pages** to be *1*.

You'll also need to import the brand colour palette as described on p. 466.

Grid

We're going to create a custom grid design for the background of our slip. This can be done fairly easily by setting up a grid for our document and then tracing over it using the **Pen Tool**.

Enabling the grid

1. Go to **View > Show Grid**.
2. On the **Toolbar**, click the down arrow on the **Snapping** option, and ensure **Enable snapping** and **Snap to grid** is checked.

Setting up the grid

1. On the **View Menu**, go to **Grid and Axis Manager**.
2. On the **Preset** pop-up menu, select the *1cm Square* grid.
3. Increase the grid's **Spacing** to *11 mm*. This gives a 9-row grid that fits perfectly into the 99 mm document height.

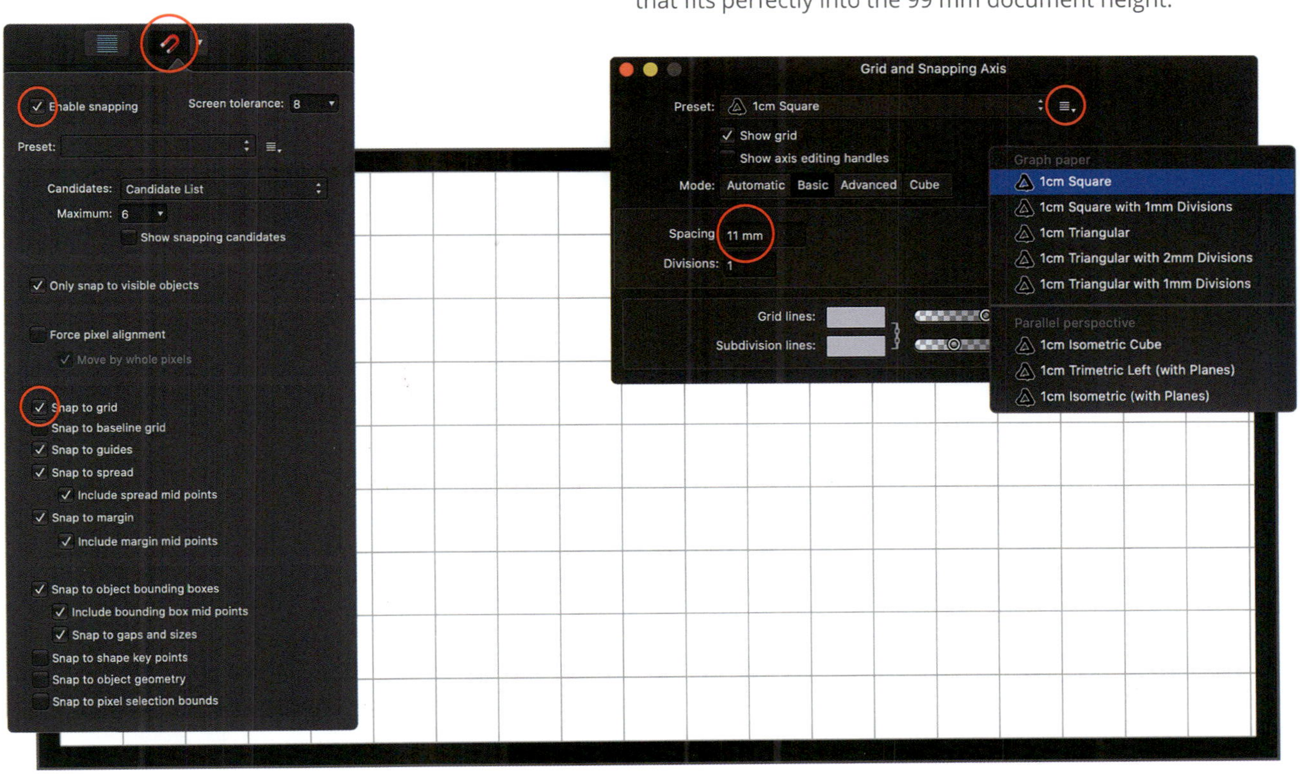

Making the grid

Now that our grid has been established, we can begin drawing lines over it.

1 With the **Pen Tool** (P) selected, draw a single line vertically down the left page edge to the bottom of the page that follows the grid.

2 With the **Move Tool** (V) selected and the cmd ⌘ key or ctrl key (Win) pressed, select the line and duplicate it by dragging it right to the next vertical grid line; power duplicate the line 15 times using cmd ⌘ + J (Mac) or ctrl + J (Win) to complete the vertical lines. This should leave around a fifth of the white space on the right-hand side of the page empty for your copy.

3 Repeat the process for the horizontal lines, drawing the initial line along the top edge of the page that meets the outmost vertical lines.

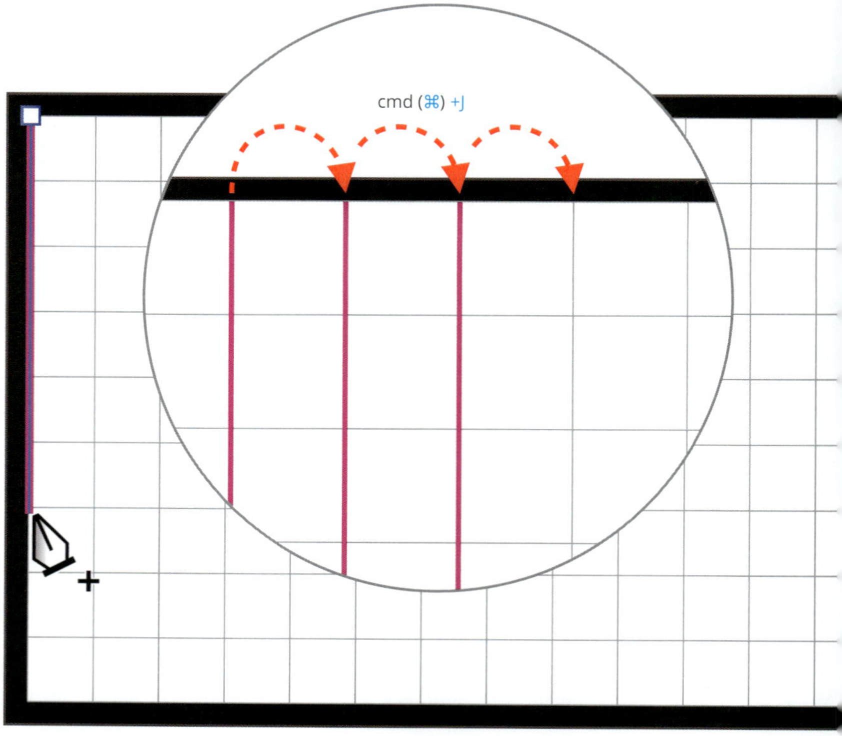

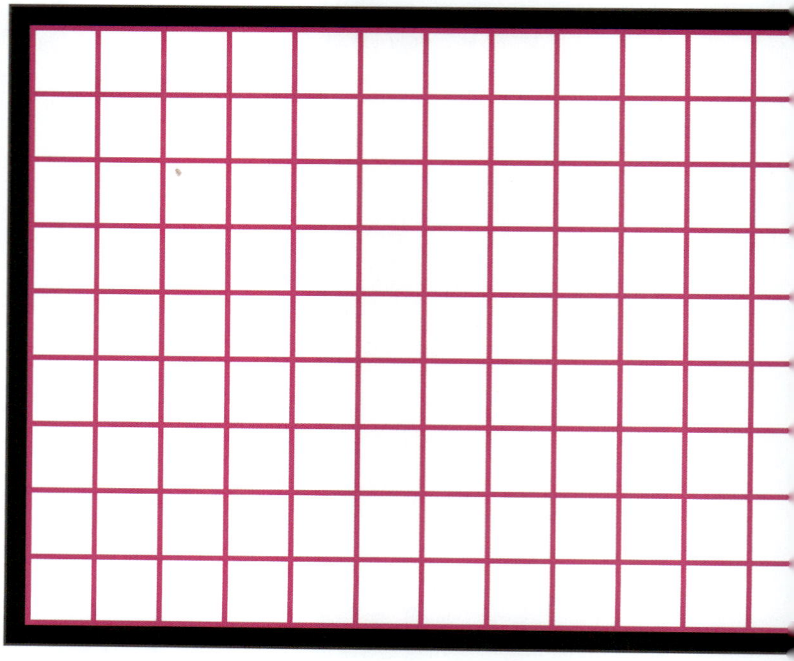

Tweaking your new custom grid

We want our completed grid design to be 'branded' and made less visible so that it doesn't clash with messages written on the compliments slip.

1 Choose **Select All** on the **Select Menu**.

2 On the **Swatches Panel**, ensure the Stroke colour selector is active and apply the *Blue* global colour.

3 On the **Stroke Panel**, change the stroke **Width** to *0.2 pt*.

4 On the **Layers Panel**, drop the **Opacity** down to *20%*, making the grid more transparent.

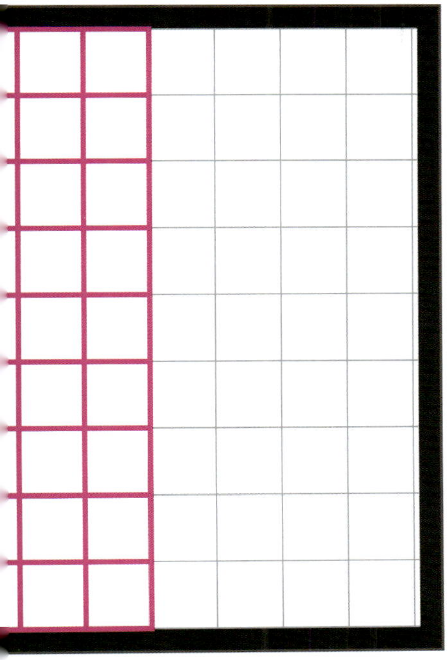

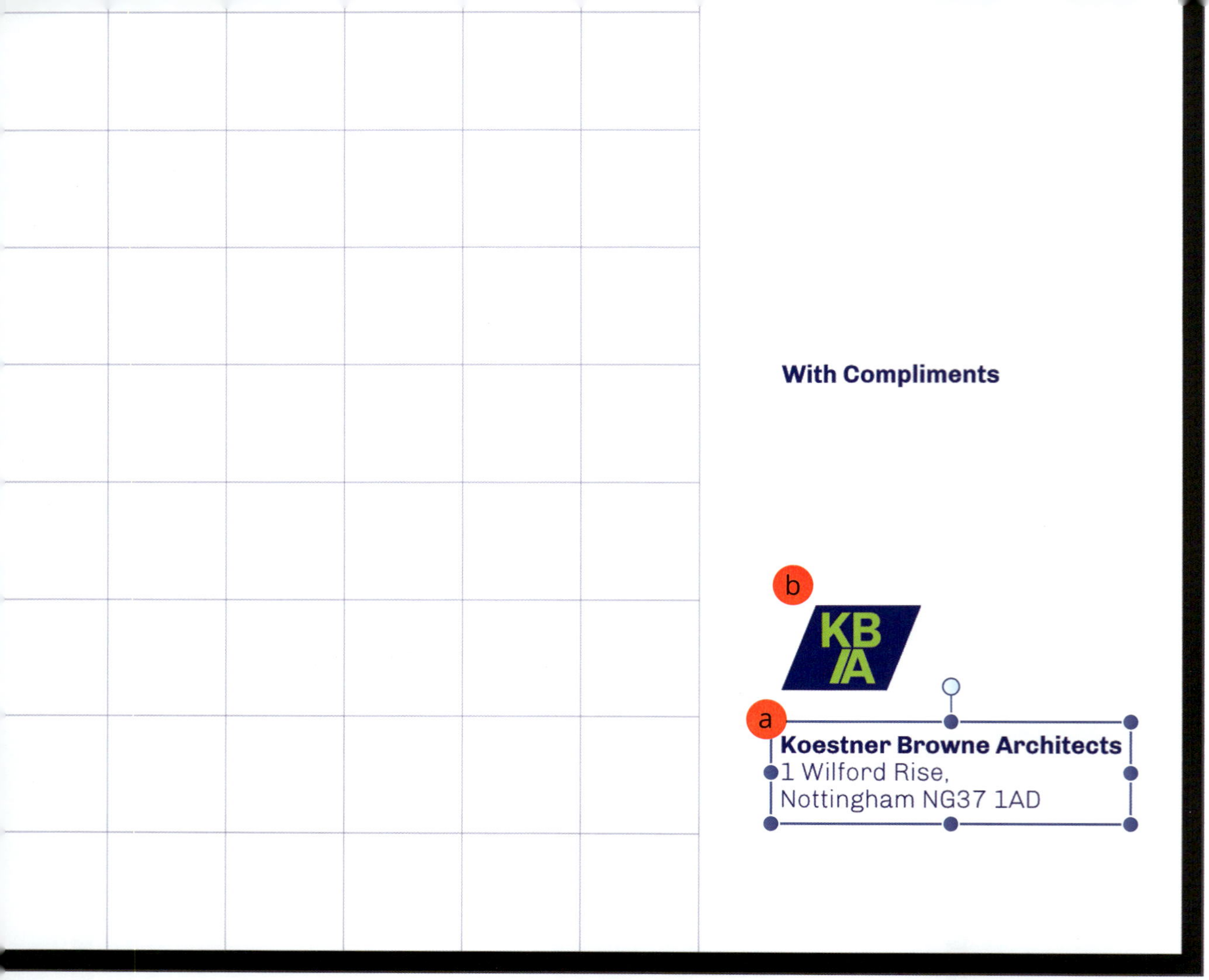

Text

The compliments slip copy should be set to a small size and kept simple, being mindful of the page edges and overall legibility. Our text should not be too large and distracting, or too small to be read properly. There should also be ample space on the slip to include a message.

Adding salutation text and company address text (a)

1 With the **Frame Text Tool** active, set your preferred text settings on the context toolbar.

2 Drag a small text frame out in the centre of the blank area on the right of your page and type your salutation text into the text frame. Add company address text to a second text frame.

As with our other stationery projects, we'll use the *Blue* global colour to keep our branding consistent.

Ensure plenty of space is left between the text frames for a personalised message, as well as our company logo.

Emphasising text details

- With your salutation and company name text selected, apply the *Bold* Font Style on the context toolbar.

Placing the company Logo

For our compliments slip, let's use a version of our logo that introduces both brand colours.

Placing the company logo (b)

1 Go to **File > Place**.

2 Using the KBA_logos.afdesign file as before (p. 467), select the **Artboard** called *KBA Logo Blue and Green* on the context toolbar once placed.

3 Move the logo so it snaps in vertical alignment to the left edge of both text frames.

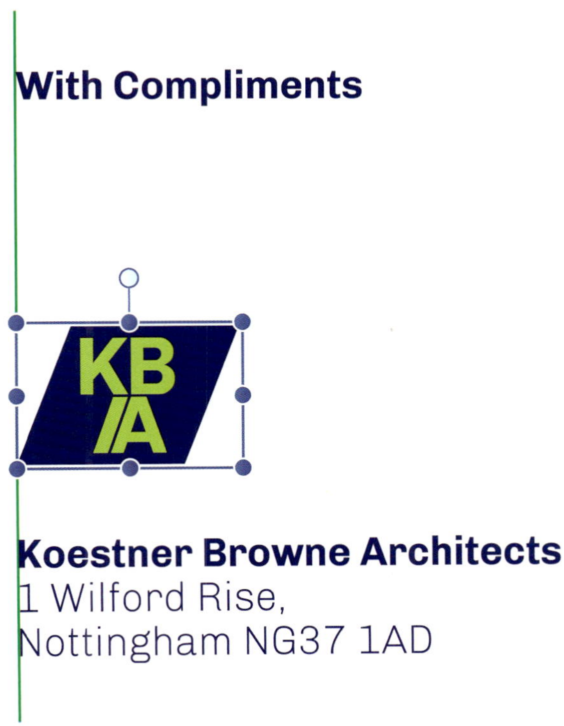

EXPORTING AS PDF

The CMYK document setup for all three stationery deliverables makes it easy to export as press-ready PDF files for hand-off to your print company.

The export process is identical to that for exporting the KB/A Brand Guide (p. 455).

This KB/A Stationery project focussed on two main aspects for all three deliverables: simple design and maintaining the brand. The next project continues this in the development of a KB/A Annual Report.

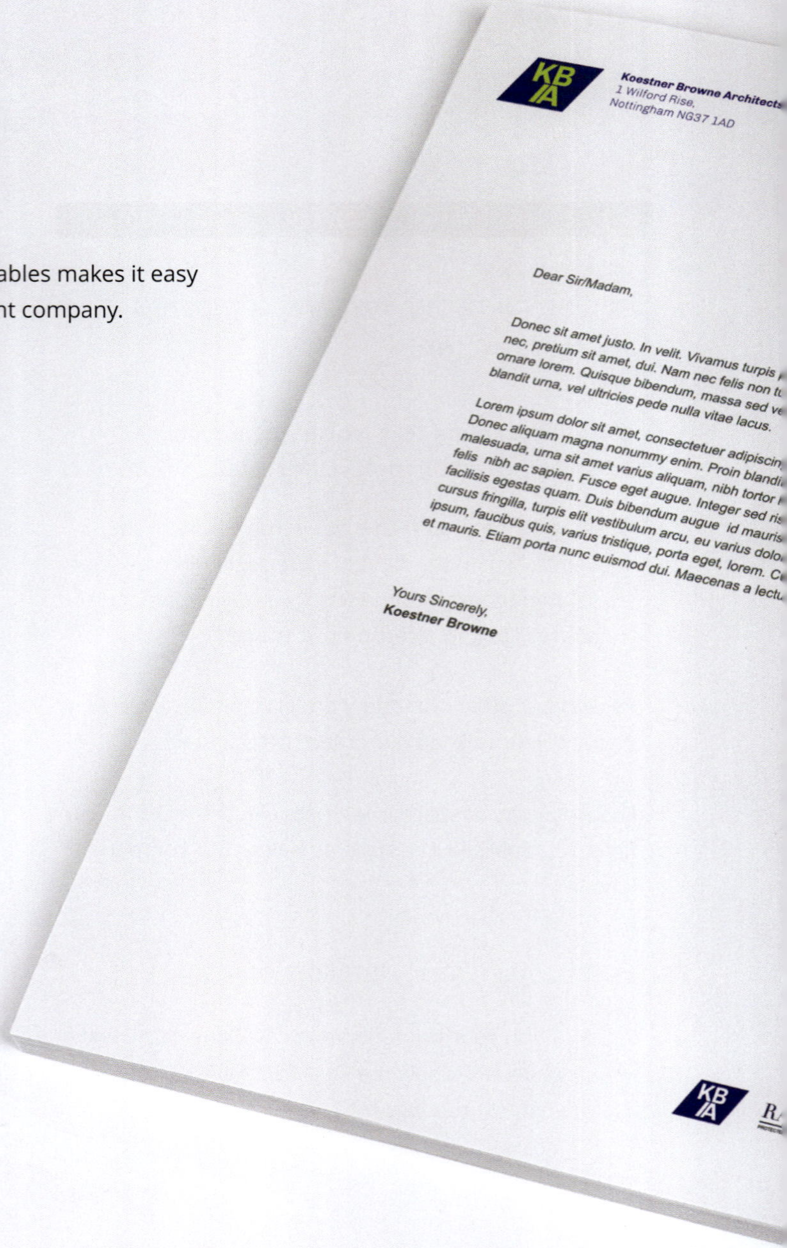

With Compliments
Koestner Browne Architects
1 Wilford Rise,
Nottingham NG37 1AD
Nadia Koestner
Co-Founder
Tel: +44 1632 960421
Mail: n.koestner@kba.com

3

KB/A Annual Report

Designing a corporate annual report to brand guidelines by *David Hussner*

An annual report enables a business to communicate its activity and direction to stakeholders and potential investors. It's critical that the document reflects the company's brand design and values.

In this project, we'll produce a multi-page document containing text and data that's typical of an annual report, with an eye-catching cover design.

The report will use approved logos and colours from the earlier KB/A Brand Guide project.

KB/A
Koestner Browne Architects.
Annual Report 2020
Delivering over 20 years of architectural growth and award-winning architectural designs.
Koestner Browne Architects
Annual Report
2019 Financial Summary
Three-year financial overview
Company Highlights
Meet the Team
The Board of Directors
Our Offices
Location

BEFORE YOU GET STARTED

Resources

You can get all the resources that are referenced in this project from: https://affin.co/KBAAnnualReport

Knowledge of Affinity Publisher

To get the most from undertaking this project, you will need to:

- Be familiar with the interface of Affinity Publisher. You can learn more about the interface in the Interface Tour chapter, starting on p. 14.
- Have good core skills. See the skills table below to see which additional aspects of Affinity Publisher you need to be confident with to complete this project:

Pages and Master Pages	p. 82
Object Control	p. 106
Working with Text	p. 112
Picture Frames	p. 124
Adding Content	p. 130

INTRODUCTION

For this project, we will design a 16-page annual report. The report's design will make extensive use of KB/A's mandated green and blue colour swatches and logos (solidi) to reinforce the brand identity.

We'll build on that foundation by using advanced capabilities of Affinity Publisher to add visual flourishes that spark the reader's interest.

STARTING THE DESIGN PROCESS

Before starting the layout process in Affinity Publisher, I like to begin projects offline. On sheets of paper, I sketch different design and layout options. I get a better feeling for a project by testing some variations of grids, sizes and arrangements in this way.

When you're ready with design concepts and have a good idea of your direction, take a deeper look at the available content. Ensure it is divided into clear sections that help readers to navigate the document.

We have content for the sections listed in the table. I've shown the final page counts to help simplify your path through the project. In reality, you would have to estimate at this stage.

Section	Page count	Speculative page numbers
Company Principles	1	2
Brand Story	1	3
Message from the Board of Directors	3	4, 5, 6
Company Highlights	1	7
Current Year Financials and Rankings	2	8, 9
KB/A in the News	2	10, 11
Meet the Team	2	12, 13
Our Offices	2	14, 15
Total (including front and back covers)	**16**	

For an effective start to the design and layout process, plan what is needed for functional and professional layout. Think about the necessary assets for your design—fonts, colours, images, etc. For this project, the KB/A Brand Guide provides much of this foundation.

Resource

KBA Global Swatches.afpalette
KBA_annual_report_text_styles.afpub
KBA_annual_report_document_setup.afpub

DOCUMENT SETUP

Let's create an Affinity Publisher document for the annual report.

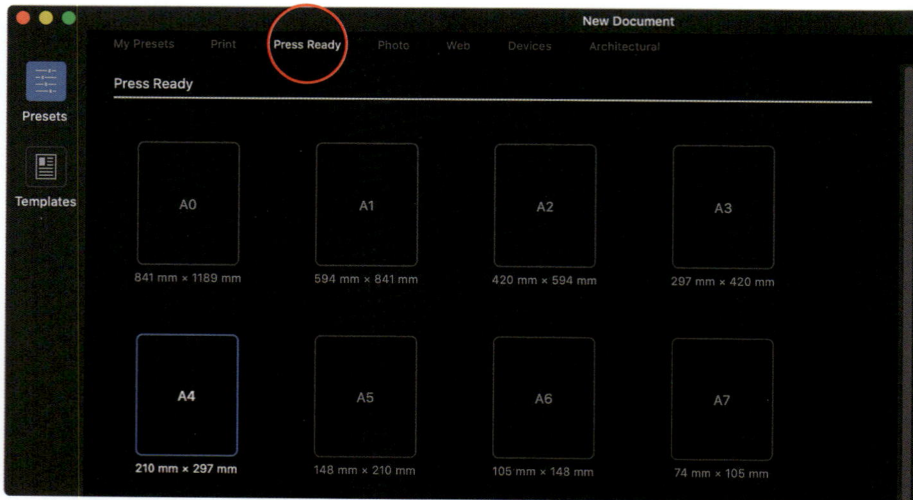

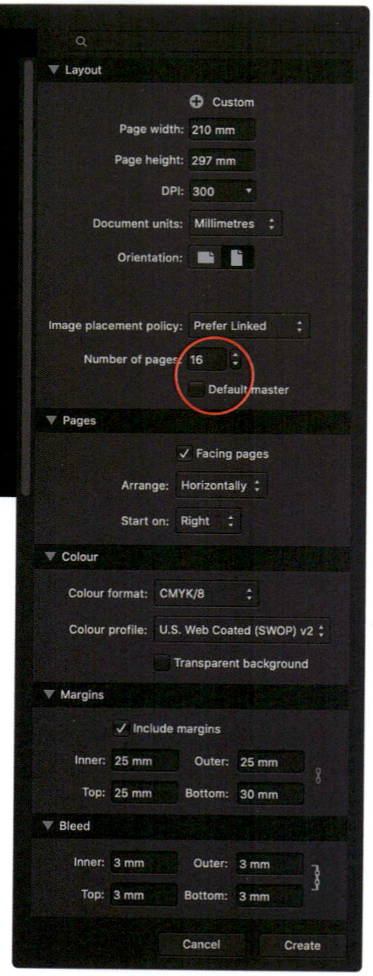

1 Select **File > New**.

2 On the dialog, select **Presets** and **Press Ready**.

3 Select the *A4* preset.

4 Set **Number of pages** to *16* and uncheck **Default master**.

5 Click **Create**.

For this project, we know the pagination of my final design. When designing from scratch, you might add pages as you go. The important thing is that your completed annual report, if it's to be professionally printed, has a total page count that's divisible by four.

Importing colours and text styles

Many of the annual report's elements will use the KB/A brand's approved PANTONE® colours. Import these to your document, along with text styles I've already created for the annual report.

1. On the **Swatches Panel**, go to Panel Preferences and select **Import Palette > As Document Palette**.
2. Locate and open KBA Global Swatches.afpalette.
3. Select **Text > Text Styles > Import Text Styles** and open KBA_Annual_Report_text_styles.afpub.

Having done this, throughout this project you can apply the brand's approved green and blue colours from the *KBA Global Swatches* palette on the **Swatches Panel**. The text styles will show in the **Text Styles Panel**.

About my text styles

Each of my paragraph styles' names is prefixed either *Headline* (section headings, subheadings and text on the report's covers) or *Copy Text* (small text, such as body copy).

Several headline styles might use the same font family, colour and tracking but a different size or leading, so I include the key values that differ in my style names.

This gives me greater orientation within the **Text Styles Panel**, ensuring I can find whatever size/spacing I need to apply.

You'll also apply my five character styles for quick, consistent application of colour to text. Text Bold Black also applies a marginally heavier font style.

The most commonly used paragraph styles in this project are:

Headline 27/31 Left is for section headings at the top of pages.

Section Heading

Headline 13/15 Left is for subheadings, especially within body copy.

Subheading

Copy Text 08/14 Left is for most body copy, especially long passages.

Body copy. Body copy. Body copy.

DESIGN THE FRONT COVER

Resource
KBA_logos.afdesign KBA_cover.rtf KBA_annual_report_1.afpub

Let's create a master page with margin and column guide settings and a coloured background, which we'll apply to the report's front and back covers.

1 On the **Pages Panel**'s upper window, click **Add Master**.

2 Name it *Cover* and click **OK**.

3 In **View > Guides Manager**, set **Columns** to *12* and **Gutter** to *5 mm*.

4 Set the margins to *21.8 mm* on the bottom and *21.2 mm* on the other sides, then click **Close**.

5 In **View > Baseline Grid Manager**, check **Use Baseline Grid** and set **Grid Spacing** to *5 pt*.

We'll use the same column guide and baseline grid settings throughout the report.

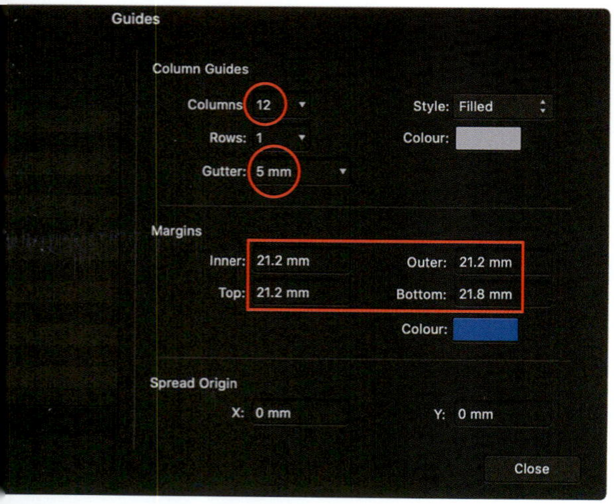

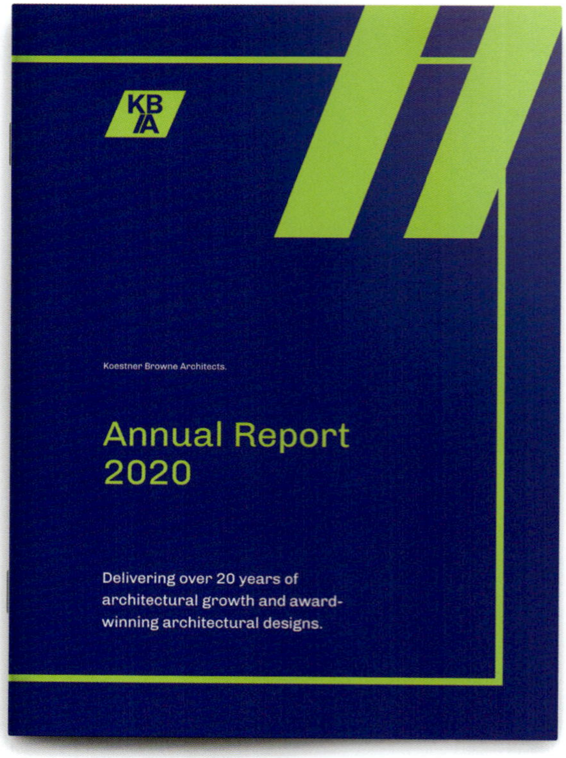

Colour the master page

I used the **Rectangle Tool** (M) to draw a shape that covers the whole master page, including the bleed area. The shape is filled with our brand's *Blue* colour.

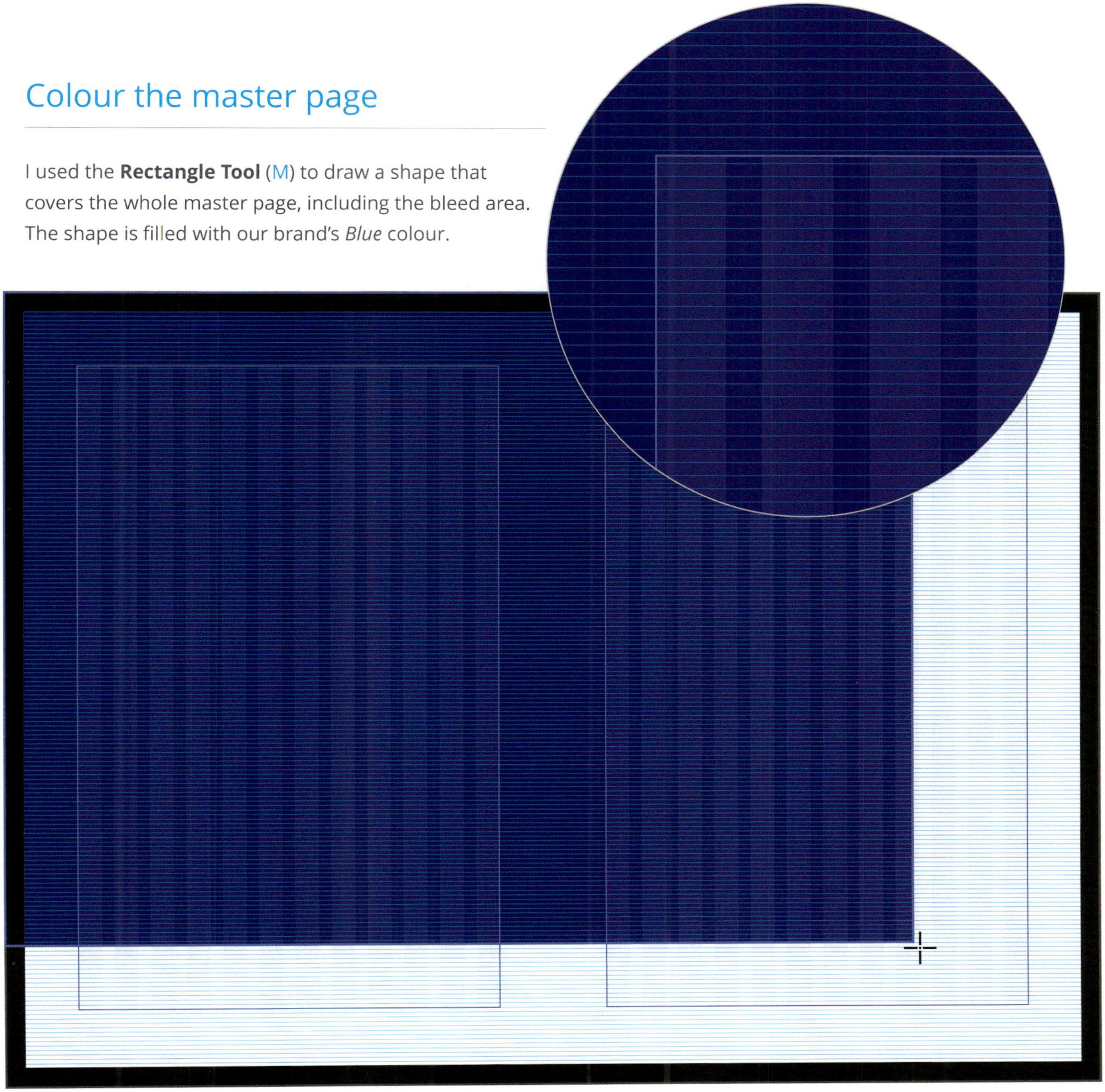

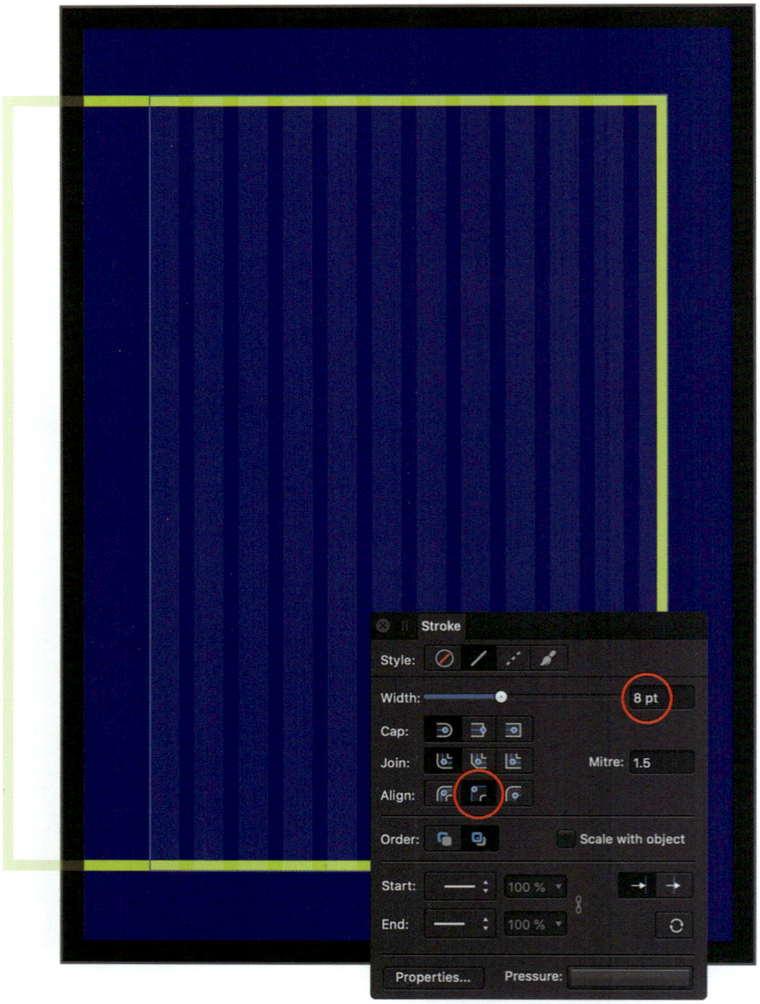

Editing the actual cover

Apply the *Cover* master to Pages 1 and 16, then double-click Page 1 on the **Pages Panel** to edit it. We'll add more brand graphics and text, starting with a border.

1 Draw a rectangle with no fill colour and our brand's *Green* swatch as its stroke colour.

2 On the **Stroke Panel**, set **Width** to *8 pt* and select **Align Stroke to Inside**.

3 Size the shape so its left edge is off the page and its other edges touch the top, right and bottom margins.

Adding brand graphics

1 Select **File > Place**, choose the KBA_logos.afdesign file, then drag across the page to place the file on it.

2 On the context toolbar, set **Artboard** to *KBA Logo Green*.

3 Resize the logo, left-align it to the second column guide and position it a few baselines down from the top margin.

4 Select **File > Open** and choose KBA_logos.afdesign and copy the shapes from the *Double Solidus* artboard in the opened document.

5 Paste on Page 1 of your annual report and apply our *Green* colour to the fill of both solidi.

6 Align, scale proportionally by holding the shift key (⇧) and position the objects as shown, so they bleed off the page near the top right.

Text	Paragraph style	Character style
Company name	Headline 10/15 Left (Head 10/15)	Text White
Report title	Headline 40/44 Left (Head 40/40)	Text KBA Green
Strapline	Headline 17/25 Left (Head 17/20)	Text White

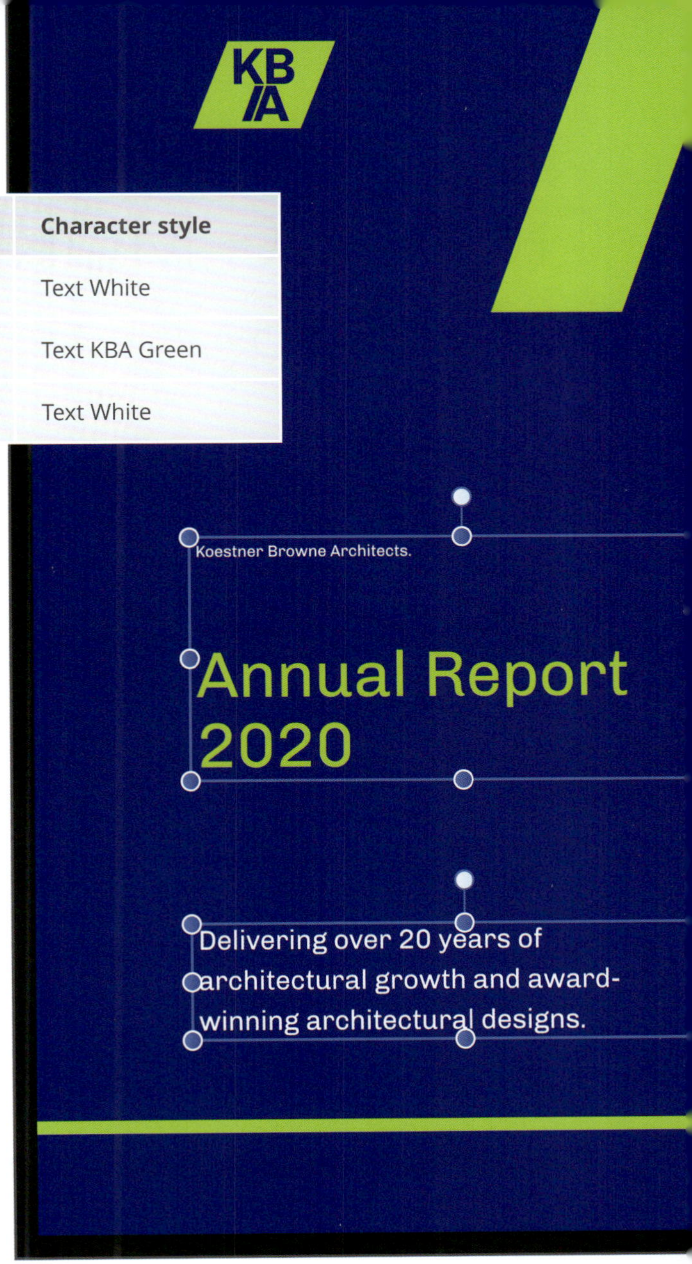

Adding the text

I drew two text frames, left-aligned to the second column guide. The upper one contains the company name and document title, and the lower one contains a strapline describing the report. Copy and paste the text from KBA_cover.rtf.

I applied the paragraph and character styles as listed in the table, creating strong contrasts. The green title connects strongly to the surrounding frame and overall brand.

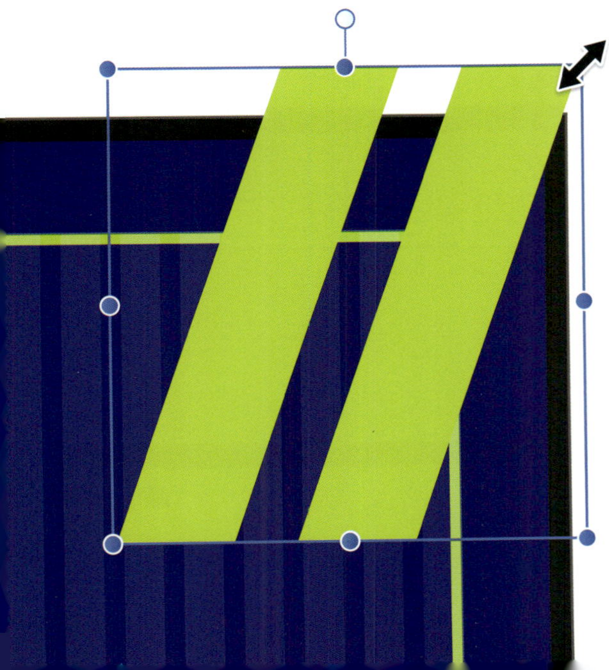

Resource

KBA_logos.afdesign
KBA_annual_report_add_masters_1.afpub

CREATING MORE MASTERS

I chose to lay out the report's interior pages against 12 column guides, but with slightly different margins than the cover.

Add a master to your document. Repeat the steps you took for the *Cover* master (p. 488) but name this one *Grid 12 Blank* and set its **Inner** and **Outer** margins to *21.2 mm*, **Top** to *26.5 mm*, and **Bottom** to *21.8 mm*.

Add another master, named *Page No*. I used the **Pen Tool** to draw a *1 pt* line in the brand's blue above the top margin (a).

The parallelogram (b) was made by opening KBA_logos.afdesign and copying the shape from the opened document's *Blue Solidus* artboard, which I widened using the **Node Tool**.

I added two text frames, the first for a page number (**Text > Insert > Fields > Page Number**) and the report title, and the other for the company name (c). I used the **Text Frame Panel** to make them ignore the baseline grid, and positioned so the field is inside the parallelogram. The *Copy Text 08/14 Left* and *Text KBA Blue* text styles were applied, then *Text KBA Green* to the page number.

Duplicate and reverse the objects' order on the facing page. Then, apply this master to *Grid 12 Blank*. We'll apply *Grid 12 Blank* and two other masters based on it—yet to be created—to interior pages, so this ensures those pages include the header.

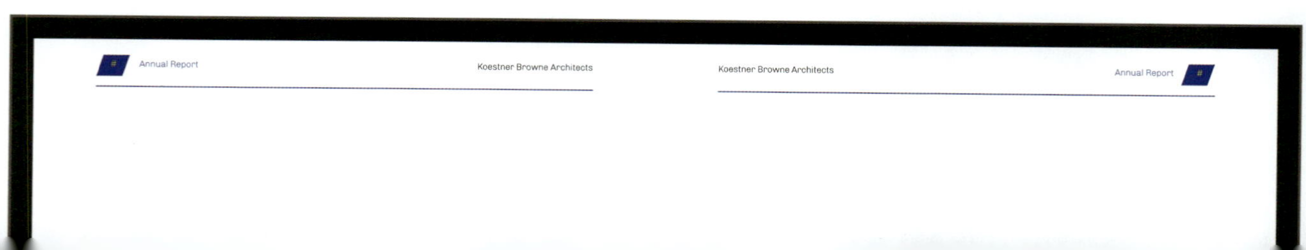

INTRODUCING THE COMPANY

Resource
KBA_logos.afdesign KBA_mission_statement.rtf KBA_annual_report_2&3.afpub

Pages 2 and 3 are used to introduce the company's principles and brand story. I've applied the *Grid 12 Blank* master page to them.

The company principles should stand out more than regular body copy later in the report.

1 On Page 2, draw a text frame and enter the *Company Principles* headline.

2 On the context toolbar, apply our *Headline 27/31 Left* paragraph style and *Text KBA Blue* character style.

3 Draw another text frame below, then copy the three principles' text from KBA_mission_statement.rtf and paste them in it.

4 Apply the *Headline 17/25 Left* paragraph style and apply a medium grey font colour (*CMYK 0,0,0,50*).

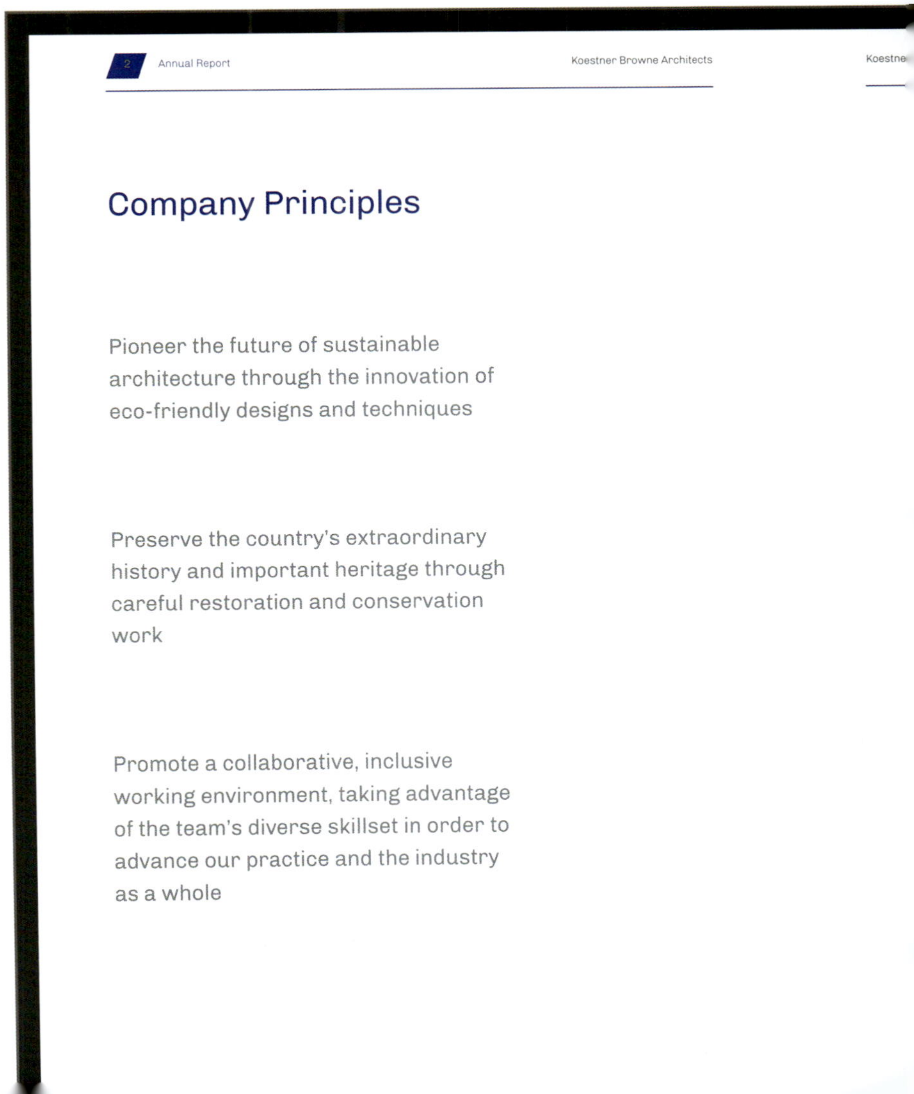

2 Annual Report Koestner Browne Architects

Company Principles

Pioneer the future of sustainable architecture through the innovation of eco-friendly designs and techniques

Preserve the country's extraordinary history and important heritage through careful restoration and conservation work

Promote a collaborative, inclusive working environment, taking advantage of the team's diverse skillset in order to advance our practice and the industry as a whole

Adding the brand story

On the right page, I drew another text frame, then copied and pasted the *Brand Story* headline and body copy from KBA_mission_statement.rtf into it.

The *Headline 27/31 Left* paragraph style and *Text KBA Blue* character style are applied to the headline.

I applied the *Copy Text 08/14 Left* paragraph style and *Text Black* character style to the rest of the text.

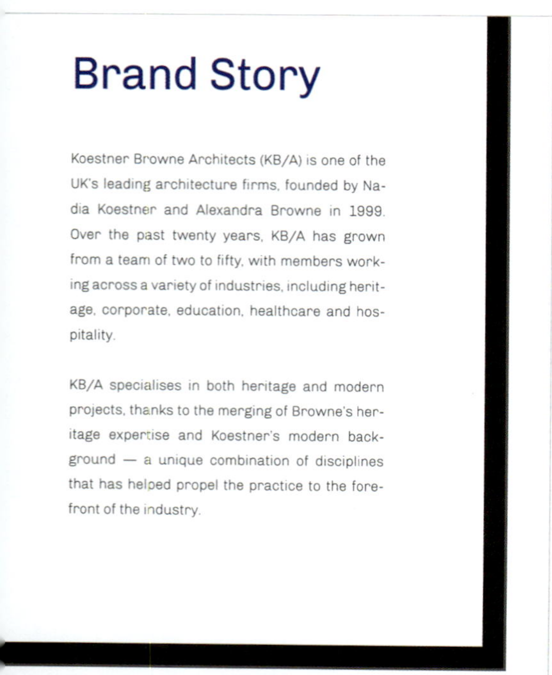
Brand Story

Koestner Browne Architects (KB/A) is one of the UK's leading architecture firms, founded by Nadia Koestner and Alexandra Browne in 1999. Over the past twenty years, KB/A has grown from a team of two to fifty, with members working across a variety of industries, including heritage, corporate, education, healthcare and hospitality.

KB/A specialises in both heritage and modern projects, thanks to the merging of Browne's heritage expertise and Koestner's modern background — a unique combination of disciplines that has helped propel the practice to the forefront of the industry.

Adding graphical elements

Due to the small amount of text on these two pages, I've used large instances of the solidus graphic in the white space. This adds structure to the spread and emphasises the all-important principles on the left page.

1 Open the KBA_logos.afdesign file.

2 Copy the shape on the *Blue Solidus* artboard to the Clipboard and close the file.

3 Paste on Page 3 of your annual report.

I scaled the solidus proportionally so it extends from Page 3's top margin to the spread's bottom bleed edge, positioned its top-left corner just left of the right page's corresponding margin corner, then made it wider.

1 Using the **Node Tool** (A), hold the shift key (⇧) and select the solidus's right-hand nodes.

2 With the key still held, drag the top-right node until it is slightly right of the corresponding margin corner. Both selected nodes will move, maintaining the edge's angle.

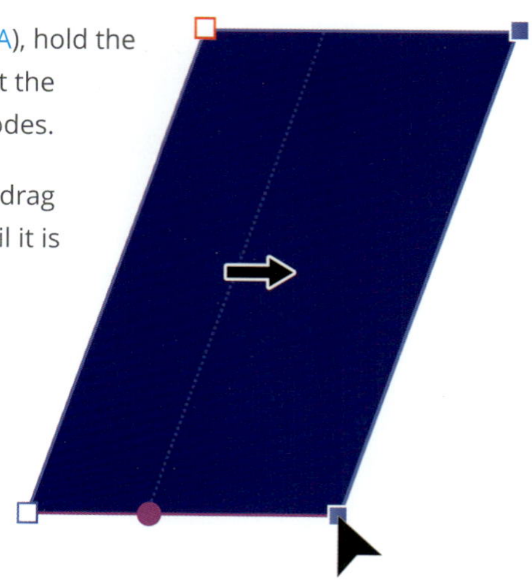

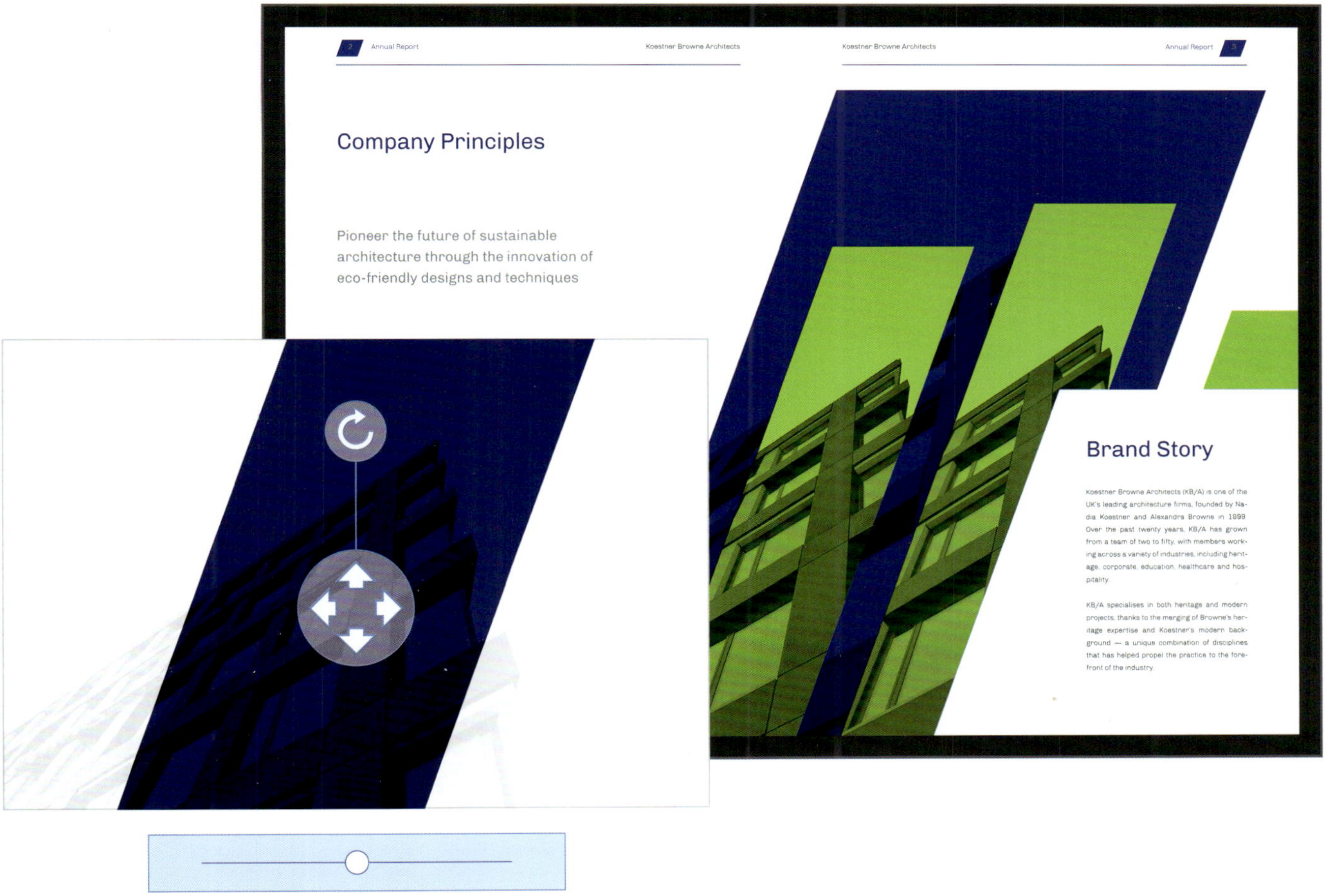

Let's add an image, reflecting KB/A's purpose, inside the solidus.

1 With the shape selected, choose **Layer > Convert to Picture Frame**.

2 On the **Stock Panel**, search for *building*. I've chosen one with clear architectural patterns and strong contrast. Drag and drop it onto the picture frame.

3 Use the overlaid controls to get the image as you want it within the shape.

4 On the **Layers Panel**, click the solidus picture frame's disclosure triangle.

5 Set the revealed image's blend mode to *Multiply* and select **Layer > New Adjustment > Black & White**. The image is tinted by its frame's fill colour.

After applying the Black & White adjustment, you can double-click its layer's thumbnail to modify its effect on the image.

Duplicate the picture frame and change its fill colour to our *Green* swatch. I duplicated this copy another two times and sized and arranged them as shown.

I made another duplicate of the picture frame, removed the image from it, and set its fill to *White* (*CMYK 0,0,0,0*). I used the **Layers Panel** to arrange it behind the brand story text and in front of the coloured picture frames.

To finish, add line breaks between the paragraphs as you want.

Resource
KBA_annual_report_add_masters_2.afpub

CREATE CONTENT MASTER PAGES

Many interior pages will display body copy across two or three columns per page. Let's create master pages for this purpose.

1. On the **Pages Panel**, click **Add Master**.
2. Name the new master *Grid 12 Col (3 text cols)* and click **OK**.
3. Apply the *Grid 12 Blank* master to this page to inherit its column guides, baseline grid, margins, and header with page numbers.

Adding a headline and brand graphic

Copy the headline text frame from Page 2 and paste it on the new master. It will appear in the same position.

Replace its contents with *Headline*, repeated till you have two lines of text.

Add the green double solidus to the right page. Scale and position it so its top-right corner touches the same margin point and its bottom edge rests on the same baseline as the headline's second row.

Adding body copy

1. On the left page, draw a text frame that spans all column guides and fills most of the space under the headline.
2. Select **Text > Insert Filler Text**.
3. Apply our *Copy Text 08/14 Left* paragraph style and *Text Black* character style.
4. On the context toolbar, set **Columns** to *3* and **Gutter** uniformly to *5 mm*. Each column of text spans four column guides.
5. With the text frame selected, ensure **Ignore baseline grid** on the **Text Frame Panel** is not checked.
6. Duplicate the frame at the same position on the right page.

For variety in the report's page layouts, we want a version of this master with two text columns per page. Duplicate it, rename the copy *Grid 12 Col (2 text cols)* and adjust each of its body copy text frames accordingly.

ADDING OUR FIRST INTERIOR PAGES

Resource
KBA_in_the_news.rtf KBA_annual_report_10&11.afpub

Let's jump further into the report to lay out Pages 10 and 11 for KB/A in the News, which I've kept simple for demonstration. We'll use our master pages more ambitiously soon.

1 Drag the *Grid 12 Col (3 text cols)* master onto *Pages 10,11*.

2 Use the right-hand **Text Flow** button on Page 10's body copy text frame to link it to the equivalent frame on Page 11.

3 Delete all of the filler text from these two frames.

4 Select either body text frame, then go to **File > Place** and choose the KBA_in_the_news.rtf file.

5 Cut the first line and use **Edit > Paste Without Format** to put it in the headline text frame.

I've put the whole headline on the second line for neatness and alignment with the double solidus.

10 Annual Report Koestner Browne Architects

Koestner Browne Architects Annual Report 11

KB/A in the News

GREEN PLANET BUILDING MAGAZINE: KB/A ONE STEP CLOSER TO MAKING THE MOST ECO-FRIENDLY BUILDING ON EARTH A REALITY

Koestner Browne Architects is one of the UK's leading architecture firms, but it's their specialisation in sustainable architecture that's really setting them apart. And now, they're one step closer to making their dream of creating the world's 'eco-friendliest' building a reality.

Founded by Nadia Koestner and Alexandra Browne in 1999, Koestner Browne Architects (KB/A) has grown from a team of two to more than 50 members of staff over the last 20 years. Headquartered in Nottingham city centre with offices in London and Durham, the KB/A team specialises in a range of disciplines and industries, including heritage, corporate, education, healthcare and hospitality. The firm's list of projects is impressive to say the least.

One of the main reasons for the company's success over the years has been its team's combined expertise in both modern and heritage projects thanks to Browne's background in heritage and Koestner's in modern architecture, something which has helped the practice transform into a sort of superfirm over the years.

"We're passionate about protecting UK heritage and have made it our mission to help preserve the UK's extraordinary history through careful restoration and conservation work," said Browne. "We want to light up the skyline with incredible buildings, while also placing a spotlight on the importance of preserving history around the UK — we can do this by restoring historical buildings and breathing a new life into them through careful conservation work."

But perhaps most importantly, and the main reason KB/A is making waves in the industry at the moment, is due to the team's commitment to protecting the environment through sustainable architecture.

"We want our legacy to be that we helped make the world a better place and were leaders in sustainable architecture. Our team is dedicated to minimising the negative impact building work naturally has on the environment and we work closely with various building and construction partners to make sure that the necessary steps are carried out from start to finish of a project," said Koestner.

"All of our buildings are designed to be eco-friendly and use sustainable products and materials wherever possible."

One of KB/A's goals has been to lead in the creation of the eco-friendliest building on earth. Having already achieved a 98% BREEAM rating on one of its major projects this year, they're not far off the mark, but now they have the project in the pipeline.

"We can't say what it is yet, but it is very, very exciting. With a prime location near the sea, we'll be tying in tidal power and other forms of renewable energy to power the building once it's complete. We'd like every single build we design to one day be fully sustainable, meaning they will all generate solar power or other renewable energy sources, harvest rainwater, produce zero net carbon emissions, incorporate adiabatic cooling systems, grey-water recycling, waste heat recycling, triple glazed windows, extra insulation, LED lighting, EV charging where relevant/possible, etc.," said Browne.

"Seeing how much the industry has transformed and the different technology that has been developed to not just help make buildings eco-friendlier, but also the practice of architecture itself, is astounding. It's such an honour to be at the forefront of the movement and help pioneer the next wave of sustainable architecture at levels that we never even imagined when we first started out."

ARCHITECT NEWS:

KOESTNER BROWNE CO-FOUNDER AWARDED ARCHITECT OF THE YEAR

Nadia Koestner was awarded Architect of the Year at the prominent Architect Awards for her work on The Emerald building in London. Named for its greenish hue, thanks to the surrounding park's reflection on the building's crystal exterior, The Emerald has been praised for its elegance, beauty and, most importantly, sustainability.

Koestner studied architecture at the University of Bath before going on to work for Gorman & Partners in London, following graduation.

While with Gorman, Koestner worked on everything from small local projects to multi-million-pound, large-

Styling the text

Apply the *Copy Text 08/14 Left* paragraph style and *Text Black* character style to all of this text.

The paragraphs starting "*Green Planet Building Magazine*" and "*Architect News*" are intended as long headings for news items, so let's style them differently.

1. Select the **Frame Text Tool** and click in the body copy text frame.
2. Hold the cmd ⌘ key (Mac) or ctrl key (Win) and quadruple-click each of the heading paragraphs to select them.
3. Apply the *Headline 13/15 Left* paragraph style for subheadings and the *Text KBA Blue* character style.

You can transform text containing lower-case characters by selecting it and applying the **All Caps** effect on the **Character Panel**'s **Typography** section.

Add paragraph breaks and column breaks (**Text > Insert > Breaks > Column Break**) as you feel is necessary to make the text look good.

Editing content only

You've replaced the contents of text frames inherited from masters; the frame and its properties can't be altered (although it's possible to do so later). This works with picture frames too. It's important to note that you can set the order in which text flows through frames *after* they've been inherited from master pages.

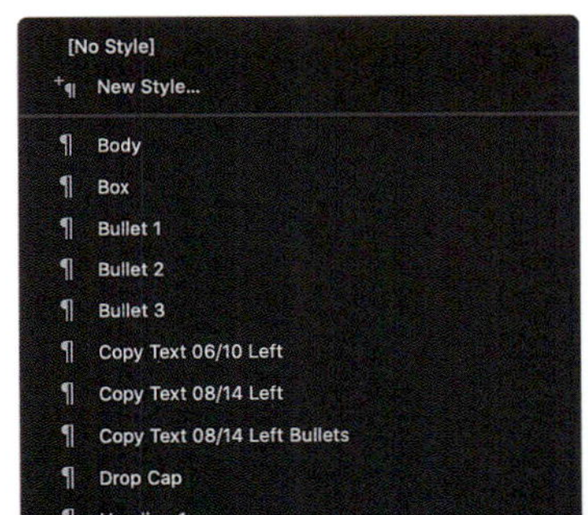

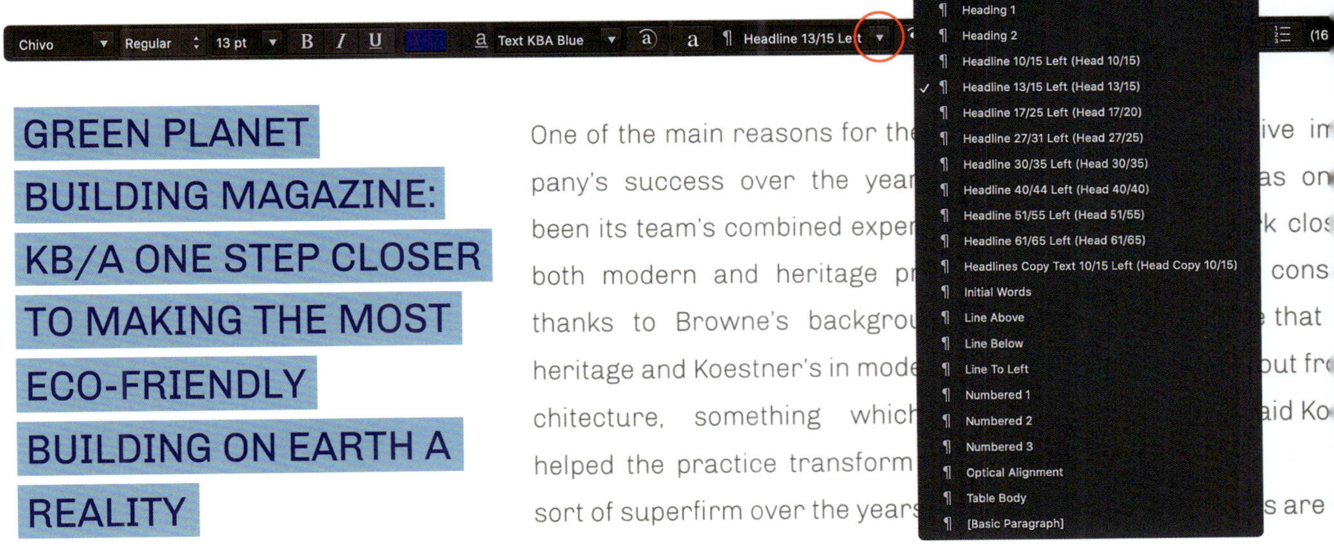

ADDING A PROPER INTRODUCTION

After the company principles and brand story, we'll use several pages to present an opening statement from the board of directors.

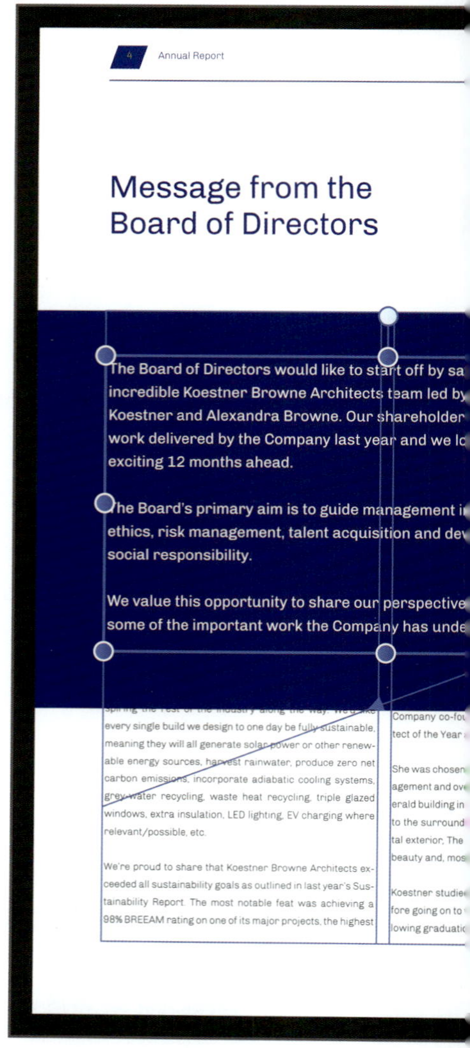

1 Apply the *Grid 12 Col (2 text cols)* master to Pages 4 through to 6.

2 On the **Pages Panel**, double-click Pages 4,5 to view them.

3 Use the **Text Flow** buttons to link the three pages' body copy text frames in page order.

4 Delete all of the body filler text.

5 Select **File > Place** and choose the KBA_message_directors.rtf file.

6 Cut the first line and use **Edit > Paste Without Format** to replace the placeholder headline.

7 For the body copy, like you did on Pages 10 and 11:

- Apply the *Copy Text 08/14 Left* paragraph style and *Text Black* character style to all text.
- Apply the *Headline 13/15 Left* paragraph style, *Text KBA Blue* character style and **All Caps** effect to the subheadings.
- Add paragraph breaks where you want them. Ensure the *Copy Text 08/14 Left* paragraph style is applied to the blank line after each subheading.

An eye-catching entry point

To make the first three paragraphs stand out, I placed them against a blue rectangle at a larger font size than body copy.

1 Apply our *Headline 13/15 Left* paragraph style and *Text White* character style to the three paragraphs.

2 Position the text insertion point at the end of the third paragraph and select **Text > Insert > Breaks > Frame Break**.

3 Use the **Rectangle Tool** to draw a shape, filled with our *Blue* colour, on the left page.

Resource
KBA_message_directors.rtf KBA_annual_report_4&5&6.afpub

4 Draw a one-column text frame in an empty area of the page. Position it over the blue shape and size to span all column guides.

5 Click the frame's right-hand **Text Flow** button and then the two-column frame that's sitting behind.

Fixing the overlap

The intro is looking good but some body copy is flowing behind it, so let's fix that. We'll use a powerful master page feature here called **Detached** (p. 92), which lets you transform master frames and edit their properties, independently of their master page, on the publication page.

1 On the **Layers Panel**, select the applied master page's layer.

2 On the context toolbar, select **Detached**.

3 Select the inherited text frame on the left page.

4 Drag its top-centre handle to a position below the blue shape. My y-coordinate is *224 mm*.

5 Click **Finish** on the orange bar.

6 To make the body copy in this frame's columns start on the same baseline, add a column break after the first paragraph, followed by a paragraph break.

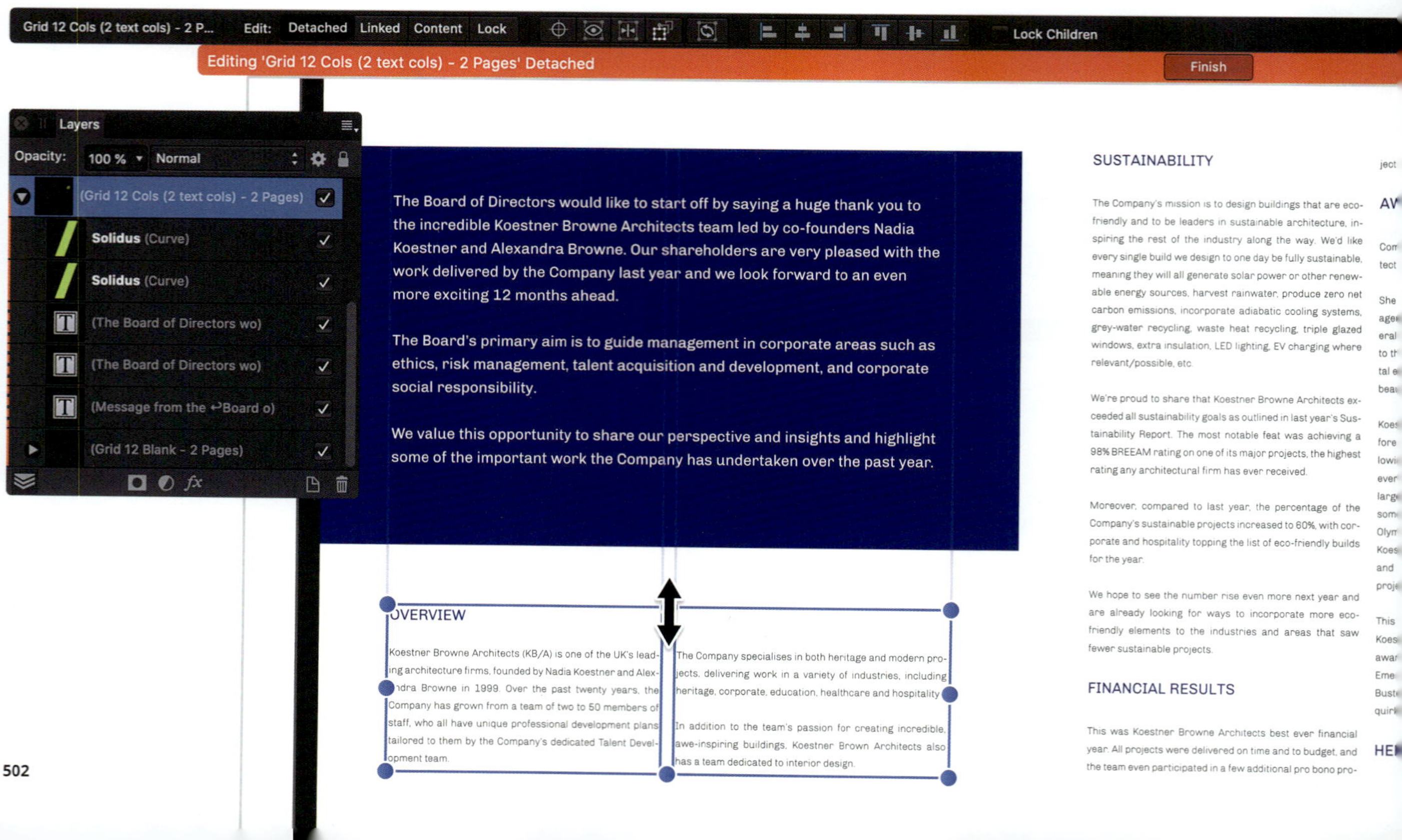

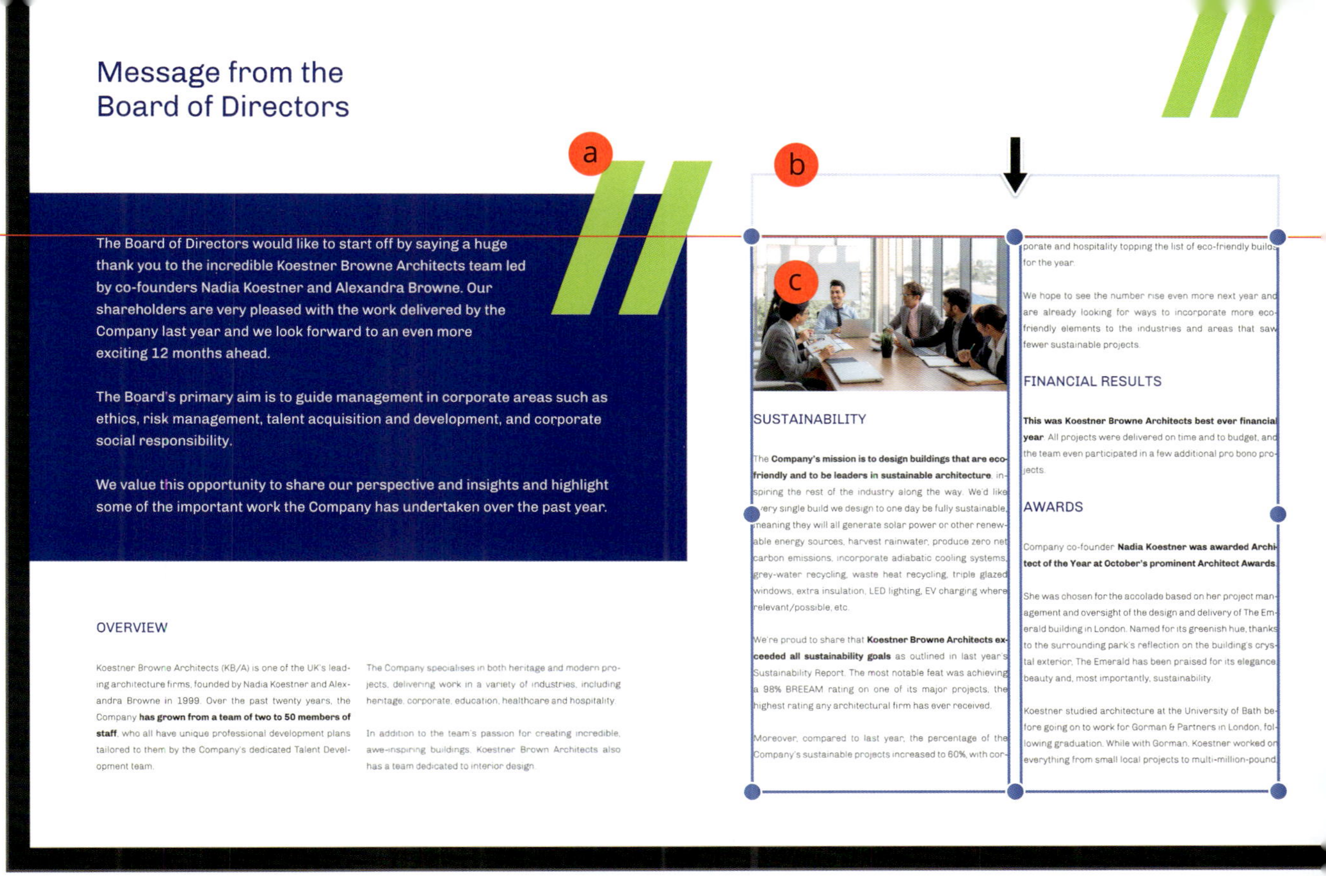

Finishing touches

1. Copy and paste the green double solidus from Page 1. Size and position it over the blue rectangle's top-right corner (a).
2. With the shapes selected, click **Show Text Wrap Settings** on the **Toolbar**.
3. Select the **Tight** wrap style and set **Distance From Text** to *8 mm* on all sides.

On the facing page, I again used **Detached** mode to drag the top of the text frame downwards into alignment with the text in the blue rectangle (b).

The picture frame at the top of the first column has the **Square** text wrap style applied, and **Distance From Text** of *7 mm* on its bottom and *0 mm* on the other sides (c).

I've drawn attention to key phrases in the body copy by applying my *Text Bold Black* character style.

On Page 6, I used **Detached** mode to hide the headline text frame and resize the larger frame to start at the top margin.

Where a paragraph style applies unwanted auto-hyphenation to a web or an email address, turn off auto-hyphenation for the affected paragraph via the **Paragraph Panel**. With long words in justified text, you may need to manually insert line breaks to eliminate large gaps between words.

COMPANY HIGHLIGHTS

Resource
KBA_company_highlights.rtf KBA_company_timeline.rtf KBA_maps.afdesign KBA_annual_report_7.afpub

There's only a small amount of text for this section, which requires creativity. I divided the page into two areas and borrowed some space at the top of Page 6.

In the first is a text frame containing the page's introduction. In the second, a timeline of important company activities from inception to the present.

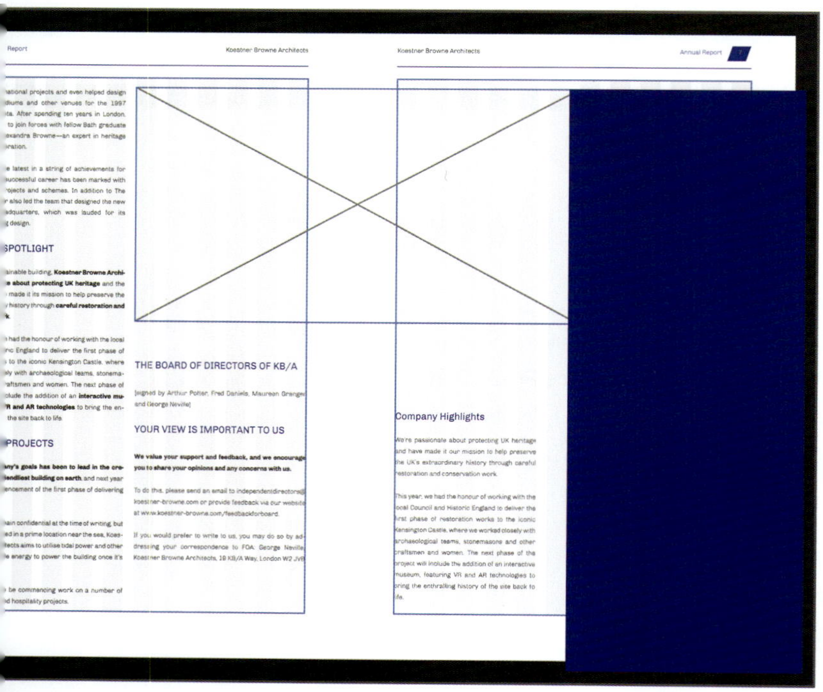

Dividing up the page

1. On the **Pages Panel**, drag and drop the *Grid 12 Blank* master onto *Page 7*.
2. Draw a rectangular picture frame, filled with our *Blue* swatch, spanning the last six column guides of the left page to the seventh column guide of the right page.
3. Give the frame a **Square** text wrap style and for its **Distance From Text** values, set **Bottom** to *10 mm* to force the final column's text out from under it.
4. Use the **Rectangle Tool** to draw a tall blue shape that fills the remaining width of Page 7 and down to the bottom-right bleed corner.

Adding the text

I placed KBA_company_timeline.rtf in a text frame over the elongated rectangle, then applied our usual body and subheading styles, the *KBA Text Green* character style to the years, and white (*CMYK 0,0,0,0*) to the rest.

In the white space at the bottom left, I added a text frame, placed KBA_company_highlights.rtf in it, and applied the same text styles used in the facing page's body.

The *Company Highlights* headline was copied from one of the master pages, moved across to Page 7, recoloured and set to ignore text wraps using the **Text Frame Panel**.

Adding graphical elements

I placed KBA_maps.afdesign, selected its *World map* artboard, and moved it into the blue area spanning Pages 6 and 7. I lowered its opacity and ensured Page 7's headline is in front of it.

To add a subtle architectural texture behind the map, I used the **Stock Panel** to find and place an image. The image inside the frame has the *Multiply* blend mode and a *Black & White* adjustment layer applied to it (p. 495).

Finally, I left-aligned a green double solidus to the first column guide, slightly overlapping the picture frame.

CURRENT YEAR FINANCIALS

Resource
KBA_financials.rtf KBA_Financial_CurrentYear.xlsx KBA_Financial_YearonYear.xlsx KBA_building_illustrations.afdesign KBA_annual_report_8&9.afpub

This section is an opportunity to use Affinity Publisher's ability to present any XLSX spreadsheet, e.g. Microsoft Excel, as a table.

Apply the *Grid 12 Col (3 text cols)* master to Page 8, and the *Grid 12 Blank* master to Page 9.

The left page is simple. Use **File > Place** to add KBA_financials.rtf file to the large text frame and cut and paste (without format) the first line into the headline text frame. Apply the usual paragraph and character styles to the subheading and body copy, and *Copy Text 08/14 Left Bullets* to the list.

Use **Text > Insert > Breaks > Column Break** to split the text so it steps down the page from left to right, as shown.

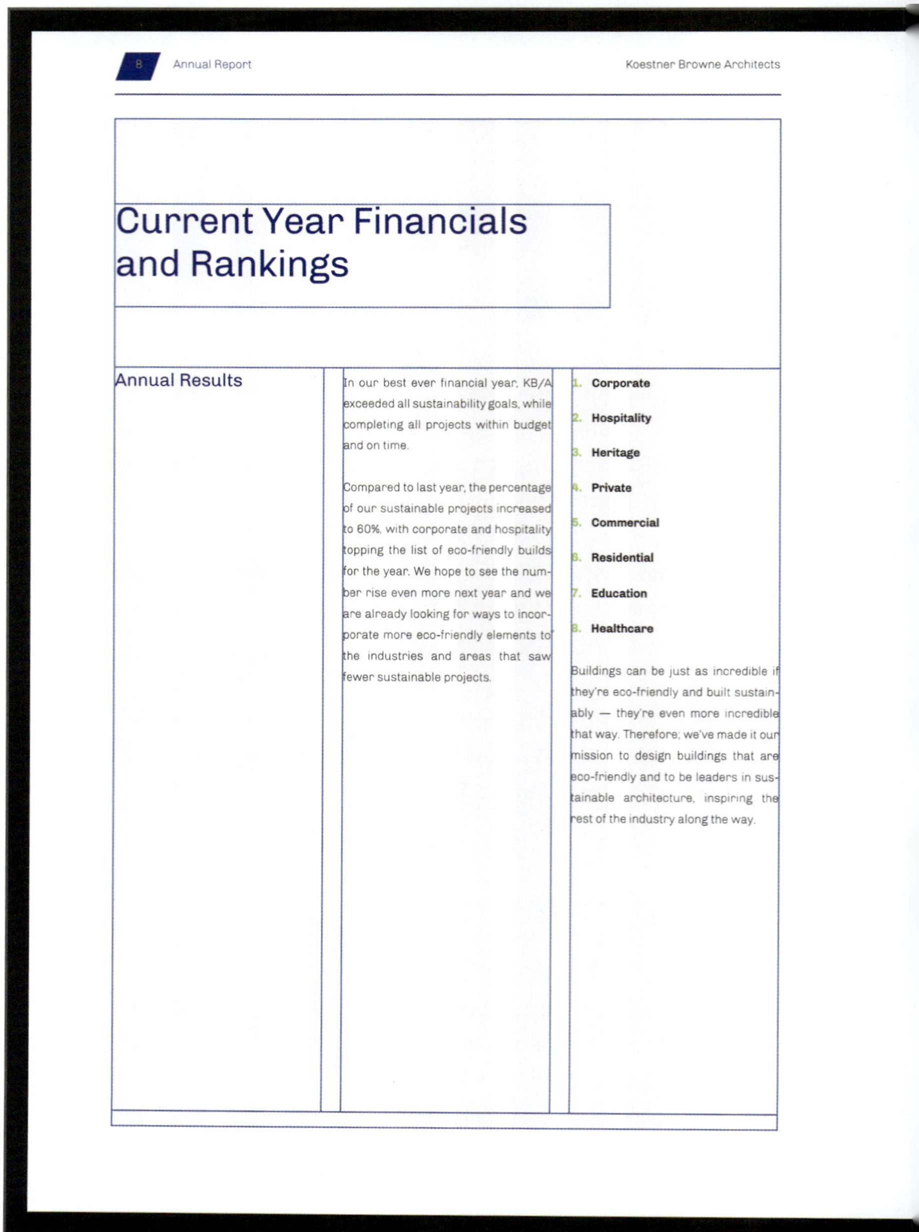

8 Annual Report Koestner Browne Architects

Current Year Financials and Rankings

Annual Results

In our best ever financial year, KB/A exceeded all sustainability goals, while completing all projects within budget and on time.

Compared to last year, the percentage of our sustainable projects increased to 60%, with corporate and hospitality topping the list of eco-friendly builds for the year. We hope to see the number rise even more next year and we are already looking for ways to incorporate more eco-friendly elements to the industries and areas that saw fewer sustainable projects.

1. **Corporate**
2. **Hospitality**
3. **Heritage**
4. **Private**
5. **Commercial**
6. **Residential**
7. **Education**
8. **Healthcare**

Buildings can be just as incredible if they're eco-friendly and built sustainably — they're even more incredible that way. Therefore, we've made it our mission to design buildings that are eco-friendly and to be leaders in sustainable architecture, inspiring the rest of the industry along the way.

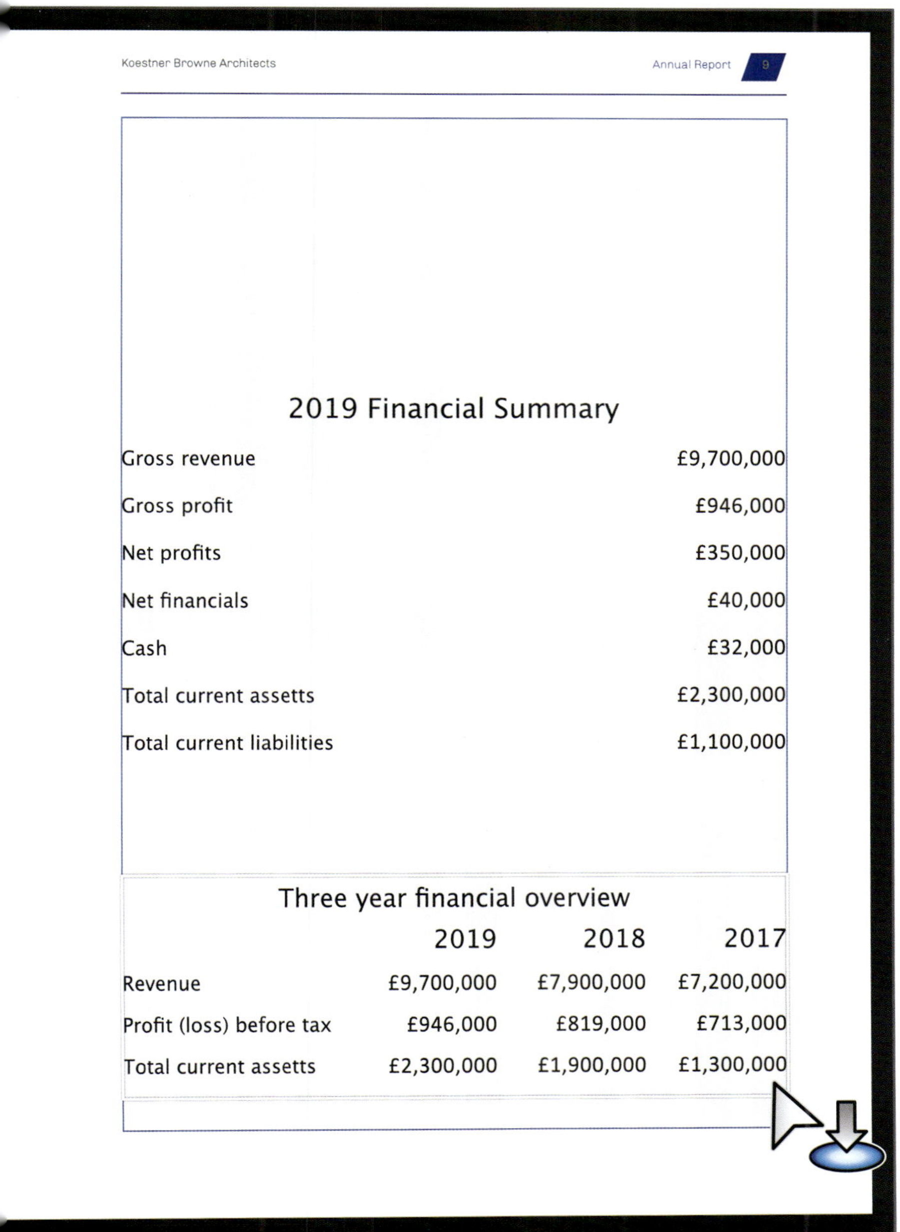
Koestner Browne Architects Annual Report 9

2019 Financial Summary

Gross revenue	£9,700,000
Gross profit	£946,000
Net profits	£350,000
Net financials	£40,000
Cash	£32,000
Total current assetts	£2,300,000
Total current liabilities	£1,100,000

Three year financial overview

	2019	2018	2017
Revenue	£9,700,000	£7,900,000	£7,200,000
Profit (loss) before tax	£946,000	£819,000	£713,000
Total current assetts	£2,300,000	£1,900,000	£1,300,000

Adding and styling spreadsheets

1 Select **File > Place** and choose the KBA_Financial_CurrentYear.xlsx file.

2 On Page 9, drag from the left margin to the right margin and then down. A preview of the spreadsheet's contents is shown throughout. Let go when it's an appropriate size.

3 Repeat steps 1 and 2 to place KBA_Financial_YearonYear.xlsx lower down the page.

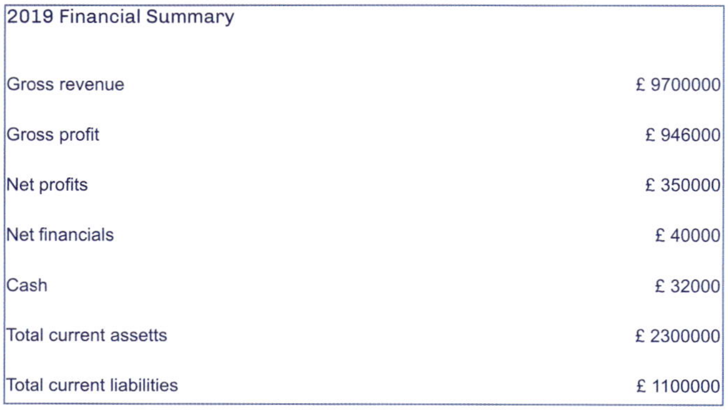

2019 Financial Summary	
Gross revenue	£ 9700000
Gross profit	£ 946000
Net profits	£ 350000
Net financials	£ 40000
Cash	£ 32000
Total current assetts	£ 2300000
Total current liabilities	£ 1100000

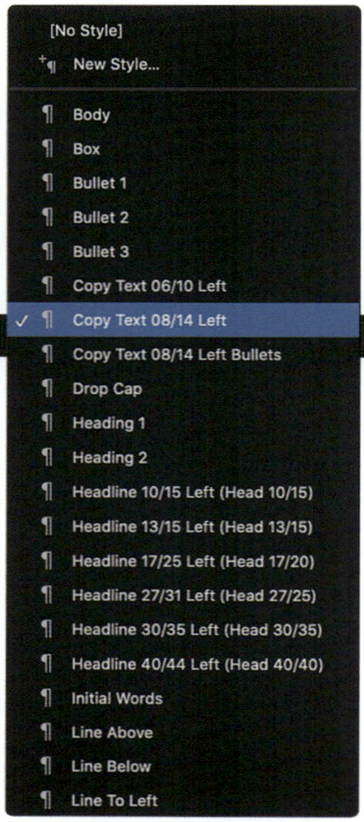

Styling the tables

Let's improve the data's presentation.

1 On the context toolbar, apply our *Copy Text 08/14 Left* paragraph style and the *Text KBA Blue* character style to the whole table.

2 Apply our *Headline 13/15 Left* paragraph style to the first row.

3 On the context toolbar, set the first row's alignment to **Top Align**.

4 Select all other rows and set their alignment to **Centre Vertically**.

5 Select each cell that contains numeric data and select **Right Align** on the context toolbar.

Adding fills and strokes

We can use cell fills and strokes to guide the reader's eyes.

1 On the first table, select the currency cells and set **Cell Fill** on the context toolbar to *CMYK 99,97,0,15* with **Opacity** of about 20%.

2 Select the bottom row and set its **Font Style** to *Bold*.

3 Select all rows except the first and, next to **Border** in the **Table Panel**'s **Stroke and Fill** section, select **All horizontal**.

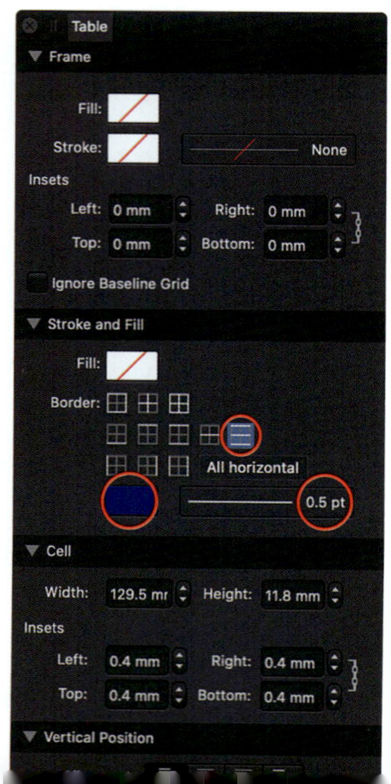

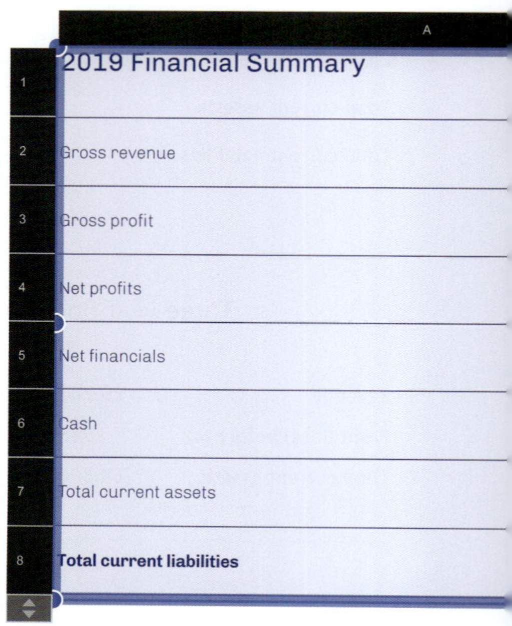

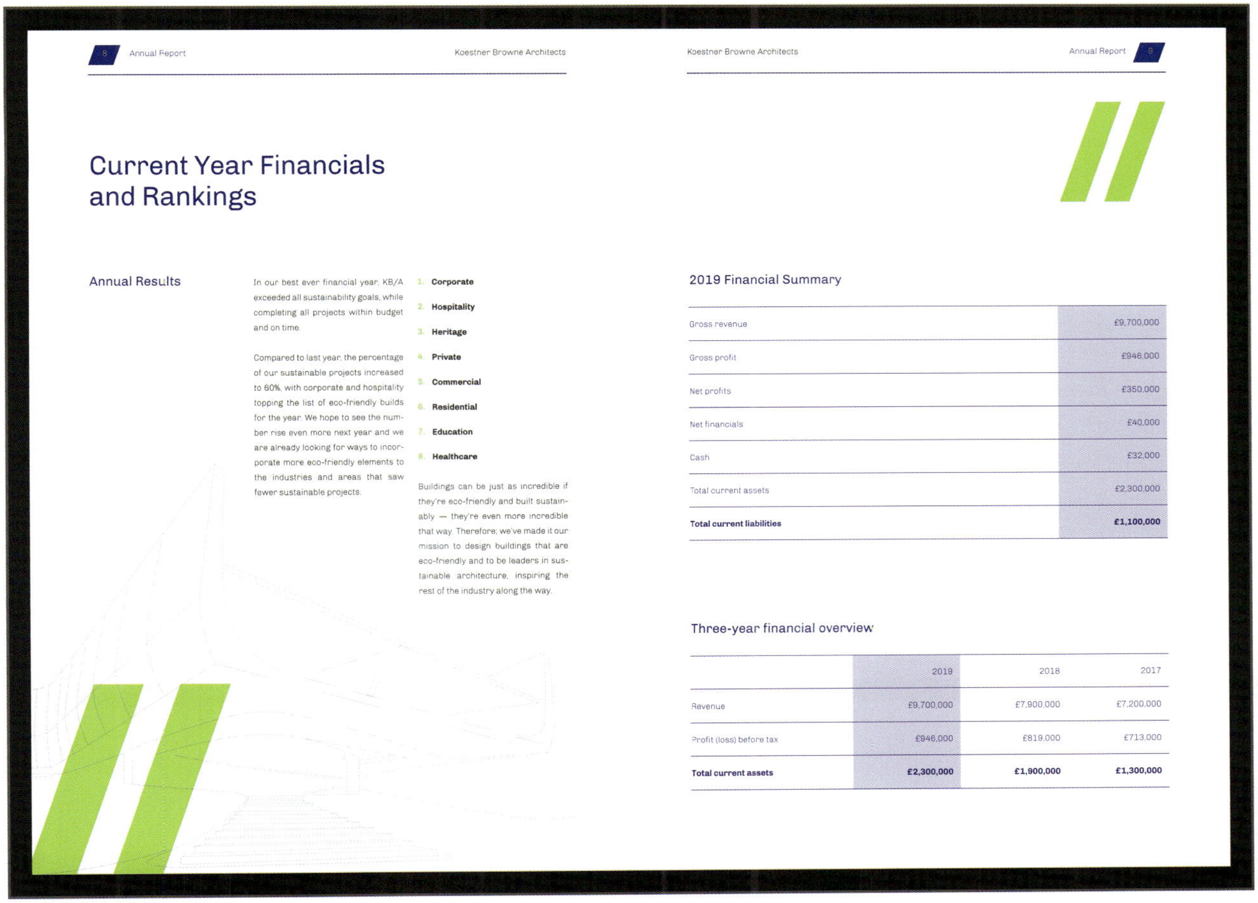

8 Annual Report — Koestner Browne Architects

Koestner Browne Architects — Annual Report 9

Current Year Financials and Rankings

Annual Results

In our best ever financial year, KB/A exceeded all sustainability goals, while completing all projects within budget and on time.

Compared to last year, the percentage of our sustainable projects increased to 60%, with corporate and hospitality topping the list of eco-friendly builds for the year. We hope to see the number rise even more next year and we are already looking for ways to incorporate more eco-friendly elements to the industries and areas that saw fewer sustainable projects.

1. **Corporate**
2. **Hospitality**
3. **Heritage**
4. **Private**
5. **Commercial**
6. **Residential**
7. **Education**
8. **Healthcare**

Buildings can be just as incredible if they're eco-friendly and built sustainably — they're even more incredible that way. Therefore; we've made it our mission to design buildings that are eco-friendly and to be leaders in sustainable architecture, inspiring the rest of the industry along the way.

2019 Financial Summary

Gross revenue	£9,700,000
Gross profit	£946,000
Net profits	£350,000
Net financials	£40,000
Cash	£32,000
Total current assets	£2,300,000
Total current liabilities	**£1,100,000**

Three-year financial overview

	2019	2018	2017
Revenue	£9,700,000	£7,900,000	£7,200,000
Profit (loss) before tax	£946,000	£819,000	£713,000
Total current assets	**£2,300,000**	**£1,900,000**	**£1,300,000**

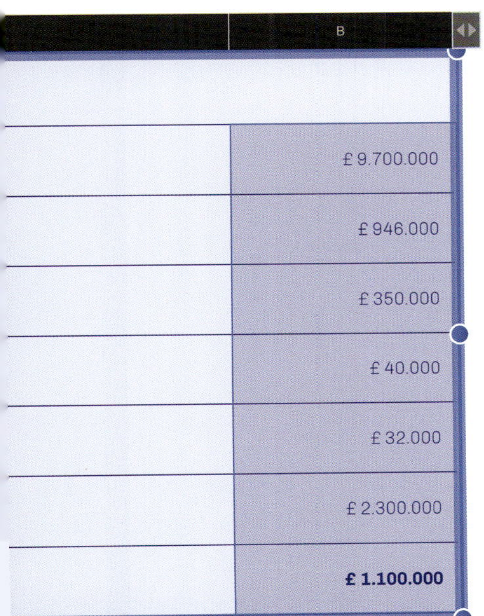

4 Set **Cell Stroke Fill** to our *Blue* swatch and **Cell Stroke** to *0.5 pt*.

Repeat these two procedures for the second table, but in step 1 of the second procedure select only the most recent year's column.

At the bottom-left and top-right corners of these pages, I've added green double solidi. The pair at the former position bleeds off the page, and the pair at the latter position was copied and pasted from the *Grid 12 Cols (3 text cols)* master page.

Finally, I've placed KBA_building_ illustrations.afdesign and selected its *Building 1* artboard as a background to the left page to fill some of the white space and add balance.

Resource
KBA_logos.afdesign KBA_team.rtf KBA_annual_report_12&13.afpub KBA_building_illustrations.afdesign

MEET THE TEAM

This section's presentation is quite different to the others. Most of Pages 12 and 13 will display KB/A's board of directors and senior team members in a grid and, for the former group, with a headshot. I applied the *Grid 12 Blank* master.

For continuity, I copied and pasted our usual headline text frame from one of the masters. On the left of Page 12 is a blue rectangle that bleeds off the page, over which I placed a text frame containing white body copy and our green solidi.

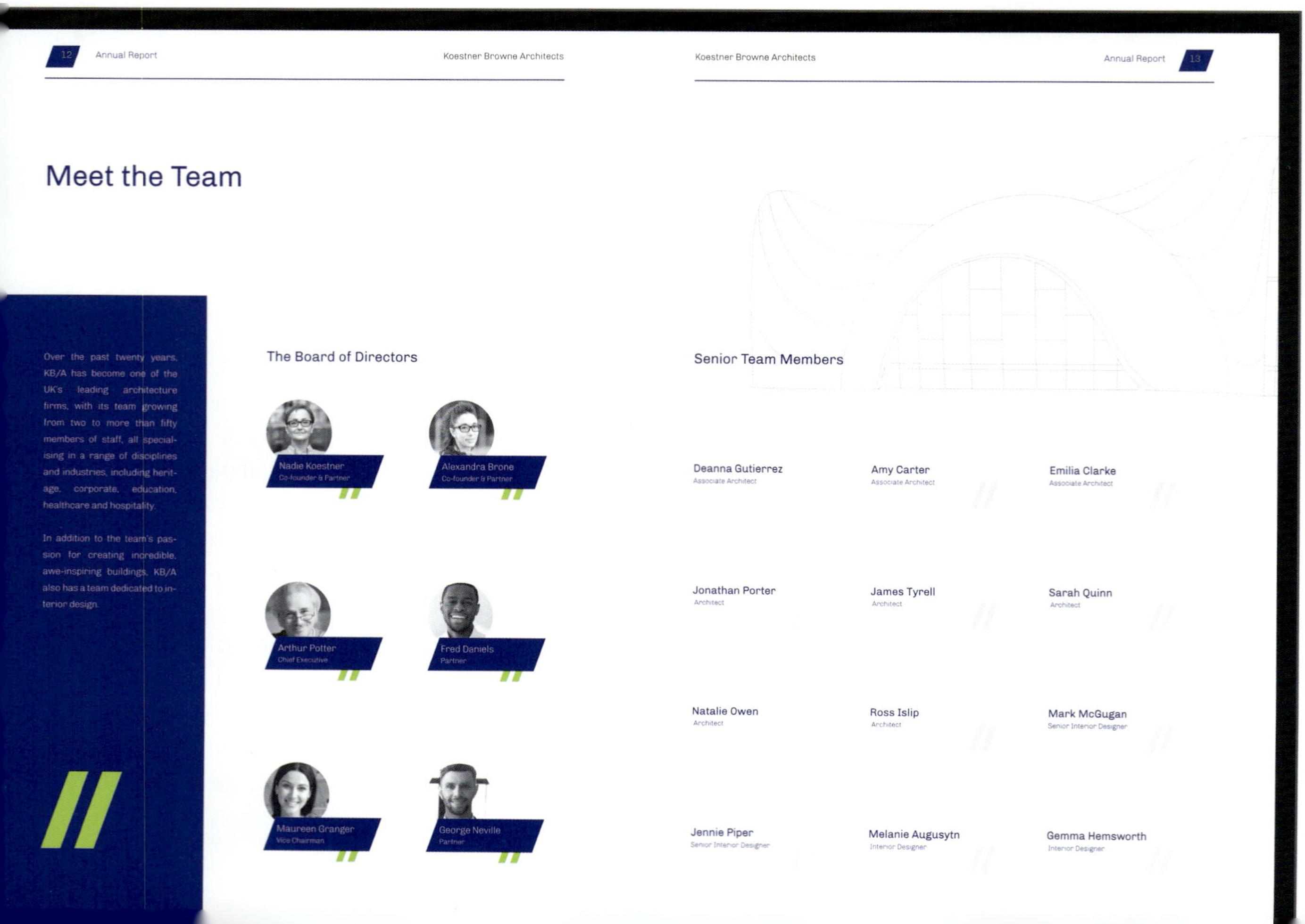

Creating the objects

We'll present each board member with a photo, their name and role inside a shape, and a double solidus.

1 Select the **Picture Frame Ellipse Tool** (F) and then hold the shift key (⇧) while drawing to create a circular frame.

2 Open the KBA_logos.afdesign file, copy the shape from the *Blue Solidus* artboard and paste on Page 12.

3 Select the **Node Tool** and turn the solidus into a parallelogram that spans three column guides. Drag selected pairs of nodes for best results.

4 Left-align the picture frame and parallelogram to a column guide.

5 Copy and paste the green double solidus from an earlier page.

6 Ensure the parallelogram's layer is in front of the picture frame and double solidus.

7 Size and position the double solidus to poke out from behind the parallelogram.

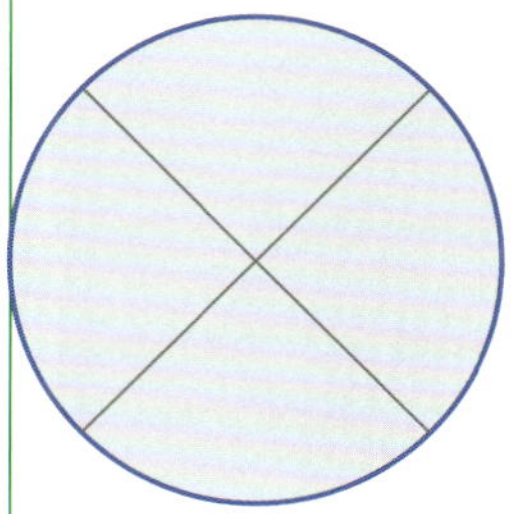

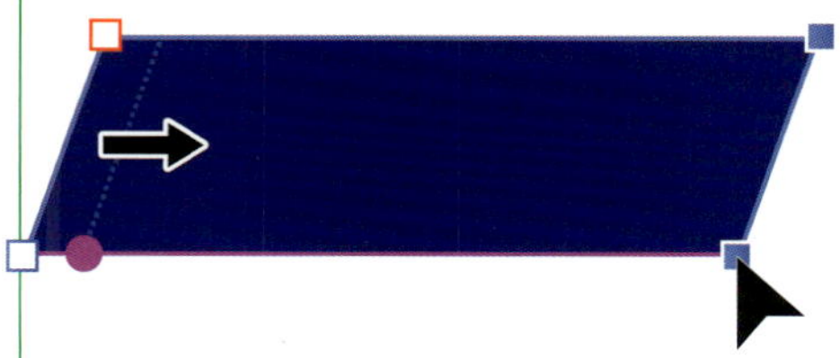

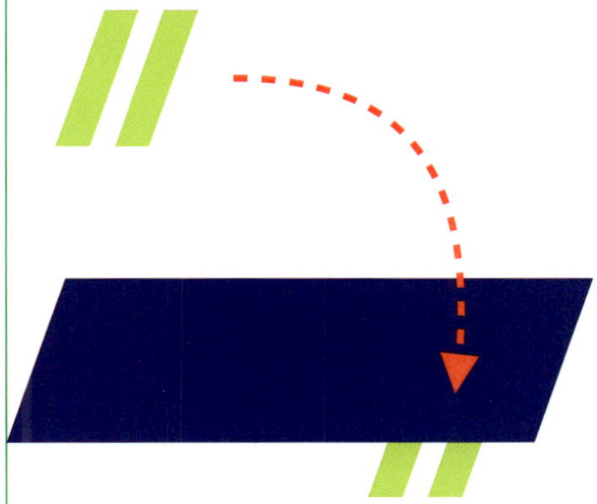

Adding name and role

1 Use the **Move Tool** to select the blue shape.

2 Select the **Frame Text Tool** and click inside the blue shape and type to create shape text.

3 On the **Text Frame Panel**, ensure **Columns** is set to *1*.

4 Apply the *Text White* character style to all of this text.

5 Type *Name*, press the Return ↵ key, then type *Role*.

6 Apply the *Copy Text 08/14 Left* paragraph style to the first line and *Copy Text 06/10 Left* to the second line.

7 On the **Text Frame Panel**, check **Ignore Baseline Grid** and set **Vertical Position** to *Centre Align*.

8 Select both rows. On the context toolbar, set **Leading** to *10 pt*.

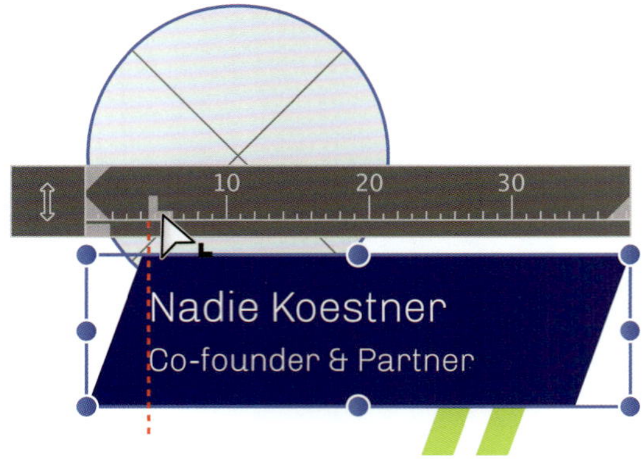

Inset the text

1 Select **View > Show Text Ruler**.

2 Select both rows of text, then click on the text frame's ruler to add a tab stop.

3 Type a tab character in front of each row.

4 Select both rows then drag the tab stop to indent and left-align, as shown.

On the left page, I arranged duplicates of these objects in a 2-by-3 grid. The resource KBA_team.rtf lists directors' names and roles that you can copy and paste (without format) to populate the text frames. Find suitable stock images by searching for *headshot*.

Many creative effects are possible using adjustments. For a consistent look to headshots, I applied **Layer > New Adjustment > Black & White**.

Adding the senior team members

Duplicate the objects for one director and move them to Page 13. I presented the senior team members a little differently, excluding the photo and coloured badge.

In a (regular-shaped) text frame, I applied the *Headline 10/15 Left* paragraph style to the first row to make it larger due to the absence of a background shape, but kept the second row's style as on the opposite page. I didn't manually adjust the leading here.

With the text frame set to have no fill colour, I applied the *Text KBA Blue* character style to the text.

I change the double solidus' fill colour to *CMYK 3,3,3,0,* and moved it further right.

I positioned duplicates of these objects in a 3-by-4 grid, with text on the top and bottom rows of team members aligned to equivalents on the facing page. To distribute the other two rows evenly in between, you can group each row's objects, select all four groups, then select **Layer > Alignment > Distribute Vertically**.

I placed a copy of KBA_building_illustrations.afdesign near the top right of the spread, again for balance, and this time selected the *Building 2* artboard.

Deanna Gutierrez
Associate Architect

Jonathon Porter
Architect

Natalie Owen
Architect

OFFICE AND CONTACT DETAILS

Resource

KBA_social_media.afdesign
KBA_location.rtf
KBA_contacts.rtf
KBA_annual_report_14&15.afpub
KBA_maps.afdesign
KBA_logos.afdesign

The last two interior pages provide company office and contact details. As with the previous spread, the *Grid 12 Blank* master page is applied to them, and a headline text frame copied and pasted on both pages.

Similar to Page 12, I placed the short introduction (KBA_location.rtf) in a text frame that's three column guides and gutters wide, in front of a blue rectangle. However, it's near the right margin this time.

The blue area bleeds off the page at the left and bottom. It's really two objects. The left portion is a picture frame containing another architectural image. The frame is filled with our *Blue* colour and has the *Multiply* blend mode and *Black & White* adjustment used earlier.

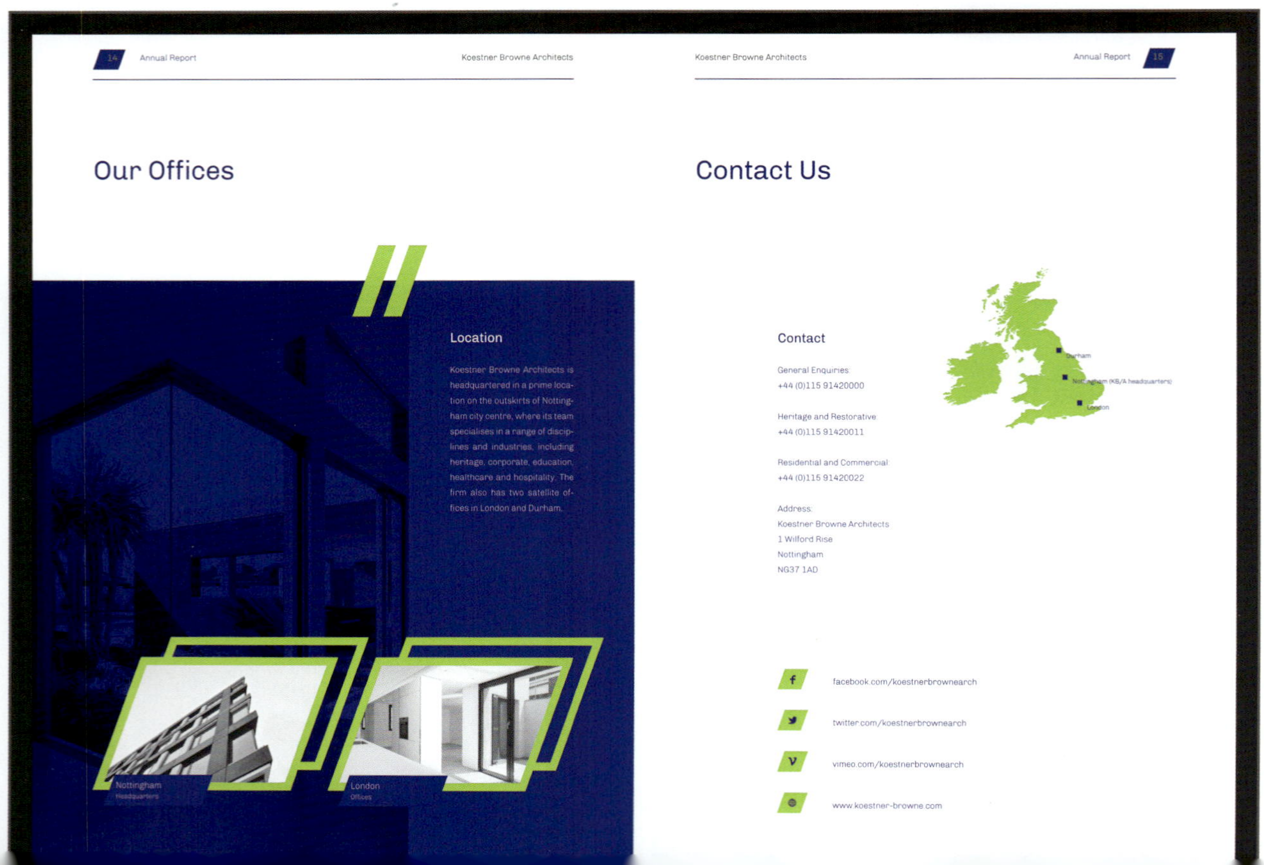

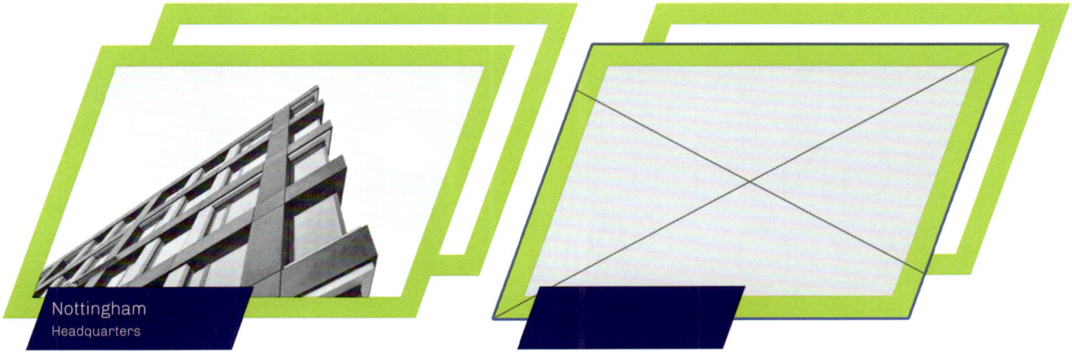

At the bottom of Page 14, I added images to represent the company headquarters and a regional office.

To present them with KB/A's look and feel, I used Affinity Publisher's ability to turn a widened solidus, or parallelogram, into a picture frame.

1 Open KBA_logos.afdesign. Copy the shape on the *Green Solidus* artboard and paste on Page 14.

2 With the shape selected, click the double-headed arrow on the **Colour Panel** to swap its fill and stroke colours.

3 On the **Stroke Panel**, set **Width** to *8 pt* and select **Align Stroke to Inside**.

4 Use the **Node Tool** to widen the shape (p. 494).

5 Duplicate this once and move the copy down and to the left.

6 With the copy selected, choose **Layer > Convert to Picture Frame**.

7 Duplicate both objects and move the copies to one side.

8 Use the **Stock Panel** to search for *office* and add a suitable image to each picture frame.

The text is styled like on the *Meet the Team* spread. Copy, paste and overwrite text from there.

Adding the final details

On the right page, I copied and pasted from KBA_contacts.rtf into text frames, then applied the *Headline 13/15 Left* and *Copy Text 08/14 Left* paragraph styles and *Text KBA Blue* character style as appropriate.

Each social network item displays an artboard (KBA_social_media.afdesign). These and the text above are left-aligned to the third column guide.

If your report will be distributed digitally as a PDF, you can use the **Hyperlinks Panel** to link the logos and text to the appropriate addresses.

For balance, I placed the *UK map* artboard from KBA_maps.afdesign. I drew blue rectangles and text frames, with *Copy Text 06/10 Left* applied, to label the company's office locations.

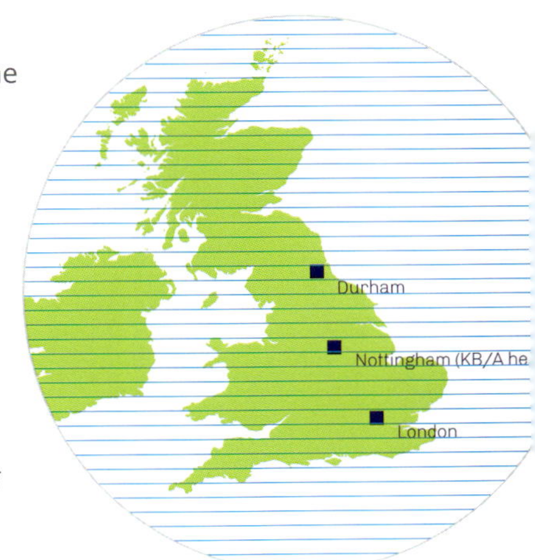

Resource

KBA_annual_report_final.afpub

DESIGN THE BACK COVER

The report's back cover is very similar to the front cover. To quickly build it, copy all objects from Page 1 and paste them on Page 16.

I changed the green-stroked rectangle to start at the left margin and bleed off the right—the report's spine edge.

I've aligned the objects on the third column guide. There are three text frames here, containing:

- The report title, with the *Headline 30/35 Left* paragraph style applied.
- The word *Contact*, set to our *Headline 13/15 Left* subheading paragraph style.
- The company name and address, set to our *Copy Text 08/14 Left* body copy paragraph style.

EXPORTING AS PDF

The CMYK document setup used for your annual report makes it easy to export a press-ready PDF file for supply to a professional printer.

The export process is the same as detailed in the KB/A Brand Guide project (p. 430). As the report makes extensive use of design elements that bleed off the page, ensure you check **Include bleed** to avoid white edges when your professional printer trims the paper to size.

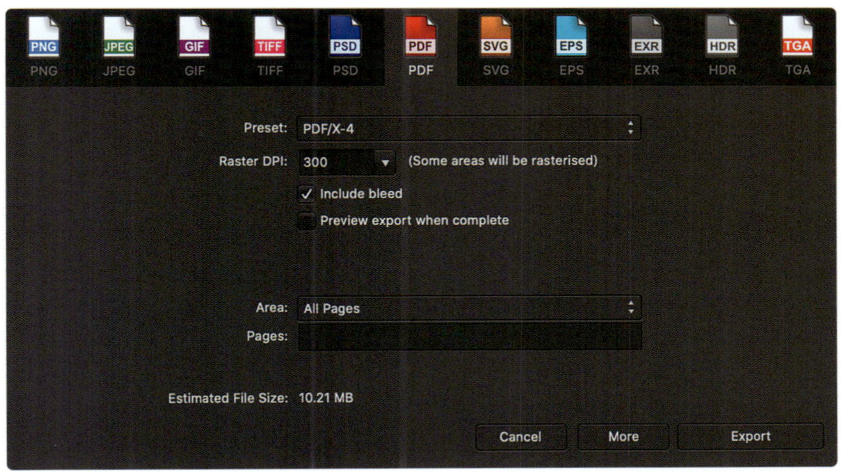

Koestner Browne Architects.
Annual Report
2020
Delivering over 20 years of
architectural growth and
winning architectural designs
14
Annual Report
Our Offices

2019 Financial Summ
Gross revenue
Gross profit
Net profits
Net financials
Cash
Total current assets
Total current liabilities
£ 40.000
£ 32.000
£ 2.300.000
£ 1.100.000
Three-year financial overview
2019
2018
2017
Revenue
Profit (loss) before tax
Total current assets
£ 9.700.000
£ 946.000
£ 2.300.000
£ 7.900.000
£ 819.000
£ 1.900.000
£ 7.200.000
£ 713.000
£ 1.300.000
Company H
Koestner Browne Architects
12
Annual Report
Meet the Team
The Board of Directors
Nadie Koestner
Co-founder & Partner
Over the past twenty years, KB/A has become one of the UK's leading architecture firms, with its team growing from two to more than fifty members of staff, all specialising in a range of disciplines and industries, including heritage, corporate, education, healthcare and hospitality.
In addition to the team's passion for creating incredible, awe-inspiring buildings, KB/A also has a team dedicated to interior design.
Koestner Browne Architects
Location
Koestner Browne Architects is headquartered in a prime location on the outskirts of Nottingham city centre, where its team specialises in a range of disciplines and industries, including heritage, corporate, education, healthcare and hospitality. The firm also has two satellite offices in London and Durham

INDEX

R

S

T

V

W

X

Z

Images used in this workbook and the accompanying downloadable resources have been created specifically for this workbook by the Affinity team and the Affinity Publisher Workbook contributors. Please see the Preface of this workbook for more information. Images supplied by contributors used in print are also credited in **Other Image Credits** in this section.

In addition, the following images have been used either under licence or with permission:

SHUTTERSTOCK CREDITS

The following images have been used under licence from Shutterstock.com

Cover	old-fashioned-barber-pole-against-red-65974987 © KennStilger47
	3d-business-building-80694952 © jl661227
	black-smoke-on-white-background-236953180 © G7 Stock
	white-ripped-art-paper-stuck-on-554221483 © alwaysloved afilm
	greyscale-head-shot-portrait-profile-beautiful-571926523 © LILAWA.COM
	acrylic-colors-water-abstract-background-isolated-618071477 © Rudchenko Liliia
	young-barber-standing-by-barbershop-682638016 © Pressmaster
	optical-art-abstract-background-wave-design-713137912 © N1chEZ
	optical-art-abstract-background-wave-design-717345820 © N1chEZ
	very-nice-young-woman-holding-big-1021598875 © AnastasiaNess
	white-paper-texture-background-cardboard-surface-1383830183 © Ton Weerayut Photograhper
	vector-abstract-geometric-design-psychedelic-swirling-1458549389 © Verlion
8-9	square-format-book-brochure-mock-template-717946594 © Gepardu
8-9, 25	technical-blue-background-drawings-details-mechanisms-797463940 © LIORIKI
10, 16-17, 74, 75	image-illustration/3d-building-86654458 © jl661227
10, 16-17, 74, 75	modern-interior-20577260 © Worldpics
10, 16-17, 74, 75	double-exposure-portrait-two-beautiful-fashion-579705169 © Tuzemka
10, 16-17, 74, 75, 135	highly-detailed-closeup-portrait-young-good-79972978 © CURAphotography
10, 16-17, 74, 75	machu-picchu-peru-southa-america-unesco-389136313 © Anton Ivanov
10, 16-17, 74, 75	hikers-backpacks-relaxing-on-top-mountain-525845020 © Dudarev Mikhail
10, 16-17, 74, 75	agricultural-terraces-sacred-valley-moray-cuzco-718031926 © Tetyana Dotsenko
10, 16-17, 74, 75	vinicunca-cusco-region-peru-montana-de-661803538 © emperorcosar
10, 16-17, 74, 75, 137	llama-macro-people-talking-background-machu-1068207905 © John Akerman
10, 16-17	long-hair-llamas-mountains-andes-peru-357551144 © Pavel Svoboda Photography
10, 16-17	view-of-the-ancient-inca-city-of-machu-picchu-298363703 © Aleksandra H. Kossowska
10, 16-17	colca-canyon-perusouth-america-incas-build-176106587 © vitmark
10, 16-17, 137	town-copacabana-lake-titicaca-during-sunset-1057096418 © Dudarev Mikhail
10, 16-17, 74, 75	portrait-beautiful-woman-flying-hair-wind-478418185 © Coy_Creek
25, 73	modern-cars-studio-room-3d-illustration-735402217 © Digital Pen
25	illustration-fictional-district-plan-quarter-residential-417486214 © shurkin_son
25, 27	cinematic-portrait-girl-pink-hair-neon-1181887693 © Roberto Vivancos
25, 27, 137	young-stylish-female-hipster-standing-near-755936482 © GaudiLab
25, 27, 137	young-stylish-woman-wearing-sparkling-jacket-1055737343 © BLACKDAY
25, 27, 137	cinematic-portrait-young-black-man-cool-1196549857 © Roberto Vivancos
27, 73, 128-129	crazy-hipster-guy-emotions-collage-magazine-1015260442 © san4ezz
27, 73	extreme-parkour-business-center-young-boy-232935316 © oneinchpunch
27, 73	skater-boy-practicing-skate-park-499900126 © oneinchpunch
27, 73	young-hipster-man-cap-standing-looking-763561555 © Mark Nazh
27, 73	portrait-pretty-sexy-young-seductive-woman-601562822 © sergey causelove
27, 73	parkour-practitioner-illustration-flat-vector-elements-778537711 © AlexeySolovyev
27	beautiful-african-american-woman-black-curly-1048199032 © MPH Photos
37	backstage-makeup-257265541 © Kokulina
37	fashion-model-walks-runway-yellow-pantsuit-624368693 © Aleksei Isachenko
37	famous-jet-set-couple-getting-out-481445731 © Corepics VOF
44, 93, 131, 148-149	black-vintage-custom-motorcycle-motorbike-caferacer-655905334 © Kaponia Aliaksei
44, 93, 131, 148-149	bag-on-wooden-background-171070082 © Yermolov
44, 93, 131, 148-149	travel-boots-vintage-shabby-shoes-old-1196768131 © Janosch Kunze
73, 134	men-watches-on-wooden-table-507857227 © Carlos Andre Santos
73	military-style-watch-brown-leather-strap-352303784 © Nor Gal
73, 137	businessman-luxury-style-men-button-on-1120961183 © Claudia K
73, 131	watch-mens-brown-leather-strap-on-617477987 © fotoliza
73	city-bicycle-fixed-gear-isolated-on-435493039 © sripfoto
74, 75	young-female-rock-climber-sunset-kalymnos-171542741 © Photobac
79	cropped-rear-view-successful-businesswoman-busy-406848577 © WAYHOME Studio
110, 111	ice-climber-green-jacket-orange-helmet-664503520 © DCrane
125	conceptual-image-light-bulb-on-background-322131167 © Sergey Nivens

125	beautiful-woman-doing-yoga-on-cliff-435680188 © Merla
133	fashion-pretty-young-woman-wearing-straw-447987058 © Rohappy
137	portrait-of-young-attractive-woman-sitting-in-lecture-hall-1029203734 © MRProduction
137	fire-show-artist-breathe-fire-in-the-dark-1164964681 © Suvorov_Alex
145, 137	male-model-walks-runway-beige-suit-1174728280 © Belish
145	fashion-show-runway-catwalk-event-backstage-402160099 © CatwalkPhotos
145	portrait-beautiful-woman-studio-backstage-187375904 © Alex Andrei
152, 444, 459, 483, 510, 512, 519	business-woman-portrait-618365528 © The Art of Pics
152, 444, 459, 510	portrait-woman-out-office-718046350 © Mamasuba
152, 449	abstract-3d-wireframe-building-1213107082 © Alesandro14
153	portrait-handsome-man-smiling-525264961 © Merla
153	modern-glass-building-157927313 © zhangyang
154-155	blank-a4-photorealistic-brochure-mockup-on-670958233 © PrimeMockup
154-155	red-hair-girl-dressed-green-shirt-1083211346 © Oleksii Dubrovskyi
154-155, 296, 297	red-hair-girl-dressed-green-shirt-1083211367 © Oleksii Dubrovskyi
154-155	green-shirt-black-dress-leather-handbag-1083211343 © Oleksii Dubrovskyi
154-155	red-hair-girl-dressed-green-shirt-1083211352 © Oleksii Dubrovskyi
156-157	group-full-body-people-620517593 © Djomas
156-157	brown-electric-guitar-amplifier-isolated-on-240529498 © jirawatfoto
156-157	guitar-amplifier-on-white-background-164432561© Garsya
157	studio-audio-instrument-cable-extending-disappearing-257748331 © optimark
158-159	vector-architectural-sketch-modern-exclusive-house-1116854846 © ornavi
158-159	scrolls-engineering-drawings-isolated-render-on-204329143 © urfin
158-159	portrait-smiling-black-woman-striped-shirt-667485685 © mimagephotography
158-159	3d-rendering-modern-cozy-house-garage-687170326 © korisbo
158-159	3d-rendering-modern-cozy-house-garage-687170329 © korisbo
158-159	3d-rendering-modern-cozy-house-garage-691354642 © korisbo
158-159	3d-rendering-modern-cozy-house-garage-704556310 © korisbo
161, 219	grand-canal-basilica-santa-maria-della-116504368 © ESB Professional
161, 219	surfer-ocean-top-view-1071223274 © Anton Watman
161, 219	girl-red-dress-amazing-tibumana-waterfall-1136038235 © Aurelia Teslaru
161, 219	traveling-asian-jungle-1278664513 © Arafat shafin99
162, 137	rearview-group-carefree-young-girlfriends-having-1075198985 © Flamingo Images
162	set-stylish-clothes-woman-summer-collage-635321216 © ivastasya
162	set-stylish-clothes-collection-collage-womens-706235647 © ivastasya
162	sunglasses-isolated-on-white-244200697 © Lifestyle Travel Photo
162	set-fashion-jeans-146514308 © Karkas
162	set-fashionable-stylish-clothes-146513426 © Karkas
167	sprinkling-chocolate-brownie-icing-sugar-horizontal-351448700 © Karpenkov Denis
167	pancakes-blueberries-on-dark-wooden-table-319683212 © Karpenkov Denis
167	chocolate-cake-on-dark-background-574305673 © thepiwko
168-169	interior-design-dining-kitchen-area3d-illustration3d-1488645683 © Ume illustration
199-202, 204, 205, 207, 209	cardboard-texture-170577635 © belkos
216-217	young-man-reading-magazine-1166326951 © Bro Crock
223, 429, 488	blank-magazine-journal-newspaper-notebook-mockup-1727514202 © Angel_AMX
244, 245, 254	koi-fish-694633309 © gunungkawi
262-263	blank-3d-illustration-magazines-mockup-on-534986113 © mileswork
265, 267, 280, 283, 286, 289	fashion-portrait-young-blond-woman-flowers-640873981 © Max Frost
265, 284-285, 290, 291	hat-beige-blouse-turqoise-pleats-skirt-1086666065 © Oleksii Dubrovskyi
265, 267, 274-277, 288	girl-model-white-dress-glasses-blue-1133304371 © Street Style Photo
267	book-blank-cover-isolated-mockup-realistic-1234147417 © David Kalosson
267, 297, 299	red-hair-girl-dressed-green-shirt-1083211367 © Oleksii Dubrovskyi
274, 278	girl-model-white-dress-glasses-blue-1133304347 © Street Style Photo
274, 287, 298	girl-model-white-dress-glasses-blue-1133304308 © Street Style Photo
274 ,288	girl-model-white-dress-glasses-blue-1133304380 © Street Style Photo
274, 279, 280, 287, 298	girl-model-white-dress-glasses-blue-1133304353 © Street Style Photo
274, 287, 298	girl-model-white-dress-glasses-blue-1133304344 © Street Style Photo
286, 288, 299	fashion-portrait-young-blond-woman-flowers-640873864 © Max Frost
290, 296, 297	outdoor-photo-beautiful-blond-woman-long-243274207 © Dari Ya
291	light-bedroom-wooden-ceiling-large-bed-552591901 © Photographee.eu
291	young-red-hair-girl-hat-dressed-1086666185 © Oleksii Dubrovskyi
291	young-red-hair-girl-hat-dressed-1086666182 © Oleksii Dubrovskyi
292	beautiful-stylish-girl-posing-trendy-living-1311811970 © Lightfield Studios
296, 297	red-hair-girl-dressed-green-shirt-1083211346 © Oleksii Dubrovskyi

296, 297	closeup-fashionable-woman-legs-wear-beige-1386912383 © Viktoria Minkova
299	girl-model-white-dress-glasses-blue-1133304374 © Street Style Photo
301	clipboard-3d-illustration-on-white-background-177953597 © Montego
301, 323	black-pencil-on-white-background-soft-1188751594 © Lifestyle Graphic
303	simple-clock-watch-on-white-tile-117918247 © Andrey_Kuzmin
303	close-stack-papers-on-white-background-129400130 © Picsfive
326-327	blank-spread-open-book-womans-hands-396277846 © Boumen Japet
366-367	samples-color-cardstock-paper-292195607 © Anton Starikov
369	close-stack-papers-on-white-background-129400130 © Picsfive
388-389, 422-423	blank-mock-vertical-street-poster-billboard-425371828 © photodonato
217, 389-423	smiling-mature-man-sitting-leaning-on-716822902 © Flamingo Images
420-421	three-white-paper-poster-mock-497244337 © Big Picture House
428	blank-a4-photorealistic-landscape-brochure-mockup-1502126720 © Hussainqev
428, 452	mockup-business-brand-template-on-gray-324563438 © mileswork
430-431	blank-a4-photorealistic-landscape-brochure-mockup-1502126744 © Hussainqev
430-431	blank-a4-photorealistic-landscape-brochure-mockup-1502126720 © Hussainqev
430, 445, 459	beautiful-modern-house-night-scene-382359508 © Alexandre zveiger
430, 450, 458, 514	luxurious-home-interior-exterior-new-empty-107394701© Image Supply
439	female-hand-holding-color-swatches-trend-1575832684 © Igisheva Maria
442, 443	3d-building-landscape-79891999 © han871111
452, 505, 483, 519	green-futuristic-skyscraper-environment-architecture-concepts-530471596 © Tostphoto
453, 514	interior-new-house-modern-white-kitchen-141908515 © Alexandre zveiger
453	modern-dark-grey-laptop-reflections-shadows-1506458510 © Yuliya Team
453	new-version-slim-smartphone-blank-white-1432609280 © Issarawat Tattong
456	open-empty-white-box-isolated-on-660629089 © Mega Pixel
460-461, 480-481	photo-template-branding-identity-graphic-designers-185706821 © Vitalliy
464	floating-business-card-mockup-isolated-on-1334268443 © sdecoret
482-483, 518-519, 458-459	blank-white-postcard-flyer-on-grey-507923374 © Ink Drop
483, 495, 514, 515, 519	modern-office-building-617520431 © Grand Warszawski
503	businesspeople-discussing-together-conference-room-during-1374784202 © Crafter
510	many-happy-diverse-ethnicity-different-young-1733872811 © Fizkes

OTHER IMAGE CREDITS

Preface, 183, 187, 365	Affinity Publisher Workbook contributor headshots used with permission of contributors
4	affinity-publisher-AOTY © Apple, Inc., used with permission
8-9, 25	Exploded Gearbox © Fernando Martins Ribeiro, used under licence and with permission
29	Stock panel 'explore', thumbnail images shown from Unsplash. Creators of images shown in thumbnails in order of appearance: Harley Davidson, Harley Davidson, Harley Davidson, Alessandro Erbetta, Andrew Neel, Bryan Minear, Jamie Street, Erico Marcelino, Andreas Chu, Joshua Earle, L B, Alin Zainescu, Tony Bertolino, Maurice Smeets, Rosan Harmenson
80	Brand Guidelines template mockup © Occy Designs. Images from Unsplash.com
80	Magazine template mockup © Luuqas Design. Images from Unsplash.com
80	Annual Report template mockup © Egotype. Images from Unsplash.com
80-81	Gemini Brochure template mockup © Slide Station. Images from Unsplash.com
80	Project Proposal template mockup © ID Vision Studio.
80, 161, 163, 219	Voyager Magazine template mockup © Visuel Colonie. Images from Unsplash.com (unless specified)
80	Architecture Portfolio template mockup © Studio Bons. Images from Unsplash.com
80	Cookbook template mockup © Occy Designs. Images from Unsplash.com
104	My Gang © James Ritson, used with permission
127	Geese © James Ritson, used with permission
132	Stock panel 'summer' thumbnail images shown from Unsplash. Creators of images shown in thumbnails in order of appearance: Sean O., Ethan Robertson, , Vicko Mozara, Angelo Pantazis, Angello Pro, Atienne Girardet, 煜翔 肖, takahiro taguchi, Aleksandr Eremin, Ali Abdul Rahman, Marissa Rodriguez, Corey Agopian, Nattu Adnan, Lionel Gustave, Alex Bunday, Simon Rae, Brooke Lark, Raphaël Biscaldi, jcob nasyr, Ian Dooley, Daan Huttinga, Mohamed Nashah, Shot On DJI, Link Hoang, Annie Spratt, Luise Schumann
132	heather-ford-1571634298-unsplash (pineapple) https://unsplash.com/photos/vAfCO8xrz0I © the_modern_life_mrs
135	Headshots of members of the Affinity Spotlight team (Charlotte Thomson-Morley, Umar Lawson, Melanie Khareghat) © Serif (Europe) Ltd.
160, 186, 187, 196, 207	rootbox-ribeiro-englishgarden.jpg © Fernando Martins Ribeiro, used under licence and with permission
160, 187, 196, 207	rootbox-ribeiro-farmersdelight.jpg © Fernando Martins Ribeiro, used under licence and with permission
160, 177, 187, 188, 196, 207	rootbox-ribeiro-paradise.jpg © Fernando Martins Ribeiro, used under licence and with permission
160, 196, 207	rootbox-ribeiro-berries.png © Fernando Martins Ribeiro, used under licence and with permission
165, 167	https://creativemarket.com/feelthis/4768929-Celen-Shadow-Mockup-Scene-Creator/ © Feel This

178,183, 199, 201-207	Root Box logo created and supplied by Matt Searston for Serif (Europe) Ltd.
183	Root Box logo concepts created and supplied by Matt Searston for Serif (Europe) Ltd.
188, 196, 207	rootbox-ribeiro-holdingbox.jpg © Fernando Martins Ribeiro, used under licence and with permission
198-199, 203, 207, 211	rootbox-ribeiro-kitchen.jpg © Fernando Martins Ribeiro, used under licence and with permission
201, 204, 207, 209-210	rootbox-ribeiro-overhead.png © Fernando Martins Ribeiro, used under licence and with permission
217, 256	Derwent Lake © James Ritson, used with permission
220-221, 223, 226, 238	magazine_profile_EleniDebo_RedCheecks.jpg © Eleni Debo, used under licence and with permission
220-221, 240, 254, 240-241	magazine_profile_EleniDebo_Ramen.jpg © Eleni Debo, used under licence and with permission
220-221, 223, 238	magazine_profile_EleniDebo_PortraitBW.jpg © Eleni Debo, used under licence and with permission
223, 238, 239, 240, 254	magazine_profile_EleniDebo_Raimondas.jpg © Eleni Debo, used under licence and with permission
239, 241	magazine_profile_EleniDebo_PublicServants.jpg © Eleni Debo, used under licence and with permission
244-245	magazine_tutorial © Moon Lotus Dreams / Roberta Burattini, used under licence and with permission
254, 257, 262-263	magazine_cover_the_final_full_artwork_by_moon_lotus_dreams.jpg © Moon Lotus Dreams, used under licence and with permission
275	Stock panel 'fashion' thumbnail images shown from Unsplash. Creators of images shown in thumbnails in order of appearance: Dom Hill, freestocks, Lauren Fleischmann, STIL, Tamara Bellis, Alexandra Gorn, Ahmed Carter, Atikh Bana, Alexi Romano, Ian Dooley, Priscilla Du Preez, Alex Blăjan, S O C I A L . C U T, Hannah Morgan, Tamara Bellis, Judeus Samson, Nordwood, Clem Onojeghuo, Jason Leung, Naeim Jafarion, Analise Benevides, Darko Mitev, Hipster Mum, Alex Iby, Brooke Cagle, Dami Adebayo, Fezbot2000, Sarah Dorweiler, Charisse Kenion, Calvin Lupiya
326-327	alice_chapter_III.png © Steve Simpson, used under licence and with permission
329, 354	alice_chapter_II.png © Steve Simpson, used under licence and with permission
329, 359	alice_chapter_VII.png © Steve Simpson, used under licence and with permission
329	alice_chapter_X1.png © Steve Simpson, used under licence and with permission
342, 343, 353, 354	alice_chapter_I-drinkme.png © Steve Simpson, used under licence and with permission
344, 360	alice_chapter_IX-gryphon.png © Steve Simpson, used under licence and with permission
364-365	Steve Simpson illustrations © Steve Simpson, used under licence and with permission
365	Steve Simpson portrait © Steve Simpson, used under licence and with permission
368	alice_chapter_IV.png © Steve Simpson, used under licence and with permission
363, 372-375, 380-381, 383, 385-387	artwork_alicecover.jpg © Steve Simpson, used under licence and with permission
374	ZTF Logo © Zeune Type Foundry, used with permission
443	Stock panel 'architecture' thumbnail images shown from Unsplash. Creators of images shown in thumbnails in order of appearance: Alex Wong, Lance Anderson, Joel Filipe, Maarten Deckers, Anders Jildén, 贝莉儿 Danist, Tobias Keller, Luca Bravo, Marc Olivier Jodoin, Jimmy Chang, Joel Filipe, Joel Filipe, Joakim Nådell, Riccardo Oliva, Christian Perner, Farhan Khan, Ricardo Gomez Angel, Simone Hutsch, Matthew Henry, Sandro Katalina, All Bong, Kimon Maritz, Luca Bravo, Verne Ho, Etienne Beauregard, Guillaume Bolduc, Colin Carter, bantersnaps, Scott Webb, Christian Perner

FONT COPYRIGHTS

Special Elite © 2011, Astigmatic
Caladea © Carolina Giovagnoli and Andres Torresi
Crimson Pro © 2010, Sebastian Kosch (sebastian@aldusleaf.org), with Reserved Font Name "Crimson Text"
Chivo © 2011, Omnibus-Type (www.omnibus-type.com | omnibus.type@gmail.com)
Poppins © 2014, Indian Type Foundry (info@indiantypefoundry.com)
DM Serif Display © 2014 Adobe (http://www.adobe.com/), with Reserved Font Name "Source"
Muli © 2011 by Vernon Adams (vern@newtypography.co.uk), with Reserved Font Name "Muli"
Wallington Pro © 2014, Zeune Ink Foundry (https://ink.creativezeune.com) with Reserved Font Name "Wallington Pro"
Istok Web © Andrey Panov
IBM Plex Sans © 2017, Mike Abbink, IBM BX&D, in collaboration with Bold Monday

NOTES

NOTES (CONTINUED)

AFFINITY Publisher Mac

PUBLISHER PERSONA SHORTCUTS

For Designer Persona and Photo Persona keyboard shortcuts, refer to the first pages of the respective cheat sheets at:

affin.co/afdmacshortcuts
affin.co/afpmacshortcuts

AFFINITY Publisher | Windows

PUBLISHER PERSONA SHORTCUTS

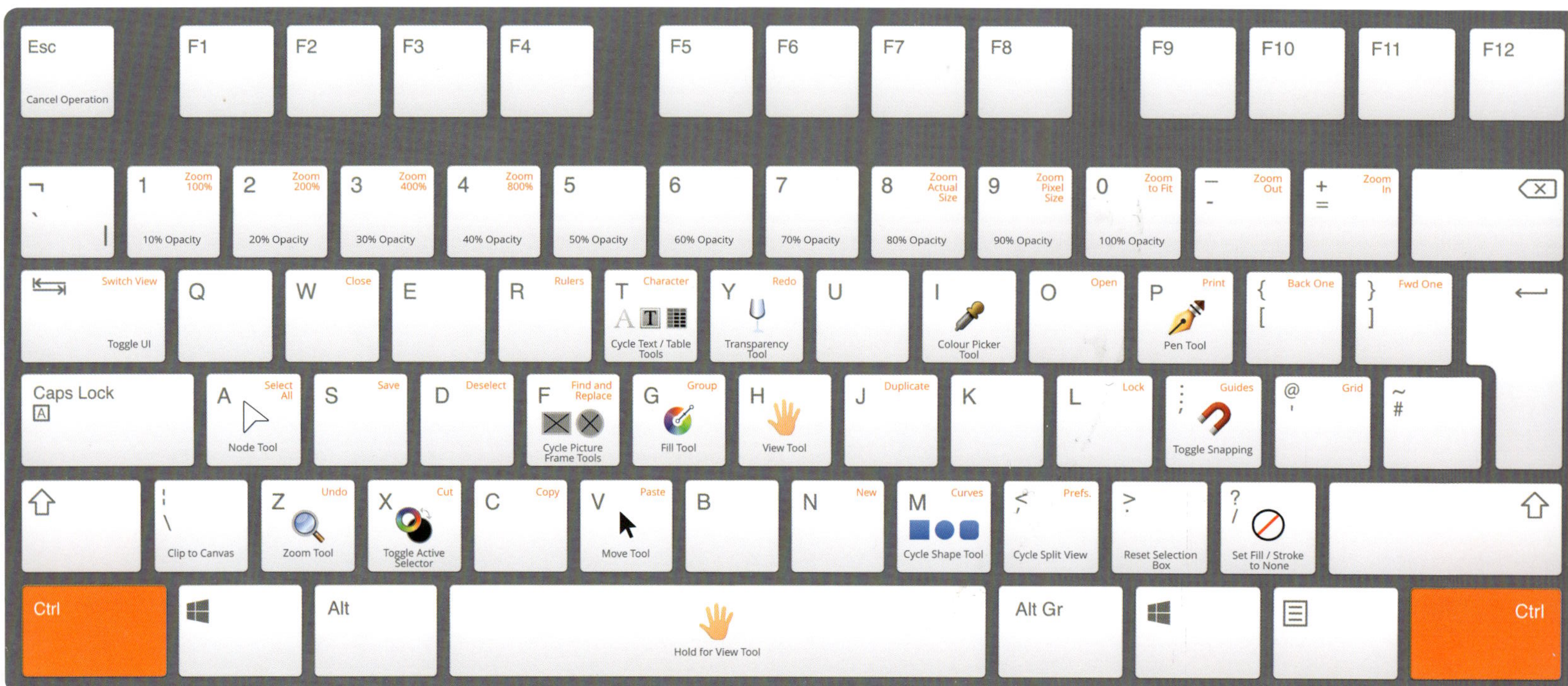

For Designer Persona and Photo Persona keyboard shortcuts, refer to the first pages of the respective cheat sheets at:

affin.co/afdwinshortcuts
affin.co/afpwinshortcuts

ADVANCED TEXT

Press buttons for various actions
Alt ⌥ Cmd ⌘ Shift ⇧ Ctrl ^

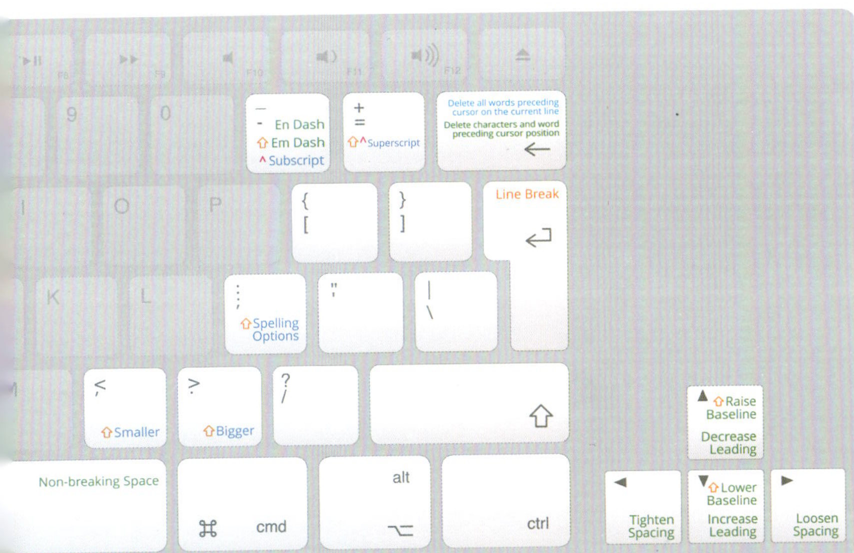

Add ⌘ to arrow key shortcuts to adjust step size
(Increases for ◄ & ►, decreases for ▲ & ▼)

⌘ + F Find & Replace Panel
⌘ + T Character Panel
⇧ ⌘ + T Typography Dialog

⌘ + B Bold
⌘ + I Italic
⌘ + U Underline

⌥ ⌘ + L Align Left
⌥ ⌘ + C Align Centre
⌥ ⌘ + R Align Right

x2 Select word under pointer
x3 Select line under pointer
x4 Select paragraph under pointer
x5 Select all

EXPRESSIONS

For use in input boxes in the Transform panel (and other areas of the UI)

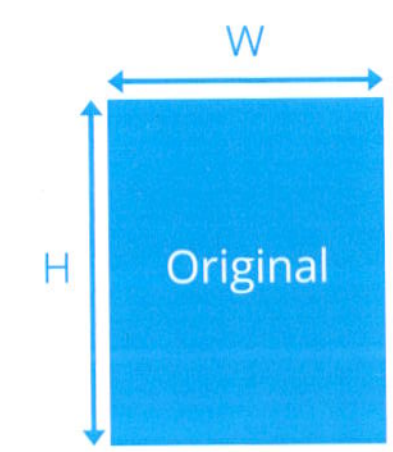

W: 120 px

H: 150 px

W: 118+55	173 px	W: *=75%	90 px
W: 37*4	148 px	W: h+30	180 px
W: +=80	200 px	W: h-5	145 px
W: -=20	100 px	W: 2*h	300 px
W: *=2	240 px	W: h/2	75 px
W: /=2	60 px	W: gr*h	242.7 px
W: *=1.4	168 px		

GESTURES

Zooming

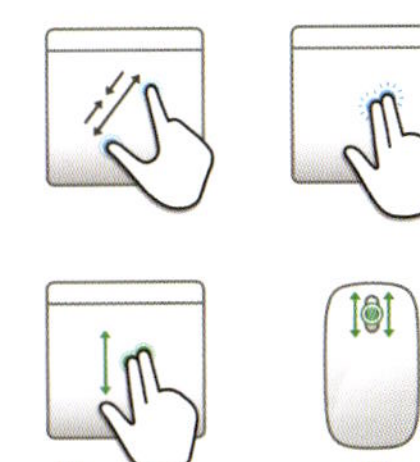

Panning

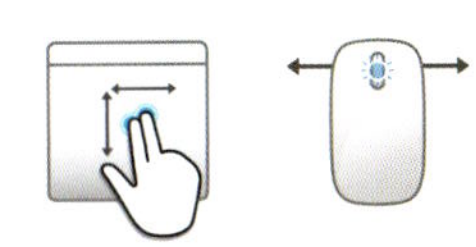

Scrolling

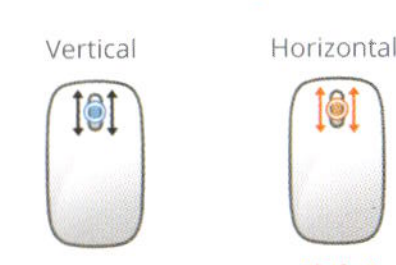

AFFINITY **Publisher** Windows

ADVANCED TEXT

Press buttons for various actions
Ctrl Alt Shift ⇧

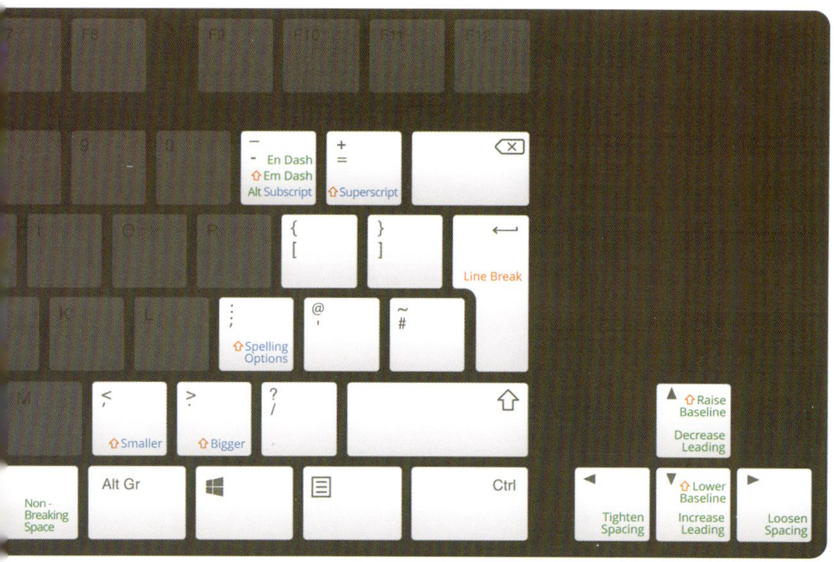

Ctrl + F Find & Replace Panel
Ctrl + T Character Panel
Ctrl + ⇧ + T Typography Dialog

Ctrl + B Bold
Ctrl + I Italic
Ctrl + U Underline

Ctrl + Alt + L Align Left
Ctrl + Alt + C Align Centre
Ctrl + Alt + R Align Right

Alt + ⇧ + ◄ Tighten Spacing More
Alt + ⇧ + ► Loosen Spacing More
Ctrl + Alt + ▼ Precise Increase Leading
Ctrl + Alt + ▲ Precise Decrease Leading

Ctrl + Alt + ⇧ + ▲ Precise Raise Baseline
Ctrl + Alt + ⇧ + ▼ Precise Lower Baseline

x2 Select word under pointer
x3 Select line under pointer
x4 Select paragraph under pointer
x5 Select all

EXPRESSIONS

For use in input boxes in the Transform panel (and other areas of the UI)

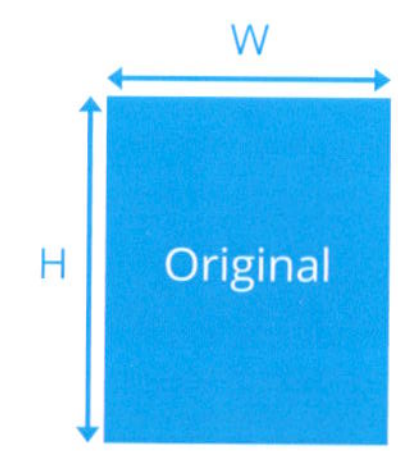

W: 120 px

H: 150 px

W:	118+55	= 173 px	W:	*=75%	= 90 px
W:	37*4	= 148 px	W:	h+30	= 180 px
W:	+=80	= 200 px	W:	h-5	= 145 px
W:	-=20	= 100 px	W:	2*h	= 300 px
W:	*=2	= 240 px	W:	h/2	= 75 px
W:	/=2	= 60 px	W:	gr*h	= 242.7 px
W:	*=1.4	= 168 px			

MODIFIERS & LAYER CONTROL

Selecting	Shift Option Drag + Ctrl Option + Drag	Selects multiple objects and layers Selects object or layer behind current selection Selects objects or layers partially encompassed Ignores initial object or layer below cursor
Moving	Cmd + Drag Shift + Drag	Duplicate object Move, constrained along 45-degree angles from origin
Rotating	Shift Ctrl	Constrain rotation to 15-degree intervals Rotates from opposite corner of layer or object
Resizing	Shift Cmd Option	Reverses aspect ratio constraint on scaling Scales from the centre of selection Ignores snapping during operation

Tables	Shift + Drag Shift Cmd	Resize column to left of dragged divider in header without resizing other columns Select multiple adjacent columns, rows, or cells Select multiple non-adjacent columns, rows, or cells
Layers panel	Layer 1 Layer 1 Layer 1	Double-click = Change layer name Double-click = Zoom to layer Alt + Click = Show selected only
Zoom Tool	Option + Click Option + Drag	Zooms out Zoom to marquee

AFFINITY **Publisher** Windows

MODIFIERS & LAYER CONTROL

Selecting	Shift	Selects multiple objects and layers
	Alt	Selects object or layer behind current selection
	Drag, then hold right button	Selects objects or layers partially encompassed
	Alt + Drag	Ignores initial object or layer below cursor
Moving	Ctrl + Drag	Duplicate object
	Shift + Drag	Move, constrained along 45-degree angles from origin
Rotating	Shift	Constrain rotation to 15-degree intervals
	Drag, then hold right button	Rotates from opposite corner of layer or object
Resizing	Shift	Reverses aspect ratio constraint on scaling
	Ctrl	Scales from the centre of selection
	Alt	Ignores snapping during operation

Tables	Shift + Drag	Resize column to left of dragged divider in header without resizing other columns
	Shift	Select multiple adjacent columns, rows, or cells
	Ctrl	Select multiple non-adjacent columns, rows, or cells
Layers panel	Layer 1	Double-click = Change layer name
	Layer 1	Double-click = Zoom to layer
	Layer 1	Alt + Click = Show selected only
Zoom Tool	Alt + Click	Zooms out
	Alt + Drag	Zoom to marquee